Praise for Joe Abercrombie

'Abercrombie writes dark, adult fantasy, by which I mean there's lots of stabbing in it, and after people stab each other they sometimes have sex with each other. His tone is morbid and funny and hard-boiled, not wholly dissimilar to that of Iain Banks... And like George R.R. Martin Abercrombie has the will and the cruelty to actually kill and maim his characters... Volumetrically speaking, it's hard to think of another fantasy novel in which this much blood gets spilled'

Lev Grossman, *Time Magazine*

'The books are good, really good. They pulled me in. Well-developed world. Unique, compelling characters. I like them so much that when I got to the end of the second book and found out the third book wasn't going to be out in the US for another three months, I experienced a fit of rage, then a fit of depression, then I ate some lunch and had a bit of a lay down'

Patrick Rothfuss

'The battles are vivid and visceral, the action brutal, the pace headlong, and Abercrombie piles the betrayals, reversals, and plot twists one atop another to keep us guessing how it will all come out. This is his best book yet'

George R.R. Martin

'Abercrombie writes fantasy like no one else'

Guardian

'Joe Abercrombie is probably the brightest star among the new generation of British fantasy writers... Abercrombie never underestimates the horrors that people are prepared to inflict on one another, or their long-lasting, often unexpected, consequences. Abercrombie writes a vivid, well-paced tale that never loosens its grip. His action scenes are cinematic in the best sense, and the characters are all distinct and interesting'   *The Times*

'Highly recommended – a funny, finely wrought, terrifically energetic work of high fantasy. Seek it out'

Joe Hill

'Joe Abercrombie has created a world able to stand alongside landscapes the likes of George R.R. Martin and J.R.R. Tolkien have created in terms of drama, political intrigue and, of course, bloodshed'   *SciFiNow*

'Abercrombie leavens the bloody action with moments of dark humour, developing a story suffused with a rich understanding of human darkness and light'   *Publishers Weekly*

'The consistently high standard of the stories in *Sharp Ends* make it a triumph. Granted, readers would be advised to acquaint themselves with their setting, but anyone who was excited by Abercrombie's debut ten years ago will feel those butterflies again. It's a masterful approach, displaying everything that's great about the short story format, from a writer at the height of his powers'   *Starburst*

'The intricately woven story never slackens its merciless grip as we follow our heroes and heroines through battlefields, boardrooms and bedrooms to their destinies – deserved and undeserved alike'
Daily Mail on *A Little Hatred*

'Witty, bloody and fun'   Nicholas Eames on *A Little Hatred*

'A tale of brute force and subtle magic set in a world on the cusp of an industrial revolution . . . a vivid and jolting tale'
Robin Hobb on *A Little Hatred*

'Goddamn magnificent'   Adrian Tchaikovsky on *A Little Hatred*

THE
TROUBLE
with PEACE

THE
TROUBLE
with PEACE

JOE ABERCROMBIE

GOLLANCZ

LONDON

For Lou,

With grim, dark

hugs

First published in Great Britain in 2020 by Gollancz
an imprint of The Orion Publishing Group Ltd
Carmelite House, 50 Victoria Embankment
London EC4Y 0DZ

An Hachette UK Company

1 3 5 7 9 10 8 6 4 2

A CIP catalogue record for this book is
available from the British Library.

ISBN (Hardback) 978 0 575 09591 5
ISBN (Export Trade Paperback) 978 0 575 09593 9
ISBN (eBook) 978 0 575 09595 3

Typeset at The Spartan Press Ltd,
Lymington, Hants

Printed and bound in Great Britain by Clays Ltd,
Elcograf S.p.A.

www.joeabercrombie.com
www.orionbooks.co.uk
www.gollancz.co.uk

PART IV

'In times of peace,
the warlike man attacks himself.'

Friedrich Nietzsche

The World's Wrongs

'I hope no one minds if we dispense with this for now?' Orso tossed his circlet down, gold twinkling in a dusty shaft of spring sunlight as it spun around and around. 'Damn thing chafes rather.' He rubbed at the sore spots it had left above his temples. There was a metaphor there somewhere. The burden of power, the weight of a crown. But his Closed Council had no doubt heard all that before.

The moment he sat they began to drag out their own chairs, wincing as old backs bent, grunting as old arses settled on hard wood, grumbling as old knees were eased under the tottering heaps of paper on the table.

'Where's the surveyor general?' someone asked, nodding at an empty chair.

'Out with his bladder.' There was a chorus of groans.

'One can win a thousand battles.' Lord Marshal Brint worried at that lady's ring on his little finger, gazing into the middle distance as though at an opposing army. 'But in the end, no man can defeat his own bladder.'

As the youngest in the room by some thirty years, Orso ranked his bladder among his least interesting organs. 'One issue before we begin,' he said.

All eyes turned towards him. Apart from those of Bayaz, down at the foot of the table. The legendary wizard continued to gaze out of the window, towards the palace gardens which were just beginning to bud.

'I am set on making a grand tour of the Union.' Orso did his best to sound authoritative. Regal, even. 'To visit every province. Every major city. When was the last time a monarch visited Starikland? Did my father ever go?'

Arch Lector Glokta grimaced. Even more than usual. 'Starikland was not considered safe, Your Majesty.'

'Starikland has always been afflicted with a restless temper.' Lord

Chancellor Gorodets was absently smoothing his long beard into a point, fluffing it up, then smoothing it again. 'Now more than ever.'

'But I have to connect with the *people*.' Orso thumped the table to give it emphasis. They needed some *feeling* in here. Everything in the White Chamber was cold, dry, bloodless calculation. 'Show them we're all part of the same great endeavour. The same *family*. It's supposed to be a Union, isn't it? We need to bloody *unite*.'

Orso had never wanted to be king. He enjoyed it even less than being crown prince, if that was possible. But now that he *was* king, he was determined to do some good with it.

Lord Chamberlain Hoff tapped at the table in limp applause. 'A *wonderful* idea, Your Majesty.'

'Wonderful,' echoed High Justice Bruckel, who had the conversational style of a woodpecker and a beak not dissimilar. 'Idea.'

'Noble sentiments, well expressed,' agreed Gorodets, though his appreciation did not quite reach his eyes.

One old man fussed with some papers. Another frowned into his wine as though something had died in it. Gorodets was still stroking his beard, but now looked as if he could taste piss.

'But?' Orso was learning that in the Closed Council there was always at least one *but*.

'But...' Hoff glanced to Bayaz, who gave permission with the slightest nod. 'It might be best to wait for a more *auspicious* moment. A more *settled* time. There are so many challenges *here* which require Your Majesty's attention.'

The high justice puffed out a heavy breath. 'Many. Challenges.'

Orso delivered something between a growl and a sigh. His father had always despised the White Chamber and its hard, stark chairs. Despised the hard, stark men who sat on them. He had warned Orso that no good was ever done in the Closed Council. But if not here, where? This cramped, stuffy, featureless little room was where the power lay. 'Are you suggesting the machinery of government would grind to a halt without me?' he asked. 'I think you over-sugar the pudding.'

'There are issues the monarch must be *seen* to attend to,' said Glokta. 'The Breakers were dealt a crippling blow in Valbeck.'

'A hard task well done, Your Majesty,' Hoff drooled out, with cloying sycophancy.

'But they are far from eradicated. And those that escaped have become... even more extreme in their opinions.'

'Disruption among the workers.' High Justice Bruckel rapidly shook his bony head. 'Strikes. Organising. Attacks on staff and property.'

'And the damn *pamphlets*,' said Brint, to a collective groan.

'Damn. Pamphlets.'

'Used to think education was merely wasted on the commoners. Now I say it's a positive *danger*.'

'This bloody Weaver can turn a phrase.'

'Not to mention an obscene etching.'

'They incite the populace to disobedience!'

'To disaffection!'

'They talk of a *Great Change* coming.'

A flurry of twitches ran up the left side of Glokta's wasted face. 'They blame the Open Council.' *And published caricatures of them as pigs fighting over the trough.* 'They blame the Closed Council.' *And published caricatures of them fucking each other.* 'They blame His Majesty.' *And published caricatures of him fucking anything.* 'They blame the banks.'

'They promote the ridiculous rumour that the debt... to the Banking House of Valint and Balk... has crippled the state...' Gorodets trailed off, leaving the room in nervous silence.

Bayaz finally tore his hard, green eyes from the window to glare down the table. 'This flood of disinformation must be stemmed.'

'We have destroyed a dozen presses,' grated Glokta, 'but they build new ones, and smaller all the time. Now any fool can *write*, and *print*, and air their *opinions*.'

'Progress,' lamented Bruckel, rolling his eyes to the ceiling.

'The Breakers are like bloody moles in a garden,' growled Lord Marshal Rucksted, who had turned his chair slightly sideways-on to give an impression of fearless dash. 'You kill five, pour a celebratory glass, then in the morning your lawn's covered in new bloody molehills.'

'More irritating than my bladder,' said Brint, to widespread chuckling.

Glokta sucked at his empty gums with a faint squelch. 'And then there are the Burners.'

'Lunatics!' snapped Hoff. 'This woman *Judge*.'

Shudders of distaste about the table. At the notion of such a thing as a woman, or at the notion of this particular one, it was hard to say.

'I hear a mill owner was found murdered on the road to Keln.' Gorodets gave his beard a particularly violent tug. 'A pamphlet *nailed* to his face.'

Rucksted clasped his big fists on the table. 'And there was that fellow choked to death with a thousand copies of the rule-sheet he distributed to his employees...'

'One might almost say our approach has made matters worse,' observed Orso. A memory of Malmer drifted up, legs dangling from his cage as it swung with the breeze. 'Perhaps we could make some gesture. A minimum wage? Improved working conditions? I heard a recent fire in a mill led to the deaths of fifteen child workers—'

'It would be folly,' said Bayaz, his attention already back on the gardens, 'to obstruct the free operation of the market.'

'The market serves the interests of all,' offered the lord chancellor.

'Unprecedented,' agreed the high justice. 'Prosperity.'

'No doubt the child workers would applaud it,' said Orso.

'No doubt,' agreed Lord Hoff.

'Had they not been burned to death.'

'A ladder is of no use if all the rungs are at the top,' said Bayaz.

Orso opened his mouth to retort but High Consul Matstringer got in first. 'And we face a veritable cornucopia of adversaries overseas.' The coordinator of the Union's foreign policy had never yet failed to confuse complexity with insight. 'The Gurkish may still be embroiled in all-encompassing predicaments of their own—'

Bayaz gave a rare grunt of satisfaction at that.

'But the Imperials endlessly rattle their swords on our western border, exhorting the populace of Starikland to continued disloyalty, and the Styrians are emboldened in the east.'

'They are building up their *navy*.' Lord Admiral Krepskin roused himself for a heavy-lidded interjection. 'New ships. Armed with cannon. While ours *rot* in their docks for lack of investment.'

Bayaz gave a familiar grunt of dissatisfaction at that.

'And they are busy in the shadows,' went on Matstringer, 'sowing discord in Westport, enticing the Aldermen to sedition. Why, they have succeeded in scheduling a vote within the month which could see the city secede from the Union!'

The old men competed to display the most patriotic outrage. It was enough to make Orso want to secede from the Union himself.

'Disloyalty,' grumbled the high justice. 'Discord.'

'Bloody Styrians!' snarled Rucksted. 'Love to work in the shadows.'

'We can work there, too,' said Glokta softly, in a manner that made the hairs prickle beneath Orso's braid-heavy uniform. 'Some of my very best people are even now ensuring Westport's loyalty.'

'At least our northern border is secure,' said Orso, desperate to inject some optimism.

'Well . . .' The high consul crushed his hopes with a prim pursing of the mouth. 'The politics of the North are always something of a cauldron. The Dogman is advanced in years. Infirm. No man can divine the fate of his Protectorate in the event of his death. Lord Governor Brock would appear to have forged a strong bond with the new King of the Northmen, Stour Nightfall—'

'That *has* to be a good thing,' said Orso.

Doubtful glances were traded across the table.

'Unless their bond becomes . . . *too* strong,' murmured Glokta.

'The young Lord Governor is popular,' agreed Gorodets.

'Damned,' pecked the high justice. 'Popular.'

'Handsome lad,' said Brint. 'And he's earned a warrior's reputation.'

'Angland behind him. Stour as an ally. Could be a threat.'

Rucksted raised his bushy brows very high. 'His grandfather, lest we forget, was an infamous bloody traitor!'

'I will not see a man condemned for the actions of his grandfather!' snapped Orso, whose own grandfathers had enjoyed mixed reputations, to say the least. 'Leo dan Brock risked his life fighting a duel on my behalf!'

'The job of your Closed Council,' said Glokta, 'is to anticipate threats to Your Majesty before they become threats.'

'After may be too late,' threw in Bayaz.

'People are . . . discomfited by the death of your father,' said Gorodets. 'So young. So unexpected.'

'Young. Unexpected.'

'And you, Your Majesty, are—'

'Despised?' offered Orso.

Gorodets gave an indulgent smile. '*Untried.* At times like this, people yearn for stability.'

'Indeed. It would without doubt be a very fine thing if Your Majesty were . . .' Lord Hoff cleared his throat. 'To marry?'

Orso closed his eyes and pressed finger and thumb against them. 'Must we?' Marriage was the last thing he wanted to discuss. He still had Savine's note in a drawer beside his bed. Still looked at that brutal little line every evening, as one might pick at a scab. *My answer must be no. I would ask you not to contact me again. Ever.*

Hoff cleared his throat once more. 'A new king always finds himself in an uncertain position.'

'A king with no heir, doubly so,' said Glokta.

'The absence of clear succession gives a troubling impression of impermanence,' observed Matstringer.

'Perhaps with the help of Her Majesty your mother, I might draw up a list of eligible ladies, both at home and abroad?' Hoff cleared his throat yet a third time. 'A *new* list... that is.'

'By all means,' growled Orso, pronouncing each word with cutting precision.

'Then there is Fedor dan Wetterlant,' murmured the high justice.

Glokta's permanent grimace became even further contorted. 'I hoped we might settle that matter without bothering His Majesty.'

'I'm bothered now,' snapped Orso. 'Fedor dan Wetterlant... didn't I play cards with him once?'

'He lived in Adua before inheriting the family estate. His reputation here was...'

'Almost as bad as mine?' Orso remembered the man. Soft face but hard eyes. Smiled too much. Just like Lord Hoff, who was even now breaking out a particularly unctuous example.

'I was going to say *abominable*, Your Majesty. He stands accused of serious crimes.'

'He raped a laundry woman,' said Glokta, 'with the assistance of his groundskeeper. When her husband demanded justice, Wetterlant murdered the man, again with the groundskeeper's assistance. In a tavern. In full view of seventeen witnesses.' The emotionless quality of the Arch Lector's grating voice only served to sicken Orso even more. 'Then he had a drink. The groundskeeper poured, I believe.'

'Bloody hell,' whispered Orso.

'Those are the *accusations*,' said Matstringer.

'Even Wetterlant scarcely disputes them,' said Glokta.

'His mother does,' observed Gorodets.

There was a chorus of groans. 'Lady Wetterlant, by the Fates, what a battleaxe.'

'Absolute. Harridan.'

'Well, I'm no admirer of hangings,' said Orso, 'but I've seen men hanged for far less.'

'The groundskeeper already has been,' said Glokta.

'Shame,' grunted Brint with heavy irony, 'he sounded like a real charmer.'

'But Wetterlant has asked for the king's justice,' said Bruckel.

'His mother has demanded it!'

'And since he has a seat on the Open Council—'

'Not that his arse has ever touched it.'

'—he has the right to be tried before his peers. With Your Majesty as the judge. We cannot refuse.'

'But we can delay,' said Glokta. 'The Open Council may not excel at much, but in delay it leads the world.'

'Postpone. Defer. Adjourn. I can wrap him up. In form and procedure. Until he dies in prison.' And the high justice smiled as though that was the ideal solution.

'We just deny him a hearing?' Orso was almost as disgusted by that option as by the crime itself.

'Of course not,' said Bruckel.

'No, no,' said Gorodets. 'We would not deny him anything.'

'We'd simply never give him anything,' said Glokta.

Rucksted nodded. 'I hardly think Fedor dan bloody Wetterlant or his bloody mother should be allowed to hold a dagger to the throat of the state simply because he can't control himself.'

'He could at least lose control of himself in the absence of seventeen witnesses,' observed Gorodets, and there was some light laughter.

'So it's not the rape or the murder we object to,' asked Orso, 'but his being caught doing it?'

Hoff peered at the other councillors, as though wondering whether anyone might disagree. 'Well...'

'Why should I not just hear the case, and judge it on its merits, and settle it one way or another?'

Glokta's grimace twisted still further. 'Your Majesty cannot judge the case without being seen to take sides.' The old men nodded, grunted, shifted unhappily in their uncomfortable chairs. 'Find Wetterlant innocent, it will be nepotism, and favouritism, and will strengthen the hand of those traitors like the Breakers who would turn the common folk against you.'

'But find Wetterlant guilty...' Gorodets tugged unhappily at his beard and the old men grumbled more dismay. 'The nobles would see it as an affront, as an attack, as a betrayal. It would embolden those who oppose you in the Open Council at a time when we are trying to ensure a smooth succession.'

'It seems sometimes,' snapped Orso, rubbing at those sore spots above his temples, 'that every decision I make in this chamber is between two equally bad outcomes, with the best option to make no decision at all!'

Hoff glanced about the table again. 'Well...'

'It is *always* a bad idea,' said the First of the Magi, 'for a king to choose sides.'

Everyone nodded as though they had been treated to the most profound statement of all time. It was a wonder they did not rise and give a standing ovation. Orso was left in no doubt at which end of the table the power in the White Chamber truly lay. He remembered the look on his father's face as Bayaz spoke. The *fear*. He made one more effort to claw his way towards his best guess at the right thing.

'Justice should be done. Shouldn't it? Justice must be seen to be done. Surely! Otherwise... well... it's not justice at all. Is it?'

High Justice Bruckel bared his teeth as if in physical pain. 'At this level. Your Majesty. Such concepts become... fluid. Justice cannot be stiff like iron, but... more of a *jelly*. It must mould itself. About the greater concerns.'

'But... surely at this level, at the *highest* level, is where justice must be at its most firm. There must be a moral bedrock! It cannot all be... expediency?'

Exasperated, Hoff looked towards the foot of the table. 'Lord Bayaz, perhaps you might...'

The First of the Magi gave a weary sigh as he sat forward, hands clasped, regarding Orso from beneath heavy lids. The sigh of a veteran schoolmaster, called on once again to explain the basics to this year's harvest of dunces.

'Your Majesty, we are not here to set right all the world's wrongs.'

Orso stared back at him. 'What *are* we here for, then?'

Bayaz neither smiled nor frowned. 'To ensure that we benefit from them.'

A Long Way from Adua

Superior Lorsen lowered the letter, frowning at Vick over the rims of his eye-lenses. He looked like a man who had not smiled in some time. Perhaps ever.

'His Eminence the Arch Lector writes you a glowing report. He tells me you were instrumental in ending the uprising at Valbeck. He feels I might need your *help*.' Lorsen turned his frown on Tallow, standing awkwardly in the corner, as if the idea of his being helpful with anything was an affront to reason. Vick still wasn't sure why she'd brought him. Perhaps because she had no one else to bring.

'Not *need* my help, Superior,' she said. No bear, badger or wasp was more territorial than a Superior of the Inquisition, after all. 'But I don't have to tell you how damaging it would be, financially, politically, diplomatically . . . if Westport voted to leave the Union.'

'No,' said Lorsen crisply. 'You do *not*.' As Superior of Westport, he'd be looking for a job.

'Which is why His Eminence felt you could perhaps *use* my help.'

Lorsen set down the letter, adjusted its position on his desk and stood. 'Forgive me if I am dubious, Inquisitor, but performing surgery upon the politics of one of the world's greatest cities is not quite the same as smashing up a strike.' And he opened the door onto the high gallery.

'The threats are worse and the bribes better,' said Vick as she followed him through, Tallow shuffling behind, 'but otherwise I imagine there are similarities.'

'Then may I present to you our unruly workers: the Aldermen of Westport.' And Lorsen stepped to the balustrade and gestured down below.

There, on the floor of Westport's cavernous Hall of Assembly, tiled with semi-precious stones in geometric patterns, the leadership of the city was debating the great question of leaving the Union. Some Aldermen stood, shaking fists or brandishing papers. Others sat, glumly watching or with heads in hands. Others bellowed over each other in at least five languages, the ringing echoes making it impossible to tell who was speaking, let alone what was being said. Others murmured to colleagues or yawned, scratched, stretched, gazed into space. A group of five or six had paused for tea in a distant corner. Men of every shape, size, colour and culture. A cross section through the madly diverse population of the city they called the Crossroads of the World, wedged onto a narrow scrap of thirsty land between Styria and the South, between the Union and the Thousand Isles.

'Two hundred and thirteen of them, at the current count, and each with a *vote*.' Lorsen pronounced the word with evident distaste. 'When it comes to arguing, the citizens of Westport are celebrated throughout the world, and this is where their most dauntless arguers stage their most intractable arguments.' The Superior peered towards a great clock on the far side of the gallery. 'They've been at it for seven hours already today.'

Vick was not surprised. There was a stickiness to the air from all the breath they'd wasted. The Fates knew she was finding Westport more than hot enough, even in spring, but she had been told that in summer, after particularly intense sessions, it could sometimes rain inside the dome. A sort of spitty drizzling back of all their high-blown language onto the furious Aldermen below.

'Seems the opinions are somewhat entrenched down there.'

'I wish they were more so,' said Lorsen. 'Thirty years ago, after we beat the Gurkish, you couldn't have found five votes for leaving the Union. But the Styrian faction has gained a great deal of ground lately. The wars. The debts. The uprising in Valbeck. The death of King Jezal. And his son is, shall we say, not yet taken *seriously* on the international stage. Without mincing words—'

'Our prestige is in the night pot,' Vick finished for him.

'We joined the Union because of their military might!' A truly mighty voice boomed out, finally cutting through the hubbub. The speaker was thickset, dark-skinned and shaven-headed with strangely gentle gestures. 'Because the Empire of Gurkhul threatened us from the south and we needed strong allies to deter them. But membership has cost us dear! Millions of scales in treasure and the price forever rises!'

Agreement floated up to the gallery in an echoing murmur.

'Who's the man with all the voice?' asked Vick.

'Solumeo Shudra,' said Lorsen, sourly. 'The leader of the pro-Styrian faction and a royal thorn in my arse. Half-Sipanese, half-Kadiri. A fitting emblem for this cultural melting pot.'

Vick knew all this, of course. She made a great deal of effort to go into every job well informed. But she preferred to keep her knowledge to herself whenever possible, and let others imagine themselves the great experts.

'During the forty years since we joined the Union, the world has changed beyond all recognition!' bellowed Shudra. 'The Empire of Gurkhul has crumbled, while Styria has turned from a patchwork of feuding city-states into one strong nation under one strong king. They have defeated the Union in not one, not two, but *three* wars! Wars waged for the vanity and ambitions of Queen Terez. Wars we were dragged into at vast expense in silver and blood.'

'He talks well,' said Tallow, softly.

'Very well,' said Vick. 'He almost has me wanting to join Styria.'

'The Union is a waning power!' boomed Shudra. 'While Styria is our natural ally. The hand of the Grand Duchess Monzcarro Murcatto is extended to us in friendship. We should seize it while we still can. My friends, I urge you all to vote with me to leave the Union!'

Loud boos, but even louder cheers. Lorsen shook his head in disgust. 'If this were Adua, we could march in there, drag him from his seat, force a confession and ship him off to Angland on the next tide.'

'But we're a long way from Adua,' murmured Vick.

'Both sides worry that an open display of force might turn the majority against them, but things will change as we move towards the vote. The positions are hardening. The middle ground is shrinking. Murcatto's Minister of Whispers, Shylo Vitari, is mounting an all-encompassing campaign of bribery and threats, blackmail and coercion, while printed sheets are flung from the rooftops and painted slogans spring up faster than we can scrub them off.'

'I'm told Casamir dan Shenkt is in Westport,' said Vick. 'That Murcatto has paid him one hundred thousand scales to shift the balance. By any means necessary.'

'I had heard . . . the rumours.'

She got the sense that Lorsen had heard the same rumours she had, delivered in breathless whispers with a great deal of lurid detail. That Shenkt's skills went beyond the mortal and touched the magical. That he was a sorcerer who had damned himself by eating the flesh of men. Here in Westport, where calls to prayer echoed hourly over the city and cut-price prophets declaimed on every corner, such ideas were somehow harder to dismiss.

'Might I lend you a few Practicals?' Lorsen peered at Tallow. To be fair, the lad didn't look as if he could stand up to a stiff breeze, let alone a flesh-eating magician. 'If Styria's most famous assassin is really on the prowl, we need you well protected.'

'An armed escort would send the wrong message.' And would do no good anyway, if those rumours really were true. 'I was sent to persuade, not intimidate.'

Lorsen was less than convinced. 'Really?'

'That's how it has to look.'

'Little would look worse than the untimely death of His Eminence's representative.'

'I don't intend to rush at the grave, believe me.'

'Few do. The grave swallows us all regardless.'

'What are your plans, Superior?'

Lorsen took a weary breath. 'I have my hands full protecting our own Aldermen. The ballots are cast in nineteen days, and we cannot afford to lose a single vote.'

'Taking away some of theirs would help.'

'Providing it is done subtly. If their people turn up dead, it is sure to harden feelings against us. Things are finely balanced.' Lorsen clenched his fists on the railing as Solumeo Shudra boomed out another speech lauding the benefits of Styria's welcoming embrace. 'And Shudra has proved persuasive. He is well loved here. I am warning you, Inquisitor – don't go after him.'

'With all due respect, the Arch Lector has sent me to do the things you can't. I only take orders from him.'

Lorsen gave her a long, cold stare. Probably it was a look that froze the blood in people used to Westport's warm climate, but Vick had worked down a half-flooded mine in an Angland winter. It took a lot to make her shiver. 'Then I am *asking* you.' He pronounced each word precisely. '*Don't* go after him.'

Below them, Shudra had finished his latest thunderous contribution to noisy applause from the men around him and even noisier booing from the other side. Fists were shaken, papers were flung, insults were grumbled. Nineteen more days of this pantomime, with Shylo Vitari trying everything to twist the outcome. Who knew how that would turn out?

'His Eminence wants me to keep Westport in the Union.' She headed for the door with Tallow at her heels. 'At any cost.'

A Sea of Trouble

'**W**elcome, one and all, to this fifteenth biannual meeting of Adua's Solar Society.'

Curnsbick, resplendent in a waistcoat embroidered with silver flowers, held up his broad hands for silence, though the applause was muted. The members used to raise the roof of the theatre. Savine remembered it well.

'With thanks to our distinguished patrons – the Lady Ardee and her daughter Lady Savine dan Glokta.' Curnsbick gave his usual showman's flourish towards the box where Savine sat, but the clapping now was yet more subdued. Did she even hear a few tattletale whispers below? *She's not all she was, you know. Not one half of what she was . . .*

'Ungrateful bastards,' she hissed through her fixed smile. Could it only have been a few months since they were soiling their drawers at the mention of her name?

'To say that it has been a difficult year . . .' Curnsbick frowned down at his notes as though they made sad reading. 'Hardly does justice to the troubles we have faced.'

'You're fucking right there.' Savine dipped behind her fan to sniff up a pinch of pearl dust. Just to lift her out of the bog. Just to keep some wind in the sails.

'A war in the North. Ongoing troubles in Styria. And the death of His August Majesty King Jezal the First. Too young. Far too young.' Curnsbick's voice cracked a little. 'The great family of our nation has lost its great father.'

Savine flinched at the word, had to give her own eye the slightest dab with the tip of her little finger, though no doubt any tears were for her own troubles rather than a father she had hardly known and certainly not respected. All tears are for oneself, in the end.

'Then the terrible events in Valbeck.' A kind of sorry grumble around the theatre, a stirring below as every head was shaken. 'Assets ruined. Colleagues lost. Manufactories that were the wonder of the world left in ruins.' Curnsbick struck his lectern a blow. 'But already new industry rises from the ashes! Modern housing on the ruins of the slums! Greater mills with more efficient machinery and more orderly workers!'

Savine tried not to think of the children in her mill in Valbeck, before it was destroyed. The bunk beds wedged in among the machines. The stifling heat. The deafening noise. The choking dust. But so awfully orderly. So terribly efficient.

'Confidence has been struck,' lamented Curnsbick. 'Markets are in turmoil. But from chaos, opportunity can come.' He gave his lectern another blow. 'Opportunity must be *made* to come. His August Majesty King Orso will lead us into a new age. Progress cannot *stop*! Will not be *permitted* to stop! For the benefit of all, we of the Solar Society will fight tirelessly to drag the Union from the tomb of ignorance and into the sunny uplands of enlightenment!'

Loud applause this time, and in the audience below, men struggled to their feet.

'Hear! Hear!' someone brayed.

'Progress!' blurted another.

'As inspiring as any sermon in the Great Temple of Shaffa,' murmured Zuri.

'If I didn't know better, I'd say Curnsbick has taken a stiffener himself,' said Savine, and she ducked behind her fan and sniffed up another pinch. Just one more, to get her ready for the fight.

Battle was already joined beneath the great chandeliers in the foyer. A sparser melee than at recent meetings. Less buoyant. More bitter. Hungrier dogs, snapping over leaner pickings.

The press reminded her of the crowd in Valbeck when the Breakers brought food around the slum. They wore silk rather than rags, they stank of perfume rather than stale sweat, the ever-present threat was of ruin rather than violence, but the jostling and the hunger were very much the same. There had been a time when Savine was as comfortable in this crawling activity as a queen bee in her hive. Now her whole body tingled with chilly panic. She had to smother the urge to lash out with her elbows and run screaming for the door.

'Calm,' she mouthed to herself, trying to let her shoulders relax so her hands would stop shaking, instantly losing all patience and flexing every muscle instead. 'Calm, calm, *calm*.'

She squeezed her face into a smile, snapped out her fan and forced herself into the midst of the press with Zuri at her shoulder. Eyes turned in her direction, expressions harder than she was used to. Assessing, rather than admiring. Scornful, rather than envious. They used to crowd around her like pigs around the one trough in the farmyard. Now the most tempting morsels went elsewhere. Savine could scarcely see Selest dan Heugen through the swarm of gentlemen competing for her attention. Only a flash of that garish red wig. A snatch of that hideous, brash, overdone laugh that other women were beginning to imitate.

'By the Fates, I despise that woman,' muttered Savine.

'The highest compliment you could pay her,' said Zuri, with a warning glance up from her book. 'One cannot despise a thing without acknowledging its importance.'

She was right, as always. Selest had enjoyed success after success since she invested in that scheme of Kaspar dan Arinhorm's, the one that Savine had so pointedly turned down. Her own interests in Angland's mines had taken quite the beating since he began to install his new pumps across the province.

And those were far from her only disappointing investments of late. Once she made businesses bloom just by smiling at them. Now every apple she bit into turned out rotten. She was not left alone, that was sure. But her fan was busier beckoning the suitors in than waving them off.

She was obliged to talk to old Ricart dan Sleisholt, who had some mad fantasy of making power by damming the Whiteflow. You could tell at a glance he was one of life's losers, the shoulders of his jacket liberally dusted with dandruff, but it was vital that she look busy. While he blathered on, she sifted the flood of conversation around her for opportunities as a prospector sifts the Far Country's icy streams for gold.

'...cutlery and drapery and crockery and clocks. People have money and they want things...'

'...heard Valint and Balk called in his loans. Magnate in the morning, beggar by afternoon. Salutary lesson for all of us...'

'...property in Valbeck. You wouldn't believe the price I got on some vacant land. Well, I say vacant, but these scum are easily moved...'

'...impossible to know which way the Closed Council is going to fall on tax. There's a hell of a hole in the finances. The entire treasury's a hole...'

'...told 'em if they wouldn't do the work, I'd bring in a crowd of brown bastards who would, and they soon got back to their machines...'

'...nobles furious, commoners furious, merchants furious, my wife isn't furious yet, but it never takes much...'

'And so you see, Lady Savine,' Sleisholt was working up to a grand finale, 'the power of the Whiteflow is languishing unharnessed, like a stallion unbridled, and—'

'If I may!' Curnsbick caught Savine's elbow and steered her nimbly away.

'Unbridled, Lady Savine!' Sleisholt called after her. 'I am available to discuss it further at your convenience!' And he dissolved into a coughing fit which faded into the chatter.

'Thank the Fates for you,' murmured Savine. 'I thought I'd never escape that old dunce.'

Curnsbick glanced away while rubbing significantly at his nose. 'You have a little *something* just here.'

'Fuck.' She dipped behind her fan to wipe a trace of powder from the rim of her sore nostril.

When she came up, Curnsbick was looking worriedly at her from under his grey brows, still flecked with a few stubborn ginger hairs. 'Savine, I count you as one of my closest friends.'

'How lovely of you.'

'I know you have a generous heart—'

'You know more than me, then.'

'—and I have the highest regard for your instincts, your tenacity, your wit—'

'It takes no great wit to sense a "but" coming.'

'I'm worried for you.' He lowered his voice. 'I hear *rumours*, Savine. I'm concerned about . . . well, about your *judgement*.'

Her skin was prickling unpleasantly under her dress. 'My judgement?' she whispered, forcing her smile a tooth wider.

'This venture in Keln that just collapsed, I warned you it wasn't viable. Vessels that size—'

'You must be delighted at how right you were.'

'What? No! I could scarcely be less so. You must have sunk thousands into financing the Crown Prince's Division.' It had been closer to millions. 'Then I hear Kort's canal is hampered by labour problems.' Utterly mired in them was closer to it. 'And it's no secret you lost heavily in Valbeck—'

'You have no *fucking* idea what I lost in Valbeck!' He stepped back, startled, and she realised she had her fist clenched tight around her folded fan and was shaking it in his face. 'You . . . have no idea.' She was shocked to find the pain of tears at the back of her nose, had to snap her fan open again so she could dab at her lids, struggling not to smudge her powder.

Never mind her judgement, it was getting to the point where she could hardly trust her own eyes.

But when she glanced up, Curnsbick was not even looking at her. He was staring across the busy foyer towards the door.

The eager chatter fell silent, the crowd split and through the midst came a young man with a vast retinue of guards, officers, attendants and hangers-on, sandy hair carefully arranged to give the impression of not having been arranged at all, white uniform heavy with medals.

'Bloody hell,' whispered Curnsbick, gripping Savine's elbow, 'it's the bloody king!'

Whatever the criticisms – and there were more than ever, regularly circulated in pamphlets revelling in the tawdry details – no one could deny that King Orso looked the part. He reminded Savine of his father. Of *their* father, she realised, with an ugly twisting of disgust. He chuckled, slapped arms, shook hands, traded jokes, the same beacon of slightly absent good humour King Jezal had once been.

'Your Majesty,' frothed Curnsbick, 'the Solar Society is *illuminated* by your presence. I fear we had to begin the addresses without you.'

'Never fear, Master Curnsbick.' Orso clapped him on the shoulder like an old friend. 'I can't imagine I would have been much help with the technical details.'

The great machinist produced the most mechanical of laughs. 'I am sure you know our sponsor, Lady Savine dan Glokta.'

Their eyes met only for an instant. But an instant was enough.

She remembered how Orso used to look at her. That mischievous glint in his eye, as if they were players in a delightful game no one else knew about. Before she learned they had a father in common, when he was still a crown prince and her judgement was considered unimpeachable. Now his stare was flat, and dead, and passionless. A mourner at the funeral of someone he had hardly known.

He had asked her to marry him. To be his queen. And all she had wanted was to say yes. He had loved her, and she had loved him.

Their eyes only met for an instant. But an instant was all she could stand.

She sank into the deepest curtsy she could manage, wishing she could keep sinking until the tiled floor swallowed her. 'Your Majesty . . .'

'Lady Selest!' she heard Orso say, his heel clicking sharply as he turned away. 'Perhaps you might show me around?'

'I'd be *honoured*, Your Majesty.' And the bubbling of Selest dan Heugen's victorious laughter was as painful as boiling water in Savine's ears.

It was a slight no one in the entire foyer could have missed. Had Orso knocked her down and trodden on her throat, he could scarcely have done more damage. Everyone was whispering as she stood. Scorned, by the king, at her own function.

She walked to the doors through swimming faces, smile plastered to her burning cheeks, and stumbled down the steps into the twilit street. Her stomach roiled. She pulled at her collar, but she could sooner have torn through a prison wall with her fingernails than loosened that triple stitching.

'Lady Savine?' came Zuri's concerned voice.

She tottered around the corner of the theatre into the darkness of an alley, doubled up helpless and sprayed vomit down the wall. Puking made her think of Valbeck. Everything made her think of Valbeck.

She straightened, dashing the burning snot from her nose. 'Even my own stomach is betraying me.'

A strip of light down the side of Zuri's dark face made one eye gleam. 'When did your menses last come?' she asked, softly.

Savine stood for a moment, her breath ragged. Then she gave a hopeless shrug. 'Just before Leo dan Brock's visit to Adua. Whoever would have thought I'd miss the monthly agonies?'

Probably her ragged breaths should have turned to choking sobs, and she should have fallen into Zuri's arms and wept at the colossal mess she had made of herself. Curnsbick was right to worry, the old fool. Her judgement had turned to shit and here was the result.

But instead of sobbing, she started to chuckle. 'I'm puking,' she said, 'in a piss-smelling alley, in a dress that cost five hundred marks, with a bastard on the way. I'm fucking ridiculous.'

The laughter faded, and she leaned against the wall, scraping her sour tongue clean on her teeth. 'The higher you climb, the further you have to fall, and the greater the spectacle when you hit the ground. What wonderful drama, eh? And they don't even have to pay for a ticket.' She clenched her fists. 'They all think I'm going down. But if they think I'm going down without a fight, they should—'

She doubled over and brought up more sick. Just an acrid trickle this time. Retching and giggling at once. She spat it out and wiped her face on the back of her glove. Her hand was shaking again.

'Calm,' she muttered at herself, clenching her fists. 'Calm, you absolute *fucker*.'

Zuri looked worried. And she never looked worried. 'I will ask Rabik to bring the carriage around. We should get you home.'

'Oh, come, come, the night is young.' Savine fished out her box for another pinch of pearl dust. Just to get over the humps. Just to keep things moving. She headed for the street. 'I've a mind to watch Master Broad work.'

A Routine

'So . . . you're happy here, then?'

Liddy laughed. There'd been weeks when Broad had hardly seen her smile. These days, she laughed all the time. 'Gunnar, we lived in a cellar.'

'A stinking cellar,' said May, grinning, too. It was hard to imagine with the sunset streaming into their dining room through the three big windows.

'We ate peelings and drank from puddles,' said Liddy, forking another slice of meat onto Broad's plate.

'We queued to shit in a hole,' said May.

Liddy winced. 'Don't say that.'

'I did it, didn't I? Why fuss over saying so?'

'It's the manner of expression I'm objecting to.' Liddy was getting to act like a proper lady and enjoying every moment. 'But yes, we did it. Why wouldn't we be happy now?' She pushed across the gravy jug. Broad had never guessed there was such a thing as a special kind of jug for gravy, let alone imagined he might own one.

He smiled, too. Made himself smile. ''Course. Why wouldn't we be happy now?' He scooped up a forkful of peas, even managed to get a few in his mouth before they all fell off.

'You're not much good with a fork,' said May.

Broad nudged his food around the plate with it. Just holding the damn thing made his hand hurt. Felt too delicate for his aching fingers. 'You reach an age it's hard to learn new ways, I reckon.'

'You're too young to be stuck in the past.'

'I don't know.' Broad frowned as he prodded at that slice of meat, a little blood seeping. 'The past has a way of holding on.'

An awkward pause at that. 'Tell us you're staying home tonight,' said Liddy.

'Wish I could. Got to head over to the diggings.'

'At this time?'

'Won't take long, I hope.' Broad set down his cutlery and stood. 'Got to make sure the work keeps going.'

'Lady Savine can't do without you, eh?'

May proudly puffed up her chest. 'Told me she relies on him more and more.'

'Well, tell her she has to share you with your family.'

Broad snorted as he came around the table. 'You bloody tell her.'

Liddy was still smiling as she tipped her face up, lips soft against his. She'd put weight on. They all had, since the lean times in Valbeck. She had that curve to her figure and that glow to her cheek she'd had when they first courted. That same smell she'd had when they first kissed. All that time passed, and he loved her just the same.

'Worked out all right,' she said, fingertips light on his cheek. 'Didn't it?'

'No thanks to me.' He had to talk around a lump in his throat. 'I'm sorry. For all the trouble I brought—'

'That's behind us,' said Liddy, firm. 'We work for a fine lady now. No trouble here.'

'No,' said Broad. 'No trouble.' And he trudged towards the door.

'Don't work too hard, Da!' called May. When he looked back, she was smiling at him, and that smile caught at something. Like there was a hook in his chest and whatever she did tugged at it. He smiled back. Raised an awkward hand in farewell. Then he saw the tattoo on the back and jerked it down. Worked it into the cuff of his fine new jacket.

He made sure he shut the door firmly behind him.

Broad strode through a forest of flaking iron columns, across the darkened warehouse floor towards an island of lamplight, footfalls echoing in all that inky emptiness.

Halder stood with his arms folded and his face in shadow. He was one of those men who liked his silence. Bannerman leaned against a pillar near him, that cocky tilt to his hips. He was one of those men who always had too much to say.

Their guest sat in one of three battered old chairs, hands tied to the back, ankles to the legs. Broad stopped in front of him, frowning down. 'You're Gaunt?'

'I'm Gaunt.' Didn't try to deny it, at least. Sometimes they did. Broad didn't blame them.

'Funny name for him,' said Bannerman, looking at Gaunt like he was naught but a lump of clay. ''Cause he's quite sturdy, really. Wouldn't call him fat. But I wouldn't call him gaunt.'

'Have some respect, eh?' said Broad as he took his jacket off. 'We can do this without being disrespectful.'

'What difference does it make?'

Broad draped the jacket over the back of a chair and stroked the fine cloth flat with the side of his hand. 'Makes some to me.'

'We're not here to make friends.'

'I know why we're here.' Broad met Bannerman's eye, and held it till he licked his lips and looked away. Then he shifted the chair around so it faced Gaunt and sat. He pushed his lenses up his nose, then clasped his hands. He found it helped to have a routine. Like when he swept the brewery in Valbeck. Just a job to get done, like any other.

Gaunt watched him all the while. Scared eyes, of course. Sweat on his forehead. Determined, though. Tough man to break, most likely. But anything breaks if you squeeze it hard enough.

'My name's Broad.' He saw Gaunt looking at the tattoo on the back of his hand. He let it hang there. 'Used to be in the army.'

'We all did,' said Bannerman.

'You know who we work for now?'

Gaunt swallowed. 'For Kort?'

'No.'

Gaunt swallowed again, harder. 'For Savine dan Glokta.'

'That's right. We hear you've been organising, Master Gaunt. We hear you've persuaded the workers to down tools.'

Bannerman made a disapproving *tut, tut, tut* noise with his tongue.

'Way things are in the diggings,' said Gaunt, 'the hours they work and the pay they get, they didn't need much persuading.'

Broad nudged his lenses down to rub at the sore bridge of his nose, then nudged them back up. 'Look. You seem a decent man so I'm giving you every chance I can. But Lady Savine wants her canal finished. She's paid for it. And I can tell you for a fact . . . it's a bad idea to get between her and what she's paid for. A *bad* idea.'

Gaunt leaned forward. Far as he could tied to the chair. 'A lad died the other day. Crushed by a beam. Fourteen years old.' He strained around to glance up at Bannerman. 'You know that?'

'I heard,' said Bannerman, and from the way he was looking at his nails, hadn't cared a shit.

'It's a damn shame.' Broad snapped his aching fingers to bring Gaunt's eyes back to him. 'The question is, how's *you* getting crushed going to help him?'

Gaunt stuck his chin up, still defiant. Broad liked him. They could've been on the same side. He supposed they had been, not that long ago. 'I can help the others. The likes of you wouldn't understand.'

'I might surprise you. I was in Valbeck, brother, with the Breakers. Fought the good fight there. Thought I did, anyway. Before that, I was in Styria. Thought I fought the good fight there, too. Been fighting good fights all my life. You know what it's got me?'

'Nothing?' said Bannerman.

Broad frowned up at him. 'You love to spoil the punchline, don't you?'

'You need some new material.'

'Daresay you're right. Trouble with the good fight, I find . . . once the fight starts, the good stops.' Broad began rolling up his sleeves while he thought about what to say. Slowly. Carefully. Helped to have a routine. He told himself this was for May, and for Liddy. Wondered what they'd say if they knew about it and didn't like the answer. That's why they couldn't know. Not ever.

'I've killed . . . I think . . . maybe fifty men. Maybe more. Prisoners, some of 'em. Just following orders, but . . . I did it, still. Kept a count at first, then I tried to lose count, but, well . . .' Broad looked down at the little patch of ground between Gaunt's boots. 'I'll be honest, I was drunk for a lot of it. Drunk as I could get. Bit of a blur. I remember this one fellow, in the wars. Styrian, I guess, kept gabbling at me, and I hadn't a clue what he was saying. I threw him off the wall. Wall of Musselia this was so, what, thirty strides high?' He glanced up at Halder. 'You were at Musselia, weren't you?'

Halder nodded. 'Closer to twenty.'

'High enough, anyway. He hit this cart.' Broad stuck his hand into his ribs, trying to show where. 'And it folded him right in half, sideways. Left him in a shape no living man should ever be. I mean, his feet were pointing backwards. He started making this noise.' Broad slowly shook his head. 'I swear, it was the noise hell makes. And he wouldn't stop. You see some shit out there. Changes the way you look at things.'

'It does,' said Halder.

Gaunt was staring at him. 'You think that's something to boast of?'

'Boast of?' Broad stared back, over the rims of his lenses, so Gaunt was just a sparkly blur in the lamplight. 'Fuck, no. I wake up with the sweats. I cry, sometimes. In the quiet times. Don't mind admitting it.'

'Me, too,' said Halder.

'I'm just . . . trying to get you to *see*.' And Broad nudged his lenses back up his nose, back into that little groove. 'To see where this is going before we get there and find out . . . we really didn't want to get there.' He winced. That'd come out all wrong. Wished he was better with words, but, being honest, words alone rarely got this kind of job done. Malmer had been a good talker. Look where he'd ended up. 'What I'm trying to say—'

'Master Broad?'

He turned, surprised. There was a single light burning in the office, built up on columns at the back of the warehouse. A figure stood by the steps leading up to it. A woman's figure, tall and slight and graceful.

Broad felt an ugly twist of fear in the pit of his stomach. Small women troubled him a lot more than big men these days.

'Just . . . hold on,' he said as he stood.

'He's not going anywhere.' And Bannerman patted Gaunt on the side of his face and made him flinch.

'Respect.' Broad strode across the warehouse floor, footsteps echoing. 'Not like it costs anything.'

It was Zuri. She looked worried, and that made him worried. She was about as hard to rattle as anyone Broad had ever met.

'What's wrong?' he asked.

She nodded up the steps towards the office. 'Lady Savine is here.'

'She's here now?'

'She wants to watch you work.' That sat there for a moment, between them, in the darkness. Doing it was one thing. He could tell himself he had to. Choosing to watch it was another. 'Perhaps you could . . . persuade her not to?'

Broad winced. 'If I could persuade people just by talking I wouldn't have to persuade 'em the other way.'

'My scripture teacher used to say that those who strive and fail are as blessed as those who succeed.'

'That ain't been my experience.'

'Trying cannot hurt.'

'That ain't been my experience, either,' muttered Broad, following her up the steps.

From the door, Savine looked her usual, perfectly controlled self. Close up in the lamplight, he could tell something was wrong. There was a sore pinkness around the rims of her nostrils, an eager brightness to her eyes, a strand of hair stray from her wig. Then he spotted the streak of faint stains on her jacket, as shocking as no clothes at all might've been on someone else.

'Lady Savine,' he said. 'Sure you want to be here for this?'

'Your concern is ever so sweet, but I have a strong stomach.'

'I don't doubt it. I'm not thinking o' you.' He dropped his voice. 'Truth is, you bring out the worst in me.'

'Your problem, Master Broad, is you confuse your best with your worst. I need work to continue on the canal first thing tomorrow. *First* thing. I need it open and making me *money*.' She snarled the last word, teeth bared, her fury setting his heart thumping. She was a head shorter than him. He'd have been shocked if she was half his weight. But she still scared him. Not because of what she might do. Because of what she might get him to do. 'Now make it happen, there's a darling.'

Broad glanced over at Zuri, her black eyes gleaming in the darkness. 'We all are fingers on God's hand,' she murmured, with a sorry shrug.

He looked down at his own hand, knuckles aching as he slowly curled it into a fist. 'If you say so.'

Broad strode back across the warehouse floor, footsteps echoing, towards that pool of light. He told himself he was trying to look eager. To act the part. But he'd never been much of an actor. The truth was he couldn't wait to get there.

Gaunt saw something in Broad's eye, maybe. He twisted in his chair, like he could twist away from what was coming. But neither of them could. 'Now wait a—'

Broad's tattooed fist thudded into his ribs. The chair rocked back and Bannerman caught it, shoved it forward again. Broad's other fist sank into Gaunt's other side and twisted him, eyes bulging. He stayed like that, quivering, face turning purple, for a moment. He got one little wheezing breath in before he puked.

It spattered in his lap, spattered the warehouse floor, and Bannerman stepped back, frowning down at his shiny new boots. 'Oh, we got a gusher.'

Took an effort, not to keep punching. Took an effort, for Broad to keep some kind of grip on himself and speak. When he did, it was strange how calm his voice sounded. 'Time's up on the civilised approach. Bring him out.'

Halder came from the darkness, dragging someone with him. A young lad, roped up, gurgling into a gag.

'No,' croaked Gaunt as Halder shoved the lad down and Bannerman started tying him to a chair. 'No, no,' a string of drool still hanging from the corner of his mouth.

'A man can take a lot, when he thinks he's fighting the good fight. I know that.' Broad rubbed gently at his knuckles. 'But seeing it done to your child? That's something else.'

The lad stared around, tears tracking his face. Broad wished he could have a drink. He could almost taste it, on his tongue. A drink made everything easier. Easier at the time, anyway. Harder afterwards. He pushed the thought away.

'Doubt I'll be boasting 'bout this, either.' Broad checked his sleeves were rolled up right. That seemed important, for some reason. 'But when you toss it into all the other shit I done, it hardly even shifts the level.'

He glanced up towards the office. Maybe he'd been hoping Savine would be waving at him to stop. But there was no one there. Just the light, to say she was watching. A man has to be able to stop himself. Broad had never been any good at that. He turned back.

'I'd like to get home.'

He took his lenses off, tucked them into his shirt pocket and the lamplit faces all turned to smudges.

'But we've got all night if we need it.'

The lad's fear, and Gaunt's horror, and Bannerman's carelessness, made muddy blurs Broad could hardly tell one from another.

'I need you to imagine . . . the state you two will be in by then.'

The lad's chair squealed on the warehouse floor as Broad shifted it to just the spot he wanted it.

'Daresay you'll both be making that noise soon.'

Tweaked his sleeves one more time. Routine, routine, routine.

'The one hell makes.'

Broad knew how he'd have felt, if he'd been tied helpless in one chair and May in the other. That was why he was pretty sure it'd work.

'There'll be no strike!' gasped Gaunt. 'There'll be no strike!'

Broad straightened up, blinking. 'Oh, that's good news.' Didn't feel like good news. Deep down inside it felt like quite the disappointment. It was an effort, to make his fists unclench. An effort, to take the lenses from his shirt pocket, hook them back over his ears. Too delicate for his aching fingers. 'Your son'll stay with us, though, just to make sure you don't have a change of heart.'

The lad wriggled as Bannerman dragged him back across the warehouse floor into the darkness.

'Respect!' called Broad, carefully rolling his sleeves down.

Important to have a routine.

The Art of Compromise

'**P**recision, you dolts!' Filio leaped from his bench to yell at the two swordsmen, their steels drooping as they gaped at him. 'Speed is nothing but faff and bluster without *precision*.'

He was in his late fifties, but quick and handsome still. Vick might've had more grey in her hair than he did. He dropped back beside her, muttering a few more Styrian curses under his breath before switching to common. 'Young men these days, eh? They expect the world served to them with golden cutlery!'

Vick glanced over at Tallow. He looked like he might never have seen cutlery, let alone been served with the golden kind. Even dressed smartly in Practicals' black, he reminded her of her brother. That apologetic hunching of the shoulders, as if he was always expecting a slap. 'Some have to handle hardship,' she said.

'A little hardship would do my nephew no harm.' Filio shook his head as he watched the swordsmen shuffle about the training circle, boards polished smooth by generations of soft fencing shoes. 'He has fast hands, good instincts, but so much to learn.' He groaned at a wayward lunge. 'I hope he might represent our city in the Contest in Adua one day, but talent is useless without *discipline*—' He leaped up again. 'Come on, you donkey, think about it!'

'You competed in the Contest yourself.'

Filio gave her a sly grin as he sank back down. 'Have you been checking up on me?'

'You lost to the future King Jezal in the semi-final. Took him to a last touch, as I recall.'

'You were there? You can't have been ten years old!'

'Eight.' A good liar sticks to the truth whenever possible. She had been eight when that bout took place, but she'd been huddled in the blackness of a stinking ship's hold, shackled to a great chain with her family and a few-score other convicts. All on their way to the prison camps of Angland, from which only she would return. She doubted that memory would've brought quite the same delight from Filio, though, his eyes shining at the memory of past glories. People are rarely made happy by *all* the truth.

'The cheering crowd, the scrape of steel, the Circle laid out before the grandest buildings of the Agriont. The proudest day of my life!' He was a man who admired the pomp and structure of the Union. A man who appreciated precision and discipline. That was why Vick had worn the full dress uniform of an Inquisitor Exempt, boots buffed to a mirror gleam, hair parted with a ruler and ruthlessly bound back. Filio waved towards the flashing blades. 'So, you are a devotee of the beautiful science?'

'Who isn't?' Though in fact she wasn't.

'And I suppose you have come to gather votes?'

'His Majesty is extremely keen that Westport remain where it belongs, in the Union.'

'Or His Eminence is?' murmured Filio, eyes never leaving the swordsmen as they jabbed and parried. 'And who else have you spoken to?'

'You are my first call.' He was the fourth, but in Vick's experience, you had to take care with the pride of moderately powerful men. They bruised much more easily than the truly mighty. 'Superior Lorsen spoke of you in glowing terms. A senior Alderman, well respected on all sides. Someone who could be a unifying voice.'

'I'm flattered, of course, but the Superior is too kind. If unity was simply a matter of the right voice ... Westport might not be so terribly disunited.'

'Perhaps we can help bring your city together. I know you believe in the Union.'

'I do! I have, all my life. My grandfather was one of those who brought us in to begin with.' Filio's smile faded. 'But there are difficulties. King Jezal was a known quantity but King Orso is young ...' Filio winced as his nephew gave a showy flourish of his steels. 'And has, by reputation, a surfeit of all the young man's faults. Your bungling in the wars against Styria was far from helpful. And then we have Solumeo Shudra!' Filio clicked his tongue. 'Have you heard him speak?'

'Briefly.'

'So *persuasive*. So *compelling*. So very ... what's that word ... *charismatic*. Loved as only politicians free from power – and therefore from disappointment – ever can be. He's brought a lot of people around to his way of seeing things. The Union side have no one in his class. All rather stodgy. But then it's difficult, isn't it, to make a passionate argument for what you already have? So boring. Whereas the delightful alternative? A bouquet of promises! A sackful of dreams! A glorious ship of fantasies, undamaged by collision with actually getting anything done.'

'So His Majesty can count on you to vote the right way?'

'I wish I could give you an uncompromising Union *yes*. But I fear, for now . . .' Filio scrunched up his face with distaste. 'I can only go so far as the traditional Styrian *perhaps*. Here in Westport, at the Crossroads of the World, balanced between the Gurkish and the Styrians and the Union, we have been obliged to make an art of compromise. I have not lasted so long in the politics of the city by sticking too closely to any one set of principles.'

'Principles are like clothes,' said Vick, straightening her jacket. 'You have to change them to suit the audience.'

'Precisely so. In due course, perhaps we can discuss my price for wearing one set of colours or the other? But it would be folly to pick a side too early. I might put myself on the losing one!'

Vick supposed she could hardly blame the man. If she'd learned one thing in the camps, after all, it was that you stand with the winners.

'Then we should talk again. As the future takes shape.' Vick stood, ignoring a sudden twinge through her bad hip, snapped her heels together and gave a stiff bow.

Filio looked rather pleased with it. But not pleased enough to promise his vote. 'I hope so. But let us not waste each other's time until we are sure of our arithmetic— Ah!' He sprang up as his nephew's heel scuffed the edge of the Circle. 'Watch your back foot, you fool! Precision!'

A rare breeze washed through Westport's public gardens, smelling of resin, flowers and spice from the market over the wall. It made a hundred varieties of foliage flap, rustle and whisper. It flung a cloud of spray from the fountain in which the bright spring sun made a short-lived rainbow. Then a shadow fell across Vick.

'Might I sit?' A broad-shouldered woman stood over her, dressed in loose linens in the southern fashion. Dark-skinned, strong-featured, with a fuzz of clipped grey-black hair.

'I'm afraid I don't speak Styrian,' said Vick, in common. Half a lie. She could make herself understood but might not catch every nuance, and in negotiations as delicate as these, she couldn't risk a mistake. That, and she preferred to be underestimated.

The woman sighed. 'How typical of the Union authorities to send a negotiator who cannot even speak the language.'

'I thought this was the Crossroads of the World, where all tongues are spoken. You must be Dayep Mozolia.'

'And you must be Victarine dan Teufel.'

'I have that misfortune.' Vick had reckoned the aristocratic overtones of her full name, however awkwardly it fit her now, would suit this meeting best. Mozolia was said to be a hard-headed woman of business, so Vick had chosen to present herself as a practical Aduan lady on a trip abroad. Hair neatly braided, coiled and pinned. Top button left undone, for a hint of relaxed approachability. It had been a while since she wore a skirt, and she felt no more comfortable in it than she did in her name. But then, feeling comfortable is a luxury spies are better off without.

'How do you like the public gardens?' asked Mozolia.

'Beautiful. If a little thirsty.'

'They were a gift to the city from a childless heiress to a vast merchant fortune.' Mozolia took her time arranging her long body on the bench. 'She travelled the Circle of the World hoping to gather one of every kind of tree that God has made.' She waved towards a towering fur, its lower branches entirely bare, its upper ones still clinging to a few dry needles. 'Sadly, not everything flourishes in our climate.' And she glanced at Tallow, wilting in servant's livery, blotchy face beaded with sweat.

It had been a bad idea to bring him. Vick knew she was better off alone. A lesson learned fresh in the camps with every family member gone in the frozen ground. Her father, shivering, lips turned blue, shortened fingers turned black. Her mother, always asking what she'd done to deserve this, as though deserve had anything to do with it. All the sweat and pain it had taken to get that medicine for her sister. Turning up with the bottle gripped tight to find her stiff and cold under the threadbare blankets, her brother still holding her hand. Only the two of them left. Vick and her brother. His big, sad eyes, just like Tallow's.

You'll never hold up someone who can't swim for themselves. In the end, they'll drag you down with them.

Mozolia sighed, stretching one arm across the back of the bench. 'But I daresay you have not crossed the Circle Sea to discuss trees.'

'No. To discuss the forthcoming vote.'

'People here talk of little else. A momentous decision. But not one that you and I can take any part in. Women cannot be Aldermen, after all.'

Vick snorted. 'Women might not sit in the Assembly, but they can still control the men who do. You have at least five votes in your pocket.'

Mozolia shrugged her heavy shoulders. 'Six. Possibly seven.'

'I wonder if you might be persuaded to cast them for the Union.'

'I might be. But not easily. I had one grandparent from Yashtavit, one from Sikkur, a third from Ospria and a fourth from the Old Empire. I am welcome, or perhaps equally unwelcome, at five different temples in the city. I sometimes forget which version of God I am supposed to be praying to. In other nations I would be called a mongrel. In this mongrel city I am the norm.' She smiled out at the yellow lawns, where people of every shape and colour walked, sat, chatted in the shade of every strange and wonderful tree God had made. 'A merchant in fabrics cannot afford to take a narrow view. My business stretches across the Circle of the World. Suljuk silks and Gurkish linens, Imperial cottons and woollens from the North.'

'Not to mention all those fine new textiles spooling from the mills of the Union.'

'Not to mention those.'

'It would be a shame, for a merchant in fabrics to be cut off from the largest market in the world.'

'There would be frustrations, of course, but, like water, commerce always works through the cracks in time. And becoming a part of Styria would offer its own opportunities.'

'I understand the Serpent of Talins can be a domineering mistress.'

Mozolia's turn to snort. 'As several Union generals have discovered to their cost. But when people are willing to compromise, she can be reasonable. Look how the citizens of Talins have prospered under her rule! And I rather like the idea of a woman in charge, don't you? Even a domineering one. We women really should do everything we can to work together.'

'Or should we do exactly what the men do, and put sentiment to the side, and follow the greatest profit?'

Mozolia smiled, ever so slightly. 'Fancy that. You speak Styrian after all. I hope His Eminence sent an unsentimental sum of money along with you.'

'Something better.' Vick flicked open the letter and held it out between two fingers. The signature of Arch Lector Glokta lurked at the bottom, the lethal punchline. 'Trade rights once controlled by the Guild of Mercers, managed by His Majesty's Inquisition for these last thirty years. His Eminence is prepared to cut you in, quite handsomely.'

Mozolia took the letter and weighed every word. Vick didn't rush her. She closed her eyes and tipped her face towards the sun, breathed in the perfumed air. So rare, she had a moment to just sit.

'A nice, neat bribe.' Mozolia lowered the letter. 'Well judged.'

'I understand that here in Westport, you like to be honest about your corruption.'

'I take it all back, you are positively fluent.' Mozolia rocked her weight forward and stood, casting Vick into shadow again. 'I shall consider your offer.'

'Don't take too long. We women really should do everything we can to work together.'

Vick nudged the over-heavy drapes aside to peer into the street. The sun was setting on a largely wasted day, a muddy flare above the maze of mismatched rooftops, the thirsty treetops, the puffing chimneys, the spires of a hundred temples to a dozen versions of the Almighty. She wondered if it helped, to believe in God. Whether it was reassuring or terrifying, to look at all this shit and know for sure it was part of some grand plan.

Vick pressed her thumb into her aching hip as she watched the candles being lit at some Thondish shrine, the lights twinkling in the windows, the bobbing torches of guides who led foreigners to Westport's best hostelries, best eateries, best back-alley muggings. The low murmur of voices passed the door, a coquettish giggle tinkling off down the hallway.

Tallow frowned around the room. It was an idiot's idea of how a palace might be decorated, all velvet and peeling gilt. 'What kind of arsehole arranges to meet in a brothel?'

'One who likes whores and making people uncomfortable,' said Vick. Sanders Rosimiche, by all accounts, loved both. A strutting loudmouth, but one who'd voiced support for the Union in the past, and a vote was a vote. People often say that bullies should be stood up to, but Vick usually found it more productive to let them bully her. That was why she'd made a rare visit to a dressmaker, in the hope of looking as feminine and yielding as possible. Hair down and combed with oil in the Westport style. She'd even worn perfume, Fates help her. The one thing she'd refused was high shoes. In her line of work, you never knew when you might have to run for your life. Or kick someone in the face.

'Fuck these things,' she grunted, hooking a finger into her corset and trying vainly to wriggle into a comfortable position. Despite being made to measure, it fit her incredibly badly. Or perhaps it was cut to fit the woman people would like her to be, not the one she was.

She wondered what Sibalt would've said if he'd seen her dressed like this. *I wish I'd met you sooner*, maybe. *Things might have been different.* And she'd have said, *You didn't and they're not.* And he'd have given that weary smile of his and said, *You're a hard case, Vick*, and he'd have been right. She caught herself missing him at the oddest times. Missing the warmth of him, the weight of him in her arms, the weight of his arms around her. Missing having someone she could touch.

But Sibalt cut his own throat when she betrayed him. Thinking about what he might've done was a waste of time.

She let the drapes fall and turned back into the room, caught Tallow frowning at her, as if at a puzzle he couldn't quite find the answer to.

'Do you have to keep staring?' she snapped.

'Sorry.' And he shrank back like a puppy got a kick. 'It's just, you look...'

'Absurd?'

'Different, I guess—'

'Don't forget it's the same woman underneath. The one who's got your sister for a hostage.'

'Not likely to forget that, am I?' he snapped, a hint of sullen, useless anger showing. Even that reminded her of her brother. The look he used to have when he told her they had to help people, and she told him they had to help themselves. That wounded righteousness. 'Why are you even here?'

'You know why. The Union's weak. Enemies everywhere. If we can't hold on to what we already have—'

'I'm asking why you care a shit. Sent you to the camps, didn't they? If I was you, I'd laugh while the Union sunk in the fucking sea. Why are *you* here?'

Her mouth twisted to spit the answer. Because she owed a debt to His Eminence. Because blackmail and betrayal was the only profession she'd ever excelled at. Because you stand with the winners. She had half a dozen answers to hand. It was just that none of them were any good. Truth was, she could have done anything. Run off to the Far Country like she and Sibalt had always joked about. But the moment His Eminence said, 'Westport,' she'd started packing. She was still standing there, mouth half-open but nothing quite coming out, when the door swung wide and Rosimiche strode in.

He hadn't made quite the effort that she had. He wore a dressing gown left carelessly open to the waist and apparently nothing else, a slice of hairy belly and chest on display.

'Sorry to keep you waiting,' he blustered, not sounding sorry at all.

She forced out a smile. 'No need to apologise. I know you are a busy man.'

'You're right. I was busy fucking.'

Keeping that smile was an effort. 'Congratulations.'

'I would like to get back to it, so let us be brief. Westport will be joining Styria. We share a coastline and a culture. One cannot argue with geography *and* history. I intend no disrespect.' A phrase people only use when they intend as much as possible.

'Disrespect doesn't bother me,' she said, giving her voice the slightest edge. 'But it might bother the Arch Lector.'

'There was a time when men would soil themselves at the mere mention of the Cripple.' Rosimiche sneered over at her as he poured himself a glass of wine. 'But the Serpent of Talins is the power in Styria now. Murcatto has bound Styria together while the Union splits at the seams. Nobility and government at each other's throats. And these Breakers...'

Disrespect didn't bother her. But that he'd rub her face in it with his brothel and his dressing gown, knowing who she worked for? That was a concern. Seemed he was convinced the Styrian faction would win. Was trying to win their favour by humiliating the Union's representative.

'One cannot have great growth without a little pain,' said Vick. 'The Union's industry is the envy of the world. Westport would be cutting herself off from her rightful place in the future. I've already spoken to several like-minded—'

'That bitch Mozolia? Ha! I hear Shudra already brought her back to his side. Better bribes than yours, I daresay. That's the thing about women, they think with their cunts. Anything that doesn't involve a cunt, they should have no opinion on. Fucking and babies, that's all.'

'Don't leave out the monthly bleed,' said Vick. 'It's a more versatile organ than men give it credit for.' She rarely allowed herself the luxury of disliking a person, any more than liking one. Either could be a weakness. But this bastard was testing her patience.

Rosimiche bristled, annoyed his ham-fisted coarseness hadn't thrown her. He swaggered over, puffed up with scorn. 'I hear Murcatto is sending Casamir dan Shenkt to the city.'

'I don't jump at shadows. Perhaps I'll panic when he gets here.'

'He may already have arrived.' He leaned close, so she could see the tiny specks of sweat on the bridge of his nose. 'They say he not only kills those he is sent for, but *eats* them.' Damn, she regretted the dress now. She was starting to wish she'd worn a full suit of armour. 'I wonder what he would eat first? Your liver, maybe?' He leered over at Tallow. 'Perhaps he would start by butchering your errand boy?'

And suddenly, all she could think of was the look on her brother's face, so hurt and so surprised, when the Practicals stepped from the shadows.

Rosimiche gave a little hoot of shock as Vick's fist smashed into his face. She'd had her brass knuckles hidden behind her, but they were on her fist now. He clutched at the curtains as he stumbled back, blood flooding from his broken nose. She punched him in the side of the jaw with a sick crunch and he fumbled his glass, spraying wine over both of them. Her knuckles caught him across the top of the head as he fell, tearing the curtains down with him.

He hunched in a ball, gasping and spluttering, and she put her knee on his shoulder and rained down punches on any part of him she could reach. She lost count of the blows.

Someone caught her arm, nearly dragged her over. Tallow, wrestling her back. 'You'll fucking kill him!'

Vick tore free, breathing hard. Her dress was wine-stained. Her arm was blood-spotted. Her hair was tangled across her face and she dragged it back, oil between her fingers. It wasn't a style well suited to beating a man. Rosimiche whimpered, still curled in a ball.

Tallow stared at him with those big, sad eyes. 'What d'you do that for?'

She hadn't even thought about it. Hadn't weighed the risks or the consequences. Hadn't even considered where to hit him, or how to make sure he couldn't hit back. If he'd been a tougher man, things could've gone very badly wrong.

'Before you brush off His Eminence, Master Rosimiche, you should consider what you owe.' Her voice was harsh now. Slum debt collector rather than city lady. She tossed the paper Glokta had given her onto the floor by his knees. 'Seven thousand scales and change to the Banking House of Valint and Balk. They don't take their friendship with the Union as lightly as you.' She nudged the paper towards him with one sensible boot and he cringed as it brushed his bare leg. 'His Eminence has arranged for them to call in the loan. They'll take your houses. They'll take your whores. Never mind Shenkt, *they'll* have your fucking liver before they're done.' Maybe some bullies need to be bullied, after all. She leaned down over him, hissing the words. 'You'll vote our way, you understand? Vote our way, or we crush you like a tick.'

'I'll vode your way,' he blubbered, holding a trembling hand over his head. The little finger was broken sideways. 'I'll vode your way...'

Vick stalked off up the darkened street in a manner not at all suitable for her wine-stained dress, the ache in her clenched fist settled to a cold throbbing, the ache in her stiff hip getting steadily worse. Old injuries. A lifetime of them.

Tallow hurried to catch her up. 'Guess you can't say he didn't ask for it.'
Silence.
'If you'd left it much longer, I might've punched him myself.'
Silence.
'I mean, he might not have noticed, but I would've punched him, still.'
'It was a mistake,' growled Vick. 'You can't change the fact the world's full of arseholes. You can only change how you deal with them.'

He gave her a weak grin. 'So you're not carved from wood after all.'
She winced as she worked her sore fingers. 'For damn sure my hand isn't.'

'Could be worse. Now folk here'll know what I've never doubted.' He gave her a stronger grin. 'That you're the wrong woman to mess with.'

She kept her face hard. It never ended well for the people she smiled at. 'Truth is we're making no progress. Two weeks left and we've lost more votes than we've gained. Solumeo bloody Shudra's too good at this.' She rubbed absently at her bruised knuckles. 'We have to take him off the board.'

'Aye, but . . .' Tallow leaned close to whisper. 'You *kill* him, everyone'll turn against us. Lorsen said so.'

'Whatever it costs,' said Vick. 'That's what His Eminence told me.'

Tallow had that worried look again. 'Easy to say for him who won't be paying.'

Some Things Never Heal

'I'm going to crush you like a tick,' growled Leo, snapping out a jab and forcing Jurand to parry. Just the sound of blades ringing made him feel better. By the dead, he'd missed the feeling of a sword in his hand.

'Like you crushed Stour Nightfall?' Jurand jabbed back and steel scraped again.

'That's right.' Leo darted forward, almost cried out at a horribly familiar twinge in his wounded thigh, had to check and pretend it had been a feint, the disappointment almost sharper than the pain.

Jurand came on, grinning. 'So you'll bleed half to death, plainly be the worse fighter and only win because I'm an arrogant fool?'

Antaup, Glaward and Jin all chuckled, of course. Leo didn't. The more time passed, the less he liked the way his friends told the tale. He preferred the more flattering story he'd read in a printed pamphlet the other day, where the peerless Young Lion had outfought Stour Nightfall, cracked a couple of jokes, then made him eat dirt in front of his uncle, all over the honour of a beautiful sorceress. In that version, there'd been no mention of his not being able to walk properly ever since.

After actual fighting, sparring had always been Leo's favourite thing in the world. He tried to find the eager smile he used to wear when he was doing it. Like a cat playing with a mouse. Maybe he wasn't as good with a sword as Stour Nightfall, but he'd always been a damn sight better than Jurand. He meant to prove it, however much it hurt.

'Ha!' He snapped Jurand's blade one way then the other with a pair of fierce cuts. That was more like it! He lined up a lunge that would hurt even with a blunted blade, then gasped as his weight went onto his bad leg and it nearly folded under him.

It was shamefully easy for Jurand to step around his feeble thrust and slash at his exposed side. Leo twisted to parry, all off balance, gave a girlish scream as pain stabbed through his thigh, then his knee buckled and he went sprawling on the rush matting, clutching at his leg.

'Bloody hell! You all right?'

'No!' snarled Leo, slapping Jurand's hand away. 'The leg's fucking worse than ever!' He was sick of pain. He was sick of sympathy. He was sick of being angry. He was sick of saying sorry for being angry. Then he saw the hurt on Jurand's face and struggled to get a grip on himself. 'I'm sorry. Always thought I could laugh off pain. But it's all the time. I wake up with it. I go to sleep with it. Getting across a room is a struggle. Leaving something upstairs is a bloody disaster.'

'Let me help.' Glaward reached for him like a father for a crying toddler.

'Get your paws off me!' snapped Leo. 'I'm not a bloody cripple!'

Jin and Antaup exchanged a worried glance. Nothing says, 'I'm crippled,' louder than the furious insistence that you're not, after all.

Leo caught Glaward's big hand before he took it away and dragged himself up, hopping on his good leg. He stood a moment, breathing hard, then gritted his teeth and accepted the inevitable.

'Bring me the cane,' he snapped at Jurand.

'You know what'd make you feel better?' Glaward gave Leo's shoulders a crushing squeeze which made him feel a good deal worse. 'Getting back in the saddle.'

'That's where you belong.' Antaup shook a fist. 'Leading the men!'

'You need a battle to lead them into,' grumbled Leo. 'Or should I lead them round and round the Lord Governor's residence?'

'There's always fighting in Starikland,' said Glaward. 'Rebels are giving Lord Governor Skald a hell of a time lately. Daresay he'd be glad of the help.'

'And people hate the Styrians more than ever,' said Antaup. 'I hear Westport's a real powder keg. One spark and... poof.' He grinned as he mimed an explosion. 'And the women over there...' He grinned wider as he mimed a bigger one.

Whitewater Jin combed worriedly at his ever-thickening beard. 'Can't say I fancy fighting the Serpent of Talins. She beat King Jezal three times and the bitch is stronger'n ever.'

'Hardly took Stolicus himself to beat King Jezal,' snapped Leo. But the man had a point. The history of reckless charges into Styria was not good.

Glaward pushed out his bottom lip. 'If it's a weak enemy you're after, I hear the Gurkish are obliging. The Empire's broken into splinters. No Prophet. Priests and princes and chiefs and governors all fighting each other for control.'

'Like the North in the bad old days,' said Jin.

The Dogman's stirring stories had all happened in the North in the bad old days. That was when names like Bethod, and Black Dow, and the Bloody-Nine were made. Names to stir the blood. 'Is that so?' muttered Leo, clenching his fists.

Antaup's brows were very high. 'The Union's got every claim on Dagoska.'

Leo raised his to match. 'That city should be ours.'

The four of them glanced at each other, teetering between joking and serious.

'Can't deny the weather's good down there.' Jin patted Leo's face with one big paw. 'Get some colour back in those cheeks!'

Leo shoved the Northman's hand away, but the idea had hold of him. Just the thought of being back on campaign was making his leg hurt less. Reclaiming Dagoska for the Union? Imagine the pamphlets they'd print of *that* story! They'd have to give him another triumph, and with a better reward than some gaudy sword this time around. 'Jurand, how would we get soldiers down there, do you think . . .'

He was somewhat put out to find his oldest friend staring at him, horrified. 'Tell me you're joking.'

'What?'

Jurand glared at the others and, like mischievous schoolboys caught out by the headmaster, one by one they were forced into sheepish submission. 'He hasn't even healed from the last duel to the death and you're falling over yourselves to talk him into another?'

'You sound like my bloody mother,' snapped Leo.

'Someone has to. It was bad enough when you were just the Young Lion. You're the Lord Governor of Angland now! You have a province full of people counting on you. You can't go charging off to any fight that'll have you because you're fucking *bored*!'

Leo stood a moment, teeth bared, ready to fight. Then he sagged. He couldn't stay angry with Jurand for longer than a breath or two. 'You're right, you bastard.'

'He's always right,' said Glaward, sadly.

'He is the clever one,' said Antaup, flicking back his dark forelock.

'Sanity prevails.' Jurand slapped the cane into Leo's hand and strode off, shaking his head.

'Shame, though,' muttered Jin.

'Aye,' said Leo. 'Shame.'

*

'We have received a letter from His Majesty—'

'From his Closed Council, you mean,' grumbled Lord Mustred.

'Or from Old Sticks and his cronies,' grumbled Lord Clensher. They were quite the pair of old grumblers, those two. They could've won grumbling contests. Which was pretty much what these meetings came down to.

Leo's mother cleared her throat. 'They ask us to raise an extra hundred thousand marks in taxes—'

'Again?' Leo's voice went shrill with dismay, while the worthies around the table shook their grey heads. The ones who weren't entirely bald, at least. They shook bald heads.

'They say since we have peace in the North revenues should rise, and Angland will not need so large an army—'

'We have peace *because* we have an army!' Leo tried to leap up, winced at a stab through his leg and had to sink back, clenching his teeth, clenching his fists, clenching everything. 'What about the cost of the war – are they paying that, at least?'

Leo's mother cleared her throat again. 'They . . . do not mention it.'

'Are we the king's subjects or his bloody livestock?' snapped Mustred. 'This is unacceptable!'

'Disgraceful!' growled Clensher.

'Outrageous!'

'What the *shit*?' Leo smashed at the table with a fist and made the papers and most of the old men jump. 'The bloody arrogance of the bastards! In war, all they sent were good wishes and in peace all they send are demands! I swear they'd ask for my fruits in a bag if they thought they could get a good price for the damn things!'

'My lords.' Leo's mother turned smiling to the room. 'Do you suppose you could give us the chamber for a moment?'

With tired voices and tired legs, the old lords of Angland shuffled to the door. They could hardly have looked more tired than Leo felt. As Lord Governor he was buried in responsibilities. If he didn't spend four hours a day at his desk, he'd drown in paperwork. He hardly knew how his mother had done it. No small part of him wished she was *still* doing it.

'We support you, Lord Brock.' Mustred's moustaches vibrated with loyalty as he paused in the doorway.

'We support you *whatever*.' Clensher's jowls trembled as he nodded agreement. '*Damn* those bastards on the Closed Council!' And he pulled the doors shut.

The gloomy room was silent for a moment as Leo's anger drained away and he worked up the courage to look at his mother. To see that slightly disappointed, slightly exasperated, slightly resigned look she'd been perfecting ever since he could remember.

'Another bloody lecture?'

'Just an entreaty, Leo.' She took his hand, squeezed it in hers. 'I share your annoyance, really I do, but you're Lord Governor now. You have to be patient.'

'How can I?' He couldn't bear to sit a moment longer. He twisted his hand free and struggled up, half-hopped to the narrow windows and wrestled one open, desperate to feel fresh air on his face. He looked out across the rain-shiny roofs of Ostenhorm towards the grey sea, rubbing at his sore leg. 'Are you sure I'm cut out for this? Managing petty complaints? I'm happier at war than at peace.'

'Your father was just the same. But being Lord Governor is about managing the peace. The Closed Council know Nightfall respects you—'

'The Great Wolf only respects the boot across his neck! To disarm us? How can they be so *blind*? It's not half a year since we were fighting for our lives, without a shred of help from those bastards!'

'I know. But if you're furious whenever the Closed Council does something infuriating, you'll be furious all the time. Rare anger can be inspiring. Frequent anger becomes contemptible.'

Leo took a breath. Forced his shoulders down. By the dead, he was always angry these days. 'You're right. I know you're right.' The wind was chill outside. He dragged the window closed, gripped his thigh and took a few hobbling steps back to his chair – his prison – and dropped down into it.

'Perhaps you should stop training,' she said softly. 'Rest the leg—'

'I did rest it, and it hurt more. So I trained, and it got worse. So I rested it again, and that didn't help. Nothing bloody helps! I'm trapped by the fucking thing!'

'A change of scene might do you good. We've been invited to Lord Isher's wedding. A trip to Adua would present many opportunities.'

'To kiss the king's arse?'

'To make your case to him. You said he was a reasonable man.'

Leo scowled. He hated when his mother talked sense. It made it damn difficult to fight with her without talking nonsense himself. She and Jurand had him in a relentless bloody pincer movement of rationality. 'I suppose so,' he grumbled.

'Then reason with him. Build some friendships on the Open Council.

43

Make some allies among the Closed. Use their rivalries to your advantage. You can be charming, Leo, when you want to be. Charm them.'

He couldn't help smiling. 'Could you just for once be wrong, Mother?'

'I've tried it a couple of times. It really didn't suit me.'

'By the dead, it stinks,' said Leo, face crushed up with pain and disgust as the bandages peeled sticky from his thigh.

'An odour is entirely natural, Your Grace.' The surgeon nudged his eye-lenses back up his nose with his wrist. You'd have thought a man who had to wear lenses but use his hands would at least find a pair that weren't constantly sliding down his nose, but in this, as in so much else, it seemed Leo would be disappointed. 'Some corruption has found its way into the wound.'

'Corruption? How?'

'Some injuries simply become corrupt.'

'Like everything bloody else,' hissed Leo as the man probed at the wound with his thumbs and made it weep a thick yellow tear. It looked like a red eye, lids stubbornly pressed shut in a refusal to see the truth.

'I've seen men make complete recoveries from the most terrible injuries,' mused the surgeon, as if they were discussing a scientific curiosity rather than Leo's life. 'But I've seen men die from a thorn-prick.'

'Very reassuring.'

'How long ago was it inflicted?'

'Five months?' grunted Leo through gritted teeth. 'No, six—ah!'

'And from a sword?'

'The same time and the same sword as these others.' Leo waved at the scar on his face, faded to a pale line. The one on his side. The one on his shoulder. 'But they all healed. This one . . . seems to be getting worse.'

'We'll have to drain it. That should ease the pain.'

'Whatever you have to do,' whispered Leo, wiping the tears from his cheek on the back of his arm.

'You're sure you wouldn't like husk for the—'

'No!' Leo remembered his father, at the end, raving and drooling. 'No. I need . . . to stay sharp.' Though what for? So he could watch his friends train from a chair? Sit through endless meetings about tax? He should take husk for the pain of that rubbish.

The surgeon offered a strip of leather to bite on. 'You might want to look away, Your Grace.'

'I think I will.' Flashing steel used to delight him. Now the glint of the sun on the tiny blade was making him feel faint.

He was the Young Lion! No man braver! Riding into a line of spears had been nothing. Now even the idea of moving the leg, touching the leg, using the leg, made him cringe. It was his first thought before he did anything – how much would it hurt? You would've thought the more pain you suffered, the more you'd get used to it, but it was the other way around. Hour after hour, day after day, it wore down your patience until everything was unbearable.

So rather than suffer in heroic silence, he trembled and whimpered his way through it, sobbing at every touch of the blade. At even the expectation of a touch. When it was over, he peeled the wad of leather from his teeth, strings of spit hanging off it. 'I swear it hurts more than when I took the wound in the first place.'

'Pain dulls in the excitement of combat.' The surgeon wiped Leo's thigh then wrinkled his nose at the cloth. 'The chronic is, in the end, far harder to stand than the acute.'

Leo lay back, limp as a wrung-out rag. 'When will it heal?'

'Perhaps weeks. Perhaps months.'

'Months?' He made a fist as though he might punch his own leg, but quickly thought better of it.

'But you should be aware...' The surgeon frowned as he dried his hands. 'Some things never heal.'

'It could be like this for ever?'

'It is a possibility.'

Leo turned his head away towards the window. Watched the grey rooftops and the grey sea through the distorting little rain-flecked panes. Would he be a cripple? Like that bastard Glokta, imprisoned behind his desk, burrowing among his papers like a maggot in filth?

Tears made his sight swim. He wished Rikke was with him. She would've turned it into a joke, played the fool, made him... feel *good*. It was a long time since he'd felt good.

'All done for now.' And the surgeon began to wind a fresh bandage around Leo's thigh, hiding that puckered red eye.

He'd dreamed of leading armies and winning great victories, just like in the stories. He'd dreamed of fighting in the Circle and being reckoned a great warrior, just like in the songs. He'd dreamed of stepping from his mother's shadow into the sunlight of renown and being cheered as Lord Governor of Angland. He'd done it all.

And look where it had left him.

That's the trouble with songs. They tend to stop before it all turns to shit.

With the Wind

D ownside frowned towards the burned-out shells of hovels and houses. Couple of chimney stacks still stood, couple of charred beams poked at the pink morning sky. He cleared his throat, worked the results around his mouth like he was tasting ale, then spat 'em out. He loved a good spit, did Downside. Might've been his favourite pastime. After killing folk.

'Just like the village I came from, this,' he said.

'Aye,' said Clover, 'well. Villages all look much the same when they're burned.'

'You say that like you've seen a few.'

'There was a time back in the wars...' Clover thought about it and gave a sorry grunt '...'fore you lot were born, I daresay, when burned villages were a more common sight in the North than unburned ones. I'd hoped those days were behind us but, you know. Hoping for a thing often seems the best way o' bringing on the opposite.' There was another gurgling retch behind and Clover turned to look. 'How can you have any puke left?'

'It's just...' Flick straightened up, wiping his mouth. 'A sort o' snot coming out now.' And he peeked at the display from the corner of his eye, as if looking sidelong might make it prettier.

You could tell it had been people once. A hand here. A face there. But mostly just bits of meat, nailed up high or dangling in the burned trees at the centre of the village, where the rain had washed the ash into a black slurry. There was something coiled snake-like around a trunk which Clover had an unpleasant sense might be someone's guts. A scene from a nightmare, and no mistake.

'Fucking flatheads,' muttered Flick, then he hunched over and coughed up another string of drool.

'Chief?'

'By the dead!' shouted Clover, near jumping in the air with fright. Sholla had slipped out of the bushes, silent as regrets, and was squatting not a step to his side, one eye big and white in her ash-smeared face and the other just a gleam behind her tangled hair. 'Creep up on *them*, girl, not on me! I near shat myself!' He was worried he might've, just a streak.

'Sorry.' She didn't look sorry at all. She never looked much of anything. Deadpan as an actual pan, this girl.

'I should hang a bell on you,' muttered Clover, bending over and trying to calm his racing heart. 'What is it?'

'The flatheads left tracks. Took some sheep with 'em. Wool tufted on the trees. Tracks all over. Couldn't have left bigger ones if they'd driven a wagon. I could track 'em easy. Want me to track 'em? I'll track 'em, shall I?' Maybe she spent so much time on her own, only trees for company, that she'd poor judgement now on quantity of words. It was either too few in little stabs or too many in a flurry. 'Want to follow, Chief?'

Clover still didn't much like being called chief. The tallest flower is oft the first clipped, and no one he'd called chief down the years had lived to enjoy a pleasurable retirement. 'No, I don't much want to follow, as it happens.' He held a hand out to the nailed-up offal. 'Adding my own innards to such a display in no way appeals.'

There was a pause. Sholla's one visible eye, and the gleam of the one hidden, slid to Downside, and he shrugged his great shoulders. They slid to Flick, who groaned, and straightened, and wiped his mouth again. They slid to the display, which still sat there in the trees, of course. They slid back up to Clover. '*Shall* we follow, though?'

Clover puffed out his cheeks. They'd been puffed out ever since Stour gave him these scrapings from the pot and told him to hunt Shanka. But when your chief gives you a task, you get to it, don't you? Even if it's far from the task you'd have picked.

'Aye,' he grunted. 'We shall.'

'Chief?'

'Huh?'

Flick knelt in the wet brush, twisting his spear nervously in his pale fists. 'What you thinking about?'

Clover stood, trying to find a gap in the leaves so he could peer into the valley, grunted as he stretched one aching leg, then the other, then squatted down again. 'The past. Choices made. Things done.'

'Regrets, eh?' Flick nodded sagely, like he knew all about regrets, though if he'd seen sixteen winters Clover would've been surprised.

'Might be a parade o' triumphs and successes, mightn't it?'

'Didn't look that way.'

'Aye, well.' Clover took a long breath through his nose. 'You've got to blow with the wind. Let go of the past. Dwelling on your mistakes does no one any good.'

'You really think that?'

Clover opened his mouth to speak, then shrugged. 'It's the sort of shit I always say. Keep talking and I'll more than likely crack out the one about choosing your moment.'

'Habit, eh?'

'I'm like a wife who's served the same stew every night for years, and hates it more each time, but can't cook aught else.'

Downside looked up from checking his axe to grunt, 'Who wants to marry that bitch?'

Clover puffed out his cheeks again. 'Who indeed?'

That was when Sholla came bounding up the gully, springing from rock to rock, making no effort to stay quiet this time. She flung herself into the bushes and slid to a stop in the undergrowth beside Clover, breathing hard and her face shining with sweat but otherwise not looking much bothered by a deadly chase through the woods.

'They coming?' asked Flick, voice shrill with fear.

'Aye.'

'All of 'em?' asked Downside, voice growly with excitement.

'Pretty much.'

'You sure?' asked Clover.

She glanced at him through her hair, which had a couple of bits of twig stuck in it. 'I am irresistible.'

'No doubt,' he said, with the ghost of a grin. It was the sort of thing Wonderful might've said.

Then Clover heard 'em, and the grin faded fast. A howling first, like a pack of wolves far off, making the hairs on his neck prickle. Then a clattering and clanking, like armoured men coming on the rush, making his mouth turn dry. Then a mad snuffling and gibbering and hooting somewhere between a crowd of hungry hogs and a gaggle of angry geese, setting his palms to itch.

'Ready!' he hissed, men shifting in the undergrowth all around him, gripping their weapons tight. 'And as Rudd Threetrees used to say, let's us get them killed, not the other way around!' He gave Sholla a nudge with the rim of his shield. 'To the back, now.'

'I can fight,' she whispered. He saw she'd pulled out a hatchet and a wicked-looking knife with a long, thin blade. 'I can fight better than your champion puker here.'

Flick looked a little hurt, but he looked a little green, too.

'I've got plenty o' folk can fight,' said Clover, 'but just the one who can sneak up on a squirrel. Get to the back.'

He saw a flicker of movement in the trees, then another, then they burst from the branches and into the open, swarming up the gulley, funnelled between the steep rocks and straight towards Clover. Exactly the way he'd planned. Though the plan didn't seem such a clever one right then.

A vile mass they were, whooping and warbling, skittering and scuttling, limping on legs of different lengths, all teeth and claws and mad fury. All twisted and misshapen, mockeries of men, squashed from clay by children with no knack for sculpting.

'Fuck,' whimpered Flick.

Clover caught his shoulder and gripped it hard. 'Steady.' At a moment like that, everyone's thinking about running, at least a bit, and it only takes one doing it to convince 'em all it's the best idea. Before you know it, you're being hunted through the woods instead of celebrating a victory. And Clover's knees were getting far too stiff for doing the hunting, let alone for being the prey.

'Steady,' he hissed again as the Shanka scrambled closer, sun glinting on the jagged edges of their crude weapons and the plates and rivets they'd bolted into their lumpen bodies.

'Steady,' he mouthed, watching, waiting, feeling out the moment. He could see their faces now, if you could call 'em faces. One at the front wore a bloodstained woman's bonnet and another waved a man's rusted sword and a third had a horse's skull over its own face and a fourth a helmet made of spoons bent in a fire or maybe they were nailed into its skull, the rough flesh swollen around the strips of metal.

Grab the moment, 'fore it slips through your fingers.

'Spears!' roared Clover, and men popped from the undergrowth, long spears all pointed down the gully so there was nowhere for the flatheads to run to. They checked and clawed and skittered, surprised by that thicket of bright blades. One couldn't stop and went tumbling onto the spears, took a point right through the throat and hung there, spitting dark blood and trying to turn around and looking somewhat surprised that it couldn't.

Clover almost felt sorry for it. But feeling sorry's always a waste of time, and specially in a battle.

'Arrows!' he roared, and men leaned out over the rocks at the sides of the gully. Bows sang and shafts fluttered down among the Shanka, bounced, rattled, stuck into flesh. He saw one flathead flailing, trying to reach with one twisted arm to where an arrow was sticking from its neck. The archers drew and strung and shot, easy as shooting lambs in a slaughter-pen. A spear went flying up the other way but bounced from a rock, harmless.

The flatheads were shook up, now. Seems Shanka and men don't behave all that differently when they're bottled in a gully with shafts showering down on 'em. One tried to climb the rocks and caught three arrows, dropped off on top of another. A third charged at the spears and got stuck through the guts, ripped open all up its side and a metal plate torn from its shoulder, bloody bolts showing underneath.

Clover saw one flathead dragging another that had an arrow in its chest, trying to get it to the back. Almost like something a person might do. A better person than he was, anyway. Made him wonder if flatheads had feelings like people, as well as blood and screams much the same. Then an arrow stuck into the head of the one doing the dragging and it fell with the other one on top and that was that for the demonstration of human feelings. On either side.

Clover got the sense they were ready to break.

'Axes!' he bellowed, and the spearmen split apart, pretty neat. Not too far from what they'd practised, which was quite the wonder under the circumstances. The best fighters Stour had given him came pouring through the gap, mail and shields and good axes smashing into the flatheads from uphill with a sound like hail on a tin roof.

Downside was right at the front, of course. He was a bad bastard. Mad bastard. Fought with that total lack of concern for his own safety that men usually grow out of fast or die of even faster. Hell of a fighter, but no one wanted him 'cause he'd a habit of getting carried away and not really caring who he smashed on the backswing. Or even the frontswing.

Still, when you're sent to fight monsters, it's a good idea to have a monster or two of your own. That, and the way he was never happier'n when he was charging at the Great Leveller reminded Clover of himself twenty years past, when they still called him Jonas Steepfield and misfortunes hadn't taught him to tread lightly. He was just congratulating himself on staying well clear of the action when a spearman gave a screech, dropped clutching at his shoulder, and a giant flathead came roaring out of the pack, a great studded club in its fists.

Clover never saw a Shanka so big nor so covered in iron. They liked to rivet any metal they could find into their skin, but this one was covered all over with hammered plates. A mist sprayed from its mouth as it bellowed, and it sent a man reeling with its club. Others scrambled back, and Clover was not ashamed to say he was with them, jaw well lowered and shield well raised.

The great Shanka took a step forward, lifting its club, then squawked and dropped wobbling on one knee. Sholla had slipped up behind, now set her knife between two of the plates on its head and smashed the pommel with the back of her hatchet calm as hammering a nail. Made this hollow *bonk* and drove the knife into the Shanka's skull to the grip, popped one of its eyes right out of its metal-cased head.

'Fuck,' said Clover as it crashed down at his feet with a sound like a chest full of cooking pots.

'Told you I could fight,' said Sholla.

Looked like that was the end of it. The last few flatheads were running. Clover saw one cut down in a shower of blood, another fall with an arrow in its back, a couple bounding away down the gully even quicker than they came.

'Let 'em go!' Clover roared up at the archers. 'They can take the message back. They stay north of the mountains, we'll have no quarrel. They come south, the Great Leveller's waiting.'

Downside watched 'em run, eyes wide and wild, spit in his beard and blood streaking his face. No one wanted to tell him to stop and honestly Clover didn't much, either. But that's the thing about being chief. You can't just throw your hands up at everything and say it's someone else's problem.

So Clover stepped towards him, one palm raised, the other just tickling the grip of the knife in the back of his belt. There's no bad time to have one hand on a knife, after all.

'Easy, now,' like he was trying to calm a mean-tempered dog. 'Calm.'

Downside stared at him, quite mildly, if anything. 'I am calm, Chief,' he said, and wiped blood out of his eyes. 'Bleeding, though.'

'Well, your own face is a poor choice of weapon.' Clover let go his knife and surveyed the axe-hacked, spear-stuck, arrow-pricked corpses clogging the gully. Fight won, and he hadn't even needed to swing in anger.

'By the dead,' muttered Flick. There was a flathead spitted on the end of his spear, still twitching.

'You got one,' said Downside, putting a boot on its neck and hacking its skull open.

'By the dead,' muttered Flick again, then he dropped his spear and was sick.

'Some things don't change,' said Sholla, busy trying to prise her dagger out o' the big Shanka's skull.

'Worked out just the way you said, Chief.' Downside rolled a dead flathead over with his boot and left it goggling at the sky.

'You should never have doubted me,' said Clover. 'The first weapon you bring to any fight ain't a spear or an arrow or an axe.'

Flick blinked at him. 'Sword?'

'Surprise,' said Clover. 'Surprise makes brave men cowards, strong men weak, wise men fools.'

'Ugly fuckers, ain't they?' said Sholla, tugging, tugging, then nearly falling over backwards as her dagger suddenly came free.

'I find myself on shaky ground when it comes to criticising others' looks. Weren't you a butcher's boy once, Downside?'

'I was.'

'Reckon you can take the lead on carving these bastards, then.'

'What d'you want from 'em, sausages?'

Some of the others laughed at that, ready to laugh at anything now the fight was done and they likely had a fat gild coming.

'Trouble with sausages is you can't tell what's in 'em,' said Clover. 'I want no one to be in any doubt. Make us a display like they did with those folk at the village. We might not speak the same tongue as Shanka, but heads in trees gets the point across in every language. Toss a few in that sack for Stour while you're at it.'

'You want to impress a girl, take a bunch o' flowers.' Flick gave a sad sigh. 'You want to impress a King o' the Northmen, bring a sack o' heads.'

''Tis a sorry observation,' said Clover, 'but only the truer for that.'

'Don't think much o' flowers myself,' said Sholla.

'No?'

'Never saw the point of 'em.'

'They've got no point. That's the point.'

She tipped her head to the side, thinking that one through.

Downside was frowning at the Shanka corpses, weighing his axe and wondering where to start. 'Never thought o' myself as a man who fills sacks with heads.'

'No one sets off in that direction,' said Clover, puffing out his cheeks one more time. 'But before you know it, there you bloody are.'

Visions

'She's coming back.'

'Thank the dead,' Rikke heard her father say in the fizzing blackness, and she groaned as she pushed the spit-wet dowel out of her mouth. 'But that's four times this week.'

'Fits are getting worse,' croaked Rikke. Her teeth ached. Her head was splitting. She prised one eye open, then the other, saw Isern and her father looking down at her. 'Least I didn't shit this time.'

'To shit you have to eat,' said Isern, hard-faced as ever. 'What did you see?'

'I saw a river full of corpses.' Bobbing and turning, face up and face down. 'I saw two old men fight a duel in the Circle, and two young women hold hands under a golden dome.' Applause echoing in the gilded spaces. 'I saw a flag with an eye upon it, standing behind a high chair.' And someone sitting in the chair... who had it been? 'I saw an old woman...' Rikke winced and pressed her hand against her left eye, burning hot, and shuddered at the memory, still faint on the inside of her lids. 'And her face was stitched together with golden wire. She spoke to me...'

Isern sagged back on her haunches. 'I know this woman.'

'You sure?' asked Rikke's father.

''Tis a distinctive look, d'you not think? She is a witch.' Isern took up the dangling necklace of runes and fingerbones she wore, tattooed knuckles whitening as she squeezed it tight. 'She is a woman much loved by the moon, or perhaps much hated.' Rikke never saw Isern-i-Phail look anywhere near scared before, and it made her feel scared. Even more scared than usual. 'She is a sorceress who returned from the land of the dead.'

'None escape the Great Leveller,' muttered Rikke's father.

'None escape. But they say some few...' Isern's voice faded to a scratchy whisper. 'Are sent back.' She leaned close, hard hands gripping Rikke's shoulders. 'What did she tell you?'

'That I had to choose,' whispered Rikke, feeling cold all over.

'Choose what?'

'I don't know.'

Isern bared her teeth, tongue stuck in the hole where one was missing. 'Then we must pick a path up into the High Places. There is a forbidden cave there, beside a forbidden lake. That's where she lives. If you can use the word about a dead woman.'

Rikke's father stared. 'Do we really want help from a corpse stitched together with golden wire?'

'Help with strange problems comes from strange people.'

'I guess.' Rikke's father helped her up, the horribly familiar pain pulsing away behind her eyes. 'You should eat something.'

Her gorge rose at the thought. 'I'm not hungry.'

'You're skin and bones, girl.'

'I just need some air. Just need to breathe.'

Isern pushed the door creaking open and bright daggers glittered along its edge, stabbing, stabbing. Rikke closed one eye altogether and the other to a slit, groaning as they helped her through the doorway. She felt weak as a newborn calf. Everything hurt. The soles of her feet. The tips of her fingers. The inside of her arse.

They helped her onto her father's favourite bench in the overgrown garden, with the view of Uffrith's steep streets sloping down to the glittering sea. 'Oh, the sun's a bastard,' she muttered, but she managed to smile as the salt breeze came up and kissed her clammy face. 'But the wind's a good friend.'

'Other way around where we're going,' said Isern, dumping a sheepskin about Rikke's shoulders. 'Up into the hills.'

'Everything's a matter of where you stand.' Rikke's father took both her hands in his. 'I have to get back to this bloody moot. If I'm not there, they'll argue.'

'They'll argue more if you *are* there. They're like bloody children.'

'We're all like children, Rikke. The older you get, the more you realise the grown-ups won't suddenly walk in and set things right. You want things right, you have to put 'em right yourself.'

'With your bones and your brains, eh?'

'And your heart, Rikke. And your heart.'

She squeezed her father's hands, so thin and crooked. 'I worry they'll wear you down.'

'Me?' He gave a smile that was convincing no one. 'Never.'

'They already have.'

He smiled again. Truer this time. 'That's what it is to be chief. You make the hard choices so your people won't have the trouble of 'em.' He glanced about at the weed-choked beds as he stood, brushing off his knees. 'One day I'll tame this bloody garden, you'll see. You just sit in the breeze, now. Sit and rest.'

Wasn't like she had much choice. Didn't have the strength to do much else. She sat and listened to the gulls squawking on the rooftops and the bees busy at the garden's first ramshackle hints of blossom. She watched the fishermen on the wharves, the women at the well, the carpenters still mending the wounds Stour Nightfall had cut into Uffrith. She wondered if her father would live to see it put right again, and the thought made her feel sad. Sad and lonely. Who'd she be when he was gone?

She closed her eyes again and felt tears prickling. She hardly dared look these days in case she saw something that wasn't there yet. Hardly dared breathe in case she choked on years-old smoke. Isern had always told her that you cannot force the Long Eye open, but she'd tried, when Leo fought his duel against Stour Nightfall. She'd tried, and seen a crack in the sky. She'd tried, and seen too much, and now she couldn't force the Long Eye closed again.

'Hear tell you had a fit.'

A shaggy shape loomed over her, a dull glint where one eye should be. 'Hey, hey, Shivers,' she said.

He sat beside her, looking out towards the sea. 'Hey, hey, stringy.'

'That's rude.'

'I'm an infamous killer. What d'you expect?'

'One can still kill politely.' It was then she noticed a building not far away was on fire. Going up like a torch, it was, flames gouting from the windows and burning straws whirling from the thatch.

Rikke gently cleared her throat. Even that made her head pound. 'That building over there . . .' She watched a fire-wreathed figure stagger from the doorway and flop down near the well, no one taking much notice.

'What, the inn?'

'Aye. Is it . . . would you say . . . on fire, at all?'

Shivers raised his brows at it. Or he raised the one that worked, at least. 'Not that I can tell. Does it look on fire to you?'

She winced as the tottering chimney stack collapsed into the charred rafters in a gout of sparks. 'Little bit. But I've a habit of seeing things that aren't there.'

'Getting worse?'

'Despite my efforts to look on the sunny side, it seems so.' Rikke felt tears in her eyes and had to wipe them away. The left one was hot again. It was always hot, now. 'Isern says there's someone up in the mountains might help. A dead witch whose face is stitched together with golden wire.'

'That's your help?'

'Help with strange problems comes from strange people.'

'I guess,' he said.

'At this point, I'll take any I can get. What've you been up to?'

'I was sitting in this moot of your father's. They're talking of the future.'

'And what's in it?'

'You're the one with the Long Eye.'

Rikke stared at that burning building that wasn't really burning. The one next door had caught fire, too, now, just patches among the thatch. By the dead, she wanted to reach for a bucket, but how do you put out flames that aren't there yet? Or that burned out long ago? 'Fire and discord,' she muttered.

Shivers gave a grunt. 'Takes no magic to see that coming. Red Hat thinks the Protectorate should be part o' the Union, with seats on their bloody Open Council and everything, I daresay.'

'Hard to imagine.'

'Oxel thinks we should kneel to Stour Nightfall.'

Rikke curled her lip and spat, but weak as she was, she got most of it down her front. 'Give it all away before he tears it from us?'

'Or bargain for something while we've still got something to bargain with.'

'What about Hardbread?'

'He can't decide one way or the other, so he agrees with whoever's talking. No one reckons we can stay as we are once your father's gone. And no one reckons he'll be around much longer.'

Rikke blinked at him. 'That's harsh.'

Shivers' metal eye twinkled with the colours of fire. 'I'm an infamous killer. What d'you expect?'

By the dead but the whole of Uffrith was burning now, clouds lit orange and yellow and red and the air heavy with screams and clatters of war, and Rikke gave a groaning sigh, right from her hollow belly, and closed her smarting eyes, and clapped her sore hands over 'em, but even then she could feel the heat pressing on her face, the smoke harsh in her nose.

Something was forced between her jaws and she gagged, tried to twist in a sudden panic but couldn't move, gripped tight as swelling ice might grip a drowned corpse.

'She's coming back.'

'Thank the dead,' Rikke heard her father say in the fizzing blackness. 'But that's four times this week.'

She jerked up, pain stabbing behind her eyelids, and spat out the dowel. 'Fits are getting worse!'

She was in her room again. Her teeth ached. Her head was splitting. She stared up bleary at her father's worried face, trying to make sense of it.

'What did you see?' asked Isern. Again.

'The river of corpses and the old men fighting and the young women holding hands and the flag with the eye and an old woman . . .' blathered Rikke, pressing her hand against her left eye, burning hot. 'And her face was stitched together with golden wire.' The same words slobbering out. The same words as before. 'She said I had to choose.'

Isern sagged back on her haunches, just like last time, and her jaw squirmed as she worried at the hole in her teeth with her tongue. 'What does that mean?'

'You know what it means,' snapped Rikke, every word another stab through her head. 'You already told me.'

'What did I say?'

'That she's a witch who was sent back from the land of the dead. That she's much loved or hated by the moon. That she lives in the High Places in a forbidden cave beside a forbidden lake. You told me we had to go and see her.'

Isern looked more and more scared with every word. Rikke never saw her look scared before. Except just before, in the vision. It made Rikke feel even more scared than the last time it happened.

'Can't very well disagree with myself, can I?' muttered Isern.

'Do we really want help from a corpse stitched together with golden wire?' asked Rikke's father, again.

Isern shrugged. 'Help with strange problems—'

'—comes from strange people,' Rikke finished for her.

Man of the People

'Snake!' screamed a woman, and Vick recoiled, then realised it wasn't a warning but a sales pitch. 'Best snake meat!'

She waved something like a length of red rope in Tallow's horrified face and Vick barged past, shoving people out of the way. Politeness got you nowhere in Westport. It didn't get you far anywhere.

'Never been nowhere so busy in my life,' gasped Tallow, dodging a stringy Suljuk woman juggling gourds. Westport was always too hot but with the ovens, braziers and cook-fires of a dozen different cultures burning all around them it was stifling.

A bearded man loomed up with blades in his hands and Vick went for her pocket, but they were only skewers covered in singed lumps of meat.

'You never tasted lamb so tender!' he roared in Tallow's face.

'Thanks, but—'

'Don't speak if silence will do,' grunted Vick, dragging him on. 'To these folk, "no" is the start of a conversation. *There* he is.'

She caught a glimpse of Solumeo Shudra through the shimmering haze above a great pan of rice, three guards sticking close to him. Two were Styrians, big men but none too skilled by Vick's reckoning. The third was a Southerner with busy eyes and a scarred sword through his belt. The most dangerous of the three. The most likely to move fast. But no one can be ready all the time. Especially in a crowd like this. All it would take was a moment to brush close. A quick movement of the blade. Then away into the chaos before anyone realised that the man who might've led Westport out of the Union was dead.

'You sure about this?' Tallow caught her by the elbow, hissing in her ear over the rattle of pans, spoons, knives, the calls of the hawkers. 'Lorsen told us to leave him be.'

'If I always did what I was told I'd still be down a mine in Angland. Or dead.'

Tallow raised his brows. 'Or both?'

'Probably.' She jerked her arm free and battled through a crowded archway after Shudra and his guards, into a spice-market as blinding, deafening and choking in its own way as a Valbeck mill. Baskets and barrels stood in teetering towers, shelves stacked with gleaming jars of oil. The colours were vivid in the sunlight, powders bright red, orange, yellow, leaves every shade of green and brown. Weights and coins rattled and clinked, men and women haggling in a dozen languages, screaming out that they had the best goods, the cheapest prices, the fairest measures.

Shudra was ahead, talking with one of the traders in Styrian, then with another in some Kantic tongue, switching between the two and making them both laugh, shaking their hands, clapping their shoulders. Vick pretended to look at a stall covered in sticks of incense, hardly able to breathe for their reek, keeping one eye on Shudra through the seething crowd. He scooped up a handful of bright red buds from a basket and gave them a deep sniff, beamed at the merchant as though he never smelled anything so fine.

'Man of the people, eh?' muttered Tallow.

'Very likeable,' said Vick. That's what made him such a threat. She felt the metal in her pocket knock against her stiff hip as she turned to follow him. 'But knives kill likeable men just as easily as unlikeable ones.'

'Easier, if anything.' Tallow shrugged as she glanced around at him. 'The likeable ones don't tend to be watching for it.'

A great sedan chair was heaved in front of them and Vick ducked under it, nearly knocking one of the carriers over and making the whole thing teeter, pushing on into a flood of people while the passenger screamed abuse after her.

There was a blood-curdling roar and Tallow jerked back from a cage, would've fallen if Vick hadn't caught him. There was a damn tiger inside. She'd never seen one before, could hardly believe the size of it, the power of it, the weight of bright fur and muscle, twisting angrily with its huge teeth bared.

'Bloody hell,' squeaked Tallow as Vick dragged him up by one wrist. It was an animal market. A screeching, hooting, snarling menagerie. A boy shook a sad little monkey in Vick's face and she brushed it out of her way.

'Fuck you, then!' he spat in a thick accent, and was gone among the faces.

Vick bent down, trying to catch sight of Shudra through the forest of legs, then up on tiptoe. She waved towards a rooftop. One of her hired men was on a scaffold there, pretending to work at a crumbling chimney. He caught her eye, nodded at an alley.

'This way.' Vick swung towards it, making sure not to run. Between the high buildings it was suddenly dark, slogans daubed on walls topped with rusted spikes. Eyes gleamed in doorways, watching them hurry past. A sunburned Northman slumped in a heap of rubbish shouted something, waving a bottle after them.

Down steps three at a time, fetid water splashing with each footfall, the alley so narrow Vick had to turn sideways to slip through. Chanting echoed from up ahead, then a babble of raised voices, then they burst out onto an expanse of worn paving.

The Great Temple of Westport rose up at one side, six tall turrets like the Valbeck chimneys, but capped with golden spikes rather than plumes of smoke.

Platforms were scattered in front. Stages where men and women stood in robes, in rags, festooned with talismans and beads or brandishing books and staffs. Wailing in broken voices to little crescents of curious onlookers, tearing at the air with their hands, pointing skywards with clawing fingers, eyes popping with passion and certainty, promising salvation and threatening damnation. Each insisting all the rest were frauds, and they alone were the one with all the answers.

Vick scorned them, pitied them, but underneath, well hidden, she envied them, too. Wondered what it would be like, to believe in something that much. Enough to die for it. Like Sibalt had. Like Malmer had. Like her brother had. How wonderful it must feel, to be certain. To know you stand on the right side, instead of just the winning one. But you can't just choose to believe, can you?

'What the hell is this place?' muttered Tallow.

'Another market,' said Vick, staring around for Shudra and his men.

'What are they selling?'

'God.'

Now she saw him, gently nodding as he listened to one of the calmer prophets, his bodyguards distracted, unwary.

'This is the place,' said Vick. Just crowded enough. Plenty of escape routes. But so much confusion that a little more would hardly raise a brow. Not until it was far too late.

She started towards Shudra, not too fast, not too slow, not looking right at him, no one to remark upon, easing one hand into her pocket. She strode past a woman stripped to her waist on a platform, on her knees in front of a crudely lettered sign, eyes brimming with ecstasy as she whipped herself, bare back a mass of new scratches and old scars.

'Repent!' she was screeching with every crack of the whip. 'Repent!' She twisted around, raised a trembling finger. 'Repent, sister!'

'Later,' said Vick as she strode past.

And now she saw the hooded figure. Just where she'd guessed he'd be. Walking towards Shudra, not too fast, not too slow, not looking right at him, no one to remark upon.

'There,' she hissed.

'He doesn't look like much,' said Tallow.

'He'd be a poor assassin if he stood out.' She cut sideways through the crowd then around a platform where a blistered old man was yelling at the heavens.

She fell in behind the hooded figure, keeping pace as he slipped towards Shudra. Hoods are good for hiding you from others, but they hide them from you, too. She eased her brass knuckles on, feeling the reassuring tickle of cold metal between her fingers.

She saw the flash of steel as the hooded man pulled something from his pocket, held it down beside his leg, half-hidden in the folds of his clothes.

She quickened her pace, closing on him as he closed on Shudra, heart thumping hard now and her breath coming fast as she thought out how she'd do it.

Shudra clapped as the prophet finished his sermon, turned smiling to say something to one of his guards, caught sight of the hooded man coming, frowned slightly.

The hooded man stepped towards him, lifting the blade.

Doesn't matter how skilled, or tough, or big a man is if he doesn't see you coming.

Vick caught his wrist as the knife went up and hauled it down, pulling him backwards and punching him as hard as she could in the side of his knee.

He gave a shocked gasp as his leg went from under him. She twisted his arm, knife clattering down, dragged him around as he fell and shoved him on his face on the stones, her knee in the small of his back.

She hit him quick and hard, barking with each punch, in the kidney, in the armpit, in the side of his neck, and he quivered, back arched, gave a breathy wheeze then went limp.

'Casamir dan Shenkt, I presume,' she forced through her gritted teeth. She looked up at Shudra, who was staring down at her with wide eyes, his guards only now fumbling out their weapons. 'No need to worry. You're safe.'

Her hired men were shoving through the crowd, one of them snapping manacles shut on the assassin's wrists while the other dragged him groaning up under one arm.

'But you might want to head home and bar the door,' she said as she stood, frowning into the crowd for any other threats. 'Maybe stay off the streets until the vote.'

'You saved my life,' breathed Shudra. 'Did the Styrians send you?'

Vick snorted. 'The Union sent me.' She was pleased to see he looked more shocked than ever as she nodded towards the assassin, swearing noisily as her men dragged him away. 'The Styrians sent *him*.'

Safe Hands

'Your Majesty!' Wetterlant started forward, pressing his face to the bars. He was a handsome man with a playful head of dark curls, but something missing about the eyes. 'Thank the Fates you're here. They've been treating me like a dog!'

'We've been treating you like a prisoner, Lord Wetterlant,' grated out Glokta as the Practical wheeled him to a halt and retreated into the shadows. Shadows were one thing of which there was no shortage down here. 'This is the House of Questions, not an inn. These are some of the best quarters we have.'

'You have a window.' High Justice Bruckel pointed through the bars at it. A tiny square of light, up near the ceiling. 'He has a window!'

'*I* barely get a window,' said Glokta.

'You dare to talk to me about windows, you crippled remnant?' snarled Wetterlant. 'Your Majesty, please, I know you are a reasonable man—'

'I like to think so,' said Orso, stepping into the light. 'I understand you have requested the king's justice. *My* justice,' he corrected. He would still on occasion forget that he was the king, in spite of the phrase *Your Majesty* being flung at him five thousand times a day.

'I have, Your Majesty! I fling myself upon your mercy! I am ill-used! I am falsely accused!'

'Of the rape or the murder?'

Wetterlant blinked. 'Well . . . of everything! I'm an innocent man.'

'The murder, as I understand it, was witnessed by . . . how many, Glokta?'

'Seventeen witnesses, Your Majesty. All sworn statements.'

'Seventeen bloody peasants!' Wetterlant gripped the bars in a sudden fury. 'You'd take their word over mine?'

'Look at the *number* of them,' said Orso. 'Your groundskeeper has already been hanged on the strength of their testimony.'

'It was all his idea, the bastard! I tried to talk him out of it. He *threatened* me!'

Glokta sucked air disgustedly through his empty gums. 'We've only been here a minute and you've gone from innocent to coerced.'

'Few moments more,' murmured the high justice, 'he'll be the victim.'

'Can we speak alone?' Wetterlant's voice was growing increasingly shrill. 'Man to man, you know. Orso, please—'

'We were never on first-name terms,' snapped Orso. 'I can't see us getting there now, can you?'

Wetterlant looked from Glokta to Bruckel to Orso, and evidently found little cause for encouragement. 'Things have got entirely out of hand. It was simple high spirits.'

'From innocence, to coercion, to high spirits,' said Glokta.

'You understand, Your Majesty. You've embarrassed yourself often enough.'

Orso stared at him. 'Embarrassed myself, without doubt. But I never bloody *raped anyone*!' He found he had screamed the last words at the very top of his voice. The high justice took a nervous step back. Glokta ever so slightly narrowed his eyes. Wetterlant blinked, and his lower lip began to wobble.

'What will become of me?' he whispered, eyes suddenly brimming with tears. It was a strange about-face, from frothing outrage to melodramatic self-pity in a breath.

'The traditional punishment,' pattered the high justice. 'For such crimes. Is hanging.'

'I'm a member of the Open Council!'

'You'll find we all hang much the same,' said Glokta, softly.

'You *can't* hang a member of the Open Council!'

'From innocence, to coercion, to high spirits, to immunity.' Orso leaned towards the bars. 'You demanded the king's justice. I mean to give it to you.' And he turned on his heel and stalked away.

'Your Majesty!' wailed Wetterlant as the Practical wrestled Glokta's chair around, one of its wheels shrieking. 'Orso, please!'

The door was shut behind them with a clunk like the fall of a headsman's axe. Orso gave the faintest shiver as he strode away, deeply grateful to be on the right side of it.

'Oh, hell,' hissed Bruckel. A formidable-looking woman, black hair streaked with iron grey and her angular dress incorporating more than a hint of armoured steel, ploughed towards them with the determination of a warship under full sail.

'Who's this?' muttered Orso.

'The bastard's mother,' grunted Glokta, from the corner of his mouth. 'Oh, hell.'

'Your Majesty.' Lady Wetterlant's rigid curtsy bespoke barely contained fury.

'Lady Wetterlant.' Orso had no idea of the right tone to strike and ended up trapped between a funeral guest and a boy caught stealing apples. 'I . . . er . . . wish we were meeting under happier circumstances—'

'You have the power to make them happier, Your Majesty. Do you plan to dismiss this ridiculous case?'

He was almost tempted, just to avoid this interview. 'I . . . fear I cannot. The evidence is compelling.'

'The word of jealous commoners? My son is infamously used! Slandered by unscrupulous enemies. You would take their side?'

'This is not a question of sides, madam, but of justice.'

'You call this justice? He is imprisoned!'

'He has,' said Bruckel, 'a window.'

Lady Wetterlant turned a glare on the high justice that might have frozen milk. 'Mine is an old family, Your Majesty. We have many friends.'

Orso winced as if into a gale. 'A great comfort for you, and them, I am sure, but it does not bear upon the guilt or innocence of your son.'

'It bears upon the consequences of the verdict. It bears upon them quite considerably. You have a child, Your Eminence.'

Glokta's left eye gave an ugly twitch. 'Is that a threat?'

'A humble entreaty,' though made in the very tone one might have used for a threat. 'I would ask you to look into your heart.'

'Oh, mine's a very small one. People who seek for anything of much significance in there are inevitably disappointed.'

Lady Wetterlant wrinkled her lip. 'Be in no doubt, I will do everything in my considerable power to ensure my child goes free.'

'Everything within the law,' squeaked Bruckel. 'I trust.'

Lady Wetterlant eased towards him. 'A mother's love for her child transcends the law.'

'Don't count on it.' Glokta jerked his head at the Practical wheeling his chair, who shoved it forward with sufficient violence to run Lady Wetterlant down, had she not stumbled aside. Orso seized the opportunity to hurry past in his wake.

'Do the right thing, Your Majesty!' Lady Wetterlant shrieked after him, her voice so sharp it made him hunch his shoulders. 'I beg you, for my sake. For *your* sake. Do the right thing!'

'I intend to,' muttered Orso. But he doubted he and Lady Wetterlant meant the same by that particular phrase. No one does. That's the problem with it.

The First of the Magi was standing in the gardens when Orso returned, among well-manicured beds in which the first blooms were just peeping from their buds, frowning towards the House of the Maker, its stark outline showing over the battlements of the creeper-covered palace wall.

'Lord Bayaz.' Orso's greeting came out with more than a dash of resentment. 'Still with us?'

'Your Majesty.' The First of the Magi smiled as he bowed, but his green eyes stayed hard. 'I will soon be taking my leave, in fact.'

'Oh? Oh.' Orso had been desperate to get rid of the old meddler, but now it came to it, he found he was sorry to see him go. Perhaps he wanted someone to blame. Now, as usual, he would have to blame himself.

'I had not intended to stay so long but, with your father's death, I wanted to see the crown ... smoothly transferred.'

'Chaos in Westport, chaos in Valbeck, chaos among the commoners, chaos among the nobility?' Orso gave a sorry grunt. 'Things could be smoother.'

'Your father and I passed through rougher seas together.' Bayaz took a long breath through his nose, winced and cleared his throat. The air was always bad when the wind blew from the west, sharp with smoke from the chimneys that towered ever higher over the Three Farms and the Arches. 'Times change.' And Bayaz began to stroll through the gardens, giving Orso no choice but to scrape after him, the paths a shade too narrow to walk abreast, leaving him feeling more like a butler than a king. 'I am pleased to have played my part in ushering in the new age but ... I confess I feel like something of a relic in Adua. And there are other issues that demand my attention. I judge the Union to be in safe hands.'

'What, mine?'

Bayaz spared him a glance. 'Let us say safe enough. What was your opinion of Fedor dan Wetterlant?'

Orso gave an explosive snort. 'Guilty as the plague and an utter shit to boot. I'm not sure I ever in my life met so loathsome a man.'

'Your Majesty has been fortunate in his acquaintance,' said Bayaz, feet crunching in the perfect gravel. 'I have known many of his type.'

'He's like the villain in some tawdry play.'

'I must confess I have always had some sympathy with villains. Heroism

66

makes fine entertainment but sooner or later someone has to get things *done*.'

'Well-written villains, maybe. You wouldn't believe Wetterlant in a book! How the hell does a man end up like that?'

'Being given everything he wants all his life. Being asked for nothing in return.'

Orso frowned. He could have said much the same about himself. 'It stings me that we must waste so much effort on so worthless a man. The Breakers, in Valbeck—'

'Traitors, Your Majesty.'

'But at least they had *reasons*. At least they *thought* they were doing right. What the hell can Wetterlant's excuse be? He doesn't even bother to make one. He doesn't even see the *need* to make one. I bloody *hate* hangings, but a man like that presents a sore temptation. I just wish we could find our way to some compromise.'

'You are welcome to try, of course.'

'Am I?'

'Each generation must make its own choices.' Bayaz stopped, smiling down at a perfect white flower, the first in the garden to fully show its face to the spring sun. 'If all we do is stick to what we know, how can we make progress?'

'You couldn't solve it all with . . .' Orso waved feebly towards the House of the Maker. 'A spell, or something?'

'Magic fades from the world. I destroyed the Prophet's indestructible Hundred Words. Those few of his Eaters that remain skulk about the South, trying to hold together the shreds of their ruined empire. A man is measured by his enemies. Worthy ones can be more missed than friends.' Bayaz gave a sigh, then a shrug. 'Magic fades from the world but, in truth, most problems have always been better solved with a few sharp words. Or a little sharp steel.'

'So I must be a rock, eh?'

'As your father always tried to be.'

Orso felt a pang of sadness at that. 'I used to think he could do whatever he pleased, and chose to do nothing out of fear, or weakness, or incompetence. Now I see he was dragged in so many different directions at once that it took all his energies to stand still.'

'It is not an easy role to fill.' Bayaz reached out to touch that flower with his fingertip, ever so gently brushing a few specks of glittering dew from its petals. 'Living kings are always objects of derision. But people cannot wait to worship the dead ones. Someone must lead. Someone must make the hard choices. For everyone's benefit.'

'I somehow doubt they'll thank me for it,' muttered Orso.

Bayaz showed his teeth for an instant as he nipped that bloom off with his thumbnail and slipped the stalk through his buttonhole. 'Thanks would be too much to ask.'

'Lord Isher, thank you for coming.'

'Of course, Your Majesty, the moment I received the message.'

Orso had an urge to ask Isher what army his overblown uniform belonged to, as he'd certainly never served with the Union one. But then Orso was wearing an even more overblown uniform himself, and the only military action he had seen was surrounding one of his own cities and hanging two hundred of his own subjects. When it came to impostors, he was surely the worst in the whole Circle of the World, so he smiled wide and resisted the temptation to make himself a hypocrite into the bargain. He was getting better at resisting temptations, all in all. Or so he told himself.

'An astonishing room,' murmured Isher, suitably awestruck as he gazed up at the ceiling, carved in the minutest detail as a forest canopy, gold and silver clockwork birds dotted among the branches. They had sung, once, when fully wound, though the mechanism had failed long ago. It was, without a doubt, impressive, which was why Orso had picked it for this interview. He could not escape the thought, however, that whatever monarch constructed the place could simply have frolicked in one of the dozens of real forests he owned and put several hundred thousand marks into paying off his debts.

'They call it the Chamber of Leaves,' he said. 'For obvious reasons.'

'I had no idea it existed.'

'There are probably a dozen rooms just as grand in the palace that I have no idea exist, and I'm supposed to own the place.' Orso thought about how that sounded as he gestured Isher to a chair. 'Or . . . at least be its custodian, for a generation. There's a hall in the east wing so big my mother used to ride in there. She even had it turfed at one point.'

'Your Majesty, might I extend my condolences on the death of your father. I have not had the chance to do so personally and – though I confess we had our differences – he was a man I always very much admired.'

'Thank you, Lord Isher. And might I offer my congratulations on your forthcoming wedding. We have had too few happy events to look forward to, of late.'

'Difficult times, Your Majesty. Nothing for me.' As a well-powdered footman leaned towards him, silver tray expertly balanced on his fingertips.

'Nor me.' Orso waved the man away and shuffled to the edge of his chair. 'In my youth I loved to dance, but since taking the crown I prefer to get straight to the matter. I wish to speak to you, man to man, on the subject of Fedor dan Wetterlant.'

'A terrible business.' Isher grimly shook his head. 'And one that has the prospect of doing serious harm. Discord between the Closed Council and the Open is like discord between a man and his wife—'

'It has not been the happiest of marriages in recent years, then,' observed Orso, thinking of his father's grinding teeth during their fencing sessions.

Isher only smiled. 'The Open Council can be a somewhat shrewish bride, I confess.'

'And the Closed Council a domineering and neglectful husband. No one knows that better than I, believe me.'

'Older men on both sides have, perhaps, become entrenched in their positions. Sometimes it takes younger men to find new ways forward.'

Orso nodded along. 'Honestly, my advisors feel the nation's interests would be best served if a trial were never to happen. If Wetterlant were to rot away in the empty ground between innocence and guilt.'

'It is a solution that makes sense from their perspective, but . . . if I may?' Orso waved him on. 'It would satisfy no one. Wetterlant would continue to bleat for justice from his cell, and his friends in the Open Council would bleat on his behalf, and his mother would be a continual thorn in everyone's side—'

'Doubtless.'

'—while the common folk would see no justice done and harbour further resentment. And then . . . I hope you will not think me naïve, but there is a *moral* question. It would be a victory of expediency over principle.'

'We have had far too many of those.' This was going better than Orso had dared hope. 'You speak my very thoughts!'

'With your permission, Your Majesty, might I suggest a compromise?'

'You think you can find one?' Orso had expected to coax or threaten or barter his way to it, and here Isher was offering it up as a gift.

'I took the liberty of speaking to Lords Heugen and Barezin. Influential old allies of mine. And my friend Leonault dan Brock will soon be arriving in the city. He is new to politics but tremendously popular.'

'Mmm,' murmured Orso. The Young Lion's tremendous popularity was something he could hear less about, overall.

'I believe, with their help... I could get broad support in the Open Council for a lengthy prison sentence.'

'Wetterlant committed rape and murder.'

'That is the *accusation*.'

'He scarcely even bloody denies it himself!'

'When I say lengthy... I mean without end.'

Orso raised his brows. 'The Open Council would countenance a life sentence for one of their own?'

'Most of them are every bit as disgusted at his behaviour as we are, Your Majesty. They are keen to see justice done.'

'His mother most decidedly is not.'

'I know Lady Wetterlant well, and this bluster is merely the tigress's desperate defence of her cub. She is fierce, but no fool. I believe when she realises the alternative... she will help me secure an admission of guilt.'

'A confession?'

'A full and contrite confession with no need for the Arch Lector's... *intervention*. The trial could be a formality. A demonstration of your justice done, firmly but fairly. Of your power exercised, without delay or dispute. Of a new spirit of cooperation between the Open Council and the Closed.'

'Well, that would be a fine thing.' It might have been the first time Orso had enjoyed discussing official business. 'It's supposed to be a damn Union, isn't it? We should strive to find our way to common ground. Perhaps some good can come of this after all.' Orso sat back, grinning up at the gilded birds as he considered it. 'I certainly do hate hangings.'

Isher smiled. 'What kind of monster enjoys them, Your Majesty?'

An Ambush

*S*queak, *squeak*, *squeak*, went the wheel of her father's chair. Savine narrowed her eyes at it. Gritted her teeth at it. Struggled with every turn of that wheel not to scream.

She had been walking her father to work, then wheeling him to work, once a month since she was a girl. The same route down the Kingsway, between the statues of Harod and Bayaz that began the frowning parade of the Union's heroes. The same conversation, like a fencing match in which you were never sure whether the steels were blunted. The same laughing at the misfortunes of others. She saw no reason to change her habits simply because her life was falling apart around her, so she mimed the old routines. Still walking, like a ghost through the ruins of the house she died in. Still wriggling, like a snake with its head cut off. Not laughing at misfortunes so much, mind you. One's own bad luck is so much less amusing than other people's.

'Something on your mind?' asked her father. Though he wasn't really her father, of course.

'Nothing much,' she lied. Just a string of failing investments, a network of souring acquaintances, a calamitous love affair with her own brother, the ruin of all her dearest ambitions, a constant feeling of nagging horror, an aching chest, occasional waves of weariness, a near-constant need to spew, and the minor detail that she was a bastard carrying a bastard who had become a terrified impostor in her own life. Other than that, all good.

Squeak, squeak, fucking *squeak.* Why the hell had she ever asked Curnsbick to build this shrieking contraption?

'How's business?'

Ever more disastrous. 'Good,' she lied as she pushed the chair through the giant shadow of Arnault the Just. 'If they keep digging at this rate, the canal will be completed within the month.'

'You let Kort off with a warning? I thought you might have had him skinned as an example to your other partners.'

'Skinned men generate no revenue. And Zuri says forgiveness is neighbour to the divine.'

'She has you quoting scripture now? Is she your companion, or are you hers?'

'She's my friend,' said Savine. The only one she trusted. 'Introducing us may be the best thing you have ever done for me.'

'We all need someone we can rely on.'

'Even you?'

'Please. I can't get out of bed without your mother's help.'

Savine ground her teeth. What she really wanted was to wheel her father off a bridge and stop somewhere for another sniff of pearl dust, even though her face was still numb from the last one. But the parapets on the bridges were too high, and there was nowhere private to snort on the Kingsway, so for the time being the torture would have to continue. It was what her father was known for, after all. Truly, as he loved to say, life is the misery we endure between disappointments. She wheeled him on, between the magnificent sculptures of Casamir the Steadfast and his Arch Lector, Zoller.

'You should try not to blame her.' Her father paused a moment, and Savine watched the breeze stir the white hairs on his liver-spotted pate. 'Or at any rate, you should blame me just as much.'

'I have more than enough blame to go around, believe me.'

'I thought forgiveness was neighbour to the divine?'

'Zuri thinks so but I couldn't say. Neither of them lives anywhere near me.'

The scaffolding was coming down from the final statue before the shimmering greenery of the park. The king most recently deceased. Jezal the First, that personification of vaguely well-meaning indecision, rendered grimly commanding by the royal sculptors. The sight of his face made Savine more nauseous than ever. Her uncle, Lord Marshal West, stood opposite, with a hint of her mother in a mood about his frown as he glared off towards the sea, as though he saw the Gurkish fleet there and would sink them with pure force of dislike. Beside him Bayaz towered again, a statue very much like the one at the other end of the Kingsway. Seven hundred years of Union history, topped and tailed by the same bald bastard.

'A charming picture!' A sturdy man in a superbly tailored coat was blocking their path. Bayaz himself, Savine realised, sun gleaming from his hairless pate, looking less like a legendary wizard than a highly prosperous merchant. 'My own brothers and sisters are forever feuding. It warms my heart to see a father and daughter enjoying each other's company.'

Or, indeed, a torturer and an unrelated woman barely speaking to one another.

'Lord Bayaz.' Savine's father sounded distinctly uncomfortable. 'I thought you were returning to the North.'

'Interrupted on my way to the docks by these new statues.' And he waved up towards King Jezal. 'I knew all the men in question and wished to make sure their likenesses were faithful to the facts. I am supposed to be retired, but as an owner of businesses, I am sure you know, Lady Savine, it is nigh impossible to find people who can manage things properly in one's absence.'

'Good budgeting is key,' said Savine, stiffly. 'When Angland needed help the treasury was empty. Yet we can afford statues.'

'I need not lecture you on the importance of investing wisely. A bright future rests on a proper respect for the past. The seeds of the past bear fruit in the present, eh, Your Eminence?'

'In my experience, they never stop blooming.' Her father reached around to put his hand on Savine's. 'We should not take up too much of your time—'

'I always have time to meet the leading lights of the new generation. The future belongs to them, after all.'

'Even if we must tear it from the grip of the old,' said Savine, twisting her wrist free of her father's hand.

'Very little worth anything is ever given away. I am sure you know that, too.' Bayaz smiled at Savine's father. The one in the chair, not the one immortalised in stone. 'I have no doubt your father will stand here one day. Who has sacrificed more for the Union, after all? Except perhaps your uncle.' Bayaz turned to look up at the statue of Lord Marshal West. 'Who gave his life defending it.'

'I thought we were being faithful to the facts?' Savine was in no mood to flatter this old fool. 'I understand he survived the Gurkish attack but died of the sickness you released when you destroyed half the Agriont.'

'Well.' Bayaz's good humour did not so much as flicker. 'If this row of statues tells us anything, it is that there are many ways to tell the same story.'

'Clearly,' said Savine, glancing from the real First of the Magi, shorter than she was with her boots on, to his colossal statue.

'Savine,' murmured her father, a warning note in his voice.

'Such a spirited young woman.' Bayaz gave her the kind of look she might have given the men of the Solar Society, wondering which was worthy of investment. 'The Union will need someone with good sense and a strong stomach to take charge one day. One day soon, perhaps. Someone who does not flinch from what must be said. What must be done. The Breakers and Burners must be *dealt* with.' The first hint of real anger in his voice, and for some reason it made Savine flinch. 'You were in Valbeck. Do you know the first thing they broke and burned there?'

She swallowed a wave of sickness. *Calm, calm, calm.* 'I—'

'The Banking House of Valint and Balk! An attack on *enterprise*. On *progress*. On the very *future*! If the current administration cannot get a grip on the situation . . . we must find someone who can.'

'I hope to serve the Crown for many years to come,' grated her father. 'King Orso will need just as much guidance as his father did.'

'Guidance does not have to be given in the White Chamber. It can come in theatre foyers, or comfortable living rooms, or even, who knows, in writers' offices.' That choice of words could hardly be an accident. Savine felt the heat spreading up her collar. Bayaz smiled at her, but it did not get as far as his eyes. 'We should have a talk some day, you and I. About what I want. And about what you want. Who knows? You might be the first woman to be immortalised on the Kingsway! As the only person with two statues here, you can take my word for it – when it's *you* they're sculpting, it all starts to seem like an excellent use of funds.'

Savine was not often lost for words, but she hardly knew how to reply. 'I had no idea you picked the leaders of the Union.'

Bayaz only smiled wider. 'Recognising one's own ignorance is the first step towards enlightenment. Lady Savine. Your Eminence.' He gave them a brief nod and strode off jauntily down the Kingsway, the tails of his expensive coat flicking behind him.

Savine's heart pounded as she watched him go. As if she had parried a few thrusts to the heart, rather than replied to a few strange remarks. She used to be razor-sensitive to the subtext of every conversation. The dangers lurking beneath the surface, like rocks to the unwary vessel. But she hardly trusted her own instincts any more.

'What exactly was he offering me?' she muttered.

Her father gave a bitter snort. 'The First of the Magi never gives, only takes. That was not an offer to you, it was a threat to me.'

'Threats, and blackmail, and banks?' It was one of those moments when you realise the world may not be quite what you had thought it was. She had been experiencing a lot of those lately. 'What kind of wizard is he?'

Her father frowned up at Bayaz's towering statue. 'The kind you obey.'

'I've been made some outrageous proposals,' Savine threw over her shoulder to Zuri as she pulled off her gloves, 'but that must be the first time a statue on the Kingsway has been put on the table...'

She became aware of the muffled burble of conversation from the door to her mother's parlour. Odd, that she should have a visitor so early. It usually took something special to get her out of her bedroom before lunch.

Zuri had her black brows significantly raised. 'I believe Lady Ardee might have an outrageous offer of her own to put to you.'

'My mother and I are not on the best of terms at the moment.'

'I realise. But the scriptures say those lost in the desert should take such water as they are offered.' She gently swung open the door. 'No matter who it comes from.'

Her mother's voice spilled out as Savine stepped suspiciously into the room. '...my husband might as well be dead, as far as *that* department goes, and then— Savine, you're here!' She smiled over from the cabinet where she was, it hardly needed to be said, pouring herself a glass of wine. 'We've a visitor.' Another woman was rising from a chair, something of a military cut to clothes mud-spotted about the hem from riding. 'This is Lady Finree dan Brock.'

Savine prided herself on being hard to rattle, but Leo dan Brock's mother in her own mother's parlour was not an easy thing to write off as coincidence. Especially when she was currently carrying the woman's grandchild.

'Savine.' Lady Finree took her hand in both of hers, and a fearsomely firm grip it was, too. 'I've heard so much about you.'

'All good, I hope.'

'Mostly.' Finree dan Brock had an unflinching stare that even Savine found slightly intimidating. 'But a woman who produced only good reports would not be fighting hard enough. I am a great admirer of your achievements as a lady of business.'

Savine assumed her sweetest smile while she tried to work out what was going on. 'As I am a great admirer of yours as a Lady Governor.'

'All I did was mind the shop for a few years.' Finree dan Brock sat as if for a business discussion rather than a social call. 'My son Leo governs Angland now.'

Savine refused to react. 'So I hear. What brings you to Adua?'

'An invitation to Lord Isher's wedding.'

'It'll be the event of the season,' said Savine's mother, 'though if you're asking me, the man's a bloody viper. Wine, Savine?'

The conversation with Bayaz had felt somehow dangerous. This felt even more so. Savine had a sense she would need her wits intact. 'Not for me.'

'Lady Finree?'

'No, but don't let me stop you.'

'You won't stop mother drinking unless you brought a few fathoms of chain with you.'

Savine's mother plopped herself down on a chair, making a perfect triangle of the three of them, wiped a streak of wine from the side of her glass and sucked her fingertip. 'You're salty this morning.'

'I don't care for the feeling of being ambushed,' said Savine, looking from one woman to the other, both formidable in their own ways and as a pair positively daunting.

They exchanged a glance. 'You go,' said her mother. 'I'll chime in if needed.'

'My son has inherited a weighty responsibility,' said Lady Finree. 'One that he is in some respects well suited for, but in others . . . less so.'

Savine could well imagine. 'He's hotheaded, ignorant and reckless, you mean?'

'Exactly.' Savine should not have been surprised. A woman who had faced down an army of screaming Northmen was unlikely to be put off by a little plain-speaking. 'You, meanwhile, are known to be cool-headed, calculating and patient. It seems the two of you are complementary.'

'Fire and ice!' threw in Savine's mother between sips.

'My son likes to think he can do it all but, like his father, he has always needed someone beside him. Someone to give good advice and make sure he takes it. Someone to guide him to the right decisions. There comes a time when a mother can no longer do that for a son.' She raised her brows expectantly.

Savine did not like the way this was going. 'I'm not sure what I—'

Her mother gave an explosive sigh. 'Don't be obtuse, Savine. Lady Finree and I have been discussing a match between you and Leo.'

Savine blinked. 'A marriage?'

'Well, not a bloody fencing match.'

Savine stared from her mother to her prospective mother-in-law. It *was* an ambush. An expertly prepared pincer movement, and she was outflanked on both sides.

She lifted her chin and played for time. 'I'm not sure the two of us are suited. He is a good deal younger than—'

'I understand you felt differently when he last visited Adua,' said Lady Finree, looking at her significantly from under her brows.

It took a moment for the implications to sink in. 'He told you that?'

Savine's mother raised a hand. 'I told her that.'

'How the hell did you find out?'

'Don't be cross and don't be coy. Neither suits you. Zuri is worried for you, as a good servant should be. As a good *friend* should be. She is thinking of your best interests. We all are, believe it or not.' Her mother leaned forward, holding her eye, and put a reassuring hand on Savine's knee. 'She told us about your . . . *situation.*'

Savine's face burned. She found she had put a hand to her stomach and angrily snatched it away. She was used to stabbing other people with their secrets. She did not at all enjoy being impaled on one of her own.

'Forgive me if I am blunt,' said Lady Finree. 'I have spent much of my life around soldiers—'

'Fancy that,' snapped Savine. 'So did mother, in her youth.'

'It's a shame youth has to end,' sang Savine's mother, fluttering her eyelashes. Then she gave Savine's knee a parting pat and sat back, murmuring out of the corner of her mouth, 'You see that bluntness won't be a problem.'

'Then let us speak plainly,' said Lady Finree. 'It will not be long before your condition becomes difficult to hide.' Savine angrily set her jaw, but she could hardly dispute the facts. The laces of her corsets already needed even more brutal handling than usual. 'It could be a disaster for you. Or it could be an opportunity. Turning disasters into opportunities is what an investor does, isn't it?'

'Wherever possible,' muttered Savine.

'My son has title, fame, courage and loyalty.'

'And is a damnably handsome fellow,' observed Savine's mother.

'You have wealth, connections, cunning and ruthlessness.'

'And in the right light can look rather well yourself.'

'I doubt there is a more eligible young man in the Union,' said Lady Finree. 'Unless you were to marry the king, I suppose.'

Savine's mother coughed wine down her dress. 'Damn it. Silly me.'

'Your pride is well earned,' said Finree, 'but the time has come to put it aside.'

Her mother was dabbing at herself with a handkerchief. 'Really. You could be the most envied couple in the Union! You're far too clever not to see the sense of this.'

'And certainly far too clever to raise a bastard alone when you have such an advantageous alternative. By all means lead my son a little dance if you please, no man values what he gets too easily. But there really is no need to drag this charade out any further between the three of us.'

Savine slowly sat back. There had been a golden moment when her fingertips had brushed the crown. Her wildest ambitions, so nearly in her grasp. Her August Majesty the High Queen of the Union, before whom all must kneel or suffer! But, she had to admit, Her Grace the Lady Governor of Angland was not a bad second best. She had tried following her heart, and it had led her straight to shit. She and Leo dan Brock were an excellent match in every way that counted. He would need some moulding, some steering, some discipline. But who could argue with the quality of the raw materials? A wedding to a famous hero might be the very thing to turn her fortunes around.

Savine had spent her whole life scheming, plotting, striving to control events. There was a certain relief in yielding to the inevitable. 'No,' she said, almost a sigh. 'I don't suppose there is.'

She had been made many proposals of marriage, but this was the first she had actually accepted. And the only one made not by the prospective husband, but by his mother.

'I think I'll take that drink now,' she said.

'I, too.' Lady Finree issued a neat little smile. 'Since we've something to celebrate.'

Savine's mother grinned as she trotted to the cabinet.

Gentle Temperaments

The Lords' Round was an awe-inspiring space, all marble and gilding and friezes of noble forebears. Heart of the Union and all
that, light streaming from the stained-glass windows, through the
echoing vastness, to splash the tiled floor where the great noblemen of
the past once set the course of the future.

But all Leo saw were the steps down through the empty banks of
seating.

Before his duel and the damn leg wound, he'd never noticed how many
steps there were in the world. He'd sprung up them three at a time and
gone blithely on his way. No more. They were everywhere. And down
was worse than up, that was the thing people never realised. Going up,
you couldn't fall that far. He took the usual moment to curse the Circle,
swords and Stour Nightfall, then set off slightly sideways, grumbling with
each lurching stride.

'Leo!' Isher ignored the offered hand at the bottom of the steps and instead folded him in a hug. '*Wonderful* to see you again!' A bit overfamiliar
given they'd spoken no more than three times, but better too friendly
than the opposite.

'Congratulations on your forthcoming marriage.' Leo winced at a
twinge in his leg as he broke free. 'Haven't seen my mother this excited
in years.' He turned slowly around, looking up towards the gilded dome
high, high above. 'Doubt you could find a grander venue.'

'Nor a bride with better pedigree.' Isher stroked at the air as though
they were discussing a racehorse. 'Isold dan Kaspa, do you know her?'

'Don't think I've had the pleasure.'

'Excellent blood. Good old Midderland stock. Wonderfully gentle
temperament.'

'Wonderful,' said Leo, without much joy. To him, a woman with a
gentle temperament was like a sword without an edge.

Isher frowned down at Leo's cane. 'How's your leg?'

'Fine.' Along with the constant pain was the constant need to pretend you weren't in pain at all, as though the worst thing about your agony was that it might put other people out. 'Sword wounds can take some time to heal.'

'Ah, yes. Sword wounds.' As though Isher knew a damn thing about swords or wounds. He leaned close. 'Things have *not* been going well since your last visit.'

'No?'

'I hate to be unpatriotic,' he murmured, as if he could hardly wait, 'but King Orso proves to be every bit the empty vessel we were expecting.'

'There's nothing unpatriotic about the truth,' muttered Leo, wondering whether there might be.

'He offers not the slightest check to Old Sticks and the rest of those withered bastards on the Closed Council. It's all liars and swindlers in the White Chamber.'

'Always has been,' muttered Leo, wondering if it had been.

'They're set on limiting the powers of the Open Council. Stripping us of ancient rights. Clawing land back to the Crown. Taxing us to the bloody balls.'

'Huh,' grunted Leo. 'I feel your pain there. Angland's being squeezed hardest of all.'

'And if anyone's earned some clemency, it's you, who held back the savages alone, with no help from the Crown!'

'We fought the king's war. We *won* the king's war! We *paid* for the fucking . . .' Leo brought his voice back down, with some difficulty, '. . . king's war. And what did we get back?' He slapped angrily at the lion-head pommel of the commemorative sword he'd so proudly accepted from King Jezal last year. 'One sword. And it's not even properly bloody balanced!'

'It's a scandal.'

'It *is* a scandal.' Leo wondered whether he was saying too much but couldn't help himself. 'A breach of the contract between the Crown and the provinces. There are folk back home asking if we're subjects or livestock.' Jurand had told him to be careful what he said in Adua, but Jurand was a long way away, sadly, and the truth was the truth. 'There are folk on the verge of bloody *rebellion*,' he hissed, grinding the end of his cane into the tiles.

'A *bloody* scandal,' lamented Isher. 'Still. Nothing compared to what they're doing to poor Fedor dan Wetterlant.'

'Who?'

'You never met?'

'Don't think I've had the pleasure...'

'One of us, Wetterlant. Seat on the Open Council, estates down near Keln. Good old Midderland stock, you know.'

'Gentle temperament?'

'Little wild, truth be told, but we've known each other for years. I believe he's a fourth cousin of mine or some such. Once removed, maybe?'

'Never really understood how all that once removed stuff works...'

'Who does? The charges are trumped up, without a doubt. Some ruse of Old Sticks'. I hear he's confessed but no doubt it's under torture.'

'They tortured a member of the Open Council?' Leo could scarcely believe it. 'I didn't think Orso was the type.'

'I'm telling you, the man's a cipher! He has no idea what's done in his name and wouldn't do a thing about it if he did. They've got Wetterlant locked up in the bowels of the House of Questions, away from friends, away from family. Not even a window! His poor mother is beside herself. Cousin of a cousin as well, it's taken quite the toll.'

'By the dead,' murmured Leo, then realised it was a Northern saying and meant nothing here.

'He's appealed for the king's justice. Anyone with a seat on the Open Council has the right to a trial here with His Majesty as the judge but, well... I doubt there's any justice to be had in the Union these days.'

'By the *dead*! I mean, bloody hell.'

'Even members of the old families, even members of the Open Council, even patriots like you or I aren't safe. It hardly feels like our country any more.'

Leo rubbed at his thigh, the simmering pain a spur to his simmering anger. 'Someone should do something,' he growled.

'Someone should.' Isher nodded sadly. 'But... who has the courage?'

Leo tried not to limp as he walked back down the Kingsway, past the statues of the great men of history. Kings loomed on one side. *Real* kings. Harod the Great. Arnault the Just. Casamir the Steadfast. Great figures from their reigns loomed a little lower on the other.

Leo wondered if a statue of him would stand here one day. Holding sword and shield in recognition of great victories, gazing sternly across the roadway to a taller and more impressive statue of King Orso. That thought hardly filled him with joy. He was paying for his glories with every step and didn't fancy sharing with a man he was losing all respect for.

Crown Prince Orso had struck him as a good enough sort, but the throne only amplifies a man's bad qualities, and his Closed Council were the same corrupt old worms who'd driven King Jezal's reign into the ditch. What the Union needed was men of courage, men of passion, men of *action*.

Men like him.

The quarters he and his mother had been given were high up, blessed with views but cursed with steps. When he finally got to the top, his leg was on fire. He had to pause to settle his breath, mop away sweat and force his grimace into a carefree smile. He told himself he didn't want his mother to worry. In truth, he didn't want to prove her right.

'How was your meeting with Lord Isher?' she asked as he strode in.

'Well enough. He'd a bastard of a story about this poor fellow Wetterlant. There's a rot in the Agriont, but no one's got the courage to . . .' There was someone behind him. A woman perhaps a few years older than his mother but still rather handsome, a lopsided smile on her lips as if she knew secrets he didn't.

'This is Lady Ardee dan Glokta.'

'Oh . . .' By the dead, he saw the resemblance to her daughter now. That direct, searching, slightly mocking look was just the same. He was blushing to the roots of his hair. 'Wonderful to meet you, of course—'

'The wonder is all mine, Your Grace. A genuine hero, adorned with the scars of great deeds. Will you catch me if I faint?'

'Well . . . I'd do my best—'

'I understand you know my daughter, Savine.'

At that moment, it seemed more likely he'd faint than she would. 'We've . . . met. Just the once.' The same number of times they'd fucked. Might've been better not to think of that, but now he couldn't stop. 'When I was last in Adua. Four months ago, was it? She struck me as a very attractive . . .' Terrible choice of word! 'I mean . . . *formidable* woman.'

'Please, you're embarrassing me. And certainly yourself.' Lady Ardee laid a familiar hand on his arm. Everyone in Adua was too familiar. 'I'm sorry to put you in a corner but I know the two of you were intimate.' She nodded towards Leo's mother. 'We both do.'

'You . . . do? Oh. Oh.' Damn, he sounded lame. He was a Lord Governor, wasn't he? Not some stuttering schoolboy. 'I assure you I didn't . . . take advantage of her . . . in any sense—'

Lady Ardee laughed. 'The man isn't made who could take advantage of my daughter. I've no doubt it was quite the other way around.'

'What?' He wasn't sure whether that was better or worse, only that he wanted this conversation to end, but his mother had blocked the doorway. There was no escape.

'You know how much I love you, Leo,' she said. 'You're a wonderful leader. Brave, honest, loyal to a fault. I could not be more proud. I have the Young Lion for a son!'

'Rawrrrr,' said Lady Ardee, grinning at him sidelong.

'But lions are not suited to administration. I know you want to do it all, but the last few months have proved to us both that you cannot govern Angland on your own.'

'You are the head of a great family,' said Lady Ardee, 'and great families must be sustained. You may want to do it all, but I very much doubt you'll be bearing any heirs yourself. You need a wife.'

He struggled to put the parts of this conversation together but could only see one way to do it. 'You want me . . . to marry . . . your daughter?' The whole thing had an air of unreality.

'Whyever not? She's a beautiful, wealthy, refined, intelligent, impeccably connected and widely admired lady of taste.'

Leo's mother nodded along. 'I was most impressed with her.'

'You've met her?' asked Leo. 'I feel a bit . . . ambushed.'

'A famous warrior? Ambushed by two mothers?'

'Two *grand*mothers,' muttered Lady Ardee, for some reason. 'Can you honestly deny anything we've said?'

Leo swallowed. 'Well, I won't deny I'm not suited to administration. I don't deny I need help. I can't deny Savine's beautiful, tasteful, refined and all the rest of it, I mean, she's . . .' He thought back to that night, and not for the first time. 'A *hell* of a woman.'

'It would be folly to deny that,' said Lady Ardee, tossing her head.

'And no one can deny a man needs a wife, especially a Lord Governor, it's just . . .' Both of them were giving him a slightly pitying smile, as though waiting for a moron to comprehend the obvious. 'Anyone'd think you've booked the date and invited the bloody guests!' Lady Ardee and Lady Finree exchanged a loaded glance. Leo felt the cold shock creeping further up his throat. 'You've booked the date and invited the guests?'

'Lord Isher has kindly agreed to make his grand event a double wedding,' said Lady Ardee.

'Kindly agreed to bask in your reflected glory,' murmured Leo's mother.

'But . . .' squeaked Leo, 'that's next week!'

'You are no longer a carefree young man. You are a great lord of the realm. When did you expect to marry?'

'Not next bloody week!'

'We realise it's a lot to take in,' said Lady Ardee, 'but delay serves nobody's interests. Regardless of who took advantage of whom, you have placed my daughter in a difficult position.'

'She is pregnant,' chimed in his mother, 'with your bastard.'

Leo opened his mouth but only a choked-off gurgle came out. 'But . . . how . . .'

Lady Ardee rolled her eyes. 'I'd hoped you'd be versed in the basics but, if we must. Have you ever noticed that girls and boys have different things between their legs?'

'I know where babies come from!'

'Then you appreciate the responsibilities that emerge with them.' Lady Ardee took a nip from a flask she'd produced as if by magic, then offered it around. 'Drink?'

'Reckon I'd better,' he said numbly, taking a little swig. It proved to be a very good brandy. He stared off hopelessly into the corner as its warmth spread down his throat. He'd known real adulthood was advancing on him, but he'd assumed it was still some way off. Now it had fallen from a great height and squashed him flat. 'Can I at least ask her myself?'

'Of course.' His mother stepped aside and gestured towards the tall windows.

'Wait . . .' Leo felt a new stab of nerves. 'She's *here*?'

'On the terrace,' said Lady Ardee. 'Waiting for your proposal.'

'I don't even have a—'

His mother was holding a ring out, blue stone glinting in the sunlight. 'The one your father gave me.' She took his wrist, turned his hand over and dropped it into his palm while Lady Ardee nudged the window open with her boot-heel, a cool breeze washing in from the terrace and stirring the curtains.

Leo's only options were a courageous advance or to run screaming from the room, and with the state of his leg he doubted he could outrun his mother. He closed his fist tight around the ring, drained the flask and handed it to Lady Ardee. 'My thanks.'

'My honour.' She plucked a speck of dust from his jacket and gave his chest an approving pat. 'We'll be here if you get into trouble.'

'What a comfort,' he murmured as he stepped out into the sunlight.

Savine stood at the parapet, the Agriont spread out below her as if she owned it. Somehow, he'd expected her to have turned matronly, rosy-cheeked, bloated out with child. But she was every bit as sleek and dignified as the day they met. Not rattled by the long drop beyond the short parapet at her back, or their whirlwind courtship, or her delicate condition. Apparently impossible to rattle at all. His first thought was what a portrait they'd make together.

She sank into a curtsy with a rustling of skirts. Very formal. Very clean. Except, perhaps, for the slightest playful smirk at the corner of her mouth. 'Your Grace.'

He'd thought about her often since that night in the writer's office, but somehow it didn't prepare him for seeing her again in the flesh. 'Call me Leo,' he said in the end. 'I think we're past titles.'

She put a hand on her stomach. 'Well, Leo, we have made a child together.'

It wasn't funny, on the face of it, but he had to smile. The polish of an empress with the candour of a sergeant-at-arms.

'So our mothers tell me.'

'They make quite the pair, don't they? As complementary as a long and a short steel.'

'And just as deadly.' He put his fists on the lichen-spotted stonework beside her, the ring digging at his palm. Was he really going to do this? Could he possibly do this? The whole thing felt like a dream. But far from a nightmare.

'I can only apologise for the ambush,' she said, turning to look at the view. The statues standing proud on either side of the Kingsway, the wide expanse of the Square of Marshals, the glinting dome of the Lords' Round. 'If it's any consolation, they did the same to me. I was somewhat . . . surprised at first.'

'So was I, I'll admit.'

Her eyes came to rest on his, her chin raised in a challenge which he found, for some reason, deeply attractive. He thought of what his friends would say, when he presented a famous beauty as his wife. *That*'d wipe the smile from Antaup's face. 'I enjoyed our moment together a great deal.'

'So did I.' He had to clear his throat at the roughness in his voice. 'I'll admit.'

'But I had thought that would be all it was. A moment.'

'So had I.' Leo found himself smiling. 'I'll admit.' He'd expected this to be a painful duty, but he was starting to enjoy it. It had the feel of a dance. A ritual. A duel.

'Does my father worry you?'

His eyes widened. It hadn't even occurred to him that he was getting Old Sticks for a father-in-law. It occurred to him now, the way the slaughterman occurs to the pig. The most feared man in the Union, a master torturer with an army of Practicals, an enemy of all Leo stood for. 'I get the sense he . . . doesn't like me very much.'

'He doesn't like anyone.'

'But I get the sense I don't like him very much—'

'That would be terrible. If you were planning to marry him.' She raised one brow. 'Are you planning to marry him?'

'I don't think your mother would like it.'

'My father doesn't own me. Not even a percentage. If we marry, my loyalty will be to you. But you should know I am my own woman and do things my own way. I do not plan for that to change.'

'Wouldn't want it to.' He admired her spirit. So independent. So determined. So fierce, even. Isher might like a gentle temperament but Leo couldn't think of anything worse.

'It might help if you look at it as a business arrangement.'

'Is that how you're looking at it?'

'Force of habit. And it does make excellent sense. A partnership, be-tween your title and my wealth. Between your fame and my connections. Between your leadership and my management.'

Put that way, it *did* make excellent sense. He enjoyed listening to her talk. So sharp. So confident. So commanding, even. He liked a woman who could take charge. He imagined the admiration when she spoke on his behalf.

'I can share the burden,' she said. 'Take the politics and the paperwork off your hands. You can focus on the military aspects. The things you enjoy. No more dusty meetings.'

He thought of that stuffy room, those tottering heaps of papers, those endless grumbles with Mustred and Clensher and the rest. 'Doubt I'll miss them.'

She didn't seem to take anything so tasteless as steps, but still she drifted closer. He enjoyed watching her move. So graceful. So precise. So regal, even. He liked a woman with pride, and Savine dripped with it. With her on his arm, he'd be the envy of the world.

'Look at it as . . . a political alliance,' she said. 'You are popular. You are celebrated. You are loved. In Midderland, in Angland, in the North, even. But you do not know Adua.' She was looking at his mouth as she came closer. Looking at it in a way he very much enjoyed.

'It's true,' he murmured. 'I'm a lost little lamb here.'

'Let me be your shepherdess. I can help you get your way.' By the dead, she was close now. 'With the Closed Council. With my father. With the great men of the realm.' He could smell her. That sweetness, that heady sharpness. 'I know everyone worth knowing. And how to use them.' Her scent brought all the excitement of that night rushing back.

He found he had held up his open palm, blue stone on the ring twinkling in the sun. 'My mother gave me this.'

'It's beautiful,' said Savine softly.

'Best I could do on the way from the room to the terrace, anyway— ah.'

To his surprise, but by no means disappointment, her hand was between his legs. Already halfway hard, and it took no time for her to get him the rest of the way. It only made it more exciting that they were in full view of half the Agriont with their mothers not ten paces distant.

'Look at it . . .' she whispered urgently in his ear, her breath tickling his cheek, 'as a business arrangement . . . and a political alliance . . . that makes superb sense.' She kissed him, ever so gently, while her hand worked less than gently down below. 'Then anything . . . we can get from it . . . on a personal level . . .' She bit his lip, pulled it and let it flap back. 'Let's call it a bonus.'

'Let's.' He caught Savine's free hand and slid his mother's ring onto her finger. It proved too tight to go over the knuckle, but he didn't care a shit.

He caught her in his arms and kissed her, the Agriont spread out below them.

To anyone watching, they must have looked truly spectacular.

Minister of Whispers

'How was the vote?' asked Vick as Lorsen stepped into his office and shut the door to the gallery.

Apparently, the Superior had remembered how to smile. His thin lips had a noticeable bend. 'The vote was the most fun I have had in *some time*. They're already arguing over points of procedure down there, but that's what they do when they know they've lost. One hundred and fifty-nine votes to stay in the Union. Fifty-four to leave.'

Vick couldn't keep the slightest curl of satisfaction from her own mouth. 'Not even close.'

'Never mind Shenkt, *you* must have some unnatural powers.' Lorsen pulled a cork and poured an ungenerous measure of wine into two glasses. 'Shutting that bastard Shudra up was more than I hoped for, but to bring him over to our side? It could only be sorcery!'

Vick shrugged. 'There's no magic for changing your mind like a glimpse of the knife meant to kill you. The Styrians hoped to make him a martyr for their cause. Vitari knew she could win far more votes by killing him and blaming us than by killing any number of our Aldermen. I pointed out that Murcatto did much the same thing in Musselia. I mentioned the purges that came after, with some help from a couple of eyewitnesses. All I did was show him what ruthless bastards the Styrians really are. Shudra was happy to change his vote.'

'And that was the start of a landslide! Credit where it's due!' And Lorsen wagged a finger at her. 'It was clever thinking, to be watching over him.'

Vick shrugged again. 'I asked myself what I'd have tried, if I'd been in Vitari's place. Anyone could've done it.'

'Not just anyone could have caught the famous Casamir dan Shenkt.'

Vick shrugged one more time. Shrugs cost nothing, after all. 'Infamous killers and nobodies, they all go down much the same when you punch them in the knee.'

'It seems the more far-fetched rumours about him were just that. Rumours.'

'Perhaps. The Arch Lector wants him taken back to Adua. His Eminence has some questions.'

'If we'd lost the vote, it might have been me going back to answer the Arch Lector's questions. I freely confess I *much* prefer it this way.' Superior Lorsen raised his glass. 'You have my thanks, Inquisitor, for what they're worth.'

Vick drank. Lorsen's wine was as thin and sour as he was. But it was wine. She'd counted clean water an impossible luxury once. She never let herself forget it.

Solumeo Shudra was waiting on the gallery, his thick fists propped on the railing as he watched the Assembly at work below.

'Sounds like they're arguing as fiercely as ever,' said Vick, stepping up beside him.

'The swamps will run out of flies,' said Shudra, 'before politicians run out of arguments. They are already splitting into new factions over the latest issue.'

'Which is?'

'Spending on sewers. I wanted to thank you once more, before you left. I have . . . never owed anyone my life before.'

'You get used to it.' Shudra glanced at her, brows raised. More than she should have said already, perhaps. But she felt as if she owed him some honesty. 'His Eminence the Arch Lector once gave me a chance.'

'Not a man known for giving chances.'

'No. But without that . . .' She remembered the sound of rushing water, in the darkness, the day the mine flooded. She thought of her brother's face as they dragged him away, heels leaving two crooked trails through the dirty snow. 'I hear the Aldermen voted to remain in the Union?'

'They did. I never thought I would be happy to say so.' Shudra took a long breath through his nose. 'It is easy, perhaps, in the earnest desire to look for something better, to dismiss the virtues of the allies one has and overlook the faults of the alternatives.'

'The Union is far from perfect. We have our rivalries, our greed and our ambition. That is why we need honest, upright, passionate people. People like you.'

Shudra snorted. 'I could *almost* believe you, Inquisitor. But I am not too proud to admit that I misjudged the situation. I misjudged the Union. I misjudged you.'

Vick smiled. She couldn't help a small one. The satisfaction of a loyal servant at a job well done. 'It takes a strong man to admit his weakness, Master Shudra.'

'Did you have to hit me so bloody hard?' asked Murdine, rubbing at the great bruise on the side of his neck.

'I told you to pad your knee.'

'Three layers of saddle leather! I can still hardly walk!'

'It had to look good. You can't expect the infamous Casamir dan Shenkt to go down easily.'

'I am the world's most fearsome assassin.' Murdine twisted his mouth in a pouting sneer, narrowed his eyes and snarled the words. 'Cower in fear, Aldermen of Westport, for none are safe from my deadly blade! A shame I will never be able to take credit for one of my finest performances.'

'A little overacted, if you're asking me.'

'Pfffft. Everyone's a bloody critic.'

'Well, you convinced Shudra.' Vick slipped the purse from her pocket, weighed it in her hand, silver clinking. 'He was the only audience that counted.'

Murdine grinned at her. 'If you ever need someone to take a punch again, you know my rates.'

'Doubt I'll be through here any time soon,' said Vick. 'The climate doesn't suit me.'

'You never know, I may see you in Adua. I've a feeling it might be wise to clear out of Westport for the time being. There will no doubt be recriminations following the recent shift in power. Debts to be paid and scores to settle.' Murdine glanced nervously about the tavern and twitched his hood further down. 'I wouldn't want to be mistaken for Shenkt a second time.' He gave a little shiver. 'Or, for that matter, to run into the real one.'

'Very wise.'

'They say Styria's the home of culture, but when it comes to theatre, all they want is flash and sparkle.' Murdine waved it away with flamboyant disgust. 'I want to get at the *truth*.'

'The truth is overrated.' Vick let the purse drop into his hand. 'An actor should know that.'

It was early, the sun an angry clipping over the hills in the east, the rigging of the ships casting a cobweb of long shadows on the quay. It was early, but the sooner they were at sea and she was out of this endlessly crowded, superstitious, suffocating city, the happier she'd be.

Or the less unhappy, at least.

Two Practicals followed Vick and Tallow along the seafront, lugging her trunk between them. They were big men, but they were sweating. There was almost as great a weight of clothes, powders and props inside as Savine dan Glokta might have taken on a trip abroad. The many different Victarine dan Teufels she might need to slip into. Made her wonder who the real one was. If there was such a thing any more.

'He was an *actor*?' muttered Tallow, for about the fifth time, his one little bag slung over his shoulder.

'An actor *and* acrobat. He's very particular on that point.'

'You didn't think to tell me?'

'You can't let slip what you don't know.'

'What if, well . . .' He mimed a stabbing motion. 'I'd killed him. Or something?'

'Then there are always more actors.' She gave a sigh that tasted of salt and sea rot and the acrid smoke from the tanneries down the coast, just starting up for the day. 'Every idiot wants to be one.'

'Was the real Shenkt even in the city?'

'Who says there even is a real Shenkt? People like things that are simple. Black and white. Good and evil. They want to make a choice and tell themselves they were *right*. But as His Eminence is fond of saying, the real world is painted in greys. The truth is complicated, full of mixed emotions and blurred outcomes and each-way bets. The truth . . . is a hard sell.'

They'd reached the ship, now. An unappealing tub in need of a good careening, but it was sailing the right way. The two Practicals set down Vick's trunk with a clatter. One unceremoniously planted his arse on it while he stretched out his back, the other pulled his mask aside to wipe his sweaty face.

'It helps to give people a straightforward story, with villains to boo and heroes to root for.' Vick narrowed her eyes as she looked out to sea. 'In my experience, that means making them up.'

'But who's—'

Doesn't matter how sharp you are. No one can be ready all the time.

Something flashed past. One of the two Practicals. He didn't make a sound. He didn't have time. Just flew a dozen strides and crashed into the side of a boat, staving in the planking in a cloud of splinters.

Tallow shrank back, hands over his head. Vick whipped around to see the other Practical tumbling across the quay, limbs bonelessly flopping. She caught a glimpse of a black figure against the rising sun, coming impossibly fast. She was just raising her arm, she hardly even knew what

91

to do, when it was caught with irresistible strength. She was jerked off her feet, the world reeled, and the quayside smashed her in the chest and drove her breath out in a choking wheeze.

She saw boots through the blur. Well-worn old work boots. Then something was over her face. Darkness and her own booming breath. Hands tied behind her. Scrape of her toes as she was dragged along under the armpits. Hiss over the cobbles. *Clack, clack, clack* over the boards of a wharf.

She gathered herself, trying to think through the throbbing in her head, the burning ache in her shoulder. She might only get one chance. She might not even get one chance. She shoved a boot down, tried to twist free, but she was gripped tight as barrel bands. Pain stabbed up her arm, made her gasp through gritted teeth.

'Better not,' said a man's voice in her ear. A soft, bland, bored-sounding voice.

A door clattered open, then shut. Boots clonked and rattled on a loose floor. She felt herself dumped into a chair. A creak of wood and a hiss of rope as her hands were tied fast to the back, her ankles to the legs.

'All right, take it off.'

The bag was pulled from her head.

Some gloomy shed with a tar-and-fish stink. Shafts of light shone through the cracks between the timbers of its walls. Slimy lobster cages were stacked to one side. Vick wondered if this was the place she'd die. She guessed she'd seen worse.

A tall woman perched on a table with arms folded, looking down at Vick through narrowed eyes. Her grey hair was short and spiky, her sharp face deeply lined. Late fifties, maybe. Calm and professional. Not trying to be menacing. There was no need.

'Know who I am?' she asked. A Styrian accent, but she spoke common well. Like someone who'd spent a lot of time in the Union.

Vick's head was thumping where it had hit the quay. Blood tickling her scalp. Her shoulder was throbbing worse and worse. But she made sure to show as little pain as possible. Show hurt, you're asking to be hurt. 'I've a guess,' she said.

'Well, don't keep us in suspense.'

'You're Shylo Vitari, Minister of Whispers for the Serpent of Talins.' If Old Sticks had an opposite number on this side of the Circle Sea, here she sat.

'*Very* good.' Hard wrinkles showed around Vitari's eyes as she smiled. 'I like her already. You like her?'

The bored man gave a non-committal grunt. As if liking or disliking things wasn't really his business. He finished tying Tallow to his chair the way he'd tied Vick to hers. Quick and practised, like he'd done it many times before.

'Know who this is?' Vitari nodded towards him as he tested the knots on Tallow's bonds.

Vick hardly wanted to answer. 'I've a guess.'

'Let's see if you can make it two of two.'

'He's Casamir dan Shenkt.'

'The real one,' said Vitari. 'Imagine *that*.'

Styria's most infamous killer, if it really was him, gave Vick a watery, slightly apologetic smile. Few men had ever looked so ordinary. Gaunt and colourless, with dark rings around his eyes. But then awesome looks put people on their guard, and that's the last thing a killer wants. He leaned back against the wall and pulled something from a pocket. A piece of wood, roughly carved. He began to whittle it with a little curved knife, blade flashing, white shavings scattering about his worn boots.

'Do you go by Victarine?' asked Vitari. 'It's quite the mouthful. Maybe your friends call you Vick?'

'Maybe they would. If I had any.'

'You've got at least one.' She grinned down at Tallow and he stared back at her with those big, sad eyes, and grunted something into his gag no one could understand.

Vick didn't like the thought that he'd ended up in that chair because of her. 'No need to hurt him,' she wanted to say, and, 'It's me you want,' and all the bloody clichés, but that would've been good as telling them this stringy fool was a chink in her armour. So Vick didn't even glance in his direction. She treated him like he was nothing. It was all she could do for him.

'Do you know the irony, Vick?' Vitari slowly sat forward, wrists on her knees and her long hands dangling. 'We were *there*. In the Temple Square, waiting for Shudra, so we could kill him and pretend you'd done it.'

When you've nothing to add, stay silent.

'Then we saw you coming, and we thought, if you're fool enough to kill him yourself... why not let you save us the trouble?'

More silence.

'But you weren't there to kill him. You were there to pretend we'd tried, so you could pretend to save him. I watched the whole thing with a growing sense of annoyance, then a growing sense of admiration. It was very neat, wasn't it?'

Shenkt's only contribution was the soft scraping of his knife.

'Who was he? Your fake assassin? An actor?'

'And acrobat,' said Vick. 'I found him in a circus.'

Vitari grinned. 'Nice touch. Well, he can take a punch. You gave him quite the beating.'

'He was a bit upset about it.'

'So am I,' said Vitari, her grin vanishing. 'The Grand Duchess Monzcarro is going to be quite irked. And believe me, you haven't really seen irked until you've seen the Serpent of Talins irked. Do you think you're clever?'

Vick tried to shift her throbbing shoulder into a more comfortable position, but there was none. 'I've felt cleverer.'

'I think you're clever. I don't often find people who can get the better of me. When I do, I'd rather have them work for me than work against. Or dead, I guess. But dead would be a waste, wouldn't it?'

Shenkt gave that grunt again, as though it was the same to him either way.

'So, how about it?' Vitari looked sideways at her. 'After a new job? You could tell me secrets. What the Union's planning, where they're weak, where they're strong, that kind of thing.'

Thump, thump, thump went the pulse in Vick's head and the blood tickled at her scalp and it occurred to her this might be one of those turning points. Like in the mine, when she chose to run. Or in the camps, when she chose to tell. Or in Valbeck, when she chose to stay. Her mouth felt very dry all of a sudden.

'I've already got a job,' she said.

Vitari's brows drew in. Grey brows, with just a few orange flecks in them. 'I used to work for Old Sticks, you know. Back before he was Old Sticks. Young Sticks, would you say?'

Shenkt shrugged, as though he wouldn't say much about anything, and pursed his lips, and blew a puff of dust from his carving.

'We were in Dagoska together, during the siege.' Vitari gave a faraway sigh. 'So many happy memories. He's a clever bastard. Fearless. And ruthless. Understands pain like no one else I ever knew. Lots to admire. But it's not as though he really pulls the strings himself, is it?'

She narrowed her eyes slightly, as if she was waiting for Vick to chime in. She'd a feeling there was some piece to this conversation she was missing. But when you've nothing to add, stay silent.

'Bayaz.' Shenkt pronounced both syllables crisply in Vick's ear, and his breath felt chill, like the draught through a window on a winter evening, and it made the hairs on her neck rise almost painfully.

'The First of the Magi?' The idea of that self-satisfied old bastard pulling anyone's strings seemed hard to credit.

'The Union has been his tool since he first brought it together in the days of Harod the Great.'

'You want ruthless?' Vitari gave a low whistle. 'Should've seen Adua after he was done with it. He already has you dancing to his tune, I reckon.'

'I never even met the man.'

'And yet you came to Westport with more than a trunk full of clothes.' Vitari leaned closer, voice dropping to a breathy murmur. A voice for secrets. A voice for threats. 'You came with Valint and Balk's debts. With Valint and Balk's trade rights. With Valint and Balk's *money*.'

'What have Valint and Balk got to do with Bayaz?'

'They're three names for the same thing,' murmured Shenkt.

Vitari slowly shook her head. 'Dark company you keep.'

'Really?' Vick jerked her head towards Stryia's most infamous assassin. 'I heard he eats people.'

'As rarely as possible,' he said, without a trace of irony. 'That bank chomps up dozens a day.'

'So how about it?' Vitari stuck her lips out in a pout. 'Come work for me. Stand with the righteous. Or as close as the likes of us will get.'

Vick looked down at the ground, the blood *thump, thump, thumping* in her skull louder than ever. 'I owe Glokta.' It surprised her, that she said it. It surprised her, how sure she sounded. 'Reckon I'll stick with him. Till the debt's paid.'

Tallow made a high-pitched squeak into his gag. Vitari gave a long sigh. Shenkt issued that indifferent grunt one more time. Vick bared her teeth, back prickling, expecting the blade. Any moment now. The brittle silence stretched, almost unbearable.

'That's interesting,' said Vitari.

'Mmm,' said Shenkt, slipping his carving away but keeping the knife out.

'You could've told me yes, then when you got back home, never followed through. Or tried to work me somehow. Someone clever as you would've seen that right off. So why not just tell me yes?'

Vick looked up at her. 'Because I want you to believe me.'

'Huh.' Vitari smiled wide. Good teeth she had, for a woman her age. 'I like that. Do you like that?'

'I do,' said Shenkt.

Vitari pulled out a slip of paper, and folded it, and pressed the fold sharp with her thumbnail, then she opened Vick's shirt pocket, and slipped the paper inside, and gave it a pat. 'Once you realise how things really are, go to this address. The barman there will have what you need.'

'He has what everyone needs,' said Shenkt.

'Until then, if I was you . . .' Vitari stood and strolled towards the door, wagging one long finger. 'I wouldn't come back to Styria.'

'We're in Westport,' said Vick. 'This is the Union.'

'For now.' Vitari drew the bolt and opened the door. Shenkt slipped away that little curved knife, pulled up his hood and walked out, humming faintly to himself, leaving nothing but a scattering of pale shavings on the boards.

It looked like Vick would live out the day after all.

'How do we get free?' she called, still trussed up tight.

Vitari paused, a long, black shape in the bright doorway. 'You're the clever one. You work it out.'

Late

'You are late, Rikke.'

She opened her eyes. Candle flames in the darkness. Hundreds of flames, like stars prickling a night sky. Or were they the ghosts where candles once burned, long ago?

'You might be too late.'

A face swam at her. Lank grey hair, and shadows in the deep lines, and candlelight glimmering on the golden wire.

'There is no time left.'

Strong fingers pressed at Rikke's face, pressed at the sore flesh around her burning left eye, and she grunted, squirmed, but she was too weak to move.

'There must be a price.'

A hand lifted her head, the rim of a cup pressed to her mouth. She coughed on something bitter, shuddered as she swallowed.

'You have to choose, Rikke.'

She felt afraid. Terrified. She tried to twist away but strong hands held her down, held her tight.

'Which will it be?'

The woman reached for her. Something glittered in her hand. A cold needle.

'No,' whispered Rikke, closing her eyes. 'This hasn't happened yet.'

Shivers held her hand. Held so tight it hurt.

'Can't lose you, Rikke.' The grey stubble on his grey cheek shifted as he clenched his jaw. 'Can't do it.'

'Not planning to be lost.' Her tongue felt all thick and clumsy, she could hardly make the words. 'But if I am you'll get through it. Lost your eye, didn't you, and you were a good deal closer to that.'

'I've got another eye. There's just one o' you.'

It was dawn, she thought. Slap and suck of water on shingle. Cold light on rocks streaked with damp. A cobweb fluttered in the breeze, glittering dewdrops dancing.

'You don't know what I was.' Shivers fussed at that ring with the red stone he wore on his little finger. 'I cared for nothing. Hated everything. Came to serve your father 'cause of all the men I hated, he was the one I hated least. I walked in a nightmare.' He shut his eyes. Or the one that could see. The other showed a slit of gleaming metal still.

'You were so sick, then. No one thought you'd last another winter. Your mother dead and your father grieving. So sick, but so full of hope. You trusted me. Me, with nothing in him to trust. You sucked goat's milk from a cloth, in my arms. Your father said I was the least likely nursemaid he ever saw. Said I brought you back from the brink.' He looked at her then, and a tear streaked from his good eye. 'But it was you brought me back.'

'You soft fool,' she croaked through her cracked lips. 'You can't cry. Not you.'

'When I was a boy, my brother called me pig fat, I cried so easy. Then I forgot how. All I wanted was to be feared. But you never feared me.'

'Well, you're not so scary as they all make out.' Rikke tried to shift, but nothing was comfortable. She felt her eyes drifting closed, and Shivers squeezed her hand so hard it made her gasp.

'Hold on, Rikke. She's coming.'

'No,' she said, tears stinging her lids. 'This hasn't happened yet.'

Two great stones loomed into the evening, black fingers against the pink sky. Ancient, they were, splattered with moss and lichen, carved with symbols that time had pitted and smudged all meaning from. There was a hint of drizzle in the air and the hair was stuck to Rikke's face and everything had a watery sheen.

A pair of guards stood by the stones, holding crude spears, so still Rikke took them for statues. As Shivers carried her closer, she saw there was something wrong about them. Misshapen.

'By the dead,' croaked Rikke. 'They're flatheads.'

'That they are,' said Scenn. The hillman stood grinning next to one of the Shanka and it narrowed its already narrow eyes at him while it used a splinter of bone to pick at one huge tooth. 'They guard the witch. She can speak to 'em. Sings to 'em, some say. They're tame. Long as we behave.'

'I always behave,' said Isern, frowning at those two flatheads with her grip tight on the dark haft of her spear. Far as Shanka have expressions beyond just a lot of teeth, these ones seemed to frown back. 'Let's go, then.'

Scenn shook his head. 'I go no further.'

'I know you to be many things, Scenn, and most of 'em bad, but I never took you for a coward.'

'Take me for whatever you like, sister, but I know where I belong, and it's on this side of the stones. My task was to bring you and my task is done. I don't pretend to be—'

'Shit on you, then, you hill of blubber,' and Isern elbowed him out of their way and strode on.

'Just the three of us.' Shivers grunted as he shifted Rikke higher up his shoulders. Made her feel like a child again, being carried like this, his hands around her ankles. On between the stones and down a steep path through trees. Old, old trees with whispers in their high, high branches and their jealous roots delving deep, deep, knotted like misers' fingers.

Around a bend and Rikke saw the shore. Grey shingle stretching down to grey water, blurred reflections of the tall trees prickled by rain-ripples. A few strides out, all was lost in a mist, and beyond that Rikke could see nothing, and somewhere a lonely owl hooted at the sunset.

'The forbidden lake,' said Isern. 'Not far to go now.'

'Always has to be a mist, doesn't there?' grunted Shivers.

Isern set off, her boots crunching in the shingle. 'I guess nothing looks so magical, d'you see, as what can't be seen at all.'

'No,' whispered Rikke, closing her eyes. 'This hasn't happened yet.'

Night, and firelight danced on the gathered faces. Withered old faces and fresh young ones. Faces pricked with the swirling tattoos of the hillmen. Faces that weren't there yet, maybe, or had been there long ago. Rikke could hardly tell today from yesterday from tomorrow any longer. Meat spat and sizzled. The cold, crisp air of the hills on the back of Rikke's head but the warmth of the fire on her face and she grinned at the simple pleasure of it, snuggled into a smelly old fur.

'I don't like it,' said Scenn, shaking his great fat head.

'You've confused me with someone who'd spare a turd on what you like or don't,' said Isern.

Two siblings could hardly have been less alike. Isern, spear-hard and dagger-faced with her crow-black hair in a long tangle. Scenn, huge as a house with hands like hams and a face like a pudding, hair shaved back to a red fuzz on his creased scalp.

'Don't like going up there,' he said, frowning northwards, between the firelit hovels to the archway of crooked branches. 'It's forbidden for a reason.'

'I need you to take us, not voice your opinions. They're as bloated with wind as you are.'

'You need not be so harsh about it,' said Scenn, kneading at his belly and looking a touch hurt. He frowned over at Shivers. 'She's harsh as a whipping, ain't she?'

Shivers raised his brows. Or the one he had, anyway. 'You say that like it's a bad thing.'

'She has to go up there and that's all there is to it,' snapped Isern, harshly. 'This girl matters, Scenn. She's beloved of the moon. I've always known it.'

'You've confused me with someone who'd spare a turd on what you know or don't,' said Scenn. 'I'm not taking her just 'cause you say so.'

'No, you're taking her because she has to go.'

'Because she has the Long Eye?'

'Because she has the Long Eye so strong it's killing her.'

Scenn looked over at Rikke, then. Small, dark eyes he had, but she saw the sharpness in them. Beware of clever men, her father told her once. But beware most of clever men who look like fools. 'What do you say, girl?' And he spat a bit of gristle into the fire and pointed at her with the stripped-bare bone. 'If you can see the future, tell me mine.'

Rikke leaned forward then, the fur slipping from her shoulders, and she turned her burning left eye on him and opened it wide. He flinched back as she raised her left hand, pointing with her forefinger towards the glittering stars, and spoke in ringing tones her prophecy.

'I . . . see . . . you're going to get fatter!'

Laughter around the fire at that. An old woman with just one tooth laughed so hard she nearly fell over, and a young one had to slap her on the back till she coughed up a shred of meat.

Shivers tapped his ale cup against hers and Rikke took a swig and settled back into her fur. There weren't a lot of things would bring someone to Slorfa, but they made good ale, the hillmen, her head was dizzy with it. Or maybe that was the sickness of the Long Eye. Hard to tell the difference. Scenn frowned, settling his bulk cross-legged.

'She has a sense of humour, then. She'll need that, up in the High Places. There are few laughs at the forbidden lake.' He frowned towards Isern again. 'Do you really think this little shred of gristle, this little snot with the ring through her nose, is beloved of the moon?'

Isern spat ale in the fire and made it hiss. 'What would you know about it, Scenn-i-Phail, who carries our father's hammer?'

Scenn stuck his beard out at her. 'I'd know as much as you, Isern-i-Phail, who carries our father's spear. Just because he loved you best, don't think you learned the most from him.'

'You're joking, you sheep-fucker! Our father hated me.'

'He did. He loathed the guts and face and arse of you, head to toe.' Scenn paused a moment. 'And you were his favourite.'

And the two of them burst out laughing together. They might not have looked much alike but their laughter was the same. Mad, cackling peels that sounded halfway to wolves howling while overhead the full moon hung fat and round, and they smashed their cups together and sent up a fountain of ale and drained what was left and carried on laughing.

Shivers watched them, face in shadow. 'This'll be a long month, I reckon.'

'No,' said Rikke, snuggling into that smelly fur and shutting her eyes. 'This hasn't happened yet.'

'Always upwards,' gasped Rikke, shading her eyes against the sun and squinting uphill.

'That's going into the hills for you.' Isern wasn't even out of breath. Nothing ever tired her.

'Where are we headed, exactly?' asked Shivers, his boots crunching on the dirt path.

'To the forbidden lake.'

'That much I know. I'm asking where it is.'

'If they told everyone where it was, it wouldn't be very forbidden, would it?'

Shivers rolled his eyes. Or eye, at least. 'Do you have any straight answers, woman?'

'What use are straight answers in a crooked world?'

Shivers gave Rikke a glance, but she was too out of breath to do much more than shrug. 'How ... do we get there ... then?' she asked between her wheezes.

'My brother Scenn knows the way. He is a turd in the shape of a man, but he'll help. We'll head to his village first, which is a turd in the shape of a village. Slorfa, they call it, at the head of the valley four valleys on.'

'Sounds ... a long way,' muttered Rikke.

'One foot in front of the other will get it done with time.'

'How many brothers do you have?' asked Shivers.

'Eleven of the bastards, and each more like a dog's arse than the last.'

Rikke raised her brows. 'You don't ... talk about 'em much.'

'We all had different mothers,' said Isern, as though that explained the whole business. 'My upbringing was less than happy. An ordeal, d'you see? Living through it once was bad enough but had to be done. Remembering it is a thing I aim to avoid.'

Isern stopped on a heap of rocks, and pulled out a flask, and splashed water over her head and some more in her mouth and offered it to Rikke.

By the dead, she was weary. She stood, swallowed water, wiped sweat from her forehead. It was springing out about as fast as she could drink it. Her vest was soaked through. She reeked like a haystack after the rains. The air was cool, but her eye, her eye was always hot. Burning in her head. There'd been a time, she was sure, when she could run and run and never stop. Now a few paces had her panting, and her head pounding, and her sight swimming, ghosts haunting the edges of her vision.

She looked back the way they'd come, out of the hills over the crinkling valleys towards the lowlands. Back down the long miles walked towards Uffrith. Into the past.

'Let's make some footprints,' grunted Isern, turning back to the steeply climbing trail. 'The forbidden lake won't be coming to us, will it?'

Rikke blew out so hard she made her lips flap and wiped a fresh sheen of sweat from her forehead.

'Need to ride on my shoulders?' asked Shivers. Most folk couldn't even have told he was smiling. But she knew how to tell.

'Never, you old bastard,' she growled, setting off. 'More likely I'll be carrying you.'

'That I'd like to see,' Isern threw over her shoulder, and stones scattered from the heel of her scuffed boot and down the bald track.

'No,' muttered Rikke, closing her eyes. 'This hasn't happened yet.'

'Found you!' shouted Leo in that piping voice with the strange accent, catching hold of Rikke's foot and dragging her out of the hay.

She'd soon realised they'd be man and woman grown by the time he found her if she'd stayed in her first hiding place, up among the rafters where the pigeons nested. She'd enjoyed looking down on him hunting around the barn, but when he wandered off to look elsewhere she got bored and dropped down, burrowed into the hay and left one boot sticking out where he could see it. Games are only fun if they're close, after all.

'Took you long enough,' she said.

He was pretty, Rikke thought, even if he wasn't the cleverest. And he had an odd manner and talked strange. But being brought up in the Union would do that to a boy, maybe, and for pretty you could forgive a lot.

She was glad he was here, anyway. Nice to have someone her age to play with. She liked to pretend she was happiest on her own, but no one is, really. Her da was always busy having the long talks with the grey-bearded bastards where everyone frowned and shook their heads a lot.

Shivers would tell her stories sometimes, about his travels around the Circle of the World and all the different styles o' strange folk he'd killed there, but she felt there was something odd about a friendship between a little girl and one o' the most feared warriors in the North. He said he didn't mind but she didn't want to push it.

There weren't many children in Uffrith and those there were thought she was cursed and wouldn't come near her on account of the fits. Leo didn't seem worried about the fits. Maybe he would be once he saw her having one. Specially if she shat herself during, which was more often than not, sadly. But there wasn't much she could do about that. About the fits or the shits.

Rikke had sworn an oath not to worry about the things she couldn't change, and she took an oath very seriously. Her father always said there was nothing more important than your word, usually while frowning and shaking his head. It was a shame he frowned so much, 'cause when he smiled it lit the world up.

'My turn to hide!' shouted Leo, and he dashed off, slipped and fell, rolled in a shower of hay dust, then scrambled up and disappeared through the barn door. Made Rikke sad, for some reason, to see him go. So sad.

'No,' she said to herself, closing her eyes. 'This happened long ago.'

An Infinite Supply

'How's my stance?' asked Flick, peering over his shoulder at his back foot.

'We'll get to your stance,' said Clover.

'In about a year, at this rate,' muttered Downside, holding the edge of his axe up to the sunlight then polishing away at it again.

'If you last a year.' Sholla frowned as she tried to cut the finest slice of cheese imaginable with that long, thin knife of hers.

'Don't listen to this sorry pair,' said Clover. 'We'll get to your stance. But always bear in mind, if your sword's drawn, you've already made at least one mistake.'

'Eh?' said Flick, squinting at Clover over the wobbling point of his blade.

'Unless you're cleaning it, or sharpening it, or maybe selling it.'

'What if you're in a battle?'

'Then you've made at least two mistakes, possibly a lot more. A battle's no place for a self-respecting warrior. But if you must attend one, at least have the good taste to be where the fighting isn't.'

'What if some bastard tries to kill you?'

'Ideally, you'd have worked that out a while back and done 'em first, preferably while they're asleep. That's what knives are for.'

'That and slicing cheese,' said Sholla, lifting her knife towards her mouth with furious concentration, a cheese-shaving so fine it was almost see-through clinging to the flat. A spring gust came through the courtyard just as it was getting to her lips and blew it away like thistledown, left her clutching helpless at the air.

'That's the thing about knives,' said Clover. 'Cheap to get and with endless applications. Swords are dear as all hell and they've got just the one, and it's one every man should avoid.'

Flick crunched up his face. 'You're sort of talking yourself out of a job here, far as the teaching of sword-work goes.'

'Aye, but life being what it is, mistakes happen. That's when an understanding of sword-work might save your worthless hide from an unsightly hole or two, as it's saved mine on a couple of regrettable occasions. So, to the stance—'

'Clover!'

Greenway came strutting across the yard like he was the one that built it and was highly delighted with the achievement, thumbs in his belt and his elbows pointing out, as if you could tell a man's quality by the amount of space he took up.

'I fucking hate this prick,' murmured Sholla as she tried to shave an even thinner slice from the edge of the cheese block, then clicked her tongue in disgust as it crumbled.

'You're a fine judge of character,' said Clover, giving Greenway a cheery wave hello as he approached, sneering at Flick. Since Magweer's untimely demise, he'd taken on the role of Stour's chief sneerer.

'Who's this?' he sneered.

'This is Flick. I'm teaching him how to use the blade. Or how not to.'

'He looks a bloody idiot,' said Greenway.

'Aye, well, there's a short supply of men clever as you. Have to make do with what we're given. Stour ready for me?'

'The king, you mean.'

Clover stared back blankly. 'Aye, the king I do mean. Stour is the king and the king is Stour. We were both there when he hung the chain round his neck, weren't we?' They'd both been there and they'd both been bloody.

Greenway shifted his thumbs in his sword-belt. 'One o' these days you'll say too much, Clover.'

'Well, the mud's waiting for us all. Worse ways to get there than excessive conversation. Now, shall we take the news to the Great Wolf?' He nodded at the sack, which had drawn the attention of at least half of Carleon's flies. 'Bring that along, eh, Flick?'

The lad wrinkled his nose. 'You sure? It's got quite the odour.'

'That's the way of things, lad, we all end up stinking. And yes, I'm sure. It's not for my benefit, I can tell you that.'

'Stay out o' trouble, eh, Chief?' grunted Sholla, eyes fixed on her knife and her cheese.

'Believe it or not, I've spent fifteen years trying.'

'What the bloody hell are you about, anyway?' Downside was asking as Clover went to answer the king's call.

'If you get it right,' murmured Sholla, 'it just melts on your tongue...'

Flick looked like he was about to swing the sack over his shoulder, saw the stains and decided against. He wasn't strong enough to hold it at arm's length, though, so it ended up knocking against one knee as he walked with a wet clumping. 'Never met a king,' he said.

'No?' said Clover. 'I'd have thought you'd be in daily contact with royalty.'

'Eh?'

'Just keep your mouth shut and smile.'

Flick made a gurning rictus of the lower half of his face.

'Smile, I said. You're not trying to sell him your teeth.'

There was a lot that hadn't changed in Skarling's Hall since Skarling's time. The big creaking doors with their great iron hinges, the high rafters, the tall windows, the bright, cold sun beyond and the sound of rushing water far below. Skarling's Chair was the same one Bethod, and Black Dow, and Scale Ironhand had sat in, hard and simple, paint worn off the time-polished arms and flaking from the back.

The man sitting in it was new, though. Stour Nightfall, who men called the Great Wolf, with his left leg hooked over one of the arms and the bare foot gently swinging, a very fine wolfskin cloak about his shoulders and grinning like a wolf indeed. Why wouldn't he smile? Got everything he wanted, hadn't he? No longer king-in-waiting but king all the way, and all he'd had to do was stab his uncle in the throat.

Everything boiled over with menace in there. The faces of the young warriors, unsmiling, like life was a contest at having the least fun. The flames in the great fireplace stabbed angrily. Even the cups on the tables seemed to be nursing a slight. There was this horrible quiet, everyone holding their breath, expecting violence to strike like lightning any moment.

'You should be kneeling,' growled Greenway as they stopped in the midst of that wide stone floor in front of Stour.

Clover raised his brows. 'Thought I'd at least walk in first. Guess I could shuffle in on my knees but that'd wear quite considerably on my trousers and everyone's patience.' He twirled his finger around, turning back towards the door. 'But I'll happily head back out and start again if there's a better way to go about it—'

'You don't need to kneel, Clover,' said Stour, waving him closer. 'Old friend like you? Don't be a cunt, Greenway.'

Greenway gave an epic sneer which made him, in Clover's opinion, look more of a cunt than ever. Some men just can't help themselves. All the ones in this room, certainly. It was then he noticed there was a new cage in the corner, hanging from one of the high rafters, gently turning. Didn't seem a good sign. There was someone in it, too, naked and beaten bloody but with eyes still open. That seemed an even worse sign.

'Unless I'm mistook,' said Clover, 'you've got Gregun Hollowhead in a cage.'

Stour narrowed his eyes. 'I've a room full of bastards to tell me what I know already.'

'I could've sworn he was on our side.'

'I had my doubts,' said Stour, curling his lip at the cage. 'When I raised his taxes, he didn't want to pay. Felt quite angry about it. Made other folk angry.'

'How's he feeling now, d'you reckon?' asked Greenway.

Clover scratched gently at his scar. 'Bit sore, by the look o' things.'

'My father was always for buying him off,' said Stour. 'Him and men like him.'

'Black Calder's a great one for compromise.'

'I'm not.'

'No,' said Clover. 'I see that.'

'Men are greedy, aren't they? No gratitude. They don't think about what they've already got from you, only about what they can get next.'

'There's a lot of arseholes about, all right,' said Clover, letting his eyes sweep across Stour's closest.

'And Hollowhead and his sons and all those shits from the West Valleys, they're closer to Uffrith than Carleon. Don't trust 'em.'

'Do you trust 'em more now?'

'At least we all know where we stand.'

'The Nail's one of his sons, no? Dangerous man, that.'

The warriors ranged about the walls competed to look more dangerous themselves. 'You scared?' asked Greenway.

'Constantly,' said Clover, 'but that's probably just my age. What you going to do with Hollowhead?'

Stour glowered at the cage and gave a great sniff. 'Still thinking. Let him go so he can pay the taxes or cut the bloody cross in him as an example.'

'He'll have taught folk a good lesson whichever you choose,' said Greenway.

Clover had his doubts as he watched that cage gently turn. Hollowhead was a popular man. Lot of friends and family all over those valleys on the border with Uffrith. Lot of hard fighters who'd be less than happy about that man being in a cage. Black Calder had spent years stitching the ripped-up North together with threats and whispers and debts and favours. Can't do it just with fear alone. But it was hardly Clover's job to say so.

He looked away from Hollowhead and smiled. 'Well, I wish you joy of the outcome, whatever you decide.'

'Huh.' Stour's wet, sly eyes slid back to Clover. 'And how about you? Get some joy out o' the Shanka?'

'Joy is not the word I'd pick, my king, but when your chief gives you a task, as old Threetrees used to say, you get on with it, so we bowed to the inevitable. You know me, I don't mind bowing. Specially not to the inevitable.'

'Got no pride, eh, Clover?'

'Used to have, my king. Used to have a fucking surfeit. Like a field in spring can draw too many bees. But I found when you're struggling, there's not a lot you can buy with the stuff. Pride, that is, not bees. So I shed mine. Don't miss it in the least.'

Stour narrowed his eyes at Flick. 'Who's this?'

'This is Flick.' And Clover clapped a hand down on the lad's scrawny shoulder. 'He's my best man.'

'He looks a good one,' said Stour, and his arseholes laughed. More arseholes than there used to be. The North had an infinite supply.

'Man should have friends, I reckon,' said Clover.

'Definitely. Need someone to stab, don't you?'

More laughter. Took an effort for Clover to smile, but he managed it. He jerked his head sideways at Flick. 'Need me to stab him, my king?'

'Nah. Y'already proved what you are, Clover. I'd hate to take your best man away. What's he got there?'

'Little present for you.' Clover took the bag from Flick and upended it, and the Shanka heads bounced and rolled out across the floor. He wished those had been the first scattered across Skarling's Hall, but he'd a sorry sense severed heads had been quite a frequent decoration down the years.

Greenway took a step back with his arm across his face. 'They fucking stink!'

'Don't be a cunt, Greenway.' Stour sprang eagerly from his chair and trotted over to look down at 'em, still a trace of a limp when he moved from the Young Lion's sword-cut. 'So you taught the Shanka a lesson, eh?'

'Not sure flatheads really learn lessons,' said Clover.

'Not these ones, anyway.' Stour nudged the half-rotten heads around with one bare foot so he could see their leering faces. 'Ugly bastards, eh?'

'I find myself on shaky ground when it comes to criticising others' looks,' said Clover.

'And we none of us look our best dead,' added Flick, then cleared his throat and looked down at the ground. 'My king.'

'Oh, I don't know,' said Stour, giving him that wet-eyed stare. 'I can think of quite a few folk I'd prefer as corpses. I'm heading down to Uffrith, Clover. Like you to come along.'

'To fight?'

'No, no, no.' Which was something of a relief, as Clover couldn't say he'd much enjoyed their last war with the Union. 'Gave my word in the Circle, didn't I? Swore a solemn oath to the Young Lion! Think I'd break my word?'

'Honestly, my king, I haven't a fucking clue what you'll do one moment to the next.'

Stour grinned. 'Well, wouldn't life be dull if you could see everything coming? You know a fellow called Oxel?'

'One o' the Dogman's War Chiefs. Wouldn't trust him to hold the bucket while I pissed.'

'Sometimes a shifty bastard's what you need, though, eh? Dogman's on the way out. Old. And sick, I hear. When he's gone, Uffrith needs to go to someone. Oxel wants it to be me.'

'And what about that solemn oath in the Circle?'

Stour shrugged. 'Swore not to take it. Didn't say a thing about it dropping in my lap. Uffrith wants to be part o' the North, who am I to argue?'

'And if there's some don't want to join?' asked Clover.

Stour nodded towards the cage. 'I can get more o' those. Off you go, now.'

'And take your stinking heads with you,' hissed Greenway.

'Don't be a *cunt*!' roared Stour, spraying spit, and all around the hall men jerked up, stepped forward, put hands to their weapons, like dogs might bare teeth at their master's anger. Greenway backed off, white and trembling, no doubt thinking the Great Leveller had a hand on his shoulder.

Then Stour grinned bigger'n ever. And he squatted down on his haunches, that beautiful wolfskin cloak dragging in the mess the heads had left. He took the biggest one in his hands and set it right-side up, its great spiked helmet still on and its great long bloated tongue hanging from its oversized jaws.

'I want to look at 'em.'

The Demon That
Breaks All Chains

'By all the dead,' croaked Rikke as she lifted her head. Her mouth tasted like graves, her empty stomach squelched and bubbled. Felt like there was a mace hanging behind her eyes, bashing painfully against the inside of her skull with every movement. But at least time was going all one way.

She'd been sleeping in a nest of furs but with hard rock underneath, and she dragged a dusty old deerskin around her shoulders, stumbling from the darkness, eyes almost closed against the stabbing light.

It wasn't raining but there was a chilly damp in the air that turned everything dark. No wind. No sound. Everything still as the land of the dead. Tall trees, black wood and black needles. Jumbles of black rock jutting on the slopes. Tall black mountains in the far-off distance, white-bearded and white-capped like grumpy old warriors. Dark shingle sloped down from the cave-mouth to the dark water, and in its mirror the trees and the rocks and the mountains all reflected, still and perfect and darker than ever. A woman stood there, tattered skirts tucked into her belt, up to her thin, pale, veiny calves in the lake. Stood so still she didn't make a ripple.

Rikke puffed out her cheeks. When she bent to roll up her trouser legs, her head throbbed so hard she nearly fell. She hitched the bald hide up around her shoulders then tottered towards the water, crunching shingle sharp between her bare toes. It was that cold it surely should've frozen. But it's better to do it than live with the fear of it, as her father occasionally told her, so she sloshed out, wincing and shivering, ripples catching the peaceful trees, and the still mountains, and shattering them into dancing fragments.

'Chilly as winter's arse,' she gasped as she wobbled up next to the woman. From the side she looked about normal. Old and deep-lined, cool blue eyes fixed on the horizon.

'The cold has a wonderful way of clearing the mind.' Not the witchy croak Rikke had expected. A young voice, smooth and full of music. 'It fixes you on what counts. Draws your attention inwards.'

'So . . . you do it to gather your magic . . . or something?'

'I do it because fools rarely follow a woman into cold water with their problems.' She turned, and Rikke could only stare, because her face was just the way she'd seen it in her vision.

A great pink-grey scar ran down the centre of her buckled forehead, from hairline to mouth, one eye and one brow higher than the other, as though her skull had been entirely split and set back together by a drunken surgeon. There was a crazy zigzag of stitches through the puckered skin. Stitches of golden wire that gleamed in the morning sun.

'I am Caurib,' she said, in that soft, soft voice. 'Or I was. A sorceress, from the utmost North. Or I was. Now I am the witch of the forbidden lake.' She turned back to the horizon. 'I find that suits me better.'

Rikke had grown up in the North where a man with no scars was no man at all, but she never before saw a scar the like of this. She looked down at the water, already settling around her own sharp shin bones and holding a dark reflection of herself. 'What happened to you?'

'An axe happened, as axes do.'

'Didn't see it coming, then?'

Caurib slowly raised one brow. Looked like it took some effort, skin stretching around the stitches. 'I do not need to tell you that the Long Eye comes when it comes. If you are hoping it will keep you safe from all life's axes, you will be disappointed. But then it is the fate of hope to end in disappointment, as it is the fate of light to end in darkness and life in death. They are still worth something while they last.'

Rikke wiggled her numb toes and watched the ripples spread. 'Bit of a bleak message.'

'If you sought optimism from a hermit whose head is stitched together with golden wire then you are a bigger fool even than you look. Which would be quite an achievement.'

Rikke stole a glance sideways, but Caurib was looking ahead again. 'I thought what I saw in the visions, the golden wire, might be, you know . . .'

'I do not know. Try saying the words.'

'A metaphor?'

'For what?'

'I just see the visions, I don't understand them.'

The witch gave a hiss of disgust. 'It is not the seer's task to *understand* her visions, girl, any more than it is the potter's task to *understand* her clay.'

'I'm guessing...' Rikke winced as she tried to shift her foot on the slippery lake bed and caught her toe on a pointed rock. 'We're not actually talking about pots now? Or are we talking about pots now?'

The witch gave a hiss of disappointment. 'It is the potter's task to impose her *will* upon the clay. To *shape* the clay into something useful. Or something beautiful.'

'So... I have to impose my will upon my visions? Shape them into something beautiful?'

'Ah! A ray of sunshine penetrates the long night of your ignorance.' The witch gave a hiss of scorn. She could do a lot with a hiss. 'And I only had to waste half my morning explaining it to you.'

'But—'

'I am not your mentor, girl, nor your teacher, nor your wise grandmother. You want me to give you the rules, but there are no rules. You are like those old fools the magi, who want to chain the world with laws. You are like those old fools the Eaters, who want to cage the world with prayers. You are like these new fools who want to bind the world with iron and make it obey. The Long Eye is *magic*, girl!' She raised her withered arms, screaming it towards the mountains. 'It is the devil that cannot be caged! It is the demon that breaks all chains!' She let her arms drop. 'If there were rules it would not be magic.'

'Guess I'll have to find my own answers, then,' said Rikke, mournfully.

Caurib looked down at her feet, hidden in the lake. 'Fear is like cold water. A little is a fine thing, it fixes you on what counts. But too much will freeze you. You must make a box inside your mind, and put your fear inside, and lock it.'

'That sounds a lot like something a mentor would say.'

'No doubt I'd be a wonderful one. But I'm not yours.'

Rikke heard crunching footsteps behind, turned with a smile thinking to see Shivers or Isern walking down the shore. Instead she saw a Shanka, coming with a lurching gait as it had one leg longer than the other, clawed foot sending a shower of shingle sideways with each step. It had fish threaded onto a spear, one still twisting and flipping, scales glinting silvery in the morning sun.

'Ah!' Caurib smiled, and the great scar through her top lip stretched about the wire in a way Rikke found most unsettling. 'Breakfast.'

'How did you make the Shanka serve you?' asked Rikke as it shoved its fish-laden spear point-down near the water's edge. Her father always talked of the flatheads as if they were animals. A plague that couldn't be reasoned with. And here was one snuffling around for sticks to build a fire like any fisherman on the beach. Well, any fisherman with spikes hammered into his head.

'The same way you make anyone serve you,' said Caurib. 'By offering them what they want.'

Rikke watched that flathead grunt and slurp to itself, tongue wedged in its great teeth as it carefully stacked twigs on a patch of shingle blackened by years of fires. 'They're like people, then?'

'Oh no.' And Rikke felt Caurib's hand on her shoulder, light but firm, and her soft voice in her ear. 'They can be *trusted*. It is them I have to thank for my life.'

'What, the Shanka?'

'Yes. If thanks are appropriate for what hardly seems a life.'

Rikke watched the flathead fumbling with a flint and tinder and juggling it all over the beach. 'Wouldn't think they had the fingers for pretty stitching.'

'Does this look pretty to you?'

Rikke cleared her throat and thought it best to say nothing.

'The Shanka don't like baths and they've no sense of humour at all, but they understand the meeting betwixt flesh and metal. They learned that much from the Master Maker.' And the Shanka bent down, crooked lips pursed, and coaxed a flame into life with its breath.

'What happened to the others?' asked Rikke.

'The man with the steel eye and the woman with the iron temper? They sat a while beside you, each pretending to be less worried than the other, but after a few days they tired of fish. Neither would trust the other to hunt so they went off together.'

'Hold on,' said Rikke. 'Days?'

'Four days you slept. They are good companions. A woman who is to be taken seriously as a seer should have some colourful folk about her.'

'I didn't pick 'em for their colour.'

'No, they picked you, which speaks to your quality and theirs.'

'Speaks of good quality, or poor?'

Caurib didn't answer. Just turned her bright blue eyes on Rikke and said nothing. Rikke didn't much care for being looked at in that way, specially not by a witch, and specially not one with wire through her face.

'Reckon I'll eat if you don't mind sharing your breakfast.' The Shanka had his fish over the fire now and was making quite the mouth-watering smell. First time Rikke felt hungry in weeks, and she rubbed at her aching belly. Not much to rub these days. Her clothes were hanging off her like rags off a scarecrow. 'When my colourful friends get back we'd best start home. Long way down to Uffrith.'

'Going so soon?'

Gave Rikke a worried feeling, the way Caurib said it. Like there was an unpleasant surprise coming. Pleasant surprises seemed to get rarer as you got older. 'Aye, well . . . I feel better now.' Rikke put her palm a little nervously to her left eye. Cool and clammy, just like the other. Just like anyone's. 'Whatever you did worked.'

'I have painted runes about your Long Eye. Runes to keep it caged.'

'Caged, eh? Grand.' Since she woke, she'd seen no visions of things past and no ghosts of things to come. The world looked more ordinary than any time since the duel, when she'd forced the Long Eye open. Aside from standing in a magic lake with a woman sent back from the land of the dead while flatheads cooked breakfast, that was. Rikke took a long breath, puffed up her chest and blew it out. 'I'm all good.'

'For now.'

Rikke felt her shoulders sag. 'It'll get worse again?'

'The runes will fade, and it will get worse again, then worse still. We must paint the runes so they will not fade. We must tattoo them into your skin with a crow-bone needle and chain the Long Eye for as long as you live.'

Rikke stared at her. 'I thought it was the demon that breaks all chains?'

'Yet we must chain it. With eleven wards and eleven wards reversed, and eleven times eleven. A lock strong enough to hold shut the gates of hell themselves.'

'That . . . doesn't sound like something you want on your face.'

'You should eat. Then you should rest. You should drink plenty of water.'

'What's the water for?'

'One should always drink plenty of water. The tattooing will take several days. It will be draining for you and even more so for me.'

Rikke brushed her cheek with her fingertips as she watched the smoke from the cook-fire drift across the lake. She thought of the hillmen, and the hillwomen, and those bastards from past the Crinna she'd seen sometimes with their blue painted faces. She gave one of those sorry sighs made her lips flap. 'There's just no going back from tattoos on your face, is there?'

'There has never been any going back for you.' Caurib shrugged. 'Though you could always leave it, and let the visions get madder and madder until you are sucked into the darkness and your mind bursts apart into a million screaming fragments. That would save me some work.'

'Thanks for that option.' Rikke felt a bit teary, had to sniff back hard. But it's better to do it than live with the fear of it, and all that. 'Reckon I'll go for the tattoos, then. If that'll fix it.'

The witch gave a hiss of impatience. 'Nothing is ever *fixed*. From the moment it is born, from the moment it is built, everything is always dying, decaying, drifting into chaos.'

'I could stand a mite less philosophising and a couple of actual answers in the conversation, if it's all the same to you.'

'Look about you, girl. If I had all the answers, do you think I would be standing in a freezing lake with my head stitched together?'

And the witch held up her skirts and sloshed back towards the shore, leaving Rikke scared and shivering, up to her calves in the frosty water.

'Oh!' Caurib had turned back to shout at her. 'And if you need to shit, make sure you do it well away from the cave!'

The King's Justice

'**S**poke to the king myself, at length.' Isher lounged on the front bench as if he was in his drawing room. 'Orso's every bit his father's son.'

'None too bright.' The Lords' Round was full, but Barezin hardly seemed to care if they were overheard. 'And ever so easily led.'

Open disdain for not one but two kings felt a mite disloyal to Leo, especially here at the heart of government, attending a trial where a man's life would hang in the balance. His mother would've been most displeased to hear it. But then, sooner or later, a man has to stop making everything about pleasing his mother.

'Last year, outside Valbeck, Crown Prince Orso presided over the summary hanging of two hundred supposed revolutionaries,' said Isher. 'Without trial or process.'

'Their gibbeted bodies were used to decorate the road to Adua.' Barezin stuck his tongue out and mimed a hanging. 'As a warning to other commoners.'

'Now they want to do the same to a member of the Open Council.'

'As a warning to other noblemen.'

Heugen leaned in close. 'He may've inherited his mother's mercy along with his father's brains.'

Barezin's eager whisper could scarcely contain his amusement. 'He certainly got her weakness for the ladies!'

'By the dead,' breathed Leo. He found neither the Queen Dowager's preferences nor the king's brutality a laughing matter.

Isher shook his well-groomed white head. 'At this rate, not even the best of us will be safe.'

'It's the best who are in the most danger,' said Heugen.

Barezin grunted agreement. 'Wetterlant hasn't a bloody chance. Bet you they present no evidence at all.'

'But ... *why?*' asked Leo, struggling to find a position on the hard bench where his leg didn't nag at him.

'Wetterlant has no heir,' said Isher, 'so his estates will be forfeit and the Crown will sweep them up. You'll see.'

Leo stared in disbelief at the chamber's stained-glass windows. The proudest moments of Union history. Harod the Great bringing the three kingdoms of Midderland together. Arnault the Just throwing off tyranny. Casamir the Steadfast taking law to the lawless in Angland. The Open Council lifting King Jezal to the throne, uniting behind him to defeat the Gurkish. The noble heritage his father once loved to talk of. Could the corruption really have spread so deep?

'They wouldn't dare,' he breathed. 'In front of the whole Open Council?'

'You'd be a bold man to bet on what Old Sticks wouldn't dare,' said Isher as the announcer struck his staff upon the tiles for order.

'My lords and ladies, you are commanded to kneel at the approach of His Imperial Highness...'

The announcer's voice echoed through the gilded doors and into the stuffy darkness of the anteroom, and Orso hooked a finger inside his stiff collar and tried to get some air in. His regalia was bloody stifling, in more ways than one.

'...the King of Angland, Starikland and Midderland, the Protector of Westport and Uffrith...'

Orso twisted the considerable weight of the crown this way and that. Given the hours the royal jewellers had spent measuring his skull, one might have hoped they could have made the damn thing fit. Perhaps his head was simply the wrong shape for a crown. No doubt there were plenty who thought so.

'...His August Majesty, Orso the First, High King of the Union!'

The vast doors were heaved open, the crack of light down the middle gradually widening. Orso set his shoulders in what he hoped was a regal bearing, plastered on a smile, realised that was utterly inappropriate to the occasion, swapped it for a solemn frown and stepped through.

It was far from his first visit to the Lords' Round, of course. He remembered being mildly bored when his father had shown it to him as a building site, rather impressed when his father had shown it to him largely completed, then exceedingly bored when his father had presided over the first meeting of the Open Council there.

But Orso had never seen it from this angle – the way an actor might a theatre. An ill-prepared understudy, in his case, suddenly called on to face an audience of hostile critics. The curved benches brimmed with lords and proxies, all weighty furs and weighty frowns and weighty chains of office. The original Lords' Round, the one Bayaz destroyed, had boasted only the one public gallery. The architects of the replacement had clearly felt a speaker might not be sufficiently overawed, so they had added another above. Both were now crammed to the rails with brightly dressed onlookers, frothing with anticipation at the delicious prospect of a stranger's downfall.

There could easily have been a thousand in attendance. There could easily have been more. All kneeling or sunk into curtsies at his approach, of course. But the aristocracy of the Union could kneel and radiate contempt simultaneously. They had centuries of practice at it.

'Bloody hell,' he murmured under his breath. He could have sworn that by some acoustic sorcery, it was carried about the entire vast chamber and echoed back to his ear as he shuffled across that lonely expanse of tiles to the High Table, dragging a mighty weight of cloth of gold cloak behind him.

Bloody hell, bloody hell, bloody hell . . .

He flinched as he felt hands reaching around his neck, but it was only Gorst, unfastening the golden clasp and whisking the royal vestment away, while one of his legion of footmen did the same with the crown. Orso wasn't even sure he knew the man's name. He wasn't even sure he *had* a name.

Bloody hell, bloody hell, bloody hell . . .

Orso cleared his throat as he sank into the great gilded chair, had a momentary panic as he wondered whether he should have been sitting somewhere else, then reminded himself that, however improbable it felt, he was king. He always got the biggest chair.

'All rise!' bellowed the announcer, making him startle.

There was a rustling wave through the crescents of benches as lords took their seats, a muttering and whispering and grumbling as they discussed the forthcoming business. Clerks dumped monstrous ledgers at either end of the table and heaved them thumping open. High Justice Bruckel took his seat on one side of Orso. Arch Lector Glokta was wheeled into place on the other and gave the great collection of lords and their proxies a suspicious glare.

'What's Isher doing over there?' he murmured.

As one of the foremost of Midderland's old nobility, he should have been sitting in the middle of the front row, but instead he had shifted to the right, beside the representatives from Angland, whispering in the ear of an unhappy-looking Leo dan Brock.

Bruckel raised his straggling brows. 'Isher and Brock? Intimate friends?'

'Or close conspirators.' Glokta nodded to the announcer, who lifted his staff and struck it on the tiles, filling the hall with crashing echoes.

'I call this meeting of the Open Council of the Union . . .' The announcer let it hang there as the noise gradually faded into weighty silence. 'To order!'

'Good morning, my lords and ladies!' Orso gave a smile that felt more like the accused trying to ingratiate himself with the judge than the judge himself. 'It is my honour to preside over this meeting. We have only one item of business today—'

'Your Majesty, if I may?'

'The Open Council recognises Fedor dan Isher!' thundered the announcer.

An instant interruption was the last thing Orso wanted, but he had to start as he meant to continue, generous and easy-tempered. Perhaps this was all part of Isher's plan to bring monarch and nobility together, after all. 'Of course, Lord Isher, proceed.'

Isher pranced from his bench onto the tiled floor like a man stepping from his favourite chair to give his fire a poke, the echoes of his highly polished boots snapping in the vast domed space above.

'Before we turn to today's . . . sorry work, I hope my esteemed colleagues of the Open Council can join me for a moment in some happier business.'

Glokta leaned towards Orso to mutter, 'Here's a bastard who loves the sound of his own voice.'

'I wish to congratulate one of the most celebrated of our number, His Grace Leonault dan Brock, the Lord Governor – and, if I may say, the undoubted saviour – of Angland . . . on his forthcoming marriage!'

An excited muttering swept the Lords' Round. There could be few more eligible bachelors in the Circle of the World, after all. Perhaps King Jappo mon Rogont Murcatto of Styria, although rumour had it he preferred swords to sheaths, as it were. Perhaps Orso himself, though his romantic reputation, admittedly, was less than glowing. But the dashing young Lord Governor of Angland would be right up there on the wishlist of any ambitious young heiress. It was a roster with which Orso, thanks to his mother's constant quest for a bride, had more than a passing familiarity. He wondered absently which one of them had staged the coup.

'To none other . . .' Isher gestured towards the lower public gallery, lords twisting around on their benches to peer upwards. And there she was, sitting at the rail. There was no mistaking that poise, that elegance, that offhand pride. Orso could have sworn she was looking straight at him. But perhaps he was only desperate that she would. 'Than Lady Savine dan Glokta!'

It was not like being stabbed in the heart. It was much more gradual. An odd shock, first. Some mistake, surely? Then, as the clapping began, a spreading realisation, cold as the grave. It was like having one great stone after another loaded upon his chest.

Her refusal had left no room for doubt, but Orso had not realised until that moment how hard he had been hoping. As a marooned sailor hopes for rescue. Now, even for a man as unrealistic as he was, hope was suddenly snuffed out.

The whole chamber was filled with thunderous applause. The high justice was leaning across him to congratulate the Arch Lector. Orso became aware he was clapping himself. A limp-wristed flapping that made almost no noise at all. Clapping at his own funeral. Down on the front row, lords had clustered around an awkward-looking Leo dan Brock to slap him on the back.

There was no excuse for it, he knew. They had been involved, once, on a casual basis. She had given him a great deal of money and he had come by a roundabout route to her rescue. He had somehow convinced himself that they loved each other and she had sharply disabused him of the notion. It really should have come as no great surprise that she had chosen someone else.

So why did he feel so utterly betrayed?

It was surely a triumph.

With one deft move, Savine had catapulted herself back to the very summit of the endlessly subsiding slag heap that was Union society. Those who had sneered at her with smug scorn, with self-righteous con-descension, even with infuriating pity, those who had written her off as yesterday's woman, all gaped at her now in stunned envy. Perhaps they would never kneel to her and whisper, 'Your August Majesty,' but they would have no choice but to bow and say, 'Your Grace.'

In the parlours of Adua, the ladies would wonder how Savine dan Glokta, well past her most marriageable age, had snared the Young Lion, and they would whisper the kind of unkind rumours one only whispers about people too important to ignore.

It was a triumph, and after the misfortunes, the reverses, not to mention the life-threatening horrors of the previous few months, it was one she sorely needed. She should have been revelling in the attention. Relishing the jealousy of her many enemies. Letting the world see just a hint of her self-satisfied smirk over her fan.

But she did not care at all for the manner of the announcement. She had supposed that her engagement would be a matter of supreme indifference to Orso, but the intensity of the look he had given her told a different story. She wished she could somehow have let him know about it sooner. And she could not have trusted the self-appointed announcer less. Lord Isher was entirely too pleased with himself, too friendly with her husband-to-be and too willing to share the glory of his wedding with them. As he smiled up towards her and gave a flourishing bow, she did not reckon him a man to give anything away.

That and, a few chairs further down the gallery, Lady Wetterlant was glaring at her with unconcealed hatred. Clearly, it was not a happy day for everyone.

But it *was* a triumph. Savine would be damned if she did not at least *look* like she was enjoying it.

So she ignored Lady Wetterlant, simpered at the envious crowds with girlish innocence, blew a kiss down to her embarrassed husband-to-be and wondered what the hell that snake Isher was up to.

'Are you sure about this, Your Majesty?' murmured Glokta. 'We could postpone.'

'Delay,' offered Bruckel, from the other side. '*Always* popular.'

As the good wishes for the marriage of the year faded, Orso did his best to tear his thoughts away from Savine and back to the pressing business at hand – three hundred or so of the most powerful and privileged noblemen in the land, accustomed to seeing the king and his Closed Council as their adversaries.

If Isher had filled the Lords' Round with friends, they were hiding their warm feelings towards him remarkably well. But if he postponed now, he would look a coward and a ditherer. He would confirm all the worst things they said about him. All the worst things he thought about himself.

'It's all arranged,' he grunted. Wetterlant would confess and beg for clemency, and Orso would offer a life sentence and look merciful as well as authoritative. Old enmities would be put aside and the Union could take a collective step towards a better politics, just as Isher had promised. 'Let's get this over with.'

'Bring in the accused!' barked Glokta.

A side door was flung open with an echoing bang. There was a rustling as lords and proxies twisted to see, people in both public galleries leaning out dangerously far in their eagerness to glimpse the prisoner. The hall fell quiet. There was a scraping, tapping, clinking sound, and Fedor dan Wetterlant emerged from the darkness.

At first, Orso barely recognised the man. He had abandoned his fine clothes and dressed in penitent's sackcloth. He had shaved off his curls and looked wan and hungry. One side of his face was badly bruised, scattered with fresh scabs. He wore only the lightest of chains, but he walked so as to make them rattle as loudly as possible. The pampered fop Orso had met in the House of Questions had transformed into an abused martyr. There was a collective gasp at the sight of him, then a shriek of rage from the public gallery. Looking up, Orso saw Lady Wetterlant standing at the rail, white with fury. There was a gradually increasing grumble from the lords and an ever-more-excited murmur from the onlookers as her son shuffled out before them.

'What the *shit*?' hissed Orso through gritted teeth.

'What did I tell you?' whispered Isher in Leo's ear. 'Next, one of the old leeches will offer a false confession as though that closes the case. You'll see what passes for the king's justice these days.'

'Your Majesty!' someone shouted from near the back. 'I most *strongly* protest!'

'This man has been tortured!'

'To treat a member of the Open Council in this manner...'

The announcer struck his staff for order but couldn't stem the mounting anger as Wetterlant was herded out onto the floor before the High Table.

Heugen shook his fist towards Glokta. 'Your Eminence, I am disgusted!'

'To disgusting people I readily confess,' drawled the Arch Lector, 'but any fool can see I did not torture this man. He looks *far* too pleased with himself.'

'Why is no one doing anything?' muttered Leo, gripping his throbbing thigh as he sat forward.

'Order, my lords! Order!' bellowed the announcer. If the atmosphere had been hostile when Orso arrived, it was rapidly swinging towards outright rebellion. He had an unpleasant sensation that the wheels were already coming off his plan as it careered down a steep slope at high speed, and by no means towards a better politics. But he could hardly disembark now.

High Justice Bruckel sat forward, clearing his throat. 'Fedor dan Wetterlant! You stand accused. Most serious crimes.' The wattle beneath his chin wobbled as he fired off phrases, the clerks' pens scratching desperately as they struggled to record them for posterity. 'As a member of the Open Council. You have requested and now receive. In the sight of your peers. The king's justice. How do you plead?'

Wetterlant swallowed. Orso caught him glance up towards his mother. She gave him the faintest nod in return, her jaw clenched. A reassurance, perhaps. A nudge in the right direction. An urging to make the agreed-upon confession and take his agreed-upon punishment and—

'I am innocent!' shrieked Wetterlant in ringing tones. A collective gasp from the public gallery. 'I have been dreadfully wronged! Fearfully abused! I am innocent of all charges!'

The hall erupted more angrily than ever.

'That fucker,' hissed Orso as he stared at Wetterlant. 'That *fucker.*' He looked to his supposed new best friend in the Open Council, but Isher had brows raised and palms helplessly spread, as if to say, *I'm as astonished as anyone.*

In one moment, Orso's carefully laid plans went up in flames and his hopes for a better politics sank into the depths. Now he realised why his father had always despised this place.

'Oh. Dear,' murmured Bruckel. Uselessly.

Leo had never seen so clear an injustice. He sat with his jaw hanging open.

'Are we to hear no evidence?' called out Heugen.

'Will there be no witnesses?' shouted Barezin, thumping a fat fist into a fat palm.

'Witnesses have been presented. Exhaustively interviewed.' High Justice Bruckel struggled to make himself heard over the anger. 'The Closed Council is satisfied!'

Unsurprisingly, that satisfied no one, and Wetterlant's mother was the least satisfied of all. 'I demand justice for my son!' she screamed from the balcony. 'The king's justice!'

Glokta held up a sheet of parchment, an illegible scrawl at the bottom. 'The accused has confessed! In full!'

'I was forced!' wailed the accused.

'Shut him up!' snapped Bruckel, and Wetterlant cringed as the two Practicals turned on him.

'There is no need to waste more of the Open Council's time!' shouted Glokta.

'Waste our time?' whispered Leo. Isher had brows raised and palms helplessly spread, as if to say, *What did I tell you?* Behind him, in one of the great stained-glass panels, the Open Council rose up united against the tyranny of Morlic the Mad, and all because Arnault had the courage to stand first, alone.

'Waste our time?' said Leo. Everyone else on the Open Council might be too craven to say what they could all see, but the Young Lion was no coward.

'Waste our time?' shouted Leo, lurching to his feet. Damn it, his leg hurt. It was as if he were being stabbed again and he almost fell, had to clutch the back of the bench to steady himself as the announcer struck his staff on the floor for order.

'The Open Council recognises—'

'They know who I bloody am! This...' Leo floundered for words. Everyone was staring at him. Everyone in the whole great chamber. But this had to be done. For his father. For his country. 'This is a *disgrace!*'

'What is he doing?' muttered Savine. Ladies were stuck to the rail all around her, staring down, eyes bright, fans fluttering like excited butterflies. Better drama than the theatre and all free of charge.

'I'm no lawyer!' called Leo, his Angland accent sounding particularly pronounced. 'But... even I can tell this is a *travesty.*'

Savine watched with growing horror. A man who knows he is no lawyer should also know to keep his bloody mouth shut during a trial. But the Young Lion was not a man to keep his mouth shut.

'My father,' he bellowed, in an ever angrier and more broken voice, 'always told me Union justice was the envy of the world!'

Orso frowned up towards the public gallery, looking angrier than Savine had ever seen him. She shrank back from the rail, wondering whether her own history with the two men might be aggravating things. But the Young Lion was aggravating enough without her help.

'My friends, I'm *horrified.* In the Lords' Round, of all places. Confessions got by torture? Is this Union justice or Gurkish tyranny? Styrian trickery? Northern savagery?'

'Yes!' she heard Lady Wetterlant hiss with fierce delight. There were loud shouts of agreement from the lords. One might almost have called them cheers. Isher shrank silently into his seat, lips pressed carefully together, making sure there was as much empty bench between him and Leo as possible.

'I would caution the Lord Governor to choose his next words carefully,' growled Savine's father, and she found herself in total agreement. A representative from the Angland delegation was plucking at the hem of Leo's jacket in an effort to pull him down, but Leo angrily slapped his hand away.

'Sit down, you bloody fool,' Savine forced through gritted teeth, gripping the rail of the gallery. But the Young Lion would not sit down.

'Call yourself a high justice?' he roared at Bruckel, leaning on the back of his bench with one hand and gripping hard at his thigh with the other. 'This isn't justice!'

'Your Grace,' growled Orso, 'I would ask you to return to your seat—'

'I refuse!' snarled Leo, spit flying. 'It's plain to everyone that you can't judge this man fairly! You're a puppet of the Closed Council!'

You could almost see the jaws drop. A lady clapped a hand over her mouth. Another gasped. Another gave a kind of disbelieving giggle.

'Oh no,' whispered Savine.

Orso had always thought himself the most easy-going man in the Union. He had floated over the scornful glances, the frequent insults, the scurrilous rumours. Most of them had, after all, been more or less fair. He'd never imagined he even really *had* a temper.

But perhaps he'd never before had anything to be angry about.

Whether it was the ongoing frustration of the throne, the entrenched hostility of everyone in the chamber, Wetterlant's barefaced gall, Isher's two-faced chicanery, Brock's naïve impudence or Savine's forthcoming nuptials that infuriated him most, the combination produced a feeling of utter rage such as he had never felt in his life.

'Colonel Gorst,' he managed to choke out, his throat so tight he could hardly form the words. 'Remove Lord Brock from the chamber.'

Gorst had no expression on his slab of a face as he pounded across the tiled floor towards Leo.

The Open Council didn't rise united, as they had to support Arnault in the legend. Maybe he'd spoken better than Leo. Or Morlic had been madder than Orso. Or men's principles had become so greasy, they tended to slip from their grasp at the worst moments. Or maybe the legend was balls. Everyone stared, but not one arse left its seat.

Leo took a shuffling step back and nearly fell onto his bench, grimacing at the stab of pain in his leg. 'Now, hold on a—'

Gorst caught two fistfuls of Leo's jacket.

Once, as a boy, he'd gone swimming in the sea near Uffrith and been taken by a sudden swell and dragged off his feet. He'd thrashed with all his strength, but the current had sucked him helpless over rocks, swept away by a force of nature far greater than he would ever be.

Being dragged bodily from his bench by Bremer dan Gorst felt similar. The man's strength defied belief. It felt as if he could've flung Leo from the chamber with one throw. He marched him up the aisle of the Lords' Round, through the coloured splashes of light, past gaping lords, Leo's feet kicking uselessly at the steps, tangled with his badly balanced commemorative sword.

'I'm going!' squawked Leo. 'I'm going!'

But he might as well have complained to the tide. Gorst showed no emotion as he bundled Leo from the hall, across the antechamber, then out of the Lords' Round into the daylight. He finally set Leo down with exaggerated care beside a statue of Casamir the Steadfast, feeling much the same sense of awe and relief as he had when the sea finally washed him up on that beach near Uffrith as a boy, but with an added helping of crippling embarrassment.

Gorst wasn't even out of breath. 'I hope you realise...' he squeaked, 'that this was not personal, Your Grace.' He gave an awkward smile. 'Please... pass my respects to your mother.'

'What?' muttered Leo, but Gorst was already striding back up the steps.

The doors were were shut on the Young Lion with a crash, and silence pressed in.

'Enough of this pantomime!' snarled Orso. The legs of his gilded chair gave a tortured shriek as he stood, obliging everyone in the chamber to wobble uncertainly onto their knees. He turned towards Wetterlant.

'I find you guilty of rape and murder,' he said, in the same icy tone his own mother might have used.

'But...' Wetterlant stared over at Isher, as though this was not at all what he had been expecting, but Isher had folded his arms and was meeting no one's eye. 'I am a member of the Open Council—'

'The members of this exalted body must be exemplars,' snapped Orso, glowering at the silent lords, 'held to higher standards, not lower, and subject to the same justice as any other man. The king's justice. *My* justice.' And he stabbed at his chest with a finger. 'There is no question in my mind of your guilt. I have given you every chance to show remorse and you have slapped my hand away. I therefore sentence you to death by hanging. Take him down.'

'No!' shrieked Lady Wetterlant from above.

'You can't do this!' her son wailed as he was dragged away. 'I'm an innocent man! I was compelled!' He screeched over his shoulder, bucking and twisting, 'Isher! Mother! You can't let them *do* this!'

'Get rid of him,' hissed Glokta, and the Practicals bundled him through the side door and flung it shut with an echoing bang.

'You'll pay for this!' Lady Wetterlant was screaming. 'I'll see you pay! Every one of you! Take your hands *off* me!' She was viciously beating at a guardsman with her fan as he struggled to manhandle her from the gallery.

Orso could not bear to stay a moment longer. He snatched up the crown by one pearl-studded prong, turned on his heel and strode disgustedly for the door. Caught by surprise, the Knights of the Body only had it open a crack when he got there, obliging him to wriggle through sideways.

He flung the crown angrily over his shoulder and left one of his footmen juggling the damn thing, stomped out into the daylight and off towards the palace, shocked bystanders scraping out of his way, his entourage clattering after.

Bruckel's gown flapped at his ankles as he hurried to catch up. 'Well, Your Majesty. That was—'

'Don't!' snapped Orso.

They walked in silence, one of the wheels of Glokta's chair catching on every turn with a regular *squeak*, *squeak*, *squeak* which might as well have been a saw applied directly to Orso's nerves.

He wished he had some honest men beside him. He wished he could have given Malmer a seat on the Closed Council. But he had hanged Malmer, and two hundred others, and fully earned the scorn and distrust of every commoner in Midderland. Now, in trying to find a compromise, he had somehow made enemies of the entire nobility, too, with the Union's most celebrated hero foremost among them.

And that was without even touching on the man's forthcoming marriage to the woman Orso quite evidently still loved.

'What a *fucking* disaster!' he snarled.

The high justice tried to smile but it ended up a wince. 'I suppose... It could have been... worse?'

'How, exactly?'

The Arch Lector raised one brow. 'Well, nothing's on fire.'

Savine hurried down the steps as fast as her shoes would allow.

'Leo!' she called.

Gorst had left him upright, at least, for all he was leaning against a statue's pedestal, face twisted with evident pain and his jacket in some disarray.

'What the hell were you *thinking*, you thick shit?' was what she was burning to ask, but instead she stuffed her voice with concern. 'Are you hurt?'

'Hurt? I was bloody humiliated!'

'You humiliated yourself, dunce, and me by association,' was what she wanted to say. The happy news of their engagement was entirely overshadowed now, but she bit her lip and waited for him to blow himself out.

'The whole thing was a mockery! And your *father*—'

'I know.' She spoke as softly as she could, for all she wanted to slap some sense into him. People were starting to emerge from the Lords' Round, eager for more scandal. She should have been parading the square like a peacock. Instead she was scurrying to limit the damage.

'We should get out of the way.' She came close to tug his jacket smooth. 'Before it gets busy out here.'

He nodded, then winced, all his weight on one leg. His old wound was clearly troubling him far more than he pretended. 'I left my cane in the chamber.'

'That is why you have me.' She took his elbow, one hand draped on top while the other held it firmly underneath, so she could hold him up while it looked as if she were leaning upon him, and steer him away from the Square of Marshals towards the quieter ways while it looked as if he were steering her. 'This is politics.' She smiled at passers-by as if this was the most wonderful afternoon of her life. 'You have to be subtle. There is a way to do things.'

'So I should just *sit* there?'

'That's why they have seats in the Open Council.'

'Watch a man convicted just because of who he is—'

'I have it on good authority he couldn't be guiltier,' said Savine, but Leo was not listening.

'That high-handed bastard! To have the Lord Governor of Angland dragged out like a beggar—'

'What did you expect?' she snapped, digging her fingers into his arm. 'You gave him no choice.'

'You're taking his side? We're supposed to be—'

'Leo!' She turned his face towards her so he had to look into her eyes. She spoke to him without fear or anger. With simple authority. The way one speaks to a dog that has soiled the carpet. 'Sides? Think about what you are saying. He is the High King of the Union! His is the only side that counts! He cannot allow himself to be defied before the foremost noblemen of the land. Men have ended up in the House of Questions for less.'

He stared at her, breathing hard. Then suddenly all the defiance drained out of him. 'Shit. You're right.'

'Of course,' was what she wanted to say, but she kept her silence, and tidied a loose strand of hair behind his ear, and let him get there by himself.

'Shit.' He closed his eyes, utterly dismayed. 'I've made myself look a fool.'

She turned his face back towards her again. 'You have made yourself look passionate, and principled, and brave.' And an *utter* fool, it hardly needed saying. 'All the qualities people admire in you. All the qualities *I* admire in you.'

'I've offended the king. What should I—'

'That is why you have me.' She led him on while appearing to follow, talking softly as though they were trading sweet nothings. 'I will speak to my father and arrange for you to apologise to His Majesty. You will smile and be the charming but hotheaded young hero you are. You will show how difficult it is for you to swallow your pride, but you *will* swallow it, every last bitter drop. You will explain that you are a soldier not a courtier, and say your manly passions got the better of you, but that it will *never* happen again. And it *will* never happen again.'

She smiled as they walked. The Union's most admired couple, so very well matched and so much in love. She had smiled through far worse, after all. She kept her eyes ahead, but she was conscious that he was looking at her all the way.

'I think . . .' he murmured, leaning towards her, 'that I might be the luckiest man in the Union.'

'Don't be ridiculous.' She patted his elbow. 'You're the luckiest man in the world.'

The Choice

lip, clip. Copper-brown hair scattered about her bare feet, across her bare feet. Hard fingers on her scalp, tipping her head this way and that. *Clip, clip.*

''Tis only hair, d'you see?' said Isern, pausing with the shears a moment. 'Hair grows back.'

Rikke frowned up at her. 'Hair does.'

Clip, clip, and more hair fell, like moments passed, moments lost.

Shivers set a heavy hand on her shoulder. 'Better to do it than live with the fear of it.'

'That's what my father says,' said Rikke.

'Your father's a wise man.'

'Out of all the men you hate, he's the one you hate least.'

Her father gave a sad nod. 'They'll need your bones and your brains, when I'm gone.' Old, he was, and crooked and grey. 'And your heart.'

'And my heart.' Rikke wasn't sure whether she'd meant to let go the string or not, but her arrow stuck into the lad's back, just under his shoulder blade.

'Oh,' she said, shocked how easy killing someone turned out to be. He looked around, a bit offended, a bit scared, but not half as scared as she was now.

She squeezed her eyes shut. By the dead, her head was hurting, jabbing in her face, jab, jab, jab.

'Keep it, and I see for you a great destiny. A *great* destiny. Or give it away. And be Rikke. Have a life. Push out children and teach them songs.' Caurib shrugged as she sucked fish off the bones, and the wind blew up and made sparks shower from the fire, down the shingle and out over the black water. 'Cook porridge and spin and sit in your father's garden and watch the sun go down. Do whatever it is ordinary folk do these days.'

'They do what they always do,' said Shivers. 'They die.'

Isern gripped her shoulder. 'You must choose. You must choose *now*.'

Pain stabbed through her head and Rikke screamed, screamed so hard her voice cracked and became a breathy wheeze. A long-drawn rattle. A laugh. Stour Nightfall's laugh, wet eyes on her as he grinned at the audience, dancing, mocking, and a golden snake was coiled around him.

'Break what they love!' And his sword left a bright smear. A thousand bright smears. She knew where it would be, always. She knew the sword and the arrow, too. She knew too much. The crack yawned wide in the sky and she squeezed her eyes shut. All she could hear was the clashing of steel. A thunder of voices and hooves and metal and fury.

She opened her eyes and, by the dead, a battle. A battle at night, but lit by fires so bright it looked like day. Or was it smoke? Broken pillars like broken teeth. A lion torn by the wind, ragged and stained. And a sun on a broken tower.

There was a flash like lightning, a noise like thunder, and men were ripped apart, horses flung like toys. She sank down in terror, sank among the corpses and the stomping boots and spraying mud and squeezed her eyes tight shut.

'It's already over,' said a strange, high voice. 'It couldn't be more over.'

Strong arms forced her down into the dirt and she kicked and struggled and fought with everything she had but it wasn't enough.

'Hold her! By the dead, hold her still!'

Something pressed across her chest. Pressed so hard she could scarcely breathe, iron fingers tight across her forehead, pinprick lights burning at her. Bright lights like blazing stars in a midnight sky.

'How much did I drink?' she croaked out.

'All of it, I think,' said Orso, putting down the tray. Or was it Leo? 'I brought you an egg.'

She lifted her chin a little to give him the eye. But the left eye or the right, she wasn't sure. 'Lay it yourself, did you?'

Leo smiled. Or Orso did.

'I miss you,' said Rikke. Said it to both of them. But she wasn't sure whether she missed them, or she missed who she'd been when she was with them. The Rikke who'd laughed and kissed and fucked and not had to choose.

Her face was burning. The left side of her head throbbing. Stink of herbs on the brazier, sickly sweet, so strong she could hardly breathe for it. A long, low crooning. A song in a tongue she didn't know.

'She's no better, witch!'

'I made no promises.'

'She's worse!'

'Her Long Eye is stronger than I have ever seen. It fights to be free. Hear me, girl.' Caurib's voice boomed and echoed as if from a long way off. Something slapped at her and she grunted and grumbled. 'Have you ever seen a thing entire? Through time? Have you known a thing completely?'

'An arrow,' croaked Rikke, stirring her thick tongue in her thick lips. 'From its making to its end. When it flew, I pushed it away with my finger. And a sword. And a crack in the sky.'

'What was inside?'

'Everything.'

She heard Caurib give a long, rustling sigh. 'It's worse than I feared. Or better than I hoped. The wards will not be enough. We must go further.'

'Speak another riddle,' snarled Shivers, 'and I will split your head in so many pieces no stitching will hold the shreds together.'

Hard fingers gripped Rikke's face, pulled her eyelids open, golden wire blurry in the tricking candlelight.

'You must choose,' said Caurib. 'You must choose *now*.'

She could smell fire, just beyond the mouth of the cave. But she was not in a cave but her father's hall. Burning thatch dropped from the burning rafters. Screams outside the doorway.

She saw people at the top of a high tower beneath a bloody sunset. A line of them. A queue of them. One by one they fell. One by one they hit the ground beneath, *tap, tap, tap*.

Tap, tap of the needle dipped in the ink, the needle so white and the ink so black, white as snow, black as coal, and Caurib's soft singing and the smell of sweat and spice and sickly sweet herbs burning on the brazier. *Tap, tap*. Someone held her hand. Held her hand tight and Rikke squeezed it back.

'I'm sorry,' came a whispering, choking voice, breath hot on her ear. 'But it must be done.'

A burning pain in her cheek and she snapped and snarled but could not move even a hair's breadth. Stabbing, stabbing in her face, around her burning eye, and men spilled over a snow-patched hill, an army, while shadows swarmed across the land from the racing clouds above.

'Yes. Hold her tight. Calm, now, calm.'

She stood upon a wharf, rain falling, clothes clammy on her, and a ship rocked and tossed on the unquiet sea, shields on its top strake battle-scarred, oars struggling like the legs of a woodlouse tipped over as it crawled closer.

'Time to settle some scores,' said the Nail, all shoulders and elbows and fierce grin, and behind his back he held a knife.

'Scores have to be settled,' said Shivers, grey hair plastered to his scarred face with the rain. 'But don't expect it to feel good.' And he charged towards a gate, and men charged after him, their boots hammering on a wooden bridge, *tap, tap, tap.*

Tap, tap. Like nails hammered into her forehead and she gasped and twisted and spat.

'I can't stand it!' she whimpered. 'Let me up, I can't stand it!'

'You can and you will.'

The bench had ropes around it. And on the polished-smooth cave floor salt had been scattered. Circles and lines and symbols in salt. Candles burning in the darkness. A joke of a witch's cave.

'Here is your couch, girl,' said Caurib.

'Looks like a joke,' whispered Rikke as she walked towards it, stone cold under her bare feet.

'You will not be laughing.'

Clip, clip, and the hair scattered across her bare feet.

'Fucking a crown prince is no great distinction,' Orso laughed. 'But being brought breakfast by one...'

She closed her eyes, strained up towards him and he kissed her lids, kissed her forehead, kissed her cheek, and his kisses became a numb pressing, then a sharp jabbing, then a brutal stabbing, and she growled and twisted but she was so weak. Steaming waves on the shore. Footprints, burning footprints in the shingle.

'Hold her, then, she's twisting like a salmon!'

'I *am* bloody holding her.'

'This is fine work. It *must* be fine work.'

The bench hard against her hard shoulder blades and her body rigid and trembling and the jab, jab, jabbing at her face, and she could see a wagon made of bones, rattling along behind skeleton horses. She heard Caurib clicking her tongue.

'That one is done. That one will hold.'

Hiss of more herbs on the brazier and her face stung and sweated and stung and she was so thirsty, so thirsty, her eye burned. A wolf ate the sun and a lion ate the wolf and a lamb ate the lion and an owl ate the lamb.

'By the dead, it hurts,' she croaked.

'Did she speak?'

'She said it hurts.'

'You can tell that just by looking, d'you see?'

'Shut up and light that candle.'

'Why did I ever trust you?'

Old men gathered around a bed. A deathbed. A dead king, and her eye burned.

'Hang a hide in the mouth of the cave to keep the wind out. Now!'

A woman stood on a high wall. A terrible woman holding a terrible knife. A man leaned beside her on the stones, and she smiled as she raised the blade. 'Break what they love,' she said, merciless, ruthless, and Rikke screamed as the needle jabbed at her face, merciless, ruthless.

'Send him down, then.'

'I've changed my mind!' she screeched, slobbering, desperate, eyes fixed on the needle, trying to twist away.

'Too late now, girl.'

She sat down beside Shivers, frowned across the fire at the Shanka, gathered in a half-circle, light dancing in their black eyes. One got up, and Shivers reached for his sword, but all it did was sprinkle salt on the cooking fish. A little flick of salt, with a neat flick of its crooked wrist.

'I can't tell what's real and what's a vision,' Rikke heard herself say. 'I can't tell what's then and what's to come. It all runs together like paints in the water.'

She gasped at another stabbing twinge through her eye. Gasped, and retched, but there was nothing to come up. Felt like she'd puked out everything she'd ever eaten. Everything anyone had ever eaten. A great building burned. A high dome crumbled inwards, sparks showering into the sky, showering down the shingle.

'You must make of your heart a stone,' said Isern.

Candle flames glinted in Shivers' metal eye. 'I'm sorry. I'm sorry.'

So cold around her feet. The lake to her calves. She saw her own reflection, a knobbly clipped head against the racing clouds. Turned her face this way and that. Something written there. Eleven wards, and eleven wards reversed, and eleven times eleven.

'How does it look?' she asked.

'Never mind how it looks,' said Isern, frowning. 'Will it work?'

'One eye fights the other.' Caurib lifted the needle. 'You must choose. You must choose *now*.'

Silence for a moment. Stillness for a moment. Rikke stared up at them, the cold fear spreading through her.

'Choose . . . an eye?'

Let Ring the Bells

Savine studied her face in the mirrors from every angle, no fewer than nine maids fluttering nervously about her: Freid with powder and brush, Metello with comb and scissors, Liddy with a mouthful of pins, May with four different colours of thread woven around her fingers. Aside from a wrinkle or two about the eyes – and unless great Euz could turn back time for her there was no help for that – she saw no opportunity for improvement.

'Perfection,' said Zuri, with the quiet pride of a painter placing the last brushstroke on a masterpiece.

'Hardly.' Savine took one last surreptitious sniff of pearl dust then carefully brushed clean the rims of her nostrils. 'But as close as we'll get under the circumstances.'

She had never worked so hard as she had in preparation for this event. There were a great many things that fell short of her standards, but then she had only been given a few days to prepare for seven hundred and fourteen guests, and at this particular wedding she was not the only bride.

Indeed, the thing that fell furthest short of her standards was the other one.

Isold dan Kaspa, soon to be Isold dan Isher, was waiting at the vast, inlaid doors, breathing faster than an untried soldier about to meet a charge of horse. She was very young and rather chinless, with a scattering of freckles across her nose and big, brown eyes that looked constantly on the point of brimming with tears.

'I . . . never saw such a dress,' she murmured as Liddy stooped to make some tiny adjustment to Savine's train.

'My dear, you're so kind. But it really was thrown together.' And it had been, in six days. By two corset-makers, a goldsmith, three dealers in pearls, an expert in working with them, and nine seamstresses going through the night by candlelight. 'You look magnificent, too.'

Isold blinked down doubtfully at herself. 'Do you think so?'

'I do.' Savine did not. Isold's dress was a triumph of optimism over taste and accentuated all her worst features. But its inferiority to her own would be so utterly obvious to anyone watching there was no point in saying so.

'That's such an unusual necklace.'

'Runes.' Savine stretched out her throat as Zuri gave an infinitesimal tweak to the way they sat. Everyone here had diamonds, after all, but these gave her a dash of the exotic. She was the least superstitious person alive, but they felt like good luck, somehow. 'They were a gift from...' An old lover of my husband's did not sound quite right, so she settled for, 'A friend from the North.'

'Will your parents be here?'

A more complicated question than Isold probably realised, since one of Savine's fathers was dead and the other not actually her father. She settled for, 'Both of them.'

'You're so lucky. I have hardly any family left. My uncle died before I was born, on campaign in the North, then my father last year, and my mother a few months after. I never had any siblings.' Leaving her, no doubt, with quite the inheritance. Savine began to divine what made her so irresistible to Lord Isher. 'I only wish one of them had lived to see this...'

'I am sure they would have been proud.' And somewhat relieved to be rid of her. Savine took her gently by the shoulders. 'Today you will gain a whole new family. I know your husband to be a good man.' She suspected him of being a devious scorpion. 'And from the way he talks, he is very much in love with you.'

Isold blinked up at her. 'Do you think so?'

Savine did not. 'How could it be otherwise?' she asked, chucking Isold under the chin and making her smile. 'Zuri, could one of the girls help Isold with her powder?'

'Blessed is she who gives succour to the needy, Lady Savine...'

'I'm sorry...' croaked out Isold as May attended to her face, 'I don't mean to be a burden—'

'Don't be ridiculous,' said Savine. 'I should be the one apologising, for stealing half of your big day. And with so little notice. It has been... quite the whirlwind.'

'It's good to have someone to share it with.' Isold looked down at her shoes. 'To take some of the attention.'

'I understand entirely.' Though there had never been enough attention in the Circle of the World to satisfy Savine.

'The Lords' Round.' Isold stared at the huge doors. Beyond they could hear the vague murmur of the gathering witnesses. Almost as many as had witnessed Wetterlant's trial. 'So many people watching.'

'Everyone who's anyone.' Savine had spent several hours poring over the guest list with Zuri and her mother in order to make absolutely sure of it.

'The *king* is here,' whispered Isold.

Savine found her nonchalance slipping a little at that. 'Yes.'

'Do you know him?'

'We . . . have met. He is a good man, regardless of what you hear.'

'My husband-to-be doesn't seem to think so.'

For some reason, that caused Savine a stab of anger. 'Luckily, I am not obliged to agree with Lord Isher.'

'I am,' said Isold, in a tiny voice.

By the Fates, her eyes were already brimming again, making her powder run. It can be pleasant to have someone weak leaning on you. It can make you feel strong. But there comes a point when they become a dead weight to carry. Savine was happy to play big sister but she drew the line at motherhood. She would have her own child to worry about soon enough.

'You are being married to the man,' she said, less gently now, 'not sold to him.'

'I suppose.' Isold took a heavy breath. 'I wish I had your . . . *grit*.'

Savine was far from sure that grittiness was the quality most sought for in a bride. She took Isold by her limp little hands. 'Act as if everything is going exactly according to your plans. As if you are the most confident person in the world. As if you never had a doubt in your life.' Savine forced her shoulders back, her chin up and faced the door. 'It works for me.'

'Does it?' asked Isold. 'Really?'

Savine paused a moment, mouth half-open. Then she slipped the box of pearl dust from her sleeve and offered it out. 'There's always this.'

'Ready, my friend?' asked Isher.

Leo forced a watery smile towards High Justice Bruckel, standing by to officiate, his robes trimmed with so much fur he looked like a giant, disapproving badger. 'Can't wait.'

Leo had always reckoned himself the bravest man in any company. They called him the Young Lion, after all. But standing here, on the marble floor of the Lords' Round, well dressed, well fed, well attended and in no danger of violent death, he was terrified.

There are different kinds of courage, maybe, and the kind that lets you fling yourself into a thicket of spears has nothing to do with the kind that lets you stand smiling in front of a thousand people and give your life to a woman you hardly know.

He wished his friends were there. His *real* friends. Antaup, with his endless chatter about women, and Glaward, with his endless chatter about weapons, and Whitewater Jin with his beard and his belly laugh, and good old Jurand, most of all. Jurand, with his caution and good sense. Jurand, with his endless patience and support. Jurand, with the fine shape of his jaw, and his hair falling in that artless mess, and the perfect definition of his lips... Leo shook himself. He even wished he could hear Barniva wax on about the horrors of war one more time but, as if to prove his own point, the poor bastard had got himself killed. In a war.

And none of them were invited anyway. There had been no time to send for them. Leo had come to Adua to attend Lord Isher's wedding and make new friends. Not to make an enemy of the king and get bloody married himself.

He felt another surge of nerves. Could you call it cowardice? He found he was glancing about for some route of escape, more little rabbit than Young Lion. He caught sight of his mother, who gave him an encouraging nod. Then Lady Ardee, who gave him an encouraging wink. Then her husband the Arch Lector, who gave him a bitter glare which entirely undid all the ladies' support. Finally, King Orso, slouching on his cushions in the middle of the front row, jaw angrily clenched.

Leo turned his back on them, mouthing the over-rehearsed apology Savine had arranged for him to give later. 'Your Majesty, I'm a soldier, not a courtier. A *simple* soldier. I can *only* apologise. I let my passions get the better of me. No excuse. Will *never* happen again—'

'Please rise!' bellowed Bruckel.

There was a rustling as the hundreds of witnesses stood, an echoing fanfare from the gallery garlanded with spring flowers, and a mighty creaking as the doors were heaved open and the two brides stepped into the light.

Whenever Leo saw Savine she was somehow more than he remembered, but now, in ten thousand marks or more of Suljuk silk, Osprian lace and pearls from the distant Thousand Isles, advancing so proudly, so gracefully, so dauntlessly down the aisle, he couldn't take his eyes away.

No one could. The future Lady Isher was a simpering little girl by comparison, the blushing maid beside the peerless empress. Savine was doing her best not to outpace her, to hold her hand, to show her off to best advantage, but poor Isold was utterly upstaged at her own wedding.

It didn't help that she appeared to be constantly suppressing an urge to sneeze.

It was as if all these people were the setting of the ring in which Savine was the jewel. As if the Lords' Round had been built especially for this moment. Perhaps you can borrow courage from someone else. As Savine joined him at the High Table, Leo's doubts were wiped away. With her at his side, there was nothing he couldn't do. He was the Young Lion again.

She gave him a look up and down, nodded approvingly and raised one perfectly plucked brow. 'You came, then?'

'Are you joking?' Leo turned to the high justice and gave him a grin worthy of a famous hero. 'I wouldn't miss this for the world.'

The spring sun shone on the park, turning every dewdrop to a diamond. Dappled shade danced on the manicured lawns under trees that had been ancient in Casamir's reign. A gentle breeze brought only the slightest scratch in the throat from the chimneys that towered over the Agriont on every side. Everything crisp and bright and ready to burst forth with new possibilities.

Lady Finree dan Brock and Lady Ardee dan Glokta, mothers to one of the happy couples, glided about the gathering arm in arm, an all-conquering double act, the one imposing military precision on the serving staff, the other administering risqué anecdotes to every guest. So many different styles of laughter. Hearty guffaws and bubbling chuckles from the gentlemen. Silvery giggles and tinkling titters from the ladies.

A truly wonderful time was being had by all. With one notable exception, of course.

Orso would rather have been anywhere else. The dungeons of the Emperor of Gurkhul held more appeal at that moment. It was hard to imagine greater torture, after all, than the glorious wedding of the woman he loved to a man he decidedly didn't, where the guests consisted of a range of sneering enemies, bowing and scraping to his face then spitting scorn as soon as he was out of earshot.

With every day that passed, he was coming to understand, even to admire, his father more. The man had played the eternally losing hand of being king about as well as was possible.

He lifted his glass, and glumly watched the way the sunlight sparkled through it. The oblivion of the bottle, then. Wine had never let him down. More importantly, he had never let it down.

'Your Majesty?'

It was one of the grooms. Not the one he hated. The one he utterly despised. Lord fucking Isher, even more immaculately polished than usual.

'I wished to give you my unreserved apology for the events in the Open Council. I am devastated. Who could have known that Lady Wetterlant would renege on her commitments and turn on us both?'

Orso had spent a great deal of time pointlessly rehearsing the events of that day and, though he could prove nothing, he strongly suspected Isher had orchestrated the whole thing. To Lady Wetterlant, he blamed Orso; to Orso, he blamed Lady Wetterlant; then he teased out Leo dan Brock's little performance and imagined he would come through greatly empowered and still everybody's friend.

The desire to punch him in the face was almost irresistible. But breaking his treacherous nose in front of several hundred guests, though satisfying for a moment, would only have played into Isher's hands, and Orso had done that quite enough already. Plainly, Isher thought him an utter fool. Better he keep doing so.

'You have nothing to apologise for!' Orso tossed his empty glass into the bushes and folded Isher in a tight embrace. 'I know you did everything you could. Those bloody Wetterlants stabbed us *both* in the back.' He held Isher at arms' length and smiled, smiled, smiled. 'Some dogs are a danger to everyone. Have to be put down for the general good. And you can hardly be blamed for Lord Brock's outburst.' Although he most certainly could be and most certainly was.

'The man has a soldier's temperament,' said Isher. 'I know how desperately he wants to apologise for his behaviour.'

'Not everyone is a politician, eh? Heart of a lion, and so forth. It's a shame how things went, but— Ah!'

And Orso snatched two glasses from a passing waiter's tray and pressed one into Isher's hand. 'There's as much need for cooperation between the Crown and Open Council as ever. More! I hope we can work together again to bring it about. This time . . . with a happier outcome?' Such as Isher's neck in the noose rather than Wetterlant's, for example. 'To your happiness, my friend, and that of your charming bride, of course!'

Isher gave a slightly surprised smile. 'Of course.'

Their glasses chinked pleasantly together, and Orso thought about how much he would have loved to smash his in Isher's face and grind the jagged remnant into his groin.

But all in good time.

'Cheers!'

*

Cages sprang open and songbirds swarmed into the air above the gardens, a flurry of shimmering blue and purple feathers. Imported from Gurkhul, Broad had been told, at a cost he hardly dared imagine.

Half had died on the way over. He'd watched them clean the cages out, heaping up the shiny little corpses.

May gave a delighted giggle as the survivors twittered sparkling into the sky. 'Beautiful!'

The guests clapped politely, and straight away turned to other entertainments. No doubt the birds themselves were meant to loiter in the trees and serenade the newly-weds, but they soon scattered to the wind. Broad doubted they'd last long in this climate. Only one was left on the lawn, weakly cheeping, looking almost as baffled as Broad felt.

'How much did it all cost, do you reckon?'

May winked at him. She'd held the books, had one eye on the sums, but she treated the number like a beautiful secret rather than a guilty one. 'Better not to ask.'

A lot better, probably. But he couldn't help himself. For what Savine had spent on that one dress, which Liddy would help cut her out of in a few hours and she'd never wear again, she could've paid her workers on the canal more'n they'd asked for, and got the thing dug without one bone broken.

For what her father the Arch Lector had spent on the wine today, maybe he could've built some better houses in Valbeck, and folk wouldn't have been stuck in rotten cellars, and the Breakers wouldn't have risen up, and two hundred good people wouldn't have been hanged.

For what Lord fucking Isher had spent on this dinner for seven hundred, the valley Broad grew up in could've been left as it was. He could've been herding now, the way his father had, along with all those others thrown off their land.

Was he the only one saw it? Was he the only one worried about it? Or was everyone like him? They saw, and they worried, but they somehow didn't fucking *do* anything.

'Doesn't she look beautiful?' murmured Liddy, watching Savine dan Brock sweep past with her husband, envious lords and ladies swarming after them like the tail to a comet.

'Aye,' said Broad, pushing his lenses up his nose. She did look beautiful. Everything looked beautiful. Even them. He'd never seen his wife and his daughter look so fine, so well fed, so happy. It's easy to scream about the fence when you're on the wrong side of it. Some mad twist of fortune lands you on the right side, though, the fence starts to look like it might not be such a bad idea. Might even be worth all the sacrifices. Other people's sacrifices aren't that hard to make.

'All worth it, eh?' said Liddy. She was talking about the nights she'd spent stitching by candlelight, he reckoned, not the nights he'd spent beating men by lamplight.

Had that been worth it?

'Aye,' he croaked out.

He forced the smile onto his face. He was doing that a lot lately.

Leo sat, watching his wife dance, whirl, twist, smile, flitting effortlessly from one partner to another. His *wife*. Just thinking the words gave him a guilty thrill. She was an enchanting dancer, it hardly needed to be said.

Leo would've liked to join her and soak up his share of the admiration. But he'd never been much of a dancer, even without the leg wound. Few soldiers are. Antaup, maybe. He wondered what his friends would say when he presented his bride. Speechless, most likely. How could they be anything but impressed? How could anyone?

'Not dancing, Your Grace?' It was that woman with the red hair and all the bosom he'd met last time he was in Adua.

'The leg, you know. Still a bit sore.'

'A shame. I can't remember such a spectacular wedding.'

'Thank you...' A moment of horror at not knowing her name, then a wash of relief as it came to him. 'Selest! So glad you could come.'

'Oh, Bayaz could have locked me in the House of the Maker and I'd *still* have found a way to attend!' She tapped him on the chest with her fan. 'That's *two* wonderful shows you've put on in the Lords' Round.'

Leo winced. 'You know about the other one?'

'My dear, *everyone* knows about the other one.'

'Well, I'm meeting the king later this evening. I'll say sorry, and that'll be that.'

'Of course. I suppose there was always going to be some... *friction* between you and His Majesty, given his history with your wife.'

Leo felt a coldness creeping up his spine. 'What?'

'Rumour has it they were *lovers*,' she purred. 'But I'm sure Savine told you. It's hardly the kind of secret one would want hanging over a marriage, after all.'

The music struck a false note, suddenly. Was that why Savine had been so worried about the king's feelings? So keen for Leo to apologise? He felt a surge of fury, and the pain in his leg as he leaned towards Selest dan Heugen only made it worse. He forced the words hissing through his fixed smile. 'If I hear you've spread that rumour, I'll break your fucking nose.'

She looked rather pleased with that. One of those people who count anything but being ignored as a victory. 'There's really no point getting angry with me, Your Grace. *I* didn't fuck the king.'

She left him sitting, watching his wife dance, whirl, twist, smile, flitting effortlessly from one partner to another. The sight no longer filled him with quite the same delight.

It was done. It was done, and could not be undone.

Orso drained yet another glass, wondering if there was some kind of drinking record he could aim for. Something to give his life purpose. Something more than staring at Savine and thinking about all he'd lost.

He glanced over to Brock, who for some reason appeared to be frowning angrily back, and raised his empty glass in a pointless toast. That bastard was everything Orso wasn't. Honest, decisive, likeable. Crushingly popular with both nobles and commoners. A storybook hero with no crowd of mistakes at his back. Unless you counted the one he'd made in the Lords' Round, the one he was apparently so very keen to apologise for, and that only appeared to have gilded his reputation. Hot-blooded and passionate, don't you know! Anyone would have thought the most admirable thing a man could do in Open Council these days was berate the monarch.

'Blame sticks to some men,' he murmured, under his breath. 'Others it slides right off.'

'Dinner will be served shortly, Your Majesty.' A powdered footman gestured towards his chair – the largest chair, of course – in the very centre of the great polished horseshoe of table. He wondered how many trees had died to make it possible. 'If it please Your Majesty, you are to be seated between the two brides, the grooms just without, to either side.' And he managed to back away and bow simultaneously.

Between the two brides. As though to emphasise how alone he was. He would rather have been seated between the Great Wolf and the Snake of Talins. Far rather. He did not have nearly so ugly a history with them as he had with Savine dan Glokta.

He realised he had to correct himself.

Savine dan Brock.

'Fuck,' he snarled. He could stand it no longer. He could stand himself no longer. 'Gorst?'

'Your Majesty?'

'Where might we find Corporal Tunny these days?' The Lord Governor of bloody Angland could apologise later, if he cared to. 'I think I've had quite enough of other people's happiness.'

Savine shut the doors and leaned back against them, taking a moment to breathe. Her cheeks burned from the dancing, and the compliments, and the endless smiling, and the ever-greater quantities of pearl dust. She could hardly feel her face any more. She simply had to get some air.

'So. A married woman.' The sight of her father soon cleared her spinning head. He sat in his wheeled chair on the terrace, deep-lined face tipped back, gazing at the stars. 'They say it's the proudest day of a father's life.'

'They say all sorts of nonsense.' His opinion had meant everything to her once, but she found right now she hardly cared. She was eager to shrug off the wreckage of her past life like a snake sheds its skin and sweep away smiling towards her bright new future.

'There is no guide to being a parent, Savine.' He turned his head slowly to look at her, eyes bright in the darkness. 'Especially if your parents did as poor a job as mine and your mother's did. You reel from one mess to another and chart the only course you can see at the time. We meant to tell you the truth, but . . . when is the right moment to share a thing like that? We preferred the pretence. We did not . . . want to hurt you.'

She gave a bitter snort. 'Then congratulations on your spectacular failure.'

'Hardly my first. One day, I hope you will see that we always tried to act in your best interests.'

'You could have warned me.'

'Not to bed the crown prince? Hardly advice someone of your talents should need.' Perhaps he had a point there. 'Besides, we agreed long ago that I would give you some privacy. How was I to know you would become involved with the one man who was off limits?'

'From what my mother tells me, it does rather run in the family.'

A silence, and she saw the side of his face twitch in the warm light from the party, and he reached up and wiped a streak of wet from his leaking left eye. 'Well. A life without regrets is not a life at all. It is in the past now. I know I cast a long shadow, Savine. I am glad you are ready to step out from under it. Just . . . be careful.'

'Aren't I always?'

'You will move in different circles now. As the Lady Governor of Angland, no less.'

'I'm used to hard decisions.' It felt as if her life had been one after another.

'You are used to business. This is politics. The way things are going . . . well, take care. And promise me one thing.' He beckoned her close to whisper. 'Have *nothing* to do with Bayaz. Not with him, not with any magus. Take no favours from him, owe no debts to him, make no deals with him. Do not please him. Do not displease him. Do everything possible to escape his notice *altogether*. Promise me.'

'All right,' she said, frowning. 'I promise.' If she was to have a statue on the Kingsway, she supposed she would have to win it for herself.

'Good. Good.' Her father winced as he settled into his chair, drunken applause in the background as a dance came to its end. 'The time may soon come when I cannot protect you any more.'

'Is that what you've been doing?'

'Believe it or not, I've been trying.' He frowned over the rooftops towards the dome of the Lords' Round, the great black shape soaring high into the night sky, a grand replacement for the one destroyed the year Savine was born. 'Sometimes,' he murmured, 'the only way to improve something is to destroy it, so it can be rebuilt better. Sometimes, to change the world, we must first burn it down.'

Savine raised one brow. 'Valbeck may be better in the years to come. But being there while it burned was far from pleasant.'

'The emperor's prisons were far from pleasant.' He licked at his empty gums with a faint sucking. 'But I emerged a better man. Being your father . . . is the thing I am proudest of. It's the only thing I'm proud of.'

'And you're not even my father.'

She wanted to strike some spark of anger from him. But all he did was slowly nod, a trace of a smile as he looked up at the stars, bright in the clear sky. 'That should tell you what I think of everything else I've done.' Beyond the windows, the band struck up a jaunty reel, one of her mother's favourites, people clapping and stamping and laughing in time. 'Could you wheel me back in?'

She thought about wheeling him off into the flower beds. But in the end, she took the handles of his chair and turned it about, that one wheel slightly squeaking. 'I can do that.'

Future Treasons, Past Affairs

L eo raised his fist to knock, and paused, clenching it so hard his knuckles clicked.

It was a bloody humiliation. He'd never had much respect for Orso as a man, and he'd been losing respect for the Crown as an institution for months. Now he had to spend part of his wedding night begging for forgiveness from his wife's former lover. It was an *utter* bloody humiliation.

But it had to be done. He was a leader, and a husband, soon to be a father. He had responsibilities. He was starting to see that humiliations came with the territory.

He forced on a smile, seasoned it with just a sprinkle of shame, turned the doorknob and stepped through. 'Your Majesty, I . . .'

You could've said there were a lot of kings in that vast salon. Twenty, at the least, of the Union's best, in uniforms, hunting garb, full armour, perched on gilded chairs or astride mighty steeds, sneering, smirking, pouting down at Leo from towering canvasses. But of the current throne-stuffer there was no sign.

In fact, the only living occupants of the room were Lords Isher, Barezin and Heugen, gathered around a table in one corner in a secretive huddle.

'Leo!' called Isher, raising his glass. 'It seems the king couldn't stay.'

'More important matters,' said Heugen, leaning to light his pipe at a candle.

'At the whorehouse, I understand,' added Barezin, sloshing amber spirit from the decanter and nudging the drink towards an empty chair.

Leo felt angry colour rising to his cheeks as he limped over. 'The whorehouse?' All the effort he'd put into his apology and the arrogant bastard couldn't even be bothered to hear it?

'If you ask me . . .' Heugen puffed out sweet-smelling chagga smoke. 'You've not a thing to apologise for.'

'You told the truth,' said Barezin. 'Everyone knows it. He's the one should apologise.'

'Kings don't,' grumbled Leo, dropping into the empty seat and snatching up the drink.

'Not this one, anyway.'

'Well, shit on him!' Leo drained his glass in one swallow and slammed it down in a rush of fury. 'I've had enough! We can't let things carry on like this!' He glared at a painting of Orso's father King Jezal, handsome enough but with a helpless set to his shoulders even as a young man. An ineffectual ditherer who lost every war he'd fought and achieved nothing but unmatched debts, and his reign was starting to look like a golden age. 'We can't let the Union just... slide into the fucking sewer!'

Isher gave Barezin and Heugen a significant glance. 'There comes a point,' he said with great care, 'when *talking* about a better world is simply not enough. There comes a time... when men of conscience, principle and courage must dare the unthinkable... and *fight* for a better world.'

There was a long, expectant silence. The hairs on Leo's neck prickled. A clock on the marble mantel *tick*, *tock*, *ticked*. He looked the three lords in the eye, one after another. Isher spoke far from plainly but, at the same time, left no doubt what they were discussing.

'Mightn't some men call that...' Leo licked his lips and shuffled forward on his chair, hesitating to say the word in full view of all those painted monarchs, and finally forcing it out in a breathy murmur. 'Treason?'

Heugen gave a huff of upset. Barezin's jowls wobbled in denial. Isher firmly shook his white head. 'We would be acting in the king's best interest. In the *country's* best interest.'

'We would be *freeing* His Majesty from the chains of his Closed Council,' said Heugen, his airy gestures making Leo think of liberty and honesty, and most certainly not treason.

'We need to replace those corrupt old bastards with *patriots*,' boomed Barezin, filling Leo's glass again.

'Men who can give the king the right advice.' Isher waved towards a painting of Harod the Great, who'd first forced the splintered kingdoms of Midderland together into a Union and looked exceedingly pleased about it, too. 'Guide the Union back to its founding principles.'

'Back to *glory*!' Barezin punched his palm as if it was nowhere near glorious enough. 'Men of *action*! Men who can make the Union *great* again!'

'Men like us,' said Heugen, eyebrows raised as though the idea had only just occurred.

'The Closed Council are the same self-serving liars who lost us three wars against the Styrians!' hissed Isher, and Leo could hardly deny it. 'Who nearly drove Westport out of the Union! Who turned the commoners against us to the point they burned one of our greatest cities! *They're* the enemies of the state. Ousting them is the act of *loyalists*.'

'Loyalists,' mused Leo, taking another drink and feeling its heat spreading. He'd always been fiercely loyal. No man more of a patriot. But what was he loyal *to*? A coven of greedy bureaucrats who'd sent him no help in war and only outrageous demands for tax in peace? A libertine king who'd had him thrown from the Lords' Round and, it seemed, fucked his wife?

Leo frowned up at the painting of Casamir the Steadfast, who'd ripped Angland from the clutching hands of the Northmen – strong-jawed, fully armoured and pointing out something on a map. *There* was a king. There was a *man*. He seemed to be challenging Leo with his piercing stare, as if to ask him, *What the hell are you going to do about all this?*

What would Casamir have done? What would any good man have done? Leo looked the three lords in the eye again, one after another, and drained his glass. 'Well,' he said, 'you all know I've never backed down from a fight.'

Now they huddled in close. United by a common enemy, and a shared purpose, and a righteous cause. Just talk, of course, fuelled by Leo's frustration, and jealousy, and the pain in his leg. Just talk, perhaps, but dangerous, still. Exciting, still. Just talk, wasn't it? But with each word said it became more thrillingly real.

'It might be a fight against friends,' murmured Barezin, glancing towards the window. 'Against neighbours. Against colleagues.'

'Certainly against your father-in-law,' said Isher. 'The king dances to his tune. If we on the Open Council have one enemy, it's the Arch Lector.'

'He may be my father-in-law,' said Leo, 'but I'm no friendlier with Old Sticks than you are. Less, if anything.'

'We would need a leader,' said Isher. 'A military man.'

'A latterday Stolicus!' frothed Barezin, filling Leo's glass again.

'A man whose name inspires respect on the battlefield.'

Leo's heart beat faster at the thought of strapping on his armour. He belonged at the head of ranks of cheering soldiers, not harassed and henpecked behind some dusty old desk. He smiled as he thought of the marching boots, the wind taking the flags, the ring of drawn steel, the drumming hooves of the charge . . .

'How many men could we count on?' he asked, sipping steadily. It really was a hell of a brandy.

'We three are committed,' said Isher, 'and many other members of the Open Council are with us.'

'Most,' said Heugen. 'Almost all!'

'You're sure?' Leo got the vague sense they had been thinking about this for a while.

'They have been frustrated for years,' said Isher. 'Chafing at the taxes, the infringements, the insults. Wetterlant's treatment, and yours – a genuine hero of the Union, mark you, in our own Lords' Round – was the final straw.'

'You're damn right there,' grunted Leo, clenching his fists. He couldn't tell if all this was just talk or not, but he was starting to hope it wasn't.

'Could you count on the forces of Angland?' asked Barezin eagerly.

Leo thought of Jurand and his friends' loyalty. Mustred and Clensher's fury. The soldiers cheering for the Young Lion. He drew himself up. 'They'd follow me into hell.'

'Good to hear.' Isher tapped at his glass with one well-shaped fingernail. 'But we do not want it to come to that. Even with the Open Council and the army of Angland united, we could not be sure of victory.'

'We must take them by surprise,' said Heugen. 'Field a force no one would *dare* to resist!'

'We need outside help,' said Barezin.

Leo frowned into his half-empty glass. 'The Dogman has hundreds of hardened warriors.'

'And he owes you,' said Heugen. 'For your help against Ironhand.'

'He's an honourable man. A true straight edge. He might join us . . . if it was put to him the right way.'

'Who understands the Northmen better than you?' asked Isher. 'Who has been their neighbour, fought beside them, lived among them?'

Leo gave an artless shrug. 'I've got some friends in the North.'

'Without doubt . . .' Isher glanced at Heugen, then at Barezin, and then back to Leo, 'not least the King of the Northmen himself, Stour Nightfall.'

Leo froze, glass halfway to his mouth. 'Not sure I'd call him a friend.'

'He owes you his life.'

'But there's a reason they call him the Great Wolf.' He thought of Stour's hungry smile. His wild, wet eyes. The legions of merciless Northmen they'd faced at Red Hill. 'He's savage. Bloodthirsty. Treacherous.'

'But *you* could keep him on the leash!' Barezin clapped Leo on the shoulder. 'And how many warriors could *he* call upon?'

'Thousands.' Leo tossed down the rest of his drink and pushed the glass back for a refill. 'Many thousands.'

She was there in a vast living room when he opened the door, arranged on a chaise in a great flood of cream skirts with the usual care, as if a sculptor had positioned her just so as his model.

'Your Grace,' she said.

'Your Grace,' returned Leo, sounding grumpy and drunk. 'You've been waiting.'

'Traditionally, brides do wait for their husbands on a wedding night.'

'I'm sorry,' he said, not sounding sorry at all. 'I was held up.' He glanced towards a chandelier of Visserine crystal which must have carried a hundred candles. 'These are . . . our rooms?'

'You have a dressing room through there, and a bedroom beyond.' She pointed out a distant doorway through which he caught a glimpse of manly panelling. 'My rooms are that way.' Pale paint and tapestry in the other direction, a dressing room big enough for ten, but then it probably took ten to dress her.

'We're not sharing a bed?' he grumbled.

She spread her arms across the back of the chaise. 'I suppose that depends on your mood.'

He frowned up at a vast canvas. A masterful-looking military man in a neat black uniform frowned back. 'Who's this?'

'Your grandfather.'

'Lord Marshal Kroy?' He'd commanded the Union army at the Battle of Osrung, and died when Leo was small. He only remembered the man from stories, really. But there was undoubtedly a hint of Leo's mother about his withering frown. 'Couldn't find one of my other grandfather?'

'They're in short supply. He was a famous traitor.'

Leo flinched at that. Maybe treason ran in the family. He wandered across what felt like an acre of Gurkish carpet, between carefully arranged groups of furniture, past a stuffed songbird in a glass case. This one room was the size of the Dogman's hall in Uffrith. He wondered if it had been built from scratch in the week since he proposed. Or she proposed. Or their mothers proposed. It wouldn't have surprised him. There didn't seem to be anything Savine couldn't organise. Or wouldn't organise, given the chance.

'I thought decorating might bore you,' she said. 'If there's something you'd prefer, I can change it.'

'It's fine,' he grunted, frowning at two antique swords crossed over the mighty fireplace. It was about the finest room Leo ever saw, in fact, a perfect balance of money and taste, clearly done with his feelings in mind. He should've thanked her. But he was drunk, and his leg was sore, and he was in no mood to thank anyone. Particularly not her.

'Did you speak to the king?'

Leo ground his teeth. 'He didn't bother to turn up. Had to get to the whorehouse, I hear.'

'There's kings for you. Another day.'

'Fuck him,' snapped Leo, more harshly than he'd meant to. 'I've been with Isher. And Heugen and Barezin.'

'Ah, the great minds of the Open Council.' Her total calmness was only making him angrier. It was how his mother would've behaved, but with more of an edge. 'What did they have to discuss?'

'Nothing much.' Only civil war. 'State of the government.' And its violent overthrow. 'Banter, you know.' It had been banter, hadn't it? Or had they been deadly serious? Had *he* been deadly serious? He turned away to frown out of the window, through the darkened trees towards the lights on the Middleway.

He heard the rustle as she stood. 'Is something bothering you?'

'No.' Only future treason. And past affairs.

'Come now.' She came to stand beside him. 'There should be no secrets between husband and wife. Not on the first day, anyway.'

'You're right.' He turned to look at her. 'But we hardly know each other, do we? We spent one night together.'

'Part of one night.'

'Part of one night. I know you . . . own things. Manufactories, and mills, and mines.'

'I recently acquired a large stake in the Lord Governor of Angland, in fact.'

'Huh. And he got one in you.'

She cocked her head to one side. 'Worried over your investment?'

'Not till I spoke to Selest dan Heugen.'

'I wouldn't take anything she told you too seriously. The woman hates me almost as much as I hate her.'

'She told me . . .' Leo had a feeling if he said it, there'd be no going back. But he had to know the truth. That and his leg was burning and the day and the week and the month had been full of frustrations and he felt like a fight. 'She told me you and the king were lovers.'

There was a long pause. Savine didn't so much as twitch. A woman made from porcelain could have given more away. 'And what did you say?'

'I told her if she repeated it, I'd break her fucking nose.'

'*That* I'd rather like to see.'

'Is it true?'

'Had you imagined I was a virgin?'

'Any doubts on that score were put to rest in Sworbreck's office.'

Her eyes narrowed ever so slightly. 'As I recall, you were far from a reluctant visitor.'

'Not the only one, by all accounts. Is it *true*?'

A muscle worked in her jaw. She hid it well, but he could feel the anger coming off her. He rather liked it. 'The king and I have . . . some history.' She was breathing hard, through her nose, chest rising and falling. 'But that is what it is. History. It's nothing for you to—'

'Is the child mine?' he asked.

Her eyes narrowed further, hard creases spreading around the bridge of her nose, chin angrily pointed up at him. 'How can you ask me that?'

'*Is* there even a child?'

She hit him.

Not some theatrical little tickle. She hit him as hard as she could with an open hand, and for someone of her size she hit shockingly hard.

It made a sharp smack, knocked his breath out in a sharp gasp, snapped his face sharply sideways and made him stagger against the window frame.

There was a pause which felt very long, then he turned slowly back towards her, and he stared at her, and she at him.

'Leo,' she whispered, lifting a trembling hand. 'I—'

Leo caught it by the wrist. 'Shush.' Shock had turned to excitement, and excitement to a thrill that reached every part of him. Very slowly, very deliberately, he lifted her hand up, and let go of it.

His breath came fast, almost painful in his throat. The blood had flooded to his face, making it burn and tingle, but you could've said just the same for his cock.

Very slowly, very deliberately, without taking his eyes from hers, he turned his unslapped cheek towards her. He thought he saw the slightest smile at the corner of her mouth as he said the word.

'Again.'

The next slap was no softer than the first. He would've been disappointed if it had been.

'How fucking *dare* you?' she hissed, stepping close, breath hot on his stinging face.

He gave a kind of whimper as she caught him around the throat, kissing him, biting him. Her other hand was already busy with his belt. He kissed her back, clumsily, angrily, tangled his fingers in her hair and it shifted in his hands. A wig. It came loose, skewed, she twisted it off and flung it away. She looked shockingly different without the softness of it, hair clipped to dark stubble, lips curled back in a snarl, paint smeared from one eye down her cheek in a black streak.

She shoved him. He didn't even try to stay standing. Caught his head on an occasional table as he fell, bit his tongue and sprawled on his back, surrounded by scattered ornaments. Marshal Kroy stared down at him from the heavy frame. His feelings on the business were hard to judge.

'You fucking worthless *shit*,' she hissed, ripping Leo's trousers down around his ankles. He gave a dumb moan of excitement with every breath, shivering, trembling, wriggling up onto his elbows. He could see the whorl in her hair at the crown of her shaved head as it bobbed up and down, lapping, slurping.

'Fuck...' he whimpered, dropping back. Almost painful, almost painful, then definitely painful. By the dead, his leg was on fire, trapped under her at the wrong angle. 'Fuck...' His mouth tasted of blood. He reached out desperately, caught the claw-carved leg of an armchair and gripped it like a man hanging from a cliff by a tree-root, carpet rucking up around his shoulders as he wriggled helplessly. 'Fuck... ah... ah—'

She clambered over him, dragging her skirts up around her chest with a ripping of gauzy fabric and a couple of pearls popped free and rolled twinkling away. He reached for her, wanting to drag her down, wanting to kiss her, but she caught his wrist.

'Don't *fucking* touch me!' She forced his arm down above his head, pinned it against the floor. She was strong, but not that strong. He could've flung her across the room if he'd wanted to.

He wanted nothing less.

Skirts tickled him under the chin as she straddled him, muscles twitching around her sharp collarbones as she reached down, and somewhere in that mass of rustling fabric gripped hold of his cock.

'Stay...' she breathed, lips twisted around gritted teeth, 'there.' She worked her hips in circles, she giving a little growl and he a little sob each time she pushed lower. Her face inched closer until her open mouth pressed against his open mouth.

And they bit and snapped and grunted at each other, squirming on the carpet of their meticulously decorated living room.

The King's Pimp

O rso puffed out his cheeks as he rearranged his hand. Awful hand. Utter crap. 'I suppose it's comforting, in a way,' he murmured, 'that some things don't change.'

The same table in the same little place they'd always favoured. The same overwrought furniture and the same threadbare drapery. The girls were different, and looked even more nervous than they used to, but then the girls were always different and always looked nervous. It all seemed a little sadder than he remembered. But maybe he was the sad one.

Oh, and six Knights of the Body stood about the walls, bristling with weaponry, trying to look as inconspicuous as half a dozen fully armoured men can in a brothel, which proved to be not very. Corporal Tunny didn't appear to notice. He was a man who could play cards through battle, flood or riot and, indeed, claimed to have done so on more than one occasion.

'Oh, we're still here.' And he carelessly nudged a few more coins into the pot.

'Can't see that changing,' said Yolk, filling up everyone's glasses again. Orso really should've told him not to, but he was too drunk to bother.

'Unless the king were to go to war again, of course.' Tunny raised his grey brows significantly at Orso. 'In which case, my standard-bearing services are always at Your Majesty's disposal.'

'Glad to know that my standard, if nothing else, would be competently handled.' Orso tossed his awful hand away with a flourish. 'But I think I've had quite enough of war.'

'You show more wisdom than your father, in that case.' Tunny started to rake in the pot. 'I'll have to stick to procuring whores for Your Majesty.'

'How do you feel about being the king's pimp?' Orso let go a burp. A royal burp, he supposed. He'd been drinking all day. Hadn't helped. Never did.

'Daresay there are worse jobs.' Tunny gripped his pipe between his

154

yellowed teeth as he shuffled. 'Less marching than in the standard-bearing game, at least. More fighting, mind you, but at least there's the *chance* of making people happy. Sure you won't join us, Colonel Gorst?'

Gorst shook his head, eyes eternally roving around the dim room as though a Styrian assassin might spring from the dresser at any moment. If one had, Orso never doubted Gorst would have been ready with the utmost extremes of lethal force.

'You two know each other?' Orso looked from the old bodyguard to the old standard-bearer. They were probably of an age, but otherwise could hardly have been less alike.

'Fought together at the Battle of Osrung,' said Tunny, starting to deal. 'Well, I say fought. He fought. I just sat there.'

Yolk raised a finger. 'I sat there, too.'

'So you did, boy, and you even managed to do that badly.'

Yolk grinned. 'If there's one thing I'm good at, it's doing things badly.'

'I hear you sentenced Wetterlant to dangle,' said Tunny, still flicking out cards.

'I did,' said Orso. 'Terrible decision.'

'Everyone says he's guilty,' threw in Hildi, who was sitting cross-legged on the dresser between two large candlesticks shaped like naked women.

'Guilty as hell,' said Orso.

'So . . . you should've let him off?'

'That would've been a terrible decision, too.'

Yolk's face crinkled up with incomprehension. Its usual expression. 'So . . .'

'I tried to manage a compromise in which he'd get life in prison, probably to worm his way out when nobody was looking.'

'Compromise is always a good idea,' threw in one of the whores.

Orso raised his brows at her, and she blushed, and looked at the floor. 'So I thought, but it turned out to be the worst option of all. I made the fatal mistake of trying to improve things. And of trusting Lord bloody Isher.' He scraped up his hand and started sorting through it. 'A king can only select from a range of wrong choices and bad outcomes.' Another awful hand. Even worse than the last. 'A lifetime of trying to ferret out the least worst in a mist of lies, stupidity and imperfect information.'

'Sounds like the army life,' muttered Tunny. 'Wish you'd come to me first. I could've told you Isher's a snake.'

'I should put you on my Closed Council.' Orso paused a moment, looking at his glass. 'Actually, I've heard worse ideas.'

'High Justice Tunny!' Hildi gave a giggle, and a couple of the girls laughed, and Orso thought he even heard a snort from one of the Knights of the Body.

'Charmed by the offer, Your Majesty,' said Tunny drily, 'but corporal's as high as I go.'

'Leo dan Brock would make a fine king, don't you think?' asked Orso. 'Don't you think? With those shoulders?'

'He's pretty,' said Hildi, twisting her old soldier's cap off so her blonde curls popped out in a mop, then twisting it back on.

'He's *very* pretty,' said one of the girls, and the others nodded agreement.

'Bold,' said Yolk, thoughtfully. 'Very . . . manly.'

'Reckless,' piped Gorst. Orso turned to him, surprised. It might have been the first time he'd ever heard the man volunteer a word of conversation. He shrugged, armour faintly rattling. 'Kings needs cool tempers.' And he went back to frowning about the room.

Orso turned to the table to find the madam leaning over him in an explosion of heavily daubed perfume and lightly veined bosom. 'Might one interest . . . Your *August* Majesty . . .' She traced a wiggly line on the tabletop in a manner that was perhaps intended to be arousing. 'In anything?'

Orso sighed. 'Fucking-wise?'

'It is what we do here.'

The girl who had extolled the virtues of compromise gave Orso a slightly desperate smile. His shoulders slumped.

'Do you know, I'm not sure I could even manage it. It's not you. It's not any of you. It's me. Commoners, nobles, Starikland, Angland and Midderland, everyone bloody *hates* me.'

'Hasn't Westport decided it likes you after all?' asked Hildi.

Orso ignored her. He was in a mood only for bad news. 'It's a Union indeed. United in their dislike for their king.'

'That's what a king's there for,' said Tunny. 'High or low, we all need someone to blame.'

'Who do *I* get to blame?' asked Orso.

'Whoever you like,' murmured Yolk, frowning at his cards. 'You're king.'

'My Closed Council, my Open Council, the boy who empties my bloody chamber pot, too, I shouldn't wonder, they all think I'm a fucking—'

'Who cares a shit what they think?' shouted Tunny, jerking forward and stabbing at Orso with the stem of his pipe. 'Long as they bloody obey!

You're *king*, boy! Not me, not Yolk and not Leo dan bloody Brock! You! Now, I daresay being king has its downsides but I can tell you there are worse jobs.'

'Huh,' grunted one of the girls, adjusting her bodice.

'All this bloody *self-pity*. It was fun when you were a crown prince, but fuck, it doesn't suit a king.' Tunny took a pull on his pipe, but it was dead, and he angrily smacked the ashes out on the tabletop. 'Get back to the palace and get *on* with it. We'll miss you, but these lovely ladies need to make some money and you're scaring away the guests.'

There was a long silence. Orso glanced about the room. Everyone – the girls, the knights, the madam, Hildi and Yolk, even Bremer dan Gorst, had the same expression: mouth tight shut and eyes wide open, an expression that seemed to say, *I can't believe he said it, but it definitely needed saying.*

'I see.' Orso tossed down his cards and stood, with only a small wobble. 'Gorst, we're going back to the palace. Hildi, could you see everyone paid for their time, please?'

She frowned over at him. 'You already owe me sixty—'

'I think we know I'm good for it.'

'We do?'

'I'll talk to the lord chancellor and have you written into the budget, how's that?' As the knights tramped down the stairs to leave, Orso leaned close to Tunny. 'Thank you for that, Corporal.'

Without looking up from his cards, Tunny gave a grudging nod. 'Any time, Your Majesty.'

The Darling of the Slums

'**M**orning, Your Grace,' said Leo, stepping out onto the balcony. 'Morning, *Your* Grace,' said Savine as he sat opposite her at the breakfast table and gingerly stretched out his leg.

She shifted subtly, trying not to let her own discomfort show. A comfortable corset really isn't doing its job, but her belly was most definitely starting to swell. Savine had been softening all over since she gave up fencing. Gripping a sword made her think too much of Valbeck. Scrabbling with the hilt in a sweaty panic as she tried to pull up that loose board, men screaming for her blood outside the door—

'So . . .' Leo frowned out towards the Middleway, where the morning's traffic was already busy, then gave a helpless little laugh. 'We're married, then.'

Savine banished the ugly memories and held up the new ring she had commissioned, its satisfyingly colossal stone flashing in the morning sun. 'So it would appear.'

'What happens now?'

'I recommend the trout.'

'And then?'

'Give me and Zuri a week here to put my affairs in order, and then to Angland—'

'Where you can put my affairs in order?'

'Where I can help *you* put them in order.' And people might care less about appearances and Zuri would not have to haul quite so savagely on the laces. 'Probably best that we leave before Wetterlant's hanging.'

'I might hold off on saying sorry to His Majesty as well.'

Savine winced. 'I hope my . . . *history* with the king will not—'

'If he's fool enough to let the most beautiful woman in the Union slip through his fingers, then I pity him.' And Leo gave her that big, boyish smile, the one that made a faint groove from the scar on his cheek.

She found she was smiling back, and not even having to pretend. 'That's . . . a rather lovely thing to say.'

'Don't get used to it.' He scooped a piece of trout onto his plate then sucked the fork. 'I'm not much of a flatterer.'

'Oh, I think you could prosper at anything you put your mind to.'

He smiled even wider. 'That's a rather lovely thing to say.'

'I'm one of the best flatterers in the Union, ask anyone.'

He laughed, and started eating, and she rather enjoyed watching him. So strong and healthy and handsome. No sign of last night's anger now. Except perhaps a faint pink graze her open hand had left on his cheek. The Young Lion had his moods but it seemed they passed quickly, like stormclouds sweeping over the rugged Northern valleys and just as quickly letting the sun shine again. She could work with that. Who doesn't have moods, after all? Savine had been in one ever since she got back from Valbeck.

Haroon had to squeeze his great shoulders together to fit through the door onto the balcony. 'Spillion Sworbreck is here, Lady Savine.' A few months in Adua and he had barely any accent at all.

'Thank you, Haroon, you're a treasure. Send him out.'

Leo frowned after him. 'Not sure how your servants will go down in Angland.'

'Angland will just have to get used to them. Haroon and Rabik are Zuri's brothers, and they're some of the most diligent, conscientious, trustworthy people I know. Haroon used to be an officer in the emperor's army, I believe, and Rabik's an absolute magus with horses. As for Zuri . . .' She was Savine's closest friend, and the very thought of her being unwelcome somewhere made her want to grind that place under her heel. 'She is indispensable. My business interests would suffer more without her than without me. I would trust her with our lives.'

Leo prodded at his fish. 'Just feels like there are too many *brown* faces around in Adua these days.'

'Too many for what? The people who come here are hard workers. They bring wealth and energy and new ideas. There are great thinkers among them. Great engineers. And how would you stop them, anyway? Make us less prosperous?'

Leo did not look convinced. He was not a man much moved by reason. 'We fought a war against the Gurkish,' he grumbled.

'You fought a war against the Northmen. Some of your best friends are still Northmen.'

He actually looked slightly offended. 'Not all Northmen are the same, you know.'

There was a snapping of cloth and Sworbreck swept onto the balcony, became briefly entangled in the drapes but manfully fought his way free. He was fresh from another trip to the Far Country and was affecting the facial hair of a fearless adventurer.

'Your Grace,' he intoned, giving Savine a flourishing bow. 'You look a veritable *goddess*, as always.'

'Master Sworbreck, how was your latest escapade in the unsettled West?'

'Wild and *packed* with danger. I have tales to tell which the pampered citizens of Adua will scarcely *credit*!' Savine certainly would not credit them, for she had it on good authority that he rarely strayed far from the harbour at Rostod and paid a scout to wear his clothes while riding across the plains so they would have an authentically adventured-in appearance on his return.

'And may I introduce my husband, Leo dan Brock?'

'*Your* Grace.' Sworbreck gave an even more flourishing bow. 'An absolute honour to make the acquaintance of the hero of Red Hill and conqueror of the Great Wolf!'

'I don't like to talk about that,' said Leo sternly. Sworbreck blinked, mouth slightly open. Leo burst out laughing. 'It's all I'd bloody talk about if I had my way!' And he seized Sworbreck's hand and nearly dragged the hapless writer off the balcony with the vigour of his shaking. 'I think I visited your office once.'

Sworbreck must have guessed what they had used his office for, but to his credit he gave no sign of it. 'My humble premises are forever at your disposal, as is my humble pen.'

'I have a use in mind for the latter.' And Savine nudged a chair out with one shoe so Sworbreck could sit. 'The name *Glokta* carries . . . something of a stigma.'

'A proud name, but I see Your Grace's point. There is a flavour of . . .'

'Torture?'

Sworbreck gave an apologetic smile. 'The name *Brock* has entirely different connotations. Heroism, patriotism, derring-do! Have you considered a biography, by the way, Your Grace?'

Leo paused with fork halfway to his mouth. 'I'm twenty-two years old. I hope I've a few achievements still to come.'

'Your famous victories thus far are, one cannot doubt, but a prelude, but there would be great public interest even in a first volume or two—'

'My name,' Savine reminded him.

'Of course, my apologies, new ideas *erupt* and must be thrust aside! A curse of the artistic temperament.'

Far from the only one, in her opinion. 'Savine dan Glokta was a woman of business,' she explained. 'She needed a reputation for cunning, ruthless-ness and flinty resolve.'

'She needed the confidence of investors, the respect of partners, the awe of debtors,' mused Sworbreck, 'but... Savine dan *Brock*, Lady Governor of Angland, might be... a woman of the people? A woman who balances wisdom with warmth and generosity? A woman who struggles *tirelessly* for the common good?'

Curnsbick was always saying that he suspected Savine of hiding a gener-ous heart. Perhaps the time had come to put it on public display. 'What do you think about a series of pamphlets discussing my charitable work in the Three Farms? Nothing too obvious, you understand.'

'I am *all* in the subtext.' Sworbreck sat back, considering the trees in the garden as though their branches were laden with weighty revelations. 'It would help if we could find our way to a *place of honesty*. I hope you will not think me indelicate if I suggest we might... make use of your experiences during the uprising in Valbeck?'

Savine felt a sick surge of fear, then a sting of annoyance at her own weakness. All it took was a mention of the place to set her heart thumping and turn her mouth sour, to send that tickling shiver up her back.

Her voice came strangled. 'How do you mean?'

'You lived among the common folk there.' The Broads' cramped apart-ment, her bed of rags, the cries echoing through the blistering walls. 'Their daily trials were yours.' Up to her knees in the cold river, throat raw from smoke, endlessly filling buckets to put out fires that could not be put out. 'The hunger.' Queueing for vegetable peelings, and grateful to get them. 'The danger.' The sound of the gangs outside, the screams in the night. 'The daily want.' Her wheezing breath as she dragged herself through the machinery, blood spattering the floor—

'Of course!' she barked, knuckles white as she gripped at the edge of the table. 'A place of honesty.' If Sworbreck could spin diamonds out of shit, good luck to him. Where the hell had she put her pearl dust?

'A story of personal growth,' the writer was musing. 'Of dangers faced and trials braved. A woman born to privilege, coming through the fire of struggle to understand the plight of the common man.' He took a self-satisfied breath. 'Powerful. Are you aware of Carmee Groom? She did some sketches for my *Life of Dab Sweet*. One of the best artists in Adua, but she is not in the *greatest* demand because she is...'

'A she.'

'Indeed. A few etchings can truly make a pamphlet sing. Words are powerful, but an image can shortcut the reason and speak directly in the language of the heart.'

Savine snapped her fingers. 'Done. We can visit the Three Farms this afternoon.' Once she and Zuri had calculated the precise minimum a reputation for charity could be bought for.

'Then I shall make the arrangements at once!' said Sworbreck, springing up. 'Your Grace. *Your* Grace. Do think about that biography.' And he ducked back through the window.

'So . . . that's the famous writer?' asked Leo. 'He has some of the bravest facial hair I've ever seen.'

'Despite being one of the biggest cowards in the Union.'

'I suppose if he was brave, he wouldn't need such brave facial hair.'

'And if everyone was brave, what would make you special?'

'Well . . .' He gave her that grin again. 'I am married to the cleverest woman in the Union.'

'Stop,' she said, smiling as she leaned towards him. 'By which I mean, don't.'

'I won't. But . . . pamphlets?'

'Absolutely.'

'Etchings?'

'The language of the heart.'

'Do you really think people are that stupid?'

'Darling.' She leaned closer, and kissed him gently, and touched him lightly on the tip of his nose with her fingertip. 'People are *far* more stupid than that.'

The city closed in around them and, like a rake falling into a life of debauchery, turned mean, twisted, sick and dirty. High above, so high that it seemed no one could ever reach it, a narrow crack of sky showed between the crumbling tenements.

'And so we pass into the Three Farms.' Sworbreck spoke in an urgent whisper, scribbling away in his notebook. 'Perhaps the most infamous of Adua's districts, once largely burned then brutally occupied by the savage Gurkish, now rendered into an endless night . . . no, a *perpetual dusk* by the smoke of the manufactories, and a *moral murk* even more complete in which . . . what? In which the *light of hope* is extinguished for its thousands of wretched inhabitants. Can I find a place for the word *crepuscular*, do you think?'

'I try to find a place for it in every sentence,' said Carmee Groom, her fair brows raised very high.

'Not much of a reader myself,' said Leo, leaning close, 'but he sounds a bit overwrought.'

Savine shrugged. 'That's what people consider good writing these days.'

He nodded towards a pair of ragged boys shovelling horse-dung onto a rotting wagon. 'What're they doing?'

'Making a living.'

'Out of shit?'

'All you need is a shovel and a poor sense of smell.' Savine made an utterly futile effort to wriggle some room into her overtight collar. 'And good senses of smell don't last long around here.'

'Stay close, Your Graces.' Broad went with fists clenched, frowning into the shadows. Shadows were one of the few things there was no shortage of in the Three Farms. In some of the narrower lanes, you would hardly have known it was day. 'This is no place for wealthy folk to walk alone. Nor writers and artists neither.'

'Never fear!' called out Sworbreck. 'I learned well the value of a stout escort out in the wilds!'

'Where did you find your man Broad?' murmured Leo.

'In Valbeck. He and his family took me in. I've no doubt they saved my life.'

'So you took them in.' Leo was grinning at her. 'You *do* have a heart.'

'A *generous* one, according to my friend Curnsbick. But settling one's debts is simply good business. And the Broads are all useful people.'

'No doubt. That's a Ladderman's tattoo on his hand, you know. First men onto the walls in a siege. Most deadly duty in the whole army. And four stars means he did it four times.' Leo glanced sideways at Broad. '*That* . . . is a dangerous man.'

Savine remembered him facing down six Burners that first night in Valbeck and stomping their leader's head into the cobbles. The fear she had felt. And the relief.

'Calm,' Savine whispered, under her breath. 'Calm, calm, calm.'

'We live these days in a segregated society,' Sworbreck was burbling, nudging up his eye-lenses with the end of his pencil. 'A *stratified world* where rich and poor rarely mingle! No, wait, mingle is weak . . .'

They passed under the great chimney of a salt works, walls black with crusted soot. Flies buzzed around a dead horse. Three ragged children played in the gutter. Every other building here was a jerry shop, everyone at least halfway drunk, or so ill they looked drunk. Most of the rest were pawn shops, sad little fragments of broken lives priced low in their grubby windows.

'The gap between rich and poor has never been wider. The *chasm* has never *yawned* so deep! But one woman dares to bridge the divide!' Sworbreck gave a delighted cackle. 'Bridge the divide, that's lovely. She, like few others among the wealthy and noble, *goes forth* among the people. She, like few others, *understands* their plight!'

Savine did understand it. But if she truly went to a place of honesty, all she really felt was glad she was no longer one of these wretched ghosts. All she really wanted was to get back to her palatial rooms and her conscientious servants as soon as possible. That familiar smell of sweat, piss, damp and rot, mixed with the acrid scratch of the furnaces, was hard to ignore as they worked their way deeper into the gloomy maze of streets. Strange, how smells can bring memories back so sharply. She realised she had her box of pearl dust in her hand. Forced herself to push it back up her sleeve. She was free. She was safe. She told herself so, over and over.

'Calm, calm, calm—'

'These buildings . . .' Leo gazed up at the slumping offences against architecture crowding over them, blooms of green damp flaring from their leaking gutters.

'The land is short-leased so it isn't worth the landlords' while to build well, or to repair what's built badly. The houses fall apart with the families inside.' Who would know better than Savine? She owned dozens of similar buildings herself.

'Why no window frames?'

'The tenants tear them out in the cold months and burn them for firewood.'

'By the dead . . .'

Behind them, Sworbreck scratched on in his notebook. 'We speak, of course, of none other than Her Grace – and grace is the right word, dear friends – Savine dan Brock! Wife to the Young Lion! Bride, maybe?'

'Bride is youthful,' said Carmee Groom, plucking out one of the pencils shoved through her shambolic bun and causing half of it to collapse across her face. 'Bride bursts with potential.'

'*Bride* of the Young Lion and the new Lady Governor of Angland!'

They had made it to the very heart of the slum, an unpaved square with stagnant water gathered in puddles, thick with scum and blooms of multicoloured oil. A strange building stood at one side, an ancient low house with a sagging, moss-covered roof.

'What *is* that?' asked Leo.

'One of the three farms,' said Savine, 'that stood here before the city swallowed them.'

'Hard to imagine anything ever grew here...'

One pig screamed at another as they fought in a mound of filth. Someone shouted drunken abuse in a tongue she did not recognise. A cheap flute tooted hopelessly, blending with the mindless music of steam hammers in a foundry across the way.

Zuri waited with Haroon and Rabik and two of Broad's men. She had gathered a queue of the most wretched, a lot of dark faces among them. Refugees from the collapse of the Empire of Gurkhul, seeking safety and sanity and finding little of either.

'Thank you, Zuri.' Savine swallowed her nausea. 'You've done a miraculous job, as always.'

'I fear there are no miracles down here.' Zuri frowned towards the procession of the desperate. It reminded Savine of the queues she had stood in for one of the few working pumps in Valbeck. The long walk back with the heavy buckets bruising her calves, water slopping at her legs, the unbearable aching in her shoulders with every step.

'Calm, calm, *fucking* calm...'

Rabik watchfully held her purse while she took coins from it and pressed them into filthy, calloused, broken hands. Hands missing fingers and thumbs from mishaps at machinery. Hands of beggars, children, whores and thieves.

With Haroon's help, Leo was handing out loaves from a cart, clapping people on the back, shaking his head at their thanks, throwing open his brimming heart and spraying well-wishes. Savine said nothing. She was worried if she opened her mouth she might drown the neighbourhood in spew.

'As Lady Brock moves through those darkened streets, it is as if a lamp shines. No, a *beacon*! Lighting the way to a better life for these neglected unfortunates. As if the sun breaks through the smoke of the manufactories. She gives out bread, yes, she gives out comfort, surely, she gives out silver with an open hand, but more valuable than all, she gives out *hope*.'

'Very nice,' murmured Carmee Groom, eyes flickering over the scene as she pinned her hair back up with a clip from her drawing board and began to sketch.

'Isn't it!' said Sworbreck. 'All shrouded in secrecy, though, we must make that point. We have stumbled upon her anonymous generosity!

She would blush to hear it *spoken of.* For she is the personification of humility... or modesty? Modesty or humility?'

'Why not both?'

'Is this what Valbeck was like?' Leo muttered at Savine.

'Before the uprising, maybe. Then it got worse. We picked through the dung heaps for something we could eat.'

'What can we do for them? I should've brought my purse. Never use the bloody thing.'

He really did have a big heart. It made her strangely glad to know that someone did. A big heart, but not the biggest brain. Help to these people was a coin tossed in a pool. It might make a few ripples, but they would quickly vanish as though they had never been. The bread would be gone in one swallow. The money would be wasted on drink and husk, a moment of sweet oblivion. Perhaps, at best, some tatty heirloom temporarily reclaimed from the pawn shop.

'Who, on account of her charity... no, selflessness... on account of her *remarkable* charity and selflessness, has become known among the common folk of Adua, as, hmmmm...'

A little urchin with a scabby rash across her face gazed up as Savine pressed a coin into her palm. She felt crushed, like a swineherd being smothered by hungry pigs. 'Do you need much more?' she snapped.

'Almost there,' said Carmee Groom, freckled face wrinkled with concentration as she drew.

'Benefactor?' mused Sworbreck. 'The benefactor of the Three Farms?'

'Too cold.'

Savine flinched at a shower of sparks from an open shed door. She felt trapped in this stinking gloom. She felt almost as trapped as she had in Valbeck. She had to get out.

'The... saint?' Sworbreck raised his brows high. 'Of the hovels?'

'Too religious. We're not in Gurkhul.'

'No, we are *very* much in the slums of Adua...'

That girl with the rashy face had caught Savine's skirts. Clutching at the only kindness that had ever been shown her, perhaps, no matter how much of a sham it was. Leo was watching with tears in his eyes. If they stayed much longer, he would probably adopt the little limpet. Savine's greasy skin was crawling. She wanted nothing more than to kick the girl off into the gutter. Forced herself by a towering effort of will to keep the smile nailed to her face as Rabik tried to gently peel her dirty hands away.

'How about...' Carmee Groom narrowed her eyes at the scene,

scratching thoughtfully at the side of her nose with her pencil. 'The *darling* . . . of the slums.'

'Oh, my *dear*.' Sworbreck looked up wide-eyed from Carmee's paper to Savine, holding up his hands as though framing a painting with her as its subject, that desperate orphan clinging to her feet. 'You should be a writer!'

Dead Wood, New Shoots

It was a sunny spring morning when Rikke walked back into Uffrith. She used to feel a rush of warmth passing through those weather-pitted gates, hearing the gulls and the chatter, smelling the sea. She used to reap a happy harvest of smiles and waves on the way to her father's hall. There goes Rikke – she's mad as a shield made of bread, but we like her. Coming home. By the dead, she needed that feeling then.

But things had changed since she went to the forbidden lake, and not just 'cause she kept getting surprised on her right-hand side. The left was full of sad shocks, too. Folk she'd have called friends stared as she passed like they saw the dead walk, slunk off and wouldn't meet her one good eye. Folk who used to smile looked scared, shocked, disgusted even. One woman Rikke had never been able to shut up about the weather herded her three children inside at the sight of her and slammed the door.

Till that moment, she'd been tricking herself that everything would drift back to normal, or as close to it as her life got. Five steps into town, it was clear no one would ever look at her the same again.

Stung somewhat, but she wasn't about to let it show. She buried her hurts, like grown-ups were meant to, and tried to walk the way she'd seen Savine dan Glokta walk. Shoulders back, chin up, making no apologies. Like Uffrith was hers and these bastards only got to live here 'cause she was in a good mood.

She leaned close to Shivers without letting the knowing half-smile slip. 'I look that bad?'

'You look better'n me,' he said, which was scant encouragement.

'They'll get used to it,' said Isern.

A scruffy little girl with a scruffy little dog gawped as she passed. The dog couldn't take its shocked eyes off her, either. 'People can get used to pretty much anything,' said Rikke.

'That's why they'll get used to it.'

'Rikke?'

A boy stood with a half-eaten apple forgotten in his hand, his eyes big and round and fixed on her face. She squatted down to ruffle his scruffy hair.

'You've changed some,' he said, still staring.

'Aye.'

'You used to be all twitchy.'

She lifted her hand up and held it still. It was steady as the line between sea and sky. 'Seems I'm cured of that,' she said.

'You cured o' smiling, too?'

'I can still smile, you cheeky shrimp.' Though when she forced a grin out it felt strange on her face, the skin still raw where the tattoos were drawn.

'Can you see all right?'

'Can't see at all with this eye.' She winked at him with the right, and it made no difference. She took a hard breath as she stood, watched the grey sea shifting. 'But the other sees better than ever.'

There were a lot of people gathered in front of her father's hall. There were always folk wanting something from him. Always wanting more than he had to give, whether it was silver, or men, or reassurance, or favour. They'd drained him dry of all of them, down the years.

Hardbread hastened up the cobbled road, his white hair wild. When he got close enough for his weak old eyes to get her measure he froze.

'Hardbread,' she said, giving him a nod.

'Rikke . . .' He sounded more'n a little sick. 'That you?'

'Aye. I cut my hair.'

He stared at her some more. 'Rikke, I have to tell you something.'

'It'll have to wait. Need to talk to my da.'

'That's the thing.'

'What's the thing?' she asked as she shoved the doors of the hall wide, and stopped, her weight all on one wobbling foot.

'Oh, no.' And she sagged like a scarecrow had its pole ripped out. Caurib had warned her the Long Eye wouldn't keep her safe from all life's axes. 'Oh, no.'

Her father lay on the table, his old, notched sword on his chest. His hair and his beard were white. His face and his hands were white. His eyes were closed.

'Oh, no.' Everyone watching her, silent, slipping out of her way as she walked up, like you might from someone had the plague. She stopped by the table, looking down at her father. Seemed he had the ghost of a smile about his mouth.

'He never smiled enough,' she whispered.

'Aye,' said Shivers, soft and low. 'Those were the times he lived through.'

'He done the best he could with 'em.'

'None better,' said Isern, and she took a long breath and puffed it out, ragged. 'Back to the mud.'

Rikke put her fingertips on her father's cheek. 'Peace at last, eh, Da?' she whispered, and her right eye tickled and stung and leaked. Might not see any more, but it could cry, still.

Her left stayed dry, though.

Greenway reined in hard and slithered from his saddle, got his foot caught in one stirrup in his haste and nearly fell. 'The Dogman's dead!' he screeched.

Silence, while a breeze blew up and whisked some fallen blossom across the road. Silence, while everyone wondered how Stour would take the news so they could take it the same way.

Then the young king tipped back his head and roared with laughter, and as if that was permission given, they all set to chuckling, too. All of 'em except Clover. He weren't really in the mood.

'What was it Shama Heartless said?' asked Stour, wiping his wet eyes. 'There's only one kind of good news, and that's dead enemies. Reckon those sorry bastards'll be joining the North sooner than we hoped, eh, Clover?'

'Prefer to eat the eggs I've got, my king, rather'n the ones still up in the tree.'

'Good point, Clover, good point.' Stour grinned his wolf grin and with a snapping of cloth pulled his wolf cloak around his shoulders. 'Let's take nothing for granted. We'll head straight into Uffrith, pay our respects. Or the lack of 'em. Then we can talk to Oxel. See how things stand.'

'Oxel's there,' said Greenway. 'I seen him.'

'Lovely.' Stour rubbed his palms together with a faint hissing. 'That's happy timing. *Auspicious* timing. Auspicious is the word, eh, Clover?'

'It's *a* word,' said Clover, under his breath.

'How about Red Hat and Hardbread?'

'Aye, they were there, with their long, grey faces, and I hear the Dogman's daughter, too—'

'Ha! You hear that, Clover? We've caught up to that fucking little bitch at last. This'll be fun. Ain't nothing prettier than a pretty girl crying, eh?'

There really was nothing to be said to that.

The sun was shining in Uffrith, but the place had a sullen feel. The Dogman had been loved, few men more, and it looked like his daughter weren't the only one felt they'd lost a father. Mourners gathered in a long queue, grave gifts in their hands, but Stour strode grinning past 'em, lapping up their scowls and their curses. He was one of those men loves to be despised. That treats loathing like gold, to be clawed for and hoarded up. He hadn't learned yet that hate's the one thing never runs out.

There was quite the gathering inside the hall. Named Men, fussed up in their best, gold and jewels glittering in the gloom on helms and hilts. Oxel was there, as expected, and Red Hat and Hardbread, glaring at each other almost as much as at Stour. Caul Shivers, too, though his only finery was a blood-red stone on his little finger and the only glint on him was from his metal eye. Isern-i-Phail sat on a step, slowly chewing, long spear across her knees, and as Stour strode in she made a long sucking through the hole in her teeth that spoke her scorn louder than any words.

Lots of weapons in that hall, lots of sorrow and lots of anger, and Clover made sure he knew where all the doors were. When a great man dies, those left over always take a moment working out where their loyalties are most fruitfully laid, and there's a high risk of bloodshed in the meantime. He'd seen one funeral turn into several often enough.

The Dogman himself lay pale on the long table, scarred shield under his feet, a hint of drama from a shaft of light falling on him through the smoke-hole. A woman stood over him in the shadows, back to the door. Her red-brown hair was clipped short and it made her neck look very long and very thin, blue veins standing stark up the side.

Stour strode into the silent hall, steel toes on his boots scraping. 'I just had to pay my respects!' Voice dripping contempt, not caring a shit, as usual, for anyone's feelings but his own.

Then the woman turned, and that shaft of light caught her smile, and Stour shuffled to an uncertain halt. So did his men. A dozen warriors always keen to advertise their courage, but they all checked at the sight of her, and Clover hardly blamed 'em.

'By the dead,' muttered Greenway, taking a nervy step back and near tripping over his own sword.

'The King of the Northmen!' she raised her arms in delight. 'What a joy! The gates of Uffrith stand open to you, even though last time you visited you burned the place, eh? Eh? *Eh?* The last *eh?* hissed through her gritted teeth, spit spraying.

Rumour was the Dogman's daughter was a witch. That she had the

Long Eye. Clover hadn't taken it too seriously. Now it was hard to doubt. She'd turned so lean her face was like a skull, skin so stretched you fancied you could see through it, scabbed and angry around her left eye, across her forehead, her cheek, the bridge of her nose. Clover wondered if, of the two of 'em, her father looked the healthier.

'What the hell happened to you?' muttered Stour, giving voice to the thoughts of everyone in the hall, most likely.

'A sorceress said she could make me more ordinary,' said Rikke. 'Or she could make me less. Guess which I chose?'

She strutted closer, bony shoulders tipped back, bony chin tipped up, and the mingling of that battered face and that snake-like swagger and that friendly grin and those mad, mad eyes was really most off-putting.

'I've been in the High Places. Up in the mountains, beside a lake.' And she waved a hand, runes on thongs around her thin wrist clicking and clattering. 'Fine views, but the water was a little chilly on the toes, eh, Isern?'

Isern-i-Phail, no doubt used to being the weirdest in just about any company, was of a sudden looking workaday by comparison. 'I didn't paddle,' she said, and spat some chagga juice across the floor.

'You should've. The kind of cold that burns all your doubts away. Whole business was . . .' And Rikke opened her eyes wide, so wide it seemed they might pop out of her pinched-in face. 'Eye-opening. I see right through you, now. Right through *all* of you.' And she laughed, a jagged laugh, like she'd left her senses far behind her, and it didn't help at all that she was laughing at her father's funeral.

Stour twisted his face sideways as she came close, like he was looking into a wind. Her right eye was all swollen, many-coloured bruises on the bloated lids and a great red stain all across the white of it, pupil shrivelled to a milky pinprick. The pupil of the other yawned huge and black, and Clover saw the scabbed and angry skin around it was pricked with designs. A cobweb of black lines and letters, circles and symbols, so fine it seemed it couldn't have been drawn by men at all. Clover never saw a thing looked so much like witch's work, and the warriors muttered and shifted, a dozen big men edging back fearful from one girl thin as a birch sapling.

'Fucking witch,' muttered one who came from over the Crinna, making a holy sign across his chest. 'Should be burned.'

Rikke smiled at him, pointing with one thin finger. 'But it's *you* who'll die by fire!' She smiled at Greenway. 'You on the water! And 'cause I've told you so, all the days you have left, you'll go in fear of streams and boats and wells and cups and every drop of dew shall be a terror.' She

172

wagged that finger at him. 'But the water will find you out. It will leak in through the cracks in your life no matter how you try to caulk 'em up. I see the Great Leveller coming, and there are no bargains made with him.' She stared at Stour, and took a necklace of green stones she wore and dragged them back until they made a noose, cutting into her thin neck. 'But it's steel for most of you. It takes no Long Eye to see that.' She dropped the necklace and laughed again. 'Stay! You're all welcome. Stay, and I can tell you more.'

'Not me,' muttered Greenway, who should've been called Whiteway he'd turned so pale. He blundered to the door, and saw a bucket there put under a leak, and he shrank away from it, then scrambled out into the daylight. The rest of Stour's big men weren't far behind him. Seemed this hadn't turned out quite the fun he'd promised.

The Great Wolf himself stayed to give the room a wet-eyed scowl. 'We'll be back,' he barked out. 'See *that*, witch!' And he shoved past Clover and stalked from the hall.

'How rude.' Rikke's pale eye and her red eye slid across to Clover. 'You I know.'

'We met once,' he said. 'In the woods.' And she'd come a long way from the stringy little scrap who fell at his feet then. She'd come a long, hard way by a crooked road, he reckoned.

'I remember,' she said. 'Do you want to hear what's coming, Jonas Clover?'

'Reckon I'd rather not.' Wasn't easy to meet those strange eyes, one seeming too shallow and one too deep. But he made himself do it. 'Just wanted to say I'm sorry about your father. Didn't know him well, but I wish I'd known him better. Ain't many left in the North you could say that much for.'

'Why don't you stay?' she asked, raising one brow. Seemed the other got shaved off when the tattooing was done. 'We can talk about what's coming.'

'D'you know? I wish I could.' And it was true. He'd rather have stayed with the witches and the dead than gone back out to Stour and his bastards. 'But I am what I am.' Nightfall had the power. More even than before, with the Dogman back to the mud. And Clover was done with losing sides. So he nodded to Isern-i-Phail, and nodded to Rikke, too. Then he turned for the door.

Shivers stood in his path, that metal eye glinting in the shadows. 'We still need to have that talk.'

'We do.' Clover thought about giving Shivers a clap on the arm or something, but he didn't really seem the arm-clapping type. 'More'n ever.'

Then he left.

It was raining when they put him in the mud. Thin rain, making the whole world damp. Soft as a maiden's kiss, as he used to say. Seemed right, somehow, for the occasion. The gulls and the sea and the sad voices deadened. Everything deadened, like the world was wrapped in a shroud.

Usually, when a man goes in the ground, there are a few words said. Words from his chief or his family. How good they were, how strong, how brave. How much missed they'll be by those staggering on. But today, it seemed everyone in Uffrith had words. The little garden beside the hall was packed shoulder to shoulder, mourners spilling out into the wet lanes around.

One by one they took their turn at the head of the fresh-turned earth, shuffling up to speak their piece till the whole plot was boot-mashed. Till the whole plot looked like a grave. Everyone had a story. Some kindness done. Some wisdom offered. Some little piece of courage that'd given them courage. Soft words spoke with smoking breath. Tears lost in the drizzle.

They said he'd been the best of his kind. The last straight edge. Closest friend to the Bloody-Nine, worst enemy to Black Dow, who'd fought for Bethod and fought against him, across the North and back. Red Hat shouted out a story about the fight in the High Places. Oxel barked one about the Siege of Adua. Hardbread talked of the Battle of Osrung, folk murmuring with every famous name – Curnden Craw and Whirrun of Bligh and Cairm Ironhead and Glama Golden. He started at a creaky murmur, white hair plastered to his liver-spotted pate, but by the end he was glaring lightning and bellowing thunder as he told of the high deeds done in the valleys of the past. Old men made young again in the fire of those memories, just for a moment.

Then Shivers stepped up, one hand on the grey pommel of his grey sword, and with the other he pushed the hair back from his scarred face, and spoke in that broken whisper. 'Some o' you have had the misfortune o' knowing me a long time. I used to be . . .' He ran out of words a moment, stood there silent with teeth clenched. 'I was everyone's enemy, and my own most of all. A man who'd used up all his chances and didn't deserve another. But the Dogman gave me one. In hard times, it's easy to become hard. But here was a man who always looked for the best in folk. Didn't always find it, but never gave up looking. Wasted no time polishing his own name. Singing his own songs. Didn't have to. Every man

and woman in the North knew his quality. Back to the mud, Dogman.'
And he gave the earth a slow nod. 'Feels like the best of us goes in the
ground with you.'

Quiet, then. That heavy quiet, and Isern set a hand on Rikke's shoulder.
A gentle hand, for once, soft as the rain. 'You want to speak? You don't
have to.'

'Aye,' said Rikke. 'I do.' And she slipped through the damp-eyed crowd
to the head of the grave. It was a good spot for him. In the garden he
wished he'd tended better. Looking down over the city he'd fought for
so many years. Looking down towards the sea. He'd have liked friends
beside him, she reckoned. But their lonely graves were scattered across
the North, wherever they'd died. That's a warrior's life. A warrior's death.

She looked up, saw all those sad faces turned towards her, all waiting
for her to say something worth hearing.

'Shit,' she croaked, shaking her head at that heap of ground. She'd
helped to pile it on him. There it was, dark in the grain of her hands,
black under her fingernails. Still she couldn't believe he was under there,
and wouldn't step smiling from the crowd to give the last, best word.
'Fucking shit.' She took a long, salty sniff, and rubbed the wet from the
blind side of her face.

'Been a fine thing listening to you all.' She tried to smile but it came
out all quivery and brittle. 'So many stories. So many burdens he took
a little piece of onto his own shoulders. No wonder he was crooked at
the end. No wonder. Guess we'll have to carry our own burdens now. Or
maybe all share a little o' the load between us.'

Folk held each other. Squeezed each other's hands. She wondered how
long that good fellowship would last. Not long, was her guess.

'All them battles.' Her voice had faded to a croak, she had to clear
her throat to get it going again. 'All those great names he stood beside.
Fought against. His story was the story of the North, for sixty years and
more. You'd think he was the last o' some race of giants to hear talk of his
victories but . . .' And she grinned, despite herself. 'He was a small giant,
my da. He'd rather have been growing things than killing 'em. Didn't get
much of a chance at it, as this garden'll testify. He was always going to
tend to it tomorrow. But he loved to sit here, with the sun on his face.
He could spend hours here, looking to the sea. Hoping better times might
roll in on the tide.'

She wished she had better words. Ones that somehow bound up all
he'd been to her. All the things felt but never said. All the holes he'd leave
behind. But how can you fit all that in a bit of breath?

'By the dead, I was proud to be his daughter,' she said. 'Folk can talk a lot of shit at a funeral, but even his enemies thought he was the best man in the North.' She took a damp breath and blew it out hard, her lip trembling. 'That's all I got.'

Shivers put a hand on her shoulder. 'Good words, Rikke.'

Bit by bit, with shuffling feet and hanging heads, folk started to drift back to their lives. Bit by bit, the garden emptied. Rikke stood looking at the ground, wishing she could see through it. Wishing she could force the Long Eye open and see her father's face again. But her eye stayed cold as the rain, and the sea, and the cold ground.

'You really see their deaths?' Hardbread's brow was creased with worry. 'The Great Wolf and his arseholes. You really see all that . . .' And he waved nervously towards her tattooed face. 'With the Long Eye.'

'I saw enough,' she said.

'You surely made 'em run, all right. You made 'em scamper.'

'I did, didn't I?' Caurib had been right. The power of the Long Eye wasn't so much in what you saw, but in what you made folk believe. Rikke had never felt powerful in her life till she made Stour and his men turn tail with just her eye and her words. 'But they'll be back,' she said. 'Like wolves prowling just beyond the firelight.'

'Aye.' Hardbread scrubbed unhappily at his wet wisps of hair. 'Do you see what we should do now, then?'

'Don't take the Long Eye to see that.' Red Hat had come from the ebbing crowd to stand frowning on one side of the grave. 'Stour fucking Nightfall ain't fit to rule a shit-pit.'

'He's a bastard to his enemies.' Oxel had turned up, too, not to be outdone, glowering across the dug-over earth from the other side. 'But at least he's a Northman. At least he's a warrior.'

'You don't know who his enemies'll be from one moment to the next. Not even he does! And you want us to go lick his arse?'

'Better his than some Union fool who's never drawn a sword, a thousand miles away across the sea.'

'Can't say I like the taste of anyone's arse too much,' muttered Rikke, squeezing at the bridge of her nose with finger and thumb.

'You're a woman,' said Oxel, with a sneer.

'True,' said Rikke. 'I realised that the first time I tried to piss standing up. Most disappointing day of my life.'

'My point is, you can't *lead*. But there's some who'll listen to you, still. Out o' respect for your father—'

'And my pretty smile? What about my pretty smile? I've a pretty smile, haven't I, Isern?'

'Like the sun peeping from behind a stormcloud.' And Isern picked at that hole in her teeth with a fingernail, rooted some scrap of food out of it, held it thoughtfully to the light, then ate it.

Oxel ground his teeth. 'There's a reckoning coming and it can't be put off. You all want to make sure you're on the right side of it!' And he stalked away, his warriors shooting glares about as they followed, to let everyone know they meant business.

'Stour wants Uffrith,' growled Red Hat, before they were even gone. 'He wants everything we've got and Oxel's planning how to hand it over. We have to—'

'Give it all away to the Union first?' asked Rikke.

Red Hat held his hands up. 'I'm old, Rikke. You get old, and you get to thinking – what kind o' world will I leave to my grandchildren? Do I want 'em to have to fight all the same bloody wars I fought? You were close with Brock. He's Lord Governor now. You could talk to him.'

Rikke snorted. 'I'd rather bloody talk to Stour.'

'No, you wouldn't,' said Isern.

'No, I wouldn't,' admitted Rikke. 'But neither much appeals.'

'I'm sorry about your father,' said Red Hat. 'I stood second to him most of my life. I couldn't be sorrier. But tears'll wash no one clean, my ma used to say. The Protectorate was never going to outlive him. Oxel's right about one thing. Folk'll listen to you. You'd best decide which side o' this you're on.'

He jerked his head to his men, and they tramped off after Oxel.

Hardbread was doing some head-shaking of his own as he watched them go. 'Put three Northmen together, you'll get three different ideas.'

'Unless you're one of 'em,' said Isern. 'Then you'll get two ideas and one old bastard tearing his hair out trying to choose between 'em.'

'Or trying not to,' said Rikke.

Hardbread sighed. 'Aye, well, I got my mouth smashed by Whirrun o' Bligh one time and ever since I've been trying my best to keep things peaceful.'

'Shame you can't side with everyone when everyone's on a different side,' said Shivers, arms folded. 'You have to pick one.'

Hardbread looked over at Rikke. 'So which'll you be picking?'

'Picky Rikke, eh? Ain't long since I was choosing an eye, and now I've got to choose a side?' She squinted up at the sky, where the rain was slacking off. 'I'll let the earth settle on my father, then I'll get the garden tidied, then I'll have a little think. The moment I've made my choice, I'll let you know, how's that?'

'Fine with me. 'Course it is. Just don't think too long. This is apt to get bloody.' And Hardbread and his warriors took their own share of the striding off, leaving Rikke, and Isern, and Shivers alone in the dripping garden.

'I've heard it said you can tell how great a man was by how quick folk start to argue once he's dead.' Isern thoughtfully narrowed her eyes. 'Seems your father was an even greater man than I supposed.'

Rikke gently shook her head. 'Never noticed I had a pillar propping me up till it was gone. Feels like I'd give the eye I've got left for one more talk with him.'

'That deal's not on offer,' said Isern.

'Probably just as well. I'll need all the eyes I can get to see a path through what's coming.' She set one hand on Shivers' shoulder, and one on Isern's. 'Reckon I'll need the two of you, too.'

'I'll be here,' said Shivers.

'Whatever you want,' said Isern, licking finger and thumb then rolling chagga between them into a pellet. 'But . . . what do you want?'

A good question. Rikke pressed at the raw skin around her eye with her dirty fingertips. Things would be different now. Everything would be different, and her especially. She was nowhere near getting used to losing her face, and now she'd lost her father, and it looked like her home might get took away as well. 'My da said you have to be realistic. My da said you want things right, you have to put 'em right yourself. My da said Uffrith would need my bones and my brains when he was gone.'

'In that, I judge him canny.' Isern rolled her eyes after Red Hat, and Oxel, and Hardbread. 'Those old bastards don't have one good set of bones or brains between 'em. Old men, I swear. They get weak and stubborn both at once, so they make no good ideas but won't be shifted from the bad ones.' She offered the pellet to Rikke. 'Trouble snaps 'em straight to splinters.'

'My da said they'd need my heart, too,' said Rikke, slipping it up behind her lip.

'Mmmmm,' hummed Isern, rolling another pellet for herself. 'It's a pretty notion. But you don't have your da's name, or his fame, or – let's not dress it up – a cock.'

'So if you've no cock, you can't afford a heart?'

'Not if you want to get shit done. I tell you this, Black Calder didn't get his way through kindness.' She popped the chagga in her mouth and started to chomp on it. 'You have to make of your heart a stone, d'you see?'

Rikke heaved up another sigh. 'I do. Half the eyes these days, maybe, but I see twice as clear.' She squatted down to set her hand on the fresh-turned earth one more time and gave it a pat. 'You rest now, Da.' The sun was coming out, at least, and she looked to the sea, and watched it glitter. 'I'll take care of things from here.'

PART V

'Three may keep a secret,
if two of them are dead.'

Benjamin Franklin

The Favourite Son

The ship's timbers grated against the wharf and Leo took a deep breath of that good Angland air. Felt pure after the smogs of Adua. Felt honest.

There was quite a crowd on the docks to welcome him and his bride to Ostenhorm, and the weather might've been grey but their smiles were sunny. Someone was waving a battle flag. The crossed hammers of Angland, ragged from action. It made him think of Red Hill, of the fight on the bridge, of the men marching to victory. It made him impatient to march again.

'They love you,' said Savine, staring at the cheering people.

'Well, you know how it is. They love men who win fights.'

'Leo, they *really* love you.'

'Not sure I've ever seen you surprised before.'

'I have seen angry mobs and needy throngs, but I cannot say I was ever actually *liked*.'

'I bet they'll like you now.'

She hesitantly raised a gloved hand and waved. The cheers grew louder. A little boy jumped up and down on the quayside so wildly, Leo worried he might fall in the sea. Savine laughed, and blew him a kiss, and he went so red he looked like he might pass out. 'By the Fates,' she whispered. 'I think they do.'

Alas, not everyone was so easily pleased. Mustred and Clensher advanced with weighty frowns the moment the gangplank clattered across from ship to quay. Short of diving into the brine, there was no escape.

'We need to talk, Your Grace!' snarled Mustred.

'More troubles over taxes,' growled Clensher.

'The damned Closed Council have no shame!'

'Nor pity! Someone has to draw a *bloody* line!'

Leo winced. He'd hoped at least to make it to the Lord Governor's residence before the bureaucratic bog closed over his head again. 'We'll get to that, my lords, but could I first present my wife, Lady Savine dan Brock?'

'You must be Lord Clensher.' She slipped gracefully forward to offer her hand. 'I do like your boots, are those new?'

'Well . . . as it happens, Your Grace . . .' grumbled Clensher as he bent to kiss it. He'd clearly been aiming to disapprove of Leo's choice of wife but was already finding it difficult. 'I know your father, of course.'

Savine laughed as though he was being hugely charming. 'I can only apologise for that. But I am not my father. I am your Lady Governor, and I am here to do everything I can to help. How is Lady Lizet?'

Clensher's bushy brows shot up. 'You know my wife?'

'Only by reputation, but I am keen to put that right. My friend Tilde dan Rucksted is her niece, of course, and speaks so *very* highly of her. I understood she was having troubles with her back?'

'Well . . . she—'

'I took the liberty of bringing some salts that I am told can work wonders.' And Zuri produced a jar of coloured powder from her bag.

'That's immensely thoughtful,' breathed Clensher, utterly disarmed.

'And Lord Mustred – what a magnificent moustache – I brought you a newly printed volume on the heraldry of Angland and Starikland, do you have that one?'

Mustred stroked the binding as Zuri passed it to him. 'Why . . . no, but it's always been a particular interest of mine!'

'Such a happy chance!' As if anything Savine did was by accident. She smiled even more sweetly, holding out both hands. 'And you must be Jurand, Leo's old friend and comrade.'

'Er . . .' Jurand had been giving her quite the frown, for some reason, but now he started to soften. 'Yes—'

'I heard you had all the brains around here but Leo, why didn't you tell me how very handsome he is?'

'Well . . .' Leo cleared his throat. 'I suppose that's not the sort of thing a man notices . . .'

He watched as Zuri magicked one packet after another from her bottomless bag. Savine had brought gifts for everyone. And not just any old rubbish. The kind a dear friend would bring on a special occasion. In a moment, she changed the mood from angry suspicion to baffled delight.

'It took me years to tame the old dogs,' murmured Leo's mother from the corner of her mouth. 'She has them eating out of her hand the moment she steps off the boat.'

'I own a stake in the armoury here in Ostenhorm,' Savine was saying, 'but I have never had the chance to visit. Perhaps one of you two magnates might be kind enough to show me the way?'

'It would be my honour!' shouted Mustred, offering his elbow.

'My particular pleasure, Your Grace!' shouted Clensher, offering his, and she glided off with an old lord on either side, both gormlessly grinning as they competed for her attention. For maybe the first time since he took his mother's place as Lord Governor, Leo was free of their demands. Free to limp over to his cheering people and press hands, slap shoulders, return their beaming smiles. Free to actually be a *leader*.

'Bloody hell, Leo.' Antaup stared down at a shining pair of new spurs with his family crest on the buckle. 'I think I'm in love.'

'I know,' said Leo, smiling at Savine. Everyone was smiling at her right then. 'I think I am, too.'

Steel on steel. By the dead, how Leo loved that sound. Sweeter than birdsong. He caught Jurand's sword on his, blades grinding then ringing as he flung his friend away, pressed in with a couple of cuts and made him stumble back, only just keeping his balance on the wet grass.

'Better.' Jurand was grinning as he found his stance again. 'Much better.'

'Oh, that's nothing,' said Leo, grinning, too. It was good to be back with him. Very good. And the rest of the boys, of course.

The leg was still sore, but he was learning how to manage it. He'd strapped a belt around it under his trousers, just above the knee. Made it stiffer, but a lot more solid. Jurand tried to circle but Leo watched, waited, forced him to circle back the other way. He'd had to change his style. Far less aggression. Much more patience.

Jurand darted in but Leo was ready, parried once, twice, a careful shuffle to shift his weight then a pinpoint jab, and another, and he sent Jurand stumbling back the way he'd come.

Savine had told him to look at his leg as simply a new challenge. Overcoming challenges was what he did, after all. And she was right. When wasn't she?

Jurand came on again, but he was tired from all that dancing. Leo parried the first thrust, sidestepped the second to let it slip past him, then twisted, swung, flicked the back of Jurand's leg as he blundered past and sent him rolling across the lawn with a despairing squawk.

Antaup punched the air. 'A touch to the Young Lion!'

'Damn it!' Jurand propped himself on one elbow and spat grass. 'I take it the leg's feeling better?'

'Far from healed.' Leo bared his teeth at the pain as he pulled Jurand to his feet. 'But I have to be ready.'

'For what?' asked Antaup, waggling his eyebrows. 'You're a married man. It's a different kind of sword-work that's called for.'

Whitewater Jin smirked. 'Aye. Your battle's in the bedroom now.'

They all laughed, but they'd no idea how right they were. Leo thought Savine might've loosened one of his teeth last night.

'How are the men?' he asked.

Jurand was trying to scrub the grassy stain from his fencing jacket. 'I was going to disband two regiments, now we're on a peacetime footing—'

'Don't.'

Antaup narrowed his eyes. 'Expecting trouble?'

'It's possible.'

'From who?' asked Glaward, always spoiling for a fight. 'Not the bloody Northmen again? Or are you thinking about Dagoska—'

'A good deal closer to home.' They all looked at him, curious, excited. Leo knew there was nowhere safer than the gardens of the Lord Governor's residence, no one he trusted more than these four, but even so he felt the need to draw his friends in close. Every time he whispered the words, every time he told someone new, it became that little bit more real, that little bit more dangerous. 'From the Closed Council.'

Jurand's eyes went wide. 'You can't be serious.'

'It's chaos in Adua! Far worse than I dreamed it could be. Trouble with the Breakers. Trouble with the nobles. The Closed Council is out of control. King Orso is out of his depth. They're throwing away all our *principles*. Everything we *fought* for. Everything my *father* fought for!' He was making himself angrier and angrier, and his friends' faces were getting angrier with him. 'They're dragging the country into the fucking sewer! Did you hear what happened to Fedor dan Wetterlant? Did you hear what happened to *me*?'

Jurand exchanged a worried glance with Glaward. 'We heard . . . something about it.'

'Thrown out of the Lords' Round!' snapped Leo. 'For telling the truth!'

Jin ground one big fist into his palm. 'Wish I'd been there.'

'Next time you will be,' said Leo, putting a hand on his shoulder. 'We can't let the bastards get away with it. There comes a point when talking about a better world just isn't enough. When good men have to bloody stand up and *fight* for it!'

'Damn right,' growled Glaward. 'Damn *right*.'

'Fight the Closed Council, though . . .' Jurand had that disapproving look. The one he had when Leo suggested a reckless charge, but worse. 'Fight the *king*—'

'Fight *for* the king!' Jurand's doubt was making Leo doubt, and that only made him insist the harder. 'To free him from these bloody leeches, these bloody bureaucrats. To put the Union back the way it *should* be.'

Everyone looked convinced. Except Jurand. He looked less convinced than ever. 'But you're talking about...' He dropped his voice to an urgent whisper. 'You're talking about *civil war*, Leo. You're talking about, well...' The word *treason* went unsaid, but it hung over the lawn like a bad smell even so. 'There has to be another way! Was this the Lady Governor's idea? They say she's the most ambitious—'

'This is my idea!' Well, his, and Isher's, and Heugen's, and Barezin's. 'If Savine knew about it, she'd be bloody livid. She can't know, and neither can my mother. Not yet. But when the time's right to tell them, they'll see it has to be done.' Or, at any rate, the whole thing would be too far along to stop.

'So it's not just you looking for a fight?'

'They brought the fight to us!' snapped Leo, and Antaup gave a grunt of agreement. 'They left us to die in their war.' And Jin gave a growl of support. 'They made us *pay* for their war.' Glaward nodded along harder with each point. 'They're bleeding us white with their taxes.' As Leo convinced them, he convinced himself. 'They're hanging our friends. They're shitting on our most solemn principles!'

'Bastards!' snarled Antaup, shoving back that lock of hair so it fell straight into his face again.

'No one wants a war,' said Leo, even though his heart beat faster at the sound of the word. 'We all hope it won't happen, but... if there's no other choice... we have to be *ready*. Can I count on you?'

''*Course* you can!' said Glaward, throwing his heavy arm around Leo's shoulders.

'For anything,' said Antaup, gripping Glaward around the back.

'Always!' said Jin, hooking Antaup around the neck.

'Jurand?' Leo held out his arm, beckoning with the fingers. But Jurand still stood, rubbing worriedly at his jaw.

'Jurand?' coaxed Glaward.

'Jurand, Jurand, Jurand?' wheedled Antaup.

Leo caught his eye and gave him his most wounded look. 'You wouldn't turn your back on me, would you?'

'Never!' And Jurand's smile burst out like the sun from behind a cloud. A troubled smile, but a smile even so, and he threw one arm around Leo's shoulders and the other around Jin's and closed the circle. 'I'll be there, Leo. Whenever you need me. Always. But you have to—'

'That means a lot.' Leo felt tears in his eyes, and he dragged his friends close, into a sweaty huddle. 'That means more than you can know.' Jurand gave a shocked whoop as Leo shoved him over onto his back and plucked his sword out of the turf. 'Now defend yourself, you stringy bastard!'

Patriotic Contributions

Savine walked down the echoing hallway, shaking her head. 'This building. It feels more like a prison than a palace.'

'It is a shade . . . shady,' admitted Zuri, running a fastidious finger down the top rail of the panelling.

Ostenhorm was pretty enough, if rather lacking in modern conveniences, and the air was a great deal cleaner than she was used to, but the Lord Governor's residence itself was horribly oppressive. A labyrinth of gloomy stonework and faded tapestries, displays of tarnished weaponry and armour, antique furniture old and large enough to have been used by great Euz himself, its slitted windows overgrown by ivy that let only chinks of dusty light into the murk, all smelling of fust and slow decay.

'They hardly have an excess of sun up here,' said Savine. 'You might expect them to make the best use of what there is.'

'Almost enough to make one nostalgic for the South.' Zuri neatly blew the smudge of dust from her fingertip. 'Were it not for all the civil war.'

'The whole province of Angland is trapped in the past. A *very* great deal needs to change around here.'

Nowhere was that more obvious than in the so-called governing council. It might better have been called the grumbling council, since the old men around the monstrous table in the cavernous hall treated every point of business as a problem to be avoided in the most tedious way imaginable.

The old bores tolerated Savine and Lady Finree's presence provided they sat at a rickety side table and busied themselves with something feminine. Occasionally, when some particularly dated opinion or provincial attitude was expressed, their eyes would meet and Leo's mother would roll hers to the heavens. The young Lord Governor Brock appeared entirely uninterested in the mechanics of governing, almost nodding off at times to the droning of ancient voices. Until the subject of Angland's armies came up.

'. . . since savings must be made in order to satisfy the Closed Council,' gurgled out Clensher, sounding as if he had a sockful of gravel in his throat, 'I move that we reduce Angland's standing armies by two regiments, and—'

'No!' snapped Leo, sitting up so sharply his chair's legs jumped and banged down.

Savine could not tell whether it was Mustred's chair or his joints that gave the tortured creak as he sat forward. 'Your Grace, your father could not, and you cannot, afford to maintain them in—'

'Angland has to keep her military *strong*. If anything, we should raise more men!'

Lady Finree chose that moment to set aside her needlework. 'Leo, your lords have a point. As things stand, we need money more than soldiers, and—'

Leo bashed the table with his fist, making everyone flinch. 'I've made my decision! I didn't ask for your advice, Mother.'

There was an awkward silence. Leo turned angrily away, rubbing at his leg. Lady Finree coloured as she retreated to her chair. Savine felt for her, she really did, but she was yesterday's woman. Her son might act like a child on occasion but treating him like one was a blunder. If he had to have his toy soldiers, Savine would find a way to give them to him. While he was busy playing army, she could mould Angland into the thoroughly modern province she needed it to be.

'My lords, if I may?'

Mustred cleared his throat. 'Well, actually—'

'I think I have a way to satisfy the Closed Council *and* fund the strong army that we need.'

Clensher snorted. 'Are you a sorceress, Lady Savine? Will you conjure money out of thin air?'

'In a manner of speaking.' She stood, setting her hand down on the great stack of ledgers Haroon had brought in. 'I took the liberty of examining the accounts of the province over the past ten years.'

Mustred rubbed at the bridge of his nose. 'Lady Savine, we have been preparing those very accounts for many years before that—'

'But the nature of finance, commerce, industry and law has transformed in that time.' And these old fools had barely even noticed. 'I have done a great deal of business here. Here and in Midderland, Starikland, Styria and beyond. I see many opportunities for new revenue.'

At the word 'revenue', Mustred and Clensher's brows shot up as though hoisted by a single chain. They were like any other investors, in the end. The bottom line was all that really mattered.

'With your kind permission, I would meet with some interested parties – owners of land, mines and mills, operators of penal colonies – with a view to raising more taxes.' She gave Leo's shoulder the gentlest of reassuring touches. 'I am confident you will be pleasantly surprised.'

'A pleasant surprise would be a nice change.' Leo put his hand on hers and looked across at the old men. 'Where's the harm in trying?'

Savine gave the old windbags of Angland her sweetest smile. 'Where indeed, my lords?'

'Master Arinhorm, what a tonic to see an old friend!' The sounds of the workmen putting new windows into the façade echoed faintly from outside as Rabik showed him into the room. 'I apologise for all the commotion, I am making a few changes. Bringing things up to date.'

Arinhorm leaned to kiss Savine's hand. 'Lady Savine, it's—'

'Your Grace.'

He winced ever so slightly. 'Of course, Your Grace, I apologise. It's . . . a lot to get used to.'

'Consider it from where I sit! Whoever would have thought I might find myself Lady Governor of Angland?'

Arinhorm sourly worked his mouth. 'Not I.'

'I daresay when I turned down your scheme for increasing the efficiency of mines, we supposed we would have nothing more to do with one another. Now fate forces us to become partners regardless.'

Arinhorm frowned over at Zuri, who had the book open on the desk in front of her. 'Partners?'

'Partners, *Your Grace*,' corrected Zuri, without looking up.

'You and your investors in the coal, iron and copper mines of Angland are making great profits,' said Savine. 'I know because Selest dan Heugen never stops boasting about it.'

'We have had . . . some success.'

'I *delight* in it. But while you have been thriving, others have suffered. My husband has been obliged to fight a costly war against enemies who would do us all harm, and the demands of the Crown never cease. Angland has been most welcoming to you and your partners. Not to mention all manner of mill owners, landowners, builders and innovators. It is time to spread the burden.'

Arinhorm delicately cleared his throat. 'Your Grace, these are *our* mines. They were made successful through my hard work and my investors' risk.'

'I understand the principle, I have done a little investing myself. *Of course* you own the mines. Apart from the ones I own, which are failing for lack of your new pumps. You own the mines, you own the ore mined from them, no one would deny it.'

'We are not pirates!' threw out Zuri, with a grin that might have sat quite well on a pirate.

'But you do not own the rivers and roads that carry that ore to the sea, nor the docks on which that ore is loaded for transport to Midderland. Those belong to my husband.' Savine opened her eyes very wide, as though the realisation had but that moment dawned. 'Why – I suppose that means they belong to me?'

Zuri fluttered her lashes, all innocence. 'So *much* to take care of.'

Arinhorm was looking more and more uncomfortable. 'We pay towards their upkeep.'

'Token amounts, as we both know,' said Savine. 'We have gone over the books, Master Arinhorm. I get the feeling that the worthy old gentlemen who have been in charge of Angland's government do not fully understand the books. But we do. And we see all kinds of ways to make things more . . . equitable. Ways for the industries of the province to contribute to the common good.'

'And if I refuse?'

Savine shrugged. 'I suppose you can always fly your ore across the Circle Sea.'

Arinhorm was moving from discomfort to anger. Savine rather enjoyed seeing it. 'We will simply cut off supply! In no time, the foundries of Midderland will be clamouring at you to turn the tap back on.'

'By all means let your ore rot in your warehouses, but then of course the price of ore will rocket, and I imagine my failing mines will not be failing very much longer.' Savine spread her arms comfortably across the back of the chaise. 'So you see, whichever door you open, Savine's in first. In business, Master Arinhorm, you must be realistic.'

Zuri pressed one hand to her breast. 'You *have* to be realistic.'

'Here is our suggestion. You will pay duties for every ton of ore moved over every mile of my husband's province. You will also sign over to him a one-tenth interest in all your concerns.'

'But . . . you acknowledged they're our mines!'

'Of course.' Zuri nodded earnestly. 'And, by my calculations, nine-tenths of them still will be.'

'This is *robbery!*' he spluttered at her.

'I said we are not pirates. Robbery is a much broader category. But the heading in my book is for . . .' She ran her finger down the page and tapped neatly at an entry. 'Patriotic contributions.'

'There,' said Savine. 'Doesn't that sound better? Something we can all take pride in. You will also fit your pumps to my mines at your own expense. Then we can allow you to operate.'

'Allow...?' Arinhorm stared at her, open-mouthed.

'Allow, *Your Grace*,' corrected Zuri, with impeccable timing. Savine had heard it said that it is best to beat opponents fairly, but she much preferred beating them with the deck stacked wildly in her favour.

'It has been a great regret,' she said, 'that I let your scheme slip through my fingers simply because I find you personally detestable. I am so pleased we got the opportunity to do business together in the end.'

'I will go to your husband!' snarled Arinhorm.

'You will go to the Young Lion... to complain about his wife?' Savine gave Zuri a pitying look.

Zuri gave one back. 'I imagine a man would be lucky to come away from *that* interview with his teeth.'

'I have friends on the Open Council!' snapped Arinhorm.

'I have dozens of them,' said Savine with a sigh. 'That's how I know how little good they do.'

'I will go to the Closed—'

'Let me spare you the wasted effort. The Closed Council want revenue, and they have asked my husband to find it, so he has asked me to find it. I am doing so, with the enthusiastic endorsement of everyone who counts. Speak to your investors, by all means, but my honest advice is to pay up before you make me squeeze harder. You'd be amazed at how powerful my grip has become since I married the Lord Governor. I would hate to accidently crush someone completely but...'

'It could happen,' murmured Zuri.

Arinhorm wobbled to his feet, but he had nothing to say. Savine had made sure of that. All he could do was turn on his heel and stalk from the room.

'Oh, and Arinhorm?'

He looked back in the doorway, fists, teeth and no doubt arsehole clenched. 'Your Grace?' he managed to hiss.

'When you see her, do pass on my regards to Selest dan Heugen.'

The door clicked shut and Savine settled comfortably back again. She realised she had not thought about Valbeck all day.

'Is it wrong of me to have enjoyed that one?' asked Zuri, checking the watch then marking another tick down in her ledger.

'We must take our pleasures where we can. Who's next?'

A Little Public Hanging

'I hate bloody hangings,' grunted Orso.

'Distasteful but necessary.' His mother spoke in Styrian, of course, testing the limits of the human skeleton for regal bearing and surveying the swarming humanity in front of the gibbet like a swan forced to preside over crows. 'Like so much of life.'

Orso watched the hooded executioners test their machinery, oil the lever, tug at the noose. 'A little more than distasteful, don't you think?'

'Deliver a last-minute pardon, then. Be Orso the Clement.'

'Technically possible. Politically unthinkable.' Orso looked towards the banks of seating reserved for the nobles and found more than a few of the sparse attendees glaring angrily back. At least Lady Wetterlant had stayed away. No doubt entirely consumed with plotting her revenge. 'The nobles would hate me no less,' he observed. In the great pen where the commoners were crowded, by contrast, there was a carnival atmosphere: drinking, whooping, happy children up on their fathers' shoulders. They loved seeing anyone killed, of course, but the public execution of a member of the Open Council was a dream come true. 'The commoners would hate me far more. And I'd look a wavering weakling to boot.'

'If it cannot be helped then stop complaining. Be Orso the Stoic.'

He slumped ever more sourly into his gilded chair. 'I doomed us to this when I looked for a compromise. When I tried to do the right thing.'

The Queen Dowager issued a frustrated tutting of her tongue. 'Please, Orso, you are not the tragic lead in some overwrought play. You are a king. You have no business talking about the right thing.'

'Orso the Pragmatist is beginning to see that very clearly.'

There was a ripple of noise. Hooting, booing, insults. A wave went through the crowd as they pressed towards the barriers, grim-faced soldiers of the King's Own holding them back.

Wetterlant was led up the steps to the scaffold, hands tied behind him.

He had changed again. His hair had grown back to an ugly fuzz, face gaunt and eyes sunken in dark rings. No trace of arrogance. The reality of his situation must finally have impressed itself upon him. Orso had trusted Isher and ended up looking a fool. Wetterlant had trusted Isher and it would cost him his life. The crowd jeered louder as he was dragged into the shadow of the gibbet, his wide eyes rolling up towards it.

'I almost feel sorry for the poor bastard,' muttered Orso.

His mother displayed no more emotion at the spectacle than a marble bust might have. 'If you hate hangings so much, why even attend?'

'It's the king's justice. How would it look if the king couldn't be bothered to see it done?'

'Your father was just the same. Never so happy as when he was miserable.'

Orso slumped further yet. 'I never doubted I'd be a terrible king, but I never thought I'd be my father's son so— ah!'

She gripped his wrist with a sudden strength, immaculately manicured nails digging into him. 'You are *my* son, too! So smile. And contemplate your revenge.'

'Fedor dan Wetterlant!' bellowed the Inquisitor in charge. The noise dropped back to an ugly murmur, peppered with yells and jokes. 'You have been found guilty of rape and murder and sentenced to death by hanging. Have you anything to say?'

Wetterlant blinked stupidly at the nobles. At the commoners. At Orso and his mother. He took a shuffling step forward. 'I . . .' He swallowed. 'I—'

Something spattered against his shoulder. A thrown egg, maybe. As if that was a signal there was another surge through the crowd. Soldiers shoved people angrily away from the barrier. The noise was redoubled. More thrown rubbish bounced across the scaffold. Wetterlant tried to shout something but his voice was lost.

The Inquisitor gave a grimace of distaste, then nodded to one of the executioners and he thrust the hood over Wetterlant's head from behind. His shrieks were quickly cut off as the noose was dragged tight.

'Let him speak!' roared someone from the nobles' enclosure. 'Let him—'

Something hit one of the executioners in the face and he stumbled back, catching the lever with his elbow. The trapdoor fell open but Wetterlant wasn't quite in position. He gave a muffled cry as one of his legs dropped, but his other foot stayed on the scaffold and he ended up halfway through, twisting and jerking with his knee trapped under his chin and the rope almost but not quite taut.

The crowd gave half a great cheer to see him drop, then half a great boo to see he hadn't quite dropped, then laughter and taunts and more food flung while the Inquisitor bellowed at the executioners to no effect.

Orso's mother closed her eyes, delicately pressed her middle finger to her forehead and swore softly in Styrian. Orso could only stare. This was his reign so far. When he finally decided to hang a man he hadn't wanted to hang in the first place, he couldn't even manage it without the whole business descending into farce. He jumped to his feet in a sudden rage. 'For the Fates' sakes, just get it *done*!'

But Wetterlant was wedged in the trapdoor and the executioners had no solution. One of them wrestled pointlessly with the lever, the other had the prisoner under the arms, trying to drag him out, another was kicking at the one leg still wedged above the trapdoor, trying to shove it through. Meanwhile, he was making a high-pitched squealing, the rope not quite tight around his neck and the front of his hood wildly flapping with his desperate breath.

One of the nobles from the Open Council – Barezin, maybe – was on his feet and roaring his outrage but was entirely inaudible over the screeching commoners, who were pelting the scaffold with rotten food. There was a shriek, followed by another surge through the crowd but wilder, arms flailing. A fight breaking out and quickly spreading.

People were throwing things at the nobles' enclosure now. Not only fruit but coins. Stones. Orso heard a bottle shatter. He saw someone stumbling from their seat with blood on their face.

With a final vicious kick, one of the executioners managed to free Wetterlant's leg and he vanished beneath the platform, the rope snapping taut. There was a half-hearted whoop in some quarters, but it hardly registered above the mounting chaos in the square. One could almost have described it as a riot now, a seething mass of flailing bodies with soldiers straining at the periphery, people scrambling for safety in every direction.

He thought he heard someone shout, 'The Breakers!'

A missile thudded against the sun-stitched cloth of gold that hung behind Orso. He felt wet in his hair and jerked away, shocked. A bleeding head wound might have offered some romance, but he rather suspected it was rotten fruit.

Orso's mother pushed her chin even higher, as though daring them with a bigger target. 'Are they throwing things at *us*?'

He distinctly heard a shout of, 'Down with King Orso!' but had no idea where it came from. It could have been commoner or noble. He would hardly have blamed his mother if she had chosen that moment to come out against him.

He definitely heard a scream of, 'Fuck the Young Lamb!' Black-clothed Practicals were shoving through the press, laying about them with sticks and fists, dragging struggling figures from the chaos. Orso saw a group of men break through the line of soldiers and go sprawling at the foot of the scaffold, punching and wrestling. Gorst loomed up, shielding Orso and his mother with his armoured body.

'Your Majesties,' he squeaked. 'Time to depart.'

Orso wearily nodded. 'Damn it, but I *hate* hangings.'

Old Ways, Proper Ways

Rikke sat with her boots off on her father's bench as the War Chiefs came in, trimming her toenails. Isern sat on the floor to her left with her spear across her knees, Shivers stood on her right with his thumbs in his sword-belt. By the dead, she was glad they were there. No better pair in the Circle of the World to have on your flanks, and both good and ready for their part in what was coming.

First came Red Hat, then Oxel, then Hardbread. Rikke beckoned 'em forward, friendly as she could. Men used to smile at her a lot. But the old warriors had that nervous air folk tended to have around her since she lost one eye and had the runes pricked around the other. Like if they turned their back on her she might bite their arses.

'Sorry to keep you boys waiting,' she said, though few men had ever looked less like boys, there was scarcely one dark hair on the three.

'Well,' grunted Oxel as their Named Men crowded silent and suspicious into the hall behind, 'join the Union or join the North. It's a big choice to make.'

'And up till now it's been little choices for me.' Rikke tossed her scissors down and crossed her legs. 'What song to sing or how short to trim my toenails or which eye to have pricked out o' my head.'

Hardbread winced at that. 'You've made a choice now, though, have you?'

'I was hoping for a vision to show me the way!' And Rikke raised one arm high to point at the rafters. Then she slumped back on her bench. 'Trouble with visions, though, they're like those little goats the hillmen keep. Stubborn shits, they are. There's just no rushing 'em.'

Oxel frowned over at Red Hat and Red Hat frowned back, and behind them their warriors copied their chiefs, as warriors are prone to do. It was an awful lot of frowns for that one room to hold.

'But then I realised!' Rikke sprang up on her bare feet on the bench, making 'em all jump. 'This is the North! Who needs the Long Eye? We've got ways of settling questions up here.'

'Proper ways,' croaked Shivers, red stone glinting on his finger as he shifted his thumbs around the worn buckle of his sword-belt.

'Old ways,' sang Isern-i-Phail, and she spat chagga juice and wiped her lip.

'Time-tested traditions!' Rikke wagged a finger at the old men like they'd strayed from the pasture and she was there to play shepherd. 'My father always used to say, you want things right, you have to put 'em right yourself. No better way to settle a difference of opinion . . .' And she made a ring with her finger and thumb and peered at 'em through it with the one eye that still could. 'Than in the Circle!'

There was no instant enthusiasm from the three old War Chiefs. Hardbread was light on enthusiasm, instant or otherwise, and for the other two, a fight to the death is a notion that usually takes some working up to.

'The Circle?' Red Hat rested a hand on the pommel of his sword, and the Named Men filled the hall to the rafters with a nervy murmur.

'It's a bit like a square, but with no corners,' said Rikke. 'You can step inside and settle this man to man. Ideas can contend! Then rather'n a war and all our strength wasted, we can march into the future arm in arm. For whatever my say's worth, I'll throw it behind the winner. Hardbread? You happy to do the same?'

Hardbread looked the opposite of happy. 'I'd rather find some path that don't need any more blood spilled—'

'So'd we all. But up here in the North, most paths worth taking turn out at least a *little* bloody.'

No one disagreed with that. How could they? Hardbread wearily sagged. 'I reckon. If neither o' you twain back down.'

Neither of the two old warriors looked like backing down a hair. A grey hair, obviously. Red Hat puffed up his chest and shifted his fist from his sword's pommel to its grip with a warlike rattle. 'Guess we'd better pick a time and a place—'

Isern whipped back a big canvas sheet and sent straw scattering. Underneath was the Circle she'd marked out that morning, five strides across on the floor of the hall.

She showed the gap in her teeth as she grinned. 'No time like now, my beauties!'

'No place like here,' croaked Shivers.

'You're eager to get it settled, and you're right to be eager.' Rikke turned her left eye towards the old men, who looked less eager than ever, and opened it very wide. 'It's not just me needs to know Uffrith's future.'

Isern leaned down and flicked the pommel of Oxel's sword with her fingernail. 'You've both come armed, so do we need all that pother with the choosing of the weapons? Or can we get straight to the bloodshed?'

Oxel stretched up his chin and scratched at the white beard on his neck. Plain he wasn't much enjoying this sudden rush into death's cold embrace but could see no way to stop it, either. A War Chief's fame is all built on fighting, after all. Backing down from a fight could be the end of him. 'We can get straight to it,' he growled, and drew his sword.

Red Hat drew his at about the same moment. 'Aye. Let's settle it here and now.'

'Shields for the rest o' you, then!' cried Isern, clapping her hands. 'And into the Circle with our two grey champions!'

There was none of the usual trading of insults as Oxel's men and Red Hat's slid their shields onto their arms and made a wall around the Circle's edge. All shocked into quiet at how quick this had come about.

Oxel worked his head around with a click of neck bones. Red Hat undid the golden buckle on his cloak and tossed it over his shoulder to one of his men. Both of 'em bristled like they were still as brimming with vinegar at sixty as they'd been at twenty, and both of 'em quite clearly weren't. Maybe if they had been they wouldn't have got so easily prodded into fighting each other. But then getting warriors to fight has always been easy. It's stopping the bastards that's the tougher trick.

'Well, here is a business the moon can smile upon!' called Isern. 'We all know what the matter is and we all know what hangs on the result. Get to it!' She slipped from the Circle giving no one any time for second thoughts, and the shields were locked together behind her, metal rims scraping, painted faces pointing in.

With some reluctance, the two old War Chiefs began to circle, Red Hat with his sword point up, Oxel with his out to the side. They circled closer, Oxel with his teeth bared and Red Hat's tongue working at his lower lip. They circled, closer yet, then Red Hat stabbed and Oxel parried, chopped back and Red Hat ducked away. Shield-carriers gasped, and shields scraped as the circle flexed and shifted, then the noise mounted, men behind pressing in, and calling out, and shaking their fists, then grunting and shouting and bellowing encouragement till there was a roaring in the hall might've waked Rikke's father, where he lay in the deep dark earth just outside the wooden walls.

She pulled the old sheepskin tight around her shoulders. Still smelled like him, somehow. She wished for a moment he could be woken, and thought of him striding in to see what all the fuss was about. Thought of him smiling at her the way he used to, like she was the most precious thing he had. The most precious thing there was. Then she wondered if he would smile, when he saw her blinded eye and the runes on her face. Wondered if he'd have stared, fearful and queasy like everyone else. The thought made a tear gather in her blind eye that she had to dab away.

By then, she wasn't the only one leaking. Blood was trickling from Red Hat's sleeve and tip-tapping from his fingertips, and Oxel had a red mouth from an elbow and was carrying a bit of a limp. Almost made Rikke feel bad, setting two old men to kill each other, but she had to make of her heart a stone. Someone had to steer Uffrith now her father was gone.

Steel clanged and the two old War Chiefs groaned, tottered and wrestled, tired and clumsy. Bit of an unedifying spectacle, all in all. There's a reason fighting mostly gets left to the young. Oxel's chest heaved, his sword drooped. Red Hat's twisted face glimmered with sweat as he gathered himself for one more effort, but it was clear where it'd fall. He swung overhand and Oxel stumbled out of the way. He barely even thrust, really, it was more that Red Hat slipped, and as luck would have it, he fell right onto Oxel's sword. Luck can be quite the dodgy bitch, after all.

The blade slid right through him, and Red Hat's jacket stuck out to a glinting point behind his back, then the whole thing started turning red, not just his hood. His face went pink, veins bulging from his neck, and he tried to speak, but just spluttered blood onto the ground.

Oxel ripped his blade back and Red Hat tottered, sword hanging from his hand and the point scraping the floor. He coughed and retched, like he couldn't get a breath. He gave a hissing groan as he lifted his sword one more time, and Oxel took a cautious step back, but all Red Hat did was fish at the air with it, then turn all the way around and crash onto his side. Blood trickled out of his mouth and spread down the cracks between the stones around him, and his eyes goggled at nothing.

'Reckon Uffrith won't be joining the Union, anyway,' said Isern, leaning on her spear.

Oxel's men sent up a great cheer. Red Hat's drooped, sullen and silent. Rikke had always liked Red Hat. He'd laughed at her jokes when she was a girl. He'd talked with her father into the night, firelight on their lined faces. And out of joining the Union or joining the North, she reckoned his had been much the better idea. But someone had to steer Uffrith now, and it couldn't be him.

'I win!' roared Oxel, holding up his bloody sword. 'I *fucking* win! Send word to the Great Wolf that we're joining the North and—'

'Whoa, whoa, whoa!' called Rikke, holding her palms high and bringing every face towards her. 'Let's not dash off ahead of ourselves. I never agreed to that.'

'You said you'd fall behind the winner!'

'I said ideas should contend. I didn't say there were only two.'

Oxel's face twisted. 'What the *fuck* do you mean, girl?'

'Red Hat said join the Union. You said join the North. Spat it at me over my father's grave, as I recall.' She gave it a moment, feeling her own heart thumping hard in her chest, then shrugged as if she hadn't a care. 'I say we stay as we are. As my father wanted us. Independent.'

'Who fights for that?' sneered Oxel. 'You?'

'A woman, in the Circle? Wouldn't dream o' polluting the proud institution by sticking my tits in it. First step in getting anything done is knowing what you can't do, and I wouldn't last two breaths in there wi' you. Reckon I'll leave it to my champion.' And Shivers brushed one of Red Hat's shield-carriers out of his way and stepped past, grey sword drawn and hanging by his side. 'I mean, why even have a champion if he doesn't fight your duels?'

A mutter went through the watching men. Oxel's men, and Red Hat's, and Hardbread's, and the rest. Fear, and anger, and excitement, too. The Bloody-Nine was the worst man in the world to find yourself in the Circle with. But Caul Shivers came a close second.

'You tricky bitch!' snarled Oxel.

Rikke laughed. 'Aye, Tricky Rikke. But this is the North! Tricks are a tradition even older and more proper than duels.' She let her smile fade. 'My father fought all his life so we could be free. Fought his friends and his enemies. Fought Black Dow, and Black Calder, and Scale Ironhand, and Stour Nightfall, and never lost. Gave everything for it. Gave till he was a husk. Think I'm going to give up what he gave me just 'cause you *ask?*' She curled back her lips and screamed it, spraying spit. 'You didn't even fucking ask nicely!'

Oxel worked his mouth. 'We'll see, you little cunt.'

'I do the seeing.' Rikke nodded at Shivers. 'The dead are blind.'

To be fair, Oxel gave her a shock of his own by springing forward without even waiting for Red Hat's corpse to get dragged out, lashing at Shivers' blind side with everything he had. No doubt he thought his best bet was surprise and knew his chances would wither with every swing. No doubt he was right.

It was a good effort, but Shivers was fresher, and stronger, and quicker, and Rikke never yet saw him surprised. He caught Oxel's sword with his own, metal squealing as he steered it wide to hack a long scar in one of the shields at the edge of the Circle.

Oxel righted himself as Shivers stepped back into space, weighing his sword, the bright rune near the hilt glinting on the dull blade. 'Come on, you bastard!' he snarled. 'Come on, you half-blind maggot! I'll cut a new arse in you!'

Shivers wasted no breath on hard words. Just watched. Calm as a fisherman waiting for the tide.

Oxel came on, feinted low but swung high. Rikke gasped, sure he'd caught Shivers in the face, knowing the future of Uffrith, not to mention her own, was hanging by a thread. But Shivers whipped back from the waist at the last moment, let the blade whistle past his nose, let Oxel stumble after it.

Caul Shivers wasn't Stour Nightfall. If he'd ever had a mind to show off, he'd left it far in the past with his other eye.

His sword chopped deep into Oxel's side, under his ribs, specks of blood spattering the gawping faces of his shield-carriers.

Oxel staggered sideways, giving a bubbling wheeze, clutching at his side and the blood leaking dark between his fingers. He tried a despairing lunge, all off balance, but Shivers stepped around it, pinned Oxel's right arm under his left, lifted his sword high and clubbed Oxel on the crown of his head with the pommel.

Sounded like someone hitting a pot with a hammer. Oxel's sword clattered to the ground and he dropped to his knees, blood bubbling through his hair and running down his face in red streaks. He gave a funny slurp and looked up at Rikke.

'You—'

Shivers' sword pinged as it took Oxel's head off and sent it bouncing across the circle. One of Red Hat's shield-carriers jumped out of the way to let it roll past. Shivers turned to Oxel's men as their chief's body flopped sideways. He didn't roar in triumph or throw his arms up in victory or bellow insults. Just looked at 'em, like he was making an offer, and wasn't much bothered either way whether anyone took him up on it.

No one did a thing. No one said a thing. Just a long silence as the wash of blood from Oxel's corpse became a stream, then a trickle, a great slick of it joining with Red Hat's and slowly spreading.

Rikke put her hand on Shivers' shoulder and slipped past him, padding into the centre of the Circle.

'Any more ideas need testing?' she asked, turning all the way around so everyone got the chance to speak.

She'd no idea what she'd have done if someone spoke up. But no one did a thing. No one said a thing.

'Anyone else want to go their own way?'

Her mouth was dry and her pulse thumped in her skull. But there was silence like winter. Silence like death.

'No more opinions? No one?'

The Named Men shuffled meek out of her path, shields limp on their arms, as Rikke wandered back to her bench, bare feet leaving a trail of bloody footprints across the floor of her father's hall.

'What happens now?' muttered Hardbread, staring at the two corpses and clutching at his sparse white hair.

'I know exactly what'll happen,' said Rikke, even if a lot of it was a sea of doubts, and she sat back down and dragged that sheepskin around her shoulders. 'I've seen it.'

'What have you seen?' asked one of Red Hat's men. Angry at what had happened, maybe, but with a touch of curiosity in his voice, too. A needy little whine. In the end, no matter what they say, most folk want a path to follow. Someone to tell 'em it'll all be fine. Someone to tell 'em what to do.

'I know you lot love to worry, but you can stop now.' Rikke tipped her head on one side and smiled. She didn't have to put any threat in it. The runes on her face did that for her. Well, the runes and the two corpses and Shivers standing speckled with their blood. 'All you have to do is what I tell you. You can do that, can't you?'

Like Rikke's father used to say, you want things right, you have to put 'em right yourself. She took up her scissors, and brought her knee up to her chin, and set to trimming her toenails again. The big one on her left foot had this funny little spike of skin at the corner. Always took a while to shape it nicely.

Fire with Fire

'You're a magus, then?' asked Stour.

'The Magus Radierus, at your service!' No doubt he sounded the part, making quite the meal from every 'r' passed through his mouth, and he looked the part, too. Robe with all sorts of gold thread in it, and a big long beard forked and streaked with white, and a twisted staff with a sort of crystal on the end.

'So you can do magic?' Stour had his sword drawn. He loved to keep it drawn, which seemed folly to Clover. The big advantage of a sword over an axe, after all, is that you can sheathe the bastard thing and not make everyone nervous. But making everyone nervous was one o' the Great Wolf's favourite pastimes, sword's point resting on the flagstones beside Skarling's chair, toying with the pommel, turning it so the blade flashed and flickered. Sometimes when the sun hit the windows right, he'd catch it on his sword and shine it in people's eyes, just because.

'Not *only* magic.' The old man sounded pretty confident as he wafted his staff about. 'But the High Art of Juvens!' There was quite the sheen of sweat across his forehead, though.

'Show me,' said Stour. Clover didn't much like the way this was going.

The old man closed his eyes, muttering some words Clover couldn't understand, waved his free hand with much to-do, then flung something into the air in a puff of glittering dust. It was a little bird, which flapped about a bit and ended up sitting puzzled on one of the rafters.

'That's nice,' said Clover.

Beside him, Black Calder took another swig of ale and disgustedly shook his head. 'By all the fucking dead.'

'I thought it was nice.'

Stour, it seemed, did not agree. He narrowed his eyes the way he did when someone was about to get hurt, which wasn't rarely. 'I heard tell you could disappear.'

'Well ... er ...' The eyes of the magus darted nervously about. 'Only under certain conditions, my king. Auspicious moments in the moon's cycle, you understand, when the stars align, and—'

'Hit him,' said Stour.

Greenway's fist smacked into the old man's cheek and knocked him flat on his back, robes flapping and his staff clattering down, the crystal on the end jolting loose and skittering away into a corner.

'I just do tricks!' he squealed as Greenway dragged him up again, his magnificence somewhat spoiled by a bloody mouth. 'In a travelling show! It's not magic. Not really.' His 'r' sounds weren't too clever any more. None of his sounds were. 'I'm not a magus! I can disappear, but ... it's a box with a fake bottom—'

Stour's lip curled. 'Get this old halfhead out o' my sight.'

Greenway caught the would-be magus around the neck and hauled him towards the door, heels helplessly kicking. Turned out he could disappear after all. Clover felt the twitch of a smile, almost turned around to toss the joke at Wonderful. Then he remembered he'd killed her.

Black Calder gave a great scornful snort as Radierus was dragged out, making Stour frown over. 'Something tickling you, Father?'

'Aye, rounding up magicians.' Calder snorted again. 'Quite the bloody joke.'

'You could skip to the punchline right now. Head to the Great Northern Library and bring your friend the First of the Magi to see me.'

The scorn slipped from Calder's face and left him grim. 'Bayaz is no friend of mine. No friend of anyone's. His help'll cost far more than it's worth. Cost you everything. Better off shaking hands with the plague.'

'The Dogman's daughter has the Long Eye,' said Stour, and a few of his warriors muttered and grumbled unhappily. 'I have to fight fire with fire.'

'That'll win you naught but ashes,' said Calder. 'There's not much magic left in the world, and what there is ain't worth the price. You'd best hope all you find is tricks and liars.' And he sank further into his seat and took another swig of ale. Seemed with his brother back to the mud, he was set on keeping the breweries in business himself.

Greenway was marching the next magician in, and she looked a lot less promising than the last. A sturdy woman with a ragged dress and dirty bare feet who couldn't tear her big round eyes away from the cage in the corner. Gregun Hollowhead wasn't in it any more. His head was rotting on a spike over the gates of Carleon. But one of his Named Men had come to complain about it so the cage had a new guest, starved and battered, one scabbed leg dangling from the bottom and nearly scraping the sticky stones underneath.

'Who's this one?' asked Stour, rubbing at his chin. He'd grown himself a little bit of beard, just under his mouth, while he shaved the rest. Clover couldn't understand it. Grow it or don't, but why leave bits? It was like leaving your wife half-fucked. But then, Clover had given up on trying to work out why anyone did anything, especially Stour.

'She's from a village up near Yaws,' said Greenway.

'That so?' asked the Great Wolf, considering her with his bright, wet eyes.

'Her name's Seff.'

Calder sat up, looking sharply over. 'Huh,' grunted Stour. 'That was my mother's name.'

'Good sign, I guess,' said Greenway.

'It's just a fucking name, fool. I've heard tell you can see things, Seff from up near Yaws.'

She glanced around the hard faces in the room. No one could've looked more terrified, and Clover didn't blame her. 'Well ... sometimes I do ... I reckon ...'

Calder sank back with another great snort of contempt, made his son bare his teeth in frustration. 'What do you see?'

'One time, I saw the village burning,' said Seff from up near Yaws, 'and the next day men came, and ... well, they burned the village.'

'Saved everyone, then?'

She swallowed. 'Well, no, 'cause no one believed me.'

'Guess that's their fault, eh?'

'I reckon ...'

Stour sat forward. 'You heard there's a witch down in Uffrith?'

'The Dogman's daughter?' Seff from up near Yaws nervously licked her lips. 'I heard she's got the Long Eye. Got it real and true, like back in the Old Time. Heard she can see what a man's thinking. Heard she can stay dry in the rain 'cause she knows where all the drops'll fall. Heard she's got everything that'll happen written in a golden book and all she has to do is look it up so—'

'That's all *shit!*' barked Stour, straining forward with the veins bulging from his neck, making everyone in the hall jump. 'But she *can* see things. She saw where my sword would be. Only reason I lost that duel.' He got up, pulling that fine wolfskin cloak about him, the point of his sword scraping on the old stones as he stepped down from the dais. 'If she can see things... *I* need to see things, you understand? So tell me...' Stour stopped in front of Seff, the hall all quiet. 'What do you see?'

'Nothing,' she whispered, shifting from one bare foot to the other, staring down at them all the while like she was hoping if she couldn't see Stour he wasn't actually there. 'I mean... you can't force the Long Eye to open.'

'You can't?' hissed Stour, leaning close and making her shrink away. 'Or you won't?'

'I'd help if I could, but I don't know how.' Her face crushed up and her voice got higher and higher. 'It comes when it comes. I just want... to go back to my children.' She closed her eyes and squeezed tears down her cheeks, and Clover winced and turned his face away. 'Please don't kill me.'

Stour frowned then, and he put a finger under the woman's chin and tipped her face up, so she had no choice but to look into his eyes. 'Is that what you think o' me?'

She stared at him, gooseflesh on her arms and her shuddering breath echoing around the hall.

'Look, I'll confess I kill folk,' and Stour nudged at the bloody straw on the floor like he was trying to hide the stain. 'But only when there's something to gain by it. I kill folk who wrong me. Who stand against me, like that shit in the cage over there and his fool of a chief. I don't kill folk who do what they're told. I'm not the Bloody-Nine!' And he gave that great hungry grin of his, which was anything but a reassurance. 'Greenway?'

'My king?'

'Give this girl a coin and send her back to her children, eh?' Stour patted her face and wiped some of the tears away with his thumb. 'You tried, didn't you? That's all I can ask. You see anything, you let me know, eh?'

She closed her eyes, and wiped her runny nose, and nodded, and Greenway led her shuffling out, and all the way, Clover was wincing, half-expecting Stour to run up and stab her in the back out of pure meanness. Maybe he would've, too, if someone coming in hadn't caught his eye.

They called him Dancer on account of his slick way of moving, but there was naught graceful about him then, edging around the doorway, trying and failing to be one with the shadows. There was a certain look messengers got when they had news the Great Wolf wouldn't want to hear.

'Dancer!' called Stour. 'You're back, then.'

'Aye... just got here...'

'And? What did Oxel say?'

Dancer crept out to that bloody spot on the floor of Skarling's Hall, no more eager than Seff from Yaws had been. 'Oxel's dead.'

There was a silence. Clover heard his own breath as he sucked it in. The wind sighed cold through the high windows. The river whispered at the base of the cliff beyond. Then the Great Wolf showed his teeth, and caught a fistful of Dancer's shirt, and dragged him close.

'He's fucking *what*?'

'Caul Shivers killed him! Cut his head off in the Circle!'

'How'd that old idiot get himself in the Circle with Caul fucking Shivers?'

'Rikke tricked him into it!' squealed Dancer. Before Clover saw her with the runes on her face, he would've laughed at that. But he wasn't laughing now. No one was. Specially not Dancer. 'Well, she tricked him and Red Hat into it, then Oxel killed Red Hat, *then* Shivers killed—'

'Red Hat's dead as well?'

'She's took her father's hall. She's took her father's land. She's said Uffrith's going its own way—'

'She's fucking *what*?' snarled Stour.

And Black Calder burst out laughing. Started with a snort on his ale, then became a giggle, then a chuckle, and soon enough was a full head-back belly laugh. Wasn't a sound you heard too often in Skarling's Hall these days. Unless it was Stour laughing at something dead.

'What's funny?' he snapped at his father.

'Far as the Long Eye goes, I've got my doubts,' said Calder, sighing as he stood. 'But that girl's got a sharp mind and a hard heart.' He waved over his shoulder as he headed for the door. 'Let me know when you're bored of ruining things. I'll do my best to stitch 'em back together.'

Half-Treason

'I have been *so* looking forward to seeing you again!' said Isold.

Savine leaned close to touch the back of her hand. 'I have been ticking off the moments.'

'I feel, since we were married together... we have a special bond.'

'Like the sister I never had.' The bland, talentless, uninspiring sister she never had and did not particularly want.

Isold gave Savine a shy smile, all freckly blush and eyelash. 'Fedor was desperate to visit Ostenhorm. He thinks of you and Leo as our closest friends.'

Snakes have no friends. It made Savine wonder what Isher was really up to. Most of Angland's serious business was done here in the Lady's Chamber these days, between Savine and a few chosen people, on its carefully curated furniture in the light of its new, thoroughly modern windows. But just this once she would much rather have been on the other side of the connecting door, in the panelled gloom of the Lord's Chamber, puzzling out how exactly Isold's husband meant to take advantage of hers. She had never seen Leo so agitated as he had been waiting for Isher to arrive, limping up and down the lawn like a caged lion indeed. It had made Savine feel oddly excited herself, wondering if a splash of real politics was about to upset the placid little pond of Angland.

'I hope you don't think me too forward but... might I be right in thinking...' Isold glanced down significantly at Savine's stomach.

'I am.' There was simply no hiding it any more, and Savine was rather enjoying letting it show. She had expected to be thoroughly annoyed, watching her body stolen more each day by a selfish little parasite. But there was something oddly comforting about her bulging belly. She was even finding herself singing to it, from time to time. The other day, she had felt it move. Savine raised her brows as she gently stroked it. 'Who knew the key to happiness was looser clothes? How are things in

Midderland?' she asked, trying not to sound eager. 'Sometimes I feel as if I am stranded on the island of Shabulyan! I understand Wetterlant's hanging was a fiasco.'

'A *disaster.*' Isold leaned across to give a shrill whisper. 'Queen Terez was pelted with rubbish. Breakers in the crowd, is the rumour.'

'Are they sure it wasn't members of the Open Council?'

Isold gave a guilty titter. 'Arch Lector Glokta – that is, your father – has been granted more powers, and the King's Own have been split up and sent into Keln, and Valbeck, and out on the streets of Adua. There are curfews and searches and roundings-up. It's, well . . . it's a nervous atmosphere. I'm trying to persuade Fedor to spend more time at our estates in the country, but he insists on doing everything he can to help.'

To help himself, no doubt. 'Your husband is a true patriot.'

'As is yours, of course. I should retire.'

'Really?' Isold was tepid but Savine had hoped to pick up some more gossip. She had relished the challenge of taking charge in Ostenhorm, but now she was undisputed mistress here she was teetering on the edge of boredom. She missed being at the heart of things. She missed the rush of the gamble and the thrill of the win. She missed her friends, her acquaintances, even her enemies. Her enemies most of all, perhaps. 'It's barely even dusk.'

'I know, but I hope that I might be in . . . a delicate condition myself.' Isold was turning pink at the thought, poor thing. 'My husband wants me to have plenty of rest.'

'Of course.' Though no one had ever fallen pregnant as a result of rest, as far as Savine was aware.

'Perhaps we might celebrate the births of our first children together, as well as our marriage?'

'We can hope.' Though since Savine had been with child several months before her wedding it did not seem terribly likely. She kept the smile clamped to her face until Isold was gone, then she stood, pushed the heels of her hands into her aching back, and went straight to the connecting door. She had planned to sweep through and take her share of the conversation by force, but there was something secretive to Leo and Isher's hushed tones that made her hold back. She ever so gently eased the door open a crack instead.

'. . . The Dogman's gone back to the mud.' Leo spoke in an urgent murmur. 'His daughter Rikke's in charge in Uffrith.'

'Could you get her support?' asked Isher.

Savine frowned. Was Leo planning some move against the Northmen?

As he was always saying, he was the worst man in the world at doing nothing.

'I think so. We were close once.'

'And Uffrith still needs your protection. What about Stour?'

'He owes me his life. And he's a man who loves war.'

'We need him, Leo. Find a way to bring him onto our side. Whatever it costs.'

Savine's eyes widened. They were building an alliance, but *with* the Northmen.

'What about the Open Council?' asked Leo.

'Fifteen of us committed now,' came Isher's voice, 'but we must move with the utmost care. There are laws restricting the raising of private armies, and we cannot risk making Old Sticks suspicious.'

Savine felt the hairs prickling on the back of her neck.

She had known ever since Wetterlant's trial that Isher was planning something. She had thought it strange Leo was so reluctant to disband Angland's regiments. She had guessed they were about some secret business. But she had never dreamed it might be something so audacious. So enormous. So incredibly dangerous. This was not a splash of politics, it was a great wave that might sweep everything away!

'We need to move *now*,' growled Leo. 'Every day we could be discovered.'

'Patience, my friend. Your enthusiasm is infectious, but we must not be rash. We have to gather every possible ally, wait for the clearest summer weather, then move on Adua without a backward glance.'

Savine's eyes widened. By the Fates, they were talking of revolt. Open rebellion against the Crown. Leo would be turning on Orso. He would be turning on her father. He would be gambling everything on one mad throw of the dice. Did he have any idea what he was contemplating? It was nothing less than treason!

An investor must know an opportunity when she sees it, must judge the risks and rewards in an instant. Fast now, with her breath coming sharp in her tight throat, the choices flashed through Savine's mind.

Do nothing? Retire to bed like Isold and pretend she never heard? Sit back like the good wife and let Leo manage their affairs?

No.

Reason with him, then? Enlist Lady Finree's help and persuade him to abandon this madness? Even if she succeeded, he would resent her. And she would have no control over his embittered accomplices. Their plot might still be dragged into the light. Why, Lady Brock, did you not inform the authorities of a conspiracy against the Crown?

No.

Betray her husband, then? Tell her father everything? Throw Isher and his cronies to the dogs and herself on the king's mercy? At best, her reputation would be in tatters, her title stripped away. At worst? Widowed. Banished. Ruined. Savine set her jaw.

No.

Because of her parents' folly, she had lost Orso. She had lost the crown. Now she had clawed out a new place. Dragged herself back to the top. Because of her husband's folly, was she to lose that, too?

No.

Which left one choice only.

She slipped the box from her sleeve with trembling fingers, dug out a huge pinch of pearl dust and turned from the door to snort it up. An investor must know an opportunity when she sees it, must judge the risks and rewards in an instant, and if one outweighs the other pounce upon it, commit without delay, without regret, without sentiment.

Revolt. Her mouth was dry. Rebellion. Her pulse thudded in her skull. Treason. She winced as her baby shifted. Could she really do this? Could she afford not to? Was it terrible fear she felt? Or was it an almost unbearable thrill?

'Calm,' she whispered. 'Calm, calm, calm.'

It was a risk. An awful risk. Yet she could not help but think of all there might be to gain. No less than everything, if she played her hand well . . . The Closed Council had made many enemies, within the Union's borders and without. Had her father not often listed them, discussed with her their fears and desires, their strengths and weaknesses? If they all could be brought together, pushed in the same direction at the same moment . . . It would take a delicate touch. Something Leo by no means had.

But that was why he had her.

She set her shoulders, swung the door wide and stepped through.

Savine had not changed this room. Probably no one had changed it in two centuries. Some dark oils of dead Lord Governors, some gruesome-looking Northern swords and shields looted from some old battlefield, some inexpertly stuffed hunting trophies, peering disapprovingly down with their bland glass eyes. An upset deer, an astonished stag, a baffled bear, a leering wolf. Leo had told her it was the way his father had liked it, and so it was the way he liked it, and she respected his decision. Or at least pretended to.

'My lords.' She calmly shut the door and walked smiling over, keeping a mask of dignified composure clamped over her feverish anxiety, to perch on an ancient chair that had by no means been designed for the clothes of a modern lady. Especially a pregnant one.

Leo sounded slightly choked. 'We were just talking of—'

'You were talking of gathering allies in open rebellion against King Orso,' said Savine, shocked at how levelly her own voice pronounced the outrageous phrase. 'You were talking of toppling the government of the Union and raising another.' She took the stopper from the decanter, poured herself a drink and worked her way into the most comfortable position she could find. 'You were talking of changing the world, and I have come to join the conversation.'

Isher had a superior little smile. A look men often had when she opened negotiations with them. A look she always enjoyed wiping from the faces of people who supposed themselves powerful. 'Lady Savine, I hardly think—'

'The two of you plan to risk everything you have. Therefore, you plan to risk everything *I* have. My future. The future of my child. It is clear you have already taken several steps along this path. Too far to turn back without considerable danger. Perhaps too far to turn back at all. So. It seems you have left me no choice but to commit myself to this project and do everything possible to make sure it succeeds.' She raised her chin. 'But if you think I would ever do so without voicing my opinion, you are profoundly mistaken.'

Isher narrowed his eyes. 'You would have to turn against your father—'

'That is between me and him.' Her father, if she even considered him her father, could hardly complain. He had been lecturing her about the value of ruthlessness since she was knee-high. 'Now tell me your plans.'

Leo sat forward with the eagerness of a boy keen to show off a new game. 'We have the Open Council. We have the army of Angland, the best soldiers in the Union. We'll bring Rikke and Stour and all their Northmen onto our side. We'll land on the north coast of Midderland, gather our friends as we march on Adua and take the Closed Council by surprise, forcing Orso to concede to our demands without a drop of blood spilled!'

Savine took a sip of her drink, worked it around her mouth and swallowed. 'That sounds ... optimistic.' She had managed to take her father by surprise perhaps four or five times in her life. The idea of Leo achieving it bordered on absurd. 'You rather assume that experienced politicians and soldiers will play into your hands.'

'We have a secret weapon!' Leo thumped the table. 'Lord Isher has a friend on the Closed Council.'

Isher sourly worked his mouth. Plainly he trusted her no further than she trusted him, but that hardly mattered. There were few of her many business partners she would have trusted to hold her hat, and they still made money for each other. 'A good friend,' he said, reluctantly. 'We know everything they do.'

'Orso is no soldier,' said Leo, scornfully.

'He's no politician, either. Only see what happened at Wetterlant's trial.' Isher gave a disgusted sneer. 'The man's a fool.'

'A coward.'

'He is neither,' snapped Savine. 'Indecisive, perhaps, but he is clever, and he has iron in him. The tougher things get, the tougher he will become.'

'Thought you were done taking his side?' grumbled Leo.

'Never fear your enemy,' said Savine, 'but always respect him. Stolicus, I believe? If we mean to risk everything, we cannot simply assume our enemies will fail. We must stack the deck so heavily in our favour that we can only win.' She considered the collection of battered weaponry on the walls, already working the problem through from every angle. 'The Union is flooded with idle veterans. Men who have returned from war to find a changed world in which they have no place. I suggest the Open Council asks leave to raise troops to protect their interests from the Breakers. To quash riots and root out dissent. A pretext for arming yourselves which will make the Closed Council trust you more rather than less.'

Leo raised his brows at Isher, who was moving from scornful to thoughtful. 'Neat,' he conceded.

'I will arrange for a concerted campaign of pamphlets and newsbills that can keep the embers of resentment hot. Blame the Closed Council for the state of the nation. Blame the debt to Valint and Balk. Remind the people of the hanged outside Valbeck. Remind the nobles of the injustice against Wetterlant. Queen Terez is always a popular target. King Orso, too.' It gave her a twinge of regret. But she told herself they would be fighting for their lives. No weapon could be beneath them.

Leo grinned. 'I hear that etchings speak directly to the heart.'

'The filthier the better,' said Savine. 'King Jezal was a bastard, we can dig up doubts about the line of succession.' Who would know better than she did how destructive such doubts could become, after all? 'I will write to Master Sworbreck and keep his presses hot. But even so, Lord Isher, you are right that we will need every ally. From what I heard, there are two potential ones you have left out. The Styrians. And the Breakers themselves.'

'The Breakers?' Leo looked almost as astonished as the stuffed stag's head over his shoulder. 'They're traitors!'

Savine did not make the obvious point that they were not the only ones. She rested her hand lightly on his. Not steering. Supporting. 'Leo, you are a hero to the people. We could easily persuade them to see you as a champion of the common man. You could commit to limits on the working day, protections against exploitation, representation on governing bodies. We could curb some of the most hated practices here in Angland as a demonstration.'

'I don't know anything about labour laws!'

'But I do.' She had helped develop half those hated practices, after all. 'And we need only *convince* them that you do. Lord Isher, I hear the king's forces have been spread out among the principal cities of Midderland to deter any uprisings?'

'That's true.'

'Action by the Breakers, carefully coordinated, might pin the King's Own down and prevent them from reacting to . . . other threats.'

Isher nodded, drifting from thoughtful to impressed. 'It might.'

'I have some contacts with the Breakers.' She had a notable ex-member in her employment, in fact. 'It might be that I could persuade them to support us. At least for now. I have long-standing business connections in Styria, too.'

Isher looked less sure about that. 'You really think you can bargain with the Snake of Talins?'

'No. But I understand King Jappo is keen to step from his mother's shadow . . . I might be able to arrange a meeting with him directly.'

Leo was more dismayed by every word. 'Jappo's a notorious bloody degenerate!'

'Let us overlook his taste in lovers and focus on his soldiers and his money. His help could tip the balance well into our favour. It could save lives. It could save *our* lives.'

'The idea makes me feel dirty.' Leo squirmed in his seat. 'What would it cost us?'

Savine would have liked to slap him but she settled for calm argument. 'The root of the dispute between Styria and the Union is King Orso's claim on the dukedom of Talins. We could promise to give it up. We could stop supporting Sipani's independence.' She paused a moment, considering whether to take the next step. But once you decide to rebel against the Crown, there really are no lines left to cross. 'We could offer them Westport.'

Curnsbick would have been pleased. He was forever urging her to be more charitable, and here she was giving whole cities away. 'Surrender Westport?' Leo gasped in outrage. But Savine noted that Lord Isher stayed silent.

'A paltry price to pay in return for Midderland, Angland and Starikland,' she said. 'Have you ever even been there?'

'Well, no, but—'

'A dusty slum clogged with superstitious fools. I for one will not miss it.'

'We fought three wars against the Styrians. Nasty ones. I mean...' Leo looked to Isher for support, but Isher was too busy looking at Savine, his patronising smile long gone. 'It's not very *patriotic*.'

'If looking unpatriotic worries you, then consider how being hanged for treason looks.' Savine put some iron into her voice. 'This is not a *game*. We must be *utterly* committed. Fail and we are *doomed*.'

There was a long, uncomfortable silence. A log shifted in the sooty old fireplace and sent a shower of sparks up the chimney. 'Her Grace is right,' said Isher. 'We are risking everything. We must play every card.'

'But we have to be above reproach!' Leo glanced up at the paintings of previous Lord Governors as if at a disapproving jury. 'Pure and principled. If we're willing to do anything, then how are we any better than them?' He had the wounded whine of a boy who finds the grown-ups have stolen his game and are playing it in a way he by no means approves of. 'We have to do the *right* thing!'

She wanted to tell him that they could afford no right thing, only the necessary thing. That there could be no right side, only their side. But why break down a door when you could just slip through a window? 'Leo— ah!' And she hunched over, clutching her belly.

Leo sprang to his feet. 'By the dead, are you—'

'It's nothing.' She grabbed his hand, bared her teeth. 'Ah! But could you fetch Zuri, get her to bring that tonic—'

'Of course!' And he rushed from the room as fast as his limp would allow.

Isher had half-risen, too. 'Lady Savine, can I—'

'Who do you imagine will be king when this is over?' Savine arranged herself again in her chair and coolly met his eye.

He gave a disbelieving little laugh and slowly sat himself. 'King Orso, of course. We plan to remove a corrupt Closed Council. To depose the king would be treason.'

'So you plan to stop at half-treason? Come, come. Meat half-cooked agrees with no one. Humiliate the king but leave him on the throne and you will be storing up your own destruction. Not to mention mine.' She had learned a hard lesson in Valbeck. She would never allow herself to be weak, or vulnerable, or terrified again. It gave her a surprisingly sharp pang, but her merciless logic could only lead her to one place. Perhaps she had loved Orso once, but he hated her now. Her father had lied to her all her life. And loyalty? A trick those with power played on those without to make them act against their own interests.

She met Isher's eye. 'King Orso has to go.'

He ran his tongue about the inside of his mouth, moving now from admiration to suspicion. 'I see that we are speaking plainly—'

'When speaking of treason, anything else would be ridiculous. What do you really have without us? Lord Barezin, I understand, laughs himself to the point of incontinence staging pornographic plays about Queen Terez in his private theatre. Lord Heugen, I hear, insists on steeping in a copper bath every morning to replenish his magnetic energies. Should we discuss the shortcomings of Lady Wetterlant?'

'You are well informed.'

'Knowledge is the root of power, Juvens said.'

'And what have you found out about me?'

Savine's turn to pause. 'On you, I must confess, my book has a blank page.'

'I am a careful man, Your Grace. And that unfortunate business with Wetterlant has given me great authority in the Open Council. A unity they have never had before. I will keep the lords in line, I promise you that.'

'Even so. In the army of Angland, we supply the best and most experienced soldiers you could hope for. In Stour Nightfall, we bring a decisive ally. Would you agree?'

'You leave me little choice but to agree.'

She laughed as though he had made an excellent joke. 'My aim in every conversation. My husband has fewer enemies and far more popular support than any other candidate. And he has some vestige of a legitimate claim through his grandfather. A better claim than the current occupant of the throne, some might say. He *will* be king, Lord Isher.' And she would be queen, and the ashes of that most treasured ambition blazed up suddenly again. 'If you want us to gamble everything, that is my price.'

'And when the mighty Brocks take the crown, what will remain for the rest of us?'

'Everything else. I think you would make an excellent Arch Lector and First Lord of the Open Council, Your Eminence.' Isher was good at hiding his feelings, but she caught his flicker of satisfaction at the title. 'Which would leave your magnetic and pornographic colleagues to decide who will be lord chamberlain and lord chancellor. I imagine Leo would like to choose his own lord marshals, but you could fill the other seats with friends.'

'And does all this come from your husband or from you?'

'What comes from me comes from him.'

'And yet you send him upstairs while we discuss it.'

'So that when the crown falls in his lap, he can honestly say he never sought it, but accepts it reluctantly for the benefit of all. You know he has no taste for deceit.'

'Not a problem his wife shares,' observed Isher.

'Nor his very particular friend. I daresay you would agree with me that the strongest horses often need blinkers. They are best led one step at a time.'

Lord Isher narrowed his eyes at his glass, swirled the spirit around in it, then looked up at her. She had taken him on quite a journey that evening. From scornful, to thoughtful, to impressed, through admiration, suspicion and, finally, to acceptance. An acquaintance, romance and estrangement all in one sitting. 'Your terms are acceptable.'

'Good.' Savine felt satisfied with the outcome. For now, at least. 'I look forward to working with you.'

The door burst open and Leo hurried over. Zuri was behind him, but after a glance at the way Savine and Isher were sitting, she hung back.

'Are you all right?' Leo lurched down on one knee beside her.

'No need to worry.' She took his hand, and pressed it to her belly, and smiled. 'Lord Isher has made me feel *so* much better.'

A Private Language

'I had a quick word,' said Broad.

It seemed, without ever agreeing it, that him and Savine had worked out a kind of private language, where the words didn't mean what they normally meant. What Broad meant by 'having a quick word' was that he'd knocked half the teeth out of the mouthiest worker they could find, as an example to the others. 'Everyone's back to work, night shifts, too. Don't reckon you'll have any more problems at the armoury.'

'Master Broad,' said Savine, 'you are an absolute *magus* when it comes to labour relations.'

Broad absently rubbed his sore hands together. Labour relations. That's what they were calling it. He wondered who it helped, giving ugly things pretty names. Didn't really make it any prettier. The opposite, if anything.

'Might we talk for a moment?' she asked, like they were two old friends who never got the chance to catch up. She had that glow about her, now, that women can get when they're expecting. Broad remembered that glow on Liddy, when she was pregnant with May. Long time ago, when he had all his hopes intact.

'Of course, Lady Savine. I mean, Your Grace. Sorry.'

'Don't be ridiculous, Gunnar, you never have to apologise to me. I know how much I owe you. No less than my life. Had I not happened upon you in Valbeck...' Her smile slipped for just a moment, then she took a breath and whipped out a new one, wider than ever. 'And you have been an absolute treasure since. I hardly know how I used to manage without you. You, and Liddy, and May. Your daughter is a wonder with the books. Such a credit to you.'

'Thank you, Your Grace.'

'I hope you are happy working for me. You and them.'

'We are, Your Grace.' They were, anyway, and that was what counted. 'Couldn't be happier.'

'It feels almost as if – and I hope you will not think me presumptuous – but it feels as if I am a part of your family, and you a part of mine. I would hate for us to be... split up.' She had that glow, no doubt. A healthy softness to her face, and a lively colour to her cheeks, and her hands cupping the slight swell of her belly. But that flinty gleam in her eye was the same as ever. Broad gave threats for a living. He knew how to spot one. He cleared his throat and looked down at his boots. Fine new pair of boots he had, all shiny.

'There is... one small favour I need you to do for me,' she said. 'Something very important. It needs someone strong. Someone brave. But also someone subtle. There is no one else I trust to do it.'

Broad swallowed. 'Anything I can do, you know that.'

'You were with the Breakers in Valbeck. You were one of them.'

'I... was,' he said, frowning. He didn't know where she was taking him but didn't much like the direction of travel. 'Thought I was doing right. I guess.' Hard to remember what he'd thought. Seemed like a different man who'd thought it.

'Of course you did. Is there any possibility, do you think...' And she looked up at him from under her eyelashes. 'That you could get in touch with them again?'

'The Breakers?'

'Yes. The Burners, too, even?'

She said it as though it wasn't much to ask for. Not much effort, and certainly no risk. There was that language again, where they both said one thing but meant another. They both knew it'd be a lot of effort. They both knew it'd be a hell of a risk.

'Maybe.' Broad pushed his lenses gently up his nose. Most of the Breakers he'd known in Valbeck had been left hanging from gibbets after the uprising, and the rest would be nursing deep grudges. Most of the Burners had been halfway mad to begin with. What he'd been doing for a living would not be at all popular in those quarters. Calling it labour relations wouldn't fool anyone who'd lived in a cellar. 'Maybe there's still some folk in Valbeck who could put me on the right track...'

'All I ask is that you try.'

'My best, like always.' Meaning his worst, like always. It was his turn to look her in the eye. 'Just promise me you'll look after Liddy and May, while I'm gone.' And he offered her his hand.

Her grip was surprisingly strong. Brought a twinge to his aching knuckles. 'As if they were *my* family.'

'You're not even staying for dinner?' asked Liddy. She looked worried. They both did.

'Got to leave tonight,' said Broad, tossing a few things in a bag. 'It's urgent.'

'Where are you going?'

'Midderland.' He was getting a lot better at lying than he used to be. You have to come at it sideways. Just enough truth to answer the question. Not enough to actually tell 'em anything. If he'd said Valbeck, they'd probably have set to crying. Maybe he would've himself.

May watched him from the doorway, one hand fiddling with the silver necklace she wore these days. 'It's nothing dangerous, is it?'

'Working for a fine lady, like you always say. How dangerous could it be?' And he smiled at May, and she smiled back. Either he was getting a lot better at lying, or they just wanted to believe him. He hid it with a joke. 'And don't spend too much time with Zuri's brother Rabik, I've seen how the two o' you grin at each other.'

'Shut up, Da!' Giving him a shove and blushing at the same time.

He held them both close near the doorway. When he'd gone away to Styria, he'd barely even said goodbye. So keen to leave. Now he clung on tight. Too tight, maybe.

Liddy looked up at him as they broke apart. 'You won't be long, will you, Gunnar?'

'No, I won't be long.' And he threw the bag over his shoulder. He'd always thought of himself as honest to a fault. Blunt as a hammer, ask anyone. But it occurred to him then he'd started speaking that private language with everyone. Saying one thing and meaning another. Only Liddy and May weren't in on it. 'Be back before you know it,' he said, and shut the door.

But he wondered if he would be. He wondered if he'd ever be back.

Old Friends

'You know you're more beautiful than ever.'

Savine looked sideways at him, one long-lashed eye showing under the brim of her hat, rocking gently with the movement of her horse. 'Are you flattering me, Your Grace?'

'I'm doing my bloody best,' said Leo. She rode well. What *didn't* she do well? Perched elegantly side-saddle with her whip-hand resting on the slight swell of her belly, steering her horse with the same effortless confidence she steered everything else. But he still worried. 'Sure you don't want to go in the carriage, though?'

'In the jungles of Yashtavit, women hunt while eight months pregnant. Up in the North, they work in the fields until they give birth. Honestly, it's much the same these days for the factory girls in Adua. A little ride will do no harm.'

'I reckon if a factory girl, a Northern peasant or a dusky huntress was offered a break in a carriage, they'd likely take it.'

'By all means, you can sit in it, then.' And she tapped her horse's flank with her crop and moved ahead.

Perhaps there'd been a part of him that had hoped the rebellion would never happen. That it would come to nothing more than after-dinner bluster with the fellows from the Open Council. A part that had looked forward to Savine finding out, so she could give an indulgent sigh, and pat the back of his hand, and put a sensible stop to the whole business.

But to his amazement, she'd pounced on the scheme with the total lack of doubt she brought to everything and applied all her formidable powers to making it not only a reality, but a success.

He felt hugely excited, of course. They were on a grand adventure, of course. And doing the right thing, of course. It was just that he also, sometimes, in quiet moments, felt strangely horrified. But there was no way back now. He'd look an utter fool. And once Savine got her teeth into a thing, it was happening, and that was all there was to it.

He caught her up, leaving their guards and servants behind. 'By the dead, I'm glad you came.'

'I've always wanted to see the North.'

'So you've come for the sights? Not to make sure I don't do something reckless?'

'I can do two things at once.' That one eye slipped across to him, and she nudged her mount closer to speak softly. 'This is important. We need allies.'

'I know how Northmen think,' said Leo. 'I grew up with them.'

'Of course. These are your friends. I am only here to help. Haven't I been a help to you in Ostenhorm?'

'You've been a bloody marvel in Ostenhorm.' In fact, she'd proved so good at running the governing meetings that he'd stopped attending altogether. He was still lord and master and had the last word, as she was always telling him. But why use it when her words sounded so damn good? 'I do worry about my mother, though—'

'There's no need.'

'She'll see Jurand drilling the men, raising more, she's no fool—'

'Clever people are prone to believe what they want to, Leo, just like everyone else. What your mother wants most in the world is to think the best of you.'

Leo blinked. 'Oh.'

'I told her you are growing up and taking your responsibilities seriously, and the new companies are all part of your plan for lasting peace. You are raising more soldiers because Northmen only respect force. Our talks with Stour will go that much better if he knows we are well armed. She was full of praise for your strategy.'

'Oh,' said Leo again. That was a first.

'And then I begged for her help and loaded her down with enough work on the new tax system to keep five clever people busy. What your mother wants *second* most in the world is to feel useful.'

Leo felt that witless smile on his face. The one he usually ended up with when he came to Savine with a problem, then found she'd solved it weeks ago. With her on his side, how could he fail? 'What the hell would I do without you?' he murmured.

'Luckily for you . . .' And she touched him firmly on the thigh with her riding crop and caused a pleasurable stirring in his trousers. 'It is not a problem you will ever have to face.'

And they rode from the trees into the open.

He gave a delighted laugh to see the gates of Uffrith, dappled sunlight shifting on its lichen-spattered walls. He remembered how it had felt the first time he came here, as a boy – the excitement, the romance, the freedom – to be in the North, the land of heroes!

He spurred on, through a cluster of new huts and houses, leaving Antaup and Jin and the rest behind with the carriage and the wagons. Savine kept pace with him, through the gates and clattering down the cobbled way beyond, the dirty-faced people in their colourless clothes gazing up in wonder as they passed. A lot had changed. New buildings where Stour Nightfall burned the old ones, maybe. Grander buildings, stone and slate rather than wood and wattle.

'Good old Uffrith!' He took a long breath of that familiar air. Sheep, dung, woodsmoke and sea salt, but sweet with happy memories for him. 'I spent the best years of my childhood here. I know every alley of the place!'

'That wouldn't be too difficult.' Savine gave a scornful little laugh. 'I thought you said this was one of the North's greatest cities?'

'It is.'

He had to admit, seeing it fresh through her eyes, used to the scale of Adua and the pomp of the Agriont, it looked a mean, poor, primitive place. For some reason, that nettled him. 'Things might not be so grand here as in Midderland, but they're honest,' he snapped. 'They're good people. They have a code and they stick to it. They're great fighters. Brought up with swords in their hands. Rikke will be a staunch ally. She's one of the warmest, truest, most straightforward people I know!'

Savine looked calmly away from him. 'Perhaps you should have married her.'

They rode on in silence.

Leo knew the pattern of the crooked rafters in the Dogman's hall by heart. Remembered climbing among the carved animals, trees and faces, squatting in the shadows, watching the Dogman argue with his Named Men below. The bench with the worn black sheepskin was still there, where the old chieftain used to listen to his people's complaints, pointed chin propped on one fist. The firepit still glowed, ripples of red and orange rustling through the embers, the heat pressing on Leo's face as he came close.

But there'd been changes. The hall had always bustled with life in the Dogman's day. Now there was a brittle silence which made Leo feel guilty over his every footstep. At this time, in this season, the shutters should've been wide open and the sea breeze washing in. Now hides were hung in the windows, painted with circles of runes, sinking the hall into gloom. There was a new smell, sweet and strange and sharp, like burned cakes. There were skulls on the wall in a shadowy herd. Horned and antlered skulls of ram and bull and stag and great animals he didn't know. Animals of the utmost North, maybe, where the sun doesn't shine and the world blurs into myth.

'Leo! Savine! I've missed you.' And Rikke swaggered from the shadows, arms spread wide, dangling with bracelets and thongs and charms, into the shaft of light from the smoke-hole.

Leo almost shrank back in shock. There was a great dark stain across her face. A tattoo, black runes, black lines, black arrows in a crescent from her cheek, covering one side of her forehead, to the bridge of her nose. Her right eye was turned white with just a milky pinprick in the centre, while the hungry pupil of the left had swallowed the whole iris, yawning like a grave-pit.

'Ah.' She waved a hand in front of her face. It used to be round, soft. Now it was all sharp ridges and shadowy hollows. 'All this? I forget.' She tapped at her skull with one long finger, the hair on the left all clipped back short while on the right it was grown to wild tufts and tangles. 'Can't see it from in here, but I've heard it said the tattoos and the eyes and all can be... off-putting.'

'Not at all,' croaked Leo. 'Just... unexpected.'

The gold ring through her nose shifted as she smiled. He didn't know the words for that smile, but warm, true and straightforward weren't the ones. 'You remember I used to have fits? Leo remembers, I reckon.' And she winked at him. She'd had one the first time they'd lain together, after all, both stark naked in a hay pile. 'This is the cure.'

'The cure?'

Rikke stuck her fingertip in her milky right eye. 'This eye fought the other, so it had to go. My visions come much cleaner now.' She leaned close and muttered it out of the corner of her mouth, 'Don't shit myself no more neither. And I'm still me!' She punched him on the arm. Good-natured, but hard. 'More or less.'

'Could I look closer?' asked Savine, stepping towards her, not put off in the least. 'I have seen a very great number of painted faces, but never such fine work.' And she put a finger under Rikke's chin and tipped her face gently into the light. 'I think it's beautiful.' And she traced the lines of the tattoo with her fingertips. 'It could not be more... *you.*'

Rikke gave a delighted laugh. Reminded Leo, just for a moment, of how she used to be. 'Oh, I like your wife, Leo. Best thing about you, I reckon! You kept the runes, I see.'

'They feel like good luck.' Savine touched the little wooden tablets she wore around her neck. 'And you kept the emeralds.'

'They feel like high value,' said Rikke, pulling them up with her crooked little finger so they cut white into her long, lean throat.

'I have another gift for you,' and Savine waved Zuri from the shadows, a length of cloth over her arm, a vivid red that seemed almost to shine in the muddy grey hall, golden stitching gleaming in the hem. 'This is Zuri, my companion.'

'Is it?' Rikke narrowed her eyes, then slid them, sly as a cat, towards Savine. 'Sure you aren't hers?'

'I have heard it said God puts us all where we are meant to be,' said Zuri.

'Wouldn't know,' said Rikke. 'We don't see much of Him up here.' She took the cloth and shook it out with a snap, holding it up to the light. 'Oooooooh, you give the best presents!'

'Suljuk silk,' said Savine, 'from beyond the Thousand Isles. I thought perhaps you could make a dress from it, or a hanging, or . . .'

Rikke was already wrapping it around herself, ending up with something between a scarf, a cloak and a hood.

Zuri cocked her head on one side. 'That works.'

'I love it.' Rikke smiled as she rubbed her cheek against the shining fabric. 'And I see you've got a gift for Leo, too.' She dropped down on her knees, staring at Savine's belly. 'Can I feel?'

'Well, I suppose—'

Rikke slid her arms around Savine and pressed her tattooed cheek into her stomach, making her gasp.

Savine stared at Leo, but all he could do was shrug.

'Oh,' crooned Rikke, eyes closed as she snuggled in tight. 'I'd expect something special from the two of you but this . . . *this* will change the *world*.'

'Where's your friend Isern-i-Phail?' asked Leo. 'And Caul Shivers? I swear you're the only person in the world he likes.'

'I sent 'em off to make new friends. The Protectorate's small. We need every friend we can get.'

'You should've come to us.'

'I knew you'd be coming to me.'

Leo tried to smile, but it wasn't easy. Every time he saw a hint of that gangly girl he'd played hide and seek with in this very hall, she'd flash that sly smile, and turn that strange left eye on him, and he'd feel as if she was looking right into him. Right through him. The woman he'd known was vanished, sure as her father, and he was shocked at how much he missed them.

Savine, meanwhile, gnawed at her meat, lips and fingers shiny with grease, a pile of stripped bones on the table in front of her. 'She might look like a doll,' murmured Rikke in Northern, 'but she eats like a warrior.'

Leo laughed. 'Something I should know about?' asked Savine.

'She...wonders if you want a fork.'

'When I was in Valbeck I ate with my fingers.' Savine ripped some gristle from her meat with her teeth and spat it into the firepit as neatly as any Named Man. 'When I ate at all. I came to the North to see how things are done here. Not to do things my way regardless.'

'Very open-minded,' said Rikke. 'But you didn't come here to improve your table manners. The two o' you are after something or my name's not Sticky Rikke.'

Savine's raised brow told Leo it was time to get to business. 'You're right. I wanted to see Uffrith, and I wanted to see you, but you're right. I need your help, Rikke.'

'Naught my father wouldn't have done for an old friend. And we go way back, eh? Used to wrestle on this very floor, didn't we? What do you need?'

'Your father's warriors. *Your* warriors, I mean.'

'Who are we fighting?'

'I hope they won't have to fight.'

'But we both know hopes can turn out barren. You wouldn't be asking for warriors if you didn't have a fight in mind.'

Leo glanced towards Savine one last time, almost hoping she might give the faintest shake of her head, and they could forget the whole business. But she narrowed her eyes and gave the faintest nod instead.

'We're fighting the Closed Council,' said Leo.

Rikke slowly eased back on her father's bench, puffing out her hollow cheeks. 'I know you like a scrap, Leo, but did you think of picking a smaller one?'

'Few of us get to pick our battles,' said Savine. 'The battles pick us.'

'Maybe you should let this one pick someone else.'

'You saw what they were like in the war!' Leo sat forward angrily. 'Promising everything. Giving nothing. The Union abandoned Uffrith.

Abandoned your father. Abandoned you! But Angland never did. *I* never did.' He realised as he said it, sitting beside his new wife, that Rikke might see it differently, and he cleared his throat, and frowned down at the table.

'Calling in the favours, then,' she said. 'Where's your next stop, Young Lion?'

No point trying to trick her. She could always see right through him. And honesty can be a kind of weapon, too. 'Carleon,' he said. 'As you've no doubt guessed.'

'To beg for the Great Wolf's help.' Rikke bared her teeth and snarled at him with sudden, shocking fury. 'The man who burned half this city on a whim? Who promised to send my guts to my father in a box? Who killed my friends and yours? Who'd have killed you, if my Long Eye hadn't seen it coming? Break what they love, he said. You'd have me link arms with my worst enemy?'

'Sometimes we must use one enemy to fight another,' said Savine.

Rikke curled back her lip and sucked a shred of meat from between her teeth. 'Oh, you're a clever one, Lady Brock. You could crawl through a keyhole, I reckon, even with a swollen belly. But last time we met it was on your ground. Up here, enemies aren't so easily spun into friends.'

'Oh, I doubt the rules are so very different,' said Savine. 'Uffrith needs protection. That is why it became a Protectorate. King Orso and his Closed Council have shown they will not help. Side with us, we can keep the balance between you and Nightfall. Turn us down, your time is already running out. It really is as simple as that.'

'So I risk everything, and in return I get what I've already got?' Rikke snorted. 'And a scrap of red cloth, of course. You like making deals. If you were sat on my bench, what would you say to that one?'

'I would say it's the best you'll get,' said Savine. Leo winced. He'd come to ask for help from an old friend, but now his wife was turning the whole thing into a hard-headed bargain. One with more than a whiff of blackmail about it.

He held up his hands before things got any worse. 'We're friends! I risked my life for you. For Uffrith.' He grimaced as he shifted his leg. 'I've got the scars. But I'd do the same again. I helped you against your enemies. I'm asking you to help me against mine.'

Savine sat back, sour, wiping her fingers on a cloth. Rikke sat back, sulky, hands on the bench behind her and her bony shoulders up around her ears. 'You're asking a lot, Leo. Of me and of my men. Don't pretend you're not. I need to think on it. Maybe the Long Eye'll open in the night. Show me the answer.'

'I understand. It's a big decision.' The uncomfortable silence stretched, and Leo looked down awkwardly at the floor. That was when he saw the Circle painted there, around the table where they ate. Five strides or so across. The same kind he fought Stour Nightfall in. The kind men of the North had been fighting in since before words were written. 'What's the Circle for?'

Rikke's face slid into shadow, the gleam of one eye in the darkness. 'Folk who don't agree with me.'

New Friends

Rikke woke with a lurch, flinging off the furs like they were throttling her, thoughts chasing each other around her sweaty head. Took her a moment to remember where she was. Who she was.

She still wasn't used to sleeping in her father's bed. But it was likely the best bed in the North. Huge, even though he'd been small. Always said he wanted to keep rolling and never fall out. He'd had the frame carved by the best shipbuilder in Uffrith, monsters prowling over the wood, and bought the goose-feather mattress for its weight in silver off some Styrian merchant. Other than Rikke, it was probably the thing he was proudest of in the world. Broke his heart to leave it when Black Calder took the city, filled him with joy to find it in one piece when he came back. Always said he'd spent half his life sleeping on the dirt, so he'd sleep the other half in comfort's pillowy embrace and make no apologies.

She still wasn't used to sleeping in her father's bed, but it made her feel close to him, even though he was gone. And when you're left the best bed in the North, what should you do, sleep on the floor?

She swung her feet down and wriggled her bare toes into the cold boards, nodding to herself as all the pieces dropped into place in her mind. Might be she'd had a vision, might be she'd had a dream, might be she'd just had an idea, but whether you put it down to magic, luck or wits, she saw now what had to be done. Someone had to pick the course, after all. Wouldn't be pleasant. Wouldn't be easy.

'But easy is for the dead,' she whispered, and stood.

That morning had a feel of summer, chilly but bright, curved streaks of cloud high up against the blue like dragon's ribs. Rikke shifted her chagga pellet from one side of her mouth to the other and drew that bright red cloth about her shoulders. It was quite a thing for some woven thread, so beautiful it made her feel beautiful, which was a rare feat these days.

And who should be sitting on the bench in her father's unkempt garden, watching the sunrise sparkle on the sea, but the one who gave it to her?

'Savine dan Brock herself!' said Rikke. 'You're up early.'

She seemed a different woman without all the powder and paint and costume. Younger and softer. More ordinary and more honest. Like a warrior without his mail, maybe. 'No choice,' she said, laying her hands on her belly. 'He, she or it seems intent on kicking me this morning.'

Rikke sat beside her. Watched the fishing boats rock on the waves while she gathered the courage to ask. 'Can I feel?'

Savine considered her, eyes narrowed against the low sun, then she took Rikke's hand and guided it to her stomach.

Rikke frowned. Waited. Frowned. A little knobbly pressure shifted under Savine's gown, then was gone. Just that, but Rikke found she was grinning like she'd seen High Art. 'It moved!'

'That's what it does.' Savine winced as she shifted on the bench. 'That, and the moment I piss I need to piss again.'

'Sorry I was a sour host last night,' said Rikke. That came out a little sour itself. Her pride had been hard fought for and she didn't like swallowing it, even if her father had always said pride buys nothing. 'In Uffrith, we're used to getting pushed from both sides. Being pushed brings out the worst in me.'

'Sorry I was a sour guest,' said Savine. 'I am used to fixing on what I want then treading on whoever I must to get there. Where I come from, nice wins no prizes.'

Rikke slowly nodded. 'Honestly, it's much the same here.'

'I should have told you how sorry I am about your father. Leo has spoken of him so often I almost feel I knew him. He was distraught . . . when the news came.'

'Aye.' And Rikke frowned towards her father's grave, half-hidden by the overgrown bushes. She was making even less progress on the gardening than he had. 'He's always had a big heart, Leo.'

Savine leaned close to murmur, 'He could use his heart less, I sometimes think, and his head more.'

'Why would he need his head when he's got you? I mean, he might come up with an idea you don't like.'

'Fair point.'

'And your father? What'll he feel about what you're planning?'

'My father.' Savine's face turned stony. 'You suppose he *has* feelings. He always told me that to change the world you must first burn it down.'

'He'd get on with my friend Isern, I reckon. She always says you must make of your heart a stone.'

'Sound advice. I very much admire what you have achieved here, you know. It cannot be easy for a woman to take charge.'

'Someone had to. The old men were making quite the fuck-up.'

'Honestly, it is much the same in Angland.'

'You should get a couple of the most troublesome ones to kill each other,' said Rikke. 'You wouldn't believe how thinning the pack brings the other old dogs into line.'

'*You* haven't killed each other, then?' Leo had stepped out into the sun, a worried look on his face. There was no disguise in him at all. He couldn't have hidden a tree in a forest.

His wife was craftier. Far, far craftier. 'We're better friends than ever,' she said, with a smile could've sweetened seawater.

Rikke did her best to match it, wondering whether Savine had friends, or just people that were useful to her. Then she wondered if she was any better herself. Then she wondered whether it even mattered. Long as everyone made sure they stayed useful, of course.

'I had a vision in the night!' she said, throwing up her hands then slapping them down on her thighs. 'I asked for a vision and I got one. Have to tell you that's not usually how it works. It started off with me climbing a hill of bones.'

'That . . . doesn't sound great,' said Leo.

'That was my thought! Dusty under the fingernails. But when I got to the top, the sun rose over green uplands, and there was a lion, and it wore a crown.'

Leo frowned at Savine. 'I don't want the crown. A new Closed Council and an honest government and I'll be satisfied.'

''Course,' said Rikke. 'But it's a promising sign. And when signs are sent, you've got to attend. What's the point of the Long Eye if you're not going to listen?' She thought about that. 'Or look? Anyway, my point is . . . I'm with you. The men of Uffrith will be with you. Just make sure you put us on the other wing from the Great Wolf, eh? Wouldn't want to kill that fucker at a bad time.'

Savine's smile held just a trace of suspicion. 'You don't . . . *want* anything?'

'Just a share in your bright future.' Rikke watched a pair of little white butterflies chase each other upwards in a spiral. 'You two are *going* somewhere. Not sure where, but I'm keen to find out. You helped us.' Rikke pulled Leo down onto the bench beside her, one arm about his shoulders and one about Savine's. 'You risked your life for us. You *saved* us, Leo, and my father always paid his debts. I mean to pay mine.'

'I *knew* you wouldn't let me down.' Leo looked her right in the eye. The one that couldn't see, but still. 'I can't tell you what it means... to know I've still got your friendship.'

There was the Leo she knew. Part winning honesty, part naïve recklessness. 'Well, you know me.' She had to swallow the slightest lump in her throat. 'I'm all about the friendship.'

They packed to leave soon after, which was quite the operation as Savine needed six big boxes with brass corners just to get out the door. The dead knew what she had in 'em. Secrets and lies, maybe.

Rikke gave her a hug, which was like hugging cut glass, then she gave Leo a hug, which felt very strange. She held him tight, and smelled that smell he still had, and remembered how she used to feel, snuggling into the warmth of blankets with his arms around her. Safe. She never felt safe any more, and it came to her that if things had been a bit different, maybe she'd be the one carrying his child.

Most of her knew they'd never been well matched. But there was a piece of her that'd loved him once. And that piece ached at the loss of him, and the woman she'd been with him, and the life she might've had with him, so much that tears welled up unexpected in her blind eye and she had to make out something had blown into it.

'Watch yourself,' she whispered in his ear, then slapped his arse as he was mounting up, and was pleased to see he still blushed easily.

Isern had come back that morning and stood slowly chewing, frowning after Leo and Savine and their men and their wagons as they clattered out of town. 'Doesn't bother you she stole your man, eh?'

'Stole him?' Rikke scornfully tossed her head. 'I flung him aside and she stooped to catch him.'

''Course...' hummed Isern, dragging that one word out into a whole story, then folding her arms tight. 'I trust that woman less than the weather. She is the fanciest thing I ever saw.'

'You just wish you were that fancy.'

Isern spat through the hole in her teeth and pushed her chin in the air. 'I'll confess that hat of hers would look most fine upon me. But she smells too good, d'you see? Not like a person. Like a cake. Like the best cake you ever tasted.'

'We're siding with her, not eating her. Unless you got some plans I don't know about.'

'We're siding with her husband. And if he is a lion, she is a golden serpent twisted all about him. If she told him down was up, he'd laugh at his mistake and stand on his head.'

'Probably. He's never been the sharpest. And she's cunning, and ruthless, and ambitious as the plague.' Rikke shrugged and gave that sigh that made her lips flap. 'But stupid friends won't take you far, will they?' Isern thought about that and opened her mouth. 'Don't say it!' snapped Rikke, and she slowly closed it again. 'Bring Hardbread on up here, tell him we've got to gather the warriors. Every Named Man or Carl. Every Thrall can hold a spear. And spears for 'em to hold, too.'

'And shields?'

'Aye, be nice if some of 'em came back.' Leo turned in his saddle to smile and wave, and Rikke went up on tiptoe to smile and wave back. Looked like there were some men coming the other way. At least a dozen, sun glinting on their gear, and on the metal eye of the one in the lead. 'Here's Shivers.'

'That or it's some other metal-eyed bastard. Who's that with him?'

Rikke shaded her good eye with her hand. He was very tall. Taller than Shivers, even, but with a stoop, elbows stuck out and chin stuck forward, white-blond hair sprouting in tufts. 'Unless I'm much mistook, I believe that's the Nail.'

'I believe you're right.'

'One eye, maybe.' Rikke tapped her face and gave a wink. 'But it's a sharp one. He looks angry as ever.'

'Well, his da's still killed,' said Isern, 'so I'm guessing he will be.'

'Good.' Rikke gave that fine red cloth a tweak about her shoulders and set off up the road to greet him. 'An angry man is a useful man.'

He was taller than ever when you got close, not just his beard and his brows pale but even his eyelashes. He'd a thoughtful look, but there was something in that easy slouch made Rikke think he might explode in violence any moment. She'd seen it before, after all, when he was fighting with the other side at the Battle of Red Hill. He'd seemed a terror then, blood-dotted face twisted with fury and laughter at once. But Rikke didn't scare so easily these days.

Shivers jerked a thumb sideways. 'This is—'

'I know who this is.' Rikke took the Nail's calloused hand. By the dead, it was a size, hers weren't small but they looked like a child's hands holding it. 'No less a man than the Nail, famed champion of the West Valleys and son of the great Gregun Hollowhead.'

'A sweeter introduction than I'd have dared give myself,' he said.

'Oh, don't be coy.' Rikke patted his scarred knuckles and let his hand drop. 'I saw you in the battle at Red Hill. You're a bad enemy to have.'

'Can't think o' higher praise. Saw you in the battle, too, and at the duel after. Before all this, though.' And he waved towards the left side of his face, his pale eyes still on her, taking it all in.

'Better to get looks for the wrong reason than draw no looks at all.' She turned the tattoos towards him. A little challenge. A habit she was getting, when folk stared. 'And I haven't shit myself once since it was done, which is a bonus.'

'Saves on the laundry, I expect.'

'I thought to myself, if you're going to be hideous, why stop halfway?'

'Why did you think that?' His pale brows drew in a little. 'All I see are power and wisdom. Ask me, there's naught more beautiful.'

Rikke blinked. She liked to think she was canny enough these days that flattery didn't shift her far, but she had to admit that one found the mark.

Isern leaned towards her, one hand shielding her mouth. 'I'm thinking he might be quite the find.'

'I'm thinking the same,' muttered Rikke, tidying a bit of hair behind her ear that the salt breeze had whipped free. 'What brings you down here, Nail?'

'Vengeance.'

Rikke held her hands up. 'What have I done now?'

'Ain't you a jester?' said the Nail, giving a little snort. 'Stour Nightfall killed my father. Hung him in a cage.' She heard his knuckles click as he clenched those outsize fists. 'Put his head above his gates.' The fury coming off him made her dizzy. Like a spark might jump between them and send her up in flames.

'I heard tell you'd let it go,' she murmured.

'That's what I told Black Calder. I love to fight, but I hate to lose, and the odds are long against me.'

'So you haven't let it go?'

'I have not.'

'And you've come to Uffrith looking for my help.'

'I heard *you're* a bad enemy to have. I know Stour fears you. Thought maybe, with my sword and your eye, the odds would be shorter. Uffrith and the West Valleys together. That'd be a thing no one could dismiss.'

She looked thoughtfully up at him. Quite a long way up, since she was standing downhill. 'My da told me vengeance was an empty chest you have to go bent under the weight of. He told me to let it go.'

'Your da was a tough man and a crafty man and a man to be admired.'

'No doubt,' said Shivers, quietly.

'But you don't agree?'

'I do not,' said the Nail. 'I'll have Stour's head or die trying. I saw you and him swap barbs before the duel. Thought you might feel the same.'

'Oh, I feel *just* the same!' she snarled, showing him a glimpse of the fury she kept burning. 'My father swore to see Black Calder dead, and I swore to see Stour Nightfall dead, and I mean to keep both of our words, how's *that*?' It brought a little smile from him. A little brightening of his eye. 'But I've folk to look after now.' She softened up, holding her hand out to Uffrith, looking quite pretty in the sunlight as it sloped down to the sea. 'Can't be sprinkling vengeance about willy-nilly. You see those Union guests of mine just leaving?'

'The woman wrapped up like a feast-day gift? Aye, there was no missing her.'

'Well, that was the Lady Governor of Angland. I made a deal with her and her husband.' Rikke worked her mouth like there was a bad taste in it. 'And it puts me on the same side as the King of the Northmen.'

The Nail shook his head. 'Ah, that's a shame.'

'I tend somewhat to agree. No reason you and I can't be good neighbours, though. Why don't you come inside? I'll toss a fresh log on the firepit and crack a keg of my father's ale.'

'I'd sooner have vengeance.'

'Were you going to run off to Carleon and grab it 'fore sundown?' asked Shivers.

'My da used to say only the dead can't spare time for a cup,' said Rikke. 'Let's drink and talk about the future. What might happen. What I've seen *will* happen. Uffrith and the West Valleys together, after all. That'd be a thing no one could dismiss.'

Ever so slowly, the Nail thoughtfully raised his pale brows. 'It won't last for ever, then, your deal wi' Nightfall?'

Rikke set a gentle hand on his shoulder and steered him towards the door of her father's hall. 'Nothing lasts for ever.'

The Little People

Orso took a breath of the crisp morning air and let it sigh away. It felt good to be out of the city. The vapours seemed to get worse and the demands of kingship more suffocating every day. Lord Hoff and his wearisome timetable, the pointless functions, the tedious rituals, every moment scrupulously wasted far in advance with never an opportunity to actually *do* anything. Even Orso's toilet habits were precisely circumscribed, catalogued, overseen. He would not have been surprised to find there were a bevy of highly lucrative offices for the purpose. Lord High Warden of the Royal Stool. Chief Custodian of His Majesty's Passage. Piss-Smeller General.

He twisted the circlet gently from his head and held it up, looking through it towards the gleaming track. Towards the expectant crowd. He gave a little giggle.

'Something amusing?' asked his mother, for whom nothing was ever amusing.

'I never realised before. The thing about crowns... there's nothing in them, is there?'

Orso flinched at a sudden blast of steam from the machinery, a ripple of 'oohs' and 'aahs', followed by polite applause. A band played something brassy and optimistic. Smiling children waved little Union flags. The famous device itself was a madman's nightmare of cogs, rods and rivets, a beast of brass and iron gleaming with grease, vapour puffing from its valves like smoke from a dragon's nostrils. It was mounted on a pair of polished rails that stretched across two fields to a bridge fluttering with coloured bunting. On top of it, a noted actress wore a headdress and flimsy robe that presumably marked her out as inspiration or some such abstract virtue. The sun kept going in, though, and despite her beaming smile she looked mostly rather cold.

'However does it work?' mused Orso, jamming his circlet back on. The engine might as well have been a sorcerer's wand for all he understood its workings.

'I believe a coal-fired furnace heats water in the vessel to boiling,' said Dietam dan Kort, his waistcoat straining dangerously about the buttons as he leaned across Curnsbick's empty chair. 'The formation of steam within creates pressure which drives a reciprocating piston converting expansive to rotational force, then transmitting it through a sequence of gears to the wheels. Would Your Majesty like more detail?'

Orso raised his brows. 'If anything . . . less.'

'The fire makes steam,' pronounced Queen Terez, deigning to speak a few words in the common tongue but insisting on doing so with an overpowering Styrian accent. 'The steam makes it go.'

'That,' admitted Kort, 'is the essence.'

Honrig Curnsbick, the great machinist himself, stood near his creation with tall hat and riotous side whiskers, surrounded by cheering well-wishers, shaking a fistful of drawings at his oil-blackened engineers. One of them shovelled coal furiously into the glowing maw of the machine. Another weighed a giant wrench while frowning towards the royal box with an intensity bordering on hatred. Sadly, there was nothing remarkable in that. Orso regarded anything warmer than strong dislike from one of his subjects as a delightful surprise.

'You really should have a queen beside you,' observed his mother.

He grinned sideways at her. 'I do.'

'I mean a wife, as you well know. Help me, High Justice.'

'Her Majesty. As always. Makes a fine point.' Bruckel leaned past Orso's mother to jab out a few phrases. 'See what marriage has done. For the Lord Governor of Angland.' Orso winced. He would rather have been squirted with poison than with more news of Leo dan Brock's happy union. 'The government there was paralysed. Antiquated. Incompetent. Since his wedding? Turned. Around.'

'Lady Savine is an immensely talented woman, though!' Kort leaned in from the other side to unwittingly make matters even worse. 'I must confess, I was reluctant to embrace her as a partner but, well, I couldn't have completed my canal without her. Stupendously talented.' Kort shook his head, chin vanishing into the roll of fat beneath. 'Not many like her around, Your Majesty.'

'That settles it, then,' said Orso. 'Lady Savine will simply have to marry me *and* her husband.' The real tragedy was that he would likely have clutched at that arrangement with both hands.

His mother was less taken with it. 'Don't be facetious, Orso, it's beneath your majesty.'

'I'm starting to think there's nothing beneath *my* majesty.'

'Your sisters both did their dynastic duty. Do you suppose Cathil wanted to move to Starikland?'

How often had they gone over this same conversation? 'She's an inspiration.'

'Do you think Carlot wanted to marry the Chancellor of Sipani?'

'She always seems rather pleased about it—'

'You cannot delay any longer. You are not only damaging yourself, but the whole Union.'

She detested the Union but believed hypocrisy was a thing that only happened to other people. Orso gritted his teeth. 'I'll look at the latest list again. But I want to organise this grand tour first. Get out into the country and introduce myself to the people!'

'Far better to tour with a wife, then you could introduce *her* to the people and get started on producing an heir at the same time.'

'What? Actually simultaneously?'

She glanced at him down her nose. 'At least they would see you were finally taking your responsibilities seriously.'

'Now who's being facetious?'

'My master would be *delighted* if you were to wed.'

Orso recoiled at the voice in his ear. Bayaz's stooge, Yoru Sulfur, had leaned grinning forward from the chairs behind. He was one of those people with an ugly habit of popping up at the worst moments.

'Oh really?' snapped Orso. 'Keen to buy a new dress, is he?'

Sulfur's sharp smile showed no sign of slipping. 'Anything that bears on the stability of the realm is of interest to Lord Bayaz.'

'How fortunate we are to have such a guardian. But what brings a magus to a scientific demonstration? Haven't you got . . .' Orso waved a hand. 'Something *magical* to be about?'

'There is not so wide a gulf between science and magic as some suppose.' Sulfur nodded towards the city, where the House of the Maker was still the tallest spike on the horizon. 'Was not Kanedias himself the first and greatest of engineers? And did not Juvens say that knowledge is the root of power? Lord Bayaz delights in nothing more than ideas, innovations, new ways of thinking.' He turned his bright eyes towards Curnsbick's steam-wreathed engine. 'Imagine a network of these track-roads. Iron bands binding the Union ever more tightly together, carrying a never-ceasing flood of goods and people. A wonder to rank alongside the great achievements of the Old Time!'

'It sounds a marvellous project, Master Sulfur, but ... an expensive one.' Orso began to turn away. 'I fear my treasury is not up to the challenge.'

'The Banking House of Valint and Balk has already offered to advance the capital.'

Orso frowned. It was largely due to the crippling interest on Valint and Balk's loans that the treasury was in such a lamentable state. 'That is ... uncharacteristically generous of them.'

'The bank would take the necessary land in trust and own the tracks, charging a trifling stipend for their use. I was hoping you would consent to my making the arrangements with the lord chancellor.'

'That sounds rather like the first step in selling you my kingdom piece by piece.'

Sufur smiled wider yet. 'Hardly the first step.'

'Your Majesties!' Curnsbick hurried up to the royal box, whisking off his hat and dabbing his sweaty forehead with a handkerchief. 'I hope we haven't kept you waiting.'

'Not at all,' said Orso. 'Converting expansive force to rotational is ... no easy business ... I suppose—'

The Queen Dowager issued a thunderous snort of contempt, but Curnsbick was already facing the crowds, thumping his broad fists down on the rail. The band sputtered out. The eager conversation died away. The audience turned from the engine to its creator. The great machinist began to speak.

'We have made astonishing progress in a few brief years, my friends!' Depending on who you asked, of course, Orso still heard plenty of complaints. 'With the right techniques and machinery, one man can now do the work that once took ten! Took twenty!' Though what became of the other nineteen was not made clear.

'I firmly believe that this, my latest invention ...' And Curnsbick wafted a hand towards the engine with the flourish of a pimp introducing his prostitutes. '*Our* latest invention, for it belongs to posterity, will not simply carry a few of us from Adua to Valbeck in more comfort and less time than ever before. It will carry *all* of us ... into the future!'

'The one undeniable thing about the future,' murmured Orso's mother in Styrian, 'is that it comes to you, ready or not, without need for a conveyance.'

It certainly seemed a rather overcomplicated way of crossing two fields. But Orso could only shrug and smile, which, after all, were his main contributions to any of the many events he attended. If he'd had all the answers then he supposed he could have been the great machinist, instead of merely a king.

'There are those at both ends of the social scale who would have us change direction!' Curnsbick was shouting. 'Those who would not only try to dam the river of progress but have it flow uphill! Who would break, burn and murder in the name of dragging us back into a glorious past that never truly was. A place of ignorance, superstition, squalor and fear. A place of darkness! But there will be *no* going back! I promise you that!' He raised his arm and turned to Orso. 'Your Majesty, with your kind permission?'

It always worried Orso when someone wanted to involve him in a decision, however superficially. But decisions still had to be made. However superficially. 'Carry us into the future, Master Curnsbick!' he called, grinning to the crowd.

Curnsbick turned to the engine and portentously chopped down his arm. The engineer, his smile a curve of white in his oil-smeared face, hauled upon one of the levers, and the entire world exploded.

'We have made astonishing progress in a few brief years, my friends!' bellowed Curnsbick.

'Hear, hear!' Verunice piped, and was at once rather embarrassed. One wanted to stand out from the crowd, especially after so many years in the most distant background, but one did not want to make an exhibition of oneself. Only look at Savine dan Glokta, now Brock, of course. Everyone did, after all. So audacious. Yet so feminine. The spirit of the new age! Verunice had joined all the forward-looking societies. The Fellowship for Civic Advancement, the Association for Improving the Condition of the Working Classes, the Solar Society, of course. She had already made what she considered an excellent investment with that young man Arinhorm. So polite. So attentive. He had looked at her in a way no young man had for years. Verunice felt a flush and wished she had brought her fan. But though it was summer, it was not quite fanning weather.

'With the right techniques and machinery,' Curnsbick was explaining, 'one man can now do the work that once took ten! Took twenty!'

Verunice nodded eagerly, then realised she might nod her wig loose, put a nervous hand to it and nearly knocked off her hat. She was not at all used to the headgear yet. Nor the dress. If she had been removed from it, the damn thing would probably have stood up by itself, but the dressmaker had told her this was what all the forward-looking ladies were wearing. She now found herself scarcely able to breathe, turn or move her arms, but she had acquired, as if by magic, quite an impressive bust. Her mother had always insisted that a bust was half the battle. Verunice had always wondered what the rest of the battle might be but never had the nerve to ask.

'I firmly believe that this, my latest invention...' And Curnsbick gestured towards his smouldering engine with the presence of a great actor upon the stage. Such a powerful man, those strong hands. Such a *generous* man, those impressive side whiskers. Such a *visionary*, piercing eyes behind his flashing lenses. The spirit of the age! 'Will carry *all* of us... into the future!'

Verunice applauded as eagerly as her corsetry allowed. One could see the future coming on the carriage ride out of Adua. The chimneys, the cranes, the endless building, endless creation, endless opportunity.

'There will be *no* going back!' shouted Curnsbick. 'I promise you that!'

Verunice applauded again, painfully this time but she didn't care. There would be no going back. Not to her smothering marriage or the suffocating house in the country or the stifling conversation at the village meetings. Her husband was dead and she had the money now and she'd buy herself a fucking life. She blushed, then realised she hadn't said the word, only thought it, so where was the crime? It was a new world. She could think what she liked. Could she even say what she liked?

'Fuck,' she whispered, and felt herself blushing even more deeply. She wished she had brought her fan.

The young king smiled, so carefree, so debonair, such lovely glossy hair, his golden circlet glittering in the sun. The spirit of the age! 'Carry us into the future, Master Curnsbick!'

Curnsbick chopped one broad hand down and Verunice closed her eyes, feeling the wind of freedom on her cheeks. Now she would be—

'We have made astonishing progress in a few brief years, my friends!' It was true the Union was much changed in the two decades since Muslan arrived but mostly, in his opinion, for the worse. He felt the stares when he walked the streets in his own neighbourhood. He felt the stares now. Less curiosity than there once had been, and more fear. More dislike. Insults were sometimes thrown. Objects, too, on occasion. A very pleasant young man of his acquaintance had been hit by a slate thrown from a roof and nearly killed. And he had been born in Adua! To Kadiri parents! When people are fixed on hatred they do not discriminate. But Muslan refused be cowed. He had not hidden from the priests. He would not hide from these damn fool pinks, either.

'With the right techniques and machinery,' Curnsbick blathered on, 'one man can now do the work that once took ten! Took twenty!'

Muslan gave a curt nod at that. There was much to detest about the Union. They prated on freedom but the women who toiled in the fields and the kitchens, the men who toiled in the mills and the mines, were as trapped in their lives of drudgery as any slave. A man was at least free to *think* here, though. To have ideas. To *change* things.

In Ul-Suffayn the priests had declared him a heretic. His wife had begged him to stop, but to Muslan his work was a holy duty. Others saw their holy duties differently. His workshop had been burned by people he had once called friends and neighbours, the fires of belief in their eyes. They say belief is righteous, but to Muslan only doubt was divine. From doubt flows curiosity, and knowledge, and progress. From belief flows only ignorance and decay.

'I firmly believe that this, my latest invention...' And Curnsbick wafted a hand towards the engine in the manner of a carpet-seller hoping to palm off substandard wares. 'Will carry *all* of us... into the future!'

We all are carried into the future, always. What greets us when we arrive, that is the pressing question. When the Prophet vanished, Muslan and those of his mind – the thinkers, philosophers, engineers – had hoped for a new age of reason. Instead had come an age of madness. The priests had said his work was against the laws of God. Ignorant cowards. Who made the minds of men, if not God? What was the desire to create, if not a humble imitation of His example? What was the grand idea, the great vision, the profound revelation, if not a glimpse of the divine?

'There are those at both ends of the social scale who would have us change direction!' Muslan had heard from those few friends in Ul-Saffayn who still dared write to him that the Eaters had come. They had taken his apprentices and his assistants and had burned his prototypes in the town square. He shuddered to think of it. The Eaters were belief distilled, belief without reason, mercy, compromise or regret. What could you call that, but evil?

'But there will be *no* going back!' roared Curnsbick. 'I promise you that!'

'No going back,' whispered Muslan, in his own tongue. He closed his eyes, feeling tears prickling at the lids, and spoke the words to his wife, or at least to her ashes, wishing she could hear them. 'I promise you that.'

'Carry us into the future, Master Curnsbick!' brayed their dunce of a king.

The priests supposed scriptural and scientific truth were opposed because their tightly strapped little minds had only room for one or the other. They did not realise they were one and the same. Muslan's grandfather had been a locksmith. Muslan's father had been a clockmaker. Muslan was an engineer. And so was God. So was—

'I firmly believe that this, my latest invention . . .' And Curnsbick pointed to his smoking machine like a sideshow-operator to his favourite freak, 'will carry *all* of us . . . into the future!'

Morilee frowned at that Gurkish bastard. Was that the future of the Union? Overrun by brown bastards, not even with the decency to come with drum and flag and sword so they could be properly fought and beaten, but just welcomed in at the back door by treacherous fucks wanting to sell their country for a few marks.

Thirty years ago, when this was all woods she'd come to for picnics with her grandad, King Jezal had told the people to rise up for their country. Morilee had got her father's old pike out of the shed, and put a new staff on it 'cause the old one was rotten, and she'd risen up, damn it, like the womenfolk always did when they had to. She'd fought those Gurkish bastards in the fire-blasted ruins of the streets she'd grown up in. She rubbed at the stump of her arm. Thirty years on and it still ached. But maybe the ache weren't in her arm really, but in her heart. She frowned again at that Gurkish bastard, standing proud with his little black beard like this was his country. Had she fought for this? Lost her arm for this? Lost her fucking home for *this*?

'There are those at both ends of the social scale who would have us change direction!' Morilee knew how the ones at the bottom o' the scale felt, that was sure, with their houses knocked down to make way for the mills and their gardens built over to make way for the temples and their families crowded into smaller and smaller rooms to make way for all the bastards flooding in from outside, the Gurkish and the Styrians and the Northmen and who knew what, all babbling in their own dirty tongues and forcing down the wages and forcing up the rents and choking the air with their horrible cook-smells, filth you wouldn't feed a dog, the gutters swarming with their mongrel brats.

'A place of ignorance, superstition, squalor and fear. A place of darkness!' She snorted. Curnsbick should come to the place she'd been living the past year, she'd show him squalor and darkness. She turned her head and spat. Tried to spit as far as that Gurkish bastard, but it fell short and spattered on some woman's hat. Curnsbick raised his arm and turned to Orso. 'Your Majesty, with your kind permission?'

Morilee put the one hand she still had on her heart. Maybe this new king was a clueless fucker but he was king still, and when she saw the golden sun flashing on the flags above, it still tickled the tears out. The country might be brought low, but it was still her country, in her blood, in her bones. If she was called on again, she'd fight again. Even if it meant her other arm. That was who she was.

'Carry us into the future, Master Curnsbick!' bellowed His Majesty. A fine, strong voice, and folk started to cheer and, in spite of her hurts, Morilee cheered loudest of all. Might be he was a shit king. But it's the shit kings need most cheering for.

The engineer pulled his lever and—

Blah, blah, progress, invention. High Justice Bruckel was hardly listening. He was thinking about that case yesterday. Terrible case. Regrettable business. The way the woman wept in the dock. Bruckel had wanted to weep himself. *You cry so easily*, his father used to say, *you have to present a hard front.* What would become of the children, though? It felt as if every verdict took a piece of him. Every sentence bled him. But his hands had been tied, as always. Arch Lector Glokta would demand harsh penalties. Lessons taught. Examples made.

One had to present a hard front to sit on the Closed Council. Any weakness and the vultures would be circling. Not a friend anywhere. Couldn't afford 'em. Bruckel glanced sideways. Only look at Her Majesty. Magnificent figure of a woman. Magnificent example. All the hatred flung at her. Simply bounced off, like arrows off a gatehouse. But so lonely. Like a single white tower on a blasted heath. Few truly realised how... *difficult* her position had been. Regrettable business. But Bruckel knew. And admired her hugely. Would never say so. Would be a kind of betrayal to acknowledge it. But he knew it. And she knew he knew. Was that some comfort to her? Probably not.

Curnsbick was working up to the crescendo. Blah, blah, me, me, me, change the world. Bruckel sagged back into his chair. The world did not change. Not in the ways that mattered. He was presiding over another case later today. Millworkers dead of the white lung. Not to be confused with the black lung. That was the one the miners died of. Regrettable business. But there was nothing Bruckel could do. Not with the interests lined up on the other side. Towering interests. Terrible case.

'Carry us into the future, Master Curnsbick!' called His Majesty. Bruckel wondered if Orso would make a good king. Wondered if any change could be effected. It hardly seemed likely. Not with all the interests lined up. The biggest interests of all. Valint and Balk, of course. Look at that bastard Sulfur, already easing his hooks into the king. Hooks that would rip him apart, as they had ripped apart his father. Always the vultures, circling. But the world was the world. Bruckel's hands were tied. They called him the high justice. But he was low, and there was no justice.

Curnsbick chopped down his arm with the greatest portentous self-satisfaction. Bruckel glanced sideways at Queen Terez, so endlessly impressive. He ventured the tiniest smile. She could not return it, of course. A regrettable—

'It will carry *all* of us...' screeched Curnsbick, a pygmy pretending to be a giant, the sort of man who passed for a hero in this petty age, 'into the future!'

Terez restrained a snort of contempt. Whose future? The one she had longed for had been crushed long ago. How could her fragile hopes ever have held up the weight of her father's smothering expectations, her husband's well-meaning ignorance, his subjects' mindless prejudice, the cripple Glokta's unspeakable threats?

She had sent Shalere away. Even now, Terez felt the pain of tears at the thought of her face, her smile, her warmth, the way she sang, danced, kissed. Terez kept a bottle of her scent still. Among all the gaudy trash they heap upon a queen, the one thing that was truly precious to her. Just the faintest whiff of that perfume brought it all tumbling back. That mad, romantic girl who would have fought the world for love was still trapped somewhere in this stern old body. Terez felt the pain of tears, but she had trained her eyes not to weep. She had sent her true love to safety. One must take consolation in the small things, when one has nothing else. A nearly empty scent bottle, and a few sweet memories.

She took a deep breath, used it to force herself straighter. She lived now to hold up Orso's hopes. To be his unflinching pillar. His dauntless shield against the barbs of the leering public. She had remade herself from stone and steel, an unbending, unsmiling, unfeeling sculpture of a woman, for his sake.

She could have played the game. She could have smiled, and lied, and struck deals. But her father had taught her that compromise was weakness, and weakness, death. Only far too late had she begun to wonder whether her father might not have been a giant, but a fool. Strange, how long a shadow one's parents cast. All she wanted now was to see Orso married to some fearsomely sensible woman. A woman with a strong enough grip to squeeze him into the great man she knew he could be. Then, perhaps, she could finally stop squeezing herself. Take the trip to Styria. See Shalere again, one last time...

'Carry us into the future, Master Curnsbick!' shouted Orso, with that infinitely good-humoured smile Terez's own mouth always longed to imitate.

High Justice Bruckel was looking at her, she realised, and with a deeply sad expression. Like a man watching a tragic play that, to his surprise, had struck some deep-buried nerve. As though he somehow guessed at the endless spring of sadness that welled inside her. As though—

There was a flash, Terez thought. A burst of fire. She opened her mouth to gasp in shock.

Something whizzed past. There was a loud popping sound and a strange silence.

A hot wind tore at her, twisted her back in her chair.

She could hardly see anything. Could hear absolutely nothing. Everything moved very slowly. As if she was underwater.

An armoured man blundered past, screaming silently, a smouldering shard of metal embedded in his breastplate.

There was something wet on her face. She touched it. Red fingertips. She realised High Justice Bruckel had pressed himself against her shoulder. How dare he? As she turned to remonstrate with him, she saw the side of his head was sheared away, blood spurting from the pulp inside and turning her dress red.

Probably she should assist. Very severe injury, by all appearances.

'High Justice?' she asked as he flopped into her lap, but she could not even hear her own voice. She did her best to hold his broken skull together but pieces of it slid between her red fingers.

She tried to stand, but the over-bright world tipped crazily and slapped her in the side. Dust and splinters. Boots shuffled. She saw someone staring at her. One of Curnsbick's friends, blowing bloody bubbles out of his nose. It looked as if there might be an iron rivet embedded in the side of his neck. She realised they were both lying on the floor.

She tried to stand again, thought it prudent to clutch at something for support. The railing of the royal box, its gaudy decorations now red-spotted. Curnsbick stood swaying beside her. His hat had been blown off and his grey hair stuck out at all angles.

Terez clutched at his bloody jacket. 'What happened?' Couldn't hear herself speak. Couldn't hear anything. Curnsbick clasped his hands to his face. Stared between his fingers.

Terez stuck her thumb in her ear and waggled it. It made nothing but a muffled squelching. She squinted into the sunlight. Towards the engine. Or towards where the engine had been.

There was nothing of it left now but a great claw of burning wreckage, sending up a thick plume of brown smoke. Papers fluttered down. Like the flower petals at her wedding, so long ago. Bodies were fanned out from the engine in rows. Mangled, tangled. Bodies still and bodies vaguely moving, twisting, crawling. A man wandered drunkenly. His shirt appeared to have been torn off.

There were people coming through the bodies. Not helping. Stepping over the corpses. People in dark clothes, with dark masks over their faces. One held a hatchet. One a long knife. One pointed towards the royal box with a sword. Where was Orso? By the Fates, where was Orso?

Beside her! He was beside her, staring, blood on his face. He had drawn his sword. A king should never have to touch his sword, let alone draw it. She tried to put herself between him and the assassins, but he brushed her away, pushed her back. He was so much stronger than she had expected. Had some part of her thought he was a snivelling toddler, still helpless in her arms?

Faint through the burbling in her ears she heard him speak: 'Get behind me, Mother.'

Sofee came blundering through the murk, gripping her sword so tight her hand ached, hardly able to breathe even with the cloth over her face, and stumbled to an uncertain stop.

Bodies everywhere. Bodies and parts of bodies. More and more revealed as the breeze snatched the smoke away. Things dropped. A walking stick. A hat. A broken picnic hamper, spilling broken crockery. A glove.

No. It was a hand.

The pamphlets they'd made fluttered down. The explanations, the excuses, the justifications. One fell near Sofee's boot, and began to soak up blood at one corner, and turn red. She'd been a governess for a year, before she was married, so she'd been very particular about the wording of that pamphlet. She'd wanted to convince people. To show them the truth.

Someone shoved her, near knocked her over. One of the other Burners, desperate to begin the killing. Wasn't that what she came for? All she'd wanted, for so long. To kill them. Tear them with her bare hands. Bite them with her teeth. Now she wondered who 'them' was. Whose enemy was the little boy with a fluttering pamphlet stuck across his face and his guts hanging out? She felt sick.

Brevan had been the kind of man everyone liked the moment they met him. The day they were married had been the happiest of her life. Suddenly special, when she'd been nothing since the day she was born. After they hanged him, left the crows picking at him above the road to Valbeck, it was like the sun went out for her. Such a gloom she couldn't even lift a finger. Judge had given her purpose. Lit a fire in the ashes. But now that helplessness came flooding back.

'Come on!' screeched Gus, dragging at her, and he half-pulled her over, left her kneeling in the dirt as he charged on. Charged on with the rest of them, all with a thirst for blood that would never be satisfied.

Judge had promised her she'd feel better, after this. Cleansed by righteous fire. But she saw now there was no feeling better, and for damn sure no cleansing. All she'd done was what was done to her.

Sofee had dropped her sword. She left it where it was. All those bodies. All those injured. Even if she'd wanted to help them, where would you start?

Brevan had been such a good man. Everyone loved him the moment they met him. Would he have wanted this?

She put a hand over her mouth.

What had she done?

Curnsbick's terror, when he struggled up with his hat blown off, was not for his own safety, but that he might be responsible. Or, at any rate, that he might be blamed.

'Oh, my,' he whispered. Carnage where the cheering onlookers had stood. Bodies strewn everywhere. It was as bad as that day in Crease. Worse, because then he had not been responsible. Could not possibly have been blamed.

Among engineers and investors there were many embittered failures, and he knew they must gaze enviously at him and think how wonderful it must be, to be Curnsbick. They had no idea of the pressure. Ever since his patent portable forge, with every success the weight of expectation grew heavier. For every world-changing idea there were a million duds, and until they were thoroughly tested and explored, the two could be surprisingly hard to tell apart. That was why he had founded the Solar Society, really. As a great sounding board for his worse notions. That, and he simply could not say no to Savine dan Glokta.

Someone clutched hold of him. Queen Terez? He wanted to blubber some ridiculous apology, but his voice utterly failed him. All he could do was put his hands over his face, stare between his fingers like a child at some horror and murmur, 'Oh, my.'

So when he saw the Burners coming, his first feeling was an improbable flood of relief. Someone to blame! The villains of the piece, custom made for the purpose! *Then* came the sickening concern for his own safety. There were a great number of black-clothed assassins down there. They had dispatched the disorganised guards, were converging on the royal box. They had a Knight of the Body on his knees! Were smashing at him with hammers!

'Oh, my.' Men can be brave in some ways, not in others. Curnsbick could face the unknown and summon new things into being. Could stand before a crowd of hundreds and make them believe. Could take responsibility for millions of marks and never falter. But when it came to physical danger, he had always been a hopeless coward. He missed Majud terribly, then. Brave, stingy Majud. Missed him as he had every day these past ten years. But Curnsbick had made his choices. All that remained was to live with them. Or perhaps die with them.

'If I may, Your Majesty?' That man Sulfur. He was brushing the king aside. Went smiling towards a dozen well-armed fanatics as they mounted the steps. What the hell was he about?

A Knight of the Body came stumbling from the direction of the royal box. He was stunned by the explosion, tangled with his purple cloak, and the Burners had come prepared. Judge had loved the notion of pouring Gurkish sugar through their visors and setting a match to it, but Gus had a more practical solution.

Briar threw a net and pinned his sword-arm, then Rollow and Laws, two beefy ex-diggers, went at him with hammers, aiming for knees and elbows. Once they brought him down, Gus stepped up, swung his pick high and neatly punched it right through the top of his helmet. It was some time since he had thought of himself as an engineer, but he could still take pleasure in a well-executed design.

He had been a wheelman once. A specialist in the design of water-wheels, that was. A surveyor of slopes and flows. A connoisseur of dams and sluices. His scheme for the river-driven mill at Sharnlost had been much admired. But for the important work, one had to go to Adua. So he had set out to study at the University, hoping to wear the robes of an Adeptus Mechanical himself one day, perhaps. What petty ambitions.

Gus charged through the scattering mass of panicked humanity, people running, begging, blubbing, bleeding, towards the royal box, waving his comrades forward. 'For the people!' he roared. 'For the Great Change!'

The lecture theatres of the University's grand new buildings had contained only dry whispers and dated ideas. The inspiring speeches were given in the teahouses and jerry shops on the borders of the poor districts, where the intellectuals would spring onto the tables to hold forth on the injustice of the current system, lay out bold fantasies for what could replace it, compete with each other to make the most outrageous pronouncements on behalf of the noble and oppressed commoner. The commoners themselves, it hardly needed to be said, could scarcely get a word in. Gus still remembered the excitement of those heady days. It was the first time he had ever believed in something greater than himself. *Belonged* to something greater than himself.

His pick thudded into the back of a crawling city watchman, and as he dragged the bloody weapon free, he knew he had never done such important work.

It was not until he went to Valbeck, and saw the great chimneys, the great smogs, the great slums, and heard the Weaver speak, that he began to glimpse the truth. That the Union was itself a wheel, designed not by a single engineer but by a web of mutual interest, hidden influence and collective greed, to raise up the rich and drag the poor down into the churning waters. Well, now the wheel would turn, as wheels are made to do, and drive down the privileged, and lift up the downtrodden, and there would be justice. There would be justice, and equality, and plenty for all.

He had cut the 'dan' from his name. Guslav dan Turmric had become simple Gus Turmer. Arguments with his family had borne no fruit so he had cut them off, too. He had been a stack of kindling waiting desperately for a spark. Then he met Judge, and his eyes were opened. There was no dry theory with her, no sentimental compromises, no having to be patient, no convincing the doubters. What some called madness he recognised as diamond-edged clarity. The time for arguments in the teahouse, for pretty words and fancy theories, was over. The grasping hands of the owners, the noblemen, the king and his venal henchmen could only be opened by force. Fire and steel would be the last words in their argument.

Another knight had killed two of his brothers, but they had him cornered now and were battering away at him, leaving great dents in his armour. Gus left the pick stuck in his helmet, kicked the knight over with a clatter of falling steel, pulled out his sword and charged for the royal box, its steps unguarded. He caught a glimpse of the king, mouth and eyes wide open, his Styrian mother, too, her face spattered with blood.

If he could get to them . . . what a blow for the common man! A blow that would resound across the Circle Sea and around the world as if his clenched fist were the clapper of a great bell. The history books would record *this* as the day of the Great Change, and Gus Turmer as the man who ushered it in!

Except someone stepped in front of the king as Gus laboured to the top of the steps. No armoured Knight of the Body, just a nondescript, curly haired fellow in plain clothes, with a strange, bland smile which did not quite touch his eyes. If this fool thought he could stop the changing of an epoch, rob the people, steal this moment, he was mistaken! Gus was the instrument of history! He was a torrent that could not be dammed!

He raised his sword, shouting, 'The Great Change!' The man seemed to shimmer, to blur. There was a blast of wind, and—

'Oh dear,' said Orso. Mouth all numb. Could hardly make the words.

He'd been thinking when he let the footman buckle his sword on that morning how pointless it was. How he'd never draw the bloody thing. Now he fumbled it from the sheath. He got the blade caught on the back of his chair. Realised there was a piece of metal lodged in the split wood. Must've missed his head by no more than a hand's width.

'Get behind me, Mother,' he said, pawing at her shoulder, but his voice was an echoing burble. Like water sloshing at the bottom of a very deep drain. His head hurt. His jacket felt all sticky inside. Bloody hell, was he wounded? Or was it someone else's blood? That's the thing about blood. King's or commoner's, everyone's looks much the same.

Where were the Knights of the Body? Weren't they supposed to handle this type of thing? The absolute point of the bastards, wasn't it? He saw one dead with a piece of metal through his breastplate. So he could hardly be blamed. Where was Bremer dan Gorst? Had given him the day off. Insisted on it. Terrible decision. Did Orso make any good ones? Couldn't think of any. Probably the blame was his. It usually was. A king was just a kind of bin for all the blame to go in.

No one up here would be much use in a fight. Curnsbick had his hands pressed to his horrified face. Kort had scrambled for the rear. Funny, when death's on the table, how vitally important it seems that one be killed last.

He felt very tired. As if he'd run a mile. Papers were fluttering down. Scorched pamphlets. Whole thing was like a nightmare. One was still burning as it fell beside him. He scrubbed it out under his boot. Could've been dangerous. Almost wanted to laugh at that. But not for long.

Someone was coming up the steps to the royal box. A big man wearing a dark coat. Thin yellow hair stirred by the smoky wind. A cloth wrapped around his face so Orso could only see his eyes. Hard eyes. Furious about something. There was a sword in his hand. An old, cheap sword, but cheap swords can still kill you.

All seemed so unlikely. Orso was a pleasant fellow, wasn't he? Always tried to see other people's points of view. To be polite. He could hardly believe this man had come here to murder him. There might have been a dozen killers crowding towards the steps, and none looked likely to be moved by politeness.

'Oh dear,' said Orso again. Probably the best chance was if he met them at the top of the stair. But he was worried if he took a step he might fall over. Then a hand caught his shoulder.

'If I may, Your Majesty?' It was Sulfur, brushing past and carefully, almost daintily, stepping over High Justice Bruckel's corpse. Orso had forgotten the magus was even there.

The big Burner raised his sword, the cloth over his mouth fluttering faintly as he shouted something. 'A great shame!' Orso thought it might have been, a sentiment with which he could readily agree. He narrowed his eyes, expecting that blade to swing down and split the humble representative of the Order of Magi in half.

But Sulfur had already moved. With breathtaking, impossible speed. Orso's eyes could barely follow him. His fist sank into the Burner's gut with a wet-sounding thud, so hard it folded him in half, lifted him right off his feet then dropped him on the floor of the royal box like a heap of rags, his cheap sword clattering from his hand and bouncing harmlessly from Curnsbick's leg.

The next Burner raised his shield. Sulfur's fist was a blur that turned it into flying splinters, folded the man's arm back on itself, ripped his head half-off in a spray of blood and sent him flopping like a rag doll among the benches below. Sulfur had already caught a woman by her hair, ripped her head down and smashed his knee into her face with a bang so loud it set Orso's ears ringing again.

He flinched as blood spotted the royal box, stared in horror as a man was smashed into a shape no man should ever be with one chop of an open hand. Sulfur caught another under the jaw, a board cracking beneath his heel as he flung the man high into the sky, his echoing shriek fading as if he had been shot from a cannon. Sulfur backhanded a third man and sent him tumbling bonelessly end-over-end, tangled up with fluttering festoons of the bunting that had decorated the royal box.

Orso was not sure whether he was trying to shield his mother or cling to her for support. In the space of a breath, maybe two, Sulfur reduced half a dozen assassins to flying meat. Corpses turned inside out, twisted into corkscrews, popped open or crushed in on themselves. Worse than anything the exploding engine had done to the people down near the tracks.

A man screamed through the cloth around his face as Sulfur caught the wrist of his sword-arm, the joint popping apart in his grip, and dragged him close. The scream turned to a bubbling groan, and there was a crunching, cracking, slurping, the back of Sulfur's head jolting like a famished dog's at its dinner.

'An Eater,' breathed Queen Terez. Orso made a point of never arguing with his mother. While watching a man rip into another with his teeth was no time to start. Orso's father had fought Eaters at the Battle of Adua. When Orso asked him what it was like, he had turned pale, and said nothing. Now, as the man Sulfur had thrown into the sky plummeted down and crashed into the ground thirty strides away, he finally understood why.

The last of the Burners was running. Orso caught a glimpse of her terrified eyes as she dropped her axe and bolted. Sulfur let the limp corpse fall, its throat one single glistening black wound. The air about his shoulders shimmered, like the horizon on a hot day. Orso flinched as the woman burst into flames, fell to the ground on fire, thrashing and squealing.

Perhaps they were living in the age of reason, but anyone proclaiming the death of magic had done so, it seemed, a little prematurely.

Sulfur turned towards Orso with the very same smile he had worn before the explosion. But what had been a bland salesman's grin was become a monster's leer, dotted with shreds of flesh, his mouth daubed red, different-coloured eyes twinkling with the reflected flames of the woman he had somehow set on fire.

'So, might I speak to the lord chancellor?' Sulfur asked.

Orso was not sure what word he wanted to make, but what came from his mouth was a breathy, 'Uh?'

'Regarding the funding for new track-roads, Your Majesty. Under the auspices of the Banking House of Valint and Balk.'

Orso stood staring for what felt like a very long time, one hand weakly holding his mother's limp arm, his sword dangling uselessly from the other. He would have dropped it had his fingers not been stuck in the elaborate basketwork. The first of the attackers lay on his side at their feet, the cloth twisted from his stubbly face, a steadily widening pool of blood bubbling from his nose and mouth.

'Yes,' muttered Orso. 'Yes . . . of course.'

Sulfur looked down at himself and frowned, as if he had only just now realised he was spattered red from head to toe. He dragged a hank of bloody hair from between his fingers and flicked it away.

'I should probably change first.'

Through the steady hiss in his ears, Orso could hear shouting. Sobbing of wounded. Cries for help. A breeze came up and kissed his sweaty face. Perhaps the future they were heading for was not quite the one that Curnsbick was selling. His knees felt very weak.

'Sorry, Mother,' he muttered, flopping back into his chair. 'Need to sit down.'

A Fitting Welcome

'What the hell are we all here for anyway?' grumbled Downside, uncomfortable in his finery, though his finery came down to a new cloak over his scarred mail and having cleaned his boots for the first time in six months. He hadn't even done a good job of that.

'To give the Young Lion a fitting welcome,' said Clover.

'Weren't we fighting that Union bastard a few months back? Fitting welcome for him would be an axe in the head.'

'Axe in the head is your answer to everything,' muttered Sholla, who'd borrowed some mail for the occasion she could only make fit by tightening five belts about her scrawny person.

'All too true.' Clover nodded sadly. 'And an inadequate response in affairs of state, I think it's fair to say.'

'In whats o' what?' mumbled Downside, baffled.

'This is all about presentation.' Clover nodded towards Stour's War Chiefs and Named Men, lining both sides of Skarling's Hall. The best of the best, and in their best gear, so many jewels and gildings being flaunted, Clover was half-blinded by all the glitter whenever the sun came out. 'Show o' strength. Display o' power. We don't need a fire, 'cause the day is warm, but they've banked the fire high just to show they can.' And indeed, those unlucky enough to be standing close to the blaze were sweating through their mail from it. 'It's not so much what the welcome says about the guest as what it tells the guest about the host.'

Downside looked more baffled than ever. 'What?'

'Stour wants all these bastards here because it makes him look big,' said Sholla.

'Ah. Why didn't you just say that?'

Clover sighed. 'Because I have this girl to translate into halfhead for me.'

'What the hell is this?' Greenway was pacing the room, making sure

257

everything met his standards, as if he had any. Now he'd come up to Sholla, sneering so hard it was a wonder his skull wasn't showing. 'Why the shit did you bring *her*?'

Clover heard Downside give a disgusted grunt and shot an arm out in front of him 'fore he exposed Greenway's skull for real.

'You told me bring two o' my best,' said Clover, with his usual calming grin. Felt like a keeper in a menagerie, sometimes, always struggling to stop the animals killing each other. 'You didn't want her here, you should've given more thought to what *best* meant.'

Greenway made great spectacle of sucking his teeth as he turned away. If tooth-sucking had been the measure of a man, he'd have had a place in the songs, all right. Sholla took it well. If you could say a rock takes a rain shower well. Downside, on the other hand, was a man who made a point of taking everything badly.

'Going to let that fucking arsehole sneer at one of our own?' he growled in Clover's ear.

'You sneer at her often enough.'

'She knows it's in fun.'

Sholla raised her brows. 'How would I know that?'

Downside ignored her. He ignored anything that might stop a fight from happening. 'She's three times the man that fool is. He looks over here again, I'll break his fucking head open, Skarling's Hall or no.'

'By the dead.' Clover rubbed at the bridge of his nose. Great in a fight if you kept him pointed the right way, but here was why they called him Downside. 'What do you think you'll find in his head worth having? Boy's an idiot. He'll trip over his own cock soon enough, then you can laugh at the outcome without getting your hands dirty. If I've learned one thing, it's that there's rarely any need to wade into the bitter ocean for your vengeance. It'll wash up on the shore soon enough.'

'I never been much for waiting,' grunted Downside, glaring daggers across at Greenway, who was complaining at some Named Man whose cloak-buckle wasn't to his liking. 'Time comes you have to stand up, Chief.'

'Maybe, but I'll tell you one thing for damn sure, the time's not now.' And Clover grinned about the crowded hall like they weren't dancing on the edge o' murder. 'Got to pick your moment, Downside. Can't solve every problem with your fist. Sometimes brain and mouth are better weapons.'

'Those the weapons you been using, the last few days?' asked Sholla.

'As a matter of fact. Went to meet old friends and neighbours, talk things through.'

'What friends and neighbours you got that aren't here?'

'Believe it or not, there was a time before I was nursemaid to you squabbling geese. I've had a long and varied career. Many famous chiefs down the years—'

'Didn't you kill most of 'em?' asked Sholla.

Clover's smile slipped a little. 'A few.'

Downside was busy glowering. He was every bit as deadly with a glower as Greenway was with a sneer, a great fold jutting between his brows and his little lips pressed tight together in his bush of beard. 'Say what you like. I never had a problem I couldn't solve with a big enough blade.'

'Then thank the dead you've had simple problems. You get those on the battlefield, but there's none in Skarling's Hall.'

The doors were swung open, and there was a rustle and a jingle as men shifted to see the Young Lion make his entrance. He looked quite the hero – breastplate, boots and teeth all buffed to a pretty sheen – but it was the woman beside him that really drew the eyes. She seemed to Clover to be an exception to the rule that men get more excited about a woman the less clothes she's got on. Her dress might've been spun from sunlight, glittering as she moved. Jewels on her long fingers, and jewels at her long neck, and a little jewelled sword at her hip, too. You could hardly tell what she really looked like under all that flash and flutter and dancing, prancing strut, but no one seemed to care. There was a jealous stirring among the warriors, an awestruck murmur as if some priceless gemstone had been lifted from its case rather than a woman walked in through the door.

The soldiers and servants in her wake looked somewhat concerned by Stour's fighters bearing in on every side, festooned with steel. Even the Young Lion himself, walking with a trace of a limp, for all he tried to hide it. But his wife glided down the middle like a swan down a river with roses on both banks. She'd smile at one man or another as if at a particularly handsome bloom, and he'd blink, or blush, or look down at his boots, hoary old warriors who'd laughed at red wounds humbled with a red smile.

She stopped beside Clover, and murmured something to her husband, and Clover wondered how her lips could be so pink and her eyes so dark and her skin so pale and perfect. Had to be painted on, like a face onto a Carl's shield, but done with so much craft you could hardly tell. It was the closest thing to magic he'd seen in Skarling's Hall, for all Stour's magi and seers and wise women.

Brock took a step towards them, glanced at Sholla and said in very good Northern, 'My wife is asking whether women fight here.'

Clover shook himself like he was waking from a dream. 'Well, now and again in the North we run out o' men. But we never run out o' fights.' He glanced sideways at Sholla and leaned forward to murmur under his breath, 'Then, between you and me, there are times you tell 'em not to fight and they bloody do it anyway.'

Brock rendered it into the Union tongue for his wife, and she gave a laugh as glittering as her dress. Clover wondered how long she'd practised to get it just right but still felt greatly pleased with himself that he'd been the cause of it, then greatly disappointed when she walked on. Downside stared after her like a fox at an open chicken coop.

'Watch out,' muttered Sholla. 'You might both die o' thirst from all that drooling.'

'The Great Wolf!' called Leo dan Brock, spreading his arms as he came towards the dais. 'Greater than ever! King of the Northmen, no less!' And he offered Stour his hand.

'The Young Lion!' Stour rose from Skarling's Chair. 'Not as young as you were, but no worse for that.' He caught Brock's hand, and pulled him up onto the dais, and flung his other arm around his shoulders, and slapped him on the back with an echoing clap. Then the two of 'em had one of those hugs which is halfway to a wrestling match, making out they were best of friends while each tried to drag the other off his feet.

'This is my wife, Lady Savine,' said Brock, once they'd finally fought the hugging to an ungainly draw.

And she sank down, rustling skirts spreading across the flags like a pool of gold, so smoothly it seemed she couldn't have any legs at all under there but was mounted on a well-oiled platform. 'My king. It is my honour to meet so great a warrior.'

'Oh, I know a bit about honour.' Stour grinned down at her from the dais. 'And it's *all* mine.' Her Northern might be poor, and have a heavy accent, but she'd already worked out where to tickle the Great Wolf. Not that he was too tight a riddle to untangle.

Downside leaned towards Clover, still staring at Brock's wife. 'I have *got* to get me one o' those . . .'

Sholla rolled her eyes. 'Like *you* could afford it.'

Diplomacy

By the dead, diplomacy was hard work.

'So, you see...' Leo stumbled on, 'the Closed Council have to be stopped. Before they do more damage. We need good men in charge. Honest men. Patriots.'

'Oh, aye?' grunted Stour, tossing a bone onto the floor.

The Great Wolf made no effort to hide his boredom at all this talk of tax and injustice and patriotism, and Leo hardly blamed him. When Isher spoke about this stuff it made sense right off, but Leo was always tripping on the details. And here, at a feast in Skarling's Hall, surrounded by red-handed warriors, the arguments all sounded so flimsy and ridiculous. By the dead, he was boring himself. There'd been enough bloody *talk*. What he needed to do was *do*. But one thing he'd learned over the last year – before you draw your sword, you need to know how you'll *win*.

To win, he needed the King of the Northmen.

Flattery always did the trick for Savine. Leo puffed out his cheeks, looking at the crowd of Named Men down the great horseshoe of tables. 'You've summoned quite the host,' he said. 'The North seems stronger than ever. More united than ever.'

'Why wouldn't it be?' Black Calder leaned past his son to point a frown at Leo as hostile as a drawn dagger.

'Now, now, Father.' Stour wagged a greasy finger. 'I said be polite.'

When it came to flattery, Leo was more used to taking than giving. He wished he was down there with the warriors, drinking and singing and slapping backs, with no worries but a sore head in the morning. By the dead, diplomacy was hard work.

He felt Savine's gentle touch on his arm. 'You fought the man and won,' she murmured in his ear. 'Surely you can *talk* to him?'

The thing about killing a man – you could do it in a moment. Bringing him around to your way of thinking took so much *patience*. And how could you even tell when it was done? Kill a man, he stayed dead. Change his mind, he always had the bloody chance to change it back.

'Reckon I'd rather fight him again.' He glanced over, and caught Black Calder glaring back. 'Specially with his father judging every word.'

'If I had known we were bringing overbearing parents, we could have packed some of our own.' Savine sat forward. 'I must say that you speak the common tongue wonderfully well, Lord Calder!'

She could usually slit a man right open with one compliment, but Black Calder was better armoured than most. 'My own father always said it serves a man well to learn the ways of his enemies,' he grunted.

'And even better to learn the ways of his friends. I have been trying to garner some words of Northern, but I fear I am a poor study.'

'Oh, no doubt.' Calder snorted. 'The first thing I think when I look at you is – there's a woman who's not crafty enough.'

Leo clenched his fist around his eating knife. He was damned if he'd let this old prick insult his wife, but before he could speak, Savine's hand clamped tight on his sore thigh and cut him off in a pained squeak. 'You, I think, are a man with craft to spare.' The ruder Calder got, the wider she smiled. 'Perhaps you might tell me something of the history of Skarling's Hall.'

'What am I, some bloody storyteller—'

'Father!' growled Stour. 'There isn't a man in this hall wouldn't kill for the chance to teach the Lady Governor a few words of Northern. Stop insulting my guests and make yourself useful.'

With bad grace, which seemed the only grace he had, Black Calder stood, leaned close to his son's ear and whispered loud enough for everyone to hear. 'They want something. Don't say yes because you feel you should, or because you feel you're bored, or because of anything you *feel*, you understand? Make sure they *pay*.'

'I know what to do,' snapped Stour.

Savine gave Leo a wink as she took Black Calder's bony hand and let the old man lead her from the dais. 'Black Dow fought the Bloody-Nine right there,' he was saying.

'You saw it yourself?' breathed Savine, as if she'd never been so thrilled.

Stour worked his tongue around his sharp teeth as he watched them go. 'Whatever my father says, it's quite the honour to host you, Young Lion. And your wife, who's clearly as clever as she is beautiful and I daresay knows a lot more Northern than she's letting on. But I don't reckon you suffered our roads all the way up to Carleon for my ale and my father's stories.' He licked his fingers while he looked sidelong at Leo. 'What are you after?'

Now was the moment, then. Courage, courage. He was the Young Lion, wasn't he? He leaned in, speaking in an urgent whisper. 'The Closed Council have to be stopped.'

'And you're the man who'll do it?'

'We're the *men* who'll do it.'

Stour raised one brow, as if he had his doubts.

'I want you with me on a grand adventure!' Leo tried to elbow through the detail and summon up some *passion*. 'To win glory, and set the world right, and make friends of every decent man in the Union!'

Sad to say, Stour didn't slit his hand and swear a blood oath to their alliance on the spot. Instead, he sat back, toying with his ale cup.

'So . . . you're asking for warriors of the North . . . to sail to Midderland in their thousands . . . and fight against the big king in Adua?'

'Yes!' Leo thumped his knife point-down into the table and left it wobbling there. 'You see it!'

'Who's with you?'

'The great lords of the Open Council. Isher, Heugen, Barezin and more. Famous names.' Leo paused. But he'd been honest with Rikke. Honesty would serve him best with Stour. 'And Uffrith.'

Nightfall showed his teeth. You couldn't deny he was a handsome bastard, especially when he was angry. 'Paid that Long-Eyed little witch a visit, did you? The two o' you used to be proper close, if I remember.' Stour stuck his greasy thumb in his mouth and made a little popping sound. 'You got a way with the women, Young Lion, that I can't deny.'

Leo glanced towards Savine, who was draining an ale horn while a group of warriors watched in rapt admiration. Even Black Calder had a look of some respect as she wiped her mouth and held it out for more. 'Please,' she said, 'my mother drinks more on a workday morning.'

Those men who could speak common laughed, and the ones who couldn't pretended they could and laughed even louder.

'But I'm not a woman,' said Stour, 'and my father might be quite the carper, but he knows a thing or two. So the question keeps drifting past – what's in it for me? You offering a piece of Midderland?'

Leo laughed. 'No one in the Union would ever stand for that.'

'A slice of Angland?'

Leo frowned. '*I'd* never stand for that.'

'Uffrith, then?'

'I think we settled that question in the Circle,' said Leo stiffly.

'Daresay you want me on my best behaviour, too.' Stour stuck out his bottom lip. 'Not even a little pillage on the way to battle.'

'We have to get the people of Midderland on our side,' said Leo. 'We're coming to free them, not rob them.'

'So, the way you're telling it, your grand adventure's going to *cost* me money. You're saying you'll be my friend, and your Open Council will thank me, and the people of Midderland will love me, but look around you.' And he gestured towards the hall full of warriors. 'I'm shitting friends and pissing thanks. I'm a real loveable bastard.'

'Think of it, though! The Young Lion and the Great Wolf, side by side! Our banners flying together!' Leo shook his fist between them, trying to light the fire in Stour he always felt at the thought of armoured men tramping, horses prancing, cheers of triumph. 'Think of the songs sung of our victory!'

But all Stour gave Leo was another dose of the side-eye. 'Once you've heard one song of victory you've heard 'em all. Swap the names out and it's the same spears shaken and horns blown and bodies carpeting the glen and all that shit. You see my friend Clover down there?' And he pointed out that balding bastard, the one who'd had the girl beside him with all the belts. 'That fat fool used to be Jonas Steepfield.'

'Steepfield?' Leo frowned. 'The one who held the pass at Grey Breaks? The one who killed Cairm Ironhead?'

'Aye. *That* one. He had all the glory a man could ask for. Now look at the fucker.'

'I thought you and I were the same! Men who care for nothing but *victory*.'

Stour hooked his chain with a thumb and held it up. 'I'm a king now, Young Lion. Ain't just a question of winning, it's *what* you win.'

'I'd rather not bring up your debt—'

'Don't, then.'

Leo carried on through gritted teeth. 'But there is one.'

'My life, you mean?' Stour grinned. 'The men the Bloody-Nine beat in the Circle were bound to serve him all their days, but we live in different times. And even if I was willing to clean your boots, no one else here owes you a fucking thing. You'll find no one better with a sword than me, Young Lion. You know that. But I doubt I'll beat the whole Union on my own.'

Leo took a disappointed swig of ale. 'I never expected the Great Wolf to turn coward.'

The sharpest barb he could find, and it bounced off Stour's grin. 'Coward I may be, Young Lion. But I'm a coward you need.'

Leo couldn't deny it. He slumped back and watched the warriors roar in delight as Savine called them cunts in Northern and pretended not to understand.

By the dead, diplomacy was hard work.

The Wolf's Jaws

Savine rather enjoyed watching Leo sleep.

When she agreed to marry him, she had expected to quickly become bored. To spend time on long trips. Maybe take a lover, in due course. But there was a lot to like about the Young Lion. Honesty, loyalty, courage, passion. Old-fashioned virtues, perhaps. The virtues of a really excellent dog. But virtues she was starting to appreciate. Even to admire. He was a decent man, in several ways that actually counted. Enough to make her feel almost decent when she was beside him. And that was a pleasant feeling. Certainly a refreshing one.

He shifted in his sleep, drawing the furs up around his chin. For such a strong man, such a bold fighter, he could be strangely childlike. So trusting, so optimistic, so vain. He treated the world like an implausible storybook and, though it had thus far played along, she doubted it would do so for ever. Their mothers had been right, they were well matched. The impetuous optimist and the calculating cynic. He was not weighed down with excessive cleverness, but a clever husband would only have got in her way. She was glad she had married him. The world needs heroes.

But it also needs people who will actually get things done.

She stood, and smoothed her skirts, and checked her face one more time in the distorting square of old mirror. Then she slipped out of the door and, so as not to wake her husband, ever so gently pulled it shut.

The one called Greenway was skulking in the corridor outside. It seemed when it came to Northmen, the more picturesque the name, the more of a self-regarding thug it belonged to.

He gave her a leering look up and down. 'Can't give you long.'

Gold flashed in the shaft of light from the narrow window and she pressed the coin into his palm. 'Best not waste our time, then.'

*

She heard the blades before she saw them. That familiar scrape of steel, shuffle of feet, grunting of snatched breath.

She stepped out into a narrow yard beside Skarling's Hall, a circle of patchy lawn hemmed in by grey stone walls, a training dummy in old mail and battered helm leaning against a rack of swords and spears.

Two men prowled the edge of the grass with shields and long sticks, bulky with straw matting. Stour stood between them, sword in hand, stripped to the waist, lean and muscular and shining with sweat, steaming faintly in the dawn chill. Savine wondered if this display of raw manliness was for her benefit. More than likely. Who understood the importance of appearances better than she did, after all?

The so-called Great Wolf sprang hissing at one of his training partners, so suddenly and so savagely Savine put a protective hand over her belly on an instinct. She had to force herself not to jerk back as Stour chopped at the shield and sent splinters flying, ducked the stick and darted under it, shoving the man against the wall with his shoulder and making him grunt. Stour caught the rim of the shield, kneed the man in the gut, then dealt his leg a vicious blow with the flat of his sword and dropped him mewling on the ground.

All done in a couple of breaths' worth of focused violence, so that as his other training partner lumbered up, the King of the Northmen was already prancing away on the balls of his feet. Through sweat-dark hair, his eyes slid over to Savine.

'Like what you see?' He spoke the common tongue after all. But she had guessed that at the feast, from the way he had listened to her and Leo talking.

'Who wouldn't?' She made herself step forward, around the fallen man, groaning as he clutched at his straw-padded leg. 'The Great Wolf! Grandson of Bethod and rightful King of the Northmen! The greatest warrior in the Circle of the World, they say, and I can well believe it.'

'You're almost as quick with a compliment as I am with a sword.' Stour loosed a flurry of lightning jabs at the man still standing, point gouging at his shield fast as a woodpecker and making him shuffle nervously back.

'No more than the truth.' It was a while since she'd stepped into a fencing circle herself, but she knew enough about swordsmanship to see his skill. He was even better than Leo. But even more vain, too. She wondered whether that preening arrogance would make an effective shield if Bremer dan Gorst came for him meaning business. It was something she would rather like to see.

'Can't say I don't enjoy your flattery,' he said, grinning, 'but if you want my warriors, you'll need to offer me more.'

'Of course. I will need a gift fit for a king. I was thinking, maybe... Uffrith?'

Stour froze, sword back for another jab. 'Eh?'

'A city by the sea. One of the North's greatest, I am told, though in truth it seemed a little... primitive to me.'

'Well,' he whispered, narrowing those horrible wet eyes at her. 'We're known more for our swords than our cities up here.' He dodged a swing of the stick without even looking, caught it with his free hand, slipped around the shield and clubbed the straw-strapped warrior in the face with the pommel of his sword.

The man gave a sharp cry as he fell to his knees with his hands to his bloody mouth. Stour gave a sneer of disgust as he planted his boot on the man's chest and shoved him onto his back. 'Didn't realise Uffrith was yours to give.'

'It is mine to let you take.' Savine walked closer, shrugging as if they talked of the weather. 'What's a Protectorate without anyone protecting it, after all?'

'Available.' And Stour nudged his fallen sparring partner towards the archway with a lazy kick. 'You got some bones, woman, stepping into the wolf's jaws this way. Got to admire that. But I do worry.' He rolled the man over with another kick and made him squeal. 'I worry you might be one o' those folk likes to promise everything to everyone and somehow thinks she'll never be called on to pay.'

He stepped closer, raising his sword, point towards her, and it took all her courage to stand her ground. She could tell from the murderous glint on its edge that this was no practice blade. 'I worry you can't be trusted.' And he brushed her neck gently with the point.

They called him the Great Wolf and Savine did not doubt he was well named. She could hear his growling breath. Smell his sour sweat. A wild dog indeed. And you cannot show a dog your fear. Her skin crawled, her heart thudded, but she forced herself to stand still, forced herself to meet his eye as the cold point tickled at her throat, then along her shoulder, caught something just inside her collar and eased it out.

'After all...' Dangling from the end of his sword was the necklace of runes Rikke had given her. 'Aren't you and your husband best of friends with that fucking witch?'

It was an apt word for Rikke these days. Savine had almost flinched at the sight of the tattoos inked into her bony face, one of the pale eyes she had once so admired seeing nothing, the other far too much. She thought of Rikke's hand resting on her stomach. Her delighted laugh as the baby shifted. The truest person he knew, Leo had said, and Savine felt a pang of guilt. A rare thing for her. Rarer than ever, since Valbeck. But she had chosen her path, and it led to the throne, whoever she had to step over on the way. Conscience would have been even worse to show than fear.

'Trust is a poor foundation for an alliance. Almost as poor as friendship.' Savine stared at Stour down the blade of his sword. 'Both can shake loose in a storm, and there is a storm coming. Self-interest, on the other hand, has deeper roots. We need you. And you need us. Today, and tomorrow. Rikke is useful to us today. But afterwards . . . ?'

She stepped forwards. Stepped forward so suddenly she gave Stour no choice but to stab her through the throat or pull his sword away. Close as they were he had no room, caught his arm against his body, twisted his wrist clumsily and had to let his sword drop, clattering down between the two of them.

'Afterwards, you will be lord from the Whiteflow to the Crinna and beyond. A true King of the Northmen.' She sank down, and took his sword gently by the blade, and offered the hilt to him as she stood. '*All* of them. Something I understand your father could never quite manage.'

'Well, in *that* case . . .' He wrapped his fingers around the grip, his eyes flicking about all over her face and his teeth bared in a hungry grin. 'You've got yourself a deal.'

'Of course.' She smiled as she stepped away. As if she never had any fear, or any conscience, or any doubts at all. If you think it often enough, perhaps it makes it so. 'I never offer deals until I know they will be taken.'

'Reckon I'd better gather my warriors.'

'The best you have, and plenty of them. If we lose, you get nothing.'

'I'll empty the North o' men!' growled Stour. 'A host that hasn't been seen since the days of Skarling Hoodless, how's that?'

'And, while on Union soil, their best behaviour?'

'The good folk of Midderland will hardly guess the wolves are among 'em.'

'All I could ask and more.' She turned towards the staircase. Towards her husband. Towards safety.

'I'm guessing the Young Lion doesn't know about this?' called Stour.

'There are things decent men will not do, but some of them must be done. That's why he has me.'

'And when he finds out?'

'I daresay he will be upset, but . . . by then the North will be yours.'

'And the Union yours.'

And its new king and queen would have bigger concerns.

Stour grinned. 'I like your husband. He's got a lot of heart. But do you know the thing I'm getting to admire most about him?' He turned and swung in one slick motion, sword flashing in the sunlight, and struck the dummy's head from its straw-stuffed shoulders, battered helmet clattering away into a corner. 'His taste in women.'

Questions

They'd worked on his hand.

The bruises on his face and the cut above his eye were faded. Probably happened when they blew up Curnsbick's engine. But the hand was more recent.

There was nothing artful about it. Smashed with a hammer, maybe. One of those hammers with teeth that butchers use to make meat tender. It looked like he was wearing a big, red, floppy glove. It looked like mincemeat moulded into the shape of a hand by a bored butcher. It certainly didn't look like a hand that would be attempting to kill any kings again soon. Or doing anything much ever.

'You know they've barely started,' said Vick.

His red-stained eyes crept across to her.

'What they've done there . . .' She glanced down at that mess on the end of his arm. 'Is just to show you they mean business. That's a handshake. If I'm not happy with your answers, well . . .' She leaned forward to whisper, 'I hear Old Sticks has taken a personal interest in your interrogation.'

He swallowed, the lump on his throat shifting.

'And once Old Sticks gets out the instruments . . .' She gave a long, soft whistle. 'You'll be *begging* for them to shake the other hand.'

'I told 'em everything I know,' he croaked out.

'Everyone does. But they might've missed something. You might've missed something. Something you didn't even realise mattered.'

'Will it make any difference?'

'It might.' To her, at least. For him, there was no help. His Majesty's Inquisition tended away from leniency when it came to attempted regicide. 'Who planned it?'

'The Weaver . . .' he croaked.

Vick narrowed her eyes. 'Risinau?'

271

'Never met him.' He shrugged as if lifting his shoulders took all the strength he had. 'That's what they told me.'

'Who told you?' His head was slipping sideways, eyelids fluttering. Vick snapped her fingers in front of his face. 'Who told you?'

'The Burners. Judge.'

Just the sort of bloody theatrics the woman was infamous for. 'Judge put you up to this?'

'Judge gave me the chance. I didn't need no putting up.' He worked himself taller. A touch of pride to his backbone. A spark of fire in his eye. 'My wife worked in a mill in the Three Farms. Always worried about the machinery. I told her not to, but she always worried. Foreman would make her work late some days. Asleep on her feet, but we needed that job. One day she stumbled, and the buckle on the drive belt caught her. They said it snatched her off her feet like the hand of Euz. Flung her twenty strides into the ceiling so hard she broke one of the beams. Hardly had a bone in her body wasn't shattered. Her head then looked worse'n my hand now.' He spat the words, tears starting to gather in his eyes. 'So I got *no* regrets! The Weaver gave me the chance. Strike a blow for the common man! Our blow might've missed the mark, but it won't be the last.'

'Oh, don't be too hard on yourself,' said Vick. 'Your blow didn't miss everyone. It killed dozens of honest folk who'd come to watch an engine toddle across some fields on a summer morning! What about those poor bastards, eh? What about their wives and husbands and fathers and children? We've all got sad stories, arsehole!'

'Sacrifices have to be made! Would've been worth it, if His fucking Majesty didn't have that Eater watching him.'

Vick frowned. She'd had a sense something had been cut from the reports. 'Eater?'

'We had the knights beaten! Then that little nothing-looking bastard... he killed Turmer. Killed 'em all. Flung 'em about like they were straw.'

She remembered what Shenkt had done to those two Practicals, on the quay in Westport. Big men, tossed like dolls.

'But it don't matter what devil deals you strike.' The prisoner nodded to himself, a strange little smile quivering on his lips. 'Don't matter how many Eaters you bring, or how many soldiers you hire, or how many folk have to die. There's a Great Change coming.'

Vick gave a weary sigh. 'Where's Judge?'

'A Great Change.' His bloodshot eyes had drifted beyond her, gazing into the bright future, maybe. 'And all the owners, and the bankers, and the kings, and the magi shall be swep' away!

She remembered what Vitari had told her, in that shack on the Westport waterfront. That the Union was Bayaz's tool, the banks and the Inquisition his puppets, that she was already dancing to his tune. She didn't like the thought that there might be some hidden world beneath this one. A world of Eaters, and magi, and secret powers. As if she swam out on a lake, seeing the ripples on the surface, never guessing there were hidden deeps below, ruled over by who knew what unknowable monsters. She shook the worry off. She had to stick to what could be touched, explained, offered up in evidence. 'Where's Risinau?' she growled.

'The House of the Maker will open!' he barked in a broken voice. 'And those that were first will be last, and the last first!'

She thought about smashing her fist down on that mess of a hand while she screamed the questions in his face. But he had no answers. None that helped her, anyway. She got up and left him ranting, as mad as any of the cut-price prophets in Westport's Temple Square.

'The gates shall be laid wide and Euz shall come again! And all shall be set right! You hear? A Great Change is—'

She pulled the door shut and clipped his voice back to a muffled burble. A Practical stood outside, arms folded.

'His Eminence wants you,' came hissing from his mask. '*Right now.*'

Vick strode past the eternally disapproving secretary, between the two towering Practicals and into the Arch Lector's office, the door shutting behind her with a final-sounding *click*. Time for some answers, maybe. Or at least for some questions.

'Your Eminence, I have some questions about—' She stopped with Bayaz's name on the tip of her tongue as Glokta's guest turned in his chair, raising an urbane eyebrow.

'Inquisitor Teufel!' It was only the bloody king. 'I never got the chance to thank you for your help in Valbeck. You made *me* look good, and that takes some damn doing. That note of yours saved my arse, not to mention several thousand others.' His smile faded somewhat. 'Shame it couldn't save everyone's, really. And now I hear you pulled our feet out of the fire in Westport, too!'

Vick cleared her throat. 'I am... delighted I could assist... Your Majesty.' She had slipped into the smooth, aristocratic, slightly constipated tone her mother might have used to greet the king. The full Victarine dan Teufel. Pathetic, really. The king's so-called justice had sent her family to their deaths and her to rot in Angland, and here she was grovelling before the latest occupant of the throne. That was the Union for you: nobleman, peasant or convict, deference was baked in.

'I swear, you were the one person in Valbeck who kept their wits entirely about them.' The king wagged a finger at her as she sat beside him. 'I thought then – next time I'm on a sinking ship, *that's* the woman I want rowing the lifeboat.' And he reached out as if to clap her on the shoulder, must have sensed her deep discomfort, and ended up giving the back of her chair an awkward pat instead.

She had to admit she enjoyed the gratitude. It wasn't something she tasted often and, like drink, if you only take it rarely a small measure can make you giddy. Any gratitude. Let alone a king's. But as the silence stretched, she began to consider that bit about the lifeboat and cleared her throat again. 'Is . . . the ship sinking, then?'

'There might be some bailing to be done,' came a voice from behind. Vick turned, surprised. A man was leaning against the wall beside the door. A man she somehow had no inkling was there until he spoke. An unexceptional man with curly hair. Average height, average build, average everything. The very look Vick aimed for herself, when she wanted to blend into anonymity. The exceptional ordinariness of the expert spy. Or the master assassin. It put her instantly on guard.

'Do you know Yoru Sulfur?' asked Glokta.

'We have never met,' said Sulfur, 'though I, too, am a great admirer of your work in Valbeck.' He gave her a neat little bow. 'I was once apprentice to the First of the Magi.'

Vick kept her face carefully neutral, but it was a struggle. Shenkt had said the Union was Bayaz's tool, and now she found his agent at his grinning ease with the nation's two most powerful men. 'And now?' she asked.

'His watchful eye, his sympathetic ear—'

'His punishing fist?' asked Orso.

'Let us say his guiding palm,' said Sulfur. 'By all means, pretend I am not here.'

'Not easily done,' murmured the king, holding out a folded paper to Vick between two fingers. 'I received another eye-opening note this morning. One that may give us more bailing to do than in Valbeck and Westport combined.'

Vick took it, unfolded it and began to read.

Your Majesty,
  There is a plot against you.
  Your Open Council plans to steal your throne.

They have powerful allies in the North. They look for more in Styria.
They will land their troops on the northern coast of Midderland on
the last day of summer, declare themselves patriots and march on Adua.
You should prepare. But you should have care how you prepare. There
is a traitor in your Closed Council, too.
With Best Wishes,
A Friend

Vick swallowed, her skin unpleasantly prickling. A plot. The Open Council. Allies in the North and Styria. A traitor in the Closed Council. This could be a threat to make the uprising in Valbeck look like a village dance.

'A Friend?' The writing was odd. Carefully formed. Almost a little childlike. Vick turned the letter over, studied the ink, felt the paper, smelled it, even. But there were no clues to who wrote it. 'Any idea who this friend might be?'

'None,' said Glokta. 'But people keen to declare themselves a friend are usually anything but.'

'Even enemies can tell you the truth,' said Orso. 'Relations between the Crown and the Open Council haven't been this bad since... well, the last civil war, I suppose. Probably best not to dwell on how that ended...'

Widespread murder and destruction culminating in the violent overthrow and execution of a king. She placed the letter carefully on the Arch Lector's desk. 'Who on the Open Council might have the audacity, the grievance and the resources for treason?'

'Just about any of them.' Glokta licked at his empty gums. 'Just about all of them.'

'But if I had to pick a man to declare himself a patriot while doing it, Isher would be the one.' Orso disgustedly adjusted his cuffs. 'He tricked me into that mistake with Wetterlant, and I've no doubt he manoeuvred Leo dan Brock into his little display of petulance at the trial.'

The Arch Lector was looking even more pale than usual. 'Isher and Brock were married together...' One of them to his own daughter, as they were no doubt all well aware.

'Enemies on the Open Council are one thing,' said Vick. 'Their military resources are limited. The Lord Governor of Angland is another. He commands an army of thousands. Well equipped, experienced, loyal.' That prickling sensation was spreading. 'Could Brock be a part of this?'

The king took a long breath through his nose and let it sigh away. 'Powerful allies in the North...'

'Your Majesty.' Glokta winced as he tried to straighten in his wheeled chair. 'If suspicion falls on my son-in-law, it must also fall on my own daughter. As your Arch Lector, I must be above reproach. I should tender my resignation, or at least recuse myself from this—'

Orso waved it away. 'I won't hear of it, Your Eminence. You're the one man on the Closed Council I entirely trust. You're simply far too widely hated to make a good conspirator.'

Glokta gave a weary snort. 'Immensely kind of you to say so, Your Majesty.'

'Besides, we have no evidence. The one thing I'm sure Leo dan Brock is guilty of is finding me contemptible. If that's a crime, I'll have to hang three-quarters of the country. Have you seen the latest pamphlets? About me? About my mother? About the debt?'

'Outrageous lies, of course,' threw in Sulfur.

'Yet people can't get enough of them.'

'We could arrest Isher,' offered Vick. 'I daresay we could pry the truth out of him.'

'Tempting.' Glokta shook his head. 'But after that business with Wetterlant, no one on the Open Council trusts us. We cannot afford to hand them more martyrs. We must tread carefully and bring plenty of proof wherever we go.'

'In the meantime, we take the advice of our anonymous friend and prepare,' said Orso. 'We raise our own forces, we gather every ally we can find.'

'We are spread thin, Your Majesty.' Glokta spread his thin hands. 'The King's Own are scattered across the Union keeping down the Breakers.'

'Colonel Forest helped me raise several thousand soldiers to fight in the North. The Crown Prince's Division.' Orso smiled, as if at a happy memory. 'It might be re-formed.'

'At a cost.'

'In such dark times as these,' said Sulfur, 'I have no doubt that the Banking House of Valint and Balk would prove generous.'

Again, Vick kept her face expressionless, but she nearly shivered at the memory of Shenkt's chill breath on her cheek. He had spoken of Valint and Balk, too.

'By *generous*,' said Glokta, wiping a long tear from his cheek as his eyelid flickered, 'I assume you mean further loans at even more crippling rates of interest?'

Sulfur gave a good-natured shrug. 'They are a bank, not a charity.'

'Better to put my crown in hock than have it stolen, I suppose,' murmured Orso, though Vick wondered if there was much difference.

276

'I will go to the North on the next tide,' said Sulfur. 'My master has powerful friends there. If this rebellion *is* real, it may be that I can nip it in the bud.'

'As you nipped the Burners at the demonstration of Curnsbick's engine?' asked Orso.

Was Sulfur the Eater, then? Another like Shenkt? From the white-toothed smile he gave the king, it was not that hard to imagine. 'I would hope more subtly,' he said, 'but no less decisively in defence of Your Majesty's interests.'

'As long as my interests coincide with your master's, I presume.'

'I dare not imagine where they could diverge.' And Sulfur slipped out, pulling the door shut with that final *click*.

Glokta sat forward, hands clasped. 'Inquisitor Teufel, I would like you to observe the other members of the Closed Council. Subtly, of course. If one of them is disloyal, we have to know. Employ only people you trust. Outsiders, if possible.'

'I serve and obey, Your Eminence. Your Majesty.' She stood, then paused with a hand on the back of her chair, thinking.

'Something else?' asked the Arch Lector.

'The note said they are looking for allies in Styria.'

Orso raised one brow. 'And?'

'I may know some people who could help us there.'

The address Shylo Vitari had given her belonged to a basement near the docks, odd lights glowing beyond the coloured glass in the windows, like the lights they say lure sailors into the deep. A man with a battered sea captain's hat and an even more battered moustache slumped against the crooked railings outside with hands wedged in pockets, a sign creaking above him, a woman with a spear and a bottle, a fish's tail instead of legs and a smile that said she'd seen things you couldn't dream of.

The place looked like a child's picture of a nest of Styrian spies. Vick could only assume it was a double bluff. That or their contempt for the Union was so great they weren't even bothering to hide.

The steps led to a warren of gloomy cellars and low vaults that reminded her far too much of the mines in the camps of Angland. The coloured candles were the flickering lamps as they shuffled into the dark, bent double. The clinking of glasses were the clinking of picks as they lay on their sides to nibble at the seam. The shadows writhing on the stained stone walls were her own shadow as she shoved the coal tub on with her scabbed forehead, squirming down shafts too tight to sit up in, icy water lapping at her raw knees, knowing that if the ceiling fell, if a flame caught gas, if water broke through—

She shook herself, trying to shake free of the fear. That was all long ago. That girl was gone, not trapped inside her, screaming to get out.

A man lay rocking in a hammock, tattooed arms folded behind his head, sleepy eyes following her down the tunnel. A couple swayed together to the music of a plaintive violin. It wasn't clear whether they were dancing or fucking or both, but Vick ruled nothing out. A woman shuffling cards on a ruined chaise winked, then pointed on towards a bright space where the ceiling was a little higher and Vick could stand straight.

She'd seen plenty of drinking holes, but never one so well stocked. Shelves were crowded with bottles of gleaming crystal and bland pottery, utterly plain and absurdly ornate. One filled with floating worms. One with a dagger for a stopper. One shaped like a grinning face with stones for eyes.

'At last!' The barman's accent was a strange cocktail – a slosh of Styrian and a dash of the Union with a few more ingredients which were harder to place. Tall and pale, with spiky red hair and a spiky red beard. He had a white cloth over one shoulder and a little monkey squatting on the other and he smiled a wide smile full of good teeth. 'Victarine dan Teufel graces my humble establishment.'

'Have we met?'

'We're meeting now. My mother calls me Cas.' He spread his arms to take in the vast array of bottles. 'But to everyone else I'm just the barman. You don't look like my mother.'

'I think I'd remember. Who's this?'

'My monkey. What can I get you?'

'What've you got?'

'What haven't I got?'

'Has it ever occurred to you that the more choice there is, the harder it becomes to choose?'

'It has been mentioned. But fear is a poor reason to limit your options.' He looked her discerningly up and down, like a tailor guessing a client's measurements. 'Tough day?'

'Is there another kind?'

'Have you ever tried Sworfene?' And he plucked an unassuming bottle of bubbled glass from the top shelf behind him. 'It's only made in one village near Jacra. Hard to find here.' He whipped out two glasses, wiped them with his cloth and poured two little slugs of thick, clear spirit with a practised twist of the wrist.

'What kind of barman pours himself a drink every time?'

'This kind. Don't let the revolting smell put you off.'

'I don't generally.' Vick took a sip and swilled it thoughtfully around her mouth. Up in the camps, they'd distilled every rotten vegetable they could get their hands on, but she'd still never tasted anything worse. Swallowing was against her every instinct. Afterwards, she could hardly breathe. 'What the hell's it made from?' she croaked.

'A secret more closely guarded than the colour of Queen Terez's underclothes. It's an acquired taste.'

'Why would anyone want to acquire that taste?' Vick found she was taking another sip, shuddering as she swilled it around her mouth.

'Strange, isn't it? You keep having to check how disgusting it is. Then, one day, you check and you find you actually like it. Soon after, no other drink will quite scratch that itch. I've often felt that people are the same.' He dipped the tip of his tongue into his glass and thoughtfully smacked his lips. 'The ones you like straight away rarely turn out to be your favourites. I've a feeling you might be an acquired taste, Victarine dan Teufel.'

'Are you flattering me?'

He held up his finger and thumb and peered at her through the tiny space between. 'A little. But with a subtlety and class you don't often get in Adua. Shylo Vitari doesn't like being embarrassed, but she likes people who can manage to do it. She works on the principle that it's your worst enemies that make the best friends. Have you come to take up her offer of employment?'

'No,' said Vick. 'I'm happy where I am.'

'Even though all the days are tough days?'

'Adequately unhappy.'

'So what brings you to my little patch of Styria-in-Midderland?' And the barman raised his red brows as he took a sip of that disgusting spirit. 'Or did you really just stop in for a drink?'

'My employer . . . wants to meet with yours.'

He raised his brows even higher. 'Old Sticks? Wants to meet with Vitari?'

'Let's cut out the middlemen.' She tossed back the last of the spirit. 'King Orso wants to meet with King Jappo.' Even the monkey looked shocked as she slid her empty glass back across the bar. 'Pour us another, eh?'

Tomorrow Came

The thing Broad couldn't believe about Valbeck was how much it hadn't changed.

Not a year ago, smoke poured from the mills as they burned to black shells. Now most of those shells were already demolished and the chimneys thrown up taller than before, smoke pouring from them as they worked. That same perpetual gloom, and scratching smoke, and stink of the great unwashed and unwashable. Those same showers of sparks and blooms of steam and snatches of old worksong from the foundry doorways. The river in its rotten banks was stained again from the dye-works upstream, choked with boats and churned to particoloured froth by bigger waterwheels than ever.

The destruction of the uprising hadn't put off the investors one bit, only opened up new opportunities. Scaffolds teetered everywhere, as if giant spiders were spinning webs over the city. There were barricades about, still, but made from sharpened stakes rather than broken furniture, manned not by shabby Breakers but by King's Own in bright uniforms, ready to crush any sign of disobedience with the full force of His Majesty's heavily armed displeasure. The queues of the broken and needy clogged the streets around the manufactories, rain spitting down on 'em black from soot. Only difference from the sorry processions Broad begged for work in a year before was that they were even longer.

'Any o' you know a man called Sarlby?' he asked, holding up his fist. Wasn't bothering to hide it any more. 'He'd have a tattoo like this one.'

Some flinched away. Some shook their heads. Some barely even seemed to hear him, lost in their own misery.

They'd nearly finished rebuilding the bank, and swabbed away the Burners' slogans, and cleaned up the square before the courthouse. From the three gibbets in front, though, they were doing nearly as brisk a business in hangings as when Judge was in charge. Round the corner, the whores were doing brisk business, too, a clutch of 'em in bedraggled finery, hair gathered up to show bruised necks and skirts gathered up to show pale legs and paint smudged by the summer shower.

'Any o' you girls know a fellow called Sarlby?' Broad asked, holding up a silver mark.

'You talk to those girls, it'll cost you,' said a rat-faced pimp, skulking over from an alleyway.

Broad gave him a look. 'You sure?'

The man frowned, and twitched, and skulked back into the shadows.

Broad turned his hand around to show the back. 'He'd have a tattoo like this one.'

The nearest girl shook her head. He gave her the coin anyway.

'What do you want for it?' she asked, and Broad wondered how young she was under that smeared paint. Young as May. Younger, probably.

'Just take it.'

He trudged down a slum street not far from where he'd once lived, the way just rutted dirt and ashes and rubbish flung out from the houses, dark from the buildings leaning together and the washing flapping in the gritty breeze. There were no drains, only pools of flyblown filth, fenced off in places to make pens for the squealing hogs, their run-off leaking through the slit windows into the cellars where the poorest eked out some kind of a living.

Four men came past with a coffin up on their shoulders and a sad crowd at their backs. Two women walked ahead, in good black dresses. Best clothes round here were the funeral clothes. They were worn often enough, after all. Undertakers were great ones for persuading grieving folk to spend money they didn't have. That way, debt could follow you even into the Land of the Dead.

Broad stood aside to watch the mourners pass. Wanted to give 'em something. The way they'd all chipped in when he lived on a street like this, even when they had next to nothing to give. He wanted to give 'em something but he set his jaw against it. You can't make every problem your problem, Liddy was always telling him. And she was right.

He caught an old man limping along at the back in ragged black. 'You know a fellow called Sarlby?'

'I don't know no one no more.' And he limped on.

The warehouse the Breakers once met in was a shell of blackened timbers. This was where they'd listened to Risinau, all huddling around his lies like a poor family around a one-coal fire, all staring off bright-eyed towards that better tomorrow.

And here it was. Tomorrow came, and it was much like yesterday. Just more so.

A couple of ragged boys were playing in an ash-black gutter, racing woodlice or some such. Broad squatted down beside them.

'You boys know a fellow called Sarlby?' They stared at him, big, round eyes in their thin, dirty faces, like enough to be twins. But then the starving all look the same. 'He'd have a tattoo a bit like this one,' said Broad, holding out his fist, then he turned it over, and opened it, and showed them the silver coin glinting there.

'I've a tattoo like that.'

Broad smiled, but it was hard to keep smiling once he'd turned around. 'Sarlby?' He hardly recognised the man he'd fought beside in Styria, stood beside in Valbeck. His back looked bent somehow, and his hair was clipped short and scattered with bald patches, and his face so lean you could almost see the little fibres shift in his cheeks.

'Gunnar Broad, back from the dead.' Sarlby's voice had a throaty crackle to it. Seemed he'd aged ten years in the ten months since they last spoke. 'Heard you were looking for me.'

'That I am.' Broad caught his hand and shook it, and thought how weak it felt. Like squeezing a glove full of dust.

'I thought maybe you was one of the ones they hanged,' said Sarlby.

'I thought maybe you was, too. Glad to see you're not.'

Sarlby didn't return the well-wishes. Didn't look like he had much room for 'em. 'I see you've prospered,' he said, giving Broad a long look up and down.

Sad thing was he'd picked the most threadbare clothes he could find. Maybe because he didn't want to stand out. Maybe because he was shamed about why he did. Even so, he looked like a rich man among these ghosts and beggars. He'd forgotten how bad it could get. Strange, how quick you forget.

No matter how hungry Sarlby looked, he ate slow. As if it hurt.

He was a shred of the man he'd been. A ghost of himself. Didn't matter how strong you were, or tough, or brave, this life would grind you down soon enough. The work, and the smoke, and the dust, and the sickness, and the rank water and the rotten food and the bad living and the never enough of anything.

'So where you living now?' asked Sarlby, out the side of his mouth as he chewed.

'In Ostenhorm.'

'Angland, eh? Got work up there, then?'

'Some.'

'Not mill work, I reckon.'

'No.' Broad thought about lying. But he owed Sarlby the truth, didn't he? Owed him that much. 'Been working for Savine dan Brock.'

Sarlby gave an ugly snort. 'Savine dan Glokta, you mean. The Darling o' the Slums! You ever see that pamphlet of hers?' He laughed, dry and choking, and it turned into a cough, and he had to wash it down with the thin ale they served here. 'How fucking stupid does she think we are?'

'From what I've seen she's a pretty good judge,' said Broad. 'Of that and most everything else.'

'And what does the likes o' you do for the likes o' her? Turn your hand to millinery, did you? Or have you gone from poacher to gamekeeper?'

'I've done what I had to,' growled Broad, feeling the anger coming up hot. 'I've got a wife and daughter to take care of. They're happy for the first time in years. You think I'm saying sorry for that?'

Sarlby held his eye. 'Didn't ask you to. Just want to know where you stand, is all.'

Broad realised he'd got out of his chair and was bent over the table, clenched fists trembling on the wood and his lips curled back. Realised everyone in the wretched little place was looking at him. He blinked, and slowly lowered himself again, and made his fists unclench. Seemed an effort. Like there were barrel-bands around his hands, holding 'em shut.

'I tried it your way.' He settled his lenses back on his sweaty nose, made himself breathe slow. 'Look where it got us.'

'All we done was take a first step. There'll be many more, on the road to freedom. And much more lost along the way, I don't doubt. Might be I'll never see the end of it.' Sarlby had the light of belief in his eyes. Or maybe the light of madness. Maybe there was no difference. 'But the day'll come when my kind will. Depend on that, Bull Broad. There's a Great Change coming.'

'So . . . you're still with the Breakers?'

Sarlby slowly forked up the last of his food, and slowly chewed it, and looked at Broad with narrowed eyes. 'What's it to you whether I'm with 'em or not?'

Broad paused. Felt like huddling in the trenches at Borletta, his hand on the ladder, waiting to rush at the walls. One more step, then there'd be no going back. He whispered it. 'I need to talk to the Weaver.'

He saw the muscles on the side of Sarlby's gaunt face squirm as he clenched his teeth. 'Well, you've got some fucking nerve. Savine dan

Glokta's errand boy, come back here all fat and shiny, asking to see the Weaver.'

'No one ever accused me o' too little nerve.'

Sarlby barked out a joyless laugh. 'No. No one accused you o' that.' There was silence as he slowly tore off a piece of bread, and slowly swept it around in the gravy on his plate till he'd soaked up every drop. 'But I got to warn you, the cool heads all died wi' Malmer. Feelings are running hot.'

'I need to talk to the Breakers, Sarlby. Cool heads or not.'

'I can take you to 'em.' Sarlby slowly chewed, slowly swallowed, slowly sat back. 'But what happens after ain't up to me.'

Grown Up

'Where's the damn *booze*?' bellowed Jin. He tossed his bag onto a richly upholstered chair and it slid to the floor while he threw open a chest big enough for Leo to have lain down flat in, rooting about inside.

'I'll say this for the Lady Governor,' murmured Jurand, heels clicking as he crossed the floor and gave the shimmering drapes a stroke, 'she can certainly pick a set of rooms.' He nudged the tall windows open, a warm breeze flowing in along with the slap of water and the excited Styrian babble of Sipani's evening crowds.

'How many do we have?' asked Antaup, flicking back that curling forelock as he pulled open a communicating door to another salon full of mirrored luxury.

'Must be five at the least.' Glaward gazed up at the ceiling, which was painted with a lot of smug-looking bastards eating grapes. 'Place is like a palace.'

'Like a palace,' grunted Leo, frowning at two carved cherubs among the gilded moulding. He supposed he was the Lord Governor of Angland and should demand the best of everything. His wife always did. But in truth, luxury made him nervous. Couldn't help thinking what the Dogman might've made of it. Shook his head and murmured, 'State o' this,' and given a little grunt of a laugh, most likely. Leo was carved from the same wood. Always felt happier sleeping in hay than on silk, eating with his hands than with silverware, sitting around a campaign campfire than a dining table. He kept worrying he'd blunder into something and break it.

'Here it bloody is!' Jin had flung back the doors of a vast cabinet to show a collection of spirits big enough for a small but very high-priced tavern. 'Look at *this*!' And he rubbed his hands and set to rifling through the bottles.

Antaup, meanwhile, had flopped back onto the bed with his arms out wide and a great grin across his face. 'Bloody hell, Leo, I swear you've bagged the one woman in the world who could change my mind about marriage. I mean, sending you *off*? To *Sipani*? To have *fun*? With the *boys*?' He barked a disbelieving laugh at the painted ceiling.

'Well, the wedding all happened in such a rush—'

'A reckless charge, might you say?' asked Jurand, raising one brow.

'They're what I'm known for,' said Leo. 'No time to give you bastards the send-off you deserve.' He rubbed nervously at his sweaty throat. 'And it won't be all fun.'

That caused an awkward silence, glass clinking in the background. 'When are you meeting the great King Jappo?' asked Glaward.

'After sundown.'

Antaup sat up. 'Rubs me the wrong way, making nice with one of the Union's worst enemies.' And he punched a pillow as if it was King Jappo's face.

'You know what Stolicus said about enemies, don't you?' said Jurand.

'To kill an enemy is cause for relief,' intoned Leo, in that pompous way Jurand trotted out the quotes. 'To make a friend of him is cause for celebration.'

'You actually read it?'

'Not a bloody page.'

'*Can* you read?' asked Glaward, slinging a heavy arm around Leo's shoulders.

'I can't,' said Jin, pulling a cork with a *thwop* and sniffing at the contents. 'And I'm fucking proud of it.'

Jurand rolled his eyes. 'Can we even find our way to Cardotti's? This bloody city's a warren.'

'A baking warren,' said Glaward, sniffing at the damp circle under one armpit.

'Never fear.' Antaup slipped a dog-eared book from inside his jacket. 'I've got Glanhorm's famous guide to Sipani. And I *can* read. When I've nothing better to do.' He unfolded a cumbersome map from the inside cover and squinted at it in some confusion.

'Does it show the landmarks, and so on?' asked Glaward.

'Points of historical interest?' Jurand leaned over Antaup's shoulder to turn the map all the way around. 'I have to see the ruins of the aqueduct while I'm here—'

'Glanhorm doesn't cover any of that shit.' Antaup set his brows waggling. 'Just the brothels. And Cardotti's House of Leisure is first on the fuck list.'

Jurand rubbed at the bridge of his nose. 'That I have lived to hear the words "fuck" and "list" spoken in sequence.' And he walked to the window and out onto the balcony.

'Haven't you bloody poured anything yet?' grunted Glaward, trying to shoulder Jin out of the way. They jostled each other, then Jin caught Glaward's head in a lock and they started to wrestle, barging into the cabinet and making the bottles rattle. With sorry inevitability, they worked their way down onto the carpet and started to roll about, snapping and grunting.

'D'you yield?' snarled Glaward.

'Fuck yourself!' groaned Jin.

Antaup stepped over them and plucked down a bottle, peering at the label. Leo's leg ruled out wrestling, sadly. He followed Jurand through the stirring drapes.

The sun was sinking towards the hazy maze of roofs, glinting on the water, sending pink and purple and orange flares through the heavens, bringing a hint of silver to the edges of the clouds. Below, outside some tea shop, or winery, or husk-house, or whatever it was they had here, a ragged violinist was wending between the tables, trying to saw a few coppers from the masked revellers with some sad little melody. It was sticky-hot, but there was a breeze that tasted mostly of spice and adventure and just a little canal rot, stirring the hair about Jurand's face. The man simply didn't get any less handsome. That proud, sad, thoughtful expression belonged on some statue from the Old Empire.

'Beautiful,' murmured Leo.

'I know you don't think much of Styria, but even you can't deny...' And Jurand planted his hands on the pitted parapet and looked out at the sunset. 'It's a hell of a romantic setting.'

'The very place for one last revel before a marriage.'

'The marriage happened already, remember?'

Leo frowned as he turned his wedding ring gently around on his finger. 'Hard to forget.'

Things hadn't been quite the same between him and Jurand since he came back from Adua. Since he came back with Savine. Some... *spark* missing. He'd done nothing wrong, but he felt he'd let Jurand down somehow. Broken some unspoken promise between them. He looked at Leo now, that earnest, open look that always seemed to catch him right in the heart.

'Are you sure about all this?' He dropped his voice to a whisper. 'Rebellion?'

Leo gave an impatient twitch. 'We've been over it.' A thousand times, he'd been over it. He was tired of the arguments. 'I know you're a thinker, but sooner or later a man has to get on and *do*.'

'Can we trust Isher and the rest? They're not soldiers. They've never fought a battle—'

'That's why they made me the leader.'

'I wish we weren't keeping it from your mother. She could be a hell of an asset—'

'The time comes for a man to leave his mother at home, Jurand. Along with his doubts.'

'I suppose...'

Leo stepped up to lean on the parapet beside him. Close, so their shoulders were almost touching. Almost, but with a warm chink of Styrian sky between them. 'Look, King Orso's no soldier, either. We'll be taking him by surprise. And when it comes to advice on strategy, I've got you!' And he gave Jurand's shoulder a nudge with his and brought a flicker of a smile to his face. 'Couldn't ask for a better man beside me! And lots of allies. Rikke. Stour. Who knows, maybe the Styrians, too.' He turned to look out across the city. 'If I don't make a bloody mess of it tonight...'

'Come on.' Jurand's turn to give Leo a nudge. 'You know you can be charm itself when you want to be. Just flash that smile of yours and King Jappo will be putty in your hands.' Leo grinned in spite of himself and Jurand grinned back. '*That's* the one.'

A silence, then, while the violin played on, and a pleasure-barge drifted down the grey-green canal below them, masked merrymakers lazing in each other's arms on the upper deck. One of those moments you hope might last for ever.

'I need... to thank you,' said Leo. The words were hard to find, but he had to try. 'For being such a good friend. So patient and so loyal and... I know I can be a little... self-absorbed.' Jurand gave a wry snort at that. 'I just hope you know how much I love—' That word felt oddly dangerous, of a sudden. But he couldn't think of another that fitted. 'All of you,' he added quickly, waving an arm towards the doorway, Jin and Glaward's growling coming faint from beyond. 'Glaward's my conscience, and Jin's my courage, and Antaup's my charm, and you're my—'

'Awkwardness?'

'I was going to say brains. I know how many disasters you've steered me clear of. Maybe you think I don't notice, or I'm not grateful but, well... I do, and I am. I'm just... a lot better at taking credit than giving it, I reckon. You've always been there.' He winced. 'I'm not sure... I can say the same.'

''Course you can.' Jurand's eyelashes fluttered as he looked away. As if he was blinking back tears. 'Life has leaders and followers, we all know that. I'd follow you into hell, Leo.' And he looked back, and reached up, not that far, and put his hand on Leo's shoulder.

They'd touched each other a thousand times. They'd wrestled and sparred and hugged. But there was something different about that touch. More than one old friend supporting another. Far more. Jurand's hand didn't just rest there. It squeezed, ever so lightly, and Leo felt a strange need to tilt his head and press his cheek against it. Take that hand and hold it to his face, to his heart, to his mouth.

Jurand was looking him right in the eyes, lips slightly parted. 'I want to say...'

Leo's throat felt suddenly very tight. 'Yes?'

'I... *need* ... to say—'

'Here you go!' Antaup blundered out through the window, wedged a glass into Leo's hand, another into Jurand's, spattering wine on the balcony, making them both take an awkward little step apart. 'Our boy's all grown up!' And he planted a slobbery kiss on Leo's cheek, and ruffled Jurand's already ruffled hair, and ducked back inside.

Now the violinist had seen them, prancing over to the bridge just below their balcony, grinning up and hacking out a jauntier, more marshal theme. Beside the winery, two fellows started up a noisy argument. Typical Styrians, all swagger and no action.

'Well,' said Jurand, lifting his glass. 'To the married man, eh?' And he slugged back his wine, the knobble on his long, slender throat bobbing. 'Time comes we all have to grow up.' He sounded rather bitter about it as he wiped his mouth. 'Put our silly dreams aside.'

'Aye.' Leo took a mouthful himself. 'Reckon we should get ready. If I make a mess of this, Savine'll bloody kill me.'

The spell was broken. The strange moment was gone. Leo had to admit he was relieved.

Relieved and crushed, both at once.

Grown Up

'**M**y big brother!' And she held her arms out to Orso. 'Come all the way to Sipani just to visit me!'

'Carlot. Bloody hell, it's good to see you.' And it was. She was a grown woman, of course, with a definite hint of their father about her strong cleft chin, but all he could see was the girl who used to chase him around the palace gardens in happier times. He hugged her tight, and held her head against his shoulder, and had to manfully fight down a sudden urge to cry.

She frowned as she held him out at arm's length. 'You look a little... pale.'

'Rough seas on the way over,' he lied. 'Being king suits me.'

She saw right through him, as always. 'It never suited father. It ground all the fun out of him.'

'Well, I'm not him.' Though he feared in fact he might be. 'It's brought out the responsible servant of the people in me.'

'Who would have thought you were hiding one of *those*?' She lowered her voice. 'You must tell me what urgent business has dragged the King of the Union across the Circle Sea.'

'I would if I could.'

'Let me help, Orso. I do nothing here but choose wallpaper.'

'And you've done a simply marvellous job of it,' he said, glancing admiringly about the room. 'You must choose some for me.'

She punched him on the arm. 'Come on! I never get any bloody *excitement*.'

He wanted to tell her how much trouble he was in. To moan that his subjects were united only in contempt for their king. To blurt out that a conspiracy was building against him.

To say how lonely he was.

But it would have been selfishness. What could she do about any of it?

He made himself smile. 'It's all very boring. Nothing you need to worry about.'

'Not there with the boxes, over there!' The familiar sound of their mother scolding the servants echoed from the hallway. 'And for the Fates' sakes, have a care!'

Carlot puffed out her cheeks. 'You've brought me plenty to worry about already.'

'Couldn't you have got pregnant or something?' murmured Orso from the corner of his mouth. 'That would have been a perfect diversion.'

'My womb does not exist so you can distract our mother. A sentence I had hoped I would never have to utter.' She grinned as she nudged Orso in the ribs. 'It isn't for lack of trying, I can tell you. Sotty's quite exhausted with his nightly efforts. For a big man, he's surprisingly agile.'

Sotty was Carlot's name for her husband, Chancellor Sotorius, something like the fifteenth ruler of Sipani to bear the name, only a few years younger than Orso's mother and probably twice the weight. He could be something of a bore, but he doted on Carlot and had one of the best cellars in the world, so he was all right as far as Orso was concerned. The image of the chancellor's nightly efforts with his sister was not one he wanted to be haunted by, however, agile or otherwise.

'That is . . . somewhat more detail than I required.'

'You're the one who brought my pregnancy into this. Prudery really doesn't suit you, Orso— Mother!'

As the Queen Dowager swept into the room, Carlot rushed over and administered a loving embrace. Her technique, which Orso had long admired, was to treat their mother as if she was being a tender and obliging parent regardless of her actual behaviour. 'I'm so glad you came!'

'Your husband is not here?'

'Sadly, no.' Carlot flung herself down like a tragic heroine, shrugging off her mother's displeasure with a flounce, like a duck flicking off rain. 'Sotty's got trouble with the assembly again. Sotty's always got trouble. If we eat together two nights a week we're lucky. If it isn't the assembly it's the merchants, and if the merchants are happy it's the criminals, and if the criminals take a week off it's the pimps.'

'I know just how he feels,' murmured Orso.

His mother raised a brow. 'About the pimps?'

'Not that.' He thought about it. 'Well, yes, that, but I was referring more to the demands of power.'

'Indeed?' said his mother with withering sarcasm. 'Still, I suppose we three can dine together. Apart from Cathil it will be like having the family back together.'

There was an awkward silence. 'Well, and Father,' said Carlot.

Another awkward silence. 'And him,' said their mother. In all honesty, the only times Orso could remember them dining as a family had been the weddings of his two sisters, and even then his parents had only come within arm's length of each other when etiquette strictly demanded.

'Unfortunately, I won't be able to attend, either,' said Orso. 'I have an engagement this evening. But we can dine together tomorrow. With Sotty, too, one can only hope. Then, sadly, I have to go back to Adua. Trouble with the lords of the Open Council, you know. If it's not the Open Council it's the Closed, and if the Closed are happy—'

'We can't stay longer?' snapped his mother. 'I wanted to spend some time with my daughter!'

The silence went beyond awkward and into ugly. Orso glanced at Carlot, hoping vainly that she might do the hard work for him. She gave a helpless little shrug, batting the responsibility back his way.

'What have the two of you arranged?' demanded his mother.

He gathered his courage, then puffed out his chest and met her raised chin with his own. 'Mother. For the time being, I want you to stay in Sipani.'

'Absolutely not!' Her tone was so icy, it was a surprise her breath did not smoke. 'My place is in Adua.'

'You're always telling me how much you despise Adua.'

'I despise Sipani just as much.'

'You love Sipani.'

'Did you bring me here just to get rid of me?'

'No.' Even if he had. 'Mother, listen to me—'

'I always do!'

'You *never* do!' He brought his voice back under control. 'But this time you must. At the demonstration of Curnsbick's engine, you were nearly killed.'

'Come now, don't exaggerate—'

'High Justice Bruckel was sitting beside you and had his head cut in half by a piece of flying metal. He fell dead in your lap!'

'Is that true?' asked Carlot, wide-eyed.

'It will take more than flying metal to keep me from my son.'

'Things have got no better,' said Orso. 'If anything, they've got worse. We have enemies everywhere.'

'Then you need me. You need my advice. You need—'

'What I need is to know that you're safe. And Carlot deserves some time with you.' Over his mother's shoulder, Carlot theatrically rolled her eyes. Orso ignored her. 'I've been monopolising your attention ever since I was born.'

He noticed there were grey streaks in her hair. Wrinkles around her eyes, at the corners of her mouth. When had she started to look old? It made him feel deeply uneasy. He had always supposed she was indestructible.

'Are you sure?' she asked.

'I have made my decision, Mother. I hope you will accept it.'

He had expected a ferocious dressing-down. A furious Styrian tirade. Or, worse yet, the deadly gliding off followed by days of icy silence. But all the Queen Dowager of the Union did was cock her head on one side and calmly consider him.

'You have grown up, Orso. A bittersweet moment for a mother.'

'One you were no doubt hoping would arrive a dozen years ago.'

'Better late than never. The time comes when you realise the world is not yours any more. The best you can do is pass it on to your children.' She touched him very gently on the cheek. 'You understand why I was always so demanding, don't you? Because I know you have it in you to make a great king.'

'Your approval means . . . everything to me. It always has. And there is one thing I need you to do while you are here. One thing with which I trust no one else. Certainly not myself.'

'Name it.'

'Find me a wife.' He counted the points off on his fingers. 'I only ask that she be beautiful, tasteful, passionate, cunning and superbly bred. And Carlot, make sure she has a sense of humour.'

Carlot waved it away. 'That would only be wasted on you.'

A flicker of interest had crossed his mother's face. 'A Styrian bride?'

'You know as well as I do that they make the best women in the world here. Speaking of which, has our guest arrived?'

'She has.' And Carlot gave a loud clap.

The door was swung open to reveal a tall woman in extremely impressive middle age. Orso had not seen her in ten years, but she looked every bit as elegant as the day she left Adua. If there was anyone in the world who rivalled his mother for deportment, after all, it was her oldest friend, and far more than a friend, Countess Shalere.

'Orso, you beautiful creature!' she said. 'It has been far too long.'

'Countess.' Orso snapped his heels together and gave an extravagant bow. 'Or should I say *sorceress*, since you have not aged a day.'

'And people say you have no talents!' She clasped his head and kissed him on both cheeks in a waft of perfume that took him straight back to being a boy. 'I swear there are no better liars in the Circle of the World.'

Orso's mother had not taken her eyes from Shalere since she came into the room. 'This is . . . a surprise.'

'A pleasant one, I hope.' Shalere raised one brow. 'I have been waiting for you for a long time.'

'I . . . told you not to do that.'

'Everyone must be disobeyed occasionally.'

A naïve observer might have thought it an insignificant meeting. But Orso knew his mother far better than that. He saw the slight parting of her lips, the slight glimmer at the corners of her eyes, the slight movement of her collarbones with her quick breath.

For her, that was a whirlwind of passion.

'Well,' said Carlot, making for the door and jerking her head significantly towards it. 'I have some . . . things to do.'

'As do I.' Orso felt suddenly as if he was intruding on something painfully intimate. 'Immensely important . . . things.'

No one acknowledged him. He glanced back as Carlot drew him through the door by his elbow. Long enough to see Shalere had taken both of his mother's hands, their eyes fixed on each other, unwavering. His mother was smiling. Her face lit up with it. He wondered how long it had been since he saw her smile like that. Since he saw her smile at all.

He had been desperate to escape her smothering influence for years. Now that he had finally done it, he had to push the door shut before anyone noticed the melodramatic quivering of his lip.

All Tastes, No Judgements

If there was one thing Leo valued, it was honesty, and Cardotti's House of Leisure might've been the most dishonest place in the world. A place where everything was pretending to be something else.

It was decorated like the palace of some dissolute emperor, all fake marble columns and false velvet, lulling music and forced laughter, clinking glass and whispered secrets. There were bronzes of naked people, paintings of naked people, colossal urns decorated with naked people. If it was possible to make nakedness boring, the decorators of Cardotti's had managed it.

Women glided about the hallway with high shoes and hungry smiles, with hair piled and twisted, with clinging clothes of shimmering pearl-white and glistening oil-black. Clothes that gave tricking glimpses of thigh and shoulder through slits and slashes, showed the laces and buckles of elaborate underwear.

'By the dead,' muttered Glaward.

'Very much so,' croaked Antaup, staring around with eyes wide in his mask.

Everybody wore one. A Sipanese tradition, like fog, deceit and the cock-rot. Masks of crushed crystal and lace, leering devils and porcelain dolls. Glaward's was a whale, appropriately enough, and Jurand's a bird, Jin's a gatehouse and Antaup's a unicorn complete with crystal prong. Leo had, of course, a lion. What else? It had felt foolish when he put it on but now, among so many others, it started to feel dangerous. No one knowing who anyone was. No one having to take responsibility for what they did. No one bound by the usual rules, or by any rules at all. The thought made him excited and worried both at once. His palms itched from it.

A woman swayed towards them across the mosaic floor, snake-hipped, feathers fluttering at her shoulders, holding long arms out in a showman's flourish. 'Welcome to Cardotti's House of Leisure, my lords!' she crooned in a voice overripe with Styrian song.

'Who says we're lords?' asked Glaward, grinning.

'We treat *every* visitor as if they are.' She brushed him under the chin with a gloved fingertip, then looked at Leo. 'You are the Young Lion?'

'Some people call me that.'

'It is our *honour* to entertain so famous a hero.'

He would've enjoyed the compliment more if he'd felt she was telling the truth. If he'd felt she was capable of it. 'Well, thank you—'

'King Jappo is *most* keen to speak with you but ... otherwise engaged just now. The entertainments of Cardotti's stand *entirely* at your disposal in the meantime.'

'I like the sound o' that,' said Jin, giving Leo a punch on the arm that sent his weight onto his bad side and caused him a twinge of pain. It had been a mistake to walk here. Antaup's map had led them wrong three times and the damn leg was hurting worse than ever.

'Here at Cardotti's, we cater for *all* tastes and make *no* judgements.' The greeter led them past a half-open door, three figures lurking by lamplight beyond. They were dressed, or perhaps undressed, in much the same way as the women, but they were decidedly not women. Stubbled jaws. Chiselled bodies. By the dead, did he glimpse a muscular pair of buttocks in the shadows? 'We stand ready to indulge *every* whim.'

'Perhaps we'll just gamble to begin with,' snapped Leo, disgusted. And strangely hot around the ears.

She led them into a panelled room noisy with the flutter of cards, the click of dice, the whirr of the lucky wheel, surely the unluckiest invention of all history for its players. A band with masks like leering faces stroked and tickled and kissed out music which managed to sound somehow dirty. Masked guards lurked. Masked men pushed gambling chips wearily through pools of light stained by coloured Visserine glass. Masked women hung upon them, giggled at tiresome comments, swayed with the music and caressed old grotesques as if they never saw such beautiful gallants.

The place looked like bribery, smelled like lust and sounded like blackmail.

The greeter spirited a box of chips into Leo's hand. 'Enjoy yourselves, my lords.'

'This place is vile,' he muttered as she glided off. He reached up to wipe his sweaty forehead, realised he couldn't because of the mask.

'You need to live a little!' Glaward swept two drinks from the tray of a waitress with a mask like a golden octopus and started to swill one back while holding out the other.

'I'd best stay sober. I've a deal to strike with one of the most powerful men in the world.'

'I haven't.' Antaup plucked the drink from Glaward's hand, took a mouthful, then bared his teeth. 'Bit sweet.'

'Like everything here—' Leo gasped at a touch on his shoulder and spun about. No assassin at his back, but a willowy blonde in a mask like a butterfly.

'No need to startle, my lord,' she pouted at him.

'I'm not startled!' Though he obviously had been.

She giggled as if anxious bad temper was her favourite quality in a man. 'I just wondered if I could be of any—'

'No,' he snapped, turning away.

'Yes,' said Jin, nipping in front of Antaup with surprising agility and slipping his arm through hers.

'Aren't *you* a strong one,' Leo heard her cooing as they headed for the door.

'Glad someone's enjoying themselves,' he grumbled, under his breath.

It was absurd for a red-blooded young hero to wish his wife was with him in a place like this, but he wished Savine was there. He was coming to rely on her more and more. To admire her taste, and her judgement, and . . . well, everything really. But she trusted him to do this. He couldn't let her down.

'Don't worry.' Jurand, slipping up close to speak softly. Knowing Leo's feelings without a word said, like always. He guided Leo over to the dice table. It was the right height to lean on, at least, and take the weight off his throbbing leg without showing any weakness. 'You're the Young Lion! You convinced Rikke *and* Stour to join you. United two bitter enemies under your banner! Just be honest, and strong, and generous. Just be you.' Jurand leaned closer, grinning. 'Only a bit more ruthless. This is Styria, after all.'

'You're right.' Leo took a hard breath. Good old Jurand. Always knew what to say. He *had* united Rikke and Stour. He was the great persuader, and if he could add Jappo to his alliance, the game would be won before it began.

A solid, silent, grey-haired man with a mask like a pair of dice was running the table. His eyes flicked to Leo, as blank as double ones. 'Care to throw?'

'Why not?' Leo tossed a few chips onto the baize and flung the dice.

'Two fives,' droned the dealer. 'Player wins.'

And he shuffled some chips towards Leo. As easily as that, he was the winner. Leo wanted to grab Jurand and kiss him on the forehead but, given that odd moment earlier, he threw a rough arm around him instead and put him in a manly headlock. 'What the hell would I do without you?'

He shoved a larger stack of chips out onto the table and snapped his fingers at Antaup. 'Pass me those dice!'

The greeter at Cardotti's House of Leisure was a work of art in herself, a moving sculpture of black silk, paint and feathers, the very personification of Sipani's succulent corruption. Or corrupt succulence. Whichever, really.

'Your Majesty,' she said, dropping into a deep and graceful curtsy. Almost as deep and graceful as the ones Savine used to perform, though her skirts had never split all the way to her hips in quite so mesmerising a way.

'Probably best you don't call me that,' murmured Orso, tapping the side of his nose. 'Incognito, you know.'

'*Everyone* is incognito here.' Her accent reminded him rather of his mother's, which most certainly shouldn't have been an arousing thought, but somehow rather was. 'At Cardotti's, we are *notorious* for our discretion.' She leaned close. Even masked she managed to look magnificently sly. 'Among many other things.'

'Indeed, I believe you once hosted my father?'

The greeter looked somewhat pained. 'The night of the great fire. A sad moment in a proud history.' Gorst, for some reason, gave a kind of strangled cough. The greeter took Orso by the elbow, resting against him as lightly as a fur sits on a lady's shoulder, purring in his ear. 'But the building has been *completely* rebuilt since and our security is second to none.' She gestured to six armed guards, standing still as suits of armour against the walls. 'You could not be safer locked in a vault, I assure you.'

'And we'd have a lot less fun there, eh, Gorst?'

Gorst followed in brooding silence, glaring about with fists clenched.

'King Jappo is *most* keen to speak with you but . . . otherwise engaged just at the moment. The entertainments of Cardotti's stand *entirely* at your disposal in the meantime.'

'What entertainments have you got, exactly?' asked Tunny, adjusting the fit of a mask shaped like a silver star.

'*All* of them.' The greeter led them into a dark-panelled hall where games of skill, chance and ruination were being played. Groups of men sat talking, laughing, smoking, drinking. Girls cooed and crooned and fluttered fans between them. Coloured light gleamed on fine glassware and soft skin, filtered through amber drinks and curling smoke. Rarely if ever had such a tableau of high-class debauchery been assembled in one place, and Orso had arranged quite a few himself, in his misspent youth. And his misspent adulthood, for that matter.

'Despite all my protestations to the contrary,' he said, sucking in a breath heavy with husk, musk and perfume, 'I think at least half my heart belongs to Styria.'

'Reckon I've died and gone to heaven,' said Tunny, grinning hugely, 'as the Gurkish might say.'

'To hell,' squeaked Gorst, heavy jaw firmly clenched beneath his mask of a crescent moon.

Orso had attended quite a few masked balls and learned how to handle them through pleasurable trial and error. The main rule was not to get carried away and make an utter arse of yourself. A good rule under all circumstances, in truth, but one that not everyone followed.

Four men were gathered at the dice table. One in a unicorn mask slouched against it, shirt open to show a patch of sweaty chest, waving one floppy hand in time to the band. Or, in fact, entirely out of time. 'Lovely music,' he droned, 'wonderful music.'

'I told you not to smoke that pipe,' snapped a broad-shouldered one in a lion mask as he flung the dice down the table. They were from the Union, clearly. Angland accents, maybe? Four friends, but the lion appeared to be the leader. Not unlike Orso's own party, except that Gorst never drank, while Tunny always drank but never seemed to get drunk.

The whale-masked one, who was indeed whale-sized, laughed uproari-ously at something the bird-masked one said, then lifted his glass but managed to spill most of its contents before he got it to his mouth.

'You're drunk,' growled the lion.

'It's a House of Leisure,' said the whale, spreading his hands in good-natured apology. 'Shouldn't we all be drunk?'

'We should all be as drunk as possible whenever possible.' Tunny whisked a glass from a passing tray. 'In from the Union, my lords?'

'From Angland,' said the bird. 'You?'

'From Adua,' said Orso. 'Business?'

'Of a sort,' grunted the lion as the dealer handed him the dice with a slightly pained look, as though it hurt to let go of them. 'You?'

'Business. And my sister lives in the city.' Orso lowered his voice. 'Took the opportunity to palm my mother off on her. I love the old bird but she won't stop going on at me to marry.'

'You should.' The lion tossed the dice and brought up four and six, to false delight from the girls about the table. 'Married myself not long ago. Had my doubts but it's been the best decision of my life.' The bird winced and turned away. 'Haven't looked back.'

'She's licked you into shape!' The unicorn blew a little bubble of snot as he laughed.

'I suppose it all depends on finding the right woman.' Orso gave a long sigh. 'Thought I had her. But she slipped through my fingers somehow.'

'You should work on your grip.' The lion tossed the dice one more time.

'Pair of sixes,' droned the dealer, and swept an armload of chips over while the girls cooed as though throwing one number rather than another was quite the achievement.

Now the greeter whispered something in the lion's ear and he stepped away from the table, straightening his jacket. 'Best of luck with your business. And with your mother.' He frowned over at his friends. 'I'm sure you three will keep busy while I'm gone.

The whale grinned over at the bird. 'I daresay we can think of something.'

'Lovely,' muttered Tunny, out of the corner of his mouth, as he watched the man stride away with the slightest limp.

'Real charmer.' Orso scooped up the dice and tossed them bouncing across the table.

'One and three,' said the old dealer. 'Player loses.' In much the same emotionless tone as he might have announced a win.

Orso sighed as he watched the chips gathered up. 'Why is it always the bastards who get all the luck?'

'Winning teaches you nothing,' said Tunny. 'You see what a man really is when he loses.'

Jappo mon Rogont Murcatto – Grand Duke of Ospria and Visserine, Protector of Puranti, Nicante, Borletta and Affoia, not to mention King of Styria – sprawled on a velvet chaise in front of a mural of winged women floating naked from a sunset sky and looked very pleased about it. His Suljuk silk gown trailed open to show his muscular stomach, complete with a streak of thick black hair.

A young man dressed in the style of a Gurkish slave-boy had been leaning close to light the king's pipe. Now he swaggered over to Leo, sinewy body dusted with glitter. 'Can I get you anything? Anything at all?'

'No!' snapped Leo. King Jappo's preferences were well known, but he'd never dreamed they'd be so proudly displayed. Leo had always preferred the company of men, but not in *this* way. Not *at all* in this way. He certainly wouldn't have boasted about it, if he'd been a pervert. Which he wasn't, of course. He just... found it hard to get excited unless his wife slapped him.

'Thank you for seeing me,' he managed to grate out.

'I was here anyway.' Jappo sprawled back and puffed brown smoke rings. 'You're the one who's crossed a sea.'

Not the best start. 'It was my wife's idea. Like most of my good ones.' Yes, keep it light. Charm the bastard, like Jurand had said.

'Alas, I have not met your wife, but by all accounts she's a very shrewd woman.' Jappo shook his fist. 'Very tough.' He stroked his shining gown. 'Very beautiful. I love to surround myself with beautiful things. But women?' He held up a wobbling hand and made a sound like *nyeh*. 'Mixed feelings. Hope you're enjoying Cardotti's.'

'Well—'

'No doubt you prefer the battlefield!' Jappo swung his bare feet down and sat eagerly forward, hacking at the air with his still-smoking pipe. 'You want to mount a horse rather than a lover, grip an axe instead of a bottle and have the screams of the dying for music! Am I right, Young Lion? Eh? Eh?'

'Well—'

'Chagga?'

'I like to keep a clear head.'

'I like mine stuffed with delicious dreams.' And Jappo stuck the pipe back between his teeth and puffed away. 'Come sit.' And he patted the chaise beside him.

Leo pointedly took a chair opposite. By the dead, he wished he hadn't turned down those drinks now. He couldn't have been less comfortable. But *a man shows his quality when circumstances are against him*, his father always used to say. Where was the glory in easy victories?

'So tell me, Young Lion, why did your wife send you here?'

'She didn't send me...' Had she, though? 'I mean—'

'Your wife told her friends who told my friends who told me that you're building a grand alliance! That if I were to hop aboard we could drag relations between Styria and the Union out of the bog. That after so many unprofitable wars we could forge a peace that would be the envy of the world.' Jappo grinned over. 'Anything to it?'

'Well...' Leo struggled to force his mind back onto the script. 'The only real dispute we have is King Orso's claim on Talins. His false claim, that is—'

'I think it's quite a solid claim.'

'What?'

'His grandfather was Grand Duke of Talins, then my mother murdered him and his sons and stole the city. My lawyers would no doubt differ, but if you're asking me, Orso has a much better claim to the city than I do. But then I have it, and I'm not handing it over, and every time the Union tries to take it from me, my mother gives you quite the spanking. So when it comes to claims...' And he twisted his face and made that *nyeh* sound again.

'Well... yes. I'm saying we wouldn't try again. We'd give up the claim. I'm not interested in Talins. Only the Union.'

'Indeed.' Jappo's expression was hard to gauge because of the mask. 'The Union interests you so much, you want to steal it.'

Leo worked his mouth. 'I want to *free* it.'

'I once heard a pickpocket use that defence about some purses he'd liberated. They still cut his hands off.'

'Our quarrel's not with King Orso, but with his Closed Council. Their arrogance. Their corruption. They're dragging the nation into the sewer!'

'And who is involved in this noble scheme to free the Union from its king's chosen councillors?'

Leo paused a moment, mouth half-open.

'Come, come, Young Lion. You can't expect me to join a club without knowing the quality of the other members.'

Probably Leo should have kept his cards close, but the man's constant look of slight scorn was beginning to grate on him.

'Myself and all the Lords of Angland. Lord Isher, Lord Heugen, Lord Barezin and fifteen other chairs of the Open Council, though I'm sure more will join us, they're all chafing under the Closed Council's yoke—'

'A little olive oil can help.'

'What?'

'With chafing.'

Leo soldiered on. 'Then we have friends among the commoners, and the sworn oath of the King of the Northmen himself, Stour Nightfall.'

'A far-reaching brotherhood! Can King Orso really know nothing about it?'

There was no point holding back now. It was all or nothing. And boldness had always been Leo's way.

'He doesn't suspect a thing.' Leo was trying so hard not to look at

Jappo's bare stomach, he ended up constantly glancing at it. 'A member of his Closed Council is in our pocket, warning us of every move he makes.'

'And expecting a reward, I'm sure. No doubt every one of your allies has something to gain?' If he could've seen Jappo's eyebrows, Leo expected they would've been raised expectantly.

'I can offer you Sipani.' Dismal negotiating. He was tossing away cities without even a hint of barter. Savine would've been disgusted.

'That's generous.'

'I'm a soldier, not a salesman.'

'I meant I was unaware it was yours to give. Here I am, after all, *in* Sipani, enjoying the best the city has to offer without your permission. Doing what I want. Smoking what I want. Fucking who I want.'

'Your bed, your business,' snapped Leo, but the Styrian proverb came out strangled.

'If it helps, I don't *only* fuck men.' As far as could be told through his mask, King Jappo looked faintly amused. 'Sometimes I'm fucked *by* them. Look at it this way – if you needed advice on horses, you wouldn't go to someone who never rode a horse.'

'What?'

'How could someone who never *had* a cock really know what's best to do *with* a cock? I've debated scholars the world over and no one's been able to give me a satisfactory answer on that point.'

'Some might say there's a natural order to things,' Leo forced through gritted teeth.

'If we were constrained by the natural order we would still be wriggling naked in the filth.'

'Some of us still are,' said Leo, before he could stop himself.

Jappo only gave a little snort of laughter. 'So Sipani is your final offer?'

Leo paused. They'd all agreed to offer Westport, if they had to. A superstitious slum, Savine had said. A paltry price to pay for Angland, Starikland and Midderland. He'd reluctantly agreed at the time, but now his leg was aching, and perhaps it was the chagga smoke, but he was feeling out of sorts, hot in the face and slightly dizzy. He hated Styria, hated Sipani, hated Cardotti's, hated this degenerate excuse for a king most of all. He raised his chin, trying to look haughtily down his nose, but his eyes kept being drawn to that trail of dark hair from Jappo's navel into the not entirely concealing shadows of his gown . . .

'My last offer!' he snapped, angrily.

Jappo gave a wounded pout. 'Your shrewd, tough, beautiful wife gave you nothing else to bargain with?'

'You're dealing with me!' growled Leo, further nettled. He wasn't giving up Union territory to one of the Union's enemies, especially not this one. Savine might be upset but he was the husband, the leader, the lord and master. He was the Young Lion. He'd beaten Stour Nightfall. He'd beaten Black Calder. He could beat the likes of bloody Orso without the help of some grinning Styrian pervert.

'Shame,' murmured Jappo, though whether he was talking about the offer, or who was making it, was hard to tell. 'You've given me a lot to think about.' He lay back, one arm behind his head, forcing Leo to scrupulously keep his eyes away as that bloody gown fell even further open. 'Less than I was hoping, but even so. I'll let you know my answer in due course.'

'Sooner rather than later,' said Leo stiffly. 'We move on the last day of summer.'

'Stay a while, Young Lion. Enjoy the hospitality. You seem tense. And do pass my regards to your wife!'

Leo ground his teeth as he pulled the door shut. He would've liked to fling the bastard thing closed and snarl some ugly curses after it, but the greeter was in the hallway, guiding someone else towards Jappo's door. It was that smug idiot from downstairs with a gilded sun for a mask.

'Mind out,' he snarled, barging past.

'By all means,' said Orso as the man in the lion mask shoved between him and the greeter and stomped away. 'Rather rude.'

'It was,' said the greeter.

'But being an arsehole is crime and punishment both.'

'It is.' And she eased the door open and offered him the way.

'King Orso!' Jappo Murcatto reclined on a velvet daybed in a mask sculpted like spread eagle's wings and a Gurkish robe that left nothing to the imagination. 'It is a great pleasure to make your acquaintance!'

'The pleasure is mine,' said Orso, in Styrian, giving the kind of sweeping bow his mother had always told him was popular in Talins. 'How often, after all, do two kings get to chat? It's rather refreshing, being able to speak to someone on an equal footing.' And he took his mask off and tossed it on a side table, then dropped down in a chair and poured himself a glass of wine.

Jappo frowned at the mask. 'That's really not the done thing in Cardotti's.'

'We're kings. The done thing is whatever we do. I came here for a frank discussion. By all means leave yours on, if you prefer.'

'You speak excellent Styrian.'

'I have my mother to thank. She won't bully me in any other tongue.'

'We both owe our mothers a debt, then. Mine gave me a whole king-dom.' And Jappo plucked his mask off and dropped it beside Orso's. His face was not at all what Orso had imagined. Handsome, but in a strong-boned, broad-jawed sort of way. Surprisingly pale, too, in spite of his dark curls. He looked more like a Northman than a Styrian.

'Chagga?' he asked, holding up a pipe.

'Whyever not?'

While the King of Styria charged the pipe, the King of the Union frowned up at the towering mural behind him. 'A copy of Aropella's *Fates*?'

'Well recognised!' Jappo turned to look it over. 'Worse brushwork than the great man's version but far more bare flesh, so I consider it a draw. The original's in my mother's palace at Fontezarmo.'

'I am aware. *My* mother would say it's her palace, though.'

'Really?'

'And that Aropella's *Fates* is one of the few treasures *your* mother didn't destroy when she stole the place. Mostly because, as it's on the ceiling, it was out of easy reach of the criminal scum she'd employed to help her.'

'And do you share your mother's opinion?'

'Very rarely,' said Orso. 'She tends towards the vengeful. I sometimes think she named me purely with the intention of annoying your mother. My namesake Grand Duke Orso did kill your uncle, after all, and very nearly killed your mother. Before your mother killed him. And my uncles. And half the nobility of Styria. Is that how it went?'

'Roughly.'

'So many familial murders I trip up on the details. We do have a rather... complicated family situation.'

'Most kings do, I suppose.'

'Honestly, I'd rather put it all behind me. What's the point in having new generations if all we do is pick up the feuds of the old one?'

'I'm very glad to hear you say that.' Jappo discerningly pursed his lips as he plucked the hood off a lamp and held it to his pipe, puffing up a smog of brown smoke. 'Enemies are like furniture, aren't they? Better chosen for oneself than inherited.'

'And made to be sat on.'

'My mother would agree with you there. She is a soldier.' Jappo tossed his head with a kind of fierce pride when he said it. Perhaps the first truly honest-seeming thing he'd done since Orso arrived. He handed the pipe over. 'A most formidable one.'

'Perhaps the most formidable alive,' said Orso, puffing some smoke of his own. 'Only an idiot would deny it.'

'But great soldiers become prisoners of their own success. All she thinks of is her next victory. Beating her enemies. Winning the war. She pays no mind to making friends. She has no time to win the peace.'

'And is that what you want? To win the peace?'

Jappo shrugged. 'Here in Styria we had the Years of Blood, then the Years of Fire. There in the Union you had two wars with the Gurkish and two wars against the North. Then, to cap it off, we fought three wars against each other. Half a century of destruction. No one is asking me, but if they were, I would say that we could probably take a breath. Build something! Make the world *better*!' He seemed to remember himself and sat back. 'And, you know, fuck. Make music.'

'Mmmm.' Orso blew a couple of ragged smoke rings. 'This dissolute hedonist business suits you, but I've played the role myself.'

'Really?'

'My own preference tilts towards women—'

'As does your mother's, I understand?'

'As does my mother's – she has sublime taste in that as in *so* much else – but otherwise all this is rather like looking in the mirror. I think I even had that same gown.' He pointed at it with the stem of the pipe. 'Though sadly not that stomach. So I am well aware – fun though it is – this performance is just another kind of mask.'

Jappo raised his brows. 'You'd like me to take that one off, too, would you?'

'I wouldn't ask you to strip too far for your comfort, but I think we have the best chance of a mutually beneficial discussion without it.'

A little smile curled the corner of Jappo's mouth, and he jerked his gown closed, swung his long legs from the chaise and sat forward. 'Then let's talk honestly!'

'Have you seen my friends?' asked Leo. 'One had a bird mask, and one a whale...'

The woman gave him a towering sneer, then a disgusted hiss, and turned back to the cracked mirror, touching up the paint on her mouth with furious concentration.

He limped on down the corridor, one hand on the flaking wall. He wasn't even sure how he'd ended up backstairs. Took a wrong turn somewhere. When he left Angland to ask for Styrian support, in his opinion. There was nothing you could trust in the whole damn country.

Behind the veneer, Cardotti's House of Leisure was a very different place. A warren of low-ceilinged little cells, mouldy, cheap and seething with frantic action. It reminded Leo of the preparations for a battle. The chaos and barely contained panic, the pulling on of gear and tightening of straps, the expressions of grim determination.

He glimpsed two women through a doorway, one with teeth gritted and chin raised, mask dangling from her hand. 'He fucking bit me, the bastard!' she snarled in common. 'He fucking *bit* me! Is it bleeding?'

'A little,' said the other as she dabbed at red marks on her neck with a cloth. 'You shouldn't be back here!' she snarled at Leo, kicking the door closed.

His meeting with Jappo had gone badly, he knew. Worse the more he thought about it. He wondered whether he might've made a serious mistake by not offering more. Then he felt disgusted with himself for offering as much as he had, annoyed with Savine for making him try, irritated at the world and everything in it. He'd made a grubby compromise too far by even talking to that greasy bastard and hadn't gained a thing. What use could a man like that be in a battle anyway? If you could even call him a man. Once Leo had dealt with the Closed Council, he'd have to lead an army to Styria so Union arms could finally wipe the smirk from King Jappo's face.

The thought gave him some fleeting satisfaction, but it was soon driven off by the pain in his thigh. He leaned against the wall to grip it, knead it, breathing hard through clenched teeth. He wished he'd brought his cane now, but he refused to look like a cripple. A band was tuning up somewhere, a flurry of screeching notes.

He saw a woman up on her elbows on a bench, skirts around her hips while an old man in cracked eye-lenses peered between her legs. 'You've caught the rot,' he explained to her in Northern. 'You'll need to use a powder twice a day. Don't eat it!'

'Why the hell would I eat it?' she snapped.

Leo recoiled from a blast of steam. Half a dozen dark-skinned cooks were wedged into a tiny kitchen, running with sweat as they carved meat and turned spits, one of them singing some jagged prayer as he pushed a dozen grease-caked pans around a brazier, another arranging a few morsels onto a perfectly white plate, the one clean thing in the whole place.

Leo turned to find his way blocked by a dark-haired little girl with food stains around her mouth. 'Did you hurt your leg?' she asked in very clear common.

'I did. Or, well ... the King of the Northmen hurt it. Hasn't healed. Don't know if it ever will.'

She looked up at him with that awfully solemn look children sometimes have. 'Do you know where my mother is?'

'I'm afraid ... I expect she's probably working.' Leo cleared his throat, not knowing what the hell to do with her and deciding nothing was his best bet. Somewhere a female voice screeched furiously in Styrian, an endless flow of sing-song curses. 'Do you know where the gaming hall is?'

The girl raised her skinny arm to point at a narrow door further down the hallway. 'Up the stairs.'

When Leo finally found the place, Antaup was lolling against the dice table looking even more drunk than before. 'You're back!' he called, tried to let go of the table and nearly fell.

Leo caught him by the elbow. 'Where the hell is everyone?'

'Think Glaward an' Jurand went back to the rooms ... maybe ... said we should stay. Enjoy selves. Jin, is he with that woman still? Shall we get a drink?'

'I think you've had enough,' said Leo, giving Antaup a shake. 'Jin can find his own way back.' He couldn't stand to spend another moment in this place. He needed to talk to someone clear-headed. Someone clever, who could work out how big a mistake he'd made. He needed Jurand. 'Let's go.'

King Jappo filled Orso's glass, then tapped a loose drop from the edge of the decanter. 'So what has brought you all the way across the Circle Sea?'

'Treason,' said Orso, simply. 'I may be facing a rather serious rebellion, and these rebels may be seeking your help. I want to convince you not to give it.'

'You *are* frank.'

'I expect your position, like mine, gives you limited time to relax. I would not presume to take up more of it than necessary.'

'How thoughtful.'

'Good manners are a gift that costs nothing.'

'If only the Young Lion saw things that way.'

Orso paused. Plainly that had been no slip of the tongue. 'You have ... met with Lord Brock, then?' It was a heavy blow, but hardly a surprising one. Orso wondered whether Savine knew of it. Whether she had helped plan it. Even now, the thought gave him a stab of pain so sharp he could barely hide it.

'Perhaps I *have* been approached about joining a . . . let us call it a confederation. *Conspiracy* strikes an ugly note, doesn't it?'

'Awfully tasteless,' said Orso, sucking thoughtfully on the pipe and letting the smoke curl away.

'A confederation based on freedom, patriotism and high principles.'

'Awfully taste*ful*.'

'Aimed at . . . let us say . . . altering the priorities and personnel of the Union government.'

'Just a little tweak to policy?'

'Exactly!'

'Because treason sounds *most* underhand,' said Orso, handing back the pipe.

Jappo grinned as he took it. 'Few things more so.'

'Might I ask whether you are minded to join this . . . well-intentioned group?'

'I am considering my options.' Jappo stuck out his bottom lip, twiddling absently with the pipe. 'I should say that I was offered Sipani.'

That hung between them for a moment. 'You know my sister Carlot is married to Chancellor Sotorius.'

'Does that mean,' asked Jappo, 'that you couldn't match the offer?'

Orso gave a long sigh. 'If I was willing to stab my own sister in the back, how could you possibly trust me? How could anyone? I could lie and say yes, then later renege, but I think we've all had enough of that sort of behaviour. I would rather be honest and say the best you'll get from me is that things stay comfortably familiar. I will give up my claims on Talins. I've only ever seen the place in paintings. Take it with my blessing. Perhaps in time we can even join hands across the Circle Sea and win the peace together.' He looked up at Jappo and let his smile fade. 'But if you try to take Sipani, I will fight you. I may well lose. But I will fight you. With everything I have.'

There was a lengthy silence. Then Jappo raised one long forefinger and wagged it at him. 'I thought I'd love the Young Lion and find you detestable.'

'You would hardly be alone with that opinion.'

Jappo slapped his thigh. 'That's what I mean! You're excellent value, and he's a fucking idiot! Warriors, I swear.'

'I know. They're so ridiculous, and yet they have no sense of humour.'

'Fuck him.' And Jappo handed back the pipe. 'Sipani isn't worth another meeting with that arrogant arsehole. And from what I've heard,

Stour Nightfall wouldn't know the difference between Aropella's *Fates* and a smacked arse. I very much doubt he and I would get on.'

'He was one of these patriots, then?'

'Along, I believe, with at least a dozen members of your Open Council and at least one of your Closed.'

'I don't suppose you'd fancy sharing some names?'

'I wouldn't want to spoil the game. You've played *so* well so far.'

Orso sat back, smiling. It was bad. It was as bad as he had feared. But there was a strange relief in knowing exactly how bad. 'You know, King Jappo, I think we should make this a regular thing.'

'I'm amenable, King Orso. Once you've beaten your rebels. *If* you beat them.'

'So I can rely on you to stay out of this?'

'My mother would want me to promise you yes.' Jappo grinned very wide. 'Then stab you in the back at the first opportunity.'

'I think we have probably both had enough of what our mothers want.'

'Probably.'

'So I can rely on you to stay out of this?'

'I suppose you'll find out when you don't feel the dagger between your shoulder blades.' Jappo grinned even wider. 'Or when you do.'

Orso sucked at the pipe one more time and let the smoke float from his pursed lips. 'How thoroughly Styrian of you.'

'Jurand?' called Leo as he pushed open the doors.

But the room was empty. Sounds of the city outside. Music and laughter. Gilt mouldings gleamed in the darkness, drapes stirred about the open window. That made him frown. Surely they'd shut it? Could someone have broken in? Be waiting for them? It only came to him then how dangerous this business might be. How many enemies he'd made. They should never have split up! He put a hand on the hilt of his sword.

'Glaward!' he hissed, wincing as he stepped into the room. After the walk back, his leg was burning all the way from his foot to his hip, he could hardly bend the knee.

Antaup started giggling, which didn't help. He'd been giggling all the way from bloody Cardotti's. 'Pour me a drink, eh—'

'Shush!' Leo caught him by the elbow and half-steered, half-threw him into a chair.

He sat there, shaking with suppressed laughter which, within a few breaths, turned to gentle snoring.

'By the dead,' muttered Leo. Then he saw a chink of light at the keyhole of one of the connecting doors. Jurand's and Glaward's masks dangled on the knob beside it. Whale and bird. A flood of relief. He let go of his sword, went to the door and shoved it wide. 'There you are—'

He thought at first that they were wrestling, and nearly laughed at the mismatch.

They were kneeling on the Gurkish carpet, Glaward gripping two fistfuls of the covers which he'd half-dragged from the bed, eyes squeezed shut and his mouth open. Jurand was pressed against his back with his teeth bared, one hand down between Glaward's legs, the other tangled in his hair and twisting his head around so he could bite at his ear.

Then Leo realised Jurand had his trousers down around his ankles and Glaward had his off completely, flung rumpled into a corner, their hairy thighs pressed together, and suddenly it was entirely clear what they were doing, and it wasn't wrestling.

'But...' he breathed, clapping a hand over his face, but somehow still looking through the gap between his fingers. 'Fuck!'

He reeled away, nearly tripped over Antaup's outstretched boot and stumbled from the room, out into the corridor, leg burning, face burning. He was sickened, shamed, disgusted. Wasn't he?

'Leo!' Jurand's voice echoed at him from behind and Leo flinched, kept lurching on, didn't look back.

By the dead, he wished he'd never come to Styria.

No Philosopher

They pulled the hood off and Broad was left squinting through one eye, trying and failing to bring the lamplit blurs around him into focus.

'Well, well, well. Gunnar Broad, in my back parlour.'

He knew that voice right off, and what he thought was, *Fuck*. What he said was, 'Hello, Judge.'

'Told you he'd be back, eh, Sarlby?' One of those blurs drifted towards him. 'Some men just can't help 'emselves.' Someone perched his lenses on his nose, nudged them into that familiar groove and, like magic, everything became clear. Might've been better if it hadn't.

Judge grinned down at him, Sarlby and a few others of his ilk standing around the stained walls of a cellar with not a friendly eye among 'em. Time hadn't improved her. She still wore that rusted breastplate over a ragged ballgown looked like it belonged to a baroness chased through a briar patch. Her red hair was an even madder tangle, gathered up like some parrot's crest on top and clipped to patchy stubble at the sides. She still was decked with jewels, chains of office and strings of pearls ripped from the rich of Valbeck in the uprising. But, as if she needed to look more like bloodshed personified, she'd strapped herself up with belts and bandoliers, too, knives dangling from them, hatchets tucked into them, blades enough to run a chain of butchers.

She'd made him nervous the first time he laid eyes on her, and being chained to a chair in her presence helped not one bit. Made him think of all the dead folk she'd left hanged in the yard behind the ruined court-house. He could still hear the sound of it, like a ship's rigging, creaking with the breeze.

He'd been hoping for Risinau. That would've been worrying enough. Judge was ten times worse. Worse 'cause she was far more clever and far more dangerous. Worse 'cause if she was in charge, reason was out the window and running for the hills. Worse 'cause the moment he saw her, he felt that guilty tickle, deep inside. The same one he got when he felt violence coming.

She leaned down over him, reached out and smoothed his hair with one ring-encrusted hand like a mother might smooth a wayward son's. It was the best he could do not to twist away. Twist away, or maybe twist closer.

'You know how sometimes . . .' she purred, 'you see an old lover you haven't seen in years . . . and you get that *tingle* in the crotch.' He knew what a tingle in the crotch felt like, all right, he had one now. 'And you think to yourself . . . why aren't we still together? How could something so sweet have turned so sour?'

'Might be all the hangin's,' tossed out Sarlby from the corner of the room.

Judge pushed her lips into a pout. 'Folk just don't understand me. That's my tragedy.' She snapped her fingers and one of the men slapped a bottle of spirits into her hand. 'But you do, don't you, Bull Broad? I knew it when you flung that man o' mine across my courtroom and smashed his head through a witness box. *You* see what needs to be done.'

And she curled her tongue around the neck of the bottle and drank, blotchy throat shifting with each hard swallow. She caught Broad watching and grinned as she smacked her lips. Gave the bottle a shake, that lovely tinkle of spirits sloshing inside.

'Want a drink?'

'No,' he said, wanting one worse than just about anything and not hiding it well.

'You sure? 'Cause I'm getting the feeling there's something over here you like the look of.'

Broad watched, caught somewhere between terrified and fascinated as she reached down, took the hem of her tattered skirts and pulled it up, up to show the writing tattooed around and around her thigh, long-winded quotes from some political treatise or other, and she slipped that leg over his and straddled him, knives and chains scraping against her breastplate as she perched herself on his lap.

'Sarlby tells me you want to talk to the Breakers,' she said.

Broad tried to tell himself Judge on top of him was the last thing in the world he'd want. That he was in more danger here than he'd been climbing a ladder onto the walls of Musselia, crowded with enemies. That she disgusted him.

He wasn't sure who he was fooling.

'Shame is, the Breakers melted away like snow in spring,' said Judge.

'Those they didn't hang, like your friend Sarlby here...' and she tossed him the bottle, 'have seen the light of the *fire*. Seen the folly of half-measures. Risinau's off down in Keln or some such fancy place, preaching his blather to the wide-eyed and wishful. But those of us still in Valbeck.' She leaned close, breath hot on his face. 'We're all Burners now.'

Broad tried to keep Liddy and May in his mind. It was them he was doing this for. Had to keep a grip on himself. But it wasn't easy with Judge's crotch pressing up against his half-hard prick and the reek of spirits so strong on her breath it was making his head spin.

'Breakers or Burners,' croaked Broad, 'makes no difference.'

'Suppose it wouldn't to you.' She gave a long sniff. 'I hear you've crossed the lines.'

'Gone to serve the owners,' grunted Sarlby.

'And not just any owner, but the queen bee herself! The fruit of Old Sticks' own withered loins, Savine dan fucking Glokta!'

'Dan Brock,' muttered Broad.

Judge smiled. Or at any rate showed her teeth. 'Don't try and trick a trickster. Or at least try a bit harder. The owners chisel our pay every unjust way they can and call it an honest wage. The Closed Council drafts a set of rules that make the rich richer and drive the poor to starve and call it an equality law. You know what they named the most low-lying, smog-choking, shit-stinking alley of rotten cellars in all of Valbeck?' She leaned a little closer to whisper it. 'Primrose Heights. Calling a thing a different thing don't make it a different thing, now does it?'

'Wouldn't know,' croaked Broad, who beat men for a living and called it labour relations, 'I'm no philosopher.'

'Just a *traitor*.' She barked the word, and suddenly she was standing over him with her black eyes blazing, a handful of his shirt clutched in one trembling fist and a cleaver drawn in the other. She pressed that cold metal into his neck, twisting him back in the chair, and the men around the cellar shifted and nodded and grunted their anger.

'I'm one o' you,' growled Broad, trying to scrape together as much dignity as he could with his life hanging from a thread and a badly spun one at that. 'I fought the good fight here. Stood on the barricades. Stayed to the bitter end. Chance might've landed us in different places, but we want the same thing. Food for our families. A safe place for 'em to sleep. An honest wage for honest work.' All the old slogans, puked up like he still believed them. 'Malmer was my friend. I was angry as anyone when they hanged him. But the Young Lion had no part o' that. He wants to fight the Closed Council like he fought the Northmen—'

He winced as Judge pressed that cleaver harder into his neck, right on the point of drawing blood, chair legs grinding as she started to tip him backwards. 'Is that a fact?'

'It is.' Broad's voice had a scared squeak to it. Or was it an excited one? He had to keep a grip on himself. 'The whole army of Angland. On the last day of summer, they'll land on the coast of Midderland. Thousands of Stour Nightfall's warriors, too. They'll join up with the noblemen and they'll march on Adua.'

'Rebellion against Old Sticks and his Closed Council. Against His fucking Majesty?' The cold metal was of a sudden whipped away and Judge stood, letting Broad's chair lurch forward onto its front legs. She gave a shiver all over, chains and knives rattling. 'I got chills, Sarlby. You got chills?'

'I got lice,' said Sarlby.

'Who hasn't? Well, apart from Savine dan fucking Brock. Daresay that bitch shits soap and pisses perfume.' Judge narrowed her eyes to black slits, with a gleam of flame at the corners. It was hard to look into them. Hard to look away. 'So she wants us to rise up, does she? Keep the king's soldiers busy so she can walk a carpet of flowers right into the Agriont and slip her pretty little arse onto the king's throne. Am I close to it?'

Broad glanced around at the men. 'You're Burners, no? I thought rising up was what you're all about. You'll get no better chance than this.'

Couple of them looked like they were buying it, but Judge only sneered. 'Let's say it all goes your way, and the Young Lion tears the Closed Council down and buries his wife's father and all the other vultures, what then?' She poked him in the gut with her cleaver, made him wince. 'It's the nobles backing him. The owners still. We'll have done nothing but swapped one set of users for another!'

'You'll get a say in how things are done. Might not be a Great Change, but it'll be a change for the better. The Brocks have done some good up in Angland. Limits on workers' hours. Rules to keep gears and driveshafts safe. Controls on truck shops and overseers' penalties. All sorts o' things the Breakers been after for years.'

'That's true,' said Sarlby. 'I heard about that.'

Some of the others mumbled agreement. 'Aye, my cousin's got a place in a mine, he's working three hours less a day.'

One even went so far as to mutter, 'They call her the Darling o' the Slums—'

'Do me a *fucking favour*!' Judge leaned down snarling over Broad again, lamplight gleaming on the edge of her raised cleaver. 'You must take me for some new kind o' fool.'

'No one's saying they're your friends!' Trying to stay calm in spite of his thudding heart. 'But they're the next best thing. Your enemies' enemies.' Broad tried to smile. The way Savine smiled, like she held all the cards however bad things looked. Probably didn't work too well chained to a chair, but he tried. 'Come to the docks. See what I brought with me. Then you can be... the judge.'

'Oh, I like that.' She smiled, switched back in an instant from fury to oily desire, and she settled herself in Broad's lap again, closer than ever, making him grunt through gritted teeth. 'I expected fisticuffs from you, but never wordplay.' He could hardly think for the horrible, beautiful reek of spirits on her breath. 'Did you bring me a present?' Had to keep a grip on himself. Had to. '*How* romantic.'

There was a squeal of complaining wood as Bannerman wrenched the crate open. The Burners clustered close, staring down eager as winter tramps around a brazier.

Swords glittered inside. A neat row of brand-new swords, all the same, with a long, straight, single-edged blade and a dull steel grip, fresh oiled from the foundry.

'Two-score infantry swords.' Bannerman pulled one from the crate with a practised flourish and displayed it to Judge. 'Latest pattern. Still warm from the Ostenhorm Armoury. Better than the King's Own carry.' He nodded towards some other crates. 'Two-score horseman's axes and two-score halberds, too. Two-score breastplates and two-score helms. All best Angland steel.'

Another crate screeched as Halder ripped the lid off. He pulled out a flatbow, sleek and deadly looking, even the frame made of metal, bored through with slots to make it lighter.

'Latest design with the new Wearing crank,' said Halder. 'A dressmaker could draw it and it'll still pierce the heaviest armour.' He tossed the bow across to Sarlby and he snatched it from the air, twisted it over, rattled the trigger, seeming to stand a little straighter with a weapon in his hand.

'Good?' asked Judge.

'Good,' said Sarlby, holding the flatbow to his eye and sighting down it, then slowly starting to smile. 'Very good.'

'Then there's this.' Broad ripped the top from the biggest case, dragging a fistful of wood-shavings out of the way. Dull metal shone underneath. A great dark, tapering tube three strides long, and stamped into it: *Armoury of Ostenhorm, 606.*

'What's this?' whispered Judge. 'You've got a fucking thunder pipe?'

'No. *You've* got one. The newest kind. Can throw a solid ball a mile or turn a few handfuls of ironware into a rain of death. They've taken to calling 'em cannons,' said Broad. 'From some Styrian word, I hear. But whatever you call it, it comes to the same thing.' He leaned close to whisper in her ear. 'Lightning in your pocket.'

'Never saw such a beautiful thing.' Judge stroked that metal with her fingertips, up and down with a steady swish, swish, and Broad felt that sick tickle stronger than ever, not sure whether it was Judge or the weapons or some combination of the two that dried his mouth out so.

Made him wonder, for a moment, what she might do with all this machine-sharpened steel. She who'd killed dozens in Valbeck with just a bit of rope? He told himself all he was doing was taking a thing from here to there on the orders of his mistress. Wasn't his concern what folk chose to do with it after. A tale traders in weapons been telling themselves since weapons first were made, no doubt.

Judge's black eyes rolled across to him, gleaming wetly in the echoing gloom of the warehouse. 'Well, I don't think I was ever brought nicer presents, Gunnar Broad. I thought nothing could warm me to Savine dan Brock, but she's managed to light a fire in my quim even so. Perhaps she really will be the Darling of the Slums in the end.'

'And this is just a taste,' said Broad.

'Just slipping me the tip, eh, you fucking tease?'

'I tell the Brocks we've got a deal, there's a full shipload waiting on the docks in Ostenhorm. Enough to arm a whole rebellion. And all they want is for you to speak to the Weaver, get the Breakers and Burners to do what they want to do anyway. Rise up, all at once. On the last day of summer. Throw up the barricades and fix the King's Own where they are. Make sure they can't come to help His Majesty. The Young Lion will do the rest.'

'Huh.' Judge considered him through narrowed eyes, point of her tongue showing between her teeth.

'What?'

'You know why they call me Judge? 'Cause I'm the best judge o' character. One look and I know a body better than they know themselves.' She pulled a wicked-looking axe from a freshly opened crate, all bright steel with no ornament. 'You say you're one of us. Malmer's old mate.

Good old Bull Broad, doing his best for the simple folk. But I reckon the jury's still out.'

Felt like Broad stood at a cliff-edge, one foot hovering in the empty air. But he was surrounded by angry madmen. Ones he'd just armed. There was no way back. His voice sounded husky in his ear. 'How can I convince you?'

Judge smiled wide. 'The very question I've been thirsting for. There's three dozen fellow travellers of ours been jailed after a little riot. They're being brought into Valbeck for a show trial and summary execution. Tomorrow night, is it, Sarlby?'

'Tomorrow night,' said Sarlby, holding a vicious-looking flatbow bolt up to the light.

'We're going to free those good people.'

'And you want me to help?'

'*You* want you to help. Admit it. You can't wait to get your hands bloody.'

Broad swallowed. He should've known words weren't going to get this done. 'They'll be guarded.'

'Heavily,' said Judge, the axe whistling faintly as she swung it back and forth.

'And the guards'll be expecting trouble.'

Judge nodded towards the cannon. 'Not this much.'

'Men'll die.'

'Ain't much worth doing don't involve a few dead men.' She tossed the axe over to him and he caught it by its metal shaft. 'That a point against the plan, in your mind, or in favour?'

Broad frowned as he weighed the axe in his hand. Truth was he wasn't sure.

Changes at the Top

'It seems our letter-writer may have been a friend after all,' said Orso. 'Or at least an honest enemy. King Jappo confirmed it all.'

Glokta stared bright-eyed across his desk. 'Do you trust him?'

'Not a bit. But I believe him. He told me he had been invited to join a conspiracy aimed at bringing down the Union's government and offered Sipani in return. Numerous lords of the Open Council are involved, and at least one member of the Closed.'

'Any names?'

'Only two.' Orso pronounced them carefully, dropped into the silence like great stones dropped down a well. 'Stour Nightfall . . . and Leo dan Brock.'

The Arch Lector closed his eyes. Crushing news, especially for him, but Orso could have sworn he saw a wry smile at the corner of the old Inquisitor's mouth. 'Body found floating by the docks,' he murmured.

'Sorry?'

Glokta took a sharp breath and snapped his eyes open. 'I must resign at once.'

'Your Eminence, I need your advice more than ever—'

'But we both know you cannot have it.' Glokta looked down at his white-gloved fist, clenched on the desktop. 'When you have clung to power as tightly as I have, it can be difficult to let go.' He spread his fingers out flat, the purple stone on his ring of office glittering. 'But the time has come. My son-in-law may very well be a traitor.' He curled his lips back from his ruined teeth. 'Even . . . my daughter.'

'But—'

'Superior Pike!' shrieked Glokta, so piercingly Orso was obliged to narrow his eyes as Pike walked in, black coat flapping.

'For twenty-five years, Superior Pike has been my right hand,' said Glokta. 'No one has more experience or better judgement. No one understands so well what must be done. I suggest he serves as head of the Inquisition until you appoint a new Arch Lector.'

Orso glanced up at Pike's melted mask of a face. He would have liked to choose someone else. Someone softer, gentler, more just. He remembered the hanging of the prisoners at Valbeck. Remembered Pike gazing up unfeelingly at Malmer's gibbet. He had proved himself ruthless and remorseless. A man feared and hated by all the Crown's enemies, and most of its friends.

The very qualities a king needs in an Arch Lector.

'I see no reason not to make the appointment permanent,' said Orso. Perhaps Bayaz would have other ideas when he next visited, but for now the little people would have to make their own mistakes.

Pike solemnly inclined his head. 'I serve and obey, Your Majesty.'

Orso had never liked Glokta. He was not really a man it was possible to like. But he had come to respect him. To rely upon him, even. And now, when Orso most needed support, he would be gone. 'What will you do?'

Glokta's brows went up, as though the question had never occurred before. 'Move to the country? Pin butterflies to a board? Argue with my wife? I always wanted to write a book about fencing.'

'I . . . will look forward to reading it.' Though, in honesty, Orso had never been much of a reader. 'I, and the Union, thank you for your distinguished service.'

Glokta gave a little snort of laughter. 'Only promise me one thing. Should you think me worthy of a statue on the Kingsway . . . have it stand up.' He waved a finger towards the Practical lurking behind him, and the man turned his wheeled chair towards the door.

Pike lowered his head. 'Your Eminence.'

Glokta twisted the ring from his finger, weighed it in his hand a moment, then offered it to Pike. 'Your Eminence.' He glanced around his office one last time. The bare walls. The stark furniture. The heaps of unfinished paperwork. 'I wish you both the very best of luck.'

And as simply as that, it was done. No ceremony, no medals, no grand speech and no cheering crowds. From the pinnacle of power to a toothless old cripple in one brief conversation. The chair squeaked from the room and the doors were shut upon Sand dan Glokta. The era of Old Sticks was at an end.

Arch Lector Pike stepped behind the desk. There was no chair now, of course, and so he stood, spreading his burned hands out on the leather top and frowning down at the ring on his finger. It seemed Glokta had found the one man even more monstrous than he as his replacement. But these were desperate times. And in desperate times, one must sometimes call upon the services of monsters.

'How shall we proceed, Your Majesty?' asked Pike. 'Softly, or . . . otherwise?'

Orso took a breath through his nose. 'Could you send for Inquisitor Teufel? I have some ideas.'

Colonel Forest and Corporal Tunny were waiting outside the House of Questions. Forest, typically, standing to attention in a modest uniform. Tunny, typically, sprawling on a bench with a newsbill over his face.

'Gentlemen,' said Orso. 'Would you walk with me?' He felt an irrepressible need to stay busy, and the two old soldiers fell in on either side as he strode towards the palace, his retinue of Knights of the Body clattering after.

For twenty years, he could have done anything he wanted, and he had done nothing. With his future blindingly bright, surrounded by comfort and buoyed up by every privilege, getting out of bed had sometimes felt impossible. Now, beset by enemies and with the gloomiest of outlooks, he fizzed with energy.

'How many men do we have now?'

Forest kept his voice low. 'Over four thousand, Your Majesty. Lot of 'em served with the Crown Prince's Division, keen to follow you again.'

'Really?' Orso found that hard to believe.

'You never pretended to be a general yourself, but you gave 'em pride.'

'That's . . . rather moving. Thank you.'

'Their gear was gathering dust in the Agriont's cellars in any case. It only needed passing out again.'

There was an irony. Savine had paid for the weapons they would fight her husband with. 'Where are you keeping them?'

'Some in disused barracks outside the city. Some camped in woods and valleys. Some still at their old jobs, waiting for the call. But they can be gathered quickly.'

Orso smiled. Finally, a sunny spot in the darkness. 'I knew you wouldn't let me down, General Forest.'

'I'm a colonel, Your Majesty.'

'If the High King of the Union says a man's a general, who's to deny it? Consider yourself promoted.'

'Look at that!' Tunny gave Forest a slovenly salute. 'From enlisted man to general and it only took you forty years. You should get yourself a bigger hat.'

Forest pulled off his worn fur hat, revealing his sizeable bald patch, and frowned down at it. 'What's wrong with my hat?'

'It's a fine, rugged, manly hat,' said Orso. 'Don't listen to him.'

'Only looks a little bit like a quim,' said Tunny.

Orso sternly shook his head. 'Now, now, Corporal. Any more insubordination and I'll promote *you*.'

'I'd sooner face the hangman.'

'Oh, I daresay we'll all be doing *that*.' And Orso found he had actually delivered a carefree chuckle. They came out into the park, crunching down a gravel path, shadows stretching across the dew-glittering lawns from the early morning sun. Bloody hell, had he ever been up this early before? Everything was so crisp and clean and *beautiful* at this time of day. 'It's looking likely that we'll have to fight in the not too distant future.' And he slapped a hand down on Forest's shoulder. 'Can you gather more men?'

The newly minted general glanced cautiously about, but there were few prying ears. Those without rebellions to crush were still in bed. 'I can, Your Majesty, if you can gather more money.'

'Valint and Balk put no limit on my credit. Recruit as many as we can arm, pick officers you trust and get them drilling. And secure whatever horses you can lay your hands on, too, we may have to move quickly.'

'Your Majesty.' Forest made to put his hat on, then stopped. 'Bloody thing does look like a quim.' And he strode away.

'Valint and Balk.' Tunny slowly shook his head. 'They've got a ruthless reputation.'

'A bank with a reputation for mercy is like a whore with a reputation for chastity – one fears they won't get the job done. No doubt our conspirators are watching me, though. Too many visits to my financiers might arouse suspicion. Which is why you'll be my representative to the bank.'

Tunny was not an easy man to surprise. Orso found it rather gratifying when his jaw dropped. 'I'll be bloody *what?*'

'The only real skill a king needs is to pick the best men to serve him. You may like to paint yourself as the least dependable man in the Union, but... I rather suspect it's all a front. When it comes to it, I'm not sure there's a man in the Circle of the World I trust more.'

Tunny stared at him. 'We're all doomed.'

The old bureaucrats of the Closed Council looked wild-haired and flustered, and who could blame them? They had been dragged from their beds to an unscheduled meeting in which a fully armoured Knight of the Body loomed behind each chair, even the empty chair of Bayaz, down at the foot of the table. The White Chamber felt positively cramped by so much polished steel.

Orso grimly steepled his fingers and frowned at each old face in turn. None of them gave any immediate sign of being a conspirator. But then conspirators rarely do. Not the good ones, anyway. 'My lords, I am sorry to call upon you so early,' he said, 'but we have grave issues to discuss.'

'Where is Arch Lector Glokta?' asked Gorodets, glancing nervously up at Gorst, who towered implacably at Orso's shoulder.

'I accepted his resignation just after dawn.' There was a collective gasp. Orso held out a hand to Pike, whose spotless white garments made his face look, if anything, more blighted and expressionless than his black ones had. 'Arch Lector Pike has taken charge of the Inquisition.'

'Resigned?' whispered Hoff. 'But why?'

'Because his son-in-law, Leonault dan Brock, Lord Governor of Angland, plans to rebel against the Crown.'

Brock's treachery left the room even more stunned than Glokta's resignation. Gorodets was tugging so hard at his beard Orso worried he might tear his lower jaw off. 'Can we be sure?'

'I was informed anonymously. But on my trip to Sipani I met with King Jappo of Styria.'

'You...' Matstringer looked like he might swallow his tongue. 'This is an unprecedented breach of protocol—'

'Treason takes precedence,' grated out Pike.

'It had to be an informal meeting,' said Orso. 'Off the books.' Most of the old men were looking thunderstruck. Whether at the news of imminent rebellion, or the discovery that Orso was capable of arranging something on his own, it was unclear. 'Jappo confirmed my worst fears. The Young Lion has gathered a considerable following of disaffected noblemen and means to invade Midderland.'

'By the Fates,' croaked Hoff.

'Worse still ... he has enlisted the help of the King of the Northmen, Stour Nightfall.'

'He plans to bring those savages onto Union soil?' The surveyor general's voice reached so high a pitch, it was a wonder the windows did not shatter.

'Unthinkable,' whispered Hoff, slumping back in his chair.

'Outrageous!' frothed Gorodets. 'Send to the Superior in Angland! Have Brock arrested! Have him bloody hanged!'

'Brock is loved in Angland,' said Pike, in his emotionless drone. 'We are despised. As long as he makes no move against us, he is beyond our reach.'

'Your Majesty.' Brint leaned forward with his one fist clenched, the yellow stone on his ring glinting. 'The King's Own are scattered to counter the threat of the Breakers. Lord Marshal Rucksted is in Keln with most of the cavalry. We must concentrate our forces at once so we are ready to meet any rebel threat and decisively crush it.' And he thumped the table and made several of the other old men jump.

'Agreed,' said Orso. The first useful contribution. 'Please send out the orders, Marshal Brint, to Rucksted and the rest. In the meantime, we must do everything possible to pull the noblemen's teeth.'

'The Open Council stands in summer recess,' said Hoff. 'Some members are in the city still, but most will have repaired to their estates.'

Gorodets swallowed. 'Several sought dispensation to raise extra soldiers because of fears over the Breakers. Very many extra soldiers... in some cases...'

An uneasy muttering swept the table. Brint clenched his fist even tighter. The high consul glanced furtively at Gorst. Hoff dabbed at his sweaty forehead with the fur-trimmed sleeve of his gown. The whole stuffy little room reeked of panic and suspicion. By the Fates, any one of the old bastards could have been the traitor.

'Go to your departments,' said Orso, 'and make preparations. I want our defences shored up. I want forces on high alert. I want anything disloyal rooted out.' He stood, planting his hands on the table. 'You are the only ones I can trust. My father's faithful advisors. My loyal Closed Council. If we stay together, we will yet weather this storm.'

Orso strode from the room, and with a screeching of chair legs the old men struggled up after him.

Into the Light

'You got them?' asked Vick.

'We got them,' said the Practical, voice muffled through his mask.

His black-clothed colleagues swarmed over the white-tiled bathhouse like an infestation of beetle, necks and foreheads beaded with sweat, sticks in their hands or blades wetly glinting. Men naked or wrapped in towels cringed against the walls. One lay on his side, sobbing, bloody hands clapped to his mouth. Another was sprawled face down in a dark slick, a dagger lying nearby, a pink bloom spreading into a pool beside him.

Vick stepped over the corpse and into the steamy little chamber beyond, a mosaic of intertwined snakes just visible on the floor. Appropriate. Two men sat on a bench, naked except for cloths around their waists. One was blond-haired and handsome, with moustaches he'd clearly put a lot of effort into cultivating.

'Lord Heugen,' she said.

As the steam thinned, she saw the other man more clearly. Older, grey-haired, the whole left side of his body oddly withered. His left arm was gone above the elbow, a long-healed stump.

'And Lord Marshal Brint.' Vick allowed herself the thinnest smile. 'There's one riddle solved.'

'And who the bloody hell are you?' sneered Heugen.

'Vick dan Teufel, Inquisitor Exempt.'

Brint gave a resigned sigh and ever so slowly sagged back. Heugen kept bristling. 'One of Old Sticks' cronies, eh? Well, he's gone too far this time—'

'He's gone altogether,' said Vick. 'Retired. Didn't the lord marshal tell you? I'm here on the king's personal orders. So you can forget about appealing to a higher authority. There isn't one.'

Heugen's voice had gone shrill. 'There's no law against visiting a bath-house!'

'No, but judges take a dim view of planning treason in one.'

'How dare you! The marshal and I are old friends. We've been talking of surprising our families with a joint garden party—'

'Hope I get an invite,' said Vick. 'I love an outdoor function.' She glanced over at Tallow, lurking in a steamy corner, dressed like an attendant in sandals and loincloth, almost as skinny as the mop he leaned on. 'Well? Did they talk about surprising the relatives? Or maybe giving someone else a shock?'

'Lord Marshal Brint discussed a meeting of the Closed Council this morning,' said Tallow, calmly. He was actually getting good at this. 'Said the king had discovered their plans. Then Lord Heugen talked of sending warnings to their friends, and of moving up the schedule. He also mentioned leaving the city at once and gathering his troops.'

Vick raised one brow. 'Sounds like a *hell* of a party.'

'You led them straight to us!' Heugen bared his teeth at Brint. 'You one-armed dunce!'

'The king's idea, in fact,' said Vick. 'The man's not half the fool you've taken him for. He knew someone on the Closed Council was betraying him, just wasn't sure who, so he rattled the cage and I caught what dropped loose. And here we are.' Damn, it was hot in there. Her jacket was already clinging wet from the steam. She started unbuttoning it. 'So tell me. Who else is on the guest list for your garden party? Your little conspiracy against the Crown?' She peeled her jacket off and tossed it to Tallow, leaned down over Heugen in her vest, hands on her knees. 'I want names. Now.'

'Don't tell her a bloody thing,' said Brint.

'Don't worry about *that*,' sneered Heugen. 'My lips are—'

Vick slapped him across the face, and not gently. He gasped as his head snapped sideways, turned slowly back to stare at her in stunned disbelief, one trembling hand raised to his pinking cheek. She wondered if it was the first time someone ever hit him hard. A life of luxury is poor preparation for a beating. Who'd know better than her, the pampered daughter of the Master of the Royal Mints, suddenly snatched away to the mines of Angland?

Maybe that thought put a bit more venom in her next slap, hard enough to get his mouth bleeding. 'You've given me no time to be subtle,' she hissed at him, 'so this is going to get very painful very fast.' She slapped him again, even harder, her fingers stinging and blood speckling the wall beside his face. 'Give me names.'

Tears glimmered in the corners of Heugen's eyes. The sudden pain, and the confusion, and the terrible, terrible shock of finding the world was not at all what you had thought. She knew how it felt. 'I . . . *demand*—'

Her fist thudded into his ribs and he gave a breathy grunt, eyes bulging. No doubt, safe in the armour of his wealth and status, he'd always thought himself a strong man. Now, surrounded by Practicals and with all his armour stripped away, he learned how strong he really was. Her other fist sank into his side and he twisted over, groaning, his loincloth slipping off, leaving him stark naked and helpless on the bench.

'Names!' She climbed on top of him, knee in his back, the smacks and thuds of her punches falling dead on the steamy air.

'Names!' He gasped and gurgled, tried to curl up into a ball, and she leaned over and punched him in the arse, caught his fruits and made him howl.

'Names, fucker!'

'Isher!' he squealed, sobbing. 'It was all Isher's idea!' He talked so fast he was almost sick, the names tumbling over each other. 'Isher and Barezin! They brought Brock in! And Brock brought Stour Nightfall, and that woman Rikke, the Dogman's daughter! Lots of others on the Open Council. There's Lady Wetterlant, and . . . and . . .'

'What's happened to the world?' whispered Brint as he watched Heugen spill his guts with a look of disbelieving contempt.

'Far as I can tell, it's always been like this.' Vick jerked her head towards the Practical. 'Get him to the House of Questions. See what else he knows.'

'Wait!' slobbered Heugen as he was dragged out by the wrist, trying to cover his prick with his other hand. 'I can be useful!' He clutched at the archway. 'Please! No!' With an annoyed grunt, the Practical ripped him free and he was gone.

'Have to say I'm surprised it was you.' Vick frowned over at Lord Marshal Brint. 'Always took you for an honourable man.'

'Why do you think I did it? We're supposed to be a *Union!*' He roared the last word with sudden anger, clenching his one fist, and Vick stepped back, watchful. She reckoned him far more dangerous than Heugen, however many limbs he was missing.

But all he did was sag back against the tiles. 'I fought the Northmen in the High Places, you know. Held my best friend while he died. Then again at Osrung. Lost my arm there. Lost my *wife* there.' And he looked down at the ring on his little finger. A woman's ring with a yellow stone. 'I gave my whole life for the Union. For the idea that we stand *together*. Then they attacked our Protectorate. Land the king had sworn to defend. And what did we do? *Nothing*.' He said the word as if he couldn't believe it. 'We left Lady Finree and our brothers in Angland to fend for themselves. And why? So we could make a few more payments to the Banking House of Valint and Balk? The Closed Council sold our principles for a few marks. And they *dare* talk of treason?'

He looked up at her with weary eyes. 'None of this will make any difference. The noblemen are already out of your reach, gathering their forces. The Young Lion is on his way. He'll put things right again.'

Vick gave a snort. 'You should tell the folk I saw die in the camps how right things used to be. You're going to shed a sea of blood, and the best you'll manage is to swap one set of bastards for another. Principles? I'd laugh if I had the stomach.' She frowned down at his hand. 'Now give me that ring.'

'Inquisitor Teufel.' Glokta smiled up, showing the yawning gap in his front teeth. 'Thank you for coming.'

It only occurred to her then that she could've stayed away. Could've ignored him. But obedience can be a hard habit to break. Ask any dog.

'Of course.' She sat stiffly on the bench where they had met before, more than once. It took an effort not to add *Your Eminence*.

She had never seen him without his white robes, his ring of office, his black-clad entourage. The awe-inspiring Arch Lector had become, overnight, a withered old man, heavily wrapped up even in the summer warmth, attended by just the one huge Practical who used to push his chair, awkward in simple footman's clothes and with a rash about his mouth from the mask he no longer wore. Glokta had been her saviour, her mentor, her master, her jailer. She wondered what they were now, without the office and the great desk and the vast difference in power? Friends? She had to suppress a splutter of entirely inappropriate laughter at the thought of the word.

'I hear congratulations are in order once again. Lord Heugen's faithlessness is far from surprising but it shocks me that Lord Marshal Brint would betray the Crown.' Glokta slowly shook his head. 'Ten years we sat together on the Closed Council.'

'You think you know someone ...' murmured Vick, rubbing absently at her bruised knuckles as she frowned out at the sunlight glittering on the lake. People were boating, laughing, lounging on the banks. You would never have thought a civil war was coming. But then the worst betrayals often happen in good weather. When there's a blizzard blowing, people are too busy huddling together.'

'I am leaving Adua today,' said Glokta. 'My wife thinks the country air may be good for my health. That is . . . what she tells me she thinks, anyway. I suspect she does not want us to become sad ghosts haunting the halls where we were once powerful. I suspect she is wise in this, as in so much else.' He cleared his throat. 'Before I left, I wanted to thank you.'

She looked sharply across at him. She should have been pleased to get the thanks of the man she'd served faithfully for so many years. But pleasure was not her first feeling.

'For all you have done for me,' he went on, not meeting her eye. 'Done for the Union. Especially given . . . what the Union has done for you. Or what it has failed to do. By my judgement, our new king has had few more valuable servants. So. Thank you. For your courage. Your diligence. Your . . . patriotism.'

'Diligence and patriotism.' She gave a bitter snort, slowly clenching her aching fist. 'That or lack of choices. That or being too much of a coward to find another way. That or sticking to the habits of the camps, and grabbing the chance to stand with the winners, and making the only move up the convict can see – from taking the beating to giving it.'

She wasn't sure why she was suddenly angry. Because of the things he'd made her do? Or because he wouldn't be there to make her do more?

'Well.' Glokta looked towards the summer revellers. So near to them, yet somehow in a different world. 'I have often said that life is the misery we endure between disappointments. Whatever the reasons, you have never once disappointed me. I wish I had been so reliable in return, but I fear I have let you down. I know how much you want to be . . . *need* to be . . . loyal.'

'Loyal.' She thought of all the people she'd lied to, deceived, sold out over the last eight years. It was quite the list. Malmer dangling above the road to Valbeck. Sibalt and his pathetic little dreams of the Far Country. Moor and Grise. Tallow and his sister. She could still smell the rebels' camp in Starikland, after she told the soldiers where to find them. 'I betray people for a living.'

'Yes.' He gave her a knowing glance. 'Perhaps that's why you need to be loyal. I always imagined there would be time to give you your proper reward, but . . . at the pinnacle of power, as you see . . . time runs out suddenly. Might I at least give you one piece of advice, before I go?'

She could have said no. She could have punched him in the face. But she did nothing.

He reached up to gently wipe some wet from under his leaking left eye. 'Forgive yourself.'

She sat there, on that bench, jaw clenched, breath hissing fast in her nose, while down on the banks of the lake someone gave a braying peel of laughter at some joke.

'There is no way out of the camps without His Majesty's approval.'

She could have stuck her fingers in her ears. She could have got up and stalked away. Instead she sat there, her skin turned cold and every muscle rigid.

'Your brother's little prisoners' revolution was doomed from the start.'

She remembered that last glimpse of his face. The shock and the hurt as they dragged him away. She remembered it as if it was happening now.

'It would have been easy to give in to sentimentality,' said Glokta. 'But you did the brave thing. The right thing. Turning him in. Buying your freedom.'

She closed her eyes, but her brother's accusing face was still there. As if it was etched into her lids.

'He would only have dragged you down with him. Some people . . . cannot be saved.'

Now she stood, wobbly, ready to run, almost, but Glokta caught her wrist. Caught it with surprising strength. When she turned back, his eyes were fixed on her, fever-bright.

'Everyone should forgive themselves, Vick.' He gave her wrist another squeeze then let her go, looking out towards the lake again. 'After all . . . no one else will.'

Some Men Can't
Help Themselves

Broad knelt there, in the dirt, in the darkness, axe in his fist, frowning across bare mud studded with tree stumps. Towards the road and the ruined sawmill just beyond.

He'd promised Liddy no more trouble.

Yet here he was, armed to the teeth in the moonlit brush with a crowd of bitter beggars, waiting to ambush the king's soldiers so the maddest woman he ever met would help him bring down the government. If there was such a thing as no more trouble, he'd got himself about as far from it as a man could get.

He'd promised Liddy no more trouble. But he'd promised her a good life, too. What do you do when one promise runs head first into another? He'd no choice. Had to do this. For Savine, for his family.

That, and the thing he didn't really want to think about – how the axe felt so *right* in his fist as he gripped it tighter than ever.

'They're late,' grunted Sarlby.

Broad turned to look at him, the glint of moonlight in the corners of his sunken eyes and on the edges of his loaded flatbow. 'Coming to something when you can't rely on folk to come timely to their own ambush.'

'Shhhh,' hissed Judge.

Broad shifted back into the shadows as he heard the faint sound of hoofs, rattling harness, grind of carriage wheels.

The fear sharpened, and the excitement underneath it, creeping up his throat as lamplight glimmered on the rotten tree stumps, gleamed on the puddles in the road, caught the sharpened logs of the collapsing fence and the long shed with its fallen-in roof.

The pulse thudded in his head as the first riders came through the trees into the open. Soldiers with lanterns, hint of red uniforms, helmets and breastplates gleaming. A dozen, maybe. Then a wagon of some sort. A big, black, weighty shape pulled by a team of six.

The beam of a lantern came stabbing towards the trees as one of the riders turned, Judge's tattered silhouette frozen before they all shrank into the bushes. Broad heard laughter, saw the lamplit smoke of breath as he held his own. That same feeling he'd had in the trenches in Styria, waiting for the order to charge, desperate to go.

The horsemen kept moving. The big wagon lurched after on the rutted road. More riders followed. Six more, maybe? That was all.

Broad eased closer to Judge. 'This right?' he whispered, hardly able to make the words for the tightness in his throat. 'They can't fit three-dozen prisoners in that one wagon.'

'I'll take care of the planning,' said Judge, wet teeth gleaming in her smile. 'You get the killing done.'

'Wait up!' came floating from the road, and the column clattered to an awkward halt. The officer at the front swung from his saddle, held up his lantern, beam flashing on the logs scattered across the track. Where Broad and the others had torn the sawmill's fence down a few hours before.

The wagon was still grinding forward in spite of its driver hauling on the reins, crowding the horsemen into a milling, grumbling mass. Sarlby brought up his flatbow, calmly settled the stock against his shoulder. Someone drew a sword with a soft scrape of steel, exciting to Broad as a lover's whisper. He felt a sudden urge to roll his sleeves up. Important to have a routine. But it was too late now.

'Ready...' he heard Judge say in a snarl that brought the ugly tickle in his guts to a throbbing ache. 'Ready...'

There was a flash like lightning, the great scar through the forest lit brighter than day, the broken teeth of the stumps casting strange shadows, the outline of men and horses frozen for an instant before they were flung tumbling in a spurt of fire. A crashing explosion clapped off the trees, a whizzing like angry wasps, flicking and pinging in the undergrowth. Something thudded into the trunk beside them in a spray of splinters.

Sarlby ducked down.

'Fuck!' someone hissed.

'Yes!' screamed Judge, standing up and throwing her fists into the sky.

Broad was already running. Towards the lamplight, the plunging horses, the swelling cloud of smoke. Pounding across the clearing for the road and the sawmill, the black world bouncing, the quick breath hissing through his gritted teeth, the eagerness boiling up his throat, setting him on fire.

His boot hit something in the darkness. Stump or root or rut. It spun him around, he fell and went sliding on his face in the mud. Near cut himself on his axe. Maybe he did cut himself. He was up again, running again, towards the flickering, smearing lights. Towards the great wagon. One of its six horses looked to be dead, the others had dragged it from the road, plunging in the traces, left it leaning against a stump with one wheel uselessly spinning, driver slumped in his seat.

Broad dashed around it, axe raised, ready to strike, then ducked back from flailing hooves, spraying mud. A horse was rearing and screaming and biting, maddened, flanks wet with blood, a dead man bouncing after it, one boot caught in the stirrup and his breastplate all riddled with holes.

Someone was screaming, rolling, wreathed in fire. His lantern must've got shattered in the blast, sprayed him with burning oil. A soldier dragged himself up, helmet all skewed, twisted face sticky red, trying to draw his sword. Broad's axe smashed the side of his head in.

'What happened?' someone shouted, stumbling from the smoke. Red jacket. Gold braid. An officer. 'You!' he shouted at Broad. Outraged. Not understanding. 'What *is* all—'

Broad's axe caught him right between the eyes, knocked his hat off and snapped his head back, arms flung wide as if he was offering a hug. He flopped into a puddle, blood flooding from the slice out of his forehead.

'Ambush!' someone screeched. 'Ambush!'

A rider came at him, sword raised. Broad reeled away, caught his horse in the face with his axe. It lurched sideways, toppled. The rider fell under it, yelling something. Broad hacked at him, missed and chopped deep into the horse's flank. The man tried to swing but trapped under the horse there was no venom in it, his sword just bounced off Broad's leg. Broad stepped on the soldier's sword arm, raised the axe high and stove his breastplate in with a hollow *clonk*.

He heard something behind him. Coughed. Groaned. Head hurt. He was lying on his face. Someone hit him? Tried to shake it off. Closed his hand around the cold shaft of the axe. Staggered up.

Everything was a sparkling blur. Writhing shadows. Smears of light. Lenses must've got knocked off. Only then he realised he'd even had 'em on. Shadows flickered and stabbed. He could hear Judge's voice. A demented shriek. 'Kill 'em! Kill 'em!'

A horse thundered past. He heard its hooves, felt the wind of it. He lashed with his axe, hit nothing and spun right around, nearly fell.

Someone was screaming. 'No! No! Please!' And then they were just screaming. Was it him? No, he had his teeth clenched, moaning and snarling through them, not even words, just heaved breath and sprayed spit. Couldn't think. Couldn't see. Prickling with sweat under his new breastplate.

Had a feeling two writhing shadows was one man stabbing another but he'd no idea who was who. There were no sides. Only those doing the killing and those getting killed.

He saw a man-shaped shadow against flames, stepped towards it, raising the axe high.

'Woah!' Hard to tell, but looked like the man was cringing back, holding up a hand. 'Woah, there, Bull!'

Bannerman's voice. Broad could just about recognise it through the ringing in his ears. Took an effort to lower the axe. Far more than to swing it. Felt heavy now. Hard to breathe, chest aching.

He squinted into the darkness. Started casting about for his lenses, bent over. Near tripped on something. A corpse, maybe. A horse, still weakly kicking.

He could hear someone whimpering. Judge's voice as well, dripping menace. 'Open this fucking carriage or we'll crack it open!'

'Here you go.' Halder pressed something into Broad's palm. His fingers were hurting now. A bunch of numb sausages. He was scared he'd crush his delicate little lenses in his hands. Held them to the light, squinting, almost right up against his face. Wiped them, wincing, finally fumbled them back onto his nose.

Dead men. Dead horses. Mud and blood, black in the light of fires from spilled lamp oil. That acrid smell of Gurkish sugar and charred meat he remembered from the sieges. He'd thought he never wanted to smell that again. Now he dragged it into his nostrils like a connoisseur might nose a glass of wine. Burners stood about, with their bright new arms and armour. Sarlby, grinning, empty flatbow over his shoulder.

Broad's head was throbbing. He touched his fingers to the side of it, tips came away red. *Good thing you've a thick skull,* Liddy would've said, and May would've laughed. But Broad couldn't see their faces. As blurred as if the lenses had slipped from his memory.

'Your men are dead!' Judge was screaming at the wagon. Broad saw now it was more like an armoured carriage, slit-windowed and covered in iron plates. 'Might be one or two rode off, but they don't want any more of what we gave 'em. Help's hours away. So I'm going to count to three, fucker, and if this carriage isn't open, I'll bring my cannon up here and open it the hard way. One!'

'All right!' came a muffled voice from inside. 'I'm coming out.' There was the squeaking of bolts being drawn and the carriage's iron door clattered open. Judge's men started forward, dragged someone out. A small man in neat clothes, balding hair all messed-up and a bleeding cut on his scalp, some sort of case in his hand. Or no, chained to his wrist with heavy manacles.

'Thought it was prisoners,' grunted Broad, frowning at him. 'Off to Valbeck to be hanged, you said.'

Judge shrugged. 'I say all kinds o' things.'

'You bloody fools!' the man spluttered, staring wide-eyed at the wreckage. Like all this was as unbelievable as things falling upwards or the sun not rising in the morning. 'Don't you know who this belongs to? Don't you know who I *work for*?'

Judge only grinned. 'You're the new manager of the new Valbeck branch of the Banking House of Valint and Balk.' The man's face slowly fell, outrage turning to fear, and fear to disbelieving horror. 'You've come to take up your position after I sentenced the last manager to hang and burned the last bank down. Unless I'm much mistook, you've brought funds for the building work, and look here . . .'

Two Burners clambered from the carriage, dragging a weighty chest with them, the sound of money jingling inside as they threw it on the scarred ground and started to smash at the lock with axes.

'This was about money?' Broad was having trouble thinking with the throbbing in the side of his head. Maybe he always had trouble thinking. He watched one of the Burners rooting through the pockets of a soldier's mangled corpse. Must've been close to the cannon when it went off. He hardly had anything left you could even call a head. 'What's the bank got to do with anything?'

Judge stuck her lips out in mocking pity. 'You really don't see too good, do you? Valint and Balk are the fucking enemy! Just as much as the king, or the owners, or the Closed Council, or the Open. The worst o' the lot, 'cause they hold the purse strings. Why d'you think the very first thing we did in the uprising was torch the bank?' Judge scooped coins out of the chest and let them drop jingling back. 'Every one o' these is a soldier for the cause, Bull Broad. Every single one.' Her eyes rolled towards that case the manager had chained to his wrist. 'What's this?'

'Nothing you'd want,' he said, hugging it to his chest.

Judge raised her chin so she could scratch at her rashy neck. 'I long ago tired o' men explaining to me what I want.'

'It's of no value!' he whined, voice getting higher and higher, making Broad's head ache worse and worse.

'If it's of no value, why's it locked to your wrist in an armoured carriage? Where's the key?'

He stared back. 'The whole point is I don't have one.'

Judge patted him on the cheek. 'Don't worry. I do.' And she slid her cleaver out. 'Little help here?'

Two Burners seized hold of the manager from behind and dragged him down beside a tree stump while Sarlby caught the case and the wrist it was chained to, started wrestling it towards him.

'No!' squawked the manager, struggling desperately to keep it hugged to his chest. 'You don't know what they'll do! Wait!'

'For what?' said Judge, laughter in her voice. 'The House o' the Maker to open and great Euz to spring forth wreathed in fire? 'Cause that's what it'll take to stop this.' Sarlby finally tore the case free, braced his feet against the stump and dragged the manager's arm across it by the chain while two other Burners held him, the bracelet cutting white into his wrist. A third raised a lamp high so no one missed anything, his eager grin lit from above.

'I find you guilty of offences against the people,' said Judge. 'Of usury, false dealing and profiting from misery. Of delaying the Great Change. And most of all, of selling your arse to those twin plagues Valint and Balk.'

'No!' whimpered the manager, eyes bulging. 'Please!'

Judge weighed the cleaver. 'Where's the best spot, you reckon?'

Sarlby shrugged. 'Between his hand and his elbow?'

'How dare you joke, Sarlby, this is a solemn fucking occasion.' And Judge brought the cleaver whistling down. There was a sick *thwack*. The manager gave a sobbing wail. But the blade didn't even cut through his sleeve, let alone his arm. It just bounced off.

'Shit,' said Judge. She took the cleaver in both hands, arched all the way back and swung it down with all her strength. Another thud, another howl, and it bounced off again, gouging the stump a little. Broad rubbed at the sore bridge of his nose. His head was pulsing.

'Who's in charge of keeping this sharp?' Judge held her cleaver up to the flickering firelight while the manager of the Valbeck branch of Valint and Balk sobbed and whimpered. You could see the bones in his wrist were broken. His arm was crooked as an old twig. But decidedly still attached. 'Sarlby? My cleaver's blunt.'

Sarlby watched the whole business with an expression of weary boredom. The kind they'd all had in Styria, by the end, after bearing witness to a procession of horrors. 'What am I? A knife-grinder?' The manager started howling again.

'Fuck!' snarled Broad, and his axe took the man's arm off just above the wrist with a meaty *thunk*, spattering everyone around the stump with blood.

Sarlby fell back, the case tumbling free, the manager's severed hand flopping loose in his lap.

'That's got it!' called Judge as Broad's axe smashed the case wide open with three more savage blows.

The manager took a great whooping breath as he stared at the blood welling from the stump of his arm, then the axe split his skull and cut his shriek off dead. Broad dragged it free of his ruined head, stood there with teeth bared, looking for something else to hit.

One of the two men who'd been holding the manager scrambled away. The other shrank back, eyes wide. Broad stood a moment longer, every muscle flexed tight, then with a roar that made them all flinch again, he flung the axe down and it bounced away across the road.

There was a pause, everyone staring. Then Judge gave a little giggle. 'Ouch,' she said, her eyes wide and her pale face dotted with blood, black in the lamplight. 'Always knew you belonged with us. With me. *To* me.'

Sarlby tossed the hand away and shook the contents of the case onto the muddy ground. 'Just papers,' he grunted, holding up a sheaf of documents. Judge started leafing through them by the flickering light of one of the fires.

'Deeds and contracts and legal whatever-the-fuck.' She started to drop them into the flames, paper covered in swirling calligraphy blackening and curling as it caught light. 'Won't be worth shit when the Great Change comes, eh?' And she grinned up at Broad, letting the rest slide from her fingers into the fire. 'Once our very good friends the Brocks throw down the king, we can decide afresh who owns what, who *owes* what.'

Broad stood staring at the banker's corpse, his eyes a little crossed like he didn't much approve of the gaping wound in the top of his skull. Felt like something he'd seen happen. Not something he'd done himself. He put a hand to his head again. It was hurting worse than ever. Damn, he needed a drink. But he knew it never helped. Quite the opposite.

'Look at you, you poor thing.' He felt Judge catch his face, drag it towards her so he had no choice but to stare into her gleaming eyes. 'Is it right, is it wrong, what have I done, and blah, blah, fucking blah. You done worse to better men, I've no doubt, but the truth is, there's no answers to those questions that mean a thing. Sooner you stop pretending and let go of all that shit for good, the better for you, the better for me, the better for everyone.'

'I have to go,' whispered Broad. He'd sworn no more trouble. 'I have to tell Lady Savine... to send more weapons.' Like that could ever change things for the better. 'I owe her.' Not even sure who he was talking to. 'She saved my family.'

'Nice story. She could put it in her next fucking pamphlet.' Judge picked up the fallen officer's hat and knocked out the dent Broad's axe had made. 'But don't try to trick a trickster. I don't think you care a shit about your debts. Or even about your family. I think you know there's a fight coming, and you can't stand the thought o' being left out. I think you're like me.' She perched the hat on her riot of red hair, back to front, and opened her eyes very wide. 'Only happy when you're *bloody*.'

Broad stood staring. The best judge of character, she'd said. Knew men better than they knew themselves.

'What about this lot?' Sarlby was asking, hands on hips as he frowned at all the dead men.

'We're Burners, ain't we? If in doubt, burn it.' Judge waved Broad away with a queenly waft of one red-stained hand. 'Have it your way. Tell your precious Lady Savine she's got a deal. I'll speak to the Weaver. Messengers'll wriggle out to every crew of Breakers in the Union. On the last day of summer, the king'll have an uprising to make Valbeck look like a birthday party.' She stuck her lips out in a pout. 'I almost feel sorry for the poor bastard. He'll have no friends left to fight the Young Lion. Now off you pop.'

'Just like that?' whispered Broad.

'If I'm about one thing, it's *freedom*. Why have a fucking bull if you keep it chained? We both know you'll be back.' She turned away, giving a sly grin over her shoulder, and tipped that dead man's hat at him. 'Some men just can't help 'emselves.'

A Meeting with Destiny

Savine had attended several parades with her parents and never much enjoyed them. They had always struck her as a lot of pompous guff, and her father's grumbling about the waste of time and money had hardly helped.

But she had to admit she was enjoying this one.

As dawn broke, the army of Angland filed through Ostenhorm towards the quay, where just about every vessel in the province had been pressed into service as a transport, the harbour made a shifting thicket by their masts. Drums thumped, pipes tooted, sergeants bellowed, boots tramp, tramp, tramped. The salt breeze caught flags stitched with old victories, the rising sun gleamed on gear newly forged in Savine's own armouries.

And then there was Leo, the magnificent centrepiece to all this pageantry. He was utterly in his element, magnificent in dark grey uniform and gilded breastplate, roaring lions stitched into his cloak. Like a candle flame in a dark room, every eye was drawn towards him, every cheer and salute sent in his direction. He rode constantly up and down on his snorting, pawing warhorse as though a moment still was a moment wasted, trading jokes with the men, urging them on, standing in his stirrups to wave each company aboard.

'They look good, don't they?' he asked, reining in beside her, gazing at the passing columns like a girl at her intended. 'They look *damn* good.'

'Almost as good as their general,' she said, glancing at him sidelong.

He reached out and put a gentle hand on her belly. 'I love you.'

Savine blinked at him. The truth was she had only loved one man, and he was the one they were going to war with. Love was unlucky. An encumbrance. She smiled, and pressed her hand against his, and felt their baby shift underneath it. 'I love you, too,' she said, and shut him up with a kiss. There was plenty to like about Leo, after all. Especially at the head of an army. But there were some tasks he was not suited for.

'Wherever is Jurand?' she asked as they broke apart. 'He organised most of this.' Antaup was laughing with a crowd of officers, and Whitewater Jin had stripped off his armour to help heft barrels aboard one of the transports. But she saw none of Leo's other friends. Normally it took a heroic effort to prise them from his side. 'And Glaward? He was meant to—'

'They won't be coming,' said Leo, jaw muscles working.

Savine sighed. 'Did you have some falling out in Sipani?' They could be like a gaggle of schoolgirls with their bickering. 'Honestly, Leo, we can use every man, and Jurand more than anyone, you need someone beside you who—'

'Has a brain?' he forced through gritted teeth.

Won't shit the bed in a crisis was what she wanted to say, but with Leo in this mood she settled for, 'Has a cool head and a gift for organisation. You can't let some petty—'

Leo growled each word with furious precision. 'They will *not* be coming.'

'Leo!' It was almost a shriek, and Savine's heart sank. Lady Finree was forcing her way through the baffled onlookers who had gathered beside the road.

The young lieutenant who'd been given the job of watching her hurried after, pink with embarrassment. 'I tried to keep her out of the way, Your Grace, but—'

'What's happening, Leo?' She looked pale, and scared, and much older than she had when Savine first met her, especially with her son sitting so far above her on his tall, tall horse. 'This must be half of Angland's army—'

'All of it.'

'But ... going where?'

'To war, Mother. Where else would an army go?'

'Leo, I've heard a rumour ...' She said the words in a horrified whisper. 'That you mean to move against the *Closed Council*.' She gave a desperate, quivery smile. 'Tell me it's not true!'

There was a pause. 'They've gone too bloody far!' snapped Leo. 'Someone needs to stand up to the bastards.'

Lady Finree glanced over at Savine, and Savine studiously did not meet her eye, feeling just the slightest bit guilty for the elaborate deception she had worked on the woman. 'Leo, you can't mean ...' She plucked weakly at his knee, at his saddle. 'This is *armed revolt*. This is *treason*!'

Savine felt a chill creeping up her back, then. As though, in spite of all her long preparations, because no one had actually said the words, she had not realised quite what they were about. That chill became colder yet as she recognised another familiar face. Yoru Sulfur, that humble representative of the Order of Magi, slipping through the crowds towards Lady Finree's side.

'This is patriotism!' snapped Leo.

'By the Fates, listen to yourself. You don't understand!' Finree dropped her voice, eyes darting nervously over to Sulfur and back. '*Undertakings* were made, to get us where we are. To get you where *you* are.' She dropped her voice further. 'I made promises to Bayaz—'

'Bayaz? What the bloody hell does he have to do with anything?'

'Everything,' said Sulfur, looking very directly up at Savine. She remembered the First of the Magi offering her a statue on the Kingsway. Mentioning profitable partnerships and healthy competition. Telling her that knowing one's own ignorance was the first step towards enlightenment. And she remembered promising her father she would have nothing to do with the man.

'It's not too late!' Finree was pleading. 'I can write to the king, we can appeal for his mercy—'

Leo gave a disgusted hiss and turned his horse, making his mother scramble back almost into Sulfur's arms. 'I've grovelled enough to that fool. It's high time we switched places.'

Lady Finree stared at the marching men, clutching at her chest with a thin hand, then edged close to Leo's horse again. 'Leo, please, listen to me. You're a great fighter. You're a great leader. Of course you are, but...'

'But what, Mother?'

'You're not a general!'

'I seem to remember a battle at Red Hill!' he snapped, cheeks flushed red with anger. 'I turned the tide there when no one else could!'

'You led a charge!' She caught hold of his horse's reins near the bit. 'Managing an army is a very different thing! Let me come with you, at least. Let me—'

'No!' He tore his reins from her hand. 'You've kept me in your shadow long enough. It's my time now!' And he spurred his horse savagely away.

'I wonder how long his time will last,' murmured Sulfur, gently shaking his head.

Finree stared from him to Savine. She looked so utterly distraught that it was hard to meet her eye. 'Have you thought about what you're risking? Have you thought about what happens if you *lose*?'

'There is nothing I have thought about more,' said Savine. Except what would happen if she won, of course. She already had most of the details of her coronation planned.

'People will be hurt.' Savine was disappointed to see there were tears in Finree's eyes. She really was throwing away all the respect anyone used to have for her. 'People will die!'

'And my master,' added Sulfur, 'will be seriously displeased.'

Savine looked down her nose at him. 'As my father once said, if you want to change the world, sometimes you have to burn it down.'

'But *Bayaz*,' pleaded Finree, 'our arrangement—'

'Shit on Bayaz. I did not reach my place in life by paying the interest on other people's debts.' Savine snapped her fingers at one of Leo's aides. 'Escort Lady Finree and her friend back to the Lord Governor's residence. And see that they do not interfere.'

'Your Grace.'

'Leo, please!' Finree shrieked as she was hustled away. 'Savine!'

But Savine had already turned her horse towards the ships and clicked her tongue to move him on.

She couldn't have been much over sixteen, this girl, but she strode up bold as you like. She had broad, solid shoulders and broad, solid hips and a broad, solid jaw she was intent on aiming at Shivers however far he towered above her, which was quite the distance as she wasn't tall. She planted the butt of an old spear on the ground in front of him, her broad, solid knuckles white about the time-darkened haft.

He looked down mildly at her. 'Hello?'

'I want to talk to Rikke,' she growled.

Shivers held out his hand. 'There she is.'

'What, her?'

'No,' said Isern-i-Phail. 'Rikke is the other one-eyed woman with runes tattooed on her face. Yes, her, girl, who the bloody hell else would she be?'

'Huh,' grunted the girl, walking up to Rikke. 'You're younger'n I thought you'd be.'

'Give it time,' said Rikke. 'I'll get older.'

'Or you'll get killed,' said Isern.

Rikke sighed. 'She's always trying to cheer me up. You're a well of good cheer, Isern.'

'You're Isern-i-Phail?' asked the girl, lip even more wrinkled.

'No,' said Rikke. 'Isern is the other gap-toothed, tattoo-handed, fingerbone-wearing hillwoman. Yes, her, girl, who the bloody hell else would she be?'

'You three are quite the jesters, ain't you?'

'Have a smile at breakfast,' droned Shivers, stony-faced, 'you'll be shit-ting joy by lunch.'

'Now who might you be and what might you be after?' asked Rikke.

'I'm Corleth.' The girl frowned at Rikke, then Isern, then Shivers, like she was daring them to call her a liar. 'And I want to *fight*.' She snarled the last word like a curse. Reminded Rikke of one o' those mean little dogs that'll take on anything, no matter how big.

'Then fight you shall. We can use every spear. Get this girl a shield!' she called to one of the smiths, and Corleth strutted off with her broad jaw in the air, much pleased to be a warrior.

'Don't like her looks,' said Isern, eyes narrowed.

'You don't like anyone's looks,' said Rikke. 'You're just jealous of her youth and strong hips.'

Isern propped her hands on her own hips, such as they were. 'I'm the way the moon wants me and naught wrong about it from where I stand.'

Rikke snorted. 'You're straight down like a sausage, and a gristly one at that.'

'You're a fine one to talk, Skinny Rikke. Every pinch o' meat fell off you when you went to see the witch. You're like a head stuck on a spear these days, but without the flies. Most o' the flies, at least.' And she burst out laughing.

'Harsh,' said Rikke, but by a poor stroke of luck she was obliged to wave off a fly at that very moment. She chose to rise above it as a leader should, turning away to take in the gathering.

Rikke had called, half-expecting she'd be ignored, but folk had answered and then some. They'd come in a trickle, then a flow, then a flood, from every village, farmstead and woodsman's hut in the Protectorate. The smiths and fletchers of Uffrith had worked their hands raw the past few weeks arming folk, then they'd stuck on helmets themselves and joined the throng. Some of the town's women had even took a break from nattering at the well to stitch Rikke a standard of her own. A big eye, with runes around it like the ones tattooed into her face. The Long Eye, on a red field, looking into what comes. It slapped and flapped against its pole behind her now, looking down on the greatest weapontake Uffrith ever saw.

'You sure about this?' murmured Shivers. 'Not too late to turn back.'

Rikke frowned at him. 'Never marked you as a turner-backer.'

Shivers only shrugged. He was a tough man to offend. Maybe living with a wound like his made harsh words seem harmless. 'I'm for whatever works.'

'Well, you're a big man, so you wouldn't understand. When you're small, you have to take chances. We might not get another chance like this.'

Shivers frowned at the warriors gathered, and slowly nodded. 'Aye, I reckon.'

'Besides.' And Rikke leaned close, and nudged him in the ribs with her elbow, which was something like nudging a tree trunk. 'It'll turn out sweet.' She pulled down her cheek so her left eye popped at him. 'I've seen it. Now get 'em ready, I've a mind to speechify.'

'You really seen it?' murmured Isern in her ear.

'All you know is what I say I've seen. And I say I've seen it.'

Isern winked. 'There's the Long Eye for you.'

'Listen!' Shivers was calling, but his whispery voice didn't have much poke to it and no one heard. 'Listen!' But it was quieter than last time if anything. He took another breath.

'Open your ears, you fucking maggots!' screamed Isern-i-Phail, so loud Rikke flinched at it. But silence fell, and everyone turned towards her. So many faces, choking the square and the streets about it. More of her people than she'd ever seen gathered in one place. More than she'd known she had. Made her heart swell, to see them come out on her say-so. She thought of how proud her father would've been as she clambered up on the wall beside Isern, and it gave her a lump in her throat. She pushed back the hood she'd made from Savine's red cloth and tried to scrub some life into her flattened hair with her fingernails.

'You know I'm one of you!' she screeched, voice a bit broken. 'I'll confess I look a touch odd these days, and maybe I am a touch odd, but you know I'm one of you. Born in Uffrith. Raised in Uffrith. Hope to die in Uffrith. Hope that last'll be some ways off still.' A bit of laughter at that, a whoop or two and some light drinking. Rikke waved 'em down. 'My father did all he could to keep this place free!'

'The Dogman!' someone roared, and there was a respectful mumble and grumble of his name repeated.

'Fought all his life so we could choose our own way. But here we are, still stuck 'twixt the Union and the North. It's like we've a foot on either boat, but now the two are going different ways on the current, and if we don't jump to one or the other we're apt to get torn in two.' She grimaced and grabbed her crotch. 'And in the most sensitive spot!' More laughter at that. Make 'em laugh, you're halfway there, her father always told her.

'But now we've got a chance to win our freedom for good!' She reached out, like there was something in the air she could nearly grasp. 'It's there! Right in front of us! All we need is the bones to take it! And we will. I *know* we will!' She made a ring out of her finger and thumb, and held it to her left eye, and peered at them hard through the centre. 'I've seen it!'

She flung up her arms and all those folk thrust their spears in the air and roared with one voice, all bound together in this grand adventure. All ready to risk everything to grab this chance. They were still cheering when she hopped down from the wall.

'Nice speech,' croaked Shivers, stroking his sore throat.

'Aye,' muttered Rikke, 'but no one ever died from talking a good fight.' She rubbed at her own neck like she could rub away the nerves that had gathered there. 'Fighting one's another matter.'

The rain had started coming not long after dawn, spitting down on the milling crowds of warriors. Warriors from every part o' the North where they called Stour Nightfall king. Which was pretty much all of it.

There were tough Thralls in studded leather with spear or bow. There were stout Carls in bright mail with axe and shield. There were Named Men whose helm and hilt and harness glinted with jewels. There were wild men from the distant North with furs and warpaint. There were tattooed savages from out past the Crinna with their crooked standards of bone and hide. There were thousands of the bastards.

They'd been flooding into the fields around Carleon for weeks. From up here on the roof of the gatehouse, Clover could see the muddy stain of their camps spread all the way up the far side of the valley. But the last day of summer was coming fast and the camps were emptying now, little trickles of men joining to become streams, flowing down towards the road south where they became a marching river. Steel gleamed with wet as the drizzle fell, here and there the standards of one War Chief or another flapping over the throng.

Stour watched this almighty mess with his arms folded, nodding like a baker seeing the bread rise just the way he wanted. 'Ever see a weapontake like this, did you?'

Clover shrugged. 'I've seen a few, and by and large they were about like this one. Lots of men turning up with weapons. Sort of the point of the thing.'

Stour gave him a withering glance. 'I meant, have you ever seen one so big.'

'I admit this is the biggest.' Apart from the one when Bethod went to war against the Union. Or the one when the Union went to war against Black Dow. But he doubted Stour wanted to hear that, and once you've seen a man starve one poor bastard after another in a cage, you get quite sensitive to what he wants to hear. Which Clover imagined was the point o' the exercise.

'We're going to show those Union bastards something,' snarled Stour. 'On their own ground, this time. Never fought 'em in Midderland, eh?'

'No.' Clover didn't bother to say that men usually fight harder on their own ground. He doubted Stour wanted to hear that, either.

Being honest, he wasn't sure why the young King of the Northmen kept him close. He liked to think he was looked on as some noble mixture of bodyguard, advisor and mentor. In truth, the role probably tended more towards jester. But what can you do but play the role you're given?

'You're set on this, then?' Black Calder stepped from the staircase and out onto the gatehouse roof, grey-streaked hair plastered to his pale frown by the rain. He looked sourer by the day. Like milk left out in the sun.

Stour spread his arms to gather up that whole vast host. 'Send 'em home now, they'll be so disappointed!'

'I had a visit from Master Sulfur.' Calder rubbed worriedly at his grey stubble. He'd been pouring worry, doubt and scorn on the whole business ever since the first man turned up. 'He's not happy with this. And that means his master won't be happy, either.'

Stour gave a snort. 'Just as well my business ain't making wizards happy. Be a frustrating bloody line o' work, eh, Clover?'

'I guess,' murmured Clover, who found making kings happy frustrating enough.

'Daresay you can look after things while I'm gone,' said Stour, clapping a hand on his father's back.

'Managed well enough before you arrived,' growled Calder, shaking him off. 'Though you haven't left me much to look after things with.' And he glanced about the damp roof at the smattering of greybeards, bald-chinned boys and battle-maimed cripples who'd be guarding Skarling's Hall while their king was off polishing his legend.

'Need the men. Fighting the Union's never been easy.'

True enough. Bethod, Black Dow, Scale Ironhand, they'd all found it out the hard way. The Union had been getting the better of better men than Stour Nightfall for years.

Stour seemed to guess the way Clover was thinking and gave one of those sly sideways winks of his, like they were all caught up together in the same funny secret. 'But we never had Angland on our side before.'

'We had the First of the Magi on our side,' grunted Calder, getting even sourer, if that was possible. 'Tipping all the scales. Loading all the dice.'

'When I wanted his help, you said it wasn't worth the price.'

'I said don't land yourself in his debt. I didn't say spit in his eye.' Calder shook his head grimly. 'You don't understand what he *is*.'

Understanding things was a problem for other folk, far as the Great Wolf was concerned. He gave a hiss, half-boredom, half-disgust. 'When did you turn so bloody *sour*, Father? To hear you carping, no one would ever guess you won the North!'

Calder spoke soft. 'With Bayaz's help, I won it. Like the Bloody-Nine. Like my father. If Bayaz starts helping someone else—'

'Then I'll fight 'em and I'll win!' snarled Stour, showing his teeth. The sun came out then, peeping through a patch in the cloud, and brought a sparkle from the marching men. 'Look at that!' There was a rainbow over the road south towards Ollensand. 'A good omen, I reckon. An archway we'll march through to victory!'

Cheers at that from some of the Named Men on the roof, and weapons shook, and calls of the Great Wolf. No one mentioned the one thing about rainbows that came at once to Clover – you can march at 'em for ever but you'll never actually reach the bastards.

Calder gave a disgusted sigh as he watched the King of the Northmen swagger towards the steps. 'The dead save me from the fucking *young*.'

'No getting away from 'em, sadly,' muttered Clover. 'The older you get, the more of 'em there are.'

As so often, his wit was wasted. Calder was frowning down at his fists, bunched on the grey stones of the parapet. 'This was the spot where the Bloody-Nine killed my father.'

'Mmmm.' Clover remembered it well enough. He'd held a shield in that duel, between the Bloody-Nine and the Feared, before his name was even Steepfield, let alone Clover, a mad young bastard full of fire.

'And his dream of the North united died with him.'

'Mmmm.' Clover remembered the crunching as Bethod's skull was smashed to mush. The thud as his body dropped in the Circle.

'For thirty years I've been trying to coax it back to life. Tending to it with my every breath. We're nearly there, Clover. One victory more.'

Clover had his doubts on that score. He'd seen victories enough, and they were like the false summits of a great fell. You struggle towards 'em, sure you've made the top, then the moment you get there you see another just beyond. No fight was ever the last. No victory was ever for good. But Black Calder was getting old. He wanted to see his great legacy secured before he went back to the mud. Then he could trick himself into believing it wouldn't crumble a few moments after.

He gripped Clover by the arm. He had quite the grip, for a thin man. 'You have to keep watch on him, you understand me?'

'Mmmm.'

'He's the future.'

'Mmmm.'

'We might not like it. He might not deserve it.'

'Mmmm.'

'But he's the future, and the future has to be protected.'

Clover thought of that cage in Skarling's Hall. 'How do you protect a man from himself?'

'He'll learn better, in time.'

Clover had his doubts about that, too. Sooner or later, you have to stop expecting folk to bend around your plans and fit your plans to the folk you've got. But he reckoned Calder had laboured on his plans so long they'd turned hard, and brittle, and apt to shatter. So he stuck to, 'Mmmm.' It was a contribution that worked for any circumstance. A listener could hear whatever they wanted in it.

'If things turn sour over there, do whatever you have to, you understand? Bring him back alive. Do that, I'll see you rewarded.'

'Mmmm,' said Clover, one more time. 'Well, I've always liked to be rewarded.'

And he set off towards the steps to join the great army of the North.

Orso's command tent was, being generous, a shambles. In fact, since Hildi and a group of baffled soldiers were still scratching their heads over how to put half of it up, and Orso had known nothing about leading soldiers at Valbeck a year before and learned nothing since, one could have said it was a command tent featuring neither tent nor command.

Messengers, scouts and adjutants blundered through in confusion, trampling mud, tripping over guy-ropes and tearing down canvas. Orso hardly even knew what an adjutant was, yet he had about a dozen of the bastards. The babble reminded him of a wedding party held in too small a room, except the guests were panicking and almost all men.

General Forest barked out orders, trying to impose some sanity. Arch Lector Pike fingered his melted chin, trying to sift truth from conflicting reports. Corporal Tunny watched it all from a folding field chair, the Steadfast Standard propped beside him, with an air of knowing amusement which Orso found particularly aggravating.

'Your Majesty,' Hoff was wheedling, with his trademark wringing of the hands, 'I wish you would consider returning to the Agriont where you can be protected—'

'Out of the question,' said Orso. 'Believe me, Lord Chamberlain, I would much prefer to be in my bed than my saddle, but this rebellion is like a fire in a distillery. If it is not stamped out at once it will spread. And I have to be *seen* to stamp it out.'

'So this is all about appearances?' murmured Vick.

'Being king *is* all about appearances,' said Orso. 'An endless performance with no chance for an encore and for damn sure no applause. Hildi, you do have my armour, don't you?'

''Course I do,' she grunted, without looking up from the confusion of ropes.

'You don't plan . . .' Hoff looked pale. 'To *fight*, Your Majesty?'

'Bloody hell, no. But I plan to damn well look like I might.'

There was a crash as a messenger tripped, reeled into a table and sent rolled-up maps bouncing about the tent.

'That is *enough*!' shouted Orso. 'Forest, Pike, Tunny, Teufel and Hoff, stay. The rest of you *out*.' He would not have minded ejecting a couple of those named, but he supposed he needed all the help he could get. 'Gorst, make sure we are not disturbed.'

'Buth—' muttered Hildi around a cord she was gripping in her teeth while she tried to tie two others together.

'You, too. Out!'

Hildi shrugged, let go of the ropes, and with a gentle flutter one wall of the tent billowed out and slowly collapsed to the ground. A fitting metaphor for Orso's campaign so far, he rather thought. He spoke through gritted teeth.

'Let us take one thing at a time. Your Eminence, is there any sign of the rebels?'

'No reliable sightings so far, Your Majesty,' said Pike, 'but we have eyes on every beach, bay and wharf. If Lord Heugen told us the truth, we expect them to land tomorrow.'

'Any trouble from the Breakers? Move now and they catch us with our trousers well and truly down.'

Pike glanced over at Vick, standing with arms tightly folded. She shook her head. 'All quiet, Your Majesty,' said Pike. 'We struck them a blow at Valbeck from which they have yet to recover.'

'I wish I believed it,' said Orso, 'but I have a feeling that blow only made them angrier. What about our own forces, Forest?'

'We have about nine thousand, including the resurrected Crown Prince's Division.'

'An excellent decision to raise troops in secret, Your Majesty,' broke in Hoff. 'It may have saved the Union!'

'Let's not get ahead of ourselves,' said Orso.

'There will be members of the Open Council who have stayed loyal, I'm sure of it! I have sent letters demanding their support.'

'I doubt they'll be falling over each other to help.'

'I may have implied that the rebels' estates would be redistributed to loyalists . . .'

Orso raised his brows. 'Maybe they'll fall over each other after all.'

'The King's Own are converging from all across Midderland.' Forest retrieved one of the maps and spread it out upon the righted table. 'We should link up with two regiments of foot tomorrow. Then Lord Marshal Rucksted is bringing four of horse from Keln, but there's no saying whether they'll reach us in time.'

'That cavalry could make all the difference . . .'

'We need to prepare, Your Majesty,' said Hoff. 'Tread carefully. Play for time. Gather all the troops we can.'

'But the best moment to strike would be soonest,' growled Forest, tracing the wiggly line that was Midderland's north coast with a thick fingertip. 'Before they get a foothold. Best we can tell, they'll be picking up allies of their own.'

'So we need to delay,' said Tunny, 'but also move at once.'

There was a pause while they all considered that. Orso snorted. 'Anything else?'

'The erstwhile Lord Marshal Brint,' said Pike in an emotionless drone. 'He refuses to corporate.'

Orso shook his head. 'It's always the last one you expect. I thought the man was a rock! Imaginative as a rock, but reliable as one, too. He and my father were old friends.'

'Nonetheless, he is a traitor. It might be useful to demonstrate our resolve—'

'I bloody hate hangings,' snapped Orso. 'Maybe we should demonstrate mercy for once.'

'He has been passing secrets to your enemies for months—'

'Then he should carry on,' said Vick.

Orso frowned at her. 'He's under lock and key in the House of Questions. Isn't he?'

'Awaiting the king's justice,' grated out Pike.

Vick shrugged. 'Brock doesn't know that. I could take him a message.'

'A message saying what?' asked Hoff.

'Saying the Closed Council have turned against each other. Saying the King's Own are scattered and distracted and there'll be no opposition. Saying His Majesty has fled for Gurkhul with only his standard bearer for company.'

'His standard bearer's got better sense,' muttered Tunny.

'Saying whatever you please.'

Orso considered that idea, and a rare smile began to spread across his face. 'You know, Inquisitor, I'm beginning to like you a great deal.'

Forest cleared his throat. 'Your Majesty, if that's all, we really should . . .' And he nodded towards the theoretical entrance to the tent, where Gorst was holding back a sweaty, panicky, impatient crush of messengers.

Orso sighed. 'Very well. Open the floodgates.'

As the boat's keel ground against gravel, Leo leaped into the surf. Sloshing through a few dozen strides of icy water probably wasn't the best thing for his leg, but he was burning to be first ashore. He'd been kept a prisoner behind a desk far too long, caged in ballrooms and council chambers, chained by manners and rules. Now was the time for *action*. And what was the point of a leader, after all, if he didn't actually *lead*? Directing things from a chair at the back was for King Orso and his like, not the Young Lion. Leo's headquarters would be in the saddle. At the tip of the spear. Where the blood was shed and the glory won!

It wasn't the most glorious stretch of shore, he had to admit, as his flooded boots finally crunched up onto the beach and he stood to rest his aching leg. A great grey curve of cold shingle, then a great yellow curve of wind-torn grass, then brown dunes and scrubby trees swept sideways, a few lonely birds hovering on the breeze the only sign of life. No cheering crowds waiting to celebrate their liberation from the tyranny of the Closed Council.

But Leo told himself that was a good thing. They were supposed to be landing in secret. No one in sight was a mark of success.

'Jin!' he called as the Northman jogged up onto the beach beside him. A solid presence, no one more reliable. 'Set up some pickets while the men get ashore. Antaup?'

'Your Grace?' Antaup pushed that lock of hair from his face where the wind instantly flicked it back. A good friend, who Leo was absolutely sure liked women.

'Organise some scouting parties, fan out, see if you can make contact with Isher and the rest of the Open Council's troops. Where's Stour due to land?'

'If he has good luck with the weather, maybe a few miles that way?'

'And Rikke?'

Antaup puffed out his cheeks as though it was anyone's guess. 'The other way? Maybe?'

Jurand would've known exactly where and when they were all meant to arrive, would already have been snapping out orders, making sure everything was going to plan. But Jurand . . . that image floated up again, of him and Glaward, bent over the bed, their gasping faces pressed together—

Leo clenched his teeth. 'We've got to link up with the others right away!' he snapped. 'With numbers on our side we shouldn't need to fight at all.'

'Right,' said Antaup. He took a step one way, froze, then turned back the other and hurried off up the beach.

Jin was grinning at Leo, red beard tugged by the wind. 'By the dead, it'd be a shame to go home without a battle, though.'

Leo grinned back and clapped him on his mailed shoulder. 'Maybe just a little one.'

Orders were being called now, boots splashing in the surf and scraping in the shingle, a reassuring clamour of activity as the men of Angland began to pour from the boats and onto the beach.

Leo's standard was unfurled above him, the crossed hammers and the lion, holed and torn from victories in the North but never taken by an enemy. He smiled up as the sea wind made it flap and flutter, setting his doubts to rest and his heart leaping.

'At last,' he murmured.

PART VI

'No plan survives contact
with the enemy.'

Helmuth von Moltke

Storms

The young lieutenant had looked on the point of tears when Savine refused the carriage, but it was far from the first time she had made a man cry. There was no way the damn thing was getting through the chaos on the beach, let alone the chaos getting off the beach, and she was determined to stick close to Leo and make sure her husband suffered no fatal attacks of recklessness in her absence. She had insisted on riding, and that was the end of it.

Then the rain came.

First a drizzle that beaded the weapons with dew as the first columns of Angland's army marched between the dunes. Then a steady shower that turned the proud standards to sodden rags as they struggled inland. Finally, as if the weather was fanatically loyal to King Orso, a pissing deluge that churned the narrow roads to black glue as the unhappy soldiers toiled southwards.

'Heave!' an officer roared at a set of men trying vainly to haul a wagon from a quagmire, his wet sword raised as if he was ordering a charge, and the men strained at the filth-caked wheels as the premature darkness of the storm closed in.

Savine was so used to proving there was nothing she could not do, she rarely pondered whether there might be things better not attempted. Riding while heavily pregnant at the head of a military campaign mired by foul weather proved to be in that latter category.

Her thighs burned with the effort. Her clothes were soaked through and chafing. Her hands were so swollen, she had split one riding glove and could hardly feel the reins. Her stomach was sending painful washes of acid up her throat with every jolt of her horse. If she hunched over against the rain, her great beer keg of a belly felt like it would make her aching ribs spring open. If she sat up, she got the storm full in her face and every step her horse took stabbed her in the spine. And then, in any and every position into which a heavily pregnant human body could be twisted, there was the endlessly throbbing focus of misery that was her bladder. Probably no one would have noticed had she pissed herself, she could hardly have been wetter. Probably she *was* pissing herself, an agonising slow leak with every in-breath. When she first became pregnant, she had been pathetically grateful to be free of the menses for a few months. Now it seemed she had traded the monthly agonies for constant ones.

As if to add insult to injury, her husband grinned into the elements, rain coursing down his face, never happier than when he had a simple physical obstacle to manfully wrestle with and heroically overcome. 'Can't let a bit of weather stop us!' he roared over the wind as he slapped a baffled messenger on the back and sent him to find formations that for all they knew had been washed away into the sea. 'Used to Northern storms, aren't we?' he called to a column of bedraggled Anglanders, raising a limp cheer. 'We can manage a Midderland drizzle!'

'A drizzle,' snarled Savine over her shoulder at Zuri, wishing she had taken the carriage when it was offered.

'God punished old Sippot's arrogance with a flood,' called Zuri, soaked to the perfect skin herself but facing the weather with her usual equanimity. 'Perhaps He means to do the same to us.'

There was a flash on the horizon, claws of trees caught black against the brightness. A moment later thunder crackled, and a horse reared and dumped one of Leo's aides face first into a hedge. Savine's own mount trembled, shuffled fearfully sideways, and she shushed in its ear, patted its neck, stroked her belly, trying to calm her struggling horse and her kicking baby and the rampaging storm all at once and wondering who the hell would calm her.

She flinched as Antaup spurred his horse up from behind in a shower of mud.

'No sign of Rikke?' snapped Leo.

'No sign!'

'What the hell's happened to her?'

'If her boats were caught in weather like this she could be anywhere.'

'At the bottom of the sea, maybe,' grunted Jin, peering up grimly at the streaming skies.

'If this rain gets any heavier,' growled Savine, trying to unstick her clammy dress from her shoulders under the weight of her waterlogged cloak, 'the bottom of the sea will come to us.'

They picked their way around the boggy margins of a vast puddle in the road. One could have described it as a lake without fear of contradiction, men squatting on an upended cart at one side like shipwrecked mariners, all manner of gear floating on the rain-pricked water while others waded past, weapons over their heads, or tried to force their way through the hedges to either side.

'This way!' They were led past a miserable huddle of men under a tarp and out across a darkened field. It felt good for a moment to move faster than a crawl, even if Savine had no idea where they were moving to. Then she saw flickering lights up ahead, dark shapes moving in the twilight.

'Riders!' hissed Antaup, ripping his spear from its case. Panic rippled through the knot of officers. Steel scraped as swords were drawn, shields unslung. Savine's horse was barged by another and she only just clung on to the saddle, wrenching her arm. She stared, heart in her mouth, one hand gripping the reins like death, the other wrapped protectively around her belly.

'Who goes there?' Jin roared into the night, standing in his stirrups with his great mace ready.

'Lord Isher!' came a strangled shout. 'And you?'

There was a collective gasp as men sagged in their saddles. 'It's the Young Lion!' called Leo, reassuring laughter in his voice. 'No need to piss yourselves!'

'So you say,' grunted Savine, squirming in her saddle.

'Thank the Fates!' Riders came smiling into the flickering light cast by the torches of Leo's guards. 'We thought you might be the king's men.'

'Likewise.' Leo grinned hugely as he leaned from his saddle to clasp Isher's hand.

The sight of their ally gave Savine far less comfort than she might have hoped. He had none of the self-assurance he radiated while stirring trouble in the Open Council, or discussing how they would divide the spoils in Ostenhorm. He looked gaunt and jumpy, his uniform a poor fit under his soaked oilskin, his white hair rain-flattened to a dirty grey but for one absurd tweak which stuck up like a peacock's crest.

'Barezin is somewhere behind.' Isher waved into the darkness in a way that strongly implied he had no idea where. 'I've had messages from some of the others.'

'Bloody roads are a bloody shambles,' snapped a lord with an extravagant breastplate. Savine didn't recognise him and no one seemed in the mood for introductions, least of all her.

'Lady Wetterlant's with us,' said Isher, eyes narrowed against a sudden gust, 'but her troops are strung out along five miles of boggy track and their supplies five miles behind that! Have the Northmen landed?'

'Most of 'em,' called Jin. 'Stour's somewhere to the east but half his boats drifted. In this weather, who knows where they'll wash up?'

'Bloody beaches are a bloody shambles, too,' grunted Antaup.

'Is Heugen with you?' asked Leo.

Isher's unhappy horse kept trying to turn around. Savine sympathised. He bad-temperedly jerked it back. 'You haven't heard from him?'

'No, but we can't wait. We have to push on, whatever the weather. We can't give Orso any time to gather his forces!'

They clattered through the gate of a low farmhouse, mean wooden buildings around a yard of rain-hammered mud, wind thrashing at the trees. A dog ran wild, barking at the horses, and a soldier hissed curses as he kicked it away. Savine peeled herself from the saddle and Jin helped her down. A family watched from under the dripping eaves of a barn, presumably the unfortunate owners of the place, as dozens of soldiers, wagons and one heavily pregnant woman crowded into their churned-up farmyard. Probably Savine should have felt sorry for them, but her pity was soluble in heavy rain, apparently, and what she had left she needed for herself.

The low-ceilinged front parlour of the house swarmed with men in mismatched uniforms, all gabbling at once, the windows misty with their breath. Antaup had dragged a table into the middle of the room and upended a case of damp maps onto it, rooting through them with the expression of a man trying to solve a riddle in a language he did not speak.

'Damn it!' Leo held one up to the inadequate lamplight, set flickering as someone shoved the door wide and wind whipped through the room. 'Can we get a decent light in here? Is this map accurate?'

'None of them are bloody accurate—'

'Do we know where the king's forces are?' grumbled Lord Mustred, rain dripping from his bedraggled eyebrows.

'I heard two days' march away.'

'What? We were told he was fleeing south!'

Savine winced. In business, few things went entirely to plan. In war, plans and reality barely noticed each other in passing. Panicked guesswork was the best one could hope for. The sheer scale of it. Thousands of men. Tons of supplies. Oceans of misinformation hiding infinitesimal grains of truth. Savine was used to taking charge, but how could anyone take charge of this? Especially someone who could scarcely control her own bladder.

Not for the first time, Savine wished Jurand was with them. He was the only one of Leo's friends who could really organise, who had an eye for the details, who thought less about what he wanted to do and more about what had to be done. The man was like a wagon's axle. You paid little mind to it when it was there, but take it away and things plunged rapidly off the road.

The door banged open and another cold draught swept in. A man shook water from a fur-trimmed cloak, huffing and blowing. An old white-haired Northman, with gold on his mail and rain in his beard and broken veins on his bulbous nose.

He looked about, realising all the soldiers had stopped their business to look at him, and nervously cleared his throat. 'Nice evening for it.'

'Hardbread!' said Leo, grabbing the old warrior by the hand and giving it a shake fit to tear his arm off. 'At last! Where's Rikke?'

'Still in Uffrith.'

'What?'

'Well, she was when I left. She should've left herself by now. Be here soon, I guess. There was a storm. Boats couldn't leave the harbour. Good thing it didn't come an hour later or we might've all drowned.'

Leo had lurched from the heights of relief to the depths of disappointment without taking a breath. 'How many men did you bring?'

'For now, just the ones rowed me here. 'Bout thirty?'

'Thirty?' A shocked mutter ran around the room. An officer from Angland and one of the noblemen's retainers had begun shouting at one another. A punch was thrown, they wrestled, barged the table, bellowing insults. Jin grabbed them around their necks and bundled the pair of them out into the night. The clamour and the panic and the wild eyes reminded Savine too much of Valbeck. She felt that horribly familiar sour taste, the gorge rising in her throat, her heart thudding and her head spinning as she backed into the shadows, wondering if among all these half-glimpsed faces she could see the men who had chased her through the streets—

'Are you all right?' asked Zuri, taking her gently by the elbow.

'Never mind Rikke,' Savine forced through her gritted teeth. 'Just find me a fucking bucket.'

'This way,' said Zuri, slipping through the madness to a side door.

Savine shuffled after her, one hand pressed into her back and the other under her swollen belly, into a little kitchen on the side of the building with a time-blackened fireplace and a smell of bad cooking. She pushed the door shut and leaned back on it, tried to ignore the mad babble of raised voices from beyond, fix on the rattling of the ill-fitting window, the steady drip-drip of water from a leak.

Zuri stood with hands on hips, looking down at a pair of empty milking pails, yoke still attached and propped on top.

'More than adequate,' said Savine, waddling over.

After much fumbling, she finally wriggled her drawers past her knees and with Zuri half-holding her up managed to squat over one of the pails, skirts gathered around her hips and the cold metal brushing her arse. When she heard the metallic spattering, she almost cried with relief. She shuddered at the last trickle, tried to bend down to fish up her drawers between two fingers, but could not quite reach.

'Hell,' she gasped, legs trembling with the effort. In the end, she had to stand before she fell, let Zuri drag her rain-sodden skirts out of the way and pull them up for her.

She flopped back exhausted onto a stool with a flapping of muddy cloth, shoulders against the damp plaster, boots stretched out wide in front of her.

'So much for leading an army. I can hardly get my drawers up without help.'

'A good thing for your reputation as a general that I am here,' said Zuri. 'Rabik and Haroon should be along soon with dry clothes and dinner.'

Savine shut her eyes, tears of gratitude prickling the lids. 'What the hell would I do without your family? I've no idea how you can stay so calm.'

'I was not always a lady's companion. I have seen my share of storms.' Zuri frowned off into the corner of the room, as though bad memories lurked there. 'They pass, in time.'

'If the lightning doesn't find you out,' muttered Savine, giving Zuri's hand a squeeze.

The door rattled at a thudding knock, and she gritted her teeth and worked her way into a slightly more presentable position, bladder aching again already. 'Yes?'

The door wobbled open and someone dipped his head under the low lintel.

'Broad!' The name almost came as a gasp of relief. Here was a man she had seen deal with a crisis. A rock to cling to in a storm.

'Lady Savine.' He frowned down at her, eye-lenses dotted with beads of rain and an ugly scab on one side of his head. 'Are you all right—'

'I should not have ridden and it should not have rained. Tell me you have some good news!'

He did not look like a man with good news, it had to be said. Even in Valbeck, during the uprising, even when things got bad, he had always seemed *hopeful*, at least. Now he looked grim. Brows wrinkled, fists clenched. For a moment, the sight of him, scabbed head nearly brushing the low ceiling, gave Savine the slightest twinge of fear. An echo of the terror when she first saw his great silhouette on the barricade in Valbeck.

'The Breakers'll join us,' he said, after a pause. 'And the Burners. They've been armed, like you told me. Aiming for uprisings all across the Union on the last day of summer.'

'They should already be underway,' murmured Zuri.

'That could make all the difference.' Savine closed her eyes and breathed a long sigh. 'If they can pin down the King's Own, stop reinforcements arriving, we might not need to fight at all.' She hoped, she prayed, they did not need to fight at all. 'Who did you deal with? Risinau?'

'No.' Broad took off his lenses to wipe them on a corner of his shirt. Savine got the feeling it was definitely bad news this time. 'Judge.'

'The woman who hanged all those people in Valbeck?'

Broad winced, mouth open, as though wondering how much to say. In the end, all he said was, 'That's her.'

Savine felt another surge of panic, slipped the box out of her sleeve and into her trembling hand, snapped it open. Water had got inside, the pearl dust made useless paste. 'Damn it!' she snarled, flinging it against the wall. Right away she felt foolish. 'Sorry. Not very graceful.'

'These aren't very graceful times.'

'Can this woman Judge be trusted?'

'I'd sooner trust a scorpion,' said Broad, hooking his lenses around his ears again.

'We'll just have to hope for the best.' Savine gave a little gasp as her baby shifted, put a calming hand on her stomach. 'Is war always like this?'

'It's when the enemy arrives things really turn to shit, begging your pardon.'

'Let's hope they never arrive, then,' said Savine.

'Hope can't hurt.' But Broad gave the strong impression that he did not think it would help much, either.

'Could you tell His Grace what you've told me?'

'Aye. If I can get a word in.'

Savine waved Zuri over. 'I fear I need my bucket again.'

Liar, Liar

'Lord Governor Brock's headquarters?' asked Vick, sitting easy in her saddle but with an expression that said she'd no time for nonsense. The corporal barely looked up from his sizzling pan, just waved her on. One of the soldiers gave her a weak smile, then went back to scraping mud from a boot. None of them challenged her as she nudged her horse past, but that was no surprise.

She'd always been the best liar she knew.

From as early as she could remember, little Victarine dan Teufel, doted-upon youngest daughter of the Master of the Mints, had known she didn't feel things quite the way other people did. Or at least that her feelings never made it to her face. What a solemn little child. How cold you are! Say something, Victarine, I have no notion what you are thinking.

So she had taught herself to fake it. Sat cross-legged in front of her mother's little mirror, rehearsing shy smiles and hurt frowns, squeezing out the tears, practising until she could blush on demand. Such an expressive daughter. How animated she is! Her feelings are written on her face, poor thing.

Then one day she broke a treasured vase, and blamed her brother, and maintained a perfect air of baffled innocence while he turned red and angry. Her mother punished him for her crime, and made him apologise to her for lying into the bargain, and gave her a slice of fruit tart as a reward. So little Victarine learned early what the truth is worth. Good lying isn't so much about what you say as how you say it. Amazing how far you can get if you stick to a straight line and look like you've got every reason to be there.

So Vick crossed muddy fields choked with rebels and ruined tents, not skulking on the margins, but trotting through the midst of the slimy chaos, eyes ahead. She tutted in disgust as two soldiers argued over a canteen. She hissed impatiently at a crowd trying to shift a mired wagon.

She ordered a whole queue of bedraggled men outside a slumping soup-tent to get out of her way and made them grumpily shuffle aside.

She'd always been the best liar she knew. But like anyone who wants to truly master a skill, young Victarine dan Teufel had built on natural talent with painstaking practice.

She'd made herself a student of behaviour. Noted giveaway twitches of the eyes, telltale movements of the hands, observed them in others, suppressed them in herself. She'd practised on the servants, then on her family, then on the powerful men her father met with. She'd learned to keep always as close as she could to the truth. To shape her lies to her audience like a key to a lock. To shape herself. Not only to tell them what they wanted to hear, but to be who they wanted to hear it from.

She would be dealing with nobility today, so she became nobility, shoulders confidently back, chin proudly raised. She was Victarine, with the big 'dan' in her name and disinterested scorn for anyone without it. She'd pinned her hair up. A plain dealer, hiding nothing. On reflection, she pulled a few strands free for a softening touch. Simple clothes, but not cheap. She'd decided a skirt was pushing it, but she'd opened one more button of her shirt than usual, rolled the sleeves once to show her wrists. Unguarded. Even a little vulnerable. Finally, she'd made Tallow flick her with road muck. She had been riding hard on a vital mission, after all.

'Who goes there?' snapped a sergeant, pointing a polearm and a belligerent expression.

He was guarding the gates of a fine old manor house which, judging by the lion-and-hammers standard planted in the churned-up ornamental gardens, Brock had commandeered for his headquarters. She sized the man up at a glance. Moustache waxed and breastplate polished even in the midst of this mess. A self-important stickler who took himself far too seriously.

'My name is Victarine dan Teufel.' In the smooth, clear noblewoman's accent her mother used to have. 'I need to speak to Lord Governor Brock.'

He frowned up, looking for something to distrust, but she gave him nothing.

'You could be a spy,' he said, grudgingly.

'I am a spy.'

He stared at her, caught off guard.

'On your side.' She leaned down, glancing left and right, using an urgent whisper, as if she'd picked him and only him to trust with a secret. 'And I have a message from Lord Marshal Brint that could change *everything*.'

Important news, for the important man. He puffed himself up, turned frowning to the busy yard. 'Clear a path there! This woman needs to see the Lord Governor!'

She'd always been the best liar she knew. Then the Practicals dragged her from her bed in the night, and her family was sent to the camps in Angland. Young Victarine dan Teufel had buried her fancy name in a shallow grave and become just Vick, and lying had gone from a game to a means of survival. In the years she'd spent in that freezing hell, as her family died one by one, she'd only told the whole truth once, and that was the day she got out. She'd hammered her face into a vizor of blank indifference that no shock, no pain, no terror could dent.

Which proved to be a very good thing as she was shown into Leo dan Brock's borrowed dining room. From what she'd heard, he was one of those vain men of action who can't wait to believe what they want to. But he wasn't eating breakfast alone. Standing nearby, big hands clasped, looking mightily surprised to see her wander in out of the muddy morning, was her old comrade from the Breakers, Gunnar Broad. Worse yet, sitting on the other side of the table was the heavily pregnant daughter of Vick's previous employer, Savine dan Brock.

What Vick thought was, *Shit.* What her expression said was, *Good, you're all here.*

'Victarine dan Teufel.' Savine's face might have been softened by her condition but her smile had a harder, hungrier edge than ever. 'Unless I'm much mistaken.'

Broad's heavy brows knitted with suspicion. 'The two o' you know each other?'

While Vick tried to plot a safe path through the swamp of truths and falsehoods these three knew about her, she met one question with another. 'The two of *you* know each other?'

'Master Broad saved my life during the uprising in Valbeck,' said Savine. 'And I shared the carriage there with Inquisitor Teufel.'

'Inquisitor?' Broad's wide eyes looked strangely small through his lenses. 'Thought you grew up in the camps?'

'I did. But Arch Lector Glokta offered me a way out.' Vick met Broad's eye and told all the truth she could. 'Bringing the Breakers to justice.'

'You were working for Old Sticks all that time?'

'My father once described Inquisitor Teufel as his most loyal servant.' Savine sipped delicately from a teacup, but the stare she gave Vick over the rim was flinty. 'So I must say I'm surprised to see you swagger into my parlour with a message from one rebel to another.'

There was a weighty silence, then, while everyone frowned at Vick, and Broad slowly unclasped his big hands, that Ladderman's tattoo squirming as he made fists of them. She knew it was one of those moments when her life hung by a thread. But it was hardly her first.

'Everyone's loyalties are a touch tangled these days.' She hooked out the chair at the head of the table with her foot and dropped into it, meeting Savine's eye. 'I like to think I never let your father down. He got me out of the camps. I owed him. But he's gone now.'

A flicker of doubt crossed Savine's well-powdered face. 'Gone?'

She didn't know. That was useful. A surprise might put her off balance. 'Your father had to resign. Once news got out of this little ... escapade. Retired to his country estates to write a book about fencing. Your mother thought the air would be good for his health. Or that's what she said she thought.' It rang true because it was true, and Vick took a fork and leaned across to spear a sausage from a dish. 'It's Arch Lector Pike, now.'

She noticed the muscles squirm in Broad's jaw. Saw his big fists tighten further. That was useful, too. His anger and Savine's guilt could keep them distracted, while Vick swaggered past in plain sight.

'I owed your father,' she said, 'but I don't owe Pike a thing. Lord Marshal Brint needed someone to carry a message. Someone who could slip through the lines. Someone comfortable with a lie or two.' She waved towards the window with her fork. 'Judging by all the men I passed on the way here, we may have a change in government soon enough.' She bit into the sausage and smiled as she chewed. 'If I learned one thing in the camps, it's always eat when food's on offer. But if I learned another, it's that you stand with the winners.'

She was bringing them round, she could feel it. And once you've got someone to believe, it takes a jolt to shift them. Accepting you swallowed a lie means accepting you're a fool, after all. Who wants to think that?

'You're right to be suspicious, though,' she said. 'There's a hell of a lot at stake. That's why the lord marshal gave me this.' And she twisted Brint's ring from her finger and tossed it into the dish with the sausages.

Savine held it frowning to the light, with the air of a woman who's assessed a lot of jewellery. 'It's a lady's ring.'

'He said it belonged to his wife. The one lost at the Battle of Osrung.'

There's nothing like a prop to shore up a lie. Something you can touch. Something with a story. Even if, when you *really* thought about it, she could've stolen it from a one-armed man in a bathhouse.

'Aliz dan Brint ... my mother was taken hostage with her!' Brock sat eagerly forward. 'What's the message?'

And now to forget about the truth altogether and bury the bastards in a great cargo of lies. Lies they could build all their plans out of. Lies that'd crumble as soon as any weight was put on them. 'Orso is marching against you with every man he can find, but he can't find many. He's sent for the King's Own, but they're scattered across the Union, and Brint stopped most of the orders going out. The Closed Council were taken by surprise, are off balance and all looking to save themselves. There's no help coming to the king. No friends and no reinforcements.' As she spoke, the smile spread across Brock's face, and she knew she had him. 'What are your numbers?'

'Perhaps twenty thousand,' he breathed. 'There are still men coming in.'

Worse than she'd feared. The rebels might outnumber the loyalists two to one. She smiled as though it was better than she'd hoped. 'You might outnumber him four to one.'

Leo dan Brock eagerly clenched his fist. 'We have him.'

'Take nothing for granted,' said Savine, but Vick caught the relief in her voice, the flush of triumph on her cheek. The look of a gambler who has gone all in, then been dealt the final card of a winning hand. Lady Brock was a formidable liar herself, of course. Used to flipping investors about her knuckles like a magician flips a coin. But she was nowhere near as good as she thought she was.

Vick had been staking her life on her lies for years. She'd tricked Risinau and his people, tricked Sibalt and his people, tricked Solumeo Shudra in Westport, even tricked the Minister of Whispers herself, for a few days, all while death breathed on her neck. She popped the last bit of sausage in her mouth.

'Lord Marshal Brint asked me to bring a message back. He needs to know your plans.' And she held out her hand for his ring. 'What shall I tell him?'

You Asked for Killers

'Well, here's a mess,' said Clover, wearily puffing out his cheeks. 'Just went wrong, is all.' Dancer knelt in the muddy yard with wrists tied behind him to his ankles. Not the most comfortable position, but he'd no one else to blame. His fat friend was similarly tied but he'd got knocked over when Downside slapped him and couldn't find a way to wriggle back to his knees, or maybe he'd thought better of trying. Now he was sobbing away softly on his side, one pink cheek caked in muck and the other streaked with tears. Flick, meanwhile, was being sick behind the shed. That boy could never get enough to eat, but somehow he never ran out of sick, neither.

'Just went wrong.'

'Wrong?' barked Downside, stabbing angrily at the woman's corpse with a pointed finger and making Dancer and the rest of 'em cringe. For a man who made so many corpses, he could get quite upset over the ones other people made. 'That all you got to say? Wrong?'

'We just wanted the sheep!' One of 'em bleated from the pen, as if to lend support to that part of Dancer's story if no other. 'We even asked nicely.'

Clover rubbed at his temples. Had a bit of a headache. Thinking about it, he'd had a headache for weeks. 'If those sheep were all you had in the world, would asking nicely get you to hand 'em over?'

'Would if this was the alternative,' said Sholla softly, squatting beside the old man. He was sat against the tumbledown wall with his head back like he was sleeping. Except for the arrow in his ribs and his shirt below it soggy black with blood, of course.

'We asked nicely,' whined Dancer. 'Then we asked less nicely. Think we did, anyway, you know, the language ain't my strong point.'

'Remind me what your strong point is, again?' asked Clover.

'Then the old man comes out with an axe so Prettyboy shot him.'

Prettyboy must've been named by a real wag since he was, by any standard, a thoroughly ugly man. 'Just pointed the bow,' he said, shifting awkwardly on his knees. Everything's awkward when your hands are tied to your ankles, to be fair. The bow in question lay in the mud not far away, and he gave it a filthy look like it was to blame for the whole business. 'But I fumbled the string, you know, and shot him.'

'Then the woman set to screaming and, well . . .' Dancer winced down at the mud. 'It went wrong, is all. You never had anything go wrong, Clover?'

Clover wearily puffed out his cheeks again. 'I've barely had anything go right.' A scene like this didn't make him feel sick any more, or angry, or even sad. Just tired. Maybe that's when you know you've been in the bloody business too long, when tragedies start to feel like chores. When some poor bastard's end of everything becomes your minor pain in the arse. 'Could you shut up?' he asked the fat one, and the man cut his sobbing back to snivelling, which if anything was worse.

Clover pronounced every word with care. 'It's 'cause it can all go wrong so easily that you make every effort to be sure it goes right. Like not being drunk. And not drawing your bloody bow till you want to shoot. And knowing who you're dealing with and where they are, so an old man with an axe comes as no surprise. That type o' thing!' He'd ended up shouting, and he winced and rubbed at his head, and forced his voice soft again. 'The way you came blundering at this, it's a wonder you didn't kill each other into the bargain.'

'Shame they didn't,' grunted Downside. 'Would've saved us some fucking trouble.'

Clover could not but agree. Even Dancer couldn't disagree. 'Aye, you're right,' he said, 'I know you're right, Clover. But you bring warriors to a place like this, it's the type o' thing that happens.'

'Shit warriors, maybe,' said Sholla, picking her nose.

Dancer shuffled closer on his knees. Not dancing much with his hands tied to his feet, of course. He looked up, big eyes, little voice, wheedle, wheedle. 'No chance we could let it go?'

If there had been a time when Clover was impressed by wheedling, it was far in the past. 'Not up to me, is it? If Stour lets it go, I guess it's gone.'

Dancer's smile withered like blooms in late summer, and he gave a swallow that made a *glug*, and the fat one let his face drop in the muck and set to sobbing again. Everyone knew by now. Stour Nightfall's mercy was a thin thread to hang all your hopes on.

'Just went wrong, is all,' muttered Dancer, and Prettyboy struggled to scratch his ear with his shoulder, and failed.

By then they could hear hooves, and the King of the Northmen wrenched his horse around the side of the barn, Greenway and a dozen of his bastards in a jostling crowd behind. Stour reined in savagely, of course, since there's no finer sport than mistreating the beast who carries you. He propped his arms crosswise on the saddle horn so his great chain with its great diamond brushed his wrists, and glowered at the burned-out house, and the yard strewn with rubbish, and the corpses, and the prisoners with wrists and ankles closely attached, and Clover and his people stood around them with weapons out. He slowly licked the inside of his mouth until he'd gathered what he wanted, then spat it spinning into the mud.

'Well, here's a mess.'

Dancer kept his eyes on the ground. 'Just went wrong.'

'You *fucking think?*' snarled the Great Wolf, as Greenway and the rest of his men spread out, looking down their noses at the scene with varying measures of contempt. 'Is he crying? Is he fucking simple or something? Get this cleared up, Clover, before . . . Oh, that's perfect.'

And who should burst from the trees but the Young Lion and a crowd of *his* bastards. They reined in so Stour and his lot were sneering bitter scorn from one side of the yard, Brock and his lot scowling righteous outrage on the other. Seemed the Young Lion hadn't reached the point where tragedies became chores. If anything, he tended towards too much feeling.

'What the *hell* happened?' he growled.

There was an awkward silence, which Clover for some reason felt the need to fill. What he really wanted to say was that if you don't like dead folk you shouldn't start wars, but the best he could think of was, 'I'm told it went wrong.' He'd thought when Dancer said it nothing could've sounded worse, but somehow he managed it.

'So I *see!*' The Young Lion spurred his snorting warhorse across the farmyard till it loomed over Clover and his kneeling prisoners. 'Is this your idea of best behaviour?' he snapped at Stour, pointing to the face-down corpse with the yawning sword-cut across his back.

The Great Wolf was not to be outdone on the bristling, threatening or nursing of offence. 'You're taking a high hand with me, Young Lion!' And he nudged his own horse forward till Clover had to squint up at him. 'You asked for killers. As many as I could find. You wanted dogs off the leash in your own backyard. I warned you they might run after rabbits.'

'Rabbits would be one thing.' Brock kicked his horse even closer to

Stour and Clover had to duck away lest he be squashed between the two heroes. 'Red-handed murder of Union citizens is another! Was it these bastards who did it?' he snarled at the trussed-up men, and they cringed, or wriggled, and the fat one blubbed into the mud, and Prettyboy moved his lips as he offered up some prayer to the dead which Clover very much doubted would help.

'Last I checked, I was King o' the Northmen.' Stour leaned towards Brock with that mad gleam in his wet eyes, catching hold of his chain and giving it a shake so the diamond he'd torn from his uncle's cut throat danced. 'These fuckers are Northmen. So *I'll* say what's done with 'em.'

For a moment, it looked like the Young Lion might grab the Great Wolf and they'd wrestle their way down from their saddles and set to an ugly rematch of their duel right there in the corpse-scattered farmyard. Then, looking like it took quite the effort, Brock got a grip on himself. He breathed in through manfully clenched teeth and leaned back. 'You're King of the Northmen.' With a jerk on his reins, he pulled his horse away from Stour's. 'But this is the Union. I expect to see justice done.'

'Trust me, Young Lion,' snarled Stour, looking as untrustworthy as any man ever. 'I'm *all* about the justice.'

Brock wrenched his mount around and led his glaring bastards back into the trees at a brisk trot. Clover slowly breathed out. Sholla, who'd had a cautious hand wrapped around the grip of a knife in the back of her belt, leaned to his ear to whisper, 'Seems the lion and the wolf ain't getting on.'

''Twas always a doomed romance,' said Clover, under his breath. 'Dogs and cats, you know...'

'Thanks, my king,' croaked out Dancer. 'You saved our—'

Stour gave him a little smile. 'You're fucking joking, aren't you? I came here to *fight*, not stand judge over your folly. Get these idiots killed, Clover.'

'Me?'

'I'm giving orders. It's what kings do.'

His turn to wrench his horse around and ride off, showering everyone with dirt. Dancer stared at the ground. Prettyboy frowned bitterly at his bow. The fat one set to sobbing again. The corpses, naturally, were unmoved.

'That was a lot o' bluster,' grumbled Downside, 'just to end where we started.'

'Aye, well, that's life,' said Clover. 'From mud we come, to mud we shall return. Every one of us.'

Sholla raised a brow. 'Message o' hope, then?'

'Messages o' hope would be inappropriate at an execution. Downside, get these idiots killed.'

'Me?' grunted Downside, looking somewhat put out.

'I'm giving orders,' said Clover, turning away. 'You can get Flick to help you with the burying. And best take those sheep with us, Sholla. Folk need to eat.'

Dancer was still staring at the mud as Downside pulled his axe out. 'Just went wrong,' he said, shaking his head. 'That's all.'

Good Ground

'**G**ood ground,' said Forest approvingly as they rode down the gentle slope.

Stoffenbeck nestled in a valley beside a sparkling river, a reassuringly old and solid little town of seasoned Midderland stone. Sheep lazily cropped grass in the pastures, the waterwheel of an ancient mill gently turned, soothing smoke drifted from the ornamental chimneys which were such a feature of the local architecture. It would have made a fine study for one of those nostalgic painters who turned out the good old days in bulk.

'The best ground.' Orso took a satisfied noseful of the sweet country air. 'Absolutely charming.'

'I . . . meant for a battle, Your Majesty.'

'Oh.' The thought of red-toothed war descending on the sleepy scene was far from pleasant. But then war never is pleasant to contemplate, once it comes to specific homes to be ruined, specific people to be slaughtered. Not to mention specific kings to be toppled. 'Yes, of course. Good ground.'

A gentle green hill with a few trees at the crown overlooked the town on the right. Perhaps it would have been more military to say east. Or was it west? For some reason north and south were instinctive, but the other points of the compass always took a moment for Orso to work through. On the left of the town, across the river, there was a steeper hill studded with rocky outcrops. A bluff, might a surveyor have called it?

'Good ground,' said Forest again, his scar puckering as he allowed himself the smallest smile. As if smiles were being strictly rationed and that was all they could spare.

'Hills.' Orso did his best to copy Forest's discerning expression. 'Hills are good.'

'Hills are bloody marvellous, Your Majesty. If you get up 'em first. 'Course, to *hold* them, we could use more men . . .'

'Reinforcements are on the way.' Orso tried to make sure his voice betrayed no quaverings of doubt.

'The question is,' murmured Tunny, from behind, 'will they get here before we're all killed?'

A small crowd in feast-day clothes was arranged in the square at Stoffenbeck's heart. Bunting fluttered about a singularly ugly old building with an absurdly tall clock tower, presumably the town hall.

'Go, then!' snapped a portly man with a chain of office, and a boy raised a polished trumpet and blew a salute, lacking tune but compensating with sheer volume.

'Oh dear,' muttered Orso. 'You don't suppose they've turned out for me?'

Tunny raised one brow. 'Well, I don't suppose they've turned out for me.'

'Your August Majesty!' gushed the mayor as Orso's party approached, collapsing in a bow so low his chain of office feathered the cobbles. 'I cannot find the words to describe the privilege of hosting you! The honour for me and the entire town of Stoffenbeck is quite *indescribable.*'

'Not at all, my dear sir, yours is a delightful burg.' Orso gestured towards the buildings about the square. Several fine old houses, a guildhall with a marble façade, a tavern with a half-timbered upper floor, a covered marketplace with its sagging roof held up on squat pillars. Progress had largely left this corner of the Union alone, it could barely have changed in two centuries. 'The very quintessence of rural Midderland! In happier times I would delight in a tour, but I hope you will forgive me . . .' Orso tipped his circlet towards the ladies and gentlemen and kept his horse moving ever so gently northwards. Stop for one moment, and they have you. 'Rebellions don't crush themselves, you know!'

'Of course, Your Majesty!' The mayor took a few shuffling steps after him. 'If there is anything you need, you have only to ask. Anything at all!'

'Ten thousand soldiers and an accurate weather forecast?' muttered Orso, under his breath.

'The honour is quite *indescribable.*' Tunny mimicked the mayor's delivery with uncanny accuracy.

'Believe it or not, there are still people in the world not yet sick of the sight of me.'

'I wonder if he'll reckon it such a privilege when his town hosts one of the largest battles ever fought on Union soil.'

'My dear Corporal Tunny, you underestimate the sycophancy of the stout Midderland burgher. My guess is he will still be happily genuflecting when arrows darken the sky . . .'

Jokes made him feel a little better, especially ones in poor taste, but they seemed rather foolish in light of the spectacle as they emerged from the town. There must have been thousands of men working furiously in the fields to the north. Men of the Crown Prince's Division, fortifying a great crescent between the gentle hill and the steep bluff, sharpening stakes, shoring up walls, throwing up barricades, digging trenches and pits.

Overseeing the work with the same total lack of emotion with which he had once overseen the hanging of two hundred Breakers, white clothes pristine in the afternoon sun, was Arch Lector Pike.

Orso reined in beside him, surveying the vast building site. 'Hard at work, Your Eminence?'

'Indeed, Your Majesty. I find men rarely work with such tireless dedication as when their lives depend on the results.'

On their left, the river drained into boggy shallows and was met by another stream with orchards planted on both banks. Over to the right, fields thick with ripe spring wheat sloped gently away towards woodland. In the centre, straight ahead, the crops had just been harvested, a patchwork of stubbled fields turned rich brown by the recent rains. A great cloud of starlings twisted in the sky, pouring down into the trees around a farm a mile or two away, then whirling up into the haze again.

Orso swallowed. There seemed to be something of a lump in his throat. 'So this will be our battlefield.'

'I doubt we'll find a better,' said Forest.

Orso shaded his eyes, peering north towards a single hill on the far side of the fields, a building jutting from its summit.

'What's that tower there?'

'An old fortified manor house,' said Pike. 'Belongs to a Lord Steebling. Minor nobility.'

'Bad luck for him,' murmured Orso. He thought he caught the twinkle of steel. 'We have men there? Watching for the enemy, I suppose.'

'Those *are* the enemy, Your Majesty.'

'What?'

'Their first scouts.' Forest rubbed at his grizzled jaw. 'Even with the roads in the state they are, their main body should be with us before sunset.'

'Bloody hell . . .' breathed Orso. That brought it all home, somehow. There they were, rebels fixed on his destruction, with only a few miles of flat Midderland earth between them. 'When can we expect reinforce-ments?'

'A detachment just arrived from the Siege School in Ratshoff,' said Tunny. 'They brought twenty-four cannon with them.'

'Don't those things have a nasty habit of blowing up?' The flash as Curnsbick's engine exploded was unpleasantly fresh in Orso's mind.

'I'm assured these new ones are more reliable...' Though Forest looked less than convinced. There had not been much to rely on of late.

'Three loyal members of the Open Council are a few miles away to the west.' Pike pointed off beyond the orchards. 'Lords Stenner, Crant and Ingenbeck, with perhaps a thousand men between them.'

'And we expect two regiments of King's Own from the east.' Forest stood in his stirrups and frowned towards the gentle hill, the wind making waves in the long grass on its flanks. 'Might get here during the night, maybe the morning. Lord Marshal Rucksted is bringing four more in from the south, mostly cavalry. Forced march from Keln and they've a lot of ground to cover. If we're lucky and the weather holds, they might get here late tomorrow, but... well...'

'You wouldn't want to bet a kingdom on it?' ventured Orso, turning at the sound of hooves behind. 'Ah, Inquisitor Teufel! So glad you could join us.' She did not look very glad to be joining them, but then Orso had never seen her look glad about anything. He even found it rather reassuring. Negotiation, planning or collapse of a nation, she faced them all with the same flinty resolve. 'Did you speak to the Young Lion?'

'I did,' she said. 'And to his wife, Lady Savine.'

'She's with him?' He had to cough back a ridiculous desire to ask whether she had looked well.

'Heavily pregnant but still sharp as a dagger.'

'What are we calling her?' asked Pike, with a twisting of his burned features that might have been a smile. 'The Young Lioness?'

Orso gave an unhappy grunt. An apt name, as it turned out. From what he understood of the species, the males had the big reputations but the females did all the killing.

'I told them a tale,' said Vick. 'That you're disorganised and short on men. That Brint has prevented any chance of reinforcements. The Lioness had her doubts, but her husband swallowed it whole, I think.'

'Excellent work!' said Orso. If they could have been reinforced with an-other dozen Vick dan Teufels they might have avoided fighting altogether. 'But... you look less than delighted.'

'Our rebels have struck a deal with the Breakers. They're planning uprisings across Midderland.'

An ugly pause. Orso took it with remarkable fortitude, he thought. Or perhaps he had no room to hold any more bad news. Like pouring wine into a glass already full, it simply flooded over the sides. 'Have we heard of any uprisings? Any *more*, I should say...'

'None,' said Pike, 'but...'

It was left to Tunny to say what everyone was undoubtedly thinking. 'The first warning would be when our reinforcements don't arrive.'

Orso could not help himself. He burst out in a carefree chuckle. 'Well, we can only fight one war at a time, my friends. The Breakers can be tomorrow's problem. Right now, several thousand rebellious noblemen, disgruntled Anglanders and slavering Northmen demand all my attention.'

'Twenty thousand, according to Brock's own estimate,' said Vick.

Another ugly pause. From the concerned looks on the faces about him, Orso gathered that was more than they had hoped. 'How many are we?' he asked, unable to keep a wheedling note from his voice.

'As it stands,' said Forest, grimly, 'no more than twelve thousand. But we've got the ground.'

A great deal of faith to put in earth. Orso gave a long sigh as he considered the grassy hill, the gently rising, gently waving fields of wheat before it. 'Lord Marshal Forest, I would like you to command the right wing.'

Forest raised his bushy brows. 'I'm a general, Your Majesty.'

'If the High King of the Union says a man's a lord marshal, who's to deny it? Brint's early retirement has left a seat empty on the Closed Council, and I can't think of a better man to sit there. Consider yourself promoted.' The way things were going, it might be his last official act.

Forest stared at him, mouth slightly open. 'Closed Council...'

'Congratulations,' said Tunny, punching Forest on the arm. 'You should get a baton, or something.'

'Only just got me a general's jacket.'

'Well, you're on your own there,' said Orso. 'I can pluck new lord marshals from the air, but jackets cost money.' He frowned over at the rocky hill on their left, a few more steep bluffs beyond it. The ground in front of those was more difficult, planted with overgrown orchards and cut in half by that swampy tributary of the river. 'Our left might be held by a smaller force, I think.'

'Especially if we place our cannon there,' came Gorst's piping voice.

He coloured faintly as everyone turned towards him. 'I . . . saw them used at Osrung.'

'You'd want a ruthless commander,' said Tunny, considering the hills. 'Someone who scares our men more than the enemy.'

As luck would have it, the perfect man appeared to be within arm's reach. 'Arch Lector Pike?' asked Orso. 'I believe you have experience on the battlefield?'

'In my younger days, in Gurkhul and the North,' said Pike. 'I also oversaw the first experiments with cannon in the Far Country.'

'Then I can think of no one more qualified to take charge of my left wing. Could you ensure morale there stays high?' Or at least that the demoralised troops were too scared to run.

Pike inclined his head. 'Morale is a speciality of mine, Your Majesty. With your permission, I will begin fortifying the position.'

'The sooner the better,' said Orso. Forest gave a sharp salute and spurred away towards the gentle hill. Pike turned his horse towards the steeper bluffs. Vick caught Orso's eye, gave him a firmly committed nod which he rather appreciated, then followed His Eminence.

A breeze came up, and took the Steadfast Standard, and made the white horse against the gilded sun flap and ripple. The very flag under which Casamir had conquered Angland. Witness to so many military glories down the centuries. Orso wondered if there was any chance of it presiding over another.

'You've seen a fair amount of action, Tunny.'

'I've tended more towards inaction, Your Majesty. But yes.'

'How bad is it? And bear in mind I'm a king. You should be honest.'

'Begging your pardon, but I try never to be honest with a superior, and the higher up the chain of command I go, the less honest I try to be. One could hardly be higher up than a king. Unless you've got great Euz hiding somewhere.'

'If only,' said Orso. 'An all-powerful demigod would be the very thing to balance the odds. How bad is it?'

Tunny ran his tongue around the inside of his mouth, glanced about at the hills, and the fields, and the men digging. 'It's bad.'

'But we have a chance?'

'If Rucksted arrives in time, and the enemy can't stay together, and we're lucky with the weather . . .' Tunny broke out that radiant grin of his, the deep lines crinkling around his eyes. 'There's *always* a chance. But any delay works in our favour.'

'Hmmm.' Orso narrowed his eyes towards that tower house on the hill, wondering if the Young Lion was at that very moment considering the position through his eyeglass. 'Colonel Gorst?'

'Your Majesty?'

'I would like you to conduct Corporal Tunny and his Steadfast Standard across those fields. Seek out the intrepid Lord Governor of Angland! Seek him out with the most pomp, ceremony and military bluster possible. Tunny, I want your bloody salute to take an hour minimum.'

'And once I've saluted?'

'Then you invite the Young Lion to dinner. I may not be his equal with a sword, but I flatter myself to believe that I'm more than a match for him with a fork. My father used to say a good king should attend always to the opinions of his subjects. My mother would add that he should then entirely ignore 'em. Let's hear the bastard out.' And Orso winked. 'At great length.'

The men kept digging. Out across the fields, the starlings swarmed back up into the afternoon sky.

Bad Ground

'**B**ad ground,' said Antaup, thumping a fist worriedly on the ancient parapet.

From the roof of the tower-house, Leo could see the whole valley. Stoffenbeck nestled between two hills – a rocky bluff overlooking the river to the west, a gentle ridge above ripe wheatfields to the east.

'Ground we've got to cross to reach Adua,' said Jin.

That would've been easy in peacetime. Two paved roads converged on the town from either side of the hill the tower-house stood on, met in Stoffenbeck's pretty market square and became one, then headed due south towards the capital. Trouble was, the country between swarmed with King Orso's forces. They'd fortified a wide crescent in the freshly reaped fields north of the town, bristling with stakes and gleaming spear points. There was more metal, along with a few fluttering standards, spread out across the summit of the grassy ridge. Squinting through his eyeglass, Leo could see some men on top of the bluff as well. Wagons, too, maybe. He handed the eyeglass to Antaup. 'How many men, do you reckon?'

'Hard to say. In the centre, they look well dug in, but the hills are weaker held. I see some King's Own standards. Some others I don't recognise.'

'More than we were expecting,' murmured Leo. Far more than they'd been hoping for. Looked like there might be a fight after all.

'We've still got the numbers,' growled Jin, all Northern bravado. 'Two to one, maybe.'

'Maybe.' But a good chunk of them Leo didn't trust. Isher's men were well drilled, but most of the Open Council's forces had lovely uniforms but no discipline at all. Barezin had put together what he proudly called a Gurkish Legion, but he'd taken anyone with an exotic look regardless of whether they could even speak to each other, let alone had worn armour before. A good portion of Lady Wetterlant's beggarly troops had most likely joined for a set of clothes then stolen away during the storm, taking their supplies with them. Then there was the Great Wolf, who every day seemed more likely to fight against Leo than for him.

'Might be we should attack now,' said Jin, squinting up at the sun. 'There's still a few hours o' daylight.'

Antaup handed Leo the eyeglass. 'Our men are nearly ready to go.'

'Good old Anglanders,' said Leo, watching their orderly columns tramp from the road and form neat battle lines at the base of the hill, the flags they'd fought under across the North and back flying overhead. Made him proud to see them. Made him proud to lead them. He scanned the fields they might soon be advancing across and caught sight of another flag, coming fast towards them. A white horse on a golden sun, flashing and twinkling at the head of two dozen armoured men.

'The Steadfast Standard,' murmured Leo.

Antaup raised his brows. 'Looks like His Majesty wants to talk.'

Leo couldn't have asked for a more splendid group around him: Lords Isher and Barezin and a good twenty other members of the Open Council, Lord Mustred and a dozen other noblemen of Angland, as well as Stour's man Greenway and Rikke's man Hardbread. And yet he felt very much alone as the king's standard-bearer reined in his snorting mount on the hillside, the Steadfast Standard snapping majestically with the breeze and two dozen Knights of the Body in full battle armour clattering to a halt behind. He was a grizzled old veteran with a glint in his eye and a relaxed style in the saddle, but he produced the most impeccable salute Leo ever saw. Crisp, elegant, no self-regarding flourish. The lords of the Open Council, festooned with enough braid between them to rig a fleet, could've learned a thing or two about what a real soldier looked like.

'Your Grace! My lords of the Open Council! Representatives of the North! I'm Corporal Tunny, standard-bearer to the High King of the Union, His August Majesty King Orso the First. Colonel Gorst, Commander of the Knights of the Body, I believe you all know.'

Being dragged from the Lords' Round by his boyhood hero had taken away none of Leo's admiration for the man. Had increased it, if anything. He was slightly hurt that Gorst sat frowning into the distance without even glancing in his direction.

'*Corporal*... Tunny?' Barezin's jowls trembled as he scornfully raised his chin. 'They're wasting our time!'

'It's his message that matters,' grumbled Mustred, 'not his rank.' Leo would happily have swapped a few armchair generals for corporals of long experience.

'I've dabbled with higher, my lords,' said Tunny, grinning, 'but it never suited me. Carrying His Majesty's standard is as much honour as I can manage.'

'The Steadfast Standard,' Leo found he'd murmured, with not a little awe.

Tunny grinned up fondly at it. 'The very one King Casamir rode under when he delivered Angland from the savages. Makes you think about the Union's proud history. All that the provinces owe to the Crown.'

Leo frowned. 'If men like Casamir still wore the crown, I daresay we'd have no quarrel.'

'Fancy that. No quarrel is exactly what His Majesty wants. In the hopes of getting there, he's invited you to dinner.' Tunny gave Leo's sprawling collection of allies a faintly amused glance. 'Just the two of you, though, he wouldn't want the conversation to wander too far from the matter.'

'Which would be?' asked Isher.

'Your demands and his possible concessions to those demands. The king knows men of your quality wouldn't lead soldiers against him without legitimate grievances. His Majesty is fully prepared to fight, but he wishes at all costs to avoid shedding Union blood on Union soil.'

'He's playing for time,' burst out Barezin. 'I've a mind to order my men across those bloody fields and take my dinner in bloody Stoffenbeck without his bloody invitation!'

Steebling, the old lord who owned the ruinous tower-house, sitting nearby with a gouty leg up on a stool, threw in an unhelpful snort of contempt.

'I'll give the orders,' growled Leo, and Barezin sank grumpily into the roll of fat under his chin. 'Please convey my thanks to His Majesty. He'll have my answer within the hour.'

Tunny drew himself up in the saddle to deliver that exhibition of a salute again, then whisked his horse masterfully about and bore the king's radiant standard back towards Stoffenbeck. You couldn't deny it was a hell of a flag. Perhaps when this was over it would have to go back to Angland, where it belonged.

'We should attack *at once*,' growled Barezin, with a warlike flourish of his fist. 'Eh, Isher? We should *attack!*' Some of the more aggressive lords manfully grumbled their agreement. Easy for them to say, they'd attacked nothing more dangerous than a pork chop in their lives.

Isher fidgeted with his gloves but said nothing. He'd a lot less to say on a battlefield than in a drawing room, on the whole.

'Are Stour's men ready?' asked Leo, in Northern.

Greenway's grin was almost a leer. 'Oh, we're always up for a fight.'

Jin frowned sideways at him. 'He didn't ask you to measure your cock. He asked if Stour's men are ready.'

'They're working through the woods. An hour and they'll be at the treeline. Maybe two.'

Leo winced. Maybe two could easily mean three. It wouldn't be enough to push Orso back, he had to crush him. Could they do it in the lag end of an afternoon? He shaded his eyes, trying to work through the distances, the times, but there was so much to consider, his sight danced and his head buzzed with it all. He turned to ask Jurand's opinion, then remembered, and felt the sting of disappointment and betrayal all over again. He was the only one of Leo's friends who'd ever really had an opinion worth listening to. Such a clear thinker. Such a cool head in a crisis. Why did the best man Leo knew have to be a bloody pervert? He clenched his fist.

'Isher, Barezin, what about you?'

'My men are up,' fretted Isher, sounding less than delighted about it. 'Already deploying on the right.'

'And mine are coming up!' boomed Barezin. He couldn't say a word without trying to make a threat out of it. 'My Gurkish Legion will be ready to advance within the hour!'

Steebling gave another contemptuous cackle. Leo gritted his teeth and did his best to ignore it.

'What about the rest of the Open Council?'

Barezin thumped his fat fist into his fat palm. 'Mostly up!'

'Partly up,' said Isher. 'Some are still bogged down on the bad roads...'

The roads were dried out now. It was damp command and soggy discipline that were slowing them down. They'd need more time to deploy, especially with those orchards and that river ahead. But then the bluff beyond looked only lightly held. It might be better to try to grab it now than wait...

'Damn it,' Leo muttered. As a captain, the right things to do were never in doubt. Follow orders. Care for your men. Lead by example. As a general, the right things were shrouded in fog. Everything was a best guess, a fine judgement, an each-way bet with thousands of lives staked on the outcome. The decisions he'd taken in the past had always been in the heat of the moment. He'd never had time to weigh the consequences.

Had his mother been right? Was he no general? He caught himself wishing she was with him and forced the thought away. By the dead, he was the Young Lion! But courage and a loud roar wouldn't be enough. Antaup was right, it was bad ground. Men would die taking those positions. Good men. Friends like Ritter and Barniva, killed by his recklessness.

'We have the numbers,' he mused to himself, rubbing at his aching leg. 'They have no help coming.'

'Bunch o' bloody traitors,' said Steebling, more than loud enough to be heard, swigging from a bottle and giving them a scornful stare over it. Leo would've liked to kick him off his chair and roll him down the hill, but they were here to free the Union's people from the tyranny of the Closed Council, not kick them off their chairs, however much they deserved it.

Mustred gave him a nod of encouragement. 'The men of Angland are with you, Your Grace, whatever you decide.'

That should've been a comfort. But it only brought home to Leo that the decision was entirely his. He'd always prided himself on being the definition of a man of action. Now, in command, on a battlefield with the enemy before him, the very place he'd always dreamed of being, he felt paralysed.

He found himself wishing that Rikke was there. He loved Savine, but she'd a habit of forcing her opinions on people. A subtle, velvety kind of forcing, but her opinions still. Rikke had a way of cutting through the tangle to the simple heart of things. She'd helped him see what *he* wanted.

He rounded angrily on Hardbread. 'Where the *bloody* hell is Rikke?' The old warrior swallowed and gave a helpless shrug.

High Ground

Rikke squatted in the wet woods, fretting at the old dowel around her neck, going over and over her own tooth marks with her thumbtip. Her father had spent half his life squatting in wet woods, and it was nice to feel that she was following in his footsteps, but that was poor compensation for the clingy cold spreading across her back as the pines steadily drip, drip, dripped upon her.

'There's a lot to be said for roofs,' she murmured, under her breath.

She glanced to the right. Armed men knelt among the trees, keeping low. The best men Uffrith had, scarred and war-wise, weapons ready and faces tense. Isern-i-Phail sat with her back to a tree and her spear across her knees, slowly chewing. She leaned to one side, spat and raised her brows at Rikke as if to say, *Well?*

She glanced to the left. More men. The Nail and the rest of Gregun Hollowhead's considerable family to the fore, teeth bared like wolves seen a sheep. Hundreds more in the woods behind them, she knew. All tensed like clenched fists, waiting on her say-so. Shivers was on one knee, grey hair plastered about his face with the morning dew, twisting that ring with the red stone around and around on his little finger. He raised the one brow he had at her as if to say, *Well?*

Rikke narrowed her eyes. Not that narrowing the right one made any difference. A misty night had become a misty day, which had been helpful far as not being seen went but was no help at all far as seeing where they were going now. The road was clear enough, just beyond the trees. The bridge she could see all right. But the gate was naught but a gloomy rumour.

She fiddled at her dowel, fiddled, fiddled. Truth was she hadn't needed it for months. Let alone a fit, she'd barely had a quiver since she came down from the forbidden lake with the runes on her face. She'd always hated having to wear the damn thing, but here she was hanging on to it.

Some last shred of childhood. Some hint of a past where she didn't have to make the hard choices.

She twitched at a clonking sound, craned up at a creaking over the chatter of the river and squinted towards the archway at a bobbing light. A breeze stirred the branches, and the mist shifted, and she saw two men. One had a fine crested helmet, mail gleaming under a long cloak. The other had a bald head, lamp held high in one hand as he pushed the other door wide.

And the gates of Carleon stood invitingly open.

Rikke snapped the thong with a jerk of her wrist and tossed the dowel away into the bushes.

'Go,' she hissed, and Shivers sprang up, quick and quiet with the Nail right at his heels. With a metal whisper, the first dozen were up and after them, then the next dozen, then the next.

'Come on,' Rikke whispered, nails cutting at her palms she was clenching her fists so tight. 'Come on...'

She winced at the clattering footfalls as Shivers and the rest ran out onto the wooden bridge. A moment she'd seen before, she was almost sure. Seen with the Long Eye. The cloaked man in the gateway fumbled for his sword.

His shout became a gurgle as the bald man stabbed him in the throat and shoved him back into the shadows of the tunnel. Proof once again that a little gold can succeed where a lot of steel might fail. He raised his lamp and stood politely out of the way as Shivers rushed past, leading a steady flood of armed men into Carleon.

Rikke slowly stood, wincing at the ache in her knees from all that squatting, and let her held breath sigh away. 'So that's it, then?'

'A good first step, anyway.' Isern planted one boot on a rock, grinning as a tide of warriors streamed through the misty woods around them and into the city, quiet as ghosts.

'Don't kill anyone you don't have to!' called Rikke as she set out towards the gates. She was far from the only one in the North with a taste for revenge, after all.

Things were surprisingly quiet inside the walls, for a city that just got taken.

Knots of Uffrith's Carls stood on the corners, weapons drawn and shields in hand, one or two painted with the design of the Long Eye. Some prisoners sat about, weapons down and hands bound. A few townsfolk peered scared from windows and doors as Rikke walked past.

'Don't worry!' She gave what she hoped was a reassuring grin, though the sight of her face didn't reassure anyone much these days. 'No one's going to get hurt!' She saw a corpse being dragged away by a couple of Carls, leaving a bloody smear down the cobbles. 'No one else'll get hurt!' she corrected. 'Long as you're all, you know, polite.' She wasn't sure she was helping. But at least she was trying. Trying a deal harder than when Black Calder took Uffrith, she reckoned.

The Nail was leaning against a wall, using a dagger to carefully drill a hole in the pointy end of an egg. He'd a way of standing very still, nothing moving until it had to.

'Worked, then,' he said as she walked up.

'Told you it would.'

'Not sure we've lost one dead.'

'Good news. On their side?'

'A couple. Weren't a tenth o' the men guarding the place there'd usually be.'

'Aye,' said Rikke. 'They're all off in Midderland, fighting King Orso.'

'Where you told 'em you'd be.'

'That's why I told 'em so. Reckoned we'd have a lot more fun here.'

The Nail shook his head, blade flashing as he worked that dagger back and forth. 'I knew you were a bad enemy to have.' He looked up at her from under his pale brows, his pale lashes. A long, slow look, just taking it all in. 'Now I'm wondering if you might be a bad friend to have and all.'

'I'm a bad friend to betray, I can tell you that. Savine dan Brock would've sold me out soon enough.' Rikke realised she'd put her hand to the chain of emeralds she wore and took it away again. 'She's a woman who sells everything.' The two of them smiling together, on the bench in her father's garden. Her hand on Savine's belly. The baby shifting under her fingers. 'As for her husband . . .' She thought of Leo's boyish grin, all trusting, all heart, thought of him laughing with her father, thought of the boy he'd been, playing in the barn. She wondered what'd become of him now, in Midderland, without the help she'd promised. She felt a twinge of guilt, then was annoyed with herself for feeling it. You have to make of your heart a stone.

'Have I done what I said I'd do?' she asked.

'You have,' said the Nail.

'Has it worked out the way I said it would?'

'Thus far.'

'So what's your complaint?'

'I'm not saying I've got one.'

386

'What are you saying?'

He blew a little dust from the top of his egg and his pale eyes rolled up to hers. 'I'm saying don't give me one.'

'I'll bear that in mind.' She nodded towards the big wall up ahead. The one Bethod had built on the high ground around Skarling's Hall. The strongest wall in the North, maybe. Some men were easing towards the gate with their shields up, and a couple of arrows looped down and skittered from the cobbles, made them shuffle back. 'In the meantime, we've still got work.'

'There's always work.' The Nail kept on drilling at that egg with his dagger, patient as tree-roots. 'The gates were shut when we got here. Whoever's inside don't feel like opening 'em. Keeps shooting arrows at us.'

'Not very neighbourly.'

'No. Come night-time, I was thinking I might climb over there and teach 'em better manners.'

Rikke considered the walls. Damned high, they were, and stark, and grey. 'Let's give 'em a while to consider their predicament. Meantime keep the peace, eh? Make sure no more blood gets spilled in town.'

'You're forgiving.'

'A minute ago, I was too ruthless for you. Now forgiving's a bad thing?'

'Depends who you forgive.' He squinted up towards the walls. 'In war, you seize all the high ground you can.' He lifted the egg to his lips, looking small between his big finger and thumb. 'Except the moral kind.' And he sucked the insides out through the hole. 'That ain't worth shit.'

Isern-i-Phail was in a square not far away, a row of disarmed warriors on their knees in front of her. Corleth stood nearby, proudly holding the standard of the Long Eye. Rikke walked over and planted her hands on her hips.

'I expect kneeling in the street wasn't what you were hoping for when you got out of bed this morning,' she said. 'I can only say I'm sorry for that.'

'Are you, though?' asked Isern. 'Really?'

Rikke grinned all across her face. 'Not one bit. The thought of Stour Nightfall's face when he finds we stole his city is what's been keeping me cheery these last few weeks.'

'Reckon he'll shit his britches and cry for his mummy.'

'Wouldn't be surprised,' said Rikke.

'But his mummy won't come,' said Isern, cackling away to herself, 'on account of being long years dead, d'you see, and he'll be gnashing his teeth and kicking himself, and his mouth'll pucker up like a little arsehole, and—'

'You are straying from the point, Isern.'

Isern cleared her throat. ''Tis a failing common in my family. Return us to the matter.'

'It's not Stour's mother I'm after, but his father.' Rikke turned back to the kneeling men. 'You fellows help me out, you'll find me reasonable. More reasonable than Stour fucking Shitefall, leastways.'

'Shitefall,' chuckled Isern, shaking her head.

'Now, where's Black Calder?'

The one on the left, a sour-looking old bastard with a scar through his short grey hair, lifted his head to sneer up at her. 'Fuck yourselves, you mad bitches.'

Rikke raised her brows at Corleth. Corleth raised hers back. 'Fuck yourselves, he says.'

'I heard him,' said Rikke. 'Guess there might be time for that later. Just a celebratory finger or two. But right now, I'm a little busy stealing your city. Where's Black Calder?'

'Didn't you fucking hear me?' He bared his teeth. 'I said—' Isern grabbed him by the hair and stabbed him in the side of the neck, chopped his throat out with an easy flick of the wrist and sent black blood squirting, shoved him down into the gutter with her boot on his back.

It was good to be forgiving, but this was the North still. Rikke's father never liked killing. Hadn't stopped him doing it when he had to. It wouldn't stop her, either.

'Might be there was a lot to like about him, once you broke through the gritty crust.' Rikke gave a sigh as she watched him squirm under Isern's boot. 'Might be he had a collection of interesting bird skulls, or an excellent singing voice, or a lot of love for his sadly passed sister that caused him to weep at the quiet times.' Rikke looked at the rest of the men, all of them staring over with wide eyes. 'But there's so much to feel sorry for in the world. Can't waste too much on folk who act like pricks.'

The sour-looking bastard had stopped moving and Isern reached down, wiped her dagger on the arse of his trousers, got distracted by her reflection in the bright blade, frowned as she rubbed at a smudge of something on her cheek.

Rikke stepped sideways, before the spreading pool of blood reached her feet, to stand in front of the next man. She'd always thought of herself as a figure of fun. Giggling Rikke, fountain o' laughs. Still seemed strange people might be scared of her. But she had to admit there was something satisfying about the fear in his eyes. Beat contempt, anyway.

'I like your look better,' she said, wagging her finger at him.

'Pleasant-seeming personage, this one,' said Isern, tapping him on the shoulder with her dagger. 'Family man, if I might take a guess?'

'Two daughters,' he croaked out.

'Aw,' said Rikke. 'How old?'

'Six and two.'

'Aw,' said Corleth.

'Those girls need their daddy,' said Rikke. 'I'm hopeful you'll be helpful.'

'Hopeful you'll be helpful.' Isern gave a little chuckle. 'That's got a nice balance.'

'Always had a feel for the poetry of language,' said Rikke. 'Now, where's Black Calder?'

The eyes of the father of two daughters flickered sideways, straining towards Isern's dagger, just out of sight. 'Not here,' he croaked.

'Well, don't worry, we're making progress. Where is he?'

'Went north to the High Valleys. Some of the chieftains up there are worried about the way Stour's running things.'

'Aren't we all?' said Isern. 'I mean, I'm an arsehole from a family of arseholes, but that Stour? He sets new standards.'

Rikke nodded towards the gates of the inner wall. The gates with Skarling's Hall beyond, still tight shut. 'So who's in charge in there?'

'Brodd Silent.'

Name meant nothing to Rikke. She shrugged at Isern, and the hill-woman shrugged back.

'My guess would be he don't say much,' said Corleth, which seemed a reasonable assumption.

'He ain't got many men, though,' said the father of two. 'No more'n a couple of dozen.'

'Maybe three dozen,' offered one of the others, shuffling forward on his knees. Here was a sad lesson. You can talk fine words till your tongue bleeds and never get a favour. Cut one throat and everyone's falling over themselves to be helpful.

'Three dozen's not many,' said Isern.

'No.' Rikke scratched her head as she frowned up at the black battlements against the white sky. 'But he don't need many to hold that.'

Common Ground

'*S*o sorry I'm late,' said Orso, striding into the room. The table was set for a royal dinner, silverwear gleaming. 'So much to do, you understand. Well, of course you understand, you've an army of your own to manage. And bigger even than mine! Don't get up!' Hildi struck a match and began to light the tall candles as Orso trotted over to offer his hand, smiling hugely. His mother had always told him it was important to smile. Especially at your enemies.

Brock was not much changed. Every bit the chunkily handsome storybook hero that Orso remembered. He had grown something of a beard, but then he probably grew a beard between breakfast and lunch, even those bits at the corners of the mouth that Orso could never quite get to come through. Frozen uncomfortably between rising and staying seated, Brock looked at the proffered hand with an air of puzzled disgust. Like a man who had rolled over to find a turd in his bed. Then he reluctantly reached for it.

'Not too firmly!' said Orso. 'Remember I'm no warrior!' When Brock's hand gingerly gripped his, he gave it as bone-crushing a squeeze as he could manage and was mildly gratified to see him wince. Small victories, perhaps, but Orso's father had always said one must take all the victories one can get.

Brock gestured to the two men he had brought with him, standing grimly against the wall. 'These are my aides – Antaup . . .' Lean and handsome, with that slicked-back black hair which somehow always let a rakish lock or two drop over the forehead. 'And Whitewater Jin.' A rugged, red-bearded Northman who looked to have been opening doors with his face most of his life.

Orso grinned at them, too. Grins were free, after all. 'Are there any small Northmen? I've never seen one!'

'We keep 'em at the back,' growled Jin.

'Lucky for them! I'll be at the back myself, if it comes to fighting, I can promise you that, eh, Tunny?'

Tunny gave an approving nod. 'Well in the rear, Your Majesty.'

'How about you, Young Lion? You'll be leading by example, I daresay?'

'I daresay,' said Brock stiffly.

'Corporal Tunny and Colonel Gorst you know, of course, and this is Hildi, my—' Orso frowned. 'What the hell are you, Hildi? My butler? My jester?'

'Your parasite,' she said as she lit the last of the candles and neatly wafted out the match. 'I'm only here till you pay what you owe me—'

'For the Fates' sakes, you know I'm good for it.' Orso gave a weary sigh as he dropped into his chair. 'But that's being king. Everyone wants a little piece of you. You'll find out. If you win.'

Brock paused with mouth open, then gave a kind of grimace, as though he had realised the only way to get that turd out of his bed was with his fingers. 'We don't want to depose you, Your Majesty—'

'Please don't "Majesty" me, it's faintly ridiculous at the best of times, but with armies in the field it's positively absurd. Let's talk like equals. Like friends. Just for tonight. I imagine tomorrow's events will necessitate a whole new relationship between us, in any case.'

Brock grimaced again as he pronounced the name. 'Orso, then—'

'Wine?' asked Orso, and Hildi ghosted forward with a cloth over one arm and tipped the bottle towards Brock's glass.

'Not for me.'

'I hope you won't mind if I do, it's a very good Osprian. Maybe your friends would like to—'

Whitewater Jin looked as if he might be on the point of accepting but Brock jumped in first. 'My friends want the same thing as me. To avoid a battle, if we can. That's why I'm here.'

'You're invading Midderland... to *avoid* a battle? Couldn't you have simply... stayed loyal?' And Orso took a noisy slurp from his glass, regarding the Lord Governor of Angland over the rim.

'Loyal?' Brock stared back at him, ever so slightly pale. 'No man was more loyal than me when Scale Ironhand attacked the Protectorate. We leaped to the Dogman's defence. Never considered anything else. We were outnumbered but we fought even so. We knew we had the Union behind us. We knew help would come. Any day.' He looked over at the Steadfast Standard, chest swelling with pride, as if the damn thing really was made of gold rather than just gold thread. 'Back then, I would've followed that flag into hell!'

Orso swallowed uncomfortably. This story was making his wine taste somewhat sour.

'But all we got from Midderland was well-wishes,' said Brock, nobly disappointed, 'and empty promises, and endless demands for taxes. Do you wonder why there wasn't a man in Angland who wouldn't follow me here?' His voice was growing louder and louder. Self-righteousness suited him. 'We fought your war. Men died. My friends died. *I* nearly died. My leg burns with every step and stinks like a shithouse floor and will never heal.' Brock smashed the table with his fist and made the cutlery jump. 'And all because you sat here on your fat arses while we fought for our lives!'

Orso felt Gorst shift as the echoes faded and he held up a calming hand. The room was very still. He had to admit, he had never felt more respect for Leo dan Brock than at that moment. He was a man one could envy. A man for whom everything was simple. And he had a good claim to being the injured party. It was a shame it had come to this.

'You make a very good point,' said Orso. 'No doubt it will mean nothing to you now, but I find it hard to describe my utter shame and disgust that you were sent no help. I did try, in my own rather useless way... something of an irony that most of the men I field against you now are the ones I raised to help you then. But the Breakers rose up in Valbeck, and I had to fight that fire first. And then... well. You know what happened at Red Hill and afterwards better than anyone. Suffice to say you managed without us. The Closed Council let you down. My father let you down.' He took a hard breath. '*I* let you down. But... is *this* really the remedy? Insurrection? Treason? Civil war?'

Brock glared across the table. 'You left us no choice.'

'Really? Because I don't remember anyone trying to talk to me about it. I know we have our differences, but we both, I think, believe in the Union? While there is still time – can we not find a way to satisfaction without the deaths of so many of our countrymen? Can we not find some common ground?'

'Perhaps,' said Brock coldly, 'if you were to dismiss your entire Closed Council and replace them with men of our choosing.'

'And taking a wild guess... you would choose yourselves?'

'We'd choose *patriots*!' shouted Brock, thumping the table again but with less conviction. 'Men of *quality*.' Moving away from the sun-drenched uplands of anger and into the shadowy thickets of politics, he was rather less impressive. 'Men who can... well... take the Union back to its founding *principles*.'

'But whether a man is a patriot, or for that matter of quality, all depends on who you ask, doesn't it? Our current predicament makes that abundantly clear, if nothing else. As for principles, it was Bayaz who founded the Union, and he's still on the Closed Council when it pleases him, in spite of my best efforts. You should spend some time in there. You'll find your most proudly rigid principles turn shockingly flaccid. The First of the Magi can stretch them until they fit around any outrage, believe me.'

Leo dan Brock's impressive jaw muscles worked, but to little result. He really was no philosopher. 'We have the numbers,' he grumbled. 'You have to surrender.'

'Well, I'm no general, but I believe... technically speaking... I could fight and lose? Put yourself in my place. Would you surrender?'

Orso could almost see the wheels turning behind Brock's eyes. Plainly, putting himself in someone else's place was not something he did often. Was not something he had the equipment for. Perhaps it was fortunate that Hildi barged in at that moment with a gilded tray in her hands, two bowls of Suljuk porcelain steaming on top.

'Aha!' Orso whisked up his spoon. 'My cook is called Bernille, and I know they say nothing good ever comes from Talins, but I swear her soup will change your mind.'

Brock frowned down at his bowl, then over at his friend Antaup.

'Oh, come on, I'm not going to poison you.' Orso leaned across, dipped his spoon in Brock's soup and sucked it dry. 'Now eat up, there's a good fellow. There are excuses for High Treason but letting Bernille's soup go cold is bloody unforgivable.'

Probably it was great soup. If kings don't have great soup, who does, after all? But Leo was in no mood to enjoy it. He felt angry, and worried, and with the sky almost dark outside the narrow windows, like he'd missed his chance. He'd been sure Orso would be out of his depth with soldiers in the field. That he'd be weak, and cowardly, and desperate to concede to anything. But the man couldn't have looked more relaxed. You had to admire his nerve. Anyone would've thought he was the one with the numbers.

'So...' and Orso tossed his spoon into his empty bowl. 'If I replace my Closed Council with your chosen men, I get to stay king? I honestly don't enjoy it, but all my crockery has little crowns on, and so forth. Changing everything would be...' He glanced at his strange little waiter.

She puffed out her cheeks as she filled his glass again. 'Bloody nightmare.'

'We're not usurpers,' grumbled Leo, 'we're—'

'Patriots, yes, of course,' said Orso, 'but I'm not sure you've thought this all the way through. Once the troops go home . . . what's to stop me changing my mind?'

Leo had tended to leave the thinking through to Jurand, and Savine, and his mother, and none of them was there. He frowned and said nothing.

'I am sure your friend Lord Isher *has* thought it through. He's not a man to under-plan, eh? We both know all that nonsense with Wetterlant was entirely his design.'

'How d'you mean?' muttered Leo, feeling as if he was blundering into a trap but unable to stop himself.

'He came to me. Isher. Offering to heal the wounds between the Closed and Open Councils. To orchestrate a deal that would see Wetterlant imprisoned, the commoners satisfied, the noblemen mollified and me looking like a masterful statesman.' Orso snorted. 'I should have known. Any plan intended to make me look good has to be doomed. Ah! Fish!'

Orso's blonde-haired girl came out of nowhere and whisked a steaming plate in front of Leo. 'Bernille really does work *magic* with seafood.' Orso twirled a fork around between his fingers. 'She's more sorceress than cook, even in a farmhouse kitchen. No, no, it's the small cutlery, Leo. What was I saying?'

'Wetterlant and Isher,' said Corporal Tunny.

'Ah, yes. I went into the Lords' Round that day expecting to emerge just yet merciful. Imagine my dismay when I ended up the epitome of an idiotic tyrant. But then, spare a thought for Wetterlant.' He forked up a chunk of fish and chewed with great relish. 'He was left dangling. Literally. I couldn't even make a clean job of that. Quite the ugly scene. I bloody *hate* hangings. Still, I'll confess I don't miss the man. An utterly loathsome specimen and guilty as the plague. So much for the good graces of Lord Isher, eh? He loves to play the peacemaker, but he's been sowing discord this whole time. I daresay he's the one who sold this little package to you first? Told you Wetterlant was wronged and I was a monster? Men of *quality*.' And he shook his head and chuckled.

Leo frowned, fork frozen halfway to his mouth. He'd been rather pleased with how he'd done the righteous anger, but now he wasn't enjoying himself at all. Talking to Orso was like talking to Jappo Murcatto, but with higher stakes and lower hopes of success. All his firm reasons, his noble certainties, his staunch alliances, seemed to be crumbling like castles made of sand.

'I don't know what story you've been told about reform, and freeing me from my chains and blah, blah, blah, but I'm quite certain Isher means to replace me entirely. Probably with you. Not sufficiently glorious to make a good puppet, is he? But I daresay he imagines he could pull the strings skilfully enough. And then, of course... there is your *wife*.'

Leo forced the words through gritted teeth. 'Leave her out of this.'

'Please, no one has a higher opinion of Savine than I do.' Orso gave a sad little sigh, staring off into the middle distance. 'I've been in love with the woman for years, in spite of my best efforts. But I don't think it's unfair to say she's just...' And he held up finger and thumb with a hair's breadth between them. 'A *teensy* bit ambitious. I wouldn't put money on great Juvens if he came between her and what she wanted. I never imagined she would be able to resist being queen. That's why I was so surprised that she turned me down.'

'That she what?'

'When I proposed to her.'

Leo just managed to stop himself giving a strangled squawk. If he'd been floundering in the conversation before, he was drowning in it now. Clearly his wife hadn't shared the whole truth when it came to her relationship with the king. What else might she have kept from him?

'A bolt of lightning could have struck me no more forcefully than when she said no,' mused Orso, chopping at his fish with the side of his fork. 'But... perhaps she found another way to make herself queen? I hear she is with you on campaign. She always did like to keep a close eye on her investments.'

'You've got it all wrong!' growled Leo, wondering if he actually had it all right. His chair shrieked on the stone-flagged floor as he stood, and he had to smother a gasp at the stab of pain in his leg. 'We've nothing more to discuss!'

'But we've still got the main course!'

'It's liver,' said Hildi.

'Ah! Bernille does it so it just...' and Orso closed his eyes, touched his lips and let his fingers flutter gently off, 'melts away to nothing. You know.' He opened his eyes and smiled. 'Like excuses for rebellion.'

'You mind if I...?' Hildi was already poised over Leo's half-eaten fish with a fork in her hand.

'Have at it,' he snarled as he turned for the door. 'I'll see you on the battlefield.'

Orso almost choked on his wine. 'Bloody hell, I hope not.'

Doubts and Desires

'Are you awake?' whispered Leo.

Of course she was. How could she sleep with the endless kicking of her baby, the endless noise of soldiers on the move outside the window, the endless doubts, fears, hopes chasing each other around her mind like stray dogs after the butcher's cart?

Savine had to slide her arm under her belly and half-lift it so she could wriggle over to face him. The first light was touching the sky outside, a faint gleam in the corners of his eyes, a glow on his cheek, shifting as his jaw nervously worked.

'You should go back to Ostenhorm,' he said. 'It's not safe here—'

'We're together in this, Leo.' She tried to make her voice the essence of calm. Like a mother soothing her child. Like a lion tamer trying to keep his beast on the stool. 'We have to be together in this.' She took his hand and slid it onto her belly. She wasn't sure which of them the trembling came from. 'All our futures are at stake.'

'By the dead, Savine...' His voice was the essence of panic. 'Have I made a terrible mistake?'

She felt a stab of anger, then. Everyone has doubts. The Fates knew she did. But leaders have to crush their doubts down deep inside where they cannot leak out and stain the entire enterprise. It was far too late for second thoughts. The dice were out of their hands and already rolling.

She felt a stab of anger, but losing her temper was a luxury she could not afford. 'You've done the right thing.' She made herself meet his eye, made herself sound sure. 'You've done what you had to.'

'Can I trust Isher?'

Savine would not have trusted him to carry her night-pot. 'Of course you can, he's bound to us, Leo, he has no—'

'Can I trust Stour?'

To call Stour a wild dog was unfair. Wild dogs were at least capable of loyalty. 'He respects you. And it's a little late to be—'

'Can I trust you?'

Silence. Faint cries and clatters outside as they moved up supplies by torchlight. 'How can you *ask* me that?' she snarled. She wanted to slap him. 'You're the one who chose this! All I've done is everything I can to make sure it succeeds!' And promised Uffrith to Stour, and promised the Closed Council to Isher, and promised the throne to herself. 'Orso stuffed your head with doubts, didn't he? Damn it, I told you not to underestimate him!'

Another silence. She could hear his quick breathing. She could hear her own. 'You're right,' he said grudgingly. 'You're always bloody right.' He even managed to make that sound like an accusation. 'I just don't even know where half my friends are, let alone my enemies. Rikke, and Jurand—'

'Leo—'

'What if my mother was right? What if I'm a warrior but no general? What if—'

She wished she did not always have to be the strong one. The Fates knew, she could have used some comfort. But some people need to be held up. Which means some people need to do the holding.

She clapped a hand to his head, twisted her fingers in his hair and dragged his face towards her. '*Stop*. You're not just a warrior, or a leader, or a general, you're a *hero*.' Heroes are defined not by what they do, after all, or why, but by what people think they have done. 'The cause is just.' She would be a wonderful queen. 'We have strong allies beside us.' A circle of self-serving snakes. 'We are going to win.' They had fucking better. 'And the people of the Union will win with us. They *need* us. They need *you*.' It did not matter whether she believed it, only that she made him believe. She had to blow him up with hot air until he towered over the battlefield. '*I* need you,' and she pulled him close, and gave him the softest kiss.

It had been meant just to shut him up, but it lasted longer than she had expected. When she broke away, they stared at each other in the darkness, quick breath hissing between them.

She licked her lips and went back for another. Hungrier now, and deeper, wriggling half on top of him. The constant ache between her legs had already sharpened to a pleasurable throbbing. It wasn't just her hands that were endlessly swollen. She slipped one leg over his and started to rub herself against it. Subtly at first. Then not subtly at all. Humping him like an overeager puppy.

'Are you sure?' he whispered.

'We're all awake now.' And she caught his head and pushed her tongue into his mouth.

This was one thing she had not expected about carrying a child. She had never felt less capable of coupling. Never wanted to more. Even now, with everything she had at stake. Especially now, maybe.

He was half-hard by the time she got his nightshirt up. She kept kissing him, one hand between her legs, one hand between his. Someone has to do the work, after all.

When she gave birth to this bloody thing it would be heir to the throne of the Union. That decision was made already. She would never be caught defenceless again, as she had been in Valbeck. Never be scared, never be vulnerable. If Orso had to lose, and her father, and Rikke, so be it. She would be safe. She would be powerful. If the world had to lose so she could win, so be it. The dice were already rolling.

She grunted as she heaved herself over onto her hands and knees, squirmed as she dragged her nightdress clumsily up over her hips. He knelt there, staring at her bare arse, nightshirt draped over his cock like a theatre curtain caught on a rogue piece of the set.

Ridiculous. But there it was.

She slid her elbows forward so the mattress could give some support to her over-heavy chest and pushed the side of her face into the pillow.

'Get it done, then,' she hissed.

Tallow stood with his hands wedged in his armpits as the wind bent the tall grass, shivering. He never seemed to have the right clothes for the weather. Exactly like her brother in that regard. The thought made Vick feel decidedly uncomfortable, and she drew her coat tight about her. A black Inquisitor's coat. Not something she wore often. She spent most of her time trying to look as little like a member of the Inquisition as possible. But if you didn't wear your uniform to a battle, when would you?

From up here on the bluff, the dark valley was dusted with thousands of pinprick lights. Campfires, wagon lamps, sentries' torches. You could pick out the roads, the cluster of Stoffenbeck's windows, the long battle lines cutting crooked across the hills and fields in dots of fire, a gulf of darkness lying between the two sides.

'Not often you get seats like this at the show everyone's talking about,' muttered Vick. 'Imagine how much it cost to put on.'

'Think what you could buy with it,' said Tallow, firelight glinting in the corners of his big, sad eyes. 'The folk that could be fed, and clothed, and housed. Spend it wisely, you might avoid the fight in the first place.'

'There's something wrong with the world all right,' said Vick, watching Arch Lector Pike step over to the closest cannon and sight down its barrel into the darkened valley.

He'd positioned them with the care of an emperor's butler setting table for a state dinner. Eighteen darkly gleaming, tapering tubes, set on heavy wooden trestles in a long row just below the brow of the hill. Leather-aproned engineers from the Siege School followed His Eminence down the line, cranking, adjusting, checking instruments, pointing excitedly towards the river where water glimmered faintly in the darkness.

'This one a little to the left, I think,' said Pike, then walked up to the summit of the hill to stand beside Vick, staring out at the valley. 'We have been experimenting in the Far Country for several years now.' He watched the crews drag brush around the maws of the great iron tubes to hide them from sight. 'And have found that cannons are like birthday presents. Best kept as a surprise.'

'I've never liked surprises,' said Vick.

'I suspect the enemy will feel the same.'

'Your Eminence!'

Two dark figures came across the hillside. One had a torch and a mask. The other was a boy, stumbling along with hands tied behind him. A Practical and a prisoner.

'Caught him trying to run.' The Practical shoved the lad down on his knees in front of Pike, the wind ruffling his curly hair. Couldn't have been more than fourteen. Looked younger. Tallow swallowed and slowly shrank back into the darkness.

'Dear, dear.' Pike took a long breath and squatted beside the boy, torchlight glistening on the shiny burned skin on the side of his face. 'Do you know who I am?'

The lad nodded, mouth hanging dumbly open. He looked up at Vick, and took a long sniff, then looked down at the ground between his knees. He must've known what was coming. And yet he just sat there.

'Which unit are you with?'

'Lord Crant's regiment,' he croaked out. 'I'm a loader. I load flatbows. Well, I just crank 'em.' Once he'd started talking he couldn't seem to stop. 'My friend Gert puts the bolts in, then hands 'em back to—'

'Shush,' said Pike, softly. There was silence then, and the wind stirred the grass, and Vick found she was wincing. The boy would make a good example, to keep the others at their posts. There was a tree near the summit with a low bough that would be just right. If they'll hang a boy for running, who won't they hang?

'Gert stayed,' whispered the boy, 'but I . . . I don't want to die.'

Pike turned towards those thousands of pinprick lights, twinkling in the valley. 'Faced with something on this scale, there could be no more rational response than to run away. But sometimes . . . we must do things that are not rational. Sometimes we must act on faith.' Pike stared at the lad and the lad stared back, the Practical looming dark over both. 'Sometimes . . . even as the world goes mad . . . we must crouch next to Gert and load flatbows.'

Another silence. Then the lad's knobbly throat shifted as he swallowed. 'I'd like to do that.'

'Good.' Pike set his hand on the boy's shoulder. 'Go back to Lord Crant's regiment, then.' He nodded to the Practical, and the Practical cut the ropes on the boy's wrists.

'What do I tell them?'

'That you got lost, but I guided you back to the right path. Isn't that the truth?'

The boy wiped tears on his sleeve. 'That's the truth.'

'This time, for both our sakes, you should stay at your post.'

The boy jumped up like an eager puppy. 'I'll stay there if hell comes up the hill in the morning!'

'I suppose it very well might,' murmured Pike as he watched him scurry away. 'You look surprised, Inquisitor.'

'I was expecting something . . . harsher,' said Vick. 'From your reputation.'

'I find reputations rarely fit people all that well. What are they, after all, but costumes we put on to disguise ourselves?' The mottled skin above his hairless brows twitched as he gave her uniform a glance. 'Costumes we are forced to put on. If men are to be productive, they must have something to fear. That is why we have an Inquisition. I like to tell myself that every life I have taken has saved five more. Fifty more, perhaps. Not everyone has the stomach for that kind of arithmetic.' His eyes gleamed with the Practical's torch. 'It is one thing I admire about you, Inquisitor Teufel. One cannot come through the camps without developing a very strong stomach.'

Vick said nothing as the boy vanished over the crest of the hill, a black figure against the dark sky.

'I understand cowards,' said Pike softly. 'I used to be one. Who among us never had a weak moment, after all? It cannot all be darkness. We must have a little mercy.' He leaned sideways to whisper it. 'As long as no one sees.'

Broad sat and polished his armour. Didn't need polishing. Brand new from the armoury at Ostenhorm. But it helps to have a routine. He used to do it out in Styria, the long nights before the long dawns. Kept him calm. That and the drink, anyway. And who was going to sleep now?

Scattered in every direction were other fires, other little knots of sleepless men, scraping the time away as the light leaked into the sky. Talking solemnly about the ground, or brashly about deeds they'd do tomorrow, or mournfully about families waiting back at home.

Maybe Broad should've been thinking of his family. Of May's quick look sideways when she spoke. The lines around Liddy's eyes when she smiled. But he knew what was coming with the dawn, and he didn't want it to touch them. Not even in his memory.

'That all the armour you'll wear?' asked Bannerman, firelight shifting across that little smile he liked to wear.

'Aye,' said Broad. Breastplate and steel cap. Nothing clever.

'Laddermen prefer to go light.' Halder rubbed at the tattoo on the back of his hand. Same as Broad's, but with just the one star. Some would say that was one too many. 'Quicker you get to the top, the better your chances.'

'The best armour's quick feet and high hopes,' Broad murmured. That was what they used to say to each other, while they waited for an assault. Usually while getting good and drunk.

'Defence won't save you in the press at the top o' those walls,' said Halder. 'Only attack. Only fury.' Broad kept his eyes on the steel, but his heart was thudding. 'No room to think.' He remembered what happened when you got to the top of the ladder. 'No room to breathe.' The cauldron of violence. Men made animals. Men made meat. 'Pressed in so close you'll never reach a weapon at your hip, let alone swing it.' Halder was whispering it, now. 'You need something you can use to kill a man who's close enough to kiss.'

That's why Broad wore a stabbing dagger across his chest. More a long spike than a knife, its three edges barely even sharpened. It was the point did the work, overhand, up under a helmet or into the joints in armour, or the pommel, or the heavy knuckleguard in a pinch. He remembered the feel of a cheekbone crunching, the sticky trickle of blood down the grip. Broad winced as he made his aching fist unclench. He wondered if Judge had been right. Only happy when he was bloody.

'Well, we've got no walls to climb,' said Bannerman, 'so I'll take a sword, thanks all the same.' And he drew a few inches of his own blade, then slapped it back into its sheath.

'Sword's a fine thing for riding down archers. Fighting armoured men face-to-face you can do better.' Halder nodded at Broad's warhammer, laid out on an oilcloth, waiting for its own turn to be polished. 'Hit a helmet hard with that, you can crack the skull inside without breaking the steel.'

True enough. But Broad had got more use from the bladed pick on the back. Fine thing for hooking a man who was leaning over a parapet and dragging him off. Fine thing for hooking down a shield so you could get at the flesh behind it with a dagger. And if you could find room for a proper swing, there wasn't much you couldn't punch through with it, either, if you didn't mind getting it stuck. You can't get attached to weapons in a battle any more than you can get attached to men.

Sometimes you have to leave 'em in the dirt.

Orso stared at himself in the mirror.

He had got as far as putting his trousers on before he noticed his reflection and now, even facing imminent destruction, he could not look away. No doubt an observer would have thought him immensely vain, but the truth was Orso saw no fine features in a mirror, only faults and failures.

'More reinforcements.' Hildi stood at one of the windows of the grand room the mayor had insisted Orso slept in, watching soldiers tramp past Stoffenbeck's town hall towards the front. Where they would soon be fighting. Where they would soon be dying. That was the theme of Orso's reign. The conversion of brave men into corpses.

'Three regiments came in last night,' he said, 'as well as a hugely enthusiastic group of farmers from the next valley, demanding to fight for their king.'

'Inspiring.'

'If you find stupidity inspiring.' Orso did, in fact. But he had ordered them back home regardless.

'Position's stronger, though?' asked Hildi, hopefully.

'Stronger than it was. Lord Marshal Forest still considers us well out-numbered.'

'Battles aren't always won by the biggest numbers.'

'No,' said Orso. 'Just usually.'

He placed an unhappy hand on his belly and tried his best to suck it in. One cannot suck in one's hips, though. It was reaching the point where he was considering some form of corset. Savine always looked spectacular in them, after all, and exercise was out of the bloody question. He let it all sag again with horrifying results.

'I daresay Leo dan Brock never has to hold in his belly,' he murmured.

'Wouldn't have thought so. All hard and grooved like a cobbled street, I reckon.' Hildi was gazing into the corner of the room with a dreamy expression. 'Combining the best of dancer and docker.'

'While I combine the worst of idler and innkeeper?' Orso pulled his shirt on with bad grace. 'Maybe you can get a job oiling the Young Lion's stomach once he's replaced me.'

'A girl can dream.'

'There's more to a man than his gut.'

'No doubt. You've put some weight on under the chin as well.'

Orso sighed. 'Thank you very much for that, Hildi, I'm never at risk of getting too self-satisfied with you around.'

He twitched a curtain back to watch those men marching past. Probably he should have been moved by their loyalty. His father would have flapped a half-clenched fist around and trotted out some patriotic platitude. But Orso found himself wondering what strange combination of doubts and desires compelled each individual to subsume themselves into this metal mass, plodding towards their own destruction rather than making the eminently sensible choice to run like hell the other way.

Then he found himself wondering why *he* was still there, and slapped impatiently at the side of his head. 'Damn it, Hildi, I think far too much to make a good general.'

'That and you've no military training, talent or experience.'

'Training, talent or experience would only be encumbrances to a monarch. Such petty concerns are for the little people, my dear.' From the window he could see the low ridge to the east of town, the spindly trees on top, a faint hint of dawn showing in the clouds behind. 'I don't think I can put it off any longer. When the sun comes up... I'm going to have to bloody fight.'

'Shall I get your armour?'

'I think you'd better. And tell Bernille I'm ready for breakfast.'

'Diet tomorrow, eh?'

Orso patted at his stomach. 'If I'm still alive.'

Stour Nightfall was having quite the sulk.

Flick had built a good fire for breakfast, near to the treeline where they could get news if aught happened on the hills ahead. Flick wasn't bad at building fires, and he'd built an especially pleasing one that morning.

But as Stour's mood blackened, everyone had slowly shuffled back, sidling around the trees and skulking through the bushes to get out of his eyeline, loitering at the edge of the firelight and leaving a widening empty circle about the King of the Northmen.

It seemed the only man who dared stay close was Clover himself, and that was mostly 'cause he was enjoying having his feet near the warmth. The Union was meant to be so very bloody civilised, but so far, the place was a sea of mud. His boots had got soaked yesterday and the cold had worked right into his feet. Being on campaign was far from comfortable at the best of times. He was damned if he was going to let Stour's sulking make him even less comfortable. And Clover reckoned you took more of a risk backing away from a slavering wolf than you did calmly standing your ground. So he sat there and slowly picked a leg of cold mutton down to the bone.

'We could've gone last night!' snarled Stour, and he kicked a smouldering branch from the fire and sent it spinning away, showering sparks. 'Why didn't we go last night?'

'Couldn't say, my king,' said Clover. 'Big army to manage, I reckon.'

'Big army to manage?' sneered the king, and he kicked out at a cookpot and sent it bouncing between the trees where it hit a Carl on the side of his knee and made him squeak with pain, though he kept smiling all the while, which was quite a feat.

If Stour had been an eight-year-old, he'd have got a slap from his mummy. Instead, he got every bastard bowing and grinning and pandering to him, even those he kicked cookpots at. That, of course, only made him rage the worse.

'We've joined up with a pack o' fools!' Stour said. The rest of 'em had been given no choice but to follow. 'You see that fat idiot Barezin? He came in gleeman's feast-day clothes, didn't he? You see that skinny idiot Isher? Looks like a fucking wilting cock. As for the bunch o' jesters they're leading.' He gave a snort that sent snot shooting out of his nose and angrily dashed it away. 'Fucking *Southerners*. What was I *thinking*?'

Mostly that he was bored and he wanted to fight someone, Clover imagined, and there'd been no one big enough within arm's reach.

'That cunt Rikke had the right idea! Says yes then stays home in Uffrith frigging herself. Thinks she can laugh at me, does she?'

Clover nibbled a few more shreds of meat from the bone. 'Couldn't say.'

'My king?' A wincing Carl was edging up, an eyeglass offered out to Stour like he was sticking his arm in a fire.

'What now?'

'Reckon . . . you ought to see this.'

Stour snatched the eyeglass, stomped to the treeline and trained it on the low hill beyond that long slope of darkened wheat, its shape clear now against the brightening sky.

'What the *fuck*?' he hissed.

'They were reinforced in the night,' said Jin. 'Two regiments of King's Own. Maybe three.'

The sun was peeping over the valley, long shadows stretching across the fields. Through the round window of his eyeglass, quivering slightly with the trembling of his hand, Leo could see the flags, the spears, the lines of men on top of the two hills. The rocky bluff crawled with activity now, like a distant ant heap. The long, low hill had at least twice as many soldiers on it as the night before. One flag in particular, black with a golden sun, flew above the rest. A lord marshal's personal standard.

'He took me for a bloody fool,' breathed Leo. 'He played me for time, knowing he had men on the way.'

He felt a sudden cold shock. Had that woman Teufel tricked them? Had she been loyal to the king all along, lied about his strength then taken the secrets they'd merrily blabbed to her straight back to him? Had Orso been well aware of that as he smirked across the table and tried to drive a wedge between Leo and his allies? Between Leo and his own *wife*?

'*Fuck!*' He flung the eyeglass across the hillside and it bounced once and clattered from one of the wagons with a tinkle of broken glass.

Shock turned to a reassuring fury that burned all the night's doubts away. He was the Young Lion, damn it! He'd no business dithering when there was an enemy ahead.

'What should we do?' asked Isher, plucking at a loose thread on his embroidered cuff as he stared towards those suddenly well-held hills.

'Attack!' snarled Leo. 'Now!'

'Finally!' Barezin mashed his fist into his palm. 'My Gurkish Legion will be on that bluff before lunchtime! You can depend on it!'

'I *am* bloody depending on it,' Leo forced through his gritted teeth.

Barezin gave a cavalier salute, caught hold of his saddle horn, bounced a couple of times and then, with some subtle shoving from one of his aides, hauled himself up and turned his mount towards the west.

Leo took Isher by the shoulder. 'I don't care whether it's a Gurkish legion or a phalanx of Sipanese whores,' he hissed into his pale face, 'I need men up on that bluff in force and ready to attack Stoffenbeck from the west as soon as possible. Do you understand?'

Isher wiped sweat from his forehead and gave a stiff salute. 'I do.' And he strode somewhat unsteadily to his horse.

Leo pulled Antaup close, pointed over the orchards towards the rocky hill, one flank bright with the dawn, the other cast into shadow. 'First the Open Council drive them back on the right and take that bluff.' He shoved forward with his fist, from the neat battle lines of Angland and across the open fields towards Stoffenbeck. 'By the time we attack Orso in the centre, they'll be in a position to outflank him.' He stabbed his finger towards the wheatfields, the gentle green hill beyond with those new banners at its summit. 'Before they shore up the centre, Stour will hit them on the left.'

Antaup grinned as he flicked that loose lock of hair out of his face and it dropped straight back. 'Yes, Your Grace!'

'Let the Anglanders know!' And Leo sent Antaup charging down the hill with a slap on the back. 'Greenway?'

He slouched over, giving a mockery of a Union salute. 'Young Lion.'

'Tell Stour we're attacking from right across to left. He goes last.'

'Last?' sneered Greenway.

'It's a battle plan, not a race.'

'Don't reckon Stour'll like going—'

Leo grabbed a fistful of Greenway's cloak and snarled the words in his face. 'He doesn't have to *like* it. He just has to *do* it.' And he shoved the man away and made him slither on the dewy grass. He only just righted himself before he fell, and slunk off with bad grace.

'Might not be wise to treat him with so little respect,' murmured Jin.

'I had a go at being wise,' snapped Leo. 'It doesn't fucking suit me.'

Jin laughed and thumped him on the shoulder. 'That's the spirit!'

Leo looked towards the low ridge, the high bluff, the town with the crescent of diggings in front, a fierce smile on his face. He liked this plan. Simple. Aggressive. It played to his strengths. He wished he'd done it last night, but last night wasn't coming back. They were ready now and had the whole day ahead of them. He felt like a new man.

'We could've beaten him last night.' He curled his fingers into a trembling fist. 'But we'll crush him today instead. Someone get my horse!'

Fools' Errands

Orso stood at the parapet of Stoffenbeck's clock tower, trying to frown out manfully to the north while feeling like an utter impostor in his gilded armour.

The mist clinging to the fields was clearing, the sun rising bright into a sky holding only a few lonely puffs of cloud. A rather lovely day might have been in the offing. Had it not been for the thousands of heavily armed men poised to murder each other within the next few hours, of course.

The forces of the Open Council were gathered on the far left. Yellow blocks, red blobs, blue wedges, bright flags streaming overhead. Their wondrous variety suggested a lack of coordination, but also spoke strongly to the breadth of the coalition against him.

The army of Angland was deployed below the hill on which Steebling's tower-house stood. Dark, business-like blocks so ominously neat they might have been drawn with a ruler. Men who last year had been heroes, struggling against the Union's enemies. Men Orso had done his best to help. Men he had utterly failed to help, driven now to open rebellion against him.

Of Stour Nightfall's Northmen there was no sign. Lurking in the woods, no doubt, waiting to pounce, as Northmen so loved to do. The Young Lion and the Great Wolf had been bitter enemies, fighting each other to the death but a few months before. Now Orso had achieved the apparently impossible and united them in mutual hatred for him.

By the Fates, when did he get so many enemies?

'I tried to do the right thing,' he murmured, striving to make sense of it. 'Broadly. The best I could, under the circumstances. Tried to find . . . reasonable compromises?' It would have made a feeble battle cry. *Forth, men, to reasonable compromises!*

He tried again. 'I mean to say . . . I realise that I'm hesitant, occasionally oblivious, running to fat, certainly not the most inspiring king a subject could ask for but... I'm hardly *despicable*, am I? I'm no Glustrod. No Morlic the Mad.'

Grunts and grumbles of firm denial as he glanced around the roof. But what could a king expect from his courtiers except bland agreement on every point? Tunny, he noted, stayed silent.

'If I may, Your Majesty?' offered Lord Hoff, rubbing his hands like a horse-trader spying a simpleton upon whom to palm off his lamest nag. 'The roots of this particular rebellion dig back into history. To your father's time. To *his* father's time.' Mutters of agreement. 'You, I fear, have been unfortunate enough to reap the harvest. Discontent has been swelling for many years.' Heads bobbed as men nodded. 'The seeds were sown in the war against Black Dow. The wars against the Snake of Talins. The war against Uthman-ul-Dosht, even.'

'Now *that* was a war,' came a voice.

'Master Sulfur.' Orso was less than entirely delighted to see the magus step out onto the roof of the clock tower. 'You always seem to arrive at moments of high drama.'

'Never the slightest peace, Your Majesty. I have been in the North, doing my best to put an end to this rebellion before it began.'

Orso raised a brow at the thousands of armed men facing them. 'With limited success, it would appear.'

'Alas, the younger generation refuses to honour the debts of the older. The debts that put them where they are. My master will ensure there is a reckoning, depend on that.'

'A huge comfort,' said Orso. By that point, there was every chance they would all be dead. 'I don't suppose you could do to Leo dan Brock's army what you did to the Burners at the demonstration of Curnsbick's engine, is there?'

Sulfur turned those strangely empty, different-coloured eyes upon him. 'The magic leaks from the world, Your Majesty, and there are limits to what even I can achieve. An army is far beyond my powers.'

'Just the Young Lion himself, maybe?'

'A great risk with an uncertain outcome. My master prefers safe bets.'

Orso puffed out his cheeks. 'Why he got into banking, no doubt.'

'That and so he could furnish you with the means to settle your problems by... more traditional methods.'

'For which I am immensely grateful, of course.' Orso had seen Sulfur rip a man apart with his teeth. He knew Bayaz had made a wreck of half the Agriont and killed thousands. He was sure Valint and Balk had done even more damage in the years since, with far less spectacle. Truly, he had made a pact with devils. But a man lost in the desert, as the Gurkish say, must take such water as he is offered.

Sulfur was surveying the battlefield. 'We are expecting reinforcements, I take it?'

'Imminently,' said Orso, wondering whether Lord Marshal Rucksted would reach the field before they were utterly overwhelmed. Fortunately, or perhaps unfortunately, he was spared from having to qualify the statement by a discordant mishmash of bugles, horns and shouted orders floating on the chill dawn.

'They're advancing on the left,' said Tunny.

At this distance, the Open Council's varied formations appeared to move with dreamlike slowness, inexorably southwards, through the patchwork of fields towards the tangled orchards around the river. It was hard to believe that all those tiny coloured dots were men. They seemed to flow like a fluid. Lurid shades of paint, perhaps, running together on the easel of a careless artist.

'They're attacking,' said Hoff.

Orso gave him a withering sideways glance. 'Oh, I don't know, Lord Chamberlain. Perhaps they're rushing forward to surrender.'

No one laughed, of course, not even Orso. It did not look as though it would be a day for laughs.

'Your Majesty?' A footman had appeared in purple finery, tray balanced on outstretched fingers, a selection of Visserine glassware gleaming with the morning sun. 'A drink?'

There was something faintly horrifying about a tipple while men marched to their deaths. Epic disaster as light entertainment. 'At a time like this?' asked Orso.

Officers glanced at one another, raised their brows, shrugged as if to say, *What better time could there be?*

Orso sighed. 'I'll take a sherry. Sherry, Master Sulfur?'

'Not for me, Your Majesty.'

'Of course, I forgot. Your highly specific diet...' And Orso winced as he looked back towards the battlefield.

Some of the better-disciplined formations had reached the orchards and apparently vanished. Others had scarcely moved at all, or were stuck at some hedgerow, some house, some stand of trees. Still others appeared to have twisted, drifted apart, become tangled with each other. Orso and his royal entourage watched in silence, sipping their drinks, while the movement of the great clock marked the passage of time with its steady *tick, tick, tick* beneath their feet.

'The forces of the Open Council appear to be in some confusion,' someone said.

Orso laughed so hard he snorted sherry out of his nose, had to submit to a dabbing down by his footman while he continued to helplessly giggle.

Hoff looked at him as though he had lost his reason. Perhaps he had. 'Your Majesty?'

'Oh, you know. Good old Open Council. You can always count on them to act with total disunity, disloyalty and incompetence.'

'What are they doing?' muttered Savine, clenching her swollen fists so tight they trembled. 'What the hell are they *doing?*'

She was no soldier, but it hardly took Stolicus himself to tell things had not started well. From the chaos over there, anyone would have thought the Open Council were fully engaged with the enemy rather than with some orchards and a slow-flowing tributary of the river.

'Seems your rebellion's coming apart already.' Lord Steebling lifted his gouty leg onto a stool then sat back, grinning up at her with smug satisfaction.

'I wouldn't count us out just yet,' she said, turning her back on him and stepping away.

The man was an utter shit, but Leo had insisted he be treated with every courtesy. They were here to uphold the rights of Union citizens, after all, and it was Steebling's land they were fighting on, Steebling's house they were using as their headquarters, Steebling's bed they had been clumsily coupling in last night. The memory made her feel faintly and entirely inappropriately aroused. Faintly aroused and badly in need of a piss both at once.

The great wagons carrying the cannon had been held up on the clogged roads and were only now arriving. Teams of men and horses were struggling to shift them onto their trestles and get them pointed roughly towards the enemy. Savine grimly shook her head at the thought of what each of those had cost to make. At this rate, they would be set up just in time to fire a salute to King Orso's victory.

Leo was not far away, dragging his horse impatiently back and forth, swarmed by a constantly shifting crowd of officers, messengers and panicked hangers-on. She wanted desperately to be down there with him. Being a powerless observer by no means suited her. But she knew no one would listen to her. No one was listening to anyone. Leo caught one man in the deep blue uniform of Isher's soldiers and near dragged him from his saddle.

'What the *hell* is going on over there?'

'Your Grace, it seems someone tampered with the bridges—'

'Tampered?'

'When the first units tried to cross the river, they collapsed—'

'No one thought to *check*?' Leo grabbed Antaup by the shoulder, stabbing towards the orchards with a finger. 'Get over there! I don't care if they have to raft men across. I don't care if they have to build new bloody bridges! Get over there and make sure those bastards *move*!'

'Best stay back, Lady Savine.' Broad stepped carefully in front of her as Antaup thundered past, teeth gritted. Zuri slipped a hand around her elbow and guided her ever so gently away from the milling horses, to a clear spot on the hillside.

'Shall I have Haroon bring you a chair?' she asked.

'How could I sit through this?' snapped Savine, standing with jaw, fists and bladder clenched in a paralysis of helpless fury.

Isher, Barezin and the rest were making an utter turd of it. She had been so worried about their loyalty she had not given nearly enough attention to their competence. She tore open the button at her collar. She could not get a proper breath.

'Calm,' she whispered. 'Calm, calm—'

She jumped at an almighty crash. Someone dived aside with a despairing cry as a cannon slid from its wagon and thudded to the turf, rolling down the hill and leaving a trail of wreckage, a tangle of ropes and pulleys dragged through a campfire after it.

Somewhere behind her, over the madness, she could hear Lord Steebling's laughter.

'Now, Arch Lector?' asked the chief engineer, breathless.

Pike gazed down towards the orchards. He couldn't have been calmer if he'd been timing an egg. 'A little longer.' He leaned over to murmur to Vick, 'I sent a few men down to the river last night to chisel the keystones from the bridges. I do admire a skilled mason, don't you?'

Vick had nothing to say. Her appreciation for stonework felt rather beside the point.

'I doubt they'll take the weight of more than a few men,' said Pike. 'A company of soldiers trying to cross will soon find themselves swimming. I was a quartermaster in my inglorious youth, and I can tell you for a fact that armies run on details. Without the keystones, those bridges come apart. Without the bridges, their whole plan comes apart. So much of failure is a failure to consider the *details*.'

The military chorus came oddly distorted over the distance, sounding now close, now far away. Farting bugles and bumbling drums. Voices echoed up so clearly at times Vick could hear the words, then faded to a witless burble as the wind changed.

The chief engineer glanced beseechingly at Vick, sweat glistening on his forehead. 'Now, Arch Lector?'

Pike thoughtfully narrowed his eyes. The wind picked up, whipping streams of smoke from the slow-burning match-cords in the hands of the nervous boys beside each cannon. 'Not quite yet.'

'How long'll he wait?' whispered Tallow, voice squeaky with fear.

Vick silently shook her head. From where they stood, she could just see the top of the clock tower. Hard to believe how little time had passed since the Open Council's troops began to move. The trees on the far bank were swarming with soldiers now, their order entirely gone, columns crowding haphazardly in from behind to add their weight to the confusion. But the near bank still looked as peaceful as it had at dawn.

'Now, Arch Lector?' begged the engineer. Not so much that he wanted to do it, as that he couldn't stand the tension of waiting.

Pike paused, considering the chaos around the river, hands clasped behind his back. 'Now,' he said.

The man looked taken aback, as though he'd only just realised what he'd been asking for the last half-hour. He licked his lips, then turned unsteadily towards the north.

'Cannon will fire in order from my right,' he roared, holding up his fist, 'and continue firing until the order is given to cease!'

The aproned engineers, the burly men who handled the shot and powder, the boys who held the poles and sponges, all started to screw pellets of rag into their ears. Pike was doing the same.

Stiffly, cautiously, the engineer at the first cannon took match-cord from powder boy and gingerly touched the flame to the pan. The crew all turned away, hunching down, covering their heads. Vick winced. There was a pathetic little splutter and a puff of sparks.

'That's it?' said Tallow, looking up.

The cannon jolted on its trestles, fire spurting from its mouth. There was a thunderous, barking explosion, as painfully loud as anything Vick ever heard. A moment later, the next cannon fired, and the next.

She shrank down against the hillside, clapping her hands against the sides of her head, and felt her skull buzz, and her palms tremble, and the very ground shake.

Felt like the end of the world.

'He wants you to hold,' growled out the Young Lion's pet Northman, Whitewater whatever, 'until he gives the—'

And everyone turned at a great low rumble. There was a flap and flutter as birds took off from the trees, then another rumble, and another, like thunder close at hand, loud enough Clover could feel the earth quiver through the soles of his boots. But then, they were a little worn.

'What's this?' snarled Stour, striding to the treeline and staring off across the wheatfields. Far away, on the big bluff over on the other side of the town, puffs of smoke were going up and floating out across the valley.

'Fire engines, I reckon,' murmured Clover. A few of the older fellows looked as unhappy about it as he was. They'd seen 'em used at Osrung, maybe, and hadn't much enjoyed the experience.

But Stour had slept through Osrung in his mother's belly. His eyes shone as he watched the smoke puff out. 'They call 'em cannons now,' he murmured, then turned about. 'Get the men ready.'

'Eh?' said Greenway.

'You heard me.' Stour grinned out across that sea of windswept wheat towards that sloping green ridge with the flags at the top. 'I want that hill.'

Clover winced. What the hell Stour planned to do with a hill in the middle of Midderland was anyone's guess. Graze sheep on it? But the Great Wolf wanted it. So that was that.

Whitewater was staring at 'em all like they'd parted from their senses. Which they probably had, some months before, when they all consented to Stour being king. 'Didn't you hear me? The Young Lion wants you to—'

'I fucking heard you, boy.' Stour's eyes slid across to him. 'But I've had quite enough o' the Young Lion's pleasure.' It was almost a surprise that menacing slaver didn't drip from his teeth. 'He wants me to stop, he can come over here and stop me himself. No? Didn't fucking think so.' He turned to roar into the trees. 'Weapons, lads! War cries, you bastards! Time for you fuckers to *fight*!'

And there was a great clattering and hissing as swords were drawn and shields raised and spears hefted. A great growl and murmur of war curses and prayers to the dead, shouted orders echoing from further off as the call to arms spread down the long line. A great jingle and rustle as mailed warriors crunched through the brush to the very edge of the trees. Stour brushed Brock's man out of his way and strode forward himself into the golden wheat, drawing his sword, and his gilded bastards crowded after, all falling over themselves to show how thirsty they were for blood.

'By all the fucking dead,' whispered Whitewater, staring after Stour and dragging at his red beard so hard he looked fit to tear it out of his jaw.

'Look at the sunny side.' And Clover slapped a sympathetic hand down on his shoulder. 'After today, one way or another, I doubt you'll have to deal with the idiot again.' He puffed out his cheeks as he drew his sword. 'Some of us are stuck with this madness. Downside! Get the boys ready to charge!'

The sudden cannon-thunder had turned the headquarters into a mass of plunging horses. One of Leo's guards had been thrown, dragged to the back with a broken arm. The first casualty of the day. But surely not the last.

A stone whizzed over the orchards and into the dirt, sending up a spray of mud. Another struck a tree and Leo flinched at the great cloud of splintered wood that rained down on the cowering men, now pinned more hopelessly than ever. A moment later, the great crack of the impact echoed across the fields.

'Damn it,' hissed Leo. If they waited for the Open Council to get across that river they'd be waiting till nightfall.

'What the hell?' he heard Mustred say, gazing over to their left. Leo followed his eyes.

A great mass of Northmen had emerged from the trees and was wading steadily through the ripe wheat towards the low ridge. Carls, with their round shields, and bright mail, and the sunlight glinting on the blades of axe and sword and spear.

Leo stared in mute amazement. He couldn't even find the words to swear.

The plan had been so simple. How could it have come apart so badly? Confusion in combat was one thing, but he'd lost control of his army before they'd made the slightest contact with the enemy. He stared over at the Open Council's self-inflicted chaos on the right, then at Stour's self-inflicted chaos on the left, then at the earthworks straight ahead. He took a long breath.

'Everyone!' His voice sounded surprisingly calm. He'd always been at his best when there was only one thing to do. 'Sound the advance!'

Mustred leaned closer, waving doubtfully towards Stoffenbeck. 'They're well dug in, Your Grace. They're ready for us. Without the Open Council flanking them—'

Leo clapped the old lord on the shoulder. 'We'll have to outfight the bastards.' He turned in his saddle to roar at the men around him. 'Lift the standard, lads! Beat the drums! It's time!'

He saw Savine standing on the hillside. He smiled, and raised his arm, and gave her a last wave.

Then he wrenched his horse around towards the enemy.

Bugles blared, and with a mighty tramp that shook the troubled ground, the army of Angland began to move south.

Even back here the noise never stopped now. Jolting wagons, bellowed orders, thumping hooves, the throbbing fury of the cannons. Someone kept screaming, high and thin and broken. Behind them, far from the fighting. Accident among the supplies, maybe.

Over on the left, the great mass of Northmen were forging ahead through the golden wheat, leaving it brown and flattened behind them. Over on the right, fires were burning in the orchards, black smoke from the trees meeting white smoke from the cannons and throwing a grey shroud over the whole battlefield.

'What's happening?' whispered Savine.

'I've fought in five sieges and three pitched battles,' said Broad. 'Never saw one yet where I had a clue what was happening.'

The air had a sharp smell. A tang of Gurkish Fire, and metal, and fear, and shit. Someone had dug a latrine pit way too close to camp and a couple of slumping wattle screens weren't doing much to hide the sight of men's waste, let alone the smell of it.

'Bloody traitors!' roared that old bastard with the gouty leg. 'The King's Own'll cut you to pieces!'

Broad frowned up the hill. 'He's a charmer.'

'Lord Steebling owns most of this land,' said Savine through gritted teeth. 'Leo says we're here to support his rights, not to take them away.'

'That's not why I'm here.'

'Why are you here?' asked Zuri.

Same question Broad asked himself when he climbed the ladder, time after time, and men looked at him like he was mad. He'd given up on causes in Styria. He'd given Savine all he owed and more when he risked his life speaking to Judge. He'd never promised to fight. Promised not to, in fact. And yet here he was.

'Gunnar,' said Savine. 'Could you do something for me?'

'I can try.'

'Follow my husband.' She stared off to the south. Towards where the fighting would soon be hottest, sliding her hands around her belly. She looked strangely helpless, suddenly, in the midst of all this. 'Try . . . to make sure . . .'

'I understand.' Trying to keep a man alive in a battle was the very definition of a fool's errand, but it would hardly be his first. 'Just one thing I've got to do first. Think you could look after these for me?' He unhooked his lenses from his ears, gently folded them and handed them to Zuri. She'd always struck him as a woman you could trust with something delicate. Then he strode up the blurred hillside towards the dark smudge of the tower, carefully rolling up his sleeves. Helps to have a routine.

Steebling squinted as Broad's shadow cast him into darkness. 'We Steeblings aren't easily intimidated, you— Ah!' He squawked as Broad caught him by the ear and dragged him from his chair.

The old nobleman hopped and slithered as he was marched back down the hill, whimpering whenever his weight went onto his gouty leg. Broad strode to those wicker screens and kicked one out of the way. He was glad for once that he couldn't really see, so he didn't have to look at the overflowing latrine pit in all its glory. But he could certainly smell it.

To Steebling, plainly, it was a new experience. He shrank away, one arm across his face. 'What're you—'

Broad shoved him in.

He vanished below the surface for a moment then bobbed up, his velvet cap lost somewhere under there and his grey hair plastered to his face with the shit of men he'd been laughing at a moment before.

'You bastard!' he frothed, retching as he tried to drag himself out.

Broad was already walking away, headed for Stoffenbeck, a dim ghost now through the dust of marching men.

'What should we do?' he heard Bannerman calling after him.

'Whatever you like,' he said, not even slowing.

He told himself it was loyalty. Told himself a good man has to fight. Same things he'd told himself when he headed off to Styria. But he knew a battle was no place for good men.

He took a long breath through his nose and snorted it out with a growl. Snorted it out like a bull.

When he wept at his own front door, back in the loving embrace of his family, he'd thought he was done with blood. Thought nothing could ever get him back onto a battlefield. But it seemed Judge knew him better than he knew himself. Trouble was like hunger to him. Stuffing your face till you're sick one day doesn't mean you won't want lunch the next. All you do is sharpen your appetite. And here he was, in spite of all his empty promises, back at the table again with his cutlery ready, clamouring to be served.

He slid the warhammer from his belt and felt the steel haft tight in his grip. Fit there, like a key in a lock. He bared his teeth and walked faster.

The Little People

Peck felt a slap on his shoulder and he worked his eyes open, peeled his hands from his ears and – once he'd worked out which way was up, which took longer than you'd think – looked up.

Sergeant Meyer stared back, white lines through the black soot around his eyes where he'd been squeezing 'em shut and one side of his beard a little singed, mouth moving like he was shouting at the top of his lungs. Through the rag-buds in Peck's ears and the whomp and burble of the other cannons and the rush of his own breath and the thudding of his heart and the constant high whine which seemed to be everywhere now, he heard a hint of Meyer's voice.

'Sponge 'er, Peck!'

'Oh.' He stumbled up and nearly fell and only kept his balance clutching on to one of the trestles. 'Yes.' Where'd he put the sponge? He snatched it up, tearing some grass up with it. 'Sir.' Where'd he put the bucket? He nearly tripped over it twisting around looking for it. Why was he even saying yes? He couldn't hear himself. How could anyone else?

The air was thick with the stink of Gurkish Fire, his mouth sticky with the tang of powder, his throat raw and his eyes smarting. At times, he could hardly see the next cannon along. Their crews were ghosts, crawling around their pieces, swabbing 'em, towelling 'em, loading 'em, feeding 'em powder, tending to their every screaming whim like a bunch of filth-smeared nannies to a nursery full of overgrown metal babies. Babies that spat death.

He stumbled past an engineer fiddling with some broken instrument, careful not to touch his cannon 'cause he'd already burned himself three times, it was that hot. Thick smoke curled from its mouth and he slopped water out of the bucket, dashed the crust of smouldering powder away from the maw, hefted his pole then flinched as a cannon a couple down the row fired, flame spouting, ground shaking.

It had all been such good fun at the Siege School. Good luck to end up there. Better'n working in a mill. Damn sight safer, too. Didn't seem safer now, needless to say.

Something better not thought about.

'Sponge 'er, Peck!'

He didn't like calling the cannons 'her'. Like they were women. Added a hint of the disgusting to the already unpleasant. Naught motherly about the bastard things that he could see. Murder's men's work mostly, after all.

The sponge streamed black water as he shoved it into the cannon's smoking barrel and gave it a ramming, spraying himself each time. He was soaked with sponge-water and smeared head to toe with soot and his shirtsleeves torn and flapping wet at his chafing wrists, but you leave even a smear of burning powder behind and when they put the new charge in, the lot of you will be blown to hell.

Something else better not thought about.

He could see soldiers below them, through the drifting smoke. Lord Crant's men, he thought. A ragged-looking regiment, stretched out crooked across the hillside. They'd tried to dig in but had about three good shovels between 'em and the rocky ground wasn't offering much help. No one was. They were cowering now, at the thunder of the cannons behind them and the masses of enemy somewhere in front. Trapped betwixt hell and hail, as Peck's granny used to say. They'd flung their weapons down to cover their ears, faces twisted with pain and terror. Peck had seen a couple try to run and be dragged back to their posts. Seemed a feeble sort of defence, if those rebels ever got across that river and up the rocky hillside.

One more thing best not thought about. Awful lot of those in a battle.

Like the Arch Lector, standing in his pure white coat on the summit of the hill. That hard-faced woman, too. Most frightening pair o' bastards he ever saw. Looked like they never felt a human thing between 'em. He swallowed as he glanced away, swabbed the cannon down and left it steaming.

The boy who held the smouldering match-cord was crying. Streaks through the soot on his face. Wasn't clear if it was the smoke in his eyes or he was hurt or he was crying 'cause this was so horrible. Peck slapped a hand down on his shoulder, dirty water slopping from his bucket. No point saying anything. The lad gave a helpless little smile, then Meyer snatched the match-cord out of his hand and shouted something.

'Oh, no.' Peck dropped on his knees again on the shaking hillside and clapped his hands over his ears, turning the burble to an echoing hiss, like the sound you get when you hold a seashell to your head.

The one thing you could say was that it was better to do the shooting than to be shot at. But the poor bastards their piece was pointing at were another o' those things it was better not to think about.

At a time like this, best not to think at all.

He squeezed his eyes shut.

There was a sound like a whip cracking in Suval's ear, there was a great shower of stinging splinters and he cringed as something bounced off his back. A branch fell from a tree nearby and crashed down among the wreckage.

'God help us,' he whispered, lifting his head. Someone was crying. Someone was shouting. Someone was burning. He saw him totter writhing down to the water's edge and flop in. Someone was trying to drag a limp man back by his armpits. Suval saw him fall with the wounded man on top of him, and struggle up, and struggle on. Desperate to save his friend's life. Or desperate for an excuse to save his own.

Suval picked up his dented helmet with trembling hands, put it on, dumping dirt on his head and hardly noticing. He spent a moment trying to fasten the buckle on the chinstrap before he realised it was broken. He stared about, no idea where his spear had fallen. But there was a sword nearby, so he picked that up instead. He had no idea how to use a sword. He'd never even held one before.

Murezin had said they would never have to fight, only dress up for some vain man who wanted to say he had a Gurkish Legion, and they had laughed about it while they drank bad tea together. You could not find good tea anywhere in this damned country. Murezin had been wrong about the fighting. But Murezin had also fallen in the river when the bridge collapsed, along with several others. A couple had washed up drowned on the bank, but of Murezin there was no sign.

Suval had said it was just as well the Gurkish Legion would not have to fight because he had never fought in his life and was not Gurkish and, indeed, barely even spoke their language. But it could not be worse than living in the slums in Adua where no one would hire you if you had a dark face. He had been a scribe in Tazlik, where the sea breeze had cooled his clean little office. He had copied religious texts, mostly, with some accountancy work, which was all very boring but paid well. How he prayed now that he might live to be bored again. He hunched down at another ear-splitting crack somewhere over on the left. God, that was a different life, and had happened to a different man in a different world from this one. A world that was not exploding and on fire. A world that smelled of salt sea and blossom rather than smoke and terror.

'God help us,' he whispered again. There were a lot of men praying. A lot of men crying. A lot of men screaming. One sat silent, in the dappled shade of the trees, looking exceedingly surprised, blood streaming down his face. Suval knew him a little. He had been a tailor in Ul-Khatif. No sense of humour. But senses of humour were not at a premium here.

He turned over and shuffled through a slurry of fallen fruit to a twisted tree trunk where several other Kantics were sheltering, along with a Union man in the oddest uniform, half-green, half-brown. He realised as he got close that the man was dead, and the brown half was blood from his arm, which was utterly mangled. He pushed the corpse away with his shoe and wriggled into the place it had occupied, and did not even feel ashamed at his mistreatment of the dead.

He could ask God for forgiveness later.

Someone offered him a flask and he drank gratefully, handed it back. Smoke wafted across the river. Some men had rafted over and now they were huddled trembling on the far bank with one spear between them, one of them pale and bleeding, the raft come apart and its timbers drifting away. Now and again a body would float past, face up or face down, turning gently with the current.

Furious shouting behind them, the sound of terrified horses. They were driving wagons through the carnage. They had rolled one into the river already. Trying to make a bridge, so they could get across. And what? Fight? Madness. All madness. A man they had all thought dead gave a gurgling scream as a wagon's wheel crunched over his leg.

'God help us,' whispered Suval, but God was not listening. No more than He had been when the riots started in Tazlik and his office was robbed and set on fire and he and his family spent all they had on passage to the Union. Another crash, and he wriggled back against the tree as bits of leaf and twig rained down.

Something spattered his face. Was it blood? Was he wounded? Oh, God, was this the end? He held his trembling fingertips up before his eyes.

Just plum pulp. Just rotten fruit. He wanted to laugh. But he also wanted to cry. His helmet fell off and he jammed it on again, back to front.

There was a big fat man in a big red uniform heavy with golden ropes. The one who had smiled from horseback as they set off a week before. A thin man with combed-back black hair was shouting something at him, stabbing a finger at the broken bridge, at the wagons. He wanted them to cross. But how could they cross with the world on fire? How could they even think of moving? He might as well have demanded they fly to the moon.

Suval was no soldier. He copied texts. He had a lovely hand, everyone said so. Had taken great care over his manuscripts.

'I'm not sure ... that is to say ... I don't see how ...' Barezin stared about at the ruins of the legion he had been so very proud of, mouth mindlessly opening and closing like that of a fish jerked from the river. 'My Gurk-ish Legion—' And he twisted around as another cannon-stone crashed through the trees no more than thirty strides away, his fat jowls wobbling.

Antaup had never liked the man. Never liked any of these Open Council bastards. Never trusted them. Flatterers and blowhards. But somehow, he'd bought into the big talk. And it was too late now. No choice but to work with what they had.

He grabbed Barezin by a fistful of braid and hissed the words one at a time. 'Just ... get ... them ... *across*!' He pulled his horse around. 'Now!'

He had to head back to Leo. Tell him he couldn't rely on these fools.

He shoved a low branch aside and was out from among the trees. Things were no less confused in the open. Dead and wounded everywhere. One dissolving unit was half moving forward, half back, breaking open in the middle and scattering yellow-jacketed men in every direction. A riderless horse frisked maddened through the chaos, empty stirrups bouncing at its flanks.

Antaup saw a flicker at the corner of his eye then dirt showered up in the midst of a column. Dirt and weapons and bits of people in a flailing cloud. Men were flung down like dolls, flung themselves down, covering their heads.

Antaup only just kept his seat as his horse swerved around the shattered column, soil showering down on him, pinging from his saddle, screams of injured men fading under the drumming of hooves.

That had been close.

Off to the west, through the haze of smoke, he caught a glimpse of more organised lines. Blue-uniformed troops. Isher's regiments, maybe, spared the worst of the cannon fire, still keeping some shape. But as he galloped across the fields, he saw nothing but an exhibition of cowardice. Every tree had a little clump of men huddled behind it, fighting each other for more cover. Men without weapons. Men without purpose. Wounded crawling for the rear.

A nervous company had gathered at the side of a farmhouse. You could see their terror as they gazed across the body-speckled fields towards the burning orchards and the fuming hill beyond. An officer rode up and down in front of them, waving his sword, screaming himself hoarse. 'Forward! For pity's sake, forward!' But like a stubborn herd of goats refusing the shepherd's commands, they wouldn't be moved.

Antaup gritted his teeth and dug in his heels. All bloody amateurs. And good men would be paying for it.

He jumped a hedge, jolting down, saw a set of men hiding on the other side in the midst of pulling off their brightly coloured jackets. Deserting before they'd even reached the enemy. He was tempted to turn his horse and ride the bastards down. But they weren't alone. He saw others scattering northwards across the fields, occasionally glancing back with terrified eyes.

'Bastard cowards!' he hissed into the wind.

He wished Jurand and Glaward were there. He'd always known what they were. Nothing to be proud of but they were good men still. Leo could be so bloody stubborn. Once he had an idea in his head, there was no shaking it free.

'Out of the way!' he roared, men flattening themselves against the railings of the wooden bridge as he clattered across. One messenger scarcely flung himself aside in time, a flash of his wide eyes, a snatch of his shocked whoop as Antaup whipped past him and on towards Steebling's tower-house.

He was working up a new story. Something to really gild his reputation. A nobleman's wife, this time. Lady something or other. Probably better not to think up a name, that could get him in trouble later. I'll take it to my grave and all that. Mysterious older woman. Terribly wealthy. Frisson of danger. Husband couldn't get it hard any more. They'd swallow it whole. Antaup, you dog! How do you do it? Easy when you made it up. And a lot more fun than having to actually persuade women to take you to bed. He'd no patience with women at all.

The hill the tower stood on crawled with activity, but the neat grey lines of Angland's army weren't waiting at the foot any more. He could see the dust from the formations as they crossed the stubbled fields to the south.

'Damn it,' he whispered, giving his horse a moment to rest and easing his helmet back to wipe his sweaty forehead.

Had Leo got impatient? Hardly the first time. Or had something forced his hand? He felt a guilty pricking of nostalgia for the days when Lady Finree had been in command. That sense of calm control as she considered the maps, the men, the terrain. No place for a woman, maybe, but no one ever doubted that she knew exactly what she was doing. That she knew exactly what everyone else should be doing. Now no one seemed to have the faintest idea.

He pushed down an unfamiliar feeling of panic. Get to Leo. Tell him what was happening. Do his duty. Like Ritter and good old Barniva had, if that was what it took. He pushed on south, towards the dust clouds, the rows of glinting steel. The buildings of Stoffenbeck grew closer through the gloom. The tall clock tower. He tore on past clusters of wounded men, past stretcher-bearers, past wagons laden with supplies.

He noticed bolts poking from the stubbled fields to either side now. All pointing at the same angle. Within flatbow range, then. Leo would be where the danger was, of course. It was one of the things you had to admire about the—

There was a strange little click, Antaup gasped as his horse swerved, and suddenly he was in the air. He took a whooping breath, clutching at nothing, driven out in a great groan as he hit the ground. The world tumbled and jolted as he rolled, bounced, tumbled and slid to a stop.

He lay there, looking at the sky for a moment.

The sun a bright smudge against the clouds. Peaceful.

He came back to himself with a jolt. He moved his arms and legs, wriggled his fingers. A couple of bruises perhaps, but otherwise uninjured. The ladies of the Union and, indeed, the world, could breathe again. That had been an exceedingly close thing.

His horse lay on its side, kicking weakly, a flatbow bolt buried in its flank.

'You absolute *bastards*!' he roared at no one in particular.

Canlan pulled the trigger and sent another bolt flying towards the neat blocks of Anglanders.

He didn't wait to see where it came down. That wasn't his business.

'Load!' shouted that arsehole of a lieutenant, barely old enough for a beard.

'Arsehole,' mouthed Canlan as he lowered his bow and started to crank.

Drum gave a little snigger, but he was easily amused. 'Let's have some more bolts over here!' he roared over his shoulder.

'They'll come when we need 'em.' In Canlan's experience, it didn't really help thinking about where the bolts came from and certainly not where they were going. And Canlan had a lot of experience. Been a soldier all his life, more or less. He'd shot flatbow bolts in every significant war the Union had been involved in. He'd shot 'em at Gurkish and Northmen and Styrians and Stariklanders. He'd shot 'em at Ghosts on the barren plains, at pirates on the rolling sea, even at some Imperials, once, in a desultory exchange of arrows outside of arrow range somewhere near the border of the Near Country. Now he was shooting 'em at Anglanders, who in every way that counted should've been on his side.

The string was cranked all the way now and he hefted the bow, plucked up a bolt, slotted it home, all smooth and practised. He paused a moment, wondering how many bolts he'd shot in his life. But his job wasn't to count 'em, just to put 'em in the air, calmly and carefully and quickly as possible.

He lifted the bow to his shoulder, knocked the dowel out of the trigger, lined up on the ranks of marching pikemen, their armour gleaming dully in the sun as they came on. Gave him a worried feeling, for a moment, seeing 'em like that. Weren't quite close enough to make out their faces. Weren't quite close enough to tell who they were. But they soon would be. He frowned as he lifted the bow to adjust for distance. So he was looking towards the sky, rather than towards the men. That was better. Who they were wasn't his business.

'Shoot!' said that arsehole of a lieutenant, and Canlan pulled the trigger, and put his bolt in the air, and straight away set to cranking his bow again.

Starling gasped as something bounced from his shoulder plate, flicked his helmet and clattered away behind.

'Was that a flatbow bolt?'

'Keep steady!' called Captain Longridge. 'March!'

Starling swallowed. Armour was a good thing. Armour was a very good thing.

'Come on,' someone was growling, just beside him. 'Come on.'

Bloody hell, they were getting close now. Over the shoulders of the three ranks in front, he caught a glimpse of the enemy's lines. A drystone wall, he thought. Some tree trunks with stakes hammered into them, poking out in all directions. Some trenches, maybe. Glitter of steel as a gap in the clouds passed overhead.

A man fell, screaming. As he looked around, Starling saw he had a bolt in his face. A horrible red flash of it before he went down under the stumbling men, and someone near tripped over his pike as he dropped it, everyone wobbling and clanking into each other.

'Close up!' roared Longridge. 'Close up the ranks there!'

Starling found he was marching with his eyes slightly narrowed. A shield would've been a very good thing, too, but damn, the pike was so heavy, there was no way he could've managed both.

'Forward, men!' Starling glanced over his shoulder. The Young Lion himself! On his great warhorse with his officers around him and his sword drawn. A bloody hero, like in the storybooks. Starling joined up 'cause of what that man had done at Red Hill. And beating Stour Nightfall in the Circle, and all. He'd seen the way the girls gasped when they heard the tale told and thought, *Bloody hell, that's the job for me.*

Starling puffed his chest and lifted his pike a little higher as the Young Lion rode past, but he was soon lost in the dust, and Starling's pike drooped again. Shit, the thing was heavy. You were surprised how light it was at first, but once you'd been carrying it a while, damn thing got heavier every step. He coughed. So much dust. Spat, accidently spat down himself, spit all down his breastplate, but what difference did that make? Wasn't as if he could stop to wipe it off. He was wearing gauntlets. And they weren't on parade any more.

'Come on, come on, come on,' came that voice. Couldn't tell who it was but he wished they'd shut up.

Bloody hell, they were getting close now. From the shouting over on the left, he reckoned the fighting had already started there. He flinched as a couple more bolts pinged down, rattled from helmets. He'd never fought in a battle before. Told everyone he'd been in Styria but he never went. Had a couple of brawls, one where he threw the Widow Smiler's son in the millpond, but they'd been done so fast. Some harsh words and some jostling and all over in a few silly angry moments. This was nothing like it. So big, you were carried along, helpless, like a twig by a river. And so slow. So gradual. So impersonal. All that time to think about it. More like a formal dance than a brawl. He'd much rather have been at a dance, all in all. Didn't know how to dance, but then he didn't know how to do this, either.

Wished he was in the front rank, so he could see where he was going. Then he caught sight of where they were going. That drystone wall, and men standing there, lowering their own pikes, and bloody hell was he glad he wasn't in the front rank. Everyone packed in so tight. No room, no room at all. Sort of a comfort, sort of a fear. Men protecting you, brothers at your shoulder, but how could you get out? You couldn't. That was the whole point.

'Lower pikes!' roared Longridge. 'Ready!' Grunting and scraping as men towards the front levelled their weapons, a gleaming forest of points.

Bloody hell, they were getting close now. He caught a glimpse of the enemy. Pikes and full armour. Open helmets so he could see their faces. Young faces and old. Scared faces and bared teeth. A fellow with a big moustache. Another smiling – smiling at a time like this. Another with tears on his face. Looked a lot like they did, really. Like they were advancing at a bloody mirror. It was mad, wasn't it? It was mad. He had nothing against these fools, that he had to try to kill them, and for damn sure he'd done nothing to them that they should want to kill him. Unless the Widow Smiler's son happened to be over there.

'Come on! Come on!' snapped that bastard beside him. Everyone had started growling, snarling, grunting, steeling themselves for the slow contact, and the tips of their pikes clicked against the tips of the enemy's, and the shafts met, and scraped, and slid, closer and closer. A thicket of them, slipping and knocking against each other, and deadly metal on the end.

Someone screamed on the other side. Someone gave a wail on theirs. Now they stopped walking. Boots mashing at the dirt. Starling pressed up tight against the backplate of the man in front, felt someone press up tight against him from behind. His pike had met something, he thought, but he couldn't tell what. No idea what the hell he was pushing at. He tried to look over the shoulder of the man in front. Tried to lift his pike high and push it downwards, but bloody hell, the weight of it, his shoulders were burning, haft knocking against all the others.

'Push!' roared Captain Longridge. 'Push! Kill the bastards!'

Bloody hell, the noise. The growling and spitting and swearing, the squeal and grind of tortured metal and wood, now and again a scream or a whimper or a begging gurgle.

'No!' someone shouted. 'No! No! No! No!' Getting higher and higher each time until it became a mad shriek.

Bloody hell, it was hard work, harder work than anything he'd ever done and for no reward but dead men. He snarled and shoved and strained and felt the sweat springing out of his forehead.

'Heave!' roared Longridge. 'Heave, damn it!'

Starling saw the blade coming. The man in front pulled his head out of the way and it slid past his face while he stared at it cross-eyed. He tried to twist away but he was stuck fast. Packed in like sticks in a bundle. If he'd picked his feet up off the ground, he'd have been held there by the pressure of the men all around him. The blade kept coming, or maybe he was carried towards it, and the point touched his breastplate and scraped against it. There was a squealing and it made a long, jagged scratch on the metal, right through the embossed hammers of Angland.

'Come on! Come on!'

He strained and struggled and rammed desperately with his own pike, but he couldn't even see who this one belonged to. Could hardly move his head, let alone anything else. All crushed in so tight.

'Fuck!' he snarled. 'Shit! Fuck!' He twisted and kicked ever more desperately, and the bright point of the blade scraped sideways across his breastplate, caught on the metal lip near his armpit. He stared down at it, hardly daring to breathe, begging it to somehow hold there. He let go of his pike, tried desperately to twist around but couldn't even pull his right hand free, could only get the faintest, useless grip on the shaft between finger and thumb of his left.

'Come on!'

Then with a groan the man beside him shifted, and the point jerked free, and it slid under Starling's shoulderplate and ever so gradually pierced the padded jacket he wore underneath.

'Push!' yelled Longridge, and the men behind pushed at him, and pushed at him, and pushed him onto the blade.

He gave a snarl through his gritted teeth when it pricked him. Just a cold pinch, and then a biting, and a worse, and his snarl got higher and higher until it was a desperate, slobbering shriek, an impossible, unbearable pain cutting through his chest.

Lake just shoved. Didn't know what he was shoving at, he just shoved. How could anyone know anything?

Be a man, his father had told him as he saw him off.

Damn it, his pike was stuck. He couldn't even tell on what. Lodged in some Anglander or stuck in the mud or tangled with the wall. He gritted his teeth and wrenched and twisted but it wouldn't come free.

'Come on!' someone was shrieking. 'Come on!' But he couldn't even tell which side it came from.

Be a man, he'd said, with his big calloused hand heavy on Lake's shoulder, and his bottom lip stuck right out as if he was saying something weighty.

Men were being men all around him, crowded in close, stink of sweat and blood and smoke and fear, armoured shoulders crushed together, noise like hail falling on metal, ping, scrape, scratch, and the endless yelling and the orders echoing from the rear that no one could understand. He shoved at his pike again, shoved at it, but it was shoving back at him now. Far as he could tell, beyond the ranks in front the enemy were crowding in closer. No end to them. Clouds had come across the sun and their armour had a dull sheen to it now instead of a glitter. The glitter was off the whole business.

'Get off!' The man on his right kept shouldering him. He shoved with his elbow, shoved the best he could, tried to look round, and realised the fellow was dead. Or as near dead as made no difference, head flopping sideways with his helmet skewed across his face and his eyes rolled back and his tongue hanging out and a great crimson drool of blood down his chin.

Be a man.

Then everything jolted. Lake never saw why. There was a terrible pain in the side of his face. So terrible and so sudden he vomited. Spat sick. Something in his eye. Coughed and spluttered and groaned. His helmet had fallen off. He was on the ground. How'd that happen? The pain in his face. Boots kicking at him.

He started crawling through a forest of shuffling and stomping legs, light flickering, sound muffled. He pulled his glove off with his teeth, felt at his face with trembling fingers. Sticky. Was he wounded? Cries and snarls and yells. He clutched at a leg. Dead men down here. The pain of it. Was he wounded? Was it bad? He couldn't see. Tried to open his eye but he couldn't see.

'Help,' he whimpered. No one could hear him. Be a man.

He clutched at the mud, dragged himself back. Through the boots, through the legs. Something thudded into his ribs, rolled him over, a boot caught the side of his face as it came down and he shoved at it, punched at it, dragged himself on through the feet and the mud and the corpses.

Be a man. What did that even mean?

'Help!' he squealed, hands clutched to his bloody face, and he felt himself caught by the wrists and dragged back.

It took all her strength to pull him out from there. Grown men are heavy, let alone armoured ones. Ariss gritted her teeth and heaved on his wrists as hard as she could. This was no time to be gentle. Then her foot slipped and she went down in the mud with him half on top of her. Hardly mattered, she was filthy as a miner already, her apron spattered with dirt, spotted with blood.

'Up we get,' grunted Scalla, pulling the wounded man off her and dumping him onto the stretcher. She'd almost complained when she first saw how rough he was with them. Like he was hefting sacks of coal. She'd soon learned that delicacy did no one any good. She stumbled to the foot of the stretcher, caught hold of the handles. Scalla had undone the buckle on the wounded man's helmet and tossed it bouncing away, turned around to grab his handles and looked over his shoulder to meet her eye. 'One, two . . .'

She growled as she lifted the foot end and off they went, bones jolting, teeth rattling, shoulders burning with the effort as they jogged towards the outskirts of town. Chaos here, messengers dashing, other stretcher-bearers stumbling back and forth, boys scrambling with armfuls of flatbow bolts.

Ariss had wanted to do something before she married. Wanted to do something *real*. Something to be proud of. Her uncle had fought in Gurkhul, long ago. He'd tried to warn her.

'So a battle's no place for a woman?' she'd snapped at him.

'A battle's no place for anyone,' he'd said, and she'd walked out.

Now she forced herself to look at the man on the stretcher. There was a great long slash down his face to his throat. She couldn't really see how bad it was for all the blood. She didn't really want to see how bad it was. But the blood was not a good sign. It was pouring out of him. Pooling in the stretcher around his head. Soaking through the canvas. Dripping to the dirt where her feet mashed it into the mud. So much blood. You'd be amazed how much a man holds.

He made this long, dull groan with every outbreath. Not even pained. Half-witted. Mindless.

'Shush,' she crooned, but it came out panicked and jolting with her footfalls.

She'd fondly imagined a woman's voice might help calm them, the way it had in Spillion Sworbreck's book about that dauntless frontier girl that she'd found so inspiring. But nothing calmed them. Nothing but death, anyway. She'd pictured dabbing sweaty brows, and water gratefully received, and binding the odd wound. Discreet wounds. Neat wounds. Nicks and scratches. Instead she saw bodies peeled open, hacked into, bent backwards, leaking their contents. Bodies that could never heal. Bodies that hardly looked like bodies any more.

Her uncle had been right. She'd made a terrible mistake.

They came to the garden where the wounded were laid out, sending up an awful chorus of pain and despair. Better than the wet screams coming from the tent where they did the surgery, though.

She set the stretcher down and sagged on her knees beside it, utterly spent. Her legs were trembling. Her arms were trembling. Her eyelids fluttered. She knelt there in the mud, just breathing.

The wounded man had stopped his groans, at least. The surgeon's assistant leaned down to press fingers against his throat, paused a moment, the battle roaring in the distance like a stormy sea. Like an irresistible tide coming in.

'He's dead.'

Ariss wiped her forehead on the back of her wrist, realised she'd smeared blood all over her face.

Scalla dragged the corpse off the blood-soaked stretcher. 'Let's get another.'

Ariss wearily nodded. 'I suppose.' She lurched up, stumbled as someone crashed into her. A boy who went sprawling next to the corpses, cap falling off to show a shock of blonde curls.

'Sorry! I'm sorry.' A girl, then, snatching her cap up and, with one last look back, running on.

Hildi limped for a few strides, rubbing at her bruised leg until the pain faded then upping the pace, ducking through an alley where a couple of men were getting wounds dressed by nurses. She upset a basket full of bandages as she plunged past but couldn't stop, whipping some washing out of her way and leaving it flapping behind her.

Out of the town and she ran faster, breath cutting at her chest as she hit the grassy slope up the side of the hill. Kept her eyes on her feet. Kept her mind on the few strides in front of her. Orso was relying on her. She clenched her fist tighter around the message. Volunteered to carry it, hadn't she? More or less insisted on carrying it.

Wanting to prove she was useful. Wanting to prove she was brave. She was the one always carried messages for Orso, so she'd carry this one. Realised her mistake soon as she ran from the town hall and into the madness in the street. She'd hated carrying Orso's messages to that bitch Savine dan Glokta. Her affected elegance and her gaudy taste and her superior little smirks. But Hildi's chances of getting killed carrying love letters had been very small.

'Hildi, you damn fool,' she hissed.

The sad fact was, if she was honest with herself... she loved Orso. Not *loved* loved. Not *in* love. She loved him like an older brother. Like a helpless, hopeless, hesitant older brother who just happened to be King of the Union. He was good to her. No one else ever had been. No one else had ever thought she was worth being good to. He was above everyone, but somehow he treated her, who was lower than dirt, like an equal. It would've been strange if she *hadn't* loved him.

But she could've let someone else carry the bloody message.

She paused on the hillside to catch her breath. Paused, and prised her eyes away from the grass. Made herself turn to stare out across the valley.

'Oh, fuck,' she breathed.

From here she could see the whole battlefield. The whole grand insanity of it. Over beyond the town, the steep bluff was wreathed in smoke, little plumes and puffs stabbing out. There were fires in the orchards below it, dark columns drifting into the heavy sky. Fires in Stoffenbeck, too. The air was sharp with their smoke.

Curving away from her, the great crescent of the king's lines. Glimmering metal where the fighting was. Flags limp over the press. Thickets of pikes. Blocks of dark-clothed Anglanders still crawled forward across the open fields. Horsemen moved and wheeled behind.

The lines had shifted, even she could see that, bowing back in the centre where the fighting was hottest, the massed Anglanders grinding ever so gradually in toward Stoffenbeck, weight of numbers starting to tell. Time was running out.

She turned back to the hill, forced her tired legs on. She ran past a dead horse with two arrows sticking from its side, flies already busy at the blood in the grass. Northman's arrows, long and slender, flights fluttering in the wind.

She ran past a man snarling, 'Damn it!' again and again as he fiddled with the jammed crank of his flatbow, fussing with the bolt, trying to turn the handle, fussing with the bolt, trying to turn the handle, fussing with the bolt, over and over. 'Damn it! Damn it! Damn it!'

Someone clutched at her ankle, nearly dragged her over. 'Help . . .' A man on a stretcher, blond hair turned brown with sweat stuck to his clammy pale face. 'Help . . .' She kicked free and hurried on, half-running, half-clawing at the grass with one hand while the other stayed white-knuckle tight around Orso's message.

She ran on. Up onto the brow of the hill. Breath wheezing. Legs aching. A big corporal got in her way, shoved her back so hard she bit her tongue and nearly fell. 'Where the hell are you going?'

'I have to speak to Lord Marshal Forest!' she gasped out. 'Message . . . from His Majesty.'

'That's the king's girl!' someone shouted. 'Let her through!'

She gave the corporal almost as hard a shove as he'd given her, then nearly tripped over a corpse just behind him. A Northman's corpse, fur around his shoulders matted with blood. He wasn't alone. Lots of bodies, left where they fell.

It was plain things were as much of a mess up here as they were down in Stoffenbeck. Forest's own staff had seen action. One officer's arm was in a sling. Another stood with sword drawn, staring at the edge as if he could hardly believe there was blood on it. The lord marshal himself stood with fists clenched, frowning down towards the valley, an oasis of good-natured calm, snapping out orders, clapping men's backs. Just seeing him was a reassurance. At last, someone in charge. Someone who could help.

She stumbled up, holding the message out to him, realised it was crumpled to a smudged mess in her sweaty fist. 'The Anglanders... are pushing us back... towards Stoffenbeck.' She was breathing so hard, she was nearly sick. 'His Majesty... needs support.'

Forest smiled, lines spreading across his leathery face. 'Afraid I just sent a messenger to get support from him.'

'What?' she said.

'They're coming again, Lord Marshal!' someone bellowed.

''Course they're bloody coming again!' Forest bellowed back. 'It's a battle!' He took Hildi by the shoulder and leaned close to whisper. 'If I was you, I'd run.'

And he turned away, leaving her staring.

Forest strode towards the lines, sending one of his officers off with a thump on the shoulder.

'We can't fail, Captain! Can't fail!'

They'd been mauled when the Northmen first came. Only just pushed them back. Wounded everywhere. Morale in tatters. They needed something to believe in. Someone to give 'em courage. Forest had no idea how it had happened, but it looked like that someone would have to be him.

'The king's counting on us, boys!'

Years back, when they first made him a sergeant, he'd imagined the officers must have all the answers. When he was given his commission, he'd imagined the generals must have all the answers. When King Orso made him a general, he'd imagined the Closed Council must have all the answers. Now, as a lord marshal, he finally knew it for an absolute fact. No one had the answers.

Worse. There weren't any.

The best you could do was play a long con and act as if you had them. Never show fear. Never show doubt. Command was a trick. You had to spread the illusion that you knew what you were doing as deep and as wide through your men as you could. Spread the illusion and hope for the best.

'Steady, lads!' he roared. ''Course he was scared. Any sane man would

be. But you push it down. You make yourself a rock. The king was counting on him. The king! Counting on him! He couldn't fail.

'We need the reserves!' squeaked a panicky major.

'There are no reserves,' said Forest calmly, even if his stomach was trying
to climb out of his mouth and run for the rear. 'Everyone's fighting. I
suggest you join 'em.'

And he drew his sword. Felt like the moment to do it. He'd had it
forty years. Ever since they made him a sergeant. Never swung it in anger.
Never had to. A good soldier needs to march. Needs to keep discipline.
Needs to stay cheerful. Needs, sometimes, to stand where he is. Actual
fighting was down near the bottom of the list somewhere.

But rarely, very rarely, it has to be done.

'The king's counting on us!' he roared. 'We can't fail!'

A young lieutenant stumbled past and Forest caught him by the collar
with his free hand, near dragged him off his feet.

'Lord Marshal!' he stared with wide, wet eyes. 'I was . . . I was . . .' Running for it, obviously. Forest hardly blamed him. But he had to stop him.

'Bravery's not about feeling no fear,' he said, turning the man firmly
around. 'Bravery's about standing anyway. The king's counting on us, you
understand? You going to let these Northern bastards bully us? On *our*
ground? Now get *back* there.' He gripped the young lieutenant by the
shoulder and marched him towards the line. 'And *stand*.'

'Yes, sir!' muttered Stillman, hobbling on wobbly legs back to the lines.
''Course, sir. Stand.'

Stillman had meant to stand. He *had* been standing, indeed, but then,
for some reason, his legs had carried him away up the hill. Bloody legs.

He'd dropped his sword, and clawed it up, and clawed up a handful of
sheep droppings with it. Always been so keen on his presentation. Now
he was all smeared with mud and spattered with dirt and literally left
holding a handful of shit.

Always thought he'd be one of the brave ones. Congratulated himself
on it when he was doing his jacket up that morning. You're one of the
brave ones, Stillman!

And then the Northmen had come, with their bloody horrible war
cries, and they'd killed Corporal Bland. They'd killed him all to hell,
and . . . did Stillman have that poor bastard's brains on his breastplate?
Was that brains? He wanted to be sick. He was sick a bit. Just a stinging
tickle at the back of his throat.

He stared about him at the men he was supposed to command.

Everything was a muddle now. He'd no idea where his company ended and the next began. Didn't know half the faces. Or maybe it was the mad expressions that made them strangers. The filth and the blood and the bared teeth. Animals. Savages.

Then the war cries started up again. That high wolf howling, something out of the darkness beyond the edge of the map. Stillman went cold all over. Took a shuffling half-step back.

'I . . .' he muttered, 'I . . .'

Was he crying? His eyes were swimming. Everything blurry. Bloody hell, was he a coward?

He realised he was pissing himself. Could feel the warmth of it spreading out down his trousers. Bloody bladder. Couldn't trust it any more than his bloody legs.

He knew his father, and his uncles, and his grandfather, soldiers all, would have been thoroughly disgusted to see him now, a coward.

Aliz, his wife-to-be, whose eyes had glistened so very bewitchingly when she saw him in his uniform, what would she have thought to see his shitty sword hand and the dark stain spreading out across his trousers?

The truth was he didn't care, as long as he didn't have to fight.

A man stood, teeth gritted, one hand clapped to his bloody side while he gripped his spear with the other. There was bravery.

Another stood roaring insults at the very top of his lungs. 'Fuckers! Fuckers! Come on, fuckers!' There was bravery.

Another lay shivering, staring, white as a sheet except for the red blood leaking from the corner of his mouth, one hand still weakly holding up the standard of their company. There was bravery.

But Stillman didn't care.

He heard other officers around him shouting their encouragements. 'Hold! Steady! Here they come! Stand your ground! For the Union! For the king!'

They were like phrases in a foreign tongue. How could anyone be steady with red-handed murder rushing up the hill towards them? How could anyone be steady with the Northmen's horrible yells, and the screams of dying comrades, and the endless clatter of metal, the thunder of the distant cannons echoing shrill in their ears?

Only the mad could be steady here. The already mad and the turned mad.

Arrows fluttered down. Gentle, almost. One stuck into the ground near him. Another bounced from a man's shoulder and spun away.

'Help!' someone was squealing. Bloody hell, was it him? No. No. He had his mouth closed.

He could hear them coming. The whooping, wailing war cry and the rush of steel. Rain was spitting down now, pit-pattering on metal. He stood on trembling legs, his lower lip wobbling, as though he would give some order, as though he would shout some encouragement.

'Hold?' he croaked.

He saw the men ahead of him shuffling back, boots slipping and sliding on the slick grass, spears wavering. He heard snarling shouts in Northern, voices scarcely human. They were coming. They were coming.

He saw a flash of steel and blood went up in a black spurt. One of the Union soldiers fell, arms flung wide. A gap yawned in the line, and Northmen boiled out of it.

Northmen, with their bright mail and their bright blades and the bright paint on their shields and their bright eyes full of battle madness, battle hunger. Men fixed on his death. Men made of murder. Animals. Savages.

No game. No story. They meant to kill him. They meant to rip him open and spill his guts down the hillside. They meant to dash his brains out like they'd dashed out Corporal Bland's brains, and him a very nice man with a sister in Holsthorm who'd just had a daughter.

Stillman made no decision.

Just those bloody legs of his again. He turned to run, tripped over a fallen spear and went sprawling on his face. There was an agonising pain and he realised he'd fallen on his sword and the point had gone right into his cheek.

He whimpered, trembling as he pushed himself up. Then something smashed him in the back and the ground hit him in the face again and everything was cold. His mouth was full of blood, and grass, and he coughed and gurgled and squirmed, clutching, clutching.

Downside snarled as he hacked at the man in the red jacket again, drove a great dent into the back of his helmet and knocked him limp. He was shouting something. Didn't know what. Not even words, really.

'Die, bastard, fucking die, bastard,' every breath a flood of curses, and he hacked at a shield and put a great scar through the sun pattern on it, hacked at it again and knocked the man holding it over on his back, hacked at his leg and left his foot flopping off by a flap of gristle.

Something crashed into his shoulder, knocked him sideways and he slid on the wet grass, fell, reeled up, almost smashed a man over the head before he realised it was a Northman, turned the other way, screaming, charging, rammed into someone and knocked him down. He squealed something before Downside drove the rim of his shield into his throat, and again.

A sword scraped off his mailed shoulder. Downside spun about, caught the man who'd swung it in the hip with his axe, bent him sideways, lifted his shield high and smashed the rim down on the back of his helmet, reared up and smashed his axe down in the same place so the metal was caved right in.

The fight was a mess. Lines long gone. Melted into tangles of murder. He stomped on a crawling man. Flying blood and flying dirt and flying metal. Stomped him again. Men killing each other. A Union officer with teeth bared was using his sword like a shovel, squatting on a Northman's chest and digging at his caved-in head. Downside roared as he stepped up and hacked his back wide open, blood spraying. His shield had got tangled with a dead Northman's cloak, Downside tried to tear it loose, couldn't, twisted his arm free of the straps, left it behind.

Someone came at him with a spear and Downside sidestepped, caught it below the blade, tugging on it with one hand, and was dragged around while the man who held it tried to jerk it free. He swung with his axe and hit the man in the shoulder, split him open and he gave a strange hoot, mouth a round O of surprise, and suddenly Downside was stumbling around holding the spear. Nearly stabbed himself with it. Hacked at someone and blood spattered him, eyes full of it, mouth full of it, flung the spear away, trying to wipe his face.

Someone barrelled into him and they rolled on the ground. He'd lost his axe. Or tangled on the loop around his wrist, knocking at his side. Downside came out on top, punched, kneed, snarled at the man while the man snarled back, struggling and straining. Downside punched him again, and again, smashed his nose to red pulp, got a hand around the haft of his axe and started chopping. Chopped a dent in his breastplate, chopped a great wound out of his face. Hacked at him with his axe, hacked at him, hacked at him, snorting and spitting, breath ripping at his chest, muscles on fire, blood surging so hard in his skull he thought it'd pop his eyes out.

'Die! Die! Duh—?'

He blinked stupidly as he realised his hand was empty. Loop must've broken, axe flown off who knew where. He fumbled a dagger from his belt with numb fingers and straight away dropped it as a man blundered into him, caught him, wrestled with him, the two of them staggering about, slipping on the wet grass, over the wet corpses, the fallen weapons, the fallen shields, the bits of men.

Downside growled and snarled and spat into his beard as he grabbed the man's head and twisted it, wrenched it around, twisted it, and he fumbled at Downside's clawing fingers but couldn't stop him, made a great shrill squeal, cut off as his neck bones crunched apart.

Something smashed into the side of Downside's face and the world reeled. He rolled on the ground, clawed his way up, fell back onto his hands and knees. Where was he? Clutched at someone and brought him down, clambered on top of him, punching, snapping, punching, started throttling him and his face was all twisted and his eyes bulging as he stared up at Downside, trying to push a finger up his nose. Downside twisted his head away and gave a broken howl like a mad dog slaughtered and dragged the man up and smashed him down, choking him, throttling him, crushing his throat with his hands.

Crush him till there was nothing left.

Crush 'em all.

Cold Blood

There was a sharp crack and several tons of masonry crashed into the town square, throwing out chunks of ornamental carving and a cloud of choking dust. One of Orso's guards hurled himself down. Lord Hoff shrank into a corner. One might have expected Corporal Tunny to dive for cover, or, indeed, to never have left cover, but instead he was doing his best to shield the Steadfast Standard with his body. Even Gorst flinched. But Orso found himself entirely unmoved.

'A cannon-stone must have clipped one of those lovely chimneys. A sad loss to posterity...' He brushed a few specks of plaster from his shoulder plate. Pauldron, was that the word? Or vambrace? He got them mixed up.

'Your Majesty!' piped Gorst. 'You should withdraw!'

'Nonsense, Colonel, things are just getting interesting.'

A ridiculous affectation, of course, things had gone beyond horrifying some time ago and did not look like coming back. But why attend a battle at all if you're not going to say at least one heroically imperturbable thing?

He held Lord Hoff out of the way to allow a stretcher to pass, hauled by a heavyset man in a blood-spattered apron and a gasping woman with hair sweat-stuck across her face. 'Well done!' he called after them. 'Well done!'

Contrary to all logic, Orso felt no fear at all. A great deal less than usual, in fact. He sometimes could hardly face breakfast, was alarmed by the notion of choosing a shirt, but epic disaster appeared to have finally brought out the best in him.

Even as the Northmen came pouring through the wheat to the east, then the Open Council through the orchards to the west. Even as the army of Angland advanced across the fields and engaged the Crown Prince's Division in a vicious melee, then drove them back. Even as the rebels' cannons started firing on Stoffenbeck. Even as the wounded crawled back through the streets, and the fires sprang up across the town, and the smoke billowed around the clock tower, his mood had continued to lift. As if he was somehow balanced on a set of scales against everybody else, and as their doubt and terror grew his own spirits soared.

He hoped that it looked like immense bravery, but it felt like nothing to be proud of. Immense stupidity, maybe. Immense arrogance. Perhaps that was all courage really was. Being so convinced of one's own importance one came to believe death was something only other people need worry about.

'Your Majesty!' squeaked Hoff, his voice even higher than Gorst's now. 'You really must withdraw!'

'You can, by all means,' said Orso. 'I'll catch you up.'

He squatted beside a cowering boy, not an easy operation in full armour. 'Up you get, now.' The lad's eyes went from wide with fear to even wider with astonishment as he realised who was helping him to his feet. 'You have my permission to head for the rear.' He ruffled the lad's hair, sending down a shower of broken plaster. 'Consider it a royal edict!'

Quite possibly his last, the way things were going. The thought almost brought up a snort of laughter. The Fates help him, he was enjoying himself. Was he mad?

'At least put your helmet on, Your Majesty,' whined an officer, holding out the plumed royal headpiece.

Orso waved it away. 'A king needs to be seen. And to be *seen* to be seen.' A woman was cringing in a doorway with her tangled blonde hair full of dust, gripping a drawing board tightly with one fist while she desperately sketched the carnage before her with the other. 'Make sure you get my good side!' Orso called to her. 'Can't actually remember which it is, mind you . . .'

His father had once told him that a king's job was generally just to stand there, but it was still a job one could do badly. At that moment, he felt he was doing it rather damn well. He gave his best salute as a column of spearmen clattered past, heading, he was pleased to see, towards the fighting rather than away.

'Heroes!' he called to them. 'Every one of you!'

They looked amazed to see him there but pleased, too. Proud, even. They trotted past the faster, soon lost in the rolling smoke. It appeared the rebels were using some new kind of cannon-stone which not only smashed buildings to pieces but set those pieces on fire. There's progress for you.

'Enemies!' someone screeched.

'Protect the king!' squealed Gorst, stepping in front of Orso with his shield up. He was astonished to see Tunny flinging himself into the path of danger on the other side, Steadfast Standard in one hand and sword in the other. Horsemen were indeed moving through the murk. Orso inflated his chest indignantly, exactly the way his mother might have when faced with an impudent maid.

'Friendlies!' squeaked Gorst.

Several officers from one of the Crown Prince's regiments, in fact, red jackets so soot-smeared they were hard to tell from dark Angland uniforms.

'Your Majesty! We're being driven back in the centre. The Anglanders won't stop coming!'

'Very well, Major. Give ground. Withdraw into Stoffenbeck and form another perimeter. Fight them in the streets if you must. Any chance of help from Lord Marshal Forest?' he asked as the officers clattered off to their likely dooms.

'He sent a messenger asking for help from us,' said Tunny, sheathing his sword.

'Damn it.' Orso would never forgive himself if anything happened to Hildi. 'What about Lord Marshal Rucksted? Any sign?'

Gorst grimly shook his head. Perhaps Vick dan Teufel had been right, the Breakers had risen up in Keln and their last hope had never even left.

'My leg! My leg!' A man was carried past, arms over the shoulders of two others, his leg most clearly missing below the knee. A cannon-stone struck a roof on the other side of the square and sent an avalanche of broken slates raining down, people diving for cover in all directions.

A soft touch on Orso's arm, a soft voice in his ear. 'Your Majesty.' Sulfur, leaning close. 'You really *must* withdraw.'

'Protecting your master's investment?' asked Orso.

'It will do no one any good if the king is killed by falling masonry.'

Orso took a breath and nodded. 'Especially not me.' And, he had to admit, things were starting to take on a subtle, but very distinct, flavour of defeat. 'We'll fall back a few hundred strides! No more.'

'Very good, Your Majesty,' said Tunny, hoisting the Steadfast Standard onto his shoulder.

'One moment.' Orso looked up at it. The white horse of Casamir still pranced as proudly as ever, and the golden sun of the Union still shone as radiantly. More so, if anything, in the midst of all this blood, grime and chaos. Leo dan Brock had been so very taken with it when they led that parade through Adua together, had looked so admiringly upon it at dinner. A man who placed a lot of faith in flags, one way or another. Orso slowly began to smile. 'I think my standard should probably remain.'

'But, Your Majesty . . .' A captain cleared his throat, as though to explain the obvious to a dullard. 'It must be wherever *you* are. How else will you be found on the battlefield?'

'Well, exactly,' said Orso. 'We have a few cannon left over, don't we?'

That footman was still following him, his purple livery thoroughly besmirched, cringing at the occasional impacts, his tray sheltered under one arm rather than balanced on his fingertips.

'Another sherry . . . Your Majesty?' he managed to whimper.

Orso smiled about at his entourage. 'I rather think the time has come for something stronger.'

Vick had little military experience, but when it came to self-preservation she was an expert, and as far as she could tell, they were fucked.

She dumbly twisted the buds of rag out of her sore ears. Even without them, everything was muffled. One of the cannons had burst, killing half its crew. Three others were cracked and useless. Three more had warped so badly they couldn't be fired. Another had jumped from its trestles and rolled down the hill, crushing two men before they could get out of the way. The rest had run out of stones and powder, their soot-blackened crews sprawled spent on the hillside like escapees from hell.

Gurkish Fire had left a stinking black scar through the grass, shrouding the summit in smoke as the rain started to spit down. Below, she could see the troops of the Open Council slogging steadily up the hillside under drooping flags. They were battered by cannon fire, sodden from the river, exhausted from the climb. But they were coming, and in numbers.

'What do we do?' asked Vick.

Pike surveyed the scene with the disappointed air of a cook come home to find his kitchen in a terrible mess. 'Prepare to pull back.'

Vick looked down towards Stoffenbeck, fires burning in the rubble-strewn streets, wounded trickling towards the rear. 'The king will be left with his arse in the breeze.'

'Would you rather fight?'

To her, fighting was a knee in the balls, a thumb in the eye, a punch in the throat. It was a nail hidden in a heel of bread, brass knuckles and fistfuls of soil, a sock with a rock in it. It was hurting someone as quickly and as badly as you could with whatever was to hand. None of that was any use in a battle, against armoured men and ranks of pikes. Against flatbow volleys and cannon-stones.

What would she even be fighting for? She hardly knew any more. Maybe she never had. Desperately searching for something to be loyal to, as Glokta had once told her.

'Your Eminence!' A Practical was stumbling across the grass, pointing wildly behind him. A rider was coming over the brow of the hill.

He was a beefy man with a mud-stained uniform and a great wedge of brown beard, and a lot of other riders were appearing behind him. The enemy, Vick supposed. Some lord of the Open Council, got around their flank and climbed the back of the hill, ready to finish them off.

'Good timing, Lord Marshal Rucksted!' called Pike. Vick wasn't usually slow on the uptake, but it took her a moment to make sense of things.

'Glad we didn't miss the party, Your Eminence.' Rucksted reined in beside them and frowned through the clearing smoke and the mist of rain towards the approaching troops of the Open Council. He beckoned an aide over with one finger. 'Arrange a charge and get rid of this rabble, eh? There's a good fellow.'

And Vick realised that what she'd taken for a phantom of her battered hearing was the very real drumming of approaching hooves. A very great number of hooves. It seemed reinforcements had arrived after all.

She stumbled to one of the broken trestles, her stiff hip aching.

Had to sit on her hands to stop them shaking.

Savine stared, mouth open in disbelief as, with awful, nerve-shredding slowness, all her ambitions came apart at the seams.

It felt as if it had taken days for the Open Council's cannon-mauled ranks to emerge from the smouldering orchards, then edge in multi-coloured tatters across the broken ground towards the bluff. Isher's blue lines had buckled as they reached the hill, wavered, re-formed and gradually begun to climb.

The enemy's cannon had fallen silent, while their own were finally mounted on the hill below her and began to pound steadily at Stoffenbeck, puffs of dust among the roofs marking the impacts of their stones, columns of smoke marking the fires they had set. Orso's lines bowed backwards in the centre, Stour's Northmen attacking furiously on the left.

The fierce smile had spread across her face. With that bluff in their hands, the town could not be held. The centre would give, Stour would break through on the left, the day would be theirs.

And the throne would be hers.

Then, as the veils of smoke from the cannon below her shifted, she noticed something. A glint of steel in the saddle between the rocky bluff and the one beside it. A thin rain was falling now, turning the battlefield hazy, but as she stepped forward, squinting through her eyeglass, there could be no doubt.

More steel, and more. A flood of it, spilling down from the high ground. Horsemen. A vast, dully glinting wave of them.

'No,' she whispered. They tore into the flank of Isher's ragged units, took them by surprise and broke them like blue dust, surging on towards the orchards. The red blob of Barezin's re-formed legion came apart long before they hit, scattering back towards the river.

'No,' whispered Savine again. As if the word was a prayer. But how often had she boasted to Zuri that she believed in nothing that could not be touched, and counted, and totted up in a ledger? They had been sure Orso would get no reinforcements. They had counted on it. And yet here they were, armed and eager, ripping all her plans to bits.

'No,' whispered Savine. A moment ago, she had tasted victory. Now nothing was certain. She wanted to sink to her knees. She wanted to lie down in the grass. But someone had to do something.

An engineer at the nearest cannon was just touching smouldering match-cord to powder-pan as the rest of the crew hunched away, hands over their ears. Savine started striding towards them, one hand under her belly. 'We have to get—'

There was a blinding flash. She was turning her face away, raising one hand, starting to gasp, when she was snatched off her feet and flung into the ground.

Heroics

'The bastards are running!' snarled Antaup.

'I noticed,' said Leo, watching in helpless fury as the Open Council's forces crumbled and fled for the river.

A moment ago, they'd been close to flanking the enemy on the right. Now they were in danger of being flanked themselves.

'By the *dead*,' he growled. The army of Angland had done their part. Fought for every inch of ground, forced Orso's men from their positions, bent their crescent in the centre until it touched the outskirts of Stoffenbeck. They were still fighting, through the smoke and spitting rain, the melee broken up into a dozen ugly little struggles among the buildings.

'Shit!' He smashed at his armoured leg with his armoured fist. Another hour and the day would've been theirs. But they didn't have another hour. They didn't have another moment.

'We could still pull back!' roared Antaup over the noise.

'To where?' snapped Leo. 'To what?' They'd leave Orso with the field, with the initiative, with every chance of reinforcement, while their own alliance would fall apart. He'd go from liberator to laughing stock. History would record him as a treacherous loser.

'You know what?' Jin leaned in with that huge grin of his. 'I reckon another tap might shatter the bastards!'

'The cavalry are fresh!' As if Jin's smile was catching, Antaup had one, too. 'One more throw of the dice?'

Now Leo was smiling. How could he help it when his friends were laughing at death? He had to stop himself turning to ask Jurand what he thought. He wished him and Glaward were there now. He looked up towards the king's standard. The Steadfast Standard, flapping free above the smoke and ruin on the high clock tower, the golden sun glinting as the real thing slipped through the spitting clouds overhead.

There was still time. If he could shatter Orso's centre . . . seize that flag . . . take the king himself prisoner . . . none of the mistakes would matter. Victory sponges all crimes away, Verturio said. Or was it Bialoveld? What did it matter? The day would be won with swords, not words. This was the moment he'd been waiting for. There wouldn't be a better. There wouldn't be another. It was a moment for heroes.

In battle, his father had always told him, *a man finds out who he truly is.* He was the Young Lion. And a lion doesn't slink away with his tail between his legs. A lion fights to the last.

He slid his arm through the straps of his shield. 'Tell the cavalry we charge!' he bellowed.

'Ha!' Antaup wrenched his borrowed horse around and thundered away to give the orders.

Leo could see exhausted men floundering from the river on the near bank. Across the water, the King's Own cavalry surged and whirled like the starlings above the field the day before, harrying the panicked remnants of the Open Council's forces. Corpses floated downstream, clogged into a great bobbing tangle in the boggy shallows.

But no corpses, no glory. Leo drew his sword with that faint hiss of steel that always sent a tingle across his skin, then turned his horse towards the great wedge of cavalry that was quickly forming. The men who'd ridden beside him in the North, and never let him down. The best of the best. Ordered, disciplined, fearless, their armour beaded with wet as the rain thickened.

'Men of Angland!' he roared, raising his sword high. 'Are you with me?'

Few of them could've heard the words but they got the gist, shoving their lances at the spitting heavens, letting go a rousing cheer.

'For Leo dan Brock!' roared Antaup.

'For the Young Lion!' bellowed Jin.

Leo took his place between them at the sharp end of the wedge. Where he'd longed to be ever since Isher first mentioned rebellion. Ever since Savine made it a reality. Ever since he was last here. Where he belonged. The very point of the spear.

He lifted the rim of his shield and used it to snap down his visor.

'Forward!' he roared, though it couldn't have been more than a metallic burble outside his helmet, and he gave his horse the spurs.

First at a walk, down the rutted road towards Stoffenbeck, surface turned to sticky glue by the drizzle, churned by the hooves of his horse as he urged it forward to battle.

He looked to his left. Jin never wore a visor. Leo could see his teeth in his red beard, eyes furiously narrowed, heavy mace raised. He looked to his right. Antaup, spear couched under his arm, a grin across his handsome face that made Leo grin, too.

Now at a trot, the buildings ahead growing clearer through the rain and the smoke, bodies scattered where they'd fallen as the fighting ground towards Stoffenbeck, the tangle of weapons and limp banners where the battle was still hot, all jolting with the movement of Leo's horse.

Not the first charge he'd led, but the thrill was fresh every time. The dry mouth, the aching muscles, the snatched breath. The ground sped past beneath, as if he flew. The delicious vibration, from earth to hooves to saddle and up into his very guts. The fear and the excitement building to a joy that made him want to scream. He flourished his sword, raising it high.

The ranks of Angland parted before them, officers screaming as they forced the men to wheel back, lines opening so the horses could stream through.

Now at a jolting canter, hooves drumming as the Young Lion's cavalry charged into battle once again. A battle ill-suited to horsemen, though, it had to be admitted. Leo never seemed to learn where that was concerned.

There were strong barricades across the narrower alleys: tree trunks with stakes hammered through them, heaped-up doors and rubble, bristling with pikes. But across the widest street, dead ahead, the barricades were weak, no more than scattered furniture and a few spears.

Leo pointed his sword towards them, tried to roar a command which became nothing more than echoing breath behind his visor.

Everything was pounding hooves, flying mud and billowing smoke, rushing noise and rushing wind, thudding along with his own thumping heartbeat, rattling teeth, booming breath, all seen through a slot you could hardly get a letter through.

The enemy melted before them, scattering, scurrying between the buildings. Leo whooped, cut a man down as he turned to run, sword clattering from his backplate and knocking him under the milling hooves.

They were through! Through into the square at the heart of Stoffenbeck. They'd cut the king's lines in half! A building burned on one side, smoke drawing a veil across the scattered rubbish, broken masonry, twisted corpses, a ruined fountain leaning at an angle, spilling water. He saw the town hall with its tall clock tower, one of its faces shattered, bent hands frozen at the moment its guts were torn out by a stray cannon-stone.

'Forward!' roared Leo, waving his men furiously on, but at the same time he was having to rein back. There was nothing to charge *at*. He caught a glimpse of the Steadfast Standard at the top of the clock tower.

But no sign of the King's Own, let alone the Knights of the Body. The whole place was oddly deserted. Riders spread out around him, all momentum lost, milling, rearing, clattering into one another like sheep in a pen.

He heard a shout from across the square. 'Ready!'

A breeze whipped up, brought a sudden shower into the faces of the riders, tugging the curtain of smoke aside. Long enough for Leo to see barricades across the roads that led out. No weak ones, these. Bristling with sharpened stakes, spears firmly set in a glittering tangle. The spears of men ready and waiting.

And dull metal rings, with darkness inside. The maws of cannon, Leo realised, pointed right at them.

He tried to turn his horse, ripping up his visor so he could warn his men, but it was far too late.

'Fire!'

Broad heard the crash of the volley. So loud it made his teeth buzz.

He froze, crouching in a trampled flower bed by the wreckage of a fence. Any man with half his sense would've run the other way. But Broad had proved a dozen times he had no sense at all once the fighting started, and he was in the thick of the fighting now. His head throbbed with the noise of it, the smell of it. There was no resisting its pull any more than a floating cork resists a wave.

Mess came at him blurred from the murk, sharpened under his feet, drifted into the smears behind him. Broken weapons, broken armour, broken bodies. Even the earth was wounded. Muddy ground so ripped and scarred it looked fresh-ploughed. Injured men clawed through their clothes to see how bad their wounds were. Clawed at the ground. Clawed for the rear. One was so coated in filth that even close up Broad couldn't tell which side he was on. Without his lenses there were hardly sides at all.

The cavalry had thundered through and torn the lines apart. Ripped them into shreds of bitter fighting, tattered struggles to the death, writhing in the smoke. Broad saw the blobbed shapes of three men shaken loose. King's men, he thought. Deserters, maybe. That was his best guess. In a battle, a guess is all you can afford. Time to let go, finally, and he felt the smile twist his face.

The first never saw him coming. Got his helmet staved in from the side with the warhammer.

The second turned to look. A flash of his scared eyes in his blurred face before Broad's dagger thudded into the side of his neck.

The third turned to run, got one step when Broad hooked his legs out from under him with the pick-end and brought him down. He rolled over, trembling arms held up. Before he got a word out, Broad smashed him three times with the hammer, broke his arm, caved his ribs in, caught him in the side of his face and sent teeth flying, jaw half-ripped from his head.

He squirmed in the dirt, back arched, and Broad stepped over him, looking for more, snorting breath steam-hot, teeth locked vice-tight, muscles coiled-spring tense.

Shapes rushed from the gloom and he raised his hammer. Horses, clattering past. Riderless, maddened, reins flapping, eyes rolling. One with blood streaking its flanks, another with a loose boot still caught bouncing in a stirrup.

A weak barricade across the street. Left weak on purpose. An invitation. One Brock hadn't been able to refuse. Broad was no better. He slunk through, keeping low, lips curled back, the low growl sawing at his throat.

A soldier knelt, pointing a broken spear.

'Get back!' he shouted.

Broad took one step and smashed his head open with the hammer. He'd seen men keep fighting with wounds in the body you wouldn't believe. Make the skull a very different shape, that's the best way to be sure. Flatten it, shatter it, punch holes right through it.

A window cracked, flames licking up the outside of a building. Broad coughed on smoke, prickled with sweat. Eyebrows slick with it. Blurred shapes loomed up. Pillars. What had been a covered market, its roof ripped away, slates and scorched timbers and chunks of masonry scattered.

There were dead men everywhere. Broad could hardly move without stepping on 'em. Dead men and dead horses, tangled and torn apart. Even the stonework was scarred and pockmarked. Cannons' work, he reckoned. Cannons filled with smiths' oddments. A storm of hot metal no armour, no shield and for damn sure no courage could stop. The place stank of smoke and blood, of broken men and smashed-open horses and everything they hold.

Mad fighting here. He saw a man laying about him from horseback. Another dragged from his saddle, hacked on the ground. Two men wrestled over a knife. Black figures against the fires. Devils in hell.

Broad charged into the very midst of it, caught a man full in the side with his shoulder and dumped him sprawling, sword bouncing from his hand. He reeled into someone else, spear clattering against Broad's back as he swung, too close for the hammer and Broad stabbed with his knife, overhand. It scraped on a breastplate, scratched down an armplate,

449

found the joint between the two and punched deep into flesh. The man tried to twist away, fumbling at Broad's shoulder, and Broad rammed the dagger through the slot in his helmet, left it stuck there to the hilt as he toppled back.

The first man was scrambling for his fallen sword and Broad caught his clutching hand with a swing of the hammer. Turned it to a shapeless red glove. The man took a breath to scream, bent over and Broad kicked him so hard under the jaw his helmet flew right off and went skittering across the gouged cobbles. Kicked him again, and again. Couldn't stop kicking him.

There was a cracking sound above. A great mass of stone fell crumbling, burst apart in a gout of fire. One man was flattened, others threw themselves down, reeled burning, trying to slap the flaming embers free. Broad hit another with the hammer so hard, he turned him over in the air and sent his corpse bouncing from a wall upside down.

He caught a flicker of movement, lurched back as a blade hissed past his nose. Lurched back again as the sword came at him the other way, caught it clumsily on the steel haft of his hammer.

They blundered into each other, wrestling, hints of a bearded face, teeth locked in a snarl. He butted at Broad, made him bite his tongue and filled his mouth with blood, but Broad had the wrist of his sword arm, set his weight and drove the bearded bastard back against a wall, and again, mashed his hand against the broken stonework till his sword clattered down.

He freed his hammer, snarled as he swung it at the man's face, but he slid free, the head catching the wall, twisting the haft from Broad's buzzing grip. Flash of metal as the bearded man jerked out a knife and Broad caught his hand, tripped on a corpse. They crashed over, rolling through burning wreckage.

Broad came out on top, all four of their fists clamped tight around the grip of the knife, the fire-gleaming blade quivering as they strained at it. Broad twisted it, straining, straining, clenched his jaw and put all his weight on it. The man tried to knee him, snorted as he tried to roll him, but Broad was too strong. He took a hand from the knife to claw at Broad's face, turned his head to snap desperately at Broad's hand with his teeth but it was too late.

Broad growled as he forced the blade's point up under the man's ear. Forced it up, blood turning his fist sticky, and he wrenched one hand free to peel the man's clutching fingers away from his face, then made a clumsy fist and beat at the pommel like a hammer on a nail, hammered the blade into this bastard's head till the crosspiece met his jaw.

Broad staggered up, spitting, gasping for breath. Battle was done here for now, but it'd be back, like waves up a beach. Waves of blood that left bodies as flotsam. He could hear it coming. Screams and clashes. Mad honking, squealing, like pigs rutting.

He saw a tattered standard sticking up above a heap of dead. As he got close, he could make out the lion, the hammers of Angland. One of Brock's men still held it, with one arm. Sitting propped against a dead horse. The handsome one. Antaup? He was breathing hard, a couple of little holes through his breastplate, blood leaking out to soak his trousers.

Last stand wasn't a phrase you ever wanted to use about your own side, but that was the look of it. Wounded men. Twisted faces. Desperate shouting. Someone coughed, leaning on a broken spear, coughing blood, and drooling blood, coughing again. The Northman, Jin, had a flatbow bolt in his thigh. He had Brock under the armpits even so, swearing in Northern as he struggled to drag him out from under his dead mount.

'Here,' slobbered Broad. His mouth wouldn't fit round the human word. All it wanted to do was snarl and bite like an animal. He hooked his arms under the horse's side and with a growl managed to heave its dead weight up enough for Jin to haul the Young Lion free and sag back, spent.

'Master Broad,' croaked Brock. He looked baffled. Like all this had come as quite the shock.

'Your wife sent me.' Broad frowned into the murk. Everything beyond arm's reach was blurred. Everything more than a few paces off was just wriggling smears. Crackle of flames to one side. Air full of smoke and settling dust and dying men's groans. Brock's leg was a mangled mess, armour crushed and slathered with his blood, his horse's blood, the knee-plate twisted almost flat.

'Good of you ... to come.' Brock lifted his left arm, baring pink teeth as he dragged the battered remnant of his shield from it. 'But you can see ...' A great nail had punched right through the vambrace, near the elbow, blood dripping from the end. 'There's nothing ... to be done here.'

Broad could see that. He could see that very clearly. He looked up at Jin, and the Northman looked back, and no words were any use.

'Go back ... to Savine.' Brock was panting between each phrase. 'Make sure she gets away.' Like every word was a hero's effort. 'Make sure my child ... gets away.'

Broad stood. There were shapes in the smoke. The king's men, he guessed, moving in to finish it.

He took a fallen sword and pressed the hilt into Leo dan Brock's hand. The Young Lion nodded to him, and Broad nodded back.

He could do no good here. But then he hadn't come to do good. He turned away from the killing. Slipped down a ruined side street, and away.

'Shit,' growled Clover, lowering his eyeglass and frowning down towards the smouldering wreck that used to be a town.

'What is it?' asked Flick, over the endless racket of the fighting.

'Best I can tell, the Young Lion's glorious charge came to grief. Let that be a lesson for you in the value of glorious charges.'

'What does that mean?'

'That there's naught left to fight for. We need to save what we can while there's still something to save. Stay close and stay low.' And Clover tucked the eyeglass away and drew his sword. Not so much from any desire to swing it, but because having it drawn was the done thing in a battle. Then he clenched his jaw, squared his shoulders and headed exactly the wrong way. Which was to say towards the fighting.

It was bad now. It was always bad, but it was real bad now. Everyone on the arrow-prickled, blood-smeared, mud-churned way was hurt. A Carl spluttered blood and bits of teeth into his hands. Another stared stupidly, hair clotted with blood. A Thrall clutched at the leaking stumps of two fingers, snarling curses. A Named Man sat, pale as milk, staring down at his hands as he tried to poke his guts back in through a great slit in his side. Clover caught his eye and gave him a nod. He was back to the mud, and they both knew it. A nod was all Clover could do for him.

'By the dead,' croaked Flick, wincing as if he was walking into a wind, the terrible, mindless din of it getting louder and louder.

Clover shook his head. Gripped tight to his sword. Could there have been a time he enjoyed this? Looked forward to it? Strained every muscle to get back to it as soon as he could?

'Must've been mad,' he whispered.

Some arrows fell fluttering and Clover dropped down, hunching his shoulders. Like hunching your shoulders would do any good. Who was shooting anyway? In all this, there was just as much chance of killing your side as theirs. Maybe it got so you didn't care any more. So any killing seemed a sensible notion. Everyone else was at it, why be the one fool left out?

Been a long time since Clover felt that way. The mud's cold embrace waits for everyone. Getting some poor bastard there faster just 'cause he was facing the other way hardly struck him as a thing worth risking your own life for. When there's a flood, do you waste time raging at the water? By the dead, no, you just try not to drown. Battle's no different. A natural disaster.

'Fuck,' someone was snarling, down on one knee, staring at the arrow shaft sticking from his shoulder. 'Fuck!' Like he never saw a thing so unbelievable, so unfair. Should've thought about it. Nothing more natural in a battle than getting shot with an arrow.

Least Clover had managed to keep Sholla out of it this time. Told her someone needed to bring a boat upriver, in case things turned ugly. Hadn't needed much persuading, in the end. She'd a good head on her, that girl. He'd have liked to leave Flick out, too, but there was one valuable lesson for a boy to learn here. Namely that swords do no good for the men at either end of 'em.

'Chief,' said Flick, tugging on his sleeve.

Downside knelt there on the hill, corpses all about him, leaning on a great axe he must've prised from some dead man's fingers, as if he was about to push himself up but couldn't find the strength.

He'd taken the approach to battle Clover might've when his name was still Steepfield, which was to say running for wherever the fight was wildest, raging and flailing and spilling every drop of blood he could without a thought for shield or helm or consequences. He was so red-spattered, he might as well have gone swimming in a sea of corpses, doing his best imitation of the Bloody-Nine, the mad fucker.

Still, no man can rage for ever, and he was drooping now, bloody hair hanging, mail torn and the cloth beneath ripped, jaw dangling and knuckles raw, two of the fingers on his free hand snapped crooked in opposite directions

'Had your fill, have you?' asked Clover.

Downside's eyes rolled slowly up, as if even that was too much effort, one turned bright red by a blow to the face and his cheek cut and his forehead scuffed raw and his brow opened up and weeping a dark streak.

'Aye,' he croaked out, voice raw from screaming curses. 'And more.'

'The Anglanders are finished. Reckon the day's done.'

'Aye,' croaked Downside, blowing a bloody bubble from his nose, and he held that broken hand out to Flick so the lad could help him up. 'The day's done.'

'Where's Stour?'

Downside waved a lazy hand towards the crest of the hill.

Clover saw the King of the Northman's black wolf standard bobbing over the throng, dancing in the mad tangle of spears and weapons and broken hafts, the stormy sea of heads and helms. Stour had flung himself into the midst, o' course. Up front where tomorrow's songs were made, carving himself a legend. The Great Wolf was brave, no doubt. But bravery and folly never had too big a gulf between 'em.

Clover bent down to one of the corpses, some Union man huddled on his side like a child on a cold night. He took a quick peek about but everyone was bent to their own tragedies, so he stuck his hand in the man's ripped-open jacket and flicked blood on his face, smeared it down his mail, rubbed his sword along the corpse's side to get a bit of red on it.

He realised the man was looking at him. Cheek twitched a little. Not dead, then. Clover gave him a sad little smile, a sad little shrug.

'Thanks for the gore.' Then he stood and hurried towards the madness.

Piece of luck, he didn't have to go far. He found Stour sat on a rock looking mightily disgruntled. A woman was trying to bind his bleeding leg, but he kept jumping up to shout orders, or at any rate insults, jerking the bandages out of her hands.

'Clover!' he snarled, blood on his teeth. 'Where the fuck have you been?'

'Trying to keep Downside from killing himself.' True enough, in its way. 'The Young Lion's all done. We have to pull back before they get around us.'

'You fucking *what?*'

Stour cast about him at his various young bastards, but none looked like they fancied another helping of what the Union had served 'em. They'd been a great deal more warlike leading up than in the thick, it had to be said. Greenway was gripping Stour's standard like a man who can't swim clinging to the rail of a sinking ship, flinching wild-eyed at every noise. A tough job, as the noise was constant.

'There's nothing more to prove up here, my king,' Clover shouted over the racket. 'Time to bend with the breeze. Save what we can.'

Saving things wasn't on the menu far as Stour was concerned. He was a man liked to smash things at any cost. 'The Great Wolf doesn't run,' he spat, then gave a pained grunt as the woman pulled the bandage tight.

''Course not,' said Clover. 'But he might back off when it suits him, specially from another man's fight. Wouldn't be our victory. Won't be our defeat.' He leaned close. 'The Young Lion dug this fucking hole. He can be the one buried in it.'

'The ships are back at the coast,' muttered Greenway, eyes wide.

'Told my girl Sholla to bring ours up the river. Should be no more

454

than ten miles off. I got horses waiting. Enough to whisk a few of us safe back home.'

Stour narrowed his eyes. 'Always thinking, eh, Clover?'

'Honestly, your father told me to make sure you come through whole. You're not just any man, you're the future o' the North.' Clover leaned even closer, speaking soft and urgent. 'What are we even fighting for? Glory? There'll always be more o' that for the taking. Uffrith? Without Brock to defend it, we can snatch it the old-fashioned way!'

Stour worked his red mouth a moment, frowning up towards the summit of the hill. Then he bared his teeth, and spat red, and turned away. 'We fucking pull back.'

'They're coming,' gasped Leo. Every breath was a moan through teeth gritted against the pain.

Ghosts in the smoke. Shadows in the dust. Among the corpses of man and horse, the heaps of rubble and broken spears.

'You have to go,' he hissed at Jin.

Whitewater tried to grin. There was a great wound on his head, a bit of his scalp flapping loose. 'We've come this far together. Reckon I'll finish the journey with you.' He growled as he snapped off the flatbow bolt buried in his leg. 'And I'll be running nowhere anyway.'

He dragged himself to one knee, facing the oncoming figures, holding his broken shield up, mace ready in his fist.

There was nothing Leo could do. He couldn't even stand. He twisted around, dragging himself with his one good arm, ruined leg scraping after him, fist still clinging to his sword. That commemorative sword with the lion's head pommel. The one King Jezal had presented to him. The proudest day of his life.

'Antaup!' he croaked.

The standard was upright, somehow, in the crook of his limp arm. But Antaup sat staring at nothing, blood streaked from the holes in his breastplate, that loose lock of hair still stuck to his pale forehead.

Leo dragged himself up to sit beside him, breathing hard, blowing bloody spit. 'Sorry,' he muttered. 'I'm sorry.'

'Come on, you bastards!' roared Jin in Northern.

Leo heard the rattle of flatbows and Jin tottered back, lurched down on one knee.

'No,' hissed Leo, forcing the one leg that worked underneath him, hooking his elbow around the saddle horn of a dead horse and hauling himself to a wobbling crouch.

Jin toppled over, three bolts sticking from his body.

Heavy boots crunched across the square. A big man in full armour, golden sun of the Union on his breastplate, heavy battle steels in his hands. He pushed his visor up with the back of one gauntlet. Bremer dan Gorst, great jaw clenched tight.

Jin lifted an arm to paw weakly at his ankle. Gorst frowned and kicked it away.

Leo used his sword like a crutch, weight all on his good leg, which an hour ago had been his bad leg. It hardly seemed to hurt at all now. Not compared to the other one, crushed by his horse. Not compared to his dangling arm, riddled with bits of steel from a cannon.

'Finish it.' The words tasted like blood. Did he catch a mocking flash of gold, high above, as the smoke shifted? The Steadfast Standard? A last glimpse of glory?

Gorst glanced from Leo to Jin, to Antaup, to the rest of the corpses. 'It's already over,' he said, in that little girl's voice. 'It couldn't be more over.'

Something in his total lack of feeling made Leo utterly furious. He screamed as he lurched forward, lifting his sword for a clumsy thrust.

Gorst took a step back out of reach, Leo's ruined leg crumpled and he crashed down on his side in the blood-spattered, cannon-scarred, rubbish-strewn square.

He whimpered as he wedged his good arm under him, stretched his hand out for the hilt of his fallen sword.

His fingers crawled across the flags, clutching for the lion-head pommel, half its gilding scraped away.

Gorst stepped forward and flicked it aside with his armoured boot.

It was over.

Just Talk

'Another step and you'll be arrow-pricked, all four o' you!'

Rikke stopped where she was and showed both her open hands and all her teeth.

Her father used to tell her your best shield is a smile. She'd been sceptical then. Looking up at the black battlements, with here or there a glimpse of a bow or arrow, she was sceptical now.

No one else was smiling. Shivers was a man who subscribed to the notion that your best shield is a shield. The Nail was a man who scorned the whole notion of shields, and if offered one would no doubt have gone for an extra axe instead. Corleth, meanwhile, was still working at her angry-little-dog act, fists clenched tight around the staff of the banner with the Long Eye stitched into it.

Still, good teeth were one of Rikke's few natural blessings that hadn't been covered with tattoos or blinded with a needle, so she made the best use of 'em and smiled up wide enough to compensate for all the funereal faces.

'Wouldn't want to be arrow-pricked!' she called. 'I mean, who does? You know who I am?'

A pause, and then, very sour, 'Rikke. Wi' the Long Eye.'

'Says so on the banner, eh?' And Rikke nodded towards it. 'Not to mention my face. No need to worry, I've just come to talk. I'm guessing you're Brodd Silent?'

'I am.'

'Good, good. I hear Black Calder's gone off to suck some cocks up in the High Valleys and left you holding the baby. That right?'

Silence. Though what could you expect from a man called Silent?

'I'll treat that like a yes.' Rikke nodded to the Nail, and he hefted the casket down off his shoulder and dropped it on the cobbles with a thump and a jingle. 'So I've got... what have I got? Did you count it?'

Shivers shrugged. 'I look like a banker to you?'

The Nail shrugged, too. 'Once I get past fifteen I'm all over the place.'

'Well, let's see . . .' Rikke squatted beside the box and opened it so everyone up there could get a good look at the contents. As luck would have it, the sun slipped out right then and lent the whole heap a pretty glitter. 'I've got . . . *quite* a lot of silver. Two thousand pieces, maybe?' She rooted through it with that merry clinking that somehow only money makes. 'There's some Carleon coins here, and some Union, and some Styrian scales, and . . . what's this?' She held a big coin up to the light. Had a head on both sides.

'Gurkish,' grunted Shivers. 'Emperor on one side, Prophet on t'other.'

'A Gurkish coin, how about that? All the way from the sunny South!' She stood, brushing her knees off. 'Anyway, this is for whoever opens the gates. How you split it is up to you. If Master Silent wants to open 'em, he can share it out, I guess.' She left a meaningful pause. 'Or the rest of you could. Have yourselves a wrestling match over the Gurkish one. Your business. Long as *someone* lets us in.'

'You ain't buying your way in here!' shouted Silent from up on the wall, but he sounded a little shrill over the possibility.

'Well,' she said, all innocence. 'You've got another choice . . .'

The Nail did that trick of curling his lip and whistling with just his teeth, so loud it was almost painful, and armed men showed themselves between every building, at every door and window around the walls. Battle-hardened, well-armed men of Uffrith and the West Valleys. Dozens of 'em, and adding not one smile to the tally.

'Which is I give *these* bastards the money to come over the walls and draw the bolts from that side.' Rikke pressed a hand to her chest. 'Now, I've naught but pride for how peaceful we've been so far, and when it comes to bloodshed I'd rather have a trickle than a flood. But I've seen myself sitting in Skarling's Chair, with this banner behind.' She turned her left eye towards them and tapped at her tattooed cheek. 'I've *seen* it, with the Long Eye, understand? So it's happening. That's a done deal. Whether you bastards end up rich or dead on the way, the cost's about the same to—'

There was a breathy cry and something came flying off the battlements.

'Oh,' muttered Rikke, before Shivers dragged her back and down and stuck his shield in front of her.

The Nail didn't shift a hair. He was one of those rare men goes beyond bravery to a kind of madness where there's no regard for danger at all. He just watched whatever it was plummet down, hands on hips, and didn't even flinch as it crashed into the cobbles a stride or two in front, spotting him with blood.

He peered at the mess with his brow a little wrinkled. 'Who's that, then?'

Shivers slowly stood, gently let go of Rikke. 'Brodd Silent, I expect.'

'Hold on!' someone called from the battlements. 'We're coming down!'

'They didn't think about that for long,' said the Nail, wiping the blood from his cheek.

Rikke got up, frowning at Silent's twisted corpse, the side of his face that wasn't squashed into the cobbles gawping wide-eyed with surprise.

She thought of the first time she saw a man killed. Those three she and Isern ran into in the woods the day Uffrith burned. Was it really only a year or two back? The cold shock as she let go the bowstring. The hurt look in that boy's eyes. Still gave her a shiver. Then she thought of all the death she'd seen since. The murders and the battles and the duels. The last expressions, the last words, the last breaths, all blurred into one. The blood rolled off her now, like milk off a greased pan. Isern always said you have to make of your heart a stone.

She took a breath, and kicked the casket closed.

Rikke's father had been less than complimentary on the subject of Skarling's Hall. A cold, hard, rock-carved room for cold, hard, rock-carved men. The place Bethod had seized the North. The place Black Dow betrayed the Bloody-Nine. The place Black Calder had ordered a hundred killings and thievings and petty backstabbings.

But Rikke was a firm believer that dark pasts don't have to mean dark futures, and she was pleasantly surprised by the mood in there. She felt honesty in the light streaming through the high windows. She saw strength in its bare stone walls. She heard truth in the sound of the rushing river far below. The cold, though, she could not deny. Summer was well and truly gone.

'Someone get a fire lit, eh?' she called out as the Named Men tramped into the hall. 'Before I shiver my tits off.'

'Such as they are,' said Isern, frowning down. 'A clean floor is a thing the moon despises. A clean floor bespeaks a small mind.'

'Better'n a dirty one, isn't it? Bespeaks an orderly mind, I reckon.'

'Same thing.' Isern curled her lip back, spat a long chagga stain across the stones and gave a nod of satisfaction, like she'd made a small improvement to the world. 'You never know, that might be the spot where my daddy near killed the Bloody-Nine for killing my brother.'

Shivers gave a snort. 'Ain't far from the spot where I near killed the Bloody-Nine for killing *my* brother.'

'Maybe you should've done it,' said Isern.

'Maybe's a game with no winners.' Shivers turned that ring on his little finger thoughtfully around. 'I let go o' my regrets. You'll swim better without their weight.'

There was a clash and rattle from the corner of the hall. The Nail had stalked up to the iron cage hanging in the back corner and now his knuckles were white at the bars like he'd rip it apart with his big bare hands.

'Doubt you'll pull it down without some tongs or something,' said Rikke, strolling up.

'I'll pull it down one way or another,' he snarled as he wrenched it about, chains jingling.

'I say leave it up.'

The Nail turned on her, holding one fist up under her nose, close enough she had to look at it a little cross-eyed. 'My father died in this fucking cage!'

'Aye.' She soaked his rage up with a smile, like a bundle of fresh-shorn fleece might soak up punches. 'And we might need it to hold the folk who killed him.' And she put her forefinger on that great scarred mass of fist and gently pushed it down.

The Nail blinked, like he was puzzling that through. Then he started to smile. 'I could get to like you.'

'I'm likeable. Known for it. Likeable Rikke, they call me.'

'Who's they?'

'Just, you know, *they*.'

'Would My Lady of the Long Eye care to bring her vision to pass?' Isern flicked dust from the seat of Skarling's chair, standing on its dais in the light of the great windows, polished by the arses of the great men of yesteryear.

'Guess someone's got to sit in it,' said Rikke. 'And I did come all this way, and in mixed weather, too.' And she spun about and dumped herself down. She shifted one way. She shifted the other.

'Well?' asked Shivers.

'Bit hard on the arse.'

'Was there a cushion in your vision?' asked Isern. 'You might think of finding one if you plan to perch there long.'

The Nail stretched his chin a long way forward to scratch at his throat. '*Do* you plan to perch there long?'

Rikke looked up at Shivers. He raised his brow. She looked up at Isern. She raised hers. 'Well,' she said, and noisily spat again, 'I daresay none o' Crummock-i-Phail's children would disagree with my considered opinion that . . .' She left an unnaturally long pause before finishing. 'We could do worse.'

'My thanks for that ringing endorsement,' said Rikke.

'They'll be back, you know,' said the Nail. 'Stour and all his warriors.' And he jerked his thumb towards the door as if he expected 'em to troop in any moment.

'Some will be,' said Rikke. 'But if King Orso took any notice of the letter I sent him, they'll have a much harder fight than they were expecting. So Stour'll come back with a lot fewer warriors than you were expecting. If he comes back at all.'

The Nail stared at her, mouth slightly open.

'Spent a year in Ostenhorm,' she explained, 'with what they call a *governess*.'

'What's that? Some kind o' witch?'

'A particularly boring kind o' one. But to be fair, it turns out learning to write has its uses.'

'So . . .' The Nail narrowed his eyes, counting off the points on his fingers. 'You promised the Young Lion you were going with him, then not only did you not go, you stole his ally's land while he was gone, *and* warned his enemies he was coming.'

Rikke stretched her chin a long way forward to scratch at her throat, the way he'd done a moment ago. 'Sounds somewhat underhand put that way. But once you've stabbed a man in the back, you're best off stabbing him a few more times, don't you reckon? Make sure of the job.'

'There's my girl,' grunted Shivers.

'She was listening after all,' said Isern, stretching up on her tiptoes.

The Nail gave a disbelieving little titter, staring at her with something close to admiration. 'I could *really* get to like you,' he said, and he whipped the black fur he wore off his shoulders. 'You said something about a cushion?'

'What fine manners,' said Rikke, sitting up long enough for him to slip it behind her then wriggling back into it.

'Best not get carried away with yourself,' said Shivers, nudging at the drooping lid of his metal eye with a knuckle. 'Black Calder's still out there.'

Isern nodded. 'He spent a lot of effort winkling his son onto that

461

chair, d'you see? Won't be overjoyed to hear you've wedged your skinny arse into his place.'

'He'll be ready, the moment you trip up.'

'And he's got friends all over,' said the Nail, 'and debts owed, and favours to call on. King Orso won't be ridding us of him, no matter what letters you write.'

'No,' said Rikke. 'Black Calder we'll have to deal with ourselves. And unlike his son, he's a man who earned his name.'

'Earned it with cleverness and treachery and ruthlessness,' said Isern. 'All qualities much loved by the moon.'

Shivers had his eye on Skarling's Chair. 'Trouble with being a strong man or a clever man with a big, bad name,' he said, and he ought to know, after all, 'is that folk always have their best fight ready for you.'

The Nail nodded along in sympathy. 'There are times I wish folk had never heard o' me. Look small, look foolish, got no name, well . . . that's when you're given chances.'

'Mmmm.' Rikke tapped at the arm of Skarling's Chair with her finger-nail. Picked at the scratched and faded layers of paint that centuries of rulers had picked at before her. That Skarling Hoodless himself picked at, for all she knew. 'No strength like looking weak, eh?'

'What you thinking?' asked Shivers.

'What my father would've said, once he got over the shock of seeing me here.' And Rikke looked up. 'Sitting in it's nothing special. It's staying in it that's the trick.'

The New Harvest

It was a surprise, in a way, to hear that birds still sang. To see the sun still rose and the wind still blew. But things go on. Orso took a long breath that had a faint, sickening tang of battle about it. 'Things always go on,' he murmured.

Not for everyone, mind you. The dead were everywhere. Sparsely dotted, away to the north, then more liberally sprinkled where the fighting had been fiercest, clogged up in knots. Heaps, almost. Perhaps men had felt the need to crawl towards other men while they still had the breath. Perhaps even the dead love company.

The corpse-gatherers had been labouring from before first light. Whole companies of them, dragging cadavers by hand, by stretcher and by cart into orderly piles at the corners of fields. There prisoners made unwilling gravediggers chopped away with pick and shovel in an effort to make holes big enough to hold them all. Flies, crows and human scavengers had meanwhile appeared from nowhere, flitting busily among the bumper crop of bodies while there were still pickings to be had.

The disposal of men made an industry, on the impersonal scale of the new age.

'All that work,' said Orso. 'All that effort. All that ingenuity, and courage, and struggle, to make what? Corpses.'

'Few things indeed,' mused Pike, 'seem to have so much appeal before, and so little after, as a battle.'

The fires in Stoffenbeck were out but smoke still crept from the embers to smudge the chalky sky. The picturesque town square was a ruin, several of its fine old houses blackened shells, its covered marketplace ripped open to the sky, the clock tower mangled beyond repair by cannon-stones. No bunting now in honour of Orso's visit.

Rucksted frowned towards the rocky bluff, where yesterday's cannons still poked from the hill like the prongs of an iron crown. 'The world's changing, that's for damn sure. Now a man can put a spark to some powder and a thousand strides away another man's blown limb from limb. There was a time you had to look in his eyes, at least.'

'That was better?' asked Vick.

'Victories always come with a cost,' said Sulfur, calmly. 'When my master returns from his business in the West, I do not doubt he will be satisfied with the outcome.'

'Marvellous,' murmured Orso. 'I have engineered a quantity of death to satisfy even the First of the Magi.' His eyes could hardly comprehend the carnage. He kept looking to one side, then scanning across, in an effort to take it all in. 'How many people do you think died here?'

'Hundreds,' murmured Hoff, eyes wide.

'Perhaps thousands,' said Pike, listlessly. 'But mostly on the rebel side.'

Orso took scant comfort from that. Most on the rebel side had been citizens of the Union, too. His subjects. They had fought bravely, loyally, for good reasons. But being right is of little value in war. A great deal less than being lucky, certainly. If the cavalry had not arrived when they did, it might have been Leo dan Brock shaking his head over the carnage. Except Orso doubted the Young Lion had the imagination for it.

'Can it really have been worth it?' he found he had said.

'Can what, Your Majesty?' asked Pike.

'Anything.' Orso waved a limp hand at the spectacle. 'Can anything be worth this?'

'They gave us no choice,' grumbled Rucksted. 'You were hardly the aggressor, Your Majesty.'

'I played my part,' muttered Orso, gloomily. 'If they wanted the crown so bloody badly, I could just have given it away. It's not as if I enjoy wearing the damn thing...' He glanced across the unhappy faces of his retainers. Probably not the victory speech they had been hoping for. Sulfur, in particular, was frowning thoughtfully. 'But I suppose your master takes a dim view of unauthorised abdications.'

The magus bowed his head. 'Were he to lose Your Majesty, I can only imagine his regret.'

They would have to imagine it, since Orso rather doubted Bayaz was capable of displaying any.

'There are many practical considerations,' said Hoff, hurrying to change the subject. '*Large* numbers of prisoners to consider.'

'Many from the Open Council's forces.' Rucksted gave a disdainful sniff. 'I hesitate to call them soldiers. Anglanders, too.'

'When it comes to the rank and file, I tend towards mercy,' said Orso. 'We have enough Union men to bury.'

Pike inclined his head. 'Fines, parole and forced labour may be of more value than mass executions.'

'Provided mercy does not extend to the ringleaders,' said Sulfur. 'Justice must fall on the guilty like lightning. As it did at Valbeck.'

Orso gave a grimace at that memory, but he did not disagree. 'What about the Northmen?'

'Pulling back towards their ships in disarray,' said Rucksted. 'Harried by our cavalry.'

'Let them go. I don't want to waste one more Union life on the bastards.' In truth, Orso had no appetite for any further waste of life at all: Union, Northman, dog or flea.

'We'll see every one of those swine herded from our land or buried in it.'

'Stour Nightfall himself is unaccounted for,' said Pike. 'I fear we may not have heard his name for the last time.'

'We can put down the Great Wolf another day.' Orso paused a moment, frowning. 'There was no trouble from the Breakers in Keln?'

Rucksted scratched at his beard. 'Not a whisper. If there are Breakers down there, they were quiet as mice while my men were in the city.'

'We should take no chances,' said Pike. 'Inquisitor Teufel and I will set out for Valbeck this afternoon. Ensure that the city is . . . *pure*.'

That word might have given Orso a cold shiver once, but perhaps the battle had washed away all his father's good-natured indecision and exposed a flinty core of his mother's cold-blooded scorn. The Union had to be brought together now. Whatever it took.

'Very good.' He drew his fur-trimmed cloak tight about his shoulders against the chilly autumn breeze and watched the corpse-gatherers at their work.

The door squealed open to reveal a dim chamber, walls glistening with damp, cut in half by rust-speckled gratings. Beyond, the wretched occupants of cells stuffed to bursting squinted into the light, shrank into the shadows, pressed themselves against the bars.

'Former members of the Open Council,' said the Arch Lector, with perhaps the slightest hint of satisfaction in his voice, if not his face. 'Awaiting the king's justice.'

Here they were, then. Some of the proud peacocks responsible for this epic disaster. There was little pride on display now. One listless young man had a bloody bandage wrapped around one eye. Another had hands over his face, shoulders shaking with silent sobs. The extravagant uniforms were torn and tattered, gold braid made muddy strings, glittering insignia of legions that no longer existed turned to so much trash.

'I must apologise for these quarters,' said Orso, stepping through the doorway and wrinkling his nose at the stink. 'I know they are not quite what you are used to.'

'This is all a misunderstanding, Your Majesty!' one young lordling spluttered, face pressed so hard against the bars they left livid marks in the flesh to either side. 'All a terrible misunderstanding!'

'Shut up,' snarled one of the guards, bashing the bars with a stick and making him recoil.

Orso had hoped to feel some satisfaction at the sight of his sneering adversaries from the benches of the Open Council ruined. But he felt mostly hollow, irritable and slightly disappointed that he felt nothing more. As if all meaningful emotion for the year had been used up during the battle in one profligate splurge.

'Most of those lords who rebelled are dead or captured.' Pike's burned lip wrinkled. 'Lord Isher escaped, but we will hunt him down, along with all the rest.' He gestured towards a fat man whose blond hair stuck out at all angles, his uniform so ripped it was scarcely decent, large patches of scratched and hairy skin showing. 'Lord Barezin was found tangled in a briar patch. He fell from his horse while trying to flee.'

Even having heard the name, Orso could scarcely recognise the man. Barezin drew himself up with the most dignity a man stripped of all dignity could muster. 'Your Majesty, I was hoping I might discuss with you—'

Orso had no stomach for his excuses, still less his bargaining. 'I think everything of importance was said yesterday, on the field.'

Lady Wetterlant glared from behind the bars of the cell next door. There was an angry graze up one side of her face, but she did no pleading. 'You may have won,' she snapped, 'but I have no regrets!'

Orso gave a weary shrug. 'Who cares?' he said.

'Your Majesty.' Pike leaned close to murmur. 'I suggest they all be hanged as soon as is practicable.'

Hell, Orso hated hangings. But making the things you hate come to pass seemed to be the main duty of a king.

'See it done.' He shook his head. 'What a bloody waste.'

*

466

It had been a morning of ugly shocks, but the sight of Leo dan Brock was somehow the worst of all.

A sheet was drawn up to his waist, but from its shape it was awfully clear that the surgeons had taken his left leg off above the knee. His left arm hardly looked better, wrapped in bandages to the shoulder, the dangling fingers swollen up like purple sausages. His chest, and his face, and his right arm were speckled with a hundred little nicks and scabs, stained with blue bruises. His mouth was bloated on one side, the gap of missing teeth showing through his twisted lip. He looked to have aged twenty years. All that indestructible bravado smashed out to leave him a shrivelled husk.

Orso's great rival, in more ways than one, lying hopeless and humbled at his mercy. It should have been a proud moment. But all Orso felt was sadness. To see a man who'd been so enviably handsome, so ruined. To see a man so representative of the warrior's virtues, so crushed. To see a man who'd stood so tall no room had seemed big enough, brought so horribly low.

He had been a hero to many. The Young Lion!

By the Fates, look at him now.

'Your Majesty,' he croaked out, in evident agony, his left arm useless as he tried to wriggle up his pillow to a more seemly position. As if any position was seemly for a man who had just lost half his limbs in one of the most infamous defeats in Union history.

'Your Grace.' The title was probably inappropriate now, but Orso hardly knew what else to say. He glanced up at Gorst, looming watchfully by the door. 'You can leave us, Colonel.'

'Your Majesty?'

'What will he do?' snapped Orso. 'Hop from his bed and bite me to death?'

Gorst lowered his eyes and trudged from the room, pulling the door shut. When Orso turned back, Brock had a pained grimace on his face.

'Don't you dare take exception to my fucking tone!' snapped Orso. 'Among all this suffering, you're one of the few who can truly say they brought it on themselves.'

Brock looked down, and plucked weakly at the sheet beside the stump of his leg, and said nothing.

Orso slumped into the one hard chair in the narrow room. 'Why the hell did you *do* it? You had everything. Wealth and status and admiration. Even your bloody enemies liked you! Do you really believe your cronies would have done so much better a job than mine?'

Brock opened his mouth. Then he gave a wincing shrug, and a grunt of pain, and his shoulders sagged. 'Does it matter now?'

There was a silence, then Orso slumped even lower. 'Very little.'

'My wife . . .'

Orso felt an ugly spasm through his face. The mere thought of Savine's name was still painful. A splinter he could never work free. 'Missing,' he growled. 'But Arch Lector Pike has men searching for her. She will not get far.'

'She had no part in this—'

Orso barked out a joyless laugh. 'Please. As if she ever went into anything without her eyes wide open. I've no doubt she's every bit as guilty as you are, if not more so. She doesn't even have youth, stupidity and a massively bloated sense of her own importance as excuses.'

Cruelty to a man so utterly broken in body and spirit did not help Orso in the least. It just made him feel cruel. He could be generous in victory, couldn't he? He had won, hadn't he?

So why did he feel like he lost?

'My friends . . .' croaked out Brock. His eyes looked a little wet. But perhaps that was from the agony.

'Dead,' said Orso.

Brock bared his teeth as he tried to shift back on his bed. They were pink with blood still. 'Can I ask . . . that they get a decent burial, at least?'

'In a pit with the rest. I have hundreds of loyal men to bury. I can waste no effort on traitors.' Bloody hell, he hated this. He stood, shoving back his chair, and turned towards the door.

'They were good men,' he heard Brock whisper. For some reason, it made Orso feel exceptionally angry.

'Good men and bad, they're all meat now. If it's any consolation, you won't need to worry about it long. Your hanging's within the week.'

And he strode for the door with his fists clenched.

The Truth

'**A**h!'

'My scripture teacher used to tell me...' murmured Zuri, eyes narrowed with concentration as she stitched, 'that pain is a blessing.'

'I like the man less and less.' Savine managed a watery grin. 'Not the first time your needle's come to my rescue. Usually it's been sewing on a loose button... rather than stitching my head together...' She noticed that Zuri had a rip down one side of her dress, tightly wound bandages showing beneath, and the brown dirt smeared around that rip was not dirt at all, but dry blood.

'Zuri—'

'No need to worry about me.' She did not take her eyes from her work. 'The blood is not mine.'

Savine rolled her eyes further down to look at her own dress. That same dirt was caked all down the front. 'It's mine?'

'My scripture teacher also told me...' still sewing as carefully and precisely as ever, 'that scalp wounds bleed a great deal.'

'A man of varied interests.'

'You have no idea.'

Witty back and forth, as if they were discussing business on an ordinary day rather than hiding in a muddy hollow under the roots of a fallen tree, with everything in utter ruins. Savine wrapped her arms around herself, wrapped her arms around her baby and felt it move, thank the Fates. Her shoulder, her side, her neck were one great stiff throb where she must have hit the ground. She could easily have been dead.

A cannon had burst, that's what Zuri told her. A splinter of metal had grazed her head, ripped her wig off and knocked her flat. A little lower and it would have sprayed her brains across the hillside. She had missed the chaos of the rout, bouncing unconscious in the back of a wagon. A lady of taste should appear to make no effort. The right things simply happen around her. She woke here in the woods, with the worst headache she'd ever had.

She could very easily have been dead.

But you know things are bad when you cling to that for comfort.

'Ah!' she grunted as Zuri's needle bit again.

'Best stay quiet,' murmured Broad, squatting low beside the rotten carcass of the tree trunk, light flashing on his lenses as he peered off into the woods. His voice had a rough, hollow quality. 'They'll be hunting for us.'

Meaning they would be hunting for her. 'Of course. I'm sorry.' Savine closed her eyes. How often had she said sorry before? Not often. And never really felt it. But this was a different world.

'How bad is it?' Her voice came very small. As if she hardly wanted an answer.

'Just a scratch.' There was no sign in Zuri's face that she was lying. It was Broad's face that gave it away.

'You've been stitching a long time for a scratch,' she croaked out.

'You know me, I will not stand for sloppy needlework.' Zuri leaned close to bite off the thread and sat back, frowning. 'There might be a little scar. Something to add a dash of danger.'

As if they needed any extra danger. A scar was the least of Savine's worries.

'Done?' asked Broad, standing over them. He offered one big hand. The one with the tattoo on its back. Savine noticed the knuckles were all scratched and scabbed. 'Lady Savine?'

She stayed sitting. Watched the woodlice squirm among the rotten roots. Honestly, she was not sure she could get up. 'Is my husband alive?'

'When I last saw him.'

She got the feeling there was more to that story, but she hardly dared ask. 'He was hurt?'

Broad added no sugar to it. 'Badly.'

'I see,' said Savine, cold all over. Broad, she felt, knew a bad wound when he saw one. He squatted slowly in front of her, baring his teeth as if moving was painful.

'We have to go. Can't afford to wait for dark. Have to keep off the roads, make for the coast, then to Angland. We have to go now.'

'Yes.' Savine took a long breath. 'But not towards Angland. I'm going back to Stoffenbeck.'

'What?' asked Zuri.

'I have to surrender. It's my best chance to save Leo.'

Muscles squirmed on the side of Broad's head. 'Lady Savine, from what I saw, there might be no saving him—'

'It's my only chance to save myself. We have no supplies. The king's forces are everywhere. My entourage is down to two and it's two more than I deserve. We'll never make it to the coast. Not with me the size of a house.'

'You could go to your father,' murmured Zuri.

'There's nothing he could do. He resigned. Difficult to shield the king from treason when you have a traitor for a daughter. I did this to myself.' She said it rather bitterly, for someone who had no one else to blame. 'No one can undo it. Even if I could get back to Angland, do we really think the Inquisition would not reach me there?'

'We can try,' said Broad.

'You can.' Savine took his hand and gave it an awkward pat. 'You should. Go back to May and Liddy.' She smiled up at Zuri. A queasy, hopeless smile, since she honestly had no idea how she would make it to the edge of the woods by herself, let alone back to the battlefield. 'You, too, Zuri, you have your brothers to think about. The time has come for us to—'

'I will come with you.'

Savine stared at her. She had always liked to think of Zuri as a friend, but she knew she was a paid one. Knew someone of her taste and talents must once have had far higher ambitions than being a glorified maid. Ambitions that had been destroyed by whatever horrors she had fled from in Gurkhul. She had always liked to think of Zuri as a friend but had never imagined she would carry on being one if there was nothing in it for her. When it had become a terrible risk, in fact.

She felt as if she could have taken any amount of betrayal, danger, disappointment. But loyalty was somehow more than she could bear. There was no helping it. Savine put her hands over her face and started to cry.

She heard Broad give a weary sigh. 'Reckon we're all going back.'

No one challenged them on the way to Stoffenbeck.

Perhaps those searching for her were far to the North, watching the coast for her escape. Perhaps they were looking for someone fleeing her crimes, not limping meekly back through their very scene. Perhaps – bald, bloody and bedraggled – she bore little resemblance to anyone's idea of the famous beauty Savine dan Glokta, and her own least of all.

As she toiled through the fields, sweat tickling at the burning scar on her forehead, she needed three hands. One to hold her bloated belly, one to hold her aching back, one to hold her throbbing head. She had no choice but to alternate between them, her shoulder aching with every step, breathing hard through her gritted teeth, while her baby quite literally kicked the piss out of her.

She cocooned herself in misery so she would not have to look right or left. So she would not have to see the scorched orchard, the trampled wheatfields, the smoke still crawling up from Stoffenbeck, pounded to ruins by cannon so meticulously cast in her own foundry.

All the while, she told herself she could not be blamed.

She had not wanted any of this, after all. She had wanted to marry Orso. More than anything. But she lost him because her mother once fucked a king. Curnsbick had been right, after Valbeck her judgement was no good. When Leo was served up to her, so handsome and celebrated and bursting with potential, just the delightful pastry her jaded palate needed, what choice did she have but to get her knife and fork out? And then, pregnant and puking and judgement even worse, what choice did she have but to marry him? And then, finding he was already balls-deep in conspiracy with Isher, what choice did she have but to join them and do everything to make a success of their preposterous scheme?

Making successes from men's preposterous schemes was what she did, after all.

It was terribly unfair on her, when you thought about it, that she had lost everything because of who her mother fucked, by definition some time before she was born.

And then she thought of her father. Not King Jezal, the other one. The real one, blood or no blood. Sitting in his wheeled chair, tongue touching his empty gums and a brow critically raised. Perhaps after one of her arrogant overreaches in the fencing circle. *Really, Savine?*

'What have I done?' she whispered, and she sank down to one knee in the road.

If she had really tried, if she had truly wanted to, she could have found a way to stop this. There were a thousand moments when she could have found a way to stop this.

Instead, she had fanned the flames. Instead, she had rolled the dice. And what for? Ambition. That snake twisted tight about her innards whose hunger grew sharper the more it was fed. Whose hunger could never be satisfied.

The truth was, like all gamblers who suddenly lose big, she had only thought about what there was to win. Now she saw the scale of her loss, and it was no less than everything. And she had not only lost on her own behalf, but for thousands of others. What would it mean for Zuri? What would it mean for Broad? For Haroon and Rabik? For Liddy and May? By the Fates, what would it mean for her unborn child?

'What have I done?'

She felt Zuri's light hand on one shoulder. 'My scripture teacher would no doubt have said . . .' She was frowning doubtfully out across the battered battlefield. 'That regret is the gateway to salvation . . .'

Savine gave a disbelieving snort. 'Can you really still believe in God? That this is all part of some grand plan? That it *means* something?'

'What is the alternative?' Zuri looked at her, eyes wide. 'To believe that it means nothing?'

Savine felt Broad's heavy hand on her other shoulder. 'No one makes a thing like this happen alone. We all had our hand in it.'

She slowly nodded. It would have been yet more appalling arrogance to suppose it was all her fault. She winced as she struggled to her feet, took a hard breath and, with one hand under her belly and one pressed into her back, struggled on across the wounded fields towards Stoffenbeck.

She had played her part in this.

All that remained was to pay for it.

She was not sure how long she sat there, waiting, in an agony of guilt, apprehension and, well, agony.

The pain in her head was getting no better. The pain in her bladder was most certainly getting worse. Her baby was endlessly shifting. Perhaps it was cursed with Leo's impatience. Perhaps it was infected by her panic. Perhaps, like a rat scurrying from a foundering ship, it sensed she was going down and desperately struggled to wriggle free of her.

It must have had its mother's instinct for self-preservation. Savine would have wriggled free of her own skin if she could.

From time to time, she heard guards outside the door. Muffled voices. Even laughter. She was a prisoner, then. Something she had better get used to, she supposed. Along with being universally reviled, all she had built ruined, her name used as a cheap joke or a warning lecture—

The door clattered open and she jerked up so suddenly she put a spasm through her back, nearly vomited and was trapped halfway to her feet, leaning on the chair with one trembling arm.

Orso stared at her, frozen. As if he had arranged an expression of righteous fury but on seeing her could not quite disguise his shock. Her belly, and her head wound, and her ripped and bloody clothes took some adjusting to, she supposed. The righteous fury soon returned, though.

'Don't get up,' he snapped, though it was obvious she couldn't have without block and tackle. She flopped back into the chair with all the grace of an ale keg with arms. Any trace of dignity she counted one of her least painful losses, at this point.

He shut the door, carefully not looking at her. He had changed, too. Harder. More purposeful. There was no hint of his old languid flourish as he stalked into the room with his fists clenched.

'I was surprised to hear you had given yourself up. I felt sure you'd be slithering away somewhere to hatch some new scheme.' The room was warm, but his voice was cold enough to make the hairs on her arms bristle.

'I knew that surrendering...' Her voice sounded pathetically weak. 'Was the best thing I could do...' She was used to holding all the cards. Even with Orso, she was used to holding some. Now he had the entire deck. 'For my child—'

'It's a little *late*,' he barked at her, 'to be thinking about *that*, don't you *think*? Now the dead are stacked five high in the fields?'

Savine had not supposed they would trade quips like they used to. But she had never really seen him angry before. She began to wonder if this had been a terrible mistake. If she should have run while she had the chance, and never stopped.

'Were you a part of this?' He still refused to look at her, jaw muscles squirming on the side of his face. It came to her forcefully that with a word he could have her hanged beside all the rest. She would never have dreamed he would do it until that moment. Now she was not so sure.

Lies would not help her. It had to be the truth. 'Yes,' she whispered. 'I had a full part in it.'

'I would've been amazed if you hadn't. But somehow I kept hoping.' Orso bared his teeth. 'I received a letter, some time ago, warning me of a conspiracy to steal my throne. A plot by members of the Open Council. With *friends in the North*.'

Savine closed her eyes. Rikke. It could only have been Rikke. She had not merely let them down but betrayed them. Perhaps she really had seen the future. Savine might almost have admired her tactics, had she any emotion to spare. It was very much the sort of thing she might have done herself. Not that it mattered now. When she opened her eyes, Orso was staring at her with the strangest look.

'Why?' he asked.

Savine swallowed. She had planned the best way to frame it, how to subtly shift the blame, each word picked out as carefully as an ensemble for the theatre, but now the excuses burbled out in a half-baked rush. 'They were already planning it. Isher, and the rest. I had no choice. I could only—'

'No.' Orso bit off every word. 'I mean . . . why choose *him* . . . over *me*?'

She should have known he would ask. But she had told herself he no longer cared. That it was buried and would never need to be dug up. Now she realised her error, and she stared down at the carpet, her face burning, the breath crawling in her throat.

'What did I do? To make you turn on me?' He stepped closer, lips curling back from his teeth. 'Have you even got a heart?'

She did, and it was pounding now. She felt as if her battered skull was going to split. He gripped the arms of her chair with white knuckles and she shrank back, turning her face away as he leaned down over her, snarling, spitting, stabbing at his chest with a finger.

'I *loved* you. I *still* fucking love you! How pathetic is that? After what you've done!'

'I'm sorry,' she whispered, 'I'm so sorry—'

'I don't want your sorry, I want to know *why*!' He snarled the word over and over. 'Why? Why? Why—'

'Because I'm your sister!' she screamed in his face. She was revolted. She was ashamed. She was terrified.

She was relieved.

She only realised then how the secret had eaten at her. She met his eye and gave a helpless shrug. 'I'm your sister.'

Never had she seen a man's face so contorted with different extremes of emotion within a few moments. From fury, to bafflement, to disgust, to disbelief. 'What do you mean?' He flinched back. Jerked his hand from the arm of her chair and held it up as if to ward off a blow. 'What do you *mean*?'

'I meant to say yes to you!' Her confession welled up, sickening as shit flooding from a broken sewer. 'After Valbeck. That's the truth. I wanted to. That's all I wanted. You were the one good thing . . . the only good thing . . . I went to my mother . . .' She closed her eyes, felt tears burning at the lids. A little sadness. A lot of fear. 'She told me . . . I couldn't marry you. She told me . . . she, and your father . . .' She squeezed her eyes tighter shut, had to force out the words. 'They were lovers! Before he became king. And I was the result. I'm your sister! Half-sister. That's the truth. I didn't—'

'That's a lie.' Orso's face crushed up in disbelief. 'That *can't* be true.'

'You know it is. I know it is. My father—' she gave a kind of cough, 'Arch Lector Glokta, that is, he offered to marry my mother. So she would be safe. He raised me as his own. I didn't know. Not until she told me. That's the truth. And then ... I didn't know what I could do! I couldn't marry you. I couldn't tell you why. Then seeing how you hated me for it ... it was torture!' She found she was leaning towards him, reaching out for him. 'It still is torture.'

He stumbled back, clattering into a chair and sending it over backwards.

'I lost my way after that!' She struggled up somehow, took a wobbling step towards him. 'I lost all my judgement. I was just ... pretending ... to be *me*. I was still trapped in Valbeck, somehow! I couldn't see ... past my own ambitions ... I didn't have anything else!' Pathetic excuses, mangled in her dry mouth. 'Leo ... he's a good man. He could be ... but he's so easily led. Isher and the rest brought him to this.' She closed her eyes, tears welling down her face. 'I brought him to this. Blame me. I wanted ... I don't even know what I wanted any more!'

She could hardly stand. She sank down on her knees. 'I'm begging you for mercy. For my husband. For myself. For our child.' Hands clasped, face wet with tears, nose clicking with snot. What a fucking cliché. 'I know I don't deserve it, but it's all I can do now. Please, Orso.'

He stared down at her, that hand still up as though to push her away. To push away what she was saying.

'Gorst!' he shrieked.

'No. Orso, please.' She almost clutched at his ankles. 'I didn't know. It's the truth—'

The door burst open and Bremer dan Gorst strode in. Huge. Merciless.

'Get her out of here!'

Gorst took her under one arm. Oddly gentle. But utterly irresistible.

'Please!' she blubbed as he half-marched her, half-carried her out. 'Orso!' She clutched at a table in desperation and dragged it over, a pile of books scattering. 'Please!'

The door slammed shut.

Those Names

'There's the beacon fire!' squeaked Greenway, pointing off through the mist. 'It's Ollensand!'

'Finally!' Stour stalked to the prow, shouldering Greenway aside for a better look. There was no missing the wriggling pinprick of light now, and there were smiles all around at the thought of land, and food, and warmth, Clover's big as anyone's. It had been quite the wearying voyage.

They'd scratched together a crew half his men, half Stour's young bastards who'd lived through the battle. One had a wound in his back and died after a night of groaning on the water. They'd rolled him over the side, the only ceremony Clover's observation that not everyone goes back to the mud after all. Some get the big drink instead. Greenway had looked green the whole way, and especially green at that, Rikke's prediction that he'd die on water no doubt weighing on his mind.

'Home again.' Clover shook some of the salt dew from the old blanket around his shoulders. He glanced at Sholla, sitting beside him with her arm over the tiller. 'Quite a feat o' navigation.'

'Nothing to comment on,' she said modestly, though he knew she'd spent most of the nights awake, frowning at the stars and fretting over the course. Last thing they wanted was to land in the wrong place, after all, and one bit of sea looks much like another.

All the way, Stour snapped and whined like a wounded wolf indeed. Anyone hoping a glimpse of the North would sweeten his mood was sorely disappointed. All it did was remind him that he'd left with big ambitions and a few thousand men, and was coming back with neither.

'Get the oars out and row us in, you bastards!' he snarled, that fine wolfskin cloak of his snapping as he stalked between the benches. He leaned against the mast to rub at the wound on his leg. 'Fucking thing! It's right on top o' the one the Young Lion gave me!'

'Seems a bonus,' Sholla murmured through tight lips. 'You end up with one wound not two.'

'In my experience o' the Great Wolf,' mused Clover, 'and I have about as much these days as any man alive, he's not prone to look on the sunny side. I'd best try and calm the bastard, eh?' He heaved out a sigh as he stood. 'Doubt anyone else will.' And he pulled the damp blanket off and tossed it over Sholla's head.

Men scurried about the ship as that distant light grew brighter and was joined to either side by the grey rumour of the coast. Wood clonked, rope hissed and salt spray flew as they brought in the sailcloth and leaned to the oars.

'Ready for the shore?' Clover asked Downside as he passed, and the big man gave him a wink with that bloodshot eye, red from a blow to the head in the battle. Stour was still raging, o' course, as he walked up. What else would he be doing?

'Not a moment too fucking soon! Fucking Union. Fucking disaster.' As though failure had fallen out of the sky, rather than his having any hand in it.

Clover folded his arms and looked off towards the coast. 'If no one lost, my king, where'd be the pleasure in winning?'

Stour glared at him. Seemed he found that a touch too philosophical when he was still licking his wounds in the shadow of disappointment.

Clover gave it another try. 'Aye, the Young Lion's done, and you had a good deal in common with him, a sympathetic ear in Angland and so on. No doubt his loss is a terrible shame, but... did you really like him all *that* much?'

Stour frowned as Sholla slipped around him. 'Sorry, my king, just have to get to the prow...'

She nodded at Clover, and he pulled Stour's attention back by stepping close, speaking soft, everyone's friend. 'Maybe he can't help you take Uffrith now, but, well... he can't stop you taking it, either.' Clover stepped closer yet, closer than men usually dared step to the Great Wolf. 'Aye, we lost good men back there. But we lost good men before. In your father's wars, and your grandfather's wars. There'll be more men. There'll be more wars. You got to think of any battle you come out of alive as a victory and look ahead to what comes next.'

Stour considered him. A salt wind swept chill across the deck and stirred his hair, ruffled the fine wolf's pelt about his shoulders. Ollensand was slipping from the grey up ahead, ghosts of tall masts in the harbour and low houses on the hillside, the beacon-fire burning brighter, joined by some firefly dots of torches held by a little welcoming party on the longest wharf.

The oars creaked and rattled, somewhere on the high air a gull gave a lonely call, and Clover swallowed as the King of the Northmen turned that wet-eyed stare on him. Always an uncomfortable moment.

Then, quick as the weather shifts in autumn, he grinned. 'You've been loyal to me, Clover. I know I'm not always the easiest. No, no, don't deny it.' No one had thought about denying it. 'But if any man can talk me into looking on the sunny side, it's you.' He reached out and gave Clover a slap on the shoulder. 'You'll get your reward, don't worry about that.'

Clover matched him, grin for grin. 'I know I will. And sooner'n you think.'

And Sholla slipped up from behind Stour, took the hilt of his sword and whipped it from the scabbard.

Instant later, Clover had him around the throat, butted him full in the mouth and snapped his head back. Clover snarled as he butted him again and felt Stour's cheekbone crunch under his forehead. Stour gave a shocked little hoot as Clover butted him a third time. He'd had few sweeter feelings in his life than when he watched the King of the Northmen go sprawling on his back beside the mast.

Greenway's jaw hung open. 'What—' And Downside's axe split his head in half, spraying blood. Seemed Rikke had been right about him dying on the water, and not just him. All over the boat, Clover's boys stabbed the men beside them, cut throats, smashed skulls, stuck blades in backs and fronts and sides. All done too close and too quiet and too sudden for swords. Just the way Clover always said it should be done. Far faster than when Stour killed Scale and his men. Far neater.

By the time the Great Wolf shook his head, spitting blood, Clover's boys were already rooting through the corpses of his bastards for anything worth the taking. Stour blinked, like he hadn't quite caught up yet, and found Greenway staring back at him. Well, one side of his head was, the other it was hard to tell. Stour's bloody lip twisted as he tried to sit up, but Clover put a boot on his chest and shoved him back down.

'Best stay there, I reckon.'

'You futhing traithor!' He spluttered red through his broken mouth, the chain Bethod once wore all tangled up around his neck.

'Traitor, did he say?' Clover raised a brow at Downside. Downside shrugged and set to wiping Greenway's brains off his axe. 'Traitor, did you say?' Clover shoved Stour down again and smiled. After so long under this little shit's boot, felt awfully nice to have their positions swapped about.

'You got some bones, calling me traitor,' he said. 'You, who murdered your own uncle. All I've done is what I always told you to do. Wait for your moment. Then go all the way.' He leaned down closer. 'It's just you weren't fucking listening.'

There were raised voices up near the prow. One of Stour's men left alive. Couple of the boys were arguing 'cause it seemed he was someone's cousin and a good enough fellow by all accounts and letting him live would be a fine thing for his old mother.

Clover gave Downside an impatient flick of the head, and Downside stepped up and ended the argument with his axe in much the same way he'd ended Greenway. Once you've chosen your moment, holding back is folly. Holding back is cowardice.

Stour opened his mouth again but Sholla shut him up by brushing his cheek with the point of his own sword, and Clover leaned down and undid the buckle on his cloak, and dragged it free of him, and swept it around his own shoulders.

'Always liked this,' he said, rubbing his cheek against that fine fur.

'Suits you,' said Sholla.

The men finished up their robbing of the dead and set to the oars. A skeleton crew, maybe, but enough to bring the ship in. One grey Northern city on the grey Northern coast looks much like another, but as the oars kept dipping, they could all see it wasn't Ollensand coming up out of the mist at all, but Uffrith. The light they'd seen wasn't a beacon on a hill, but a bonfire in a cage up on a high pole beside the wharf.

'*Quite* a piece of navigating,' said Clover.

Sholla allowed herself a grin rare as the Northern sun. 'Nothing to comment on.'

There were men waiting in the light of the fake beacon, just as they'd arranged. Hard-bitten men with weapons, scars and scowls in abundance. Clover knew a few faces. Named Men of Uffrith and the West Valleys, the Nail standing among 'em in that crookback slouch of his with thumbs in his sword-belt. At their front, arms folded, metal eye glinting through his long hair, stood Caul Shivers.

'You brought him, then,' he said as Clover clambered somewhat ungainly from the ship, wood of the wharf feeling unsteady under his sea legs.

'I said I would. Did you think I wouldn't?'

'I gave you about a one in three. You know the Nail?'

'By reputation,' said Clover.

The Nail grinned, all teeth and menace. 'It's a good one, ain't it?'

'It's a peach. Must say I'm sorry about your father.'

'Not as sorry as he's going to be.' The Nail grinned even wider as Downside hauled Stour from the boat, hands trussed tight behind him. 'Well, well, well!' And he gave a flourishing bow fine as any Union courtier might have managed. 'The King o' the Northmen comes home!'

'Rikke wi' the Long Eye sends her regards,' said Shivers.

'Fuck her!' snarled Stour. 'And fuck you, too, Caul Shivers!'

Stour's threats had lost a lot of their menace in the last few moments, though, and most of the men laughed, if they did anything.

'She was gutted she couldn't greet you in person.' The Nail leaned forward to poke Stour in the chest with one great big finger. '*Gutted.*'

'But she's arranged a greeting that'll make it all up to you,' said Shivers.

'She's got that cage ready for you. You remember? The one in Skarling's Hall? The one you kept my da in?'

'Aye, I remember,' spat Stour. 'Remember how he pissed himself and cried like—'

He was an odd-looking bastard, the Nail, all stringy and loose, all shoulders and elbows. But Clover never saw a man hit so fast. From nowhere, his fist crunched into Stour's ribs and the King of the Northmen doubled up, wheezing out a long string of drool, the diamond on his chain dangling.

'Ow,' said Sholla, deadpan.

'Funny,' said the Nail, back in his floppy slouch already. 'Barbs don't sting so much from a man you can slap whenever you please.'

Seemed that punch knocked out all Stour's bluster. It can get that way, with men who're always giving blows but never called upon to take 'em. 'Look . . .' Gulping and glugging as he struggled for his breath. 'I'll give . . . twice what . . . she's giving!'

Clover grinned. 'All I'm getting is the chance to butt you in the face. Well, that and the cloak.'

'Fight me, you bastards!' Stour struggled at the ropes round his wrists, provoking nothing but another round o' chuckles.

'We already fought,' said Clover. 'And you lost. You lost everything.'

'I'm the greatest swordsman in the Circle of the World!'

The Nail gave a high little titter. 'Can't see it. To be a swordsman you have to be able to stand up.' And he bent down, grabbed hold of two fistfuls of Stour's trouser legs and yanked them down hard. Yanked them right down to his ankles.

'What're you doing?' he squealed, twisting and struggling, but Downside had him under one arm now and the Nail under the other and he wasn't going far with them two holding on.

Shivers took out a knife. A small knife, it was, with a bright little blade. But a knife don't have to be big to change things. Stour stared at it, over his shoulder, his eyes wet now, all right, but with fear rather'n threat.

'What're you doing?'

Clover caught him by the jaw and hissed the words in his face. 'Giving you your last lesson. Those big names o' the past you're always wanking over. Shama Heartless. Black Dow. The Bloody-Nine. The dead know they were bastards, but they *earned* those names. They tore 'em from the world with their hands and their will. Nightfall?' Clover turned his head and spat into the sea. 'What the fuck is that? You were *born* with it. All you have you've been handed. Well, here's the thing, boy...' And he caught hold of that big diamond and tore the great chain that Bethod once wore over Stour's head. 'What's easily given... is easily took away.'

Shivers reached down and with a calm little movement, like peeling an apple, slit the tendons behind the Great Wolf's knee.

There was a silent pause, like it took a moment for Stour to realise what had happened, then his eyes bulged and he gave a great sobbing shriek, wriggling and twisting, blood running in streaks down his calf. Sholla winced and looked the other way. Downside frowned, and held Stour tight, careless as a shepherd holding a sheep for shearing. The Nail grinned like he'd never heard such a joke.

'Come on,' he called over Stour's squealing. 'Ain't fair to leave a man lopsided!'

Shivers shrugged, good eye showing no more feeling than his metal one, and he did the same to Stour's other knee.

Clover tucked the king's chain into a pocket in his new cloak and watched, arms folded. He didn't think much of vengeance, in the main, and it had been a long time since he took much pleasure in other men's pain, but he had to admit this felt good. Not so good as having Wonderful still around might have. But it was something.

'Best get him bandaged.' Shivers carefully wiped his little knife clean on a rag. 'Don't want him bleeding out.' He glanced sideways at Clover and gave him a nod. 'Glad you came to see things our way.'

'I always did.' Clover watched as the Nail dragged the King of the Northmen away, squealing and crying, his blood-streaked bare legs dragging and the jewelled buckle on his belt bouncing and clattering after. 'Just waiting for my moment.'

A Footnote to History

Climbing the steps to the platform might've been the hardest thing Leo had ever done, but he was determined to get there on his own. Determined to salvage that much pride though, the dead knew, pride had done him no favours. Pride had put him here in the first place.

He used to laugh at climbing mountains. Now he had to gather himself for each step, sweat springing from his forehead. The old wound in his right leg still hurt. Hurt worse than ever now it had to bear most of his weight. But it was nothing to the pain in his other leg. An endless, crushing, sickening throb. And the irony was, the leg wasn't even there.

He kept trying to wriggle his sore toes, work his aching ankle, put his burning foot down to steady himself. Then he remembered they were gone. His leg was crushed, the wreckage sawn off and burned, and everything he'd been was gone with it. No longer a warrior. No longer a leader. No longer a Lord Governor. He'd be a footnote to history. A man who turned himself from hero to villain with his own arrogance, and recklessness, and—

He gave a whoop as his crutch slipped on the top step and spun from his hand. He clutched at nothing, then the side of his face banged hard into the platform. He heard a few gasps, a whimper from somewhere. Maybe him.

His left arm was close to useless. With an agonising effort he could lift the hand, produce the slightest trembling twitch in the first finger, but the rest dangled limp. He barely felt a pin stuck into them. The surgeon said metal blasted from a cannon, along with bits of his shield, had riddled his arm and ruined the nerves. They'd stitched the wounds but there was nothing more to do. And the irony was, they were healing a man they were about to hang.

He worked himself up with his good arm, teeth gritted, managed to ease his right leg under him, groaning as his weight went onto the stump of his left. But once he'd made it to hands and knees – or hand and knee, at any rate – how to get further? He couldn't reach for the crutch without falling, and even if he could, how would he push himself up? There'd been a time when achieving the impossible for Leo dan Brock had meant besting the greatest swordsman of the age, or breaking an enemy's line single-handed, or turning the tide of war against the odds. Now achieving the impossible meant standing up.

He felt a firm hand under his elbow and was lifted carefully to his feet. Or foot. 'There we go.' The crutch was wedged into his armpit again. He glanced sideways to see one of the executioners. Kind brown eyes through the holes in his black mask as he helped Leo forward.

'I'm fine,' said Leo, weakly shaking the man off.

Fine. Broken, defeated, in constant agony, with a useless arm and an amputated leg, convicted of treason and already on the gallows. Fine.

He blinked about at the ruined town square of Stoffenbeck. The scene of his crime, and now of his punishment. The corpses had been hauled away but there were still heaps of rubble in every corner, only blackened pillars left of the ruined market hall where his last charge foundered. The shattered clock tower loomed above, its one remaining face with hands frozen at the moment of his downfall. The place still smelled faintly of burning.

Eleven of his fellow conspirators stood in a row on the platform, all with hands tied behind them, all watching him. Some he didn't even recognise. Lord Mustred was at the far end, bloody bandages wrapped around one eye. Lady Wetterlant, even now keeping her pointed chin high. Lord Barezin, closest to Leo, blinking about as though he could hardly believe what had happened. What was happening. At the feet of each one of them was a trapdoor. Beside each one of them was a lever. Above each one of them was a noose.

It all felt strangely bland. Strangely banal. He'd hardly known what to expect. Yet another irony. The first hanging he'd ever attended would be his own.

With jaw clenched, he hopped to the trapdoor and stood swaying, each breath a smothered groan. There was a taste in his mouth. Blood from the fall, maybe. Or a lingering sweetness from his breakfast. He licked at the grooves between his teeth, trying to root out more. Tiny pleasures seem huge when you know there's no time left. All the wonderful things he used to have, used to do, that he'd hardly noticed, let alone appreciated. Now a sweet taste on his gums was a bounty to feel thankful for.

He glanced up. The sun bright in the sky. The long beam black overhead. The nooses dangling down. His noose, right above him. He wondered how many necks had already been stretched by it. After what he'd done, there were a lot of traitors to hang. They might've done ten batches already today. From the cellars where they'd been keeping the prisoners, you could just hear the clatter as the trapdoors dropped open. The thud as the ropes stretched taut. The faint gasp of the onlookers, each and every time.

Was there dried blood on the rope? He felt vaguely affronted by that. For something so intimate, each person should surely get their own. Felt like dying in another man's underwear. Though the underwear of those who'd gone ahead was no doubt in a far worse state. People pissed and shat and leaked every fluid when they were hanged, he knew. It had seemed quite a laugh when Antaup told them all about it over drinks. Didn't seem much of a laugh now, needless to say.

'Havel dan Mustred!'

Leo looked down, blinking. It was only now that he noticed the audience. Not a large one, and most of them strangers, seated on an assortment of battered chairs dragged from the wrecked buildings about the square. It was Lord Chamberlain Hoff who spoke, droning the name from an ink-spotted list. 'You are found guilty of High Treason and open rebellion against the Crown and sentenced to death.' King Orso sat beside him, scarcely looking like he was enjoying this any more than the convicts. 'Have you anything to say?'

'I did not fight against my king,' growled out Mustred, 'I fought *for* Angland. That's all.'

On the king's other side, Lord Marshal Rucksted gave a great snort of contempt. The worms of the Closed Council. But Leo could summon up no hatred. He saw now that their tyranny had only been an excuse, and a flimsy one too. All he'd wanted was an enemy to fight. Jurand had been right about that. Jurand had been right about everything. The one consolation was that his best friend could remember him as he had been. Would never have to see him . . . like this.

It was better to imagine that Leo dan Brock died on the battlefield. It was true, in every way that mattered. He'd been a great fire, burning brightly. Why cry at the snuffing out of the feeble ember that remained?

One of the executioners offered Mustred a hood. He shook his head. He was guided onto his trapdoor, and as the noose was pulled tight, Hoff was already naming the next in the line of the doomed.

Leo's bleary eyes wandered across the faces in the audience. Not far from the king sat a gaunt woman with close-clipped hair and a bandaged forehead. He wondered for a moment why she was looking at him with such desperate intensity. Then he let out a gasp, and the one knee he still had began to tremble so badly he nearly fell again.

It was his wife.

He'd never seen her stripped of all artifice before. Without her paint, her wig, her jewels, her dozen attendants, her hundred carefully calibrated smiles. He realised now that even her appearances at breakfast had been carefully staged. Even her appearances in bed. Especially those, maybe. It seemed she'd emerged from the Battle of Stoffenbeck almost as broken as he was.

But it was her.

What should he have felt, to see her in the audience at his execution? Useless guilt, at what had become of her? Impotent anger, that she'd urged him on? Sappy sorrow, that he wouldn't see his child born? You'd have thought a man with only a few breaths left would have no time to waste on shame, but shame was what won. A crushing weight of it. At how pitiful he must look. At how badly he'd let her down. At how little was left of the man she'd married.

He could hardly bear to look at her. Even though hers was the only sympathetic face in the whole ruined square. Because hers was the only sympathetic face. At the sight of her, he might realise all he was about to lose.

Hoff was still naming the convicted. Each faced death their own way. Some raged against the world. Some tearfully begged forgiveness. Lady Wetterlant barked insults at every witness until the king ordered her gagged. One young man with broken eye-lenses started to make a speech on the deficiencies of monarchy, maybe hoping to bore a pardon from the king. Orso cut him off after a minute or two with a curt, 'If you wanted to change the world you should have won.'

There were even different kinds of silence. An obstinate refusal to speak. A baffled inability to understand what was happening. A lip-trembling, stuttering, quivering fear.

'Stevan dan Barezin, you are found guilty of High Treason and open rebellion against the Crown and sentenced to death. Have you anything to say?'

'I have,' croaked out Barezin, jowls wobbling as he turned to stare at Leo. 'It was Leo dan Brock that brought us to this! He was the instigator! He was the perpetrator! It was you that brought us to this, you bloody fool!'

There were a dozen other people who'd brought them to this. A hundred. Isher, nowhere now to be seen, had sown the seed. Heugen and Barezin himself had eagerly watered the sprouts. Savine and Stour had their parts in tending the crop. Even Rikke and the Breakers, by going back on their word, had helped bring in this harvest of hangings.

But Leo didn't have the strength to defend himself. He hardly had the strength to look up. Without him, it could never have happened. Why not shoulder the blame? He wouldn't have to carry it for long.

'I throw myself on your mercy, Your Majesty!' Barezin was almost sobbing. 'It was all Brock!'

'You damn coward!' snarled Mustred from the far end of the line.

The blubbing brought nothing but contempt from His Majesty in any case. 'Stick a hood on him,' he snapped, and Barezin squawked as the hood was shoved over his head and the noose pulled tight.

Leo saw now that his father had been wrong. *It's after the battle. That's when a man finds out who he truly is.*

He was no hero. He never had been. He was a fool. A great bloated tower of vanity. It had got his friends, his allies and hundreds who'd followed him killed. Now it would get him killed, too. He wondered for a moment if he might've become a better man for the lessons he'd learned here. He stared down at that endlessly throbbing leg that wasn't there. It hardly mattered now, did it? He'd go back to the mud, as the Northmen say, and all the hard-learned lessons with him.

'Leonault dan Brock, you are found guilty of High Treason and open rebellion against the Crown and sentenced to death. Have you anything to say?'

The whole while, as he listened to the others rage, blurt, weep, reason, all to no purpose, he'd wondered what he'd say. Now the moment came, the last moment, he found he had nothing.

He looked up at Orso and shrugged. 'I'm sorry.' He hardly even recognised his own voice any more, throaty and weak. He looked over at Savine. 'I'm sorry, that's all.' If he stood much longer, he'd fall. If he looked at her much longer, he'd weep. He shook his head as he was offered the hood. 'Let's get on with it.' And he did his best to lift his chin so it was easy to tighten the noose about his throat.

'Most kind,' murmured the executioner.

Hoff rolled up his list of names and tucked it in the pocket of his robes. Rucksted brushed dust from his shoulder. An ordinary-looking, curly haired fellow leaned forward to murmur something in the king's ear. Something familiar about him. Could he be the man who'd come to the docks with Leo's mother, begging him not to go? By the dead, his mother. Why hadn't he listened to her? King Orso gave the executioners a quick nod and they pulled the first lever.

Leo flinched as Mustred dropped with a clatter and a thud, and a set of crows that had gathered on the bare beams of a fallen roof flapped outraged into the sky.

Once they'd started it went shockingly fast. Bang, and the second man was gone, rope trembling. Bang, and the third vanished. The young lecturer in governmental theory was next. He squeezed his face tight before he dropped, like a boy jumping into a cold millpond. By some freak chance, his eye-lenses must've bounced off at the bottom, spun back up through the trapdoor to rest on the platform. One of the executioners bent and slipped them into his pocket.

Leo's life was measured in moments now. In breaths. In heartbeats. He didn't want to look, couldn't look away, winced as the executioner pulled Lady Wetterlant's lever—

She didn't drop.

He pulled the lever again, and again. The trapdoor refused to open.

'Damn it,' came muffled from behind his mask. Orso squirmed in his chair. Hoff rubbed at his temples.

Another executioner stepped forward to mutter with the first, pointing angrily at the trapdoor. Lady Wetterlant growled into her gag. Four ropes stretched taut. Seven prisoners still stood, waiting helplessly for the end.

One of the executioners started kicking at the trapdoor while another dragged pointlessly at the lever again. A third had ducked under the platform and could be heard scrabbling with the mechanism below.

Leo bared his teeth. An agony of waiting. Each moment a horror, but still a moment he was grateful for. The onlookers coughed and narrowed their eyes as a gust of wind swept grit across the ruined square. A few nooses down, one of the conspirators sobbed inside his hood.

'Fuck yourselves, you bastards!' Lady Wetterlant had worked free of her gag and now started screaming insults again. 'Damn you all, you vultures! You worms!'

King Orso jumped up. 'For pity's sake, just—'

Her trapdoor sprang suddenly open. She had been turning, fell awkwardly, scream suddenly cut off as she caught her arm on the edge of the platform and slithered through. It soon became clear that the drop hadn't killed her. The rope twitched wildly. A kind of spluttering groan came from below. Everyone stared as it became a spitty gurgle.

Leo saw piss run from the trouser leg of the man who'd been sobbing to pool on the platform around his boot.

'Proceed,' said Hoff, angrily.

The next man swooned, knees giving and dropping to the platform. One of the executioners dragged him up, slapped his hooded face, stood him straight on his trapdoor. Clatter and thud as he dropped.

As if making up for lost time, they rushed from one lever to the next. Thud, thud, thud, each sending a faint vibration through Leo's own noose.

The canvas over Barezin's face flapped faster and faster with his desperate breath. The executioner grasped his lever. 'Wait!' came muffled from under the hood. 'I—'

He dropped under the platform and with a snap his rope jerked tight. So it seemed great lords of the Open Council meet the long drop just like other men.

Leo looked up at Savine. She gave a desperate smile, tears in her eyes. Meant to give him strength, maybe. He'd never loved her like he did at that moment. Perhaps he'd never really loved her until that moment. He tried to smile back. To leave her with something good. Some glimpse of who he used to be.

He felt the executioner step up beside him. Heard him grip the lever that worked the trapdoor under his feet. Under his foot. Still wasn't used to having just the one. He closed his eyes.

Time stretched. A breeze came up and kissed his sweaty face. He took a long breath out, and held it. His last breath, he realised. He waited for the end.

'Stop.'

He thought it was Orso's voice.

He wasn't sure.

He opened his eyes again. Had to squint, somehow, as if into a wind.

The king wasn't looking at him. He was looking sideways. At Savine. And she was looking back. Everything was still, time chopped up into stretched-out moments by the thudding of Leo's heart. Someone cleared their throat. One of the crows, gathered again on the naked beams, flapped its wings. Barezin's taut rope still hummed faintly. The executioner's hand shifted on the lever.

Then Orso slumped back in his chair and gave a sharp wave of his hand. 'Leo dan Brock, I commute your sentence to life imprisonment.'

There was a collective gasp. Savine closed her eyes, tears running down her face.

'Your Majesty,' that curly headed man was saying, a warning note in his voice, 'my master will not—'

'I have made my decision!' Orso nodded towards the scaffold. 'Take the rope off him.'

And Leo felt the noose loosened, then slipped over his head. As if that had been the only thing holding him up, he slumped, crutch clattering down. The executioner was ready and caught him, lowered him to the platform.

Now he did cry. He couldn't help it. He huddled on his one knee, shoulders shaking with sobs and the tears pattering from the tip of his nose onto the rough-sawn boards. He couldn't even raise his useless left hand to wipe them.

He heard the king's chair scrape as he stood. 'Lady Brock!' he snapped. 'For pity's sake, get your husband down before he embarrasses us any further.'

Loyalties and Sympathies

It was a bright autumn day when Vick rode back into Valbeck. The place looked nothing like the last time she was there, in the final chaotic days of the uprising. No rubbish choking the streets, no burned-out shells of buildings, no sounds of distant violence, no unattended corpses. Only a few pink smears showing through the hastily applied whitewash, reminding the careful observer that these buildings were once daubed with Burners' slogans. There was even a pleasant breeze, carrying the smog of the rebuilt manufactories away inland and leaving the air halfway clean.

All quiet and orderly. Almost too quiet, the few people in the streets scurrying off to stare from alleys and doorways. But then cheering crowds might be too much to ask for when the Arch Lector of the Inquisition arrives in your city with thirty armed Practicals. Pike's last visit, after all, had left the road out of town decorated with hanged men.

'No sign of revolution,' murmured Vick.

'No,' said Pike. 'You sound ... almost disappointed.'

She looked sharply sideways. His Eminence stared straight back at her, eyes bright in his burned mask of a face. No way to tell what he was thinking. There never was. But she saw the danger hidden in the observation. Like a cake full of nails.

'No one's fought harder to stop the Breakers than I have,' she said.

'I am well aware! You scotched their schemes in Adua with impressive ruthlessness. And we could not have dealt so smoothly with the uprising here without your efforts. Nobody doubts your loyalty.'

'Good,' said Vick. She had become acutely aware how many Practicals were surrounding her.

'To Arch Lector Glokta.' And she felt the hairs stand on the back of her neck. 'He was the one who helped you escape the camps, after all. Who gave you a new life. Who moulded you into such a formidable

spy. But Glokta is gone.' Pike gave the sigh of a mourner at a funeral, if
not the tears. 'And your loyalty to me is quite another question. I, after
all, have done nothing to earn it. To count upon it so lightly would be
awfully presumptuous.'

'The Breakers are traitors,' said Vick. Stick to the official line. He could
only judge her on what she said, not what she thought. 'Enemies of the
king. There's nothing to sympathise with.'

'Nothing?' They rode beneath the towering crane at the edge of a
deserted building site, Pike's eyes hidden in the sudden darkness of its
shadow. 'Do you really think so? *Can* you really think so? A good soldier
fights in a world of black and white. He must make monsters of his
enemies. The devious Southerner, the degenerate Styrian, the barbaric
Northman, the treacherous Breaker. But a good spy must swim in an
ocean of grey, swept by unpredictable currents, far out of sight of land.
Those of us who walk, talk, sleep *with* the enemy, well – we see that they
are people. We hear their motives, their hopes, their justifications. Despite
your efforts to prove the contrary, you are not made of stone, Inquisitor.
None of us are. Proud men like Sibalt. Noble men like Malmer. How
could you not sympathise? Given where you come from?'

'Adua?' Vick kept her face neutral, but behind the mask her mind was
racing. Was he trying to trap her? Say she had no sympathy with the
Breakers, and he'd call her a liar. Say she had sympathy, he'd call her a
traitor.

'I meant the prison camps of Angland. I have come to believe . . . that
the heart of a society . . . is revealed in its prisons.' Pike rocked gently with
the movement of his horse, eyes fixed up the empty street ahead. 'I was
not there nearly as long as you, but long enough to lose my face. Honestly,
I was never a handsome man. I daresay I turn more heads now. Your scars
may not show quite so clearly, but I never doubt you have them. So I
believe I understand you.'

'Really?' In spite of all her efforts, her voice sounded strangled.

'Oh, yes. I believe I understand you better than you understand
yourself.'

It worried her that Pike was suddenly so talkative. It made her think
that he was working his way to something, and she would not like it at all
when they got there. She had the feeling, yet again, that this was one of
those moments when her life hung by a thread. But when she faced Sibalt,
Risinau, Vitari, Savine dan Brock, she had gone in with her eyes open,
had known the line she must walk. What Pike wanted was a mystery.

'It was Colonel West who pulled me from the camps,' he mused, 'without the slightest idea that we had known each other years before. In his company I even held a shield in a duel, if you can believe that. When the Bloody-Nine beat the Feared and made himself King of the Northmen! Life is . . . such a cobweb of coincidences, isn't it? West was a man one could admire.' He gave a sorry sigh. 'But the truly good men never seem to last. He died, and I began to work with Arch Lector Glokta. Even though I knew he was far from a good man. Even though he was the very man who had sent me to the camps in the first place. Does any of this sound familiar?'

It did. Not the part about holding a shield in a duel, but otherwise quite uncomfortably so.

Pike watched a nervous-looking set of labourers clear out of their way to huddle against the houses as they clattered past. 'In the name of justice, I tortured dissenters in Adua. In the name of freedom, I imprisoned rebels in Starikland. In the name of order, I spread chaos across the Far Country. I was as loyal a servant as the Crown ever had.'

Vick couldn't help but frown at that choice of words. 'Was?'

'Then the manufactories started to spring up, and the unrest began among the spinners, and I was sent here, to Valbeck, as Superior of the Inquisition.'

'You were Superior of Valbeck?'

Pike had that little curl at the corner of his mouth which was the closest he came to a smile. 'You didn't know?'

The street opened out and they rode into the square that should've been Valbeck's busy heart. It was deserted now, except for well-armed guards posted at the corners and clustered on the steps of the courthouse where Judge had tossed out death sentences. Men with fine new breastplates, fine new halberds, fine new swords, everything twinkling in the autumn sun.

A double row of them was drawn up in front of the rebuilt Valbeck branch of Valint and Balk, a temple to debt more magnificent than ever, scaffolding clinging to its pillared façade so sculptors could finish a frieze of history's richest merchants upon its giant pediment.

'Who are these?' muttered Vick. Some private militia, hired to keep the peace with the king's soldiers gone? But something didn't fit. Rough-looking men, all standing their own way. Clean armour, maybe, but unshaven faces.

Pike didn't look concerned. You might almost have called him jaunty as he led them across the empty square at a trot, past the vacant pedestals of statues torn down during the uprising to the bank's front steps. That double row of armed men parted and two figures came from the midst.

Two awfully familiar figures. One was a fat man in a well-cut suit, the other a tall, lean woman in a dress stitched from many-coloured rags, a rust-eaten breastplate over the top, her red hair pinned into a bonfire tangle.

'Fuck,' breathed Vick. Not often she was at a loss for words, but right then she had nothing better.

'Victarine dan Teufel!' called Risinau, the light of pious belief burning as brightly in his eyes as ever.

'Unless I'm much mistook,' sneered Judge, the light of angry madness burning even brighter in hers, 'which I'm not often.'

First thing Vick thought was that they'd fallen into a trap. Then Pike spread his arms wide. 'My friends!' he called as he swung down from his saddle to meet them. 'My children!' And he kissed Risinau on the forehead, and did the same to Judge, all smiling as if this was a family reunion long put off, while the armed men thumped the butts of their halberds against the steps and sent up an approving rattle.

Like every puzzle, once Vick knew the answer, she couldn't understand how she hadn't seen it right away. She was the one who'd fallen into the trap. She alone.

'You're the Weaver,' she said.

'A name I have used, at times.' Pike gestured to the soot-stained old buildings around the square, the new chimneys looming beyond their roofs. 'So much has changed since I was the Superior here. The rich have grown ever richer, but the poor . . . well. You have seen it. You have lived it. If the heart of a nation is revealed in its prisons, then you and I have seen the heart of the Union, and we know that it is *rotten*. I knew when I was in the camps, that rot had to be burned away. But it was not until I came to Valbeck that I began to dream . . .' And he closed his eyes, and took a long breath through his nose. 'That *I* would be the one to do it.'

Judge snatched a lit torch from one of the guards, its flames dancing in the corners of her black eyes. 'Can we begin?'

'I do not say we can.' Pike leaned towards her. 'I say we *must*.'

'Ha!' Judge gave a delighted giggle as she danced up the steps towards the bank's open doors.

'You must have had a long ride, Sister Victarine.' Risinau placed his soft hand on her knee. 'Perhaps you should dismount?'

Vick glanced carefully around, more habit than anything else, but she wouldn't get out of this by some mad dash on horseback. She swung her leg over the saddle and stepped down to the square.

'I called the like-minded people I gathered the Breakers,' said Pike, watching Judge set her torch to oil-soaked wood at the bank's doors. 'Not because we would break machines, though we have, but because we would break the Union. Break it, and rebuild it in a new way. A better way.' Pike watched the flames lick at Valint and Balk's fine new stonework and the armed Breakers gathered in the square gave a great cheer. 'The banks have twisted about the nation like ivy about a tree, choking all life from it, corrupting everything. So it is fitting that the destruction begins with this monument to exploitation. But it will not stop there.' He turned towards Vick. 'The uprising the Closed Council so feared . . . has already happened.'

'Three days ago,' said Risinau, rubbing his hands delightedly, 'while King Orso was winning his great victory against the rebels. They wanted us to distract the king's men for them. Instead, they distracted the king's men for us!'

'And not just here in Valbeck,' said Pike. 'By now, Keln and Holsthorm and many of the smaller cities of the Union will be in the hands of the Breakers, too.'

'In the hands of their *people*!' frothed Risinau, wagging a fat finger. 'And Adua will be next. Our day is finally come!' And the men cheered louder than ever.

Vick had smugly thought she knew how things really were. Simple as that, everything was turned upside down. 'What the hell do you want from me?' she asked.

'You served Glokta faithfully,' said Pike. 'Admirably, even. Because he was the one man who ever gave you anything. Even if it was only the chance to wear the boot, rather than having it ground into your face.' He did understand her, damn it. Maybe not better than she understood herself, but well enough. 'I would like to offer you something more.'

The silence stretched out, broken by the laughter and whoops of the armed Breakers, the crackle of flames, the tinkle of shattering glass.

'Well, don't keep me in suspense,' said Vick. Seemed to her she'd get nothing with meekness. She never had before. 'What are you offering?'

'Join us,' said Pike. 'Become a Breaker. Give the Union back to its people and shape the future. Commit yourself to a cause worthy of your loyalty.'

'I gave up on causes when I left the camps.'

'All the better.' Pike glanced at Judge, who was tossing her torch through the bank's doors and backing down the steps, a thin, black figure against the rising flames with her fists thrust up in triumph. 'A movement needs passionate believers. But it needs calculating sceptics, too.'

Vick glanced across the smiles of the armoured men on the steps, lit by the flickering fires above. No shortage of belief there. 'And my other option?'

'Leave. Go back to King Orso. Serve his corrupt regime in its dying days. Or run to distant Thond, for that matter, where they worship the sun. Go with our blessing.'

Vick thought of the long line of hanged men Pike had left outside the city, a few months before. She'd thought him ruthless then. Now it turned out they'd been his own people. A man who'll waste no time hanging two hundred of his friends . . . what might he do to his enemies? Smoke was already pouring from the windows of the bank, giving every breath the familiar char and fury stink of Valbeck she so well remembered.

Maybe he was telling the truth, and if she chose to stick with Orso they'd let her swan out of the city and off on her merry way. But she wasn't about to bet her life on it.

If she'd learned one thing in the camps, it's that you stand with the winners.

'I'm with you,' she said, simply. Why say any more?

Pike held out one burned hand towards her while behind him the Valbeck branch of Valint and Balk went up in towering flames for a second time. 'Then come, Sister Teufel! There is much to be done if we are to give the people what they need.'

'Which is?'

'Change.' Pike put that hand on her shoulder and guided her away across the square. 'A Great Change.'

Acknowledgments

As always, four people without whom:

Bren Abercrombie, whose eyes are sore from reading it.
Nick Abercrombie, whose ears are sore from hearing about it.
Rob Abercrombie, whose fingers are sore from turning the pages.
Lou Abercrombie, whose arms are sore from holding me up.

Then, my heartfelt thanks:

To all the lovely and talented people in British publishing who have helped bring the First Law books to readers down the years, including but by no means limited to Simon Spanton, Jon Weir, Jen McMenemy, Mark Stay, Jon Wood, Malcolm Edwards, David Shelley, Katie Espiner and Sarah Benton. Then, of course, all those who've helped make, publish, publicise, translate and above all *sell* my books wherever they may be around the world.

To the artists responsible for somehow continuing to make me look classy: Didier Graffet, Dave Senior, Laura Brett, Lauren Panepinto, Raymond Swanland, Tomás Almeida, Sam Weber.

To editors across the Pond: Lou Anders, Devi Pillai, Bradley Englert, Bill Schafer.

To champions in the Circle: Tim and Jen Miller.

To the man with a thousand voices: Steven Pacey.

For keeping the wolf on the right side of the door: Robert Kirby.

To all the writers whose paths have crossed mine on the Internet, at the bar or in the writers' room, and who've provided help, support, laughs and plenty of ideas worth the stealing. You know who you are.

And lastly, yet firstly:

The great machinist, Gillian Redfearn. Because every Jezal knows, deep down, he ain't shit without Bayaz.

The Big People

Notable Persons of the Union

His August Majesty King Orso the First – unwilling High King of the Union, a notorious wastrel while crown prince.

Her August Majesty Queen Terez – Queen Dowager and mother of the King of the Union.

Hildi – the king's valet and errand-girl, previously a brothel laundress.

Tunny – once Corporal Tunny, pimp and carousing partner to Orso while he was still crown prince.

Yolk – Corporal Tunny's idiot sidekick.

Bremer dan Gorst – a squeaky-voiced master swordsman who was First Guard to King Jezal, and now to King Orso.

Arch Lector Sand dan Glokta – 'Old Sticks', the most feared man in the Union, Head of the Closed Council and His Majesty's Inquisition.

Superior Pike – Arch Lector Glokta's right-hand man, with a hideously burned visage.

Lord Chamberlain Hoff – self-important chief courtier, son of the previous Lord Hoff.

Lord Chancellor Gorodets – long-suffering holder of the Union's purse-strings.

High Justice Bruckel – woodpecker-like chief law lord of the Union.

High Consul Matstringer – overwrought supervisor of the Union's foreign policy.

Lord Marshal Brint – senior soldier and one-armed old friend of Orso's father.

Lord Marshal Rucksted – senior soldier with a penchant for beards and tall tales, married to Tilde dan Rucksted.

Colonel Forest – a hard-working officer with common origins and impressive scars, commanded the Crown Prince's Division for Orso.

Lord Isher – a smooth and successful magnate of the Open Council.

Lady Isold dan Kaspa – an insipid young heiress, engaged to be married to Lord Isher.

Lord Barezin – a buffoonish magnate of the Open Council.

Lord Heugen – a pedantic magnate of the Open Council.

Lord Wetterlant – a handsome magnate of the Open Council with something missing around his eyes.

Lady Wetterlant – Lord Wetterlant's feared battleaxe of a mother.

Lord Steebling – minor nobility, gouty and bad-tempered.

In the Circle of Savine dan Glokta

Savine dan Glokta – daughter of Arch Lector Sand dan Glokta and Ardee dan Glokta, investor, socialite, celebrated beauty and founder of the Solar Society with Honrig Curnsbick.

Zuri – Savine's peerless lady's companion, a Southern refugee.

Freid – one of Savine's many wardrobe maids.

Metello – Savine's hatchet-faced Styrian wig expert.

Ardee dan Glokta – Savine's famously sharp-tongued mother.

Haroon – Zuri's heavily built brother.

Rabik – Zuri's slight and handsome brother.

Gunnar 'Bull' Broad – an ex-Ladderman wrestling with violent tendencies, once a Breaker, now handling 'labour relations' for Savine.

Liddy Broad – Gunnar Broad's long-suffering wife, mother to May Broad.

May Broad – Gunnar and Liddy Broad's hard-headed daughter.

Bannerman – a cocky ex-soldier, working with Broad.

Halder – a taciturn ex-soldier, working with Broad.

Honrig Curnsbick – 'The Great Machinist', famous inventor and industrialist, and founder of the Solar Society with Savine dan Glokta.

Dietam dan Kort – a noted engineer and bridge-builder, partner with Savine in a canal.

Selest dan Heugen – a bitter rival of Savine's.

Kaspar dan Arinhorm – an abrasive expert in pumping water from mines.
Tilde dan Rucksted – the blabbermouth wife of Lord Marshal Rucksted.
Spillion Sworbreck – a writer of cheap fantasies and scurrilous pamphlets.
Carmee Groom – a talented artist.

In Westport and Sipani, Cities of Styria

Victarine (Vick) dan Teufel – an ex-convict, daughter of a disgraced Master of the Mints, now an Inquisitor working as a spy for the Arch Lector.
Tallow – a skinny young Breaker, blackmailed into assisting Vick.

King Jappo mon Rogont Murcatto – King of Styria.
Grand Duchess Monzcarro Murcatto – 'The Serpent of Talins', mother of King Jappo, a feared general and ruthless politician, responsible for the unification of Styria.
Shylo Vitari – the Minister of Whispers, once a colleague of Sand dan Glokta, now spymaster to the Serpent of Talins.
Casamir dan Shenkt – an infamous assassin, rumoured to possess sorcerous powers.

Princess Carlot – sweet-tempered sister of King Orso, wife of Chancellor Sotorius.
Chancellor Sotorius – current ruler of Sipani.
Countess Shalere – the exiled childhood friend (and some say more) of Queen Terez.

Superior Lorsen – colourless Superior of the Inquisition in Westport.
Filio – a senior Alderman of Westport and fencing enthusiast.
Sanders Rosimiche – a junior Alderman of Westport and strutting loud-mouth.
Dayep Mozolia – a merchant in fabrics, influential in the politics of Westport.

With the Breakers and Burners

Risinau – once Superior of Valbeck, behind the violent uprising in that city, revealed to be a leader of the Breakers.

Judge – an unhinged mass-murderer or fearless champion of the common folk, depending on who you ask, the leader of the Burners.

Sarlby – an old comrade-in-arms of Gunnar Broad, now become a Burner.

In the North

Stour Nightfall – 'The Great Wolf', King of the Northmen, a famed warrior and arsehole.

Black Calder – once the true power in the North, cunning father of Stour Nightfall.

Greenway – one of Stour Nightfall's Named Men, expert sneerer.

Dancer – one of Stour Nightfall's Named Men, nimble on his feet.

Brodd Silent – one of Black Calder's Named Men. Presumably a man of few words.

Jonas Clover – once Jonas Steepfield and reckoned a famous warrior, now renowned as a disloyal do-nothing.

Downside – one of Clover's warriors, with a bad habit of killing men on his own side.

Sholla – Clover's scout, a woman who can slice cheese very fine.

Flick – an apparently useless lad among Clover's men.

Gregun Hollowhead – a Chieftain of the West Valleys, father of the Nail.

The Nail – Gregun Hollowhead's son, a feared and famous warrior.

In the Protectorate

The Dogman – Chieftain of Uffrith and famous War Leader, father of Rikke.

Rikke – the Dogman's fit-prone daughter, blessed, or cursed, with the Long Eye. Rhymes with pricker.

Isern-i-Phail – a half-mad hillwoman, said to know all the ways.

Scenn-i-Phail – one of Isern's many brothers, scarcely saner than she is.

Caul Shivers – a much-feared Named Man with a metal eye.

Red Hat – one of the Dogman's War Chiefs, known for his red hood.

Oxel – one of the Dogman's War Chiefs, known for his poor manners.

Hardbread – one of the Dogman's War Chiefs, known for his indecision.

Corleth – a girl with stout hips, keen to fight for Rikke.

From Angland

Leo dan Brock – 'The Young Lion', Lord Governor of Angland, a hotheaded warrior and famous hero, victor in a duel against Stour Nightfall.

Finree dan Brock – Leo dan Brock's mother and a superb tactician and organiser.

Jurand – Leo dan Brock's best friend, sensitive and calculating.

Glaward – Leo dan Brock's exceptionally large friend.

Antaup – Leo dan Brock's friend, renowned as a lady's man.

Whitewater Jin – Leo dan Brock's friend, a jovial Northman.

Lord Mustred – an old worthy of Angland, with a beard but no moustache.

Lord Clensher – an old worthy of Angland, with a moustache but no beard.

The Order of Magi

Bayaz – First of the Magi, legendary wizard, saviour of the Union and founding member of the Closed Council.

Yoru Sulfur – former apprentice to Bayaz, nondescript but for his different-coloured eyes.

The Prophet Khalul – former Second of the Magi, now arch-enemy of Bayaz. Rumoured to have been killed by a demon, plunging the South into chaos.

Cawneil – Third of the Magi, about her own inscrutable business.

Zacharus – Fourth of the Magi, guiding the affairs of the Old Empire.

Credits

Joe Abercrombie and Gollancz would like to thank everyone at Orion who worked on the publication of *The Trouble With Peace* in the UK.

Editorial
Gillian Redfearn
Brendan Durkin

Copy editor
Lisa Rogers

Proof reader
Gabriella Nemeth

Audio
Paul Stark
Amber Bates

Contracts
Anne Goddard
Paul Bulos
Jake Alderson

Design
Lucie Stericker
Tomás Almeida
Joanna Ridley
Nick May

Editorial Management
Charlie Panayiotou
Jane Hughes
Alice Davis

Finance
Jennifer Muchan
Jasdip Nandra
Afeera Ahmed
Elizabeth Beaumont
Sue Baker

Marketing
Lynsey Sutherland
Cait Davies

Production
Paul Hussey
Ruth Sharvell
Fiona McIntosh

Publicity
Maura Wilding
Will O'Mullane

Sales
Laura Fletcher
Esther Waters
Victoria Laws
Rachael Hum
Ellie Kyrke-Smith
Frances Doyle
Georgina Cutler

Operations
Jo Jacobs
Sharon Willis
Lisa Pryde
Lucy Brem